CW00569122

A YEAR IN
CITY OF DRAMA

An Independent Record

Greater Manchester 1994

FOREWORD BY SIR ROBERT SCOTT

Compiled by G A HAWORTH

Additional Journal entries by LYNDA BELSHAW
and NIGEL E HIGGINSON

Broadfield
Publishing

Broadfield Publishing
71 Broadfield Road
Moss Side
MANCHESTER
M14 4WE

061-227 9265

First Published: December 1994

ISBN   0 9521502 1 2

Previous Volume: A YEAR IN THE THEATRE: Greater Manchester 1993
ISBN 0 9521502 0 4
Forthcoming: A YEAR IN THE THEATRE: Greater Manchester 1994-5
ISBN 0 9521502 2 0

Typeset by the compiler on a Canon StarWriter 70, using the Humanist
font
Printed and bound by Anthony Rowe Ltd, Bumper's Farm, Chippenham,
Wiltshire SN14 6QA

CONTENTS

1

ILLUSTRATIONS

Front Cover: Gordon Wharmby as Grandad and Graham Gill as Gil, his nephew, in the Oldham Coliseum's World Premier Production of Mike Stott's My Mad Grandad (53, Journal 9 February): Photo: Valley News Pictures, 60A Huddersfield Road, HOLMFIRTH; 0484 681 362.

Back Cover: Peter Clifford as The Mad Hatter in The Wonderland of Alice, adapted from Lewis Carroll by Simon Corble and performed in Heaton Park, Haigh Hall, Dunham and many places further afield by Library Theatre with Midsommer Actors; Photo: Michael Pollard.

Contents

Contents

4

HOW THE SYSTEM WORKS

The Most Important Principle: INDEXING IS BY THE
Production Numbers given in SECTION 2

Section 2 gives the Page in Section 3 upon which Full
Programme Details can be found.

Section 3 is organised,
　　　A by Boroughs and Cities, in ALPHABETICAL
ORDER (Bolton, Bury, Manchester, Oldham ...)
　　　B with Theatres and Venues in ALPHABETICAL
ORDER within A: (Abraham Moss, Apollo, Arden, Ark ...)
　　and C, Programme Details in CALENDAR ORDER of
First Nights at each Venue.
Section 3 gives full Theatre Details for each Venue:
Address, Box Office Telephone Number, AZ Map Reference
and Access Facilities. Where a company regularly uses a
public hall, the telephone number given will often be that,
not of the hall, but of the company's Booking Secretary.

IF YOU WANT TO KNOW ANY OF THESE DETAILS OR
ABOUT A PARTICULAR PLAY AT A KNOWN VENUE:

THE EASY WAY: i) Open the book somewhere near the
middle;　　　　ii) Work your way, foreward or back,
following principles A, B and C above

Section 3 Programme Details end with
　　　　　a) giving a DATE if a production is
described in the Journal in Section 1, where entries are
given in CALENDAR ORDER
　　　　　b) Dates of coverage in the Press

The Abbreviations for Press references and for Access
facilities are explained at the start of Section 3, Page 220.

5

HOW THE SYSTEM WORKS

2. PRODUCTION NUMBERS

← THIS tells you where to find **THIS ⇒**

MEN: **Manchester Evening News**, 164 Deansgate, MANCHESTER M60 2RD; 061–832 9191

MM: **Manchester Metro News**, 2 Blantyre Street, MANCHESTER M15 4LF; 061–834 9677

OC: **Oldham Evening Chronicle**, 172 Union Steet, OLDHAM, OL1 1EQ; 061–633 2121

← The ABBREVIATIONS GUIDE is on Page 220 →

Programme Details

ROYAL EXCHANGE, St Ann's Square, M2 7DH; 061–833 9333. AZ: 101, F4; XAZ: 161, H5. H, W, + Braille & Large Print Programmes.

4. THE IMPORTANCE OF BEING EARNEST by Oscar Wilde; *16 December 1993 – 29 January 1994.* Lane/Merriman: *James Masters;* Algernon Moncrieff: *Samuel West;* John Worthing JP: *Neil Dudgeon;* Lady Bracknell: *Avril Elgar;* Hon Gwendolen Fairfax: *Zara Turner;* Cecily Cardew: *Melanie Ramsay;* Miss Prism: *Marcia Warren;* Rev Canon Chasuble DD: *John Branwell.* Director: *James Maxwell;* Designer: *Tom Rand;* Lighting: *Robert Bryan;* Sound: *Pete Goodwin;* Choreographer: *Nigel Nicholson;* Assistant Director: *Jacob Murray;* Stage Manager: *Laura Deards;* Deputy Stage Manager: *Adrian Pagan;* Assistant Stage Manager: *Jane Smailes;* Lighting Operator: *Andy Whipp;* Sound Operator: *Colin Renwick;* Deputy Head of Props and Settings: *Robert Kirkpatrick;* Set & Props: *Ged Mayo, Alan Fell, Samantha Hanks, Martin Mallorie, Imogen Peers, Jimmy Ragg, Susan Ross, Mathilde Sandberg, David Whetton;* Assistant Costume Supervisor: *Sophie Doncaster;* Men's Tailor and Cutter: *Robert Rainsford;* Cutters: *Debbie Attle, Marie Dunaway;* Costume Assistants: *Rose Calderbank, Jeanette Foster, Andrew Gilliver.*
Journal: 1/1/94 ← ←
Press: MEN: 16,17/12/93; OC: 17/12/93

ARTISTS INDEX; Section 4

PLAYS INDEX; Section 5

JOURNAL; Section 1

→ →1 JANUARY. THE IMPORTANCE OF BEING EARNEST; Royal Exchange. (4).←

This play has one of the best-known texts in the world. It has immense style but this can easily degenerate into hollow artifice and a production becoming a characterless procession of epigrams. The great triumph of **James Maxwell** and his cast at the **Royal Exchange** was for every line and the response to it to be fully motivated and to be uttered and received by completely developed characters who spoke as if every word was being coined afresh for the situation and had never been heard before.

COMPANIES INDEX

⇐ THIS tells you if there is a JOURNAL entry, & where to find

IT ⇒

JOURNAL entries are in CALENDAR ORDER

IF YOU WANT TO KNOW THE FULL YEAR'S WORK OF A PARTICULAR THEATRE ARTIST:

          a)   Sorry; you may not be able to: only the first **264** plays listed in Section 2 have been indexed in **Section 4**

          b)   For as much information as is available: i) Look up the name in **Section 4,** the Alphabetical Index of **Artists**

          ii)   This will give you the **Production Numbers** of plays in which the Artist was involved; these numbers in **Section 2** will give you the **Pages** upon which further details can be found.

IF Section 2 GIVES SEVERAL PAGES FOR A SINGLE PRODUCTION: Full Programme Details only appear on the Page given in **Bold** Print; the other pages show other places at which the production appeared.

IF YOU KNOW A PLAY TITLE BUT NOT WHERE IT WAS PERFORMED: Section 5 will give you the **Production Numbers,** from **Section 2,** where you can then learn the **Pages** giving further information.

IF YOU WANT TO KNOW ABOUT THE WORK OF A PARTICULAR COMPANY: Its **Address** and **Telephone Number,** where available, are given in **Section 6,** together with **Production Numbers** of all plays it has presented in Greater Manchester. From these you can learn the **pages** for further information, through **Section 2.**

IF YOU WANT TO KNOW ABOUT AWARDS WON THIS YEAR: See **Section 7**

GREATER MANCHESTER
BECOMES THE CITY OF DRAMA

A FOREWORD BY SIR ROBERT SCOTT

My very first visit to Manchester was in September 1967, driven by **Braham Murray** over the Snake Pass from Sheffield. It was a filthy night. He put me to stay in a dreadful hotel called the Carousel in Great Western Street, Rusholme. On that first foggy night, in damp sheets in a damp hotel in a damp city, I did not plan to be around in 27 hours' time, let alone 27 years.

As things turned out, I stayed on in Manchester a few weeks, working with **Braham Murray**'s **Century Theatre,** at the **University Theatre.** During those weeks, I also met **Michael Elliott** and **Casper Wrede** and, by the end of the year, the idea for a new professional theatre company, based in Manchester, was formed. It was to be called the **69 Theatre Company**, to demonstrate its links to the famous **59 Theatre Company** that had been based at the **Lyric Hammersmith** in 1959. I was to be the first Administrator.

The Company opened in September 1968, after a season at the Edinburgh Festival, with **Tom Courtenay** in **Hamlet** and **Wendy Hiller** in **Ibsen**'s last play, **When We Dead Awaken.** We were accused of drastically overpricing our tickets, with a top price of 17/6d. It has been calculated that in 1968 something like 4500 people per week used to go to the theatre in Manchester: – the **Palace** and **Opera House** were frequently dark and, of course, the **Royal Exchange** and all the other small theatres in the city, except the **Library**, were not even gleams in the eye. Today, over 40,000 people every week go to the city's theatres and it surprised no–one when **Manchester** was made **City of Drama 1994.**

9

1994 is not yet over but it is quite obvious that the **City of Drama** has been a great success, not least with the opening of the **Dance House**, the establishment of **Upper Campfield Market** and the quite fabulous range of visiting attractions. Many people still dream, and I am certainly one of them, of at least one new theatre: – a 1000–seat playhouse in the splendid **Theatre Royal, Bath** tradition. It is a gaping hole in our present set–up. Past experience would almost certainly suggest that there would be voices raised against it by people fearful that their own operations would be affected. Well do I remember the **Library** protests against the opening of the **Royal Exchange**. And only 10 years ago, nobody would have believed that the **Palace** and the **Opera House** could both be full together: now they are full to bursting.

Above all, we must not be satisfied with the present provision of theatres. If we are to be a true Theatre Capital of the 21st Century, we need lots more theatres. If every person living within an hour's drive of the middle of Manchester was to go to the theatre just once a year, we would need 22 more theatres the size of the **Palace**.

SIR ROBERT SCOTT
Chairman, Manchester 2002

28 October 1994

INTRODUCTION

Two years ago, after competition with other cities, **Greater Manchester** was nominated by the **Arts Council** as **City of Drama 1994**, as part of the **Arts 2000** initiative.

The **830** high quality productions detailed in this independent record are probably a greater number than could have been found in any comparable area of Great Britain. They include all those for which complete programmes could be obtained, and some information on a great many more, but the Compiler has fragmentary details on dozens of further performances which there was not time to include.

In addition, full cast details were obtained of over thirty **broadcast plays** produced in Manchester but which there was also not time to include. Some readers who sent in response cards to last year's record questioned their place in this volume, although others welcomed it. The Compiler very much regrets their omission, radio drama being a field of excellence which seems to be generally under-reported. It is one to which Manchester-produced works make a pre-eminent contribution and it would be good to see the work of the actors involved in the context of their live theatre work, recorded in this book, particularly as the **BBC** is participating formally in the **City of Drama** with it **City on Air** programme of locally written and produced plays this November

The book's most serious inadequacy in enabling the work of of actors to be seen in full is the failure to complete **Section 4,** the **Artists Index.** Only a third of the plays recorded have been covered in this index, essentially up to Number **264** but with a few of those prior to this in **Section 2** not being fully indexed, as futher details were

11

obtained at a later stage.

The Compiler would stress that **all other** indices and entries are as complete as the information obtained would permit but does recognise that the incompleteness of **Section 4** is a major shortcoming in this volume being able to provide the reader with a full picture of the work of those who create Theatre in Greater Manchester. This year the book contains almost twice as many entries as last and the publisher does not have the resources to do them justice. Given the choice between including as many productions as possible and seeing a lesser number fully indexed, the first option seemed preferable. At least the data is here and a reference library could complete the index if an assistant with a word processor was put onto it for a couple of weeks.

That the book should have to be produced by a publisher operating on a scale at which such choices have to be made is obviously not desirable but, given the outstanding nature of the theatrical achievements which this book attempts to record, it seems better to do it to the level which can be managed, rather than for the task not to be done at all. The Compiler has been much heartened by the almost universally enthusiastic responses, personal and written, which he has received to **A Year in the Theatre – Greater Manchester 1993**. If the Compiler had been able to give as much hustling time to seeking the resources for improvement of this record of a full year as many of the producers of Greater Manchester's countless small scale drama productions give to financing performances which last only a few days, more of the shortcomings known to the Compiler, as well as mentioned in review, would have been addressed. Simply compiling the yearbook had to take priority, however. The body of work recorded was impressive in performance and it is to be hoped that this volume does it some justice.

On some of the points which have been raised:

The Single-Author Journal: Essentially, this is still a case of No Alternative. The Compiler is delighted to have received the lively and well-informed additional entries donated by **Nigel E Higginson** and **Lynda Belshaw** and would have welcomed more. He is also outstandingly grateful for the Foreword contributed by **Sir Robert Scott,** whose administrative abilities and industry over the past quarter of a century have been at the heart of many of the strands of development which have brought Greater Manchester back to being the **City of Drama,** from the low point in its long and often distiguished theatrical history which it had reached by the mid-1960's.

Clearly the authorship of the Journal will have to be broadened if this volume is to cover adequately all that it seeks to record but it has been found valuable, and often highly praised, by many in its present form and among its several defenders I will quote the most general, from a vastly experienced reader: "Everyone who writes about the Theatre does so from a particular angle but, if you read enough of them, you learn how to make correction for their point of view."

"Larger Format – Fewer Pages Would Make More Manageable"; The increased number of entries has made the latter impossible and so the case for the former is probably reduced, and would have been tricky with the publisher's rudimentary resources. A more portable volume would clearly be useful to those who have discovered that it is good for "dipping into", which may help those who found the journal "less than diverse" when swallowed whole, but comprehensiveness is probably the more important criterion.

"More Eye-Catching Front Cover": The reader may judge.

Sheila Waddington is to be credited with making such striking use of the fine photograph's made available.

"Some Productions/Names Missing":   Still true and admitted, but less true than it was.   The main point to be noted from these cards was that there is a readership which does want all the detail in **Sections** 3 to 6, and more, which some have doubted.   Some readers clearly mainly value the Journal, some mainly the reference material.   The publisher will try to keep the price where those who only want half the book still get their money's worth.

"The Year": The 1993 volume, being sent to the printers at the end of October effectively petered out in the middle of that month and, therefore, began at the same time in 1992, so that readers got a full twelve–months' worth.   This volume, consequently, begins where the other left off but, although still going to press on 1 November, does make an effort to record details of productions to be expected up to the end of the year, to coincide with **City of Drama 1994.**

Mid–October to mid–October makes little sense in terms of Theatre seasons or calendar years.   Readers' opinions were requested on possible adaptations last year and almost every option was spoken for with comparable strength.   The Compiler has decided, however, that the Theatre Year is the most appropriate.   **A Year in the Theatre – Greater Manchester 1994–95 (ISBN 0 9521502 2 0)** should, therefore appear next autumn, covering, sometimes in greater detail, some productions already in this volume, – as much as may be had from 1 September 1994 to 31 August 1995.

Any reader who can do anything to ensure that any programmes for inclusion are sent to **Broadfield Publishing, FREEPOST (MR 9209), MANCHESTER M14 7DJ** will be making a most helpful contribution to the Yearbook.

"The Index." In fact most readers who sent in response cards indicated that they found the Book's Organisation "Clear", and so did some published reviews. Some others and a number of personal comments have been strongly to the contrary. Like the scurvy politician I have had to rely on an attempt at "better presentation" rather than a radical change in the system. I hope **How The System Works** and the page headings in the indices will help. The key point is that **"Indexing is by the PRODUCTION NUMBERS in SECTION 2."**

If this response to comments seems to be less than complete compliance, please do not let that discourage any reader from sending in the FREEPOST Response Card. The publisher will be endeavouring to gain the resources to raise the standard of this publication to the level its readers request. Their interest is one more item of evidence that the quality of Theatre in Greater Manchester is worthy of record.

The most public testimony to that quality is its designation as **City of Drama.** While reflecting that in the title of this year's volume, it should be noted that this book does not seek to record all the activities of City of Drama Ltd, let alone to assess them. This most industrious body has done much besides promote and publicise theatrical performances. It has stimulated the opening of new venues. It has mounted exhibitions, as on our theatre's heritage and stagecraft. There have been debates and discussions with world-famous practitioners, from many cultures. The team's brochures have also included concerts, opera and ballet. This book has made no attempt to include any record of these.

What it has tried to do is include every theatrical performance which did not clearly belong to some other category, in our most gilded palaces or most faded pubs, our urban streets or the grassy by-ways, of which the entirety of Greater Manchester includes so many. This record is not complete but it should be impressive testimony to why Greater Manchester is the **City of Drama.**

Some may think that, rather than being incomplete, a record of 830 productions includes too many, assuming much of this must be "just school and church hall stuff." Not only the Compiler's judgement but the awards they won would place among the most notable productions of the year both **The Glass Menagerie** by **St Clement's Rochdale** (39, 647, Journal 15 January) and **Roaring Boys** (123, Journal 22 July), commissioned by **Sandbach School** from **Phelim Rowland,** the only original play to be performed among the six best British Youth Theatres at the **National Theatre** in July, before being seen by us at the **Green Room** on its way to Edinburgh. Doubtless, there are some productions in Greater Manchester which might be thought unworthy of record but simply to exclude "church and school" would not be an accurate way of identifying them.

This is true even of the very youngest, as could be witnessed at the **Royal Exchange** on 20 March, at the climax of the **Manchester Schools/City of Drama Shakespeare Project (476).** There Primary School children from **Poundswick** and **Medlock** gave riveting performances of scenes from **The Winter's Tale,** showing how successfully they had been helped to find the possibly all too familiar truth of parents arguing vehemently about each other's loyalty and paternity in the presence of their child and to express it vividly in the words of an old and traditionally "difficult" play. As a tribute to skill as well as insight, it is also right to recall that the 14-year-old actress from the **North Manchester High School for Girls** who gave an electrifying performance as Capulet brow-beating his teenage daughter had not been rehearsing the part for

16

months: she played Juliet in the full production but had to switch rôles at short notice for the Sunday night extract.

These are a few brief examples of the qualities to be found throughout the length and breadth of the **City of Drama.** It is hoped that those whose work is recorded here will find it accurate, that those who saw them will find it a pleasing reminder and that both will find it impressive to see the full context in which these productions took place. May those who missed productions not only find here some idea of what transpired but be inspired to see more in future. Greater Manchester has not ceased to be the **City of Drama** simply because the year in which it has been asked to display its talent to the nation is at an end. It's infinite range of fascinating Theatre remains.

The Compiler is most grateful to those who have assisted in the supply of information and photographs. He trusts that those who did so and the book's readers will feel that these have been put to good use. Certainly the Theatre-makers of Greater Manchester have provided him and hundreds of thousands of other theatregoers with many hours of pleasure throughout the year and he hopes that this book shows something of how they have made Greater Manchester **The City of Drama.**

G A HAWORTH
Compiler

29 October 1994

17

Section 1

JOURNAL

1. JOURNAL

A ROARING START TO THE NEW YEAR: KARL SETH as Mogli and MEL TAYLOR as Baloo in NEIL DUFFIELD's skilful adaptation of THE JUNGLE BOOK at the WYTHENSHAWE FORUM.

1993

30 DECEMBER. **THE JUNGLE BOOK;** Forum. (8).

This got off to a splendidly dramatic start, with shouts around the suddenly darkened stage of "Tiger! Tiger! Hide the cubs!" and great deal of scurrying too and frow as it was shown how the baby Mowgli escaped Shere Khan and was adopted by the wolves. The strength of the tale was maintained not only with the power of **Kipling**'s language, retained in **Neil Duffield**'s skilful conflation of many of the original stories but by the lively and characterful performances: an exceptionally well-moving and cat-like Bagheera, a buffoon-like Buldeo, but one well able to make the most of his opportunities for story-telling, – **The Elephant's Child** being assimilated into the narrative to illustrate his artificial knowledge of the jungle, compared with the first-hand experience of **Karl Seth**'s personable and ever-learning Mowgli.

The original stories are interspersed with fine verses and **The Law of The Jungle** and **The Song of the Little Hunter** are effectively included here as songs. **Neil Duffield** has also ended with

21

a song, **Those Who Hunt Alone**, which sounds very Kipling-like, even though, at the end of **Tiger! Tiger!**, Kipling immediately follows Mowgli's declaration, which introduces the song here, "Man-Pack and Wolf-Pack have cast me out. Now I will hunt alone in the Jungle" by stressing "But he was not always alone" first of all hunting with the four wolf cubs with whom he had grown up and later having a family. One might have thought that **Neil Duffield**'s sympathies would be more with the earlier-cited Jungle Law, "The Strength of the Wolf is The Pack", but nevertheless this quiet, forceful song of the three loners, Baloo, Bagheera and, now, Mowgli, rather than a big production number after the great fight with Shere Khan, makes a dramatically effective ending.

1994

1 JANUARY. THE IMPORTANCE OF BEING EARNEST; Royal Exchange. (4).

This play has one of the best-known texts in the world. It has immense style but this can easily degenerate into hollow artifice and a production becoming a characterless procession of epigrams. The great triumph of **James Maxwell** and his cast at the **Royal Exchange** was for every line and the response to it to be fully motivated and to be uttered and

received by completely developed characters, who spoke as if every word was being coined afresh for the situation and had never been heard before.

The freshness did not seem to come from eliciting any particular theme in the work. The **National Theatre** production which came to Manchester in 1982 somehow did make clear why Wilde called it "A Trivial Comedy for Serious People". The word-count for "serious" in the text must be enormous and the attitude very strongly emerged that to concentrate on what the world deems serious can be deadening whereas to treat such matters as food and neckties with all seriousness can be life-enhancing. Wilde did, indeed, say in a letter with regard to this theme in the play "It has its philosophy". I noticed, with less profit, just how many German Philosophers are named in the script while being less than gripped by the flatter patches of the **Yvonne Arnaud Theatre** performance, whose incursion at the **Opera House** in 1991 led the **Royal Exchange** to postpone the production which is now so happily with us.

Although not apparently tied together by emphasising any such theme, this **Earnest** was greatly strengthened by evoking a coherent world in which its events took place. Within this, Jack and Algy could communicate much with glances during Lady Bracknell's prolonged "Wagnerian" ringing of the doorbell, **Neil Dudgeon** could glow with triumph from the beginning of her interrogation about Cecily, confident that he now held all the aces and that his opponent did not yet know this, Miss Prism's entry could suddenly turn into an attempted exit, upon her abruptly becoming aware that her Past was unexpectedly standing in front of her. Everything taking place so naturally allowed, for instance, some women in the audience to perceive enduringly accurate statements being made about their position in marriage and society but above all it gave a clear run to a fresh and very funny comedy.

13 JANUARY. THE THREE LIVES OF LUCIE CABROL; Dancehouse. (35).

After winding one's way up the crowded, freshly-painted stairways of the **Dancehouse**, noting how much more spruce it was than in its last dingy days as a multi-screen cinema, as which it closed three years ago, it was a little surprising to enter the auditorium and to see the bright orange of row upon row of cheap plastic seating. This seemed something less than the restoration of Art Deco elegance of which one had heard on the news. Looking towards the open stage, its scruffy and muddy appearance suggested that, at best, the **Dancehouse** had joined the, often distinguished, company of our theatres, such as the **Green Room**, whose builders have not quite managed to meet the agreed opening date.

These first impressions were in some measure misleading. The seating was indeed a stopgap provision and is to be replaced within the next three months. The scruffy appearance of the stage, however, had nothing to do with incomplete construction. Its covering of loose peat and its sparse wings represented the thin mountain soils below the Alpages. This was where the French peasant community of which the play built up such a detailed portrait scratched their living.

During the first few minutes of the performances I was as uncertain of the play's potential as I had been, at first glance, of that of the theatre in which it took place. The stylised parading round and introduction of the characters made me fear that we were to be presented with a production primarily concerned with form. The last **Theatre de Complicite** production which I had seen, **The Street of Crocodiles**, had contained much splendid material but it had set itself the daunting challenge of presenting the stories of **Bruno Schultz** in the context of their being the chronicle of a death foretold in the gas chambers. A work broaching such a subject must achieve an appropriate stature, worthy of those thus slain, and I did not feel that this was then quite achieved. On this occasion, however, the realities of peasant life, with its harshness, its humour and its jealousies, began vividly to appear before us. The plough horse snorted and the furrows rolled aside, showing that the actors determination to play the land and animals as well as the humans, alive and dead, was not just going to be stylised representations but the channel by which we were drawn in to mountain life.

Lilo Baur's Lucie was a vivid creation and one could well see why she proved so hypnotic, as well as daunting, to the narrator, Jean. One could also see why, with her occasional propensity for throwing the precious content of milk churns over her selfish brothers or burning their barns, they had some grounds to seek legal grounds to end her "first life" by finding quasi-legal means to exclude her from her share of the family land. The predominant motives one could see, however, were prejudice against a woman, particularly one so stunted, even recalling her soon-disappearing birthmark and, especially their reluctance to divide such a niggardly source of livelihood between more mouths in any circumstances, – they set themselves against sheltering retreating *maquisards* as instictively as Lucie welcomed and cared for them.

We only heard of her "second life", her independent existence as a smuggler, carrying mountain produce across the border to the markets on the far side in the terms in which she narrated it to Jean after his return from South America, with no more to show for his travels than enough to eke out a very humble existence until his dying day. What he does have, however, is the right to live in the village and this Lucie envies, despite the two million francs she claims to have amassed in her cottage outside. Jean shrinks from her proposal to resolve this by the same means

that she had sought to use him to secure her position fifty years before:– marriage. He shrinks from her twisted age and from the prospect of sharing his life with such a vigorous and demanding companion, just when he had got used to his own loneliness but, never-the-less, finds that she dominates his mind. This does not cease when the question of marriage is abruptly closed by the discovery of her blood-stained corpse, presumably the victim of someone seeking her alleged fortune. Her "third life" begins, her spirit drawing him, probably fatally, out along the craggy mountain tracks she had come to know so well.

Vivid though this performance needed to be, it had its power in the context of the peopling of a whole community and their livelihoods, the whole cast portraying all generations, distinctive individuals and groups of a clear character. There was much humour and much pain but, above all, the totality of a way of life.

15 JANUARY. THE GLASS MENAGERIE; Playhouse 2. (39).

Overall this became a most moving production of a notable play. I did wonder if the highly able cast were having to work a bit consciously at their accents, if there would have been ways in which to make the action a little more continuous, – even though each scene break seemed to arise from the script –, and if Laura's physical and social incapacity needed to be presented as so extreme. Of the former, **Tennessee Williams** says in the script "this defect need not be more than suggested on the stage" as though Jim's description of it as "hardly noticable" might be entirely accurate. **Joanne Devlin**, however, gave a wonderfully sustained portrayal of someone who could scarcely put any weight at all on one leg and who had devised a whole series of manouvres to avoid doing so when sitting down, stepping from a height or going through other necessary daily manouvres. The intensity of her nervousness throughout could perhaps be justified by **Williams'** description that her "separation increases till she is like a piece of her own glass collection, too exquisitely fragile to move from the shelf," although the trajectory in this performance seemed to be almost the reverse: having begun greatly incapacitated, she so recovered in her conversation with Jim that it almost seemed as if Prince Charming was to awake Sleeping Beauty, with the result that, when it was finally revealed that he was "punching two clocks" already, this news was as emotionally devastating for the audience as for her.

Williams' 1945 play seems to have been very much a trail-blazer for many dramatic skills and concerns which have become more commonplace since. One example is his allowing such symbolism as Laura's likeness to her glass menagerie not merely to be part of his conscious intentions but to be made an overt element of the dialogue, as in Tom's prologue to Scene One: "Being a memory play, it is dimly lighted, it is sentimental, it is not realistic. In memory everything seems to happen to music. That explains the fiddle in the wings. I am the narrator of the play, and also a character in it ... Since I have a weakness for symbols, I am using this character [Jim's] also as a symbol."

One way in which this production also made me see the play as prophetic was in Tom's great outburst when his mother rejects his probably completely truthful reply that the reason he is out most nights is that he's going to the movies: "I'm going to opium dens! Yes, opium dens, dens of vice and criminals' hang outs, Mother. I've joined the Hogan gang, I'm a hired assassin, I carry a tommy-gun in a violin case! I run a string of cat-houses in the Valley! They call me Killer, Killer Wingfield. I'm leading a double-life, a simple honest warehouse worker by day, by night a dynamic tsar of the underworld ..." Thus also spake **Billy Liar.**

Reminiscent of Billy as well was Tom's decision to spend money which should have been used for the light bill on a membership card for the Union of Merchant Seamen, with the result that the electricity is cut off during the all important visit of the Gentleman Caller. Living seven hundred miles from the sea, such a purchase might seem to be the pure stuff of dreams. Although Tom and Billy's mental state can been seen now as having common roots, chief among these being films and family, there are important differences. Whereas

Billy failed in his escape and could not catch a train from a station half-a-mile down the road, Tom did catch his far more distant boat. Also, where Billy was probably not aware of any other sentiment towards his mother than hate, **Ean Burgeon** in his portrayal of Tom showed a man who, though often infuriated beyond endurance, did love his mother deeply, apologised to her sincerely, though with difficulty, for his outburst and often struggled to keep himself in check and to behave as she expected him to.

Sybil Murray as the mother was often most impressive, notably in Act II when, after countless years without the opportunity to make the polite conversation at which she had diligently perfected her skills in youth, she unleashed an unstoppable deluge of it over Jim O'Connor. Even without dialogue she conveyed a great deal. From her entrance in Scene Two we knew that she had had a shattering experience, despite her determination to retain her composure in the street and before we discovered from her actions and words that she had learnt that Laura was not, in fact, attending Secretarial College.

David Lee, with his full characterisation of Jim O'Connor, enabled us to see how skilfully and perceptively the part is written. With his unfailingly polite prattle, showing his genuine belief in the social progress achievable through science and self-confidence, a character which many would doubtless have regarded as the social bedrock of

his civilisation was captured in such a way that one could feel that, despite his caring attitudes, if this was "a nice, ordinary, young man", good luck to him but thank goodness there were also desperate, muddled poets such as Tom, to prevent such blandness being cloned to infinity.

24-25 JANUARY.
ANGELS IN AMERICA;
Contact. (32).

I know nothing about **Tony Kushner**, the author of **Angels in America**. I am tempted to suppose, however, that the characters in these plays with which he identifies most are Louis and Belize, perhaps fearing that he could in some measure be like the former and wishing to be like the latter. Certainly it is in the, very one-sided, conversation between the two of them that the title phrase comes up, as Louis empties a veritable spittoonful of solecisms over the patient Belize, agonising over the nature of his country. "There are no angels in America," he claims, having found that in Holland "everyone is sort of, well, Dutch" and in London he stood out as "Sid the Yid", with a black he spoke to there, whose family had been in England "since before the Civil War, – the American one," still being regarded as an outsider. To Louis' perception, "In America, the problem isn't racism", provoking **Joseph Mydell's** Belize to raise his eyes to Heaven, interrupting his steadfast contemplation of his coffee mug.

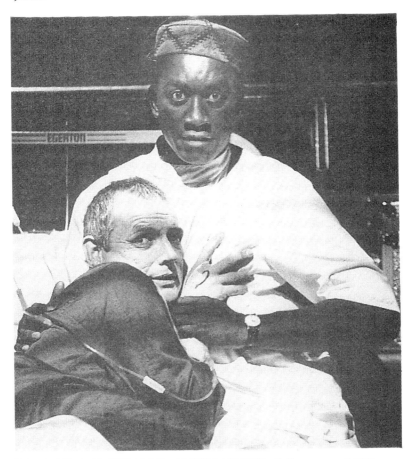

THE ANGEL AND THE DEVIL: JOSEPH MYDELL's Belize nurses DAVID SCHOFIELD's Roy Cohn through the final stages of his death from AIDS

Louis, however, needs to find what the uniting principle of his country is, since it seems to lie neither in race nor obvious culture. Both parts of the play begin with those of an older generation who look back to uniting principles: the Rabbi, burying Louis' mother at the beginning of **Part 1**, who is disconcerted to find a relative named Eric among the next-of-kin and who sets aside his standard tribute to someone he barely knew to expound 'of course I knew her, for all our generation are the same', united in the common culture of those who crossed the Atlantic from Central and Eastern Europe, and Aleksii Antedilluvianovich Prelapsarianov, the Oldest Living Bolshevik, opening **Part 2** by addressing a Gorbachev-era Praesidium: "of course there must be change, but where is the Theory to inspire your Praxis?"

Belize is nearer to **Countée Cullen**'s "America never was America for me" than **Langston Hughes**' "I, too, am America." Although finding ways to live a highly positive, loving and caring existence there, he hates the place. He rejects the need either to return to old cultures or to discover a new scheme of existence. However, the central fascination of the play with the Mormon tradition of a comparatively recent American prophet, Joseph Smith, being visited by an angel very close to New York, showing him a new revelation in a book of metal plates, presents this as an idea which the writer wants to take further. Rather than the play's specifically Mormon characters the character visited by an angel in these Latter Days is the one with the potentially longest cultural tradition, Louis' lover Prior Walter, whose family goes back to the Mayflower and the Norman Conquest. This is not a tradition upon which he specifically draws. It puts him outside Louis' Jewish culture, which helps him enjoy watching him verbally writhing in prolonged guilt over any incident, great our small, and he is agonised by the purely contemporary context of the fact that, of the tens of thousands dieing of AIDS in New York, he sees himself as the only one not to be cared for by his lover, when Louis runs out on him. The first of the visions from his sick bed in which he sees clearly-non-contemporary figures are of his Medieval and Restoration ancestors but their

main contribution to understanding are to interpret his condition in the light of the widespread ravages of the Black Death and Pox of their own days.

Prior does cite the terminal delirium of AIDS as part of its well-known trajectory and whether the fact that the Angel who eventually summons him to be a prophet is played by the same actress as his nurse is meant to suggest that the revelation was occasioned by his weakened condition causing him to confound one white-robed figure in attendance on him with another, I would not know. The nurse did once seem to utter a brief line in her "angel" voice, to which Prior seemed to respond with a minor double-take and there was the question of how much there might be significance in far less immediately recognisable doubling on parts: when Louis flees from beside Prior's bed in the hospital the rough whom he desperately picks up in the park is played by the same actor as the lover he has just deserted; when the young Mormon wife first runs from her husband, the Eskimo she throws herself upon in what she believes to be Antarctica is also played by him. The married couple's conventional greeting had been to rub noses and their unsuccessful marriage could certainly be called cold.

As the plays are subtitled "A Gay Fantasia on National Themes" there may not be too much point in trying to rationalise the fantasies. However, as the concern for National Themes would appear to be serious, it is probably proper to be ready to perceive a rationale in the method as well as the matter. We shall see what the pursuit of the Mormon "revelation" theme may yield in the third play, as the young wife ends in this one flying to Los Angeles, in a real aircraft, it would appear, rather than her previous flights of fantasy. Meanwhile it is left to Belize to represent the respect which **Kushner** clearly feels for whoever had the spirit to stitch a panel for Roy M Cohn in the AIDS Memorial Quilt, reading "Coward/Bully/Victim". He calls in Louis, both as a Jew who, he hopes, can sing the Prayer for the Dead over Cohn's corpse and as one who can smuggle out the enormous stocks of the almost unobtainable remission-granting AZT which Cohn's prized "clout" had enabled him to amass and for which Belize knows hundreds who could put it to good use. The play ends, five-and-a-half years later, with this white-robed figure, with his colourful woolly additions to his uniform, sitting before the merely metallic angel outside Bethesa Naval Hospital in a family group with Prior, still alive and reconciled with Louis, and the much-rejuvenated Mormon mother-in-law, who found getting Prior back to hospital a more worthwhile activity than trying to reconcile her son and daughter-in-law. Whatever revelation from the metal tablets may be brought in the final section of the trilogy, clearly the sort of angel who can make the health-giving waters flow once more from the dried-up fountains of America, and elsewhere, is Belize.

28 JANUARY. LES PIEDS DANS L'EAU; Royal Northern College of Music; (34).

The sun goes up and the sun goes down. In this far from elegant suburb the dawn chorus is entirely canine and the audience was much amused by the rendition of this by the as-yet-unseen cast, which we were eventually priviledged to see performed as an encore during the many curtain calls required by the prolonged applause at the end.

The first really load burst of laughter came, however, after one member of the community began her day by unloading an enormous number of wine bottles from one of the cupboards which we came to assimilate represented the dwellings of the citizens and, after she had gone, the somewhat smashed resident lurched out, even though the audience could scarcely believe that there could have been space for anything other than his formidable accumulation of glass-ware. As he settled down to replenish his liquid intake by imbibing from the reserve tank on his roof via hose-pipe, we could observe on the other side of the stage that the local recycling project was an advance on that that usually associated with Cana-in-Galilee: it turned bottles into wine. It was run not only on self-help but help-yourself principles. When the principal toper had both drained his vat and several more bottles he was able to lurch over to the engine, crank it up and, when satisfied with the quality, refill his storage tank.

This was the only evidence of quasi-economic activity. The usual operator of the machinery, with his **Buster-Keaton**-like poker face, was in fact one of the most enjoyable of the mime-artists who made up the cast. Regretably he had the smallest part, being consumed, imperturbably, half way through by his own equipment.

One might presume that many of the rest were commuters who engaged in economic activity elsewhere but what we saw was their home life and their helpful or irritating interaction with their neighbours. In many ways this was **Hulot**ville, as seen in **Mon Oncle, Jerome Deschamps**, the author, being distantly related to **Jacques Tati**. The social evolution which has taken place over the years, however, means that it is not just the richer relatives who have moved into posher housing who aspire to have unnecessary electronic gadgetry, for example, to open doors. Here, however, it is installed by Do-It-Yourself.

The play has many splendid sequences, as when the foremost home-improver, having determined, with not-entirely-reliable neighbourly help, that his garden wall is three metres long, goes into a wonderfully-sustained lengthy pencil-and-paper calculation, trying to work our what intervals he requires if he is to place five equally-spaced flower-pots upon it. This eventually proving beyond him, his

neighbour completes the task perfectly well by eye. The effect does not endure for long, however, as, inspired by his participation in a communal Wild West pageant, the neighbouring toper uses them as targets in some remarkably accurate six-gun practice.

I felt that there were one or two rather noticable gaps between some of the splendid episodes but, although I felt that the minimal dialogue was making no impossible demands upon my exiguous French, Francophone members of the audience were hooting with laughter at the conversationin such scenes as a neighbourly tea-party which seemed to me to be rather repetitiously spinning out gossip that I thought said nothing more than "He said 'Blah-Blah-Blah'", in just those terms. This was soon followed, however, by one of the most hilarious sequences, in which the DIY expert, having disasterously bitten into an unyielding biscuit, turned to and successfully undertook reconstructive dentistry upon himself, using his household drills, plastic wood and electric sanding equipment, sparks flying in all directions, from which he then emerged to champ his renovated jaw with great satisfaction.

It was a highly talented and most enjoyable evening, presenting not only splendid individual characters but creating the communal atmosphere in which they lived.

1 FEBRUARY.
PEACOCK; Green Room.
(36).

It was not until the entrance of the peacock itself, well into the play, - its head made from an inverted oil-can with the spout as its beak, surmounted by dart flights as its plume, bent teaspoons for its claws and its tail mounted on an umbrella frame -, that I was reminded of **Doo Cot's** traditional core skill of making the most fascinating puppets out of discarded fragments from other artefacts. The only reason I had come to forget this fundamental feature of my few previous opportunities to see the company's work was because up to then in this performance they had most successfully diversified into other skills.

The play began with two most characterful large hand-puppets, representing the two lovers whose story was the core of the production. After that, the tale was developed through shadow play on screens, several appearing on the detailed outline farm-house where one character lived, and where the peacock was his most prized possession, others being undisguisedly large, plain white screens, of Indonesian style, sometimes in the centre of the stage, sometimes roled to the side.

In **Doo Cot's** distinctive scrap puppetry, however, they have created such a splendid heritage of style and artistry that it gives a specifial charge to scenes when it is deployed. The next two outstanding examples were the jagged tin can, serrated to form the awful jaws of the vicious dog who eventually wreaks such terrible havoc upon the farmer's livestock, and the splendid motorbike upon which his new lover takes him on a ride to the coast.

Two further skills were prominent in creating the atmosphere of this ride: the live music, of which extensive and imaginative use was made throughout the performance, and the painted design created on a moving transparent screen as the journey took place, first evoking the beauty of the trees and hedgerows, broken by a burst of rapid overlying circles as the music speeded up and the motorcyclist did a ton.

Overall it was a highly skilful, varied and moving production. I thought the first half of the second act relied a little too unrelievedly on music and songs, with not much going on for quite some time by way of puppetry or development of the story. It did not matter, however, that the latter had little detail. Although its main features were of considerable and moving importance, as much effort was put into creating, largely through the screen images and associated sounds, the contrasting social atmospheres in which the characters lived: the mechanical roar of the impersonal city and the caring atmosphere amongst the creatures of the farm, where, however, destructive forces were not too far away.

2 FEBRUARY. TOP GIRLS; Green Room. (37).

This was a splendid production of a splendid play. It makes a lot of demands on the cast, most of whom have to play several contrasting rôles and who have to be comprehensible even when, as in the first scene, there are several separate conversations going on at once or in the blinding row between Marlene and Joyce which takes up most of the last act and in which neither feels the need to wait for the other to finish speaking before piling in with her own concerns. Much of the dialogue brilliantly captures the economic ethic of the eighties and shows its terrible consequences, whilst making full characters both out of its spokespersons and of its victims, in many ways the same people. The cast were entirely effective in presenting a wide range of powerful portraits and the play is a most perceptive and skilful picture of its times.

7 FEBRUARY. RACING DEMON; Library. (44).

After a bold opening, with the principal cleric upon his knees, railing at the eternal silence of an absent God, the first couple of scenes seemed to me to be not very profoundly satirical: a bishop casting his criticisms of a socially-conscious but God-uncertain vicar in terms of "You're not playing by the rules of the club" and extolling the "wonderful cooking" of his wife, which we later apprehend that he usually prefers to forsake for the Grill Room at the Savoy, in terms of "However much we may enjoy roast lamb, the real joy is to know that tomorrow it will be followed by meat-and-potatoe cakes." Not desperately sharp it seemed and a job which might be best done by an insider.

According to **City Life**, however, **David Hare** is as much an insider as might be necessary, "a lapsed High Anglican," and within a comparatively short space of time we are into a gripping drama with genuine insights. During the first meeting of the Brixton team ministry where the play is focussed, we not only have highly plausible glimpses of caring people doing their best amidst incursions of leaflets and paper work but are able to see that the apparently waffly vicar does have a perfectly clear grasp of principles and social realities: people turning to them during occasions of personal distress is not to be used as an opportunity to ram Christ down their throats, remaining available to them may be of some slow but genuine help but the restrictive procedures of the Social Services limit what can be done; that it is better to accept the reality of such limitations than to betray confidences and very possibly make things worse for clients, for example from potentially violent husbands, by aspiring to a more vigorous approach. **Richard Mayes'** Bishop we learn later, in a scene of passionate rage, is inspired by far more profound, if twisted, concerns than "playing by the rules of the club."

The play seemed to me to falter

again towards its end, with an excess of scenes taking various characters' concerns just a little bit further without much accumulated benefit. Their stories could be extended to infinity but as it is a play and not a drama series they could have been terminated a little earlier. If more plot was wanted it might have been more interesting if the Sunday papers had turned their attention from Gay Vicar to Randy Curate. This, in effect if not subject matter, might smack something of the Miss Prism School of Fiction but not entirely as it would probably have had to cause some embarrassment to Frances, the well-balanced pagan saint who is presented as performing straightforwardly the human ministry which the clergy are striving for but in which they often seem inhibited by their theology. Allowing the pried-upon Revd Henderson to outface the intrusions of the press, with straight talking and loyal friends, as he at first seems likely to, would probably both be less conventional fiction and as instructive a presentation of reality.

The other snag is that the purblind evangelical curate, very well played by **Stephen Mapes**, becomes as narrow in character as such people often do. It is, therefore, not very interesting to have him on stage as repeatedly as he is. **Trollope** found ways to solve this problem but I do not think **Hare** has.

He does, however, present a lot of splendid acting opportunities which are impressively taken by this vigorous cast, who present diverse characters we can genuinely care about, bringing to life the problems with which they battle. Several actors also surmount the probably significant technical problems of having formidably long speeches which they none the less find ways to make plausible and gripping, breaking them up into clearly motivated units, assisted by the re-actions of those who are present as they hold forth: **Kathryn Hunt** flinching at the hurtful callowness of the curate's laboured attempts to justify their relationship to himself; **Malcolm Raeburn** as the Suffragan, turning aside as his superior, oblivious of his presence, fulminates that he cannot be held responsible for the actions of his subordinates.

There is interesting social analysis of the church, the poorest parishes in London being staffed by clergy from the most eminent Public Schools and having trained at Cambridge, that these connections can be of some use in grappling with difficulties from the hierarchy and that these difficulties are most likely to arise if some of the most regular churchgoers in a poor parish are the Tory MPs and junior ministers, who inhabit an atypical little mews and dislike regular sermons on such topics as the morality of VAT on fuel. I do not know the accuracy of this but it is made plausible and the play certainly succeeds in drawing upon a wide variety of profound concerns and turning them into gripping and thought-provoking drama.

8 FEBRUARY.
GROUNDED; Bury Met.
(129).

One would not think, seeing this dramatically effective one-act play, that it was the product of writing by numbers. Doubtless it is not, although one might imagine that one was about to see an overtly instructional drama if one only saw the very thorough and substantial accompanying Teachers Manual, very well produced by **Dorothy Wood**, in which each of the play's 23 short scenes is cross-referenced to paragraphs in the Personal and Social Education Syllabus, with headings for discussion and back-up documents. **Eileen Murphy** has most skilfully written a fully effective piece of theatre, as always presented with the highest acting and production quality by **M6**, which incorporates a wide range of information and considerations without ever allowing these to become a pedagogic burden.

The theme of the drama is teenage pregnancy and the tale is told of how this comes about for Joanne (**Alison Darling**) at more or less the minimum age. One telling dimension is showing how the supposedly "adult" involvement of becoming "sexually active" takes place in someone still young enough for her other preferred evening activity to be dashing around a play area with other children, squirting each other with water from containers for washing-up liquid. The play's title comes from her parents' first horrified response to discovering what she has been getting up to,

which is to try and keep her confined to the house. This proves to be as painful for them as for her, as she mopes at being separated from her friends outside. The play's main steer towards a more practical response is that the girl will have to "decide for herself."

It affects to being even-handed in setting out the considerations which might lead a young girl to decide between "waiting" or "using something." It is perfectly sensible that the case for restraint is not balanced by as strong a consideration of the notional alternative option of a young person passing without intermission from the natural embrace of a parent to that of a co-eval lover. Whether such a departure from implied impartiality would be noticable or be thought suspect by the intended audiences of young adults is to be doubted. The members of the Bury Youth Theatre, who made up much of the audience on this occasion, seemed to think that most of the options worthy of consideration had been raised and joined readily in the discussion and workshop afterwards.

In this, suggested alternative courses of action were played out by the cast, who also answered questions directly "in character." As, naturally enough, the girl and her boyfriend were not the most articulate of people, this element produced more in the way of expressing attitude than the fruits of the introspection which doubtless the actors as actors could have supplied in response to questions in the form of "What did you feel when .... ?" The

34

responses given, however, were doubtless valuable enough in encouraging the young audience to discuss matters further in their own contexts, rather than in the more formal "class" consideration provided for in the Teachers Manual.

Certainly these less rehearsed elements were further evidence of the impressive skills of the actors, from **M6** veteran **Maggie Tagney** as Mum to **Chris Cooke**, only recently graduated from the **Manchester Metropolitan School of Theatre** as the boyfriend. **Katherine Hart** had the challenging task of taking all the minor parts, from other young teenage friends to adult pregnancy counsellors and medical staff, as well as leading the ensuing discussion and workshop.

All these were helped to give of their best by a script which not only provided natural and interesting dialogue and good scenes but plenty of sketched in background. The father (**Michael Atkinson**) is absorbed with plans to expand his shop, the mother has her driving test coming up. None of these other concerns suggest an improper neglect of their young daughter, with whom they are not only intelligently concerned but, overall, have good and close relations. She has to take her place, however, amongst their wide range of concerns.

It might have been of interest to have presented Joanne as having enthusiasms, besides Adam, the boyfriend, other than unstructured dashing about and shopping. The emotion that can lead to pregnancy can flourish otherwise than where there is "nothing else to do."

Nevertheless, what was presented was done vividly, as in the scenes in which the boyfriend has been allowed into the house and the probably not desperately communicative nature of their company is rendered even more stilted by the knowledge that, whether they are noisy or quiet, mum and dad will be suspicious of what they are up to. This is particularly evidenced by dad appearing at the door every few minutes, putatively to ask if they want a brew or to watch the television programme which is just beginning. Such scenes were performed with an involving blend of realism and humour.

I always think that the main "educational" benefit of **M6**'s work is the artistic experience of their bringing first class acting and plays, on whatever topic, directly to where young people are. This one also handled its chosen topic most evocatively, not least through being a very fine drama.

9 FEBRUARY. MY MAD GRANDAD; Coliseum. (53).

This play has two splendid parts: Gil, the narrator, – the small lad splendidly played by **Graham Gill** who leads us through the various anecdotes –, and Grandad (**Gordon Wharmby**) himself. The rest seems rather underwritten. If there had been more to Mum, **Sherry Ormerod** would definitely have found it. She has wonderful moments, notably the silent performance of her rage when she hears that Grandad has come back from the Home in which it was thought he was being safely kept and that the shock has killed her mum. We do not hear most of this because Grandad has warned Gil to put his fingers in his ears.

Grandad has the splendid policy, vigorously pursued: "If you see a pudden, eat it." We get a lot of fun out of this but rather less out of **Mike Stott**'s apparent principle "If you want to write a pudden, give if a speech impediment." Proprieties aside, it gets a bit monotonous. With simple Sammy, lured by the prospect of buying a "giant bantam" and then persuaded to throw all his money out of his pockets to avoid attracting the lightning during a thunder storm, it just about passes muster. Principally to characterise the much more extensive rôle of the doctor, by a one-step-forwards-two-steps-back mode of speech, – "I think, ... Do I? ... Yes! ... I do!..." – seemed to condemn **David Ericsson** to eternally dropping bricks without straw.

I strongly suspect that many incidents were entirely authentic, as of Grandad's "compulsory compassionate leave" shortly after joining up in the First World War, in order to be taken back to Rochdale as party to a wedding at which both witnesses were military police. I feel too much reliance may have been placed on the author's knowledge of the truth of his material, when more needed to be done structurally to give it appropriate dramatic impact. Some of the serious First World War recollections, however, did provide a useful strengthening element to the piece, as of coming across a sackful of ears, –"some feller must have been collecting them"–, or background on why other ranks were ready to shoot their officers. One could, perhaps, see in this some explanation of a man who subsequently led his life under the cloak of being "daft enough to know I'm daft." There was no need for such a possible interpretation to be overtly stressed but the indication of such grimmer elements was another grounds on which in would have helped to put more muscle into the structure, to get the play beyond being just a series of under-developed little tales.

It emerged, therefore, as rather a light-weight evening but what made it thoroughly entertaining throughout, as well as making one wish that it all reached the standard of the best, was the splendid performance of **Graham Gill**, playing a wonderful part to the hilt, moving in and out of being the eleven-year-old directly involved in most of the scenes and the older narrator, still in his cap and shorts, often still in his perplexed infancy, telling us the tale of the Grandad who impressed him so deeply over the short period in which he knew him.

12 FEBRUARY. **SONG OF AN HONORARY SOULMAN**; Nia. **(45).**

I do not know if **Randhi McWilliams** consciously took the style of a Seventeenth Century Tragedy, with its twisted family passions, incest, mistresses, murder, madness, revenge, complex lies and secrets within the household of a prosperous and powerful patriarch, some appealing to the heavens and some defying them. In any event, this style was a most effective evocation, conscious or otherwise, of the stresses on black individuals and communities within British society, who, having in many respects adopted the standards and ways of this culture, both find that the chances of being treated with suspicion or jailed are ever with them and, in many cases, also feel themselves proudly and eternally different from the "yeller-arsed" majority. The play does not in any way support any inclination to social separation, however. The strongest loves within it cross the colour lines.

The other style evoked by the piece is that of **The Second Book of Samuel.** The only overt reference which I noticed was when Claxton rushes back screaming from the church after hearing the preacher expound upon David and Bath-Sheba but the spirit of "Oh my son Absalom, my son, my son Absalom!" hangs over much of the play.

In fact, when his son lies dead at his feet Denzil Nathan has no such words. He is left alone with the mother and the corpse, all the rest of his household having left, for their various reasons, mostly silently. I can see the possibility of this being dramatically effective although I did not feel that, in this performance, it actually came off as strongly as the circumstances demanded. Elsewhere, the one element in the archetypes I seemed to apprehend which appeared to be missing and which I felt it would have been useful to have had was more frequent use of language with the power of **Thomas Middleton** and of the **Authorised Version.**

This, of course, is an exceptionally tall order. It is, however, a resource which available to West Indian users of English, among many of whom powerful expression is commonplace. It is also well within **Randhi McWilliams'** range. It is occasionally deployed in this play, usually in abuse, particularly from Frenchie and Mrs Willis. The **Nia** audience responded vigorously whenever vivid terms flew from the stage. Elsewhere, however, there were prolonged passages in which the dialogue was simple and clear, speakable but unstylish. There is no reason why an Antiguan writer should be constrained to write noticably "West Indian" English. As several characters were highly educated, three of them at English Public Schools, it was quite appropriate for them to speak in other terms. I just felt that, both for the power of the emotions involved and for the additional interest of the audience, some way of intensifying the style of the language more often would have been a useful tool for the actors and for the play as a whole.

This is not to say that the play ever fell far short of being totally gripping. Certainly seven finely conceived characters were thrown into the cauldron and they were all strongly performed. I felt that some impact was lost by the device which was chosen to alternate between the play's two settings: a large central piece of scenery swung as on a hinge. This may have seemed a simple and straight-forward solution but in fact, what with the lighting and extinguishing of the sitting-room candles and redisposing the few forestage furnishings, it always took a bit of time. This was not a serious drawback as it did not happen all that often and it provided occasion for some fine dramatic and foreboding covering music by **Akintayo Akinbode**. It might have been best to have gone for a design which had both settings permanently on stage. Nothing, however, stood in the way of this succeeding as a dramatic work of great power and perceptiveness.

15 FEBRUARY. THE LODGER; Royal Exchange. (47).

For me, Pollock is the problem.

This is not because he is the most overtly anti-social, dominating and threatening character. "He hasn't closed down any hospitals" Lois says in his defence. Despite the way he has treated her, she is reluctant to conspire to put the blame on him when she herself ends up in a ward bed, after being beaten up by supposedly far more respectable hands: "He's the only one who'll be waiting for me when I come out."

This fine scene brings out what I take to be the play's main purpose: a recognisable and realistic portrait of our society in which even those in as secure and well-paid an occupation as Detective Constable, with its loyal comradeship, suffer from painful isolation and are led into terrible acts of which they are ashamed. Everyone is a victim of our way of life.

The impression from this scene and several others that this is "what the play is about" is endorsed by **Lynne Greenewood**'s interview in the programme with the play's director, **Richard Wilson**. He "believes that theatre should reflect society and is confident that **The Lodger** does just that. ... He is particularly impressed by **Burke**'s dialogue. ... 'It is not often that they [Playwrights] write about people at the lower end of the social scale. But ... he has a very good ear for the way they speak.'"

This is where the Pollock problem comes in. Quite what the educational background of this indifferently effective pimp and apparently aspirant drugs baron was meant to be I would not be sure but in our "Classless Society" anyone who found that they had a taste for the incomplete literary allusions and mangled aphorisms in which he often attempts to speak would have access to a certain amount of appropriate source material through comprehensive schooling and the more cultural bits of television. One can certainly hear such fragments "at the lower end of the social scale". The congealed quantities in this character's dialogue, however, came across to me as totally unconvincing. This apparent artifice set askew my apprehension of the level upon which the play was operating.

The opening scene in which Lois, the first lodger, claimed it was she who should be asking for references of her potential landlord, not he of her, could be perceived as having an almost Monty Python-like logic to it. Were we being presented with a deliberately distorting satire? The lack of veracity in much she said, more rapidly apparent to us it seemed than to her interlocutor, despite his profession, of which we later became aware, as a detective constable, combined with the comparable untruthfulness we came to see in much that he said to her and to others, made one wonder if we were in Pinter territory, in which nothing should be taken at face value and words and actions are just being used to play artificial games. As the scenes went on one felt that at least one was being presented with material which sprang from a far more genuine concern for and understanding of the individuals and society being somehow represented, that features of common speech were there as an authentic means of expression and had not just caught the ear of outsider, as I find with Pinter, who seems to me just to use them to play stylistic games. Then, almost half way through,

in came Pollock, with the tricks of speech and menacing behaviour which seemed to cast him as the archetypical Pinter Threat. Were we in the realm of artifice afterall, with the elements of social reality just sprigs of decoration?

It is presumptuous, after one experience of a sophisticated play, to aspire to too exact an interpretation of how it chose to approach its task. Clearly it did not attempt exact documentary realism. What I think it was up was to was viewing our society at an angle which would enhance our experience of pity and terror for those involved in it and what it does to us all. Any element in this portrayal which lessened this impact, by artificialising, would seem to me to have been dysfunctional. I think Pollock did. I lay no blame for this upon the way the part was acted. All the cast and the whole effective staging seemed to me to have contributed most notably to giving all possible power to a notable play.

18 FEBRUARY. BLOOD, SWEAT AND FEARS; Nia. (69).

Once it became clear what this play was about, it followed its theme powerfully. It began with with an erratically amplified recording of the Star Trek theme, which lasted with the cast for quite sometime barely discernible on the blacked out stage but apparently in mock heroic poses, as pioneers of the Final Frontier. Then it went into a scene of frantic action in a hamburger outlet with a Star Trek motif, as the staff struggled to fulfil orders in accordance with the franchiser's formulae and, as Curtis (**Brian Morgan**) slumped across the till gasping "Have a Cosmic Day" for the umpteenth time, one assumed that the purpose of the show was to provide plenty of opportunities for his expert clowning.

The first scene having served this end quite well, one felt things were definitely flagging in the next as the central characters sat around on their break. Ashley's preference for her own health foods as against Curtis' willingness to refresh himself with the products of the establishment and the other lines of banter did not really seem to have enough laughs or other interest to be desperately promising. One needed to get a few further scenes further in to realise that the scene had not been intended as a further satiric skit but had been introducing us more deeply to the characters of a significant drama. It became significant later that part of the apparently inconsequential action involved Ben having to go to clean out the freezer and returning with severe shivers. Such tasks could be a trigger of his Sickle Cell Anaemia attacks.

This was the theme of the play. It had a great deal to communicate, both about the nature of the disease itself, about the circumstances in which it can and cannot be inherited, about the problems resulting from many in this country, the medical profession in particular but including others, such as teachers and college tutors and all of us in general, being unfamiliar with its symptoms and proper treatment, about the degree to which out-dated information still reaches sufferers and their families, about what probably are sensible and effective ways to reduce susceptibility, about the difficulty for those with the condition in following best advice, not only because of the difficulty of persuading teachers or employers of the reasons why they may occasionally be absent or should avoid duties involving, for instance, extremely cold working conditions, but because of the restriction on living a "normal" life involved in taking regular medication and avoiding certain in-takes and activities.

A very strong element of the drama concerned the limitations on what friends or relatives can do to help a victim. When Ashley (**Beverly Scarlet**), Ben's girlfriend, finds out about his condition, she throws herself into finding out all about the disease, telling Ben what he *must* do to look after himself, seeing herself as a model of loyalty and support, and getting as infuriated with him for being too feeble, as she sees it, to keep to the necessary regimen as he does with her for constant nagging. Luckily, when she manages to contact Ben's mother, Tessa, after he has been hospitalised, she manages to help Ashley to understand what she has learnt: that her even greater desperation for Ben's well-being could not be followed by keeping him on a short leash and insisting on what he must do. Ben knows the

40

risks and had to leave home and find his own balance between respecting his condition and being free to live a "normal" life.

It was good to see **Janet Spooner** given the chance to play this late key scene as Tessa so effectively, after her splendid performance last year as May Hassel in **Arden's** excellent **Accrington Pals**, when she was still a BTEC student, as it was also to see **Guy Rhys** entrusted with the part of Ben, after his notable recent performances with **Contact Youth Theatre.** There perfomances were of the highest quality and fully matched those of the longer standing professionals in the cast, most of whom also gained early experience in Manchester's excellent youth and community theatres.

The play had a considerable amount of information to convey but, while doing this effectively, once properly underway, it also succeeded in being most powerful drama. This was not only in such dramatic devices as a doctor (**Peter Kerry**) who did actually have some reasonable knowledge of the disease coming by in Out Patients just when Ben's, vividly enacted, extreme fits had developed to the point where even the "everyone's an emergency" nurse (**Karen Crook**) had had to realise that urgent treatment was necessary and Ben managing to communicate his allergy to morphine in time to avoid a further dose, when Ashley and his mother had failed to penetrate the "it's what we give to everyone" barrier. Nor was it only in the drama of

enlightenment for us as members of the audience, as we came to realise how details specifically related to Sickle Cell Anaemia are relevant to our own general social awareness and conduct. There was the profound evocation of the more general dilemmas faced by Ashley and Tessa: how can they help, and how are their emotional commitments to doing so likely to push them towards actions which are in fact unhelpful. This was the strongest drama of all. It was all set in the context of very relevant features of our current society: its institutions and our individual aspirations. Much of this was done wittily but the cast gave due strength to every aspect of the play's character.

19 FEBRUARY. STALINLAND; Green Room. (46).

This was a fine production of a splendid play.

The most obvious feature of the play's excellence was the constantly lively language, a persistent flow of usually most amusing exchanges, not only being sharply phrased but most accurately and perceptively, simultaneously capturing and demolishing the platitudes about the Westernisation of Eastern Europe and the the tacky nature of the supposedly superior and triumphing "culture", this scarcely being the correct word for the *mores* of the invaders, who see any old kitsch as saleable to tourists for "granny's mantlepiece" and who are eager to turn the material remains of the

Communist *régime* into a catch-penny "Stalinland" theme-park. The muddle-headed sculptor of the Socialist "Spirit of the Revolution" is desperate to save his art from the "spontaneous" sledgehammers of the vodka-doused masses, rallied by the youthful dissidents. It may or may not be good art but he had poured his creativity into it. Without his derided efforts to rescue it, the statue's head would not have survived to become the centre-piece of the new tourist attraction.

The second great strength of the play is the intelligence with which such elements are bonded into a mature and perceptive satire. The third is the highly effective, if intricate, structure: not only scene leading effectively to cumulative scene but simultaneous conversations, sometimes spanning the decades, not only being fascinating and enjoyable but effectively supplying us with the information we require about events in the late 1940's and in the early 1990's. The few material objects deployed are both useful structural tools and highly significant for the plays themes. These themes are of the highest value because, in showing us so clearly where we are now, as dubious in its qualities as some of the places we have previously been, often appallingly similar to them, it keeps us aware of the need to move on and helps us to be ready both to vet and, where appropriate, to accept possible means of doing so.

The excellence in the performance was not only in the vigour and style with which it powered through the lively text but in the way in which it was totally convincing that this was how it was meant to be played. Every performance was characterised by energy and detail, in speech, in expression and in gesture. Much of Karin's part, for instance, consists of the western-raised child of an emigrée dropping callow capitalist bricks over her eastern relatives. Less expertly handled it could have become repetitious and unhelpfully irritating. **Charlotte Somers** found ways, however, to vary the inflections and manner so that not only was her behaviour constantly believable, the comparative depth in the part being able to show through, but her significant part in the play's structure was able to have its full impact.

Jim Burke as the sculptor gave a particularly impressive performance, both as the man young, vigorous and believing himself to have ideals in the 1940s and as the older man who knows things went wrong in the régime which was then established but thinks he did some valuable work under it. Much of him believes that he was not to know how things would turn out and that, anyway, he was a sculptor, not a politician. He had showed clearly earlier that in 1947 he had thought himself to have political ideals, telling his wife that he thoroughly approves of her large family home being taken over to become the party headquarters, "Its what I believe in, that everyone's income should be roughly equal," but then rejecting her appeal to flee the country with her, first by saying, "I'm a Socialist sculptor. It's what I do" and then, when she says he could still be one in the West, "Yes; but it's better paid in the East."

Often **Jim Burke** had to wander round the stage alone with nothing but a glass head in which to confide, although just as ready to be spurred into shouting his self-justification or anguish at some member of the audience, but he also had to interact in the most complex ways with other cast members, usually his wife, Helena, sometimes as she alternated, line by line, between conversing with him as his youthful model and rowing with her daughters forty years later. There was an immense amount of careful detail, not ostentatious but constantly re-inforcing the text and enlivening the performance. For instance, when he and she are reconciled in the afterlife, wandering around Stalinland unseen as the ideals of the more perceptive dissidents are being betrayed, she tells him they are out of all that now and must not feel involved. She asks him if he would sculpt her again and he says they no longer have the plasticity essential to his form of expression: "Now if I had been a musician...", and he swept his finger in a way probably most like a conductor, perhaps like a very lively pianist, but in any event supplying an effective, small but vivid, piece of visual punctuation as, in countless little ways, he did through out the performance.

This was typical of the style of acting throughout the production.

Each actor, faced with a most detailed text, had found ways to make every facet of it sparkle and bear meaning. There was no question of over-elaboration. It was simply a most sophisticated application of Hamlet's advice to the travelling players. Having a splendid set of words, they made them live in action.

21 FEBRUARY. GIMME SHELTER; Green Room. (48).

Gem, the first of the three eventually linked plays which make up **Gimme Shelter,** was outstandingly the best, both in writing and performance. Set in 1975, it essentially consisted of the fragmentary conversation and antics of four disaffected junior members of the London Branch of a major accountancy firm, who, irked at having to give up their August Bank holiday to attend the prestigious annual cricket match against the Essex Division, attempt to subvert it by turning up scruffily dressed and, with ghetto-blaster, beer crate and football, disporting themselves well away from the main party but in full view. It was a considerable achievement for **Barrie Keeffe** to have written this in a way which captured their behaviour in a fully plausible manner, which was also both pointed and witty and sustained itself intriguingly for almost an hour. It was shown to be so by the entirely successful way in which the cast portrayed the four diverse characters and their interrelationships. Such behaviour is common enough in real life but it takes enormous skill to discover the reality in such dialogue when it is written on the page and then to make it full, believable and enjoyable in performance.

Gotcha, the second play I had heard of, having read reviews when it was done to considerable acclaim on television at least ten years ago. Its tale of a schoolboy taking hostage two teachers whom he found being unduly intimate in the stockroom where he had left his motor-bike had not sounded very promising to me but my hopes were raised, not only by the excellence of the first play but by the initial characterisation. The teachers' encounter was not of the simple salacity I had expected but consisted mainly of him making his excuses to leave her and the lad was not the typical aggressive thug but a rather shambling no-hoper who seemed previously to have left largely unexpressed his resentment of the school which had recognised no more in him than he in it.

Unfortunately, the bulk of the piece proved to be of far less subtlety than the previous play. The characterisation proved to be pretty rudimentary: the male teacher an archetype of the shout 'em and clout 'em school of education, she far more inclined to be listening and sympathetic but from too different a social base to be naturally effective with her pupils, the headmaster, who is drawn into the situation a vacuous prattler with interests scarcely stretching beyond school prestige and sixth form successes. After the successful naturalness of

the dialogue in **Gem**, the stilted way in which the lad was made to try and articulate his resentment at the way the new comprehensive had failed him even worse than the old seccy mod had failed his brothers not only seemed artificial but was most disappointing. It had its moments, as when the sports master exploded in protest when the head, fatuously trying to confirm that the boy could, with effort, become a brain surgeon was led on into averring that this could also, with effort, be combined with playing for West Ham. For the most part, however, the treatment of a valid subject was not very skilful or profound. If the English teacher had been able to stimulate her class into improvising a play or such a topic they could probably have done it at least as well and probably better.

It was a relief after this comparative disappointment to see that the third play, **Getaway**, was to return to the setting of the much more successful **Gem.** The two elegant deck-chairs on stage as we returned from the interval were sufficient in themselves to tell us that the main theme was likely to be that our scruffy rebels from the first play had been assimilated into the dominant culture of their accountancy firm. So it proved to be and although the dialogue as they sat in their elegant whites, waiting their turn to bat, was quite skilful in showing their social transformation, one did not feel one was actually learning much more than had been said effectively in the opening tableau.

Then the lad out of **Gotcha** shambled on as a junior groundsman and there seemed the possibility of some interesting exploration as the two cultures met. Although the way in which he had gained this position came out very plausibly in the dialogue and there was an encounter of potentially greatly effective dramatic pain, as the once rebellious accountant, who still likes to think he is "undermining from within", insists on shaking by the hand as a hero the lad of whose exploit he had read in the papers and admired as a great Protest, while the boy himself is only too relieved he had not then carried out his threats and wants to leave it all behind him.

It was a very valid, and indeed prophetic, social document, as can be seen for instance in the cult which has grown up over the past decade to celebrate Fortieth Birthdays as a *rite de passage* for those deeply imbued in the Youth Culture of the late Sixties and early Seventies, who have now adopted a lifestyle based on very different premises. I was not convinced that **Keeffe** had found quite enough to say about this to turn it into a thirty-minute play but it was well written and well performed. The lad's praise of his Juvenile Offenders Institution as against his comprehensive, - "They taught me a trade" -, might go down rather well with our present Secretary of State for Education. I would not know if **Barrie Keeffe** yet feels ready for acclaim from such a quarter.

22 FEBRUARY.
BEAUTIFUL THING;
Dancehouse. (51).

It was very good to have the chance to see another play by **Jonathan Harvey**, whose most interesting **Cherry Blossom Tree** we were able to see at the **Arden** in **Emma Wood**'s **Armadillo Company Production** from the **Liverpool Playhouse** in 1988. Although much is superficially different, the basic theme, of young people discovering themselves through a love of which others disapprove, is very similar. Then the setting was Liverpool and the star-cross'd lovers were a Catholic girl and a Protestant lad, whom she thought "so mature" until he went off to university and forgot all about her, showing himself socially very out of his depth in encountering problems in the neighborhood on his occasional returns. Here they are two fifteen-year-old lads who change from topping and tailing to "seventy minus one", again in a geographically specific location, the tower blocks of Thamesmead.

There the style was naturalistic and the outcome was tragic, - she threw herself off the roof of the Cathedral -, although there were lightening touches: "It was the Protestant Cathedral, 'cos you can't throw yourself off our one." Here the whole tone is a lot more positive: the lads' love is eventually accepted by mum and the play ends with the boys dancing soulfully together on the walkway outside the flats while mum dances with the girl next door, whom the play had begun with her calling "slag", before they all have a night out at the gay bar the boys have discovered, the mum drawn by the prospect of there being a male stripper.

At quite what level of realism this was being presented took a while to de-code. It began with **Mark Letheren** and **Sophie Stanton**, actors undisguisedly well into their twenties, sitting on the neighbouring doorsteps of the entirely naturalistic set. Fairly soon one could discern that at least the boy was still at school but as one of the items lying on the walkway was an infant's tricycle one wondered if we might be into a full **Blue Remembered Hills** intentional clear discrepancy between the ages of characters and actors. In **The Cherry Blossom Tree** premier **Harvey** was able to use young, local Liverpool actors to present quite plausibly the characters portrayed. Although nothing significant in the way of what some would interpret as "lewd and indecent acts" takes place on stage, I would not know if their occasional approximation, the need for experienced actors to sustain a long professional run and tour or an independent artistic decision led to a different style of casting on this occasion. This was not the only distancing device: **Amelda Brown**'s delivery in her early scenes often seemed almost pantomimic, one step, but only one, beyond the authentic wryness with which many of life's struggling survivors on our council estates often express their views and re-actions. **Richard Bonneville**'s Tony, his eyes glistening with illegal substances and his almost invariable response

of "Hey! That's OK ...", seemed a completely cartoon hippy.

I think the writing of his part was simply not sufficiently developed but **Amelda Brown**'s Sarah eventually came to personify the true grit and valid understanding of those who, despite being on the economic underside of our society, – working all hours to make ends meet, so getting all too little time to see the children about who they care so deeply and never succeeding in building up a full family –, yet make human achievements which the play seems to celebrate. In allowing realistic reference to the experiences of a lad who is not only disgusted and ashamed to find that the drunk whom he has to step over in the street is his dad and in showing the belt-marks on his back which make him periodically seek overnight refuge in the flat next door, **Harvey** is acting very boldly in including these in a play which is so light, often even jokey, in tone. He insists that resiliant good nature nevertheless flourishes in such an environment, its inhabitants evolving fresh and viable understandings of the social factors they experience. The lads know that their parents' lives are in some ways a moral mess but both get on with them much of the time and all concerned know how to achieve a good deal that is positive. The play is in some ways an authentic social document and is right to stress that this world contains much to celebrate as well as much to deplore.

23 FEBRUARY. YERMA; Capitol. (49).

I was particularly glad of the opportunity to see this production as in the striking Punjabi version brought to **Contact** by **The Company** last year it was obvious that there was a great deal of poetry flying about the stage to which I did not have access. How much the noted poet **Surjit Patar**, who prepared that version, translated the imagery as well as the words I still would not know but I now do have direct evidence of how important to the the piece Lorca's vivid poetry is. **The Metropolitan University's** company, in seeking out the fine translation by **David Johnson** from Belfast, equipped themselves with a powerful script, from which they presented a performance of great skill and strength, giving a convincing naturalness to the colloquial passages, notably from Juan, and clear resonance to the poetry, whether speaking individually or collectively.

Each part was made fully characterful whilst, at the same time one could see the play to be presenting a full range of options. In addition to the happy mother, which Yerma longs to be there was also the happily childless and the gladly randy, in addition to the severely spinsterly sisters–in–law. This play is very much set in the world bluntly summed up by the Mother to the Daughter in **Blood Wedding:** "You understand what marriage is: your husband, your children and a wall ten feet thick between you and all others." Despite her love of the natural world, this is a deal

which Yerma would be willing to make. What makes her life unbearable is that her husband, being so conscious of the need for wealth to ensure security amongst the poverty of their rocky, rain-starved hillside, refuses to grant her the children, seeing that they would be a drain on his wealth, preferring to labour all day in the fields and to sleep out guarding his flocks at night, even though he has so many sheep after he has bought Victor's flock that he does not know where he will be able to pasture them and even though he will have no heirs to inherit them.

Despite her ever heightening desire for a baby, however, it becomes clear that Yerma's aspiration is even more specific: it must be a child with honour. When the Pagan Woman offers her a home, where her son is vigorous enough both to father all the children she wants and to keep her husband at bay, Yerma refuses. She is very conscious of the inherited honour and reputation of her family.

24 FEBRUARY. KING LEAR; Nia. (68).

Despite the slogan on the **Nia Centre's** ticket, this was not, of course, "Britain's first Black **King Lear**." **Talawa's** programme pays proper tribute to **Ira Aldridge's** immensely popular performance in the rôle a hundred and thirty-five years ago. It may, however, be the first almost *all*-Black production. What special qualities does this bring?

47

When the first characters swept onto the stage for the opening court scene, the initial impression from the costumes was of English Medieval, although, as things went on, one could later see the influence of the Savanna tradition, with a touch of Yorubaland. This seemed a very satisfactory combination, although, as is common nowadays, it appeared not to be attempting homogeneity of period, with such modern hand props as the metal attaché case used by Lear's Doctor and Edmund, rather oddly, allotted the task of minuting the daughters' answers in the first scene with a ball-point pen on a plastic clip-board. I would not have guessed, as I noticed later from a publicity leaflet and as **The Guardian** apparently found in the later London performances, that there was any specific concern to set the play in 2000 AD, despite the somewhat futuristic design of Lear's crystalline plastic throne. The main thing one noticed about that on the first night was its tendency to fall to bits.

The style was not, therefore, ostentatiously African but I would not go along with the judgement of two white friends in the audience who praised the production in terms of the casting making "no difference."

The most general asset which many were able to bring to their parts was a splendour of voice, workshopped by **Cicely Berry**, no less; the deep rolling tones, combined with clarity and good characterisation, being ideally suited to bringing out the poetic stature of the drama. Except

where **David Webber**, as Kent, effectively utilised *patwa* for his scenes as Caius, there was nothing stereotypically "African" about this but it would have been difficult for any other race to have brought this asset consistently to the performance.

David Harewood's Edmund turned splendidly from wooing the audience through cynically direct confidences of exactly what he was about to convincingly gulling Edgar and his father in exactly the manner in which he had just told us he would. West Indian men in the audience chortled in recognition as he wounded himself with the words "I have seen drunkards do more than this in sport" and the schoolgirls who had come by coach from Stoke-on-Trent clearly agreed that, in pursuing him, Regan and Goneril were both after the right man.

These two sisters were both vividly characterised by **Cathy Tyson** and **Lolita Chakrabarti.** Their ruthlessness sprang from their determination to maintain their lifestyles, which conflicted with any resposibilities to accomodate an ageing parent. **Jeff Diamond** very convincingly portrayed Cornwall as a dangerous thug to whom violence came entirely naturally whereas **Diane Parish**'s Cordelia, physically much smaller than her sisters, dashing in, barely in time for the court session, was very plausibly her father's darling but not so close to him mentally that she could communicate effectively to him that he was asking a ridiculous question by throwing her hands wide and answering "Nothing, my lord!" in a laughing tone. She was quite taken aback by his snarled response: "Nothing?"

All this was good and interesting characterisation and, although in general terms, there was nothing peculiar to the Black community about them, they were all derived, in their particular manifestations, from that community and informed by it.

Some conceits were less happy. **Dhirendra**, perhaps seeking to find a different style in which to portray the lowest of the low than he used so brilliantly when he brought **Untouchable** to Manchester a couple of years ago, used an almost exclusively priapic mode in his manifestations as Poor Tom. This was tremendously well enjoyed by the audience and one could justify it by such means as pointing out such lines as Poor Tom's description of himself as "one that slept in the contriving of lust and wak'd to do it" and noting that his encounter with him is among the influences which lead Lear to cry out "Let copulation thrive!" There is a raft of related imagery in the play but it did not strike me as being a successful idea in practice, not least because such attention-drawing capers seemed improbable in one trying to make himself obscure. His descriptions of his lustful acts refer to his supposed past.

The more general weakness of the production seemed to me less in particular ideas like this, which clearly did succeed in some quarters and which perhaps had their rational, than in there not

being any very coherent overall view becoming apparent, to me at any rate, in the second half as to what, predominantly, the play was all about. This was odd as the whole style in the first half was very much of a play which knew where it was going. This came across not only in the vivid characterisation and the fine verse-speaking but in the boldly simple set: a wooden disk at an angle as the main acting area, with thick scarlet ropes at its perimeter, suggesting entrances. The short coming was not just on the level of First Night technical snags, like the karabiners securing the ropes not being as easy as had probably been presumed to snap open quickly to secure a supposedly simple change of pattern or the delay in executing the basically good idea of Edmund, the better fighter, apparently overcoming Edgar in the final duel but then getting his come-uppance as he sat athwart him by Edgar being able to reach the small knife hidden in the wrist of Edmund's gauntlet, which we had first seen when Edmund had used it to betray Edgar by suggesting to their father that he was under attack. It just took rather a long time for Edgar to secure it in the final scene. That was no serious problem and in fact the concept was one of the several good ideas for continuity which the production deployed: such as Lear's Doctor being prominent with his tablets among his early retainers, therefore naturally being at Gloucester's castle and available for Kent to use as his messanger to Cordelia in Dover and therefore being to hand to

49

attend to him when the distressed king finally arrived there.

With such clear thinking about the play's mechanics and so much drive and excellence in the performances it is reasonable to expect that development in the play's run will clarify its overall purview as effectively as it will clean up the trivial little slips in technicalities. The company has already demonstrated that it can perform an international classic to a standard at least to outshine such a respected production as that by the **Renaissance Theatre** 1990. If it brings all to the standard of the best, it will show that a Black British company has all the qualities to make a major production truly great.

4 MARCH. MINIMAL STORIES; Arden. (50).

"Are you dead?" "Yes."

This opening exchange from the first duologue gives a fair idea of the ambience of these **Minimal Stories**. Some are so minimal as to scarely be stories at all. Some could just about be realistic accounts, as of a mother humouring the child who rushes in with clasped hands: "Mother, Mother! I've caught the moon!" "Then put it in my hair." Other contemplations of the heavens definitely could not be found in the world as normally perceived, although this is not immediately apparent: "Look at that star!" Wide-ranging but leisurely scrutiny by her companion before the query "Which star?" "That one. By the steeple." Further lengthy study leads him to claim: "Ah

yes. I see it" and, while he stares at it vacantly, she grins quizzically and then suddenly gives a puff. The light goes out.

There was a distictively Spanish atmosphere to much that took place, abetted by a mountain-top bull silhouetted in the background against a flame-red sky, but although a father could have a perception with a classical Spanish pedigree, that the windmills his son points out to him are giants, it was made entirely natural that the son's remonstrances should be in Scouse and the despairing father could reply colloquially, "I've got problems with you, Tomás."

In front of the design at the back, the performance style was appropriately minimal, the performers dressed simply in black, with few other hand props beside the red handkerchieves which were usually kept in their pockets but for which occasional effective uses were found, most vividly when a reluctant toreador, after unsuccessful attempts at plea-bargaining with his bull, found that he could dispatch him and the crowd's cry of "Olé!" was accompanied by a cascade of red folded handkerchieves, falling as favours.

5 MARCH. BITTER 'n' TWISTED; Dancehouse. (52).

The basic conceit of this work, bringing a supposedly "typical" West Indian couple from the Brixton of 1963 into the household of the supposedly equally "typical" occupants of their flat thirty years later scarcely amounted to a play, as the plotting would not bear all that much scrutiny, but it provided occasion for a good many amusing scenes and lines. The feeling in between the most enjoyable episodes, that this was a rather over-extended series of skits, partly derived from the present-day couple being so hyper-sophisticated and ridiculuous in their attitudes as to be well beyond the plausible. They thus lost much of the social anchoring in authenticity that would have given the piece more strength. Daniel's floundering around after progressive social attitudes and Natasha's awareness of the need to crown her professional success with a Book which would lead to her access to a permanent cycle of chat-show and celebrity appearances does relate to a reality but the number of lines which captured such matters with any accuity were a bit too widely spaced. **Llewella Gideon** worked hard, flashing her eyes at remarks from her "primitive" acquaintances which flew counter to her social values and delivering straight-faced lines which were contrary to theirs, in a way which would have helped to make them very funny if the script had been consistently sharper in the first place.

The 1963 couple had much more boldly amusing material. **Wayne Buchannan** and **Angela Wynter** have had much stronger parts in their recent visits to the **Nia Centre**, in **Foxtrot in the Sand** and in **Nine Night,** but they made the best here of such

opportunities for clowning as Courtney's opening scene, in which he seeks to combine a serious evening's adultery with watching the World Cup. His companion's reservations, stemming from being not only his wife's best friend but even her bridesmaid, gave the scene additional strength, the sort of depth which the play seemed to lack elsewhere.

11 MARCH. ALL CATS ARE GRAY IN THE DARK; Arden. (55).

Wherever the World of Theatre is in need of having its swashes buckled, **Arden** stands ready, to a woman as to a man. In the magnificent fights, directed by **Renny Krupinski**, from brief passes by musketeers keen to show their prowess to full scale fracas in which the lone heroine defended herself with a brace of swords, capes and boots against three or four simultaneously, a wide range of easy proficiency was most amusingly shown.

In its other main dimension, as a specially written musical to enable the cast to develop their skills as singing actors, I am not so sure of the play's strengths. Not knowing one note from the other, I am not in the least competent to judge it musically but it seemed probable that each song was cleverly musical and particularly notable when it gave the singers scope to harmonise. I do not know if a musical today should be expected to include songs that are memorable. I could not now remember a line or musical phrase from any one of them. A lot of them seemed a bit similarish to me but that may be consistency of style with a more subtle appeal than I am equipped to meet. They carried a good deal of the fairly bulky plot. Everyone had a past as long as their rapier, going back at least two generations, and one way to pack this all in was to narrate it in song, which seemed to make information more important than felicitous phrasing.

Nevertheless, the piece succeeded in the style of being highly amusing by taking itself entirely seriously. Some grander lines might have been an asset to the actors but each of the ten characters in the cast was distinctive, if not deep, and these were all fully realised, often with significant skill. **Donna Alexander,** for instance, every inch a king last summer in **All's Well,** showed considerable range by here taking the very different part of the most diligent but also the most diffident of the young cadet musketeers, who, like so many of the characters, had a significant Secret.

12 MARCH. FULL OF NOISES; Green Room. (56).

There seems to be a minor cult at present for adaptations of **The Tempest.** **Kazzum Arts Project** brought one to the **Green Room** last November and apparently another Young People's theatre group is touring a version by **Liz Lochead.** The **Royal Exchange** is to host **Prospero's Island (476)**

on 20 March, a project involving nineteen Manchester schools and colleges.

Chris Newell's Full of Noises, presented here by a company from the **Exchange's Arden School of Theatre,** seems, like **Roar Material's Prospero at the Gates of Dawn** to be giving priority to the Spirits of the Island. That production was infested by Yellow People who interwove themselves with the action. Here the action, much more successfully, is entirely presented by similarly-suited beings, dressed from the yellow to red part of the spectrum and all wearing similar wire head pieces. A Propero voice midway pronounced "These our actors, as I foretold you, were all spirits" and I wondered if a major strand of the interpretation was a comment by the cast on their profession. When the revels indeed were ended this passage was re-emphasised again in the closing action, as they were "melted into air, into thin air" on the darkened stage, leaving only an unmasked Propero to make the one conventionally delivered speech of the evening, the Epilogue, before she followed the example of her colleagues.

I am not sure that too much should be made of this, however, as it seems that the primary inspiration of the reshaping of the text was musical, rather than the meaning of the words, this re-orchestration having come appropriately to be called **Full of Noises.** "Brrr. Umm. Ping," the much repeated sounds with which the performance began as the cast severally emerged from the shadows, came to strike me as it went on and on as much less dramatic than Shakespeare's opening, which literally starts with a bang: "A tempestouos noise of thunder and lightning." It seems to me that the lines he then wrote provide effective verbal means to echo that stage direction by an essentially musical deployment of the phrases, whilst also skilfully introducing us to some useful information about character and plot. Whether anyone who had not at some time heard Shakespeare's exposition of these matters could have made head or tail of this performance, I would not know. I am, also, not equipped to judge whether it could have been responded to on the level of pure sound.

Initially, while finding it not uninteresting, I was inclined to feel, as the performance slowly established itself, that, given the quality of the original, this re-editing was somewhat perverse. We eventually got most of the lines of Shakespeare's opening scene, several times, and one had time to reflect, as such a line as "To prayers, to prayers!" recurred in mournful tones, that it had come a long way, without much benefit, from the desperate cry of men who expected to meet their Maker within seconds. Nevertheless, as the performance established itself on its own terms, it built up its own impact and certainly was exectuted with great skill and ability.

Some of the re-editing brought out points which might be found in a more verbal interpretation of the text: the paralleling of the

attempted attack by Sebastian and Antonio upon Alonzo with Caliban's proposal of a plan to cut the wezand of Prospero; the emphasis by re-echoing of Gozalo's vision of a new Commonwealth, inspired by the Island. As I adjusted to the idea that the piece was highlighting certain themes by their selection at the expense of others, I was a little surprised in the last third to encounter, rather compactly, various characters who seemed to have been left aside in the interests of emphasis being laid elsewhere. It would be rash to claim, however, that a second hearing would not enable one to see more unity thoughout in a complex piece. It was certainly an intriguing experiment, carried through with great commitment

.

16 MARCH. VENICE PRESERVED; Royal Exchange. (58).

"Gosh, there were some irritating characters in that," said my neighbour at the play's close. "As There Are In Life," I replied.

This would not be a justification in itself for making them the subject of considerably more than two hours' traffic of our stage. However, as those who might be found most irritating, such as the perpetually woebegone Jaffeir, are so because they are as inadequate as we might be if swept into the course of events which require a decisive firmness, over-riding sensibilities, if we were to emerge with any honour, there is a bedrock of empathy which can make valuable the pain of watching such a character's

HELEN McCRORY as Belvidera and JONATHAN CULLEN as Jaffeir, the young lovers whose tragic eperiences are at the heart of this fine ROYAL EXCHANGE production of VENICE PRESERVED.

It is Jaffeir's personal experience of being pushed from poverty to ruin by the Venetian senator whose daughter he has married without his consent, despite what he perceives as his considerable deservings, which pushes him into the company of revolutionary conspirators, inspired by his best friend. He has found his deeply beloved and loving wife sitting amidst the ruins left by her father's bailiffs but, although she believes herself ready to live with him in the utmost poverty, she is revolted by the vulgar "care" of the plot-leaders with whom he leaves her and, when she discovers their intentions include the slaughter of her father, insists that Jaffeir must betray them. He is thus left disloyal to all and respected by none.

This is made deeply tragic. His ignomy is given stature by the depth of his so, incompetently expressed, love of his wife Belvedira and for his friend Pierre and by the strength of the language in which he and all other characters express themselves. The verse-speaking by all in this production is powerful throughout and gives the piece its tremendous charge.

fecklessness. We might like to identify with those who are splendidly bold in the attempt to overthrow unjust tyranny but the actual difficulty of events when once caught up in them can make it harder even to see the issue clearly, let alone to be loyal and consistent in responding to it.

Byron is quoted in the programme as naming Pierre with Shakespearean heroes as among the imperishable glories associated with Venice and this production is costumed very plausibly in or somewhat beyond his period, rather than in Otway's. It is in fact more of a revelation to hear of a proposed Revolution apparently inspired by purely secular ideals of Liberty and

Justice being penned in the Seventeenth Century than in the Nineteenth but it is assimilable for us to see how those deeply committed to such ideals are also given to posturing in swirling cloaks. If we sense some falseness in this, it does not make them inferior to the Venice which is in fact Preserved by their betrayal. The richly ironic title is emphasised in the closing moments by being projected like a coin's inscription in gold onto the rim of the now mourning houshold of the heartless Senator in which the play began. The laughableness of another Senator's demands on his whore may seem more venial but he is as ready as any to sentence the plotters to horrible torture, prior to execution. The way in which a proud cabinet of the prejudiced and the bumbling is able to do terrible damage both to individuals and to the polity is clearly shown. Helped here by a most able cast and production, the play is powerful in its portrayal of unfortunately enduring truth.

18 MARCH. PEER GYNT; Palace. (59).

The first half of this was tremendous. The two great assets ensuring this were the splendidly vigorous performance, led by **Graham Ingle,** understudying as Peer with enormous drive, and the consistently Irish style derived from **Frank McGuinness'** vivid translation and a cast well able to realise this, as those with surnames from that island formed the biggest single contingent among performers from many

origins.

It was not at first apparent that such cultural consistency was an asset which was going to be available to the production when the curtain first rose, with a blast of noise and neon, on a crowded modern amusement arcade, the signs hanging aloft advertising night spots from major cities around the globe. As the figure of Peer emerged to ponder and the gaming machines were rolled away, a giant gauze screen descended on which was projected the credits sequence of a cinematic epic, as if the earth was being approached from the Planet Krypton. When the spacecraft, which proved to be a giant onion, actually came into orbit, I wondered from its flight-path whether we were homing in on Norway but any such specific location was belied by the image of a sphere which bobbed up and down through the clouds, each time enclosing the image of a different city from around the globe.

Nevetheless, when the screen rose, although the principal scenery emerged as a giant box set designed in the style of an enormous circuit board from the electronic environment in which the play had opened, somehow the clear amplified sounds of cascading mountain streams, combined with a few clumps of marsh grass around Ase's cut-out cottage, was able to convey the mountain environment by which the action of the first half of the play is inspired, or was made to do so by the vivid way in which Peer came leaping in and excitedly cast his word-spell, portraying his vision of being dragged by the buck across the crags and lakes.

Possibly the most overtly Irish touch in this opening scene came at the end when Peer has dashed away to the wedding, leaving Ase stranded. As against the presumably-more-literal "Look, Peer Gynt/Has stuck his mother on the roof" in **Norman Ginsbury**'s translation, **Frank McGuinness** has the Second Old Woman who answers her cries for help chuckle in brogue: "Hey Ase: You've gone up in the world!" The characters on the way to the wedding and the style of the celebrations there are pure Irish and the play gained tremendously from this cultural consistency. The Troll kingdom usefully drew on wider resources, with many elements of Japanese Devils, but this was most vigorously and effectively done, with **Espen SKjønberg** handling very well the witty translation of the Troll King's lines, such as "Three-headed trolls are quite out of fashion."

An interesting question relating to the play's exploration of the human psyche was that both he and his daughter were recognisably the same actors who had just portrayed Ingrid and her father, the Bride whom Peer has just carried away from her wedding and then abandoned on the mountainside. I would not know quite what one should make of this, as I would not for much of the play, but it was certainly a question worth chewing on. For the time being however, apart from some occasional stiltedness in moving from scene

to scene, everything continued with a very satisfactory vividness and drive. It was in the more overtly interpretative second-half that it lost its grip.

The earlier parts of Act IV came across as little more than cartoon, as which they may be largely intended, but flawed even as that: unnecessary slowness in moving from scene to scene becoming even more noticable and the presumably intentionally caricature characters of the German, the Frenchman, the American and the Dane coming across as tediously thin, from actors who had shown they could give very full characterisations during the wedding scene. I have seen a, generally unenthusiastic, local review pick out the madhouse scene at the end of the act as particularly effective but it did not help me.

Perhaps this shows that it was not the performance but my attentiveness that was flagging, towards the end of a long play after a long day, although it took half-an-hour less than the four-and-a-quarter hours of which I was warned at the box office, after I had paid for my ticket. I was not the only one, however, to find the fourth and fifth acts less than gripping as little groups from the audience were constantly leaving and my neighbour was contantly looking at his watch, exclaiming "That's sooner than we will!" to his wife when Peer got an affirmative answer from the Captain to his question "Will we land by morning?"

At that point, however, I was

being kept quite interested by the portrayal of Peer's mental state, oscilating from offers of generosity to the crew to blunt tight-fistedness. It may be that those who left were like those whom I heard say at the interval "Tough going, isn't it?", "Yes; but some of the Effects are tremendous." There was certainly less of flash and bang in the second half to hold those whose tastes lay that way. When I took advantage of the interval to put on my outdoor clothing, to cope with the notorious lack of insulation at the **Palace** against cold weather, and was asked "Had enough?", at that point my answer was a very sincere "Certainly not." It may be that it was the particular tones of the Japanese actor playing the Buttonmoulder which made it hard for me to assimilate the highly significant words which he had to say but I completely failed to notice the speech in which Peer tries to find the heart of the onion, as of his own self, and finds that it has not got one. I presume that it must have been there because of the way that the image of a giant onion, like the great globe itself, was constantly used in the film episodes between scenes.

I cannot, therefore, be a reliable witness as to whether the production was seriously deficient in finding ways to make the second half of the play dramatically effective on stage. My impression is that it was. Nevertheless, there was so much that was outstandingly successful in the first half in bringing this highly wrought and hard-to-stage play to life that, overall, it was well worth seeing.

21 MARCH. ANTHONY AND CLEOPATRA; Chapman Theatre. (64).

"Nay, but this dotage of our general's/O'er flows the measure: those his goodly eyes,/That o'er the files and musters of the war/ Have glow'd like plated Mars, now bend, now turn/The office and devotion of their view/Upon a tawny front."

This is **Shakespeare's** opening and one of the great strength's of **Salford's** production is the way it used this and the following scene as the start of a clearly driven narrative towards an end such as **Aristotle** claimed is required by tragedy, "it follows naturally and necessarily" and "is about a man who is not outstanding for virtue or justice and arrives at ill fortune not because of any wickedness or vice but because of some mistake he makes. He will also be a man of high reputation who has been enjoying good fortune."

Shakespeare elaborates this by putting a woman in the same position.

By dressing the production in the military costumes of the 1940's the production immediately helps the audience to apprehend that the messages in the attaché case held by Philo are indeed likely to be of importance, that Anthony is taking serious risks in giving priority to Cleopatra over Rome. The wide arch of the rang'd empire could well fall and take him with it. This is confirmed two scenes later when he finally does take time to hear the news Philo has brought, recognises its seriousness and changes his tune from dismissing business by embracing Cleopatra with the claim "the nobleness of life is to do thus" to echoing the opening assessment of Demetrius: "These strong Egyptian fetters I must break,/ Or lose myself in dotage." But he cannot and he does. Meanwhile we have already seen the Soothsayer predict to Charmian and Iras that the outcome will be no better for Egypt: "You shall outlive the lady whom you serve/.../You have seen and prov'd a fairer former fortune/Than that which is to approach."

All this was given admirable clarity and although, once action diverged from Egypt, there were sometimes unhelpful slight delays during which a reclining rug was dragged on and off for scenes back by the Nile, in general the momentum was maintained and with it the clearness of the narrative, helped by keeping the stage admirably clear. We did not really need the rug or the indication of in whose theatre of operations we were at any time which was provided by projecting ikons of the principal characters onto the plain white enclosure. However, the projections were a trouble-free device which in general contributed to the stylish look of the production, achieved by the able positioning of the variously uniformed characters in the space.

The production was more successful in conveying the level of "one man but a man" and "no more but e'en a woman" than in suggesting that there might be a true level of greatness in the characters. The falsity of the level, suggested by the most elaborate uniforms of the triumvirate, was well exposed, as in the scene during the feast on Pompey's galley, which well conveyed as a whole the situation summarised in the removal of Lepidus: "There's a strong fellow, Menas." "Why?" "'A bears a third part of the world ..." "The third part then is drunk."

For the most part, however, Antony came across as one diverted from his duties in ways which the Sunday papers have just reminded us can still occur to a Chief of Defence Staff. One could apprehend that as such he would normally be efficient but as one responded to him on the level of a basically ordinary bloke, subject to common passions, one was taken by surprise to hear him hymned by Cleopatra as "past the size of dreaming." The performance had not suggested such a Colossus. Likewise Cleopatra, whilst both fluent and attractive, expressed her passion for Anthony on a level doubtless recognisable to countless students and shopgirls. This is powerful enough and probably one accurate dimension of identification. The play frequently, however, most notably in the description of Enobarbus, suggests that, while "e'en a woman", she had a character on a scale quite beyond "other women". I did not apprehend that in this performance nor any sense that her actions were aimed at objectives set by her being ruler of her country as well as by her personal passions.

In suggesting that certain things were not done, I am more seeking to record what was achieved than to criticise the perfomances for not being other than they were. These are parts of enormous stature and if the emphasis in these interpretations was more on the ordinary than on the supernal, they were part of a production which overall was highly succesful in making a complex work clear and accessible, not least in making it possible for members of the audience to identify clearly with the passions of the leading characters and helping that to have tremendous power and stature by enduing it with the tragedy of inevitability right from the opening moments.

22 MARCH. DEBORAH'S DAUGHTER; Library. (63).

This was very finely acted and strikingly staged. Otherwise, I could not see the point. There was a veneer of interest in Third World politics, economy and ecology, in the Rich World's relationship to these and in the condition of women but sub-title on the posters, "Intrigue and passion in a perfumed oasis!", seemed a more accurate description of what was going on, a sort of cross between Rider Haggard and Barbara Cartland. In the final scenes, when characters started to argue in page-length speeches, the style turned more to that of poor **Shaw.** There are in fact

considerable parallels of form with **Captain Brassbound's Conversion.** There are "middle-class English women who work like mules" and know exactly what is best for all denizens of North Africa, indigenous or otherwise and the play also ends with the explosion of a romance which the audience has been led to expect but, whereas this in **Shaw** progressively allowed the continued liberty of Lady Cecily, here we have the appallingly reactionary relief of Deborah Pedersen that her daughter is to marry not the Sheikh of the Desert *de nos jours* but an unparaled twit of an English marketing consultant, whose idiocies have been so galumphingly overwritten as to be neither funny nor instructive, let alone plausible.

His scenes are the only ones which are actually badly written. Elsewhere there is good characterisation and the lines are at least well-turned, fairly believable in their context and sometimes skilful, as in the utterly credible incoherence, splendidly acted by **Anna Carteret,** when Deborah staggers in physically and emotionally shattered after trying to hold onto a departing Land Rover in which she believes her daughter's Honour is to be Threatened. There is also good acting with very few lines written, notably **Nasser Memarzia's** dignified continuance with his duties, despite the crass demands and disregard of the English in his care. All this considerable skill, however, is to very little end. Whereas **Shaw** wrote an entertainment which in fact had a considerable amount of point, this professes concern with various mighty issues but has little more to it than a simple little drama.

24 MARCH. E D R; Dancehouse. (67).

There were many things which were tremendously stimulating about this performance but one of them for me was how enormously the company has progressed since I last saw them two years ago, in **Mantrail** at the **Nia Centre**. Then the company had seemed likeable and in some ways quite clever but both the material and its performance had seemed rather rudimentary. My perception of them may not have been helped both by our being a very small audience in a large theatre and also by my not being attuned to the style of mime which they were performing, this neither being entirely silent, almost amounting to a full verbal script by the latter stages, nor attempting complete realism either in sound or appearance: the "Pht! Pht! Pht!" of a football being inflated being a simplified exaggeration and also some thing I would have expected a mime artist to have conveyed silently; the invisible football, once blown up, was not then played with in such a manner that the audience could "see" it, which is an illusion of realism that it is impressive to watch some mime artists create.

Since then I have not only had the chance to see this style more widely used but I am convinced

that **Black Mime Theatre**'s use of it has matured immeasurably. The orally-produced, exaggerated sound effects and the use of words do convey useful information but primarily they are creating a virtually musical accompaniment to the actions being performed, so much so that when some actual music is introduced during a disco sequence it is this which seems at first to be breaking the bounds of the convention being used. The second sequence of the play, showing the lad thrown into jail for drug dealing dashing round his inner city estate with his colleagues on their mountain bikes, is not, if one stopped to analyse it, a realistic representation of riding a bicycle but it is exciting, physically impressive and entirely effective in representing both what is being done and the mental excitation of the lads doing it.

The other area of great advance in this production is that, whereas the Seven Ages of Man represented in **Mantrail** were recognisable, they seemed to be fairly superficial charicatures. Here a very serious topic was chosen: prison life, how people get there and the effects on there families. In fact most of the scenes were hilarious but one never doubted that the company had a deep understanding of the reality they were representing; - they had researched it in four prisons, men's and women's. When they chose to show horrors directly, usually mental horrors, they were entirely effective in doing so.

They were tremendously physical

performances. The cast wore knee protection with good reason, as they frequently threw themselves and each other about which great vigour, knowing how to land on almost any part of their bodies from almost any height, from any angle. They enthused members of the audience of all ages but it was perhaps fortunate that the company is used to doing workshops with young people, as the, quite well-mannered, thirteen-year-olds from the Whitefield dance club who had monopolised the front row were inspired not only to applaud but whistle them deafeningly through their curtain calls, with genuine enthusiasm, and then set out to pursue them for their autographs.

26 MARCH. THE MAN WHO; Contact. (60).

There seems to be a long-standing urge in many actors and writers to portray madness on stage. Although some of the resulting work, going back at least to **Sophocles' Ajax**, has been splendid theatre, I often doubt when I meet examples if these works are as interesting for the audience as they seem to be for the performers.

I never saw **Peter Brook**'s production of **Marat/Sade.** The fact that I have not been too interested by later works which I suspect were influenced by it does not mean that the original was not as great as many have claimed it to be. This did mean, however, that I did not go to **The Man Who** totally convinced that I was going to an

evening I would enjoy. I found it totally absorbing throughout.

Whether "madness" is a useful term to describe the mental disorders influencing the people we saw may be open to question. The closing sequence of the performers watching television images of the brain sectors and the occasional reference in the dialogue to such areas as the hippocampus very much related the behaviour we saw to physical irregularities, rather than to the type of earlier traumatic experiences from which many dramtic plots had ,been made.

I had heard **Peter Brook** on the **BBC World Service Meridian** programme that morning saying that the company had deliberately abandoned any narrative elements from the accounts in **Oliver Sachs'** book, saying that to have followed these would have inevitably led them into "Soap Opera" stereotype patterns of "patient/good doctor/bad doctor/ sorrow/cure", already so extensively used that an audience would gain nothing new from seeing them again. What we, therefore, got was an unbroken sequence of very persuasively recreated elicitations of different patients' peculiarities of perception. I wondered at first whether we would meet them again at a later point, when some progress had been made, but we only had the building up of the initial portraits. The one occasion upon which reference was made to any possible outcome from the doctor's enquiries was when a patient was emotionally overcome on seeing from a television monitor that he had completely failed to shave half of his face, something he had been utterly unable to see from the reverse image in a mirror, and was re-assured: "Don't worry. In a few weeks you will be much better."

Such displays of emotion were rare. One patient with an amazingly exact knowledge of his precise actions and of when he undertook them let out a cry of pain when interrupted in carrying out his declared intention "I will now leave, reaching the door in twenty-seven steps." A man with a memory grasp for recent events of barely a minute and, therefore, still thinking himself to be a twenty-three-year-old living in the nineteen-sixties was much distressed to see his grey hairs in a mirror, as was one who had believed himself to be reciting **Gray's Elergy**, a poem he much loved, when he heard a recording of himself speaking utter gibberish. Otherwise patients were as ordered and sympathetic in giving answers as the doctor was in questioning and the alternation of actors taking the doctor and patient rôles emphasised the continuum of common humanity. What we had was not a narrative nor, scarcely, a collection of narratives but a dignified and absorbing panorama of distinctive sectors of the human condition.

30 MARCH.
TEMPTATIONS – THE DRAMA; Theatre Church. (61).

This was a very courageous production, not only for the actor, **Peter Moreton**, in allowing himself to be marooned on stage for over an hour, with only a step-ladder for company and material of almost unrelieved seriousness. That material must in itself have been daunting to any actor approaching it with any degree of commitment: "an attempt to look at what must have gone on in the mind of the man Jesus as he ended his fast in the desert." The scripting of this by **Michael J Austin** was not only skilful but bold.

The skill lay both in finding ways in which to maintain a dramatic impetus over the full length of the play and in imaginatively weaving into **St Matthew**'s account of the temptations relevant material from elsewhere in the gospels. This is done much in the style of a striking African-style wall-hanging which is hung over the cross in the side chapel at **Theatre Church**. In this, not only does the trunk of the tree under which Adam and Eve stand continue downwards to bear the body of the crucified Christ but, to one side, Jesus stands amidst the animals on the ark, bringing peace and protection not only to them but to the terrified, storm-tossed disciples, rowing frantically beneath them. In the play, Jesus on the pinnacle of the temple looks down to see not only the rich worshippers proudly making their prayers but the temple merchants in the court-yard, selling their exclusive acceptable sacrificial livestock and also the poor widow bringing her two pence to the offerings chest.

The boldness comes not only in making such connections, with which few would quarrel, but in the leaps to imagine "the mind of the man Jesus" and the speculations surrounding this. The first noticably bold shaft was when Jesus, recalling what He has learnt of how countless children died at the hands of Herod's soldiers whilst He in infancy fled with His family into Egypt, asks Himself of these innocents "Did they die for me?"

The Egypt years were presented briefly as a time of slavery, which is a characterisation with a strong Biblical root. However, without knowing the actual History of the time of the man Jesus too well in this regard, I think it possible that the play has missed an opportunity here in its aspiration to "help confront contemporary human questions".

Part of our contemporary context is our multi-cultural environment: there is a thriving Islamic Community Centre less than a mile down Blackburn Road from **Theatre Church** and **Michael Austin** was among those active in the campaign to prevent the **Rahman** family being deported. When such as the present Winston Churchill visit Bolton, they portray this presence as a threat to "our traditional culture", envisioned as typified by "English spinsters bicycling to church." One way to remove the fears which lead to such weird perceptions in those who profess and call themselves Christian might be to stress how much "the man Jesus" experienced many cultures: coming as an outsider and a refugee as a child to Egypt but to a community long established there, quite possibly reasonably prosperous and fairly well tolerated but in a context where the majority faith was not their own and believers had to develop their religion in a context in which Temple worship had to be a much more rare and remote possibility than in Palestine; when He did return there it was to "Galilee of the Gentiles", with non-Jewish peoples just across the lake to the West, not far to the East, in Syro-Phoenicia, and its climate and fertility attracting a substantial Roman population, in one of whose cities, Capernaum, Matthew says Jesus immediately settled after His return from the wilderness. If we are looking for human influences on the creation of the Christian understanding, Jesus' exposure to non-Jewish cultures should be looked to as a powerful source.

Churches have split and heresies been proclaimed over variant understandings of how His thoughts and actions are those of a man and also those of God. The boldest part, it seemed to me of **Michael Austin**'s attempt to portray "the mind of the man" was his representation of Jesus first as being embarrassed by John proclaiming Him as his superior, when He had simply hoped to be baptised as one of the multitude and to return to carpentry in Nazareth, and then "feeling there was something lacking inside me" This is then defined as "something I ought to be doing", a question which has driven Him into the wilderness, to find out what and how.

One does not need to be aware of such an early assertion as "It is in Christ that the Godhead in all its fullness dwells embodied" to apprehend the nature of the question raised here. "Did the real Jesus shout?" I heard a young member of the audience whisper to her mummy as the character felt the power of the first temptation. God alone knows the answer to that question but pondering what it implies leads to consideration of the same issues as contemplating the possibility of the Godhead in all its fullness "feeling there was something lacking inside me."

Despite the historic schisms occasioned by disagreement on this issue, nowadays leading most people into contemplating it would only lead to helpful reflection. It would be only a minute atypical minority who could be led into a blinding rage by the suggestion of an answer of which they disapproved. Far more likely to lead to purblind offence being taken by such moral guardians as members of the Third and Fourth Estates and some believers, if they happened to notice, was the brief indication in the treatment of the third temptation, of Jesus seeking worldly kingship, that He apprehended the attractions of using the powers thus available to the Lord's Annointed to requisition Bathshebas for his regal pleasure. It is an old, biblical, understanding, however, that "ours is not a high priest unable to sympathize with our weaknesses but one who has been tested in every way as we are, only without sinning." If the play can help make this Jesus available

again, He is certainly relevant to our "contemporary human questions."

So is the adaptation which leads Jesus to dismiss the source of this temptation as "My Satan", a force within His human self rather than an independent being. I would believe this to be a more accurate and now more helpful understanding than any of a Devil, with or without horns, scales and cloven hooves, but it is typical of the courage of the script that it is willing, if necessary, to make this leap from text to meaning in its source material.

These are serious questions, seriously treated. Light touches were comparatively rare, as when Jesus, after reaching good religious reasons for not throwing Himself down from the pinnacle of the Temple, looked back up and gasped "Phew! No regrets, though!" For the most part, however, what was there to carry the audience through was the energy of a desperate man, fighting his way through critical problems at a turning point in his life. The audience probably needed some initial sympathy with the issues being raised but, that granted, the shape given to the material by the script and by the production and by the skill and plausibility of the performance made it a very impressive and valuable evening's Theatre.

2 APRIL. SHEER MURDER; Night & Day. (66).

This was a most skilful conflation

of four short nighteen-thirties melodramas, with music and songs of the period. The company had hoped to Thirtify more extensively the café in which they so imaginatively used all the space available. As they could hardly have expected their audience to have come in evening dress, however, they might not have got far beyond what they very successfully achieved.

The three plays which were overtly performed as such, in the small performance area at one end, were doubly framed, both by the songs and spiel of the Glissandos, acting as hosts from another platform, with their visiting *siffleur,* and by the various episodes of **The Waiter** being naturally performed between the other items amongst the tables of the café.

On the previous evening this form of enactment had led to two passing officers of the law, patrolling to ensure good order around the popular night-spots of Oldham Street and espying an apparent customer being hit over the head with a tin tray and collapsing to the floor, deciding to enter and make enquiries. Who knows if they took notice of the date when they wrote up their report.

The confident performance of **Neil Edmund** as the Waiter, boldly making his desperate soliquies in the midst of the patrons, justifiably led to his telephone number being taken after the performance by the Artistic Director of a local small scale professional company who was in the audience.

Confidence and skill, sometimes in the face of adversity, was, however, displayed by all the performers. **Gareth Beazley,** who directed the whole evening, had had to take up the part of the Host in **The Second Guest** at very short notice. Afflicted by an inadequately affixed walrus moustache, he boldly resolved the matter by using his one available hand to cast it aside with a grand gesture, as though this were part of the unmasking of his plans for revenge and without stinting the continuous menace of his lines. **Justin Edwards** as his victim unhesitatingly threw himself to his death, even though the floor was covered with the fragments of a wine bottle accidentally destroyed in the proceedings; "Don't bother to pick it up" **Beazely** had naturally interpolated earlier when the first glass fell. Later, in **A Night at The Inn**, Edwards, before he had claimed it verbally, effectively established himself as the man who forsees everything, except his Final End, by holding out his hand from behind his newspaper, ready to receive back the ruby which his colleagues had just taken away with the intention of selling it. The Green Jade Idol, whose ruby eye they had stolen, whilst patently cardboard, was, nevertheless, so huge, bold and sudden in its final apparition and movements that it very successfully achieved the intended melodramatic effect.

The knowledgeable insight and the skill with which the whole evening was conceived and performed made it a most enjoyable and successful event.

5 APRIL. BLOOD WEDDING; Octagon. (71).

To have **Henry Livings** make a translation of **Lorca** seemed likely to be an inspired idea. So it proved to be, although it led to a moment or two of initial disorientation:-

"Muther: I'm off." "What o' y' snap?" With tones and costume this opening set us clearly in the Pennines. "I'll just cut some grapes to eat while I'm in the vineyard." Eh? On *our* hills?

This was only an initial jolt on take off, however, and it was well to establish so promptly that we were neither here nor there. Culturally we were to all intents and purposes in the Pennines but it would have been a needless and improper artifice to have tried to expunge or paraphrase every detail which showed this to be a Spanish play. The production gained enormous strength from having a consistent and familiar cultural language through which to work its way to the heart of a piece whose origins are quintessentially in another nation.

It was not just a matter of having vivid natural terms, rather than rootless translationese, in which to express both the play's poetry and its colloquial dialogue, although that was impressive enough. For instance, when The Father discusses with The Mother at the wedding their various aspirations for the anticipated grandchildren, his preference for numerous boys is justified bluntly as "what this farm needs: plenty of 'ands y' don't 'ave t' pay."

What the basic style of the translation and production seemed to enable, however, while preserving the archetypical format suggested by all but one of the characters simply being identified by such titles as "The Son" and "The Bride", was a far deeper characterisation which intensified the power of the tragedy even further, beyond the terrible might of its stark basic pattern.

Perhaps because the first of my few encounters with this play was in the form of a film of a rehearsal-room run through of the wordless ballet derived from it, I have been inclined to see it as an essentially simple, though terrible, incident which just happened, everybody following long-known passions and lines of conduct to their horrible doom.

This probably is one valid perspective on what happens but this production was able to increase its force immeasurably by revealing much more particularity and depth in the events and characters. We become aware from very early on in the first scene that there is more than one character in the play with an individual name, although Leonardo is to be the only one we see. When The Son tells his Mother "A Widowed Mother goes to live with her Married Son," the terms of her refusal not only tell us that archetypical social custom is not the inevitable dictator of practice, even to someone fundamentally committed to maintaining social proprieties. It is so idiosyncratic that it shows the depths of personal torment in a very particular individual as well as introducing us to a family name with which further references in the coming scenes will make us very familiar, so that it can later be used on its own, every time carrying an enormous weight in pointing to the foreboding tragedy: if she leaves the home where she can watch the graves of her husband and eldest son "one o' them murtherin' Feylixes may die and creep in to get himself buried beside them." When she later learns that the mother of her son's intended was a Felix, we are almost as powerfully struck with foreboding as she is. This and many other references to family relationships make clear that the title **Blood Wedding** does not only refer to a wedding which eventuated in the shedding of blood. Those events at least seem to be influenced by the ancestral blood of those involved.

This is one of the elements which present the audience, far earlier than most of the characters, with a sense of tragic inevitability. Much dramatic tension is then achieved by the numerous ways in which the play and this production of it kept making one feel that the inevitable might be averted: that Leonardo's wife was going to keep close enough tabs on him to prevent the looming abduction, the times at which, during the reception, both Leonardo and the Bride were off-stage and were enquired about before one or both of them re-emerged and one saw that all was well. It was splendid Theatre when **Janet Hazlegrove** as the Wife finally

burst in to say she had seen them riding away and there was a complete transformation, the Groom's easy-going nature changing in an instant and he striding off vengefully, the last time that we would in fact see him alive, even though the play had still long to run.

The play does not shown the inevitable duel in the forest. That is too obviously in store. What we get are the poetic evocations of the bright moonlight, which will ensure that the fugitives will not be able to hide, and of the inevitable Death. **Livings** has splendid lines for the Moon, evoking, for instance, how his beams must shine brightly on the sweating flanks of the runaways' horse and the sinister clog-dance of the Foresters, banging out threatening rythms on the wooden boards of the stage took a leaf from the ballet in using such sound to create the mood. One of their lines adds to the meanings in the play's title: "If that's the way the blood leads, that's the way you go."

This further adds to the layers of inevitability and evitability in the play. Overtly it is determinist but it also shows that the characters are not living in a world of homogeneous social prescription. Just as in **Yerma** that play shows that the central character's aspirations for marriage and motherhood are not the only one's on offer, that other women in the same village have other aspirations and that there are routes to achieve them, perhaps covertly but with considerable potential support, so in **Blood Wedding** the Foresters' remarks show that the Groom and his family live in a community where an elopement can be understood in terms other than those dictating outraged and fatal revenge.

These are not options which the Groom or those speaking publicly at the disrupted Wedding Reception can recognise as open to them but never-the-less the way in which this production created distinctive characters with qualities with which we could empathise, rather than simply formulaic figures dragged to their fate, intensified the depths of our response, as we could thus feel how nearly we could be in their shoes: **Clive Moore** as the intensely likeable young Groom, entirely sincere in wishing to be completely loyal to his Mother, whilst naturally restless under some of her demands and anxious to progress to the more unrestrained love of his wife delayed by the pre-marital proprieties, which he respects; the neighbours and household sharing in the family excitement of their friends, sharing gossip or speaking bluntly as each saw proper, and relishing the propect of the festivities, greeting the musicians when these were personal friends; **Richard Mayes** and **Valerie Tilley** as Father and Mother to the couple, each with their harsh streaks, each with matters they would have preferred otherwise about the proposed marriage but, having decided to approve it, either from a sense of business or from a deep love of her son, proceeding with many decent human sentiments as well as their

reticences; the Bride who sincerely wanted to make a true and lasting marriage with the Groom but who, at the critical moment, found the appeal of Leonardo, quite profitlessly, impossible to resist.

One cared deeply for all these people, so one not only had the bleak power of a stylised portrait but the searing tragedy of terrible events involving very recognisable human beings.

6 APRIL. LA RONDE; Coliseum. (72).

The items on the open stage which one could see on entering the theatre were a large double bed, an apparently very modern camera on a stand and, also on a stand, an umbrella with a white interior, apparently in order to reflect light in photography. The relevance of the bed to this play was obvious enough. The camera and reflector, removed to the side as the action began, were to explain the nature of the punctuation between each scene in this production: the couple to appear in it posed for a flash photograph whilst a third actor announced the scene's title, such as "The Prostitute and the Soldier." The camera's use was also suggested in many of the scenes at the moments when events had reached a Certain Stage.

This seemed to me a half-good idea. The title **La Ronde**, or **Reigen**, suggests an unbroken flow of activity but to break it in a way stressing the artifice of staging, with the two actors not due to take part helping the two who were to perform in donning their new costumes and assembling their hand props at the centre of the stage, and then to begin the adoption of their new personae with a pose for the camera, seemed quite a good way to highlight what seemed to be one of the play's main themes: the enormous amount of artifice needed to bring about what some claim to be one of the most natural of acts. The photographing of that act itself has indeed developed into an increasingly major industry with the evolution of the camera and might indeed serve as a symbol of the continued artificialising of sex over the century from **Schnitzler**'s time to our own. On the other hand, as a great deal of the artifice in these scenes is occasioned by the wish to keep the liasons covert, in order to preserve a totally different surface appearance to society than that actually portrayed by the scenes' events, the idea of the parties formally posing to allow a pictorial record to be made even of their meeting did not seem an entirely appropriate device.

The influence of any short coming here, however, was entirely marginal. What made the evening, overall, a great success was the excellence of the acting, the fine style of the production and the quality of **Mike Alfreds'** translation. When I saw **Willpower**'s production two years ago I felt that The Chat Times Ten did not really have the impetus to sustain itself over its full flight, that the play had said all it had to say by about

half way through. Here I felt fresh things were emerging much more of the way. I lost interest a bit by Scene 8, The Writer and the Actress, when both characters are behaving in a totally artificial way, whereas in other scenes one is aware of the genuine concerns of at least one of the characters. However, **Melanie Deakin** in **City Life** found this the high point of the evening, both for its hilarity and finding it the acme where "the women re-assert themselves." So far as I could perceive, The Housemaid in Scene 3, with her satisfied smiles in the scullery before attending The Son's summons to the sitting-room, showed she was directing events as much to her satisfaction as the more openly dominating Actress. As artifice in sex was so much the theme, however, a couple who were both equally and openly artificial in their manner were probably a necessary part of the panorama being painted. It was well put in perspective by the final scene, moreover, in which The Prostitute is totally frank about the rigours of her working life and shows herself wearily familiar with every type of chat which may be presented to her: "... Now he says I remind him of someone." The play helps us to have a sharper perception of such realities, often in a very witty way. I took the chuckles from the predominantly female audience to be of recognition, rather than of disbelief. The play does have very serious implications but, almost regardless of the subject matter, it would have been a delight to watch this production for the aimiable expertise of the acting alone.

7 APRIL. LADY WINDERMERE'S FAN; Library. (73).

Having seen a publicity photograph of two characters from the production manifestly in drag, I had come with some dubiety as to how this play might be handled. Thus forewarned, however, that this was not to be an entirely conventional production, I was not surprized to see the dark rudimentary set in front of a black backdrop, whereas fellow audience members behind me before the performance began, who by the end appeared to be justifiably well satisfied, were discussing it in depreciating terms, doubtless thinking that **Royal Exchange**-style period glitter would have been more appropriate.

The sombre look, however, later mirrored in most of the costumes, was entirely appropriate to a production which included ample recognition that the play involved highly serious considerations. This was in no way a barrier to its main resource, the skills of its actors, being able to make the proceedings light, witty or anything else, as and when they deemed appropriate. The one colour variation in the basic set, the almost piano-key-like black and white segmentation of the steps, mirrored in the male evening dress and white ball gowns worn much of the time, was an appropriate image of the Windermeres' rigid perception of human conduct being either Good or Bad. Mrs Erlynne's eventual

appearance in a bright red costume not only reflected the general perception of her as a Scarlet Woman but showed her to be outside the categorisation which almost everyone else at least affected to perceive.

The hilarious opening of a white-faced Parker, the butler, sonorously welcoming us with a recitation of the theatre House Rules about smoking, Fire Exits and the use of cameras allowed him to conclude not only with a formal announcement of the play's title but of its sub-title, A Play about a Good Woman", drawing our attention to the play's central theme.

By the end of the play that appellation was to be attributed to quite another character but **Ali White**, then entering as Lady Windermere, open-faced and natural, as distinct from the painted Parker, the lowering Lord Darlington and the grotesque, drag, Duchess of Berwick and Lady Agatha, already imminent in the background, seemed, both from her appearance and early conversations, to be quite clearly the Good Woman and the play likely to be about the disasters that such goodness can bring.

I do not know if the inspiration for the characters played in drag came in any initial measure from the economic convenience of having a comparatively large number of rôles played by a smaller supply of actors but it certainly proved most artistically effective in itself. It was very helpful to see this production the night after **Schnitzler's** contemporaneous **La Ronde**, as that play makes explicit the salacious underbelly of the society upon which all, except perhaps Lord Darlington, in **Lady Windermere** are concerned to maintain a respectable surface. The drag characters not only made highly noticable the gulf between surface and reality but, at the party in the Second Act, when the same white-faced actors visibly exchanged male and female rôles, the frequently grotesque images helpfully conveyed the personal and social distortion involved.

In this context it was interesting that the end of the play was so much concerned with Keeping The Secret. A play at the end of this century is often concerned with battling through to a situation in which people can Tell Each Other The Truth. Here, although that is Lady Windermere's strong instinct and what she is persuaded to hide from her husband would not seem now to be the most insuperable of brief indiscretions about which to be frank, the tensions which a playwright today might emphasise, arising from the need to live with a lie, appear to be given very much second place to the possibility that not to do so would be to place a destructive burden on her husband's purblindly high ideals.

Certainly he is endowed with the most extensive range of pious speeches in the final act, rejecting Mrs Erlynne for what he believes to be her failure to maintain her "reformed" life. Whether he would have been unable to forgive in his wife the brief contemplation of the same

act as he had not only forgiven but been ready to risk his own good reputation to obliterate in her mother is a nit it is probably not worth picking.

More interesting is the parallel suggested by the quotation in the programme from **André Gide**: "The double life that it [his homosexuality] entailed was by no means a simple matter of deceit and guilt for **Wilde**; it suited the cultivation of moral independence and detachment from society that he considered essential to art." There are certainly many speeches in the play, probably an eventual excess, attacking the conventional social distinctions of moral and immoral, although the final acclamation of Mrs Erlynne as Good would seem to suggest that he saw such divisions as misplaced, rather than as non-existent. Whether he saw Lady Windermere's eventual acquiescence in Keeping Her Secret as essential for her "cultivation of moral independence" is not so clear. What is certain is that this impressively skilful production not only provided occasion for appreciating the cast's abilities and **Wilde**'s wit but the opportunity to give due consideration to his more serious concerns.

8 APRIL. BOY; Green Room. (74).

This was a notably fine play, conceived and presented with exceptional ability. One indication of its skill is that although its subject matter centres on how a young

71

homosexual lad came to the verge of suicide, there was a wonderfully light and frequently humorous feel to it, without in any way undervaluing the elements which almost led to it becoming a tragedy. Rather the reverse. As the tone was so engaging, one was draw in to appreciate the nature of the influences at work over a period of almost ten years, from beginning secondary school until Boy is about nineteen, in a way that involved one's deepest sympathies. If we had only had the agony, there would have been a limit to what we could ingest. As so much was pleasant we were able to assimilate far more, including what was most painful.

The ending was happy. The Man, – not much older, except, perhaps, in experience –, with whom we see Boy being smitten at the play's outset, not only proves to be the most sympathetic companion and pleasant character, with whom it is possible to imagine Boy going on to have a long and happy relationship and beginning to make much more positive and secure developments in his own character. Having had the experience of his first lover, at school, killing himself because he could not reconcile his homosexual love with his great popular standing as a sports hero and generally admired "manliness", Man is able to recognise Boy's desperate state and has the firmness to insist that he stays and talks, rather than rushing back to the loneliness which could have been fatal.

Other happy influences have included the Girl who took him under her wing on the production line, when he left grammar school early, without qualifications, to escape the constant bullying. She initially fancies him but, when he finds he cannot respond, is entirely supportive when she is the first person he tells that he is gay.

His Friend at school has also been a pleasant character but what provided the most continuous occasion for the witty tone, as well as the opportunity for the deepest empathy, was the central device of having Boy represented by three actors, one of them speaking for the part of him eager to assert his gay nature, one for the part determined to hide it and one for the confused individual trying to discover how to live in between. The way in which each part of his persona simultaneously responds in a completely different way to each experience or encounter is frequently very witty. It is not immediately obvious that this device is being used. In the opening scene it seems just like a gang of mates standing around, commenting variously to each other at the sight of Man on the dancefloor. It is none the weaker, however, for taking a little while to decode. Indeed, one's apprehension that there is something slightly peculiar about the way the three go around together is an effective way of drawing one into trying to comprehend the details of the proceedings.

The first time the three speak with one voice is when Boy has come to feel that he has no options. He cannot respond to Girl's invitation to be her lover. If he goes to a gay bar the importunate attempts to haul him into the lavatories are not to his taste and when he is seen emerging from one by the aggressively straight he is subject to the same bullying behaviour that drove him out of school. His mother seems to have been able to accept that he has not realised her great dreams of his academic and professional success but would clearly find it far harder to abandon also her ideal that he should "settle down with a nice girl." Girl is tremendously supportive but her ultimate counsel is "take some E and have a good time" – it works for her. For Boy, however, this is not enough. He can forsee nothing but growing old alone, in fearful isolation. Fortunately this is when he encounters Man. His three voices become discordant again on how he should respond but by the end he can leave two of them behind and go off with Man alone.

These events are not revealed chronologically but are recalled through a very intricate but apposite structure. The great skill in the writing was matched by the fluent skills in performance, whether in the interaction of the three actors representing Boy or in the others having to portray three or four different characters each and doing so distinctively and impressively.

13 APRIL. BEAU JEST; Davenport. (87).

This was a delightful evening. Attracting a largely ethnic audience, who tended to make comments like "Isn't he a ringer for Jason?" as a new character entered, created an atmosphere somewhat like a large family gathering in the foyers. The most audibly enjoyed scenes were those in which Jewish custom was treated irreverently, particularly at the attempt to deal cursorily with the Seber meal, the impatient father giving a summary response to the four questions: "We were slaves; We're free. Now: let's eat."

Although the response here was quite raucous, the humour was mostly gentle and quiet, and very well sustained, "a good light comedy" someone justifiably commented afterwards. The rather broader humour of a brief episode in which two gentile suitors simultaneously tried to outdo each other in extravagant claims as to what they were prepared to do to make themselves acceptable to Sarah's parents seemed a little out of keeping, not least because the production elsewhere gave the appearance of keeping in touch with genuine emotions and, up to a point, social realities. The love of gentile for Jew in fact creates problems which cannot all be resolved by good-heartedness and understanding: either individual commitment or the integrity of the community must lose out in some degree. This, however, was not the play in which to push such a dilemma to its conclusion, although the psychiatrist brother Joel is able to tell Sarah directly that the consequence of her stratagems to avoid hurting her parents has been the creation of a situation in which someone is bound to get hurt in some measure. While stopping short of trying to search out ultimate solutions, the play makes genuine problems easier to bear by helping to make them apparent in an aimiable and light-hearted context.

The play was all the more effective for overcoming apparent technical difficulties. The set, with a raised dining area some way behind the chairs and sofa at the front of the stage, seemed as if it was going to lead to important action taking place in an unhelpfully remote position but, in fact, the crucial meal-time sequences succeeded in being thoroughly involving. For some reason in the opening minutes it seemed as though the way any such problem was going to be resolved was by having the cast miked and one thought, surely to goodness, the **Birmingham Stage Company** must employ actors who can project, as indeed they do. Whatever led to this brief initial impression, any sign of it rapidly vanished and one of the great strengths of the production was in fact the quiet, unemphatic acting which made its impact, at some distance, by pure skill. Hearing **Libby Morris** on **GMR's It's Kosher,** shortly before the performance, describing her part as "another Jewish Momma" and seeing Sarah's panic before her appearance, at the prospect of her discovering that she had a

gentile boyfriend, one was expecting a performance which could have been quite aggressive. What we got was something much quieter and more subtle.

The all-round high quality of the acting was what gave the evening a lot of its strength, not least in the case of **Eric Loren,** acting an actor. Initially one wondered if the play's apparently simple premise was going to provide enough material for three acts. The skill with which the writing in fact made it do so was greatly enhanced by the pleasure of seeing an "actor", abruptly thrust into the rôle of representing an appropriately kosher boyfriend, improvising desperately to carry it off and taking some professional pride in harnessing his skills to do so successfully. The script's material here was in fact of greatly varying subtlety but the skill with which it was all brought off meant that the few heavier-handed elements in the often perceptive material did very little to reduce the overall pleasure to be gained from the performance and from the agreeable experience of seeing the production as a whole.

15 APRIL. ROXANA; Bury Met. (76).

I have generally been suspicious of claims for certain Eighteenth Century novels along the lines which **Defoe** made for **Roxana:** "if there are any Parts of her Story, which being oblig'd to relate a wicked Action, seem to describe it too plainly, *the Writer says,* all imaginable Care has

CLARE BARRY as ROXANA

been taken to keep clear of Indecencies, and immodest Expression; and 'tis hop'd you will find nothing to prompt a vicious Mind, but every-where much to discourage and expose it."

One's cynicism in regard to such a claim is liable to be increased by its being interwoven in **Defoe**'s preface with claims for the absolute Historical veracity of the ensuing tale which go far beyond the degree to which he very probably did draw upon certain actual events.

Nevertheless, even though this production included several occasions upon which skirts were raised and breeches lowered to portray "a wicked Action" in a manner which **Defoe** would doubtless have found represented matters "too plainly", even by the libidinous standards of the Theatre of his own day, such methods

are not beyond the bounds of what is comparatively common upon our stages today and do not hide the undoubted intention of the **Eyewitness Theatre Company** to present a moral work, their moral being apparently identical with some of the concerns of **Defoe**, represented in his own words.

If in the second half this moral seems to be presented a little too extensively and one becomes aware for the first time that it was prepared for the stage by the same pen as the company's lumbering, if allegedly popular, **Fish on a Bicycle**, which this piece so far surpasses, the degree of insistence and reinforcement is economy itself compared with the length at which **Defoe** himself frequently allows his heroine to express herself:

"But my Heart was bent upon an

Independency of Fortune; and I told him, I knew no State of Matrimony, but what was, at best, a State of Inferiority, if not of Bondage; that I had no Notion of it; that I liv'd a Life of plentiful Fortune, I did not understand what Coherence the words *Honour* and *Obey* had with the Liberty of a *Free Woman;* that I knew of no Reason the Men had to engross the whole Liberty of the Race, and make the Women, not withstanding any desparity of Fortune, be subject to the Laws of Marriage, of their own making; that it was my Misfortune to be a Woman, but I was resolv'd it shou'd not be made worse by the Sex; and seeing Liberty seem'd to be the Men's Property, I wou'd be a *Man-Woman;* for as I was born free, I wou'd die so."

That is but half of one particular exposition, midway through the book. There the whole reads with a driving power but, clearly, on the stage compression was necessary and this **Peter McGarry**'s adaptation most skilfully achieves. The basic device is to begin the tale where the book ends, in a debtors prison, but with the narration given to Roxana's maid, instead of to the heroine. When her fellow inmates learn for whom she had worked and implore her to tell the tale of this famous courtesan, she leads them in re-enacting the tale. Identity with **Defoe**'s method is restored when it is revealed at the end that the most flea-ridden and ostracised of the prisoners, whom Amy has insisted must play the part of Roxana, eventually proves to be The Fortunate Mistress

herself, fallen as the upshot of her disreputable courses.

Although **Defoe** affects to make Roxana's constant awareness "That the Pleasure of her Wickedness was not worth the Repentance" as much a part of the novel's morality as any other, **Eyewitness** would probably endorse it less than the expressions of Women's Liberty. Whereas **Defoe** ends with Roxana asserting "I was brought so low again, that my Repentance seem'd to be only the Consequence of my Misery, as my Misery was of my Crime", **Eyewitness** have her re-emerging from her rags to perform once more the Turkish Dance with which she became most famous, by winning the heart of Charles II.

This method was outstandingly successful, not only in giving scope for most actors to play many parts most ably but with impressive lines skilfully edited from the original novel and amongst which one was never conscious of a different style in the additional words which must have been interpolated from time to time.

In the first half one saw Roxana lose her first husband but then learn, through Amy's tuition, to abandon her initial concepts of respectability and to attain comfort and independence through the monetary and physical attractiveness which his endowment enabled her to maintain. By half way through it seemed as though there might be nothing left but a repetition of episodes in which smitten princes and merchants were inspired to offer themselves as her "protectors", a sequence with which we were beginning to became as familiar as she was with their words. In the Second Act, however, there was the elaboration of her arguments for rejecting those who wished to develop their relationship from being protectors to husbands, including the consideration that "A wife is treated with indifference, a mistress with a strong passion." There was also the possibility that her first child, fostered soon after birth by Amy to enhance her attractiveness when her original husband died, might re-emerge and lose her the apparent respectability which helped to make her so desirable a mistress. This last consideration and the desperate act which was undertaken to subvert it was not developed to have such clearly wide and contemporary applications as the rest but it all helped to maintain the impetus and involvement generated by this most impressive production.

18 APRIL.
COPACABANA; Palace.
(83).

This was great good fun and about absolutely nothing. The production made no bones that, as regards its vestigial plot, we had seen it all before: Boy (song-writer) Meets Girl (singer); Boy Rescues Girl. The fun was in seeing all this done magnificently, in the style of a 1940's Technicolor Hollywood musical. It looked good, with splendid and multifarious costumes ingeniously inspired by the period and imaginative mass

choreography, agilely performed. It sounded good, with a brass-dominated orchestra in constant, lively action and some very witty dialogue.

For the first twenty minutes or so I thought the spoken word was going to have no significant place in the proceedings and indeed it was, overall, a comparatively minor element. However, when **Jenny Logan** as Gladys hobbled on with her tray-full of matches we could hear that the authors were as adept at the high class verbal pastiche as they were at the visual and musical styles involved. To have a wise-cracking mature blond is a standard feature of such proceedings but to bring it off you have to be able to write, as well as perform, good wise-cracks. Some venerable denizens of the Old Jokes Home, - "Composing, ... decomposing", "... or are you just pleased to see me?" -, were incorporated as markers but much very funny original material, perfectly in style, was provided as well. **Jenny Logan** certainly knew how to make the most of it.

The noticable joins in the screens upon which the production's title design was projected while the audience entered seemed a little awkward at first but once things got going the technically advanced system of projecting all the background scenery upon screens, which moved around in many configuration without there ever being any noticable distortion of the images projected upon them, proved not only to be a most fluent method of keeping the show constantly on the move but stylistically apt for a production which avowedly owed so much to the large-screen cinema.

The main characters being intentionally so two-dimensional, although nicely played, notably by **Gary Wilmot** as Our Hero, the real stars of the show were the ever-active dancing Ensemble. I was a little sad that, as so much of the show was Cuban-set or inspired, the opportunity had not been taken to recruit more black dancers, in whose hands some numbers might have looked more appropriate. Nevertheless, it would be believable that all those actually chosen were there on merit, as they were certainly a highly talented lot who did justice to the very fine choreography. I felt the inventiveness of this was not maintained at quite the same level in the second half, the Bolero dance seeming a little routine and the Pirate act, during which the Rescue was effected, while allowing for swinging about on ropes, skittling opponents by bowling outsize stage cannon balls at them and finally letting off the cannon in their faces, was a good basic idea but as a climactic scene would have benefitted if even more vigorous elaborations could have been devised. This, however, is to carp. The show abundantly achieved its aim of providing straightforward, skilful and stylish good fun.

20, 23, 24 APRIL.
BROTHERS AND SISTERS (77) and STARS IN THE MORNING SKY (78);

Forum.

It seems that in Russia a "Small" (**Maly**) theatre is one that can put forty actors on stage with a support team of almost as many. As the company arrived in various parties over the previous week and rehearsed intensively during the final days, attendants at the **Forum** assumed that they were utilising the concourse because there was not space for them all in the theatre, not realising how extensively **Brothers and Sisters** used the whole area, advancing or departing through the auditorium as workers or soldiers returned to the village or set off for the fields or forests.

The foremost characteristic of this staging of **Abramov's** novels is how a whole community, of all generations, is recreated, including in the cast those who would have already been adult at the time of the events portrayed, immediately after the Second World War, and those who would not even have been born when this production was first mounted nine years ago. One has heard of Russian productions kept in repertory for even longer periods but sometimes in the context of them having become entirely mechanical in the process. That is the last accusation one could bring against the **Maly** company. Their productions do include elements which are more noticably stylised than the highly realistic portrayals with which they establish themselves, abetted by their universally authentic costumes and props, but they are always full of life.

If we had also been able to see **House**, their further play dealing with the same community as **Brothers and Sisters**, twenty years on, this, combined with **Stars in the Morning Sky**, which is set in 1980, would have provided us with an almost complete post-war history of the Soviet Union from the perspective of ordinary citizens. This play by **Alexander Galin** seemed to be of a very different style, having a cast of only seven and, instead of ranging over the whole stage and beyond, representing events over several years, showed incidents apparently lasting no longer than they took to perform and for most of that period confined within what seemed to a noticably solid and extremely shallow box set, right up to the edge of the stage and going back no further than the **Forum** would usually use as the far side of its orchestra pit. The basic play was of a style with which we are far more familiar, in which, crudely described, a small group of strangers brought together in difficult circumstances, – in this case Moscow prostitutes removed from the city to increase its respectability for the duration of the Olympic Games –, learn something about each other, experience agonies which break down even those most used to presenting a hard face to life's challenges and all end up on the floor in images of grotesque agony.

There were, however, significant parallels in the way all three plays were presented. Each began with exaggeratedly jolly celebratory music, with newsreels of the end of the war and, five years later, joyfully singing drivers of combine harvesters in a Sovcolour musical celebrating the joys and successes of the collective farm, watched resignedly by the villagers whose lives are unrecognisably different, at the beginnings to the two parts of **Brothers and Sisters,** and that for the 1980 Moscow Olympics, immediately before the start of which **Stars in the Morning Sky** is set. As stated, each establishes itself with an enormous amount of physical and human realism but the first half of **Brothers and Sisters** ends with a reverie replaying earlier scenes as if, instead of occasional solitary soldiers finding their way home from the war, with little but their dignity or a vodka bottle, every Ivan had come proudly marching home *en masse* and with far more valuable homecoming gifts. In the second half of **Stars in the Morning Sky** the tremendously solid-seeming back wall suddenly swings back, not revealing a star-lit sky but a totally black one, perhaps widening our perspectiove and that of the characters of the context in which their experiences take place but showing us nothing cheering, only the brutalised state in which one of the prostitutes returns after being summoned to the nearby barracks, in contrast to the false glories of the Russians Olympic theme song which is played loudly as the torch passes along the nearby road on the way to the stadium. By the end the confining wall has returned firmly to its place, even though the loud celebratory music is played again over the images of the characters' distress. This is more similar to the

79

conclusion of the second part of **Brothers and Sisters**, which contains no fantasizing element but runs its main character into the brick wall of no-one except his sister being willing to sign the petition he has drafted for the pardon of their humane Farm Chairman, arrested for being too considerate to the needs of the villagers in the impossible task of reconciling these with the purblind demands and regulations of State and Party. She insisting she must sign scares away her feckless husband, who had split on the Chairman in the first place, to raise his Party standing. When her brother apologises for thus ruining her home she has the courage to face the reality of their situation, ending the play with the words: "Let it be so. I'd rather die than live dishonoured."

In those days Stalin was still alive and active. Almost any villager is shown to look over his shoulder if he feels inclined to suggest that it might be government mismanagement rather than just the after-effects of the war which leaves them impoverished, despite good harvests, by abruptly increased grain quotas and crippling demands for state loans. Anfisa, who was Chairman during the War and has now become the wife of the new Chairman, is able to protest that it cannot just be the war: after the Civil War things had been restored within a couple of years. The promise in Stalin's 1941 radio appeal to his "Brothers and Sisters" for sacrifices to repel the invader, that prosperity would return after this effort had been made, is relayed at the beginning of the play and is constantly in the minds of the villagers throughout, the more so as the post-war years pass and more is taken from them. The Party representative does have the grace to recognise at the party which the women contrive after the first post-war sowing, by driving a cow "accidentally" in to a silo to obtain meat, as they are forbidden to butcher any livestock, that in the village it is the women who have been all the Brothers and the Sisters too, as all the able and adult males have been at the war. We only see from a flashback in the second play with what diffidence and inexperience Anfisa had taken up the Chairmanship in 1941. In the first play we just see the competence and humanity with which she has come to fill the post by 1945. Nevertheless, by the time a handful of men have found their way back, their consensus is "It is time to end the women being in charge" and matters are so contrived.

The most impressive part of the three productions, I found, was the first half of Part One, in which the whole village as it was at the War's end was established. Much of this was large group scenes but there was also very impressive small group work, most notable when the seventeen-year-old Mikhail returns, taller by a head, from six months logging in the forests. His younger brothers are eager to see him and have been picking berries in welcome but his little sister screams at the sight of this strange giant. To calm her he takes this as occasion to bring out the few

simple presents he has been able
to bring. The audience was
audibly amused at her fear and
then shared the pleasure of their
gifts. Their sounds became a
sudden silence when Mikhail came
to his "*pièce de résistance*" and
unwrapped a simple loaf of brown
bread. "What is it?" exclaimed
his infant sister.

We learn the details of the food-
hunger by incremental details
after this abrupt introduction, in
particular of the villagers learning
to make bread out of moss, so
extensively that they throught the
swamps from which they gathered
it would disappear. Moss loaves
are still being consumed five
years later and are thrust in the
face of the Party representative
as condemnation of their still
having to live so abjectly even
whilst producing copious grain
supplies which he is requisitioning
for the ever increasing national
quota. The other great hunger
is that for men, which the
women try to assuage with a
collective cuddle on the way to
the sowing. Although this is a
lack they all feel, however, they
are scandalised when the widowed
Varvara attracts the now mature
Mikhail and send Anfisa to reign
her back. "He's not yet
twenty!" she protests. "And I'm
not yet forty!" complains Varvara.
Anfisa counsels "Find some-one
your own age" to which Varvara
exclaims "But where are the men
of my own age?", leaving Anfisa
to cradle her sympathetically in
her arms. The circle is
superficially squared when Anfisa's
husband returns and she gives him
his cards, leaving him available to
leave with Varvara for the town
but in the second play we learn

that it is Varvara and Mikhail
who, years later, still remain in
each others hearts.

The episodes in the second play
seemed less fully integrated,
almost as if they were taken
from discrete short stories rather
than a novel and, perversely, I
also found their power somewhat
perverted by a familiarity with
Animal Farm. The parallel of
the diligent followers increasingly
betrayed by the leadership after
the struggle was painfully close.
In justice, however, one should
have been even more moved by
the record of actual events
recorded by those who
experienced them and presented
by actors, some of whom had
been involved in what happened
almost fifty years ago. Their
characterisation of countless
villagers was vivid and persuasive
and one had the impression of
being present while History was
re-created.

21 APRIL. TO CATCH A WHALE; Bury Met. (79).

In Greater Manchester's fecund
Theatrical environment, small new
companies frequently arise with
almost identical descriptions of
their aspirations: "emphasis on
new writing, ... some classics."
Unfortunately they then disappear,
all but as frequently. One must
hope that the notable degree of
experience and proven talent in
its production team will enable
The Company to be longer lived,
not least because of the
outstanding quality of its first
production.

SHARON POWER, KERRIE THOMAS and JANE LANCASTER (left to right) as Trish, Carol and Pauline, the three women led to review their lives in CHRIS WEBB's impressive TO CATCH A WHALE.

Its strength is rooted in the skilful effectiveness with which its insights are expressed through its theatrical form, the sureness of which makes it amazing that this is the author **Chris Webb**'s first play, although she is apparently very experienced as a short story writer and one can see that its seemingly simple little tale could also be very effective in that form.

Its action takes place in one small room, an annex to a farewell party, the basic course of which lasts no longer than the play takes to perform. Time is bent slightly, however, by one character, Trish (**Sharon Power**),

frequently stepping out of the course of events to share her recollections and reflections with us. These fill us in on some previous history but most of this is revealed to us in the very skilful dialogue, which manages, without noticable artifice, to provide occasion for two women in their forties to recount a great deal of their previous lives and to explore deeply what this means to them, whether they really wish things to be any different and, if they do, whether the time has come at which they could take radical steps to change. This is counter-pointed by the views of the young graduate daughter, about to fly overseas to "save the whale", who is still innocent enough to imagine that if her mother really does not like her job she can just change it.

The outlook of the daughter, Carol (**Kerrie Thomas**), is delineated in some detail and this is a very interesting aspect of the play as I have not seen anything else which tries to capture as fully and explicitly the views of a presumably fairly representative twenty-year old in our immediate present. The libertarianism at first seems quite similar to what was noticable twenty years ago but of a far more easy going nature: Green and veggie, believing life can be different but seeing change more as coming through personal choice than any "political" striving to re-order society, believing they can do some things more sensibly than their parents whilst being entirely affectionate towards them.

The emphasis of the play, however, is on the forty-year old mum and her best friend. Carol's expectation of easy-going freedom does lead them to ask why this has not been available to them. One answer is that they have had to flog their guts out on behalf of their children; that without this Carol would not always have been able to return to a familiar and welcoming home when it suited her, have her thesis typed and clothes cleaned. They doubt that Carol will be able to escape for ever from such commitments to her own children when, later in life than they, she too becomes a mother.

Nevertheless, they do wonder

whether some of Carol's freedom could not be for them. Pauline's surprisingly fiery response to her daughter's admonition of "if you don't like it, change it," suggesting she might not stop at seeking a new job, – she might seek a new home as well –, while unsteadying for Carol reminds Trish of the school-girl friend who had always seemed likely to dash away and do something different, who had had in her application to be an air hostess when she found she was pregnant and consequently made an abrupt start to married life, living at first in her parents' home. She sees Carol's departure as providing Pauline (**Jane Lancaster**) with the opportunity to go off independently and do all the enterprising things which had once inspired her and is keenly disappointed when Pauline comes down to earth with the confession that she needs to live with someone.

The decision that that should continue to be with her husband does not seem to have been particularly inspired by the moving farewell speech for Carol that he *ad libs,* recalling the love of their early marriage and their shared delight in their then infant daughter. She had expected him to make the prepared speech, found by Trish where he had misplaced it at the bar, full of coarse jokes inspired by such images as harpoons and sperm whales. She would probably have decided to stay with him anyway. The consequent loss of belief in Pauline's adventurousness, which emerged as seeming to provide a surrogate for

Trish, while she fulfilled her own schooldays ideal of a husband, nice home and two kids, prompts her to wonder if returning home to lie down beside her husband, after putting his suit on the hanger and puked-on shirt in the bucket, grateful that she has a man who always comes in at night, no matter how late or how drunk, is really to be the end of her story. Maybe she is the one who will decide to do something really different.

Fine acting in all rôles, as well as the fine writing, made this an absorbing as well as an often lively tale. The simple set made this all the easier to appreciate, as its main feature was two large hanging sheets of perspex, not only representing but effectively acting as mirrors. The cast could thus act towards each other however they wished, whilst we could always see their expressions clearly, reflected if not directly. This was not the only way in which the play helped us to see matters from many points of view.

22 APRIL. THE KING'S PLAYER; Bury Met. (91).

"Across parts of Europe the English companies dazzled audiences in the early seventeenth century with the liberty and style of their expression. They displayed an incredible range of skills. Dancing, singing, mime and juggling were part of every company's repertoire and they could sustain a spectacular and wordless entertainment for an hour or more before a performance." **John Retallack**

summarised information from **Jerzy Limon's Gentlemen of a Company** in these terms in the September 1993 issue of **Plays and Players**, by way of introduction to his record of how the **Oxford Stage Company** last summer repeated a recorded visit 350 years previously by an English theatre company to Gdansk, in 1643.

It is therefore entirely Historically accurate that an English vagabond minstrel could have been juggling in the streets near Elsinore castle in the years in which **Shakespeare** represents the events of **Hamlet** as taking place. Although **Trevor Gare's The King's Player** is first and foremost one big laugh, it is all the more so because it is based on the thorough period knowledge one would expect from a **Medieval Players** veteran.

As The Player King is almost as prominent as the title characters in **Tom Stoppard's Rozencrantz and Guildenstern are Dead**, the idea of a play showing the events from his point of view did not seem a terribly novel one. However, this is a completely original and most amusing work.

The most obvious difference is that, whereas **Stoppard,** as one would expect, is primarily Words, Words, Words, this is first and foremost an outstanding physical performance. This is not to deny **The King's Player** a great deal of verbal felicity: Hamlet when first encountered is described as "a bit of a mother's boy, no dress sense, looked like he'd seen a ghost ..." This can go along with deliberately awful puns: when **Gare** is representing

Elsinore castle itself, complaining of "sick building syndrome" because of all the guilt-ridden whinging it has to listen to, the introduction of the Player to the layout includes: "this 'ere's the Banqueting 'all, where you'll perform; this 'ere's the Kitchen, where you'll get a bite arterwards, and," as the promenading fingers reach the left side of Gare's head, "this ear's ..."

There is a bit of padding as the Player digresses from his conversational recollections and explanations to demonstatrate such things as different means of taking a curtain call but most of this is a skilfully absorbing narrative, as Gare represents the various characters in his tale. Though more than common tall he is well able to present himself as the small boy, dwarfed by the giant anvil in the village smithy, holding a conversation with his giant blacksmith father. The Player, having leapt at the chance to rise to the status of Honorable Minstrel by getting regular court employment and guaranteed that he can perform The Murder of Gonzago, a play of which he has never heard but is confident he can busk it he can find out the plot, Gare is well able to present both sides of the conversation as the Player starts his researches in the local pub and the bar-keeper abruptly shuts up and looks behind him when he realises the similarity of the plot to local events in Elsinore. As **John Adams** developed his production of **Hamlet** at **Bolton** from the perception that the play begins with soldiers on guard upon the battlements because they are there for a good reason, **Gare** quite authentically represented the Player as entering the streets around Elsinore to find them containing a disproportionate military presence, not conditions to be welcomed by a desperately hungry strolling player, hoping to draw a lucrative crowd with a bit of juggling near the market stalls. He was as well able to represent himself as being thrown around by such forces as to show how the Player eventually improvised The Murder of Gonzago – The Musical, having got an adequate idea of the plot through a weird sister who, not having paid close enough attention to the answer when she asked "When shall we three meet again?", had found herself on the wrong side of the North Sea and in the wrong play but able to supply a potion from her bubbling cauldron which put him in touch with a informative ghost. That all this was so much fun came both from the knowledge behind the nonsense and from the versatile performance skills with which it was all enacted.

26 APRIL. THE THREEPENNY OPERA; Contact. (75).

Streets thick with beggars, some of whom may possibly use Peachum-approved techniques, and police action endeavouring to hide their presence from more prosperous visitors on the eve of a Great Civic Event is something with which we are entirely familiar in Manchester, not least in the immediate purlieus of our theatres. This production made no explicit attempt to relate this play's subject matter to such imminent examples of its relevance. It did not go so far as to endorse the Narrator's assertion, "Such things could not happen in the here and now" but its only attempts to show matters to be local and contemporary were a little less up to the minute: the burly, bearded Chief Constable with a Wigan accent and inclined to invoke the Deity, who sometimes dined with persons as dubious as MacHeath, was a timely allusion when made by the University's **Umbrella Theatre Company** in 1988 and still apt when implied in **Kaboodle**'s 1991 **Threepenny Story** but he no longer holds sway in our city; Ratners, whose name has now been removed from our high streets, were invoked twice, – once very appositely in relation to one of **Polly**'s wedding presents, once as a simple periphrasis for a vulgar term which this translation does not hesitate to use directly and copiously elsewhere.

I cannot remember this translation, by **Robert David MacDonald**, as having any egregious shortcoming when it was used at the **Oldham Coliseum** six years ago. Given **MacDonald**'s other notable translations, including such verse as that of **Racine,** one would not expect any, least of all with the songs. I was surprised, therefore, at how more than usually tricky to sing his versions of the songs appeared to be and, more seriously, how hard one had to listed in order to hear their

points being made.

I was inclined to blame the words rather than the singers for this as although the musicality of the cast seemed to me to vary greatly, from those like **Elizabeth Mansfield** and **Josette Bushell-Mingo** who could probably have graced a more legitimate opera to those whose main abilities seemed to lie elsewhere, everyone appeared to make as good a fist of fitting the words to the music as the translation allowed.

This variety of singing talent would be entirely plausible if people from our streets did indeed gather themselves together to perform "an opera such as only beggars could imagine, staged with an economy which only beggars could afford." Performed on a wide bare stage, furnished only with a grand piano at the centre, a revolving door at one side and a fire-escape-like spiral-stair-case at the other, the walls painted a uniform battleship-grey but as if on velvet and with slightly tarnished brass hand-plates just visible on the swing doors in the far corners, as if to servants' quarters, the setting could have suggested that a group of beggars had managed to gain access to a grand hotel which had been moth-balled, – much as MacHeath's gang commandeered the Warehouse for his wedding –, and decided to perform their tale as much in keeping with the style of their surroundings as they were able. The evening dress of the narrator, the silver coffee pot from which both Mrs Peachum and Lucy Brown dispensed their occasional, dubious, hospitality and the handful of other props and furnishings could have been rifled from such a setting.

If such was the concept, however, I feel it would have helped to have made it a little bit more explicit. As it was, the production was tremendously stylish but seemed to be taking place in something of a vacuum. Now and then it seemed to me that actors such as **Robert Pickavance** and **Josette Bushell–Mingo** were having to pluck an item from their skilful repertoire of voice or eyebrow inflections just to ginger things along, rather than being able to contribute them to some more fully worked out concept for the whole production.

29 APRIL. DREAM TIME and UNITY; Bury Met. (80, 81).

The one slight short-coming in the excellent **Dream Time** devised by **Bury Theatre Works**, that its length became somewhat noticable, had an entirely proper justification: to provide good parts for all the able and well-prepared 12- and 13-year olds who took part. If the prime objective had been to produce a well-shaped drama the number of central episodes could have been reduced from five to, say, three, – which is not to say that the splendid play we got was anything like 40% overlength, as the five groups of characters had their tales interwoven in the most effective manner, which both rendered the intricate overall

narrative as compact as possible and also meant that nobody just did their bit and got forgotten about: their performances and their element of the theme were making their contribution all the way through.

The basic structure began with a central Dreamer and his chorus making claims for the general importance of dreams, with Angela, the promoter of Sweet Dreams, and Devillia, responsible for Nightmares, also stressing their rôles. Five characters in the performers' age group were then introduced: two who faced different forms of parental obtacles to attending the discos they had set their hearts on, another whose barrier to getting to parties was lack of friends willing to invite her, a bully and a lad who could neither live up to his father's aspiration that he excel in football nor get his parent to share his enthusiasm for the field in which he did perform outstandingly, the writing of essays. Dreamer, aided here especially by Devillia, first helped them to see what could be the outcome if each of them got what they wanted in these circumstances and then, with Angela, how happier results might be reached by living in a different way.

Although the underlying morals would grace a traditional Sunday School, – "Do As You Would Be Done By" and "Problems Can Often Be Resolved By a Little More Understanding On All Sides" –, there was nothing either leaden or pious about the production. Such principles emerged because they were probably the underlying instincts of the decent-spirited young people who created the show, not because any guides had brought such maxims to them with the intention of contriving a morality play in their support. There was a lot of fresh, individual, detail in the various strands of narrative, so they were no humdrum set pieces but original works, often including a lot of wit. This included a very fine curtain line:

Dreamer: And so the time has come for us to say good-bye ...
Devillia: ... Until tonight!

This is an example of some of the very manageable stylised lines but a great strength of the piece was the natural dialogue, even in the context of the fantasized scenes, which was both written and spoken to sound plausibly natural. It is all too easy for skilled efforts to be made in creating dialogue in a form that should be natural to the members of a Youth Theatre and for the result to sound clearly like the stilted speaking of a script. **Bury Theatre Works** largely avoided this and created an involving and most enjoyable play, in which every part was performed creditably and many of them outstandingly.

Dialogue was only a vestigial part of **Unity**, a piece which enterprisingly and most successfully set itself to communicate primarily through movement and music even though, it is very likely, most of the cast had not previously seen themselves as much in the way of musicians of dancers.

Presumably much credit must go to the dance company **Third Estate**, with whom they worked, for helping them to devise material which they could perform so effectively. A few who did have previously developed music skills, notably a wind player whose unity with her long-wished-for flute was made one of the main examples of the theme, were given appropriate melodies to play, which were re-inforced by several performers who had learnt to use more rudimentary percussion pieces. Not all essayed even such basic instuments but all were involved in the dance and movement, often most athletically and everyone performing what movement they had entirely convincingly.

The two liveliest dance pieces were a series of early tumbling fights and duels, presumably illustrating lack of unity, and the considerable repertory of ways in which football supporters use their scarves to demonstrate, evolved into a virtual ballet. This sequence was centred round the experience of a girl who found how much getting a scarf made her united with United. I was not entirely convinced visually by the final episode in which, after the scarf had been stolen, she was revived by the realisation that she could still feel united, even without it. As everyone went through the routines once more, but her empty-handed, it was noticable that she was the odd one out, even though fully taking part, which was presumably not quite the point. Nevertheless, it was a very fine episode.

The third main example, of Unity across the generations, was of a girl inspired by the gift of a ring from her poor grandmother, who could well have benefitted financially by selling it but preferred to use it to bind the family together, by passing it on as it had been passed to her and as her grand-daughter had now become determined to pass it on in her turn. The circle dances used to illustrate this dimension of unity were not quite so striking as some of the others but they were perfectly servicable. In amongst the effective group work which this and other episodes involved, there was also occasion for individuals to make contributions of great character, showing that Unity involved the fulfilment of distinct persons, not their loss in a general sea. It was an impressive and pleasing evening by a most worthwhile and able company.

2 MAY. WHAT THE BUTLER SAW; Royal Exchange. (82).

Kenneth Cranham begins the more accessible of this production's two programme notes on **Joe Orton** by citing **Oscar Wilde** as "one of Joe's mentors." This is very apt as the performance, especially in the first half, has a splendidly Wildean style and drive to it, turning the correct social phrases to uses which those who have usually mouthed them have never intended.

I was delighted to see this brought off in such a sustained

way, as in the couple of, good, previous productions which I have seen I have wondered if the fact that this was **Orton**'s last play meant that he had never had the chance to give it a final trimming. No such question crossed my mind on this occasion. The second act's increasingly physical humour, with accelerating dashing about, eventually augmented by shooting, was perhaps rather less distinctive but was still very well done. All rôles were fully, aptly and impressively characterised. They were cartoon-based, – a massively solid and moustachioed police sergeant, a bow-tied psychiatrist, and a bowler-hatted, impressively thick-suited, be-brief-cased and patrician-looking Whitehall inspector –, but all were filled in with ably turned phrase and facial expression.

As it is now commonplace for the institutions and types of character here satirized to be treated with such vulgar contempt, if the play is to survive it can no longer rely on its original shock value and requires the stylish standard of performance which it receives so successfully here, in order to bring out the quality of the writing.

3 MAY. TIME AND THE CONWAYS; Octagon. (84).

I saw a fine production of **Time and the Conways** at **Crompton** less than two years ago and, while thinking it a good and interesting play, wondered when I saw that it was to be performed in **Bolton** whether there was enough to it for me to want to see it again so soon. However, fine acting and interesting staging certainly made a very worthwhile evening and showed in to be a much more intricate play than I had noticed first time around. The greater detail which I noticed on this occasion, however, mostly related to the Time part of its considerations whereas the main theme I had noticed at **Crompton** had evolved more directly from the Conways half of the title. The emphasis there had emerged as on the Condition of Women, not because **Crompton** had laboured it but because of its centrality to the text. "What most women go through, all kinds of women all over the world" seemed as if it was the key line and the particular stresses on the female characters, married or unmarried, well-off or struggling, at the hands of men or of mothers were clear enough in this production.

I am inclined to think that this issue is of far greater importance than the speculations about the nature of Time. These are bound into the fabric of the play from the earliest exchanges, as to whether the young Conways' father had foreseen his death, in the same way as they have heard that some soldiers in the trenches in the recently-ended First World War could foresee theirs, and comments on how such grim considerations can be found to intrude upon a mind caught up in something happy, such as the festivities of a birthday party. If **Priestley** is here doing more than creating a largely conscious artifice with

which to structure the mechanics of the play, then I doubt if the particular form which his speculations take is really very helpful in elucidating much about aspects of human existence of which more conventional formulations may fail to take account.

More seriously, the implications drawn from this in the play seem to lay an emphasis on the virtues of stoicism, which would seem to suggest that the necessary response to the Condition of Women, or to any other social ill suggested less emphatically in the play, is to learn how to bear it, rather than how to change it: "Man was made for joy and woe;/ And when this we rightly know,/ Safely through the world we go," is repeatedly quoted from Blake. The perception that "Time ... merely moves us on – in this life – from one peep-hole to the next" might liberate us from incapacitating depression engendered by the perception that "if things were merely mixed – good and bad – that would be all right, but they get worse." To perceive that "because we think Time's ticking our lives away, that's why we snatch and grab and hurt each other" might provide us with the calm centre which would enable us to live more positively but it does not give much direction on what the nature of that positive action might be and it may even confound it by a misdiagnosis of what the sources of man's inhumanity to man may be.

The only problem with the play which I remembered from **Crompton** was a feeling that most of the Third Act seemed superfluous, as it seemed only to show us what we had already been led to expect by the Second. **Bolton** brought off the sections which had seemed unnecessary there by the excellence of the acting, making us feel very deeply with the characters as each misfortune or hubristic affirmation involved them. All it got us to in the end, however, was the intensity of Kay's personal distress, as the one who could now perceive what it would all lead to. Without wishing to undervalue the importance of the personal, this did not seem to bring to a head the wider issues which had been raised.

The whole took place in an largely absract set, founded on sky-blue building blocks, resembling the graphics now often used to represent an ether-net, perhaps suggesting the segmented apprehension of reality implicit in the Time philosophy. It provided a suitable area in which Kay could step outside the action in the Third Act, when her perceptions of events from a different Time perspective were most acute. Time's lack of fundamental influence was suggested by dispensing with any aging make-up on the actors in the different periods. Those who, in their various ways, allowed themselves to be least touched by Time, Alan and Mrs Conway, did not even change their clothes. **Rosie Cavaliero** as Carol, dead by the Second Act, was never-the-less present on stage throughout it, actively watching the behaviour of her relatives and speaking with her mother the words with which she had told her of her fatal illness. Her lively performance, noticably in showing in the Third Act how she had come to make such an impression on **Tom Higgins**'s quietly powerful Ernest Beevers, was among the many examples of fine acting which made this a notable production.

4 MAY. COTTON MATHER'S WONDERS OF THE INVISIBLE WORLD; Romiley Forum. (85).

The Glee Club's latest work is entirely delightful and among their best. Whether because of their well-deserved **New Stages** award, the production gives the impression of being more fully resourced than previous work but this is very likely because of the bright colours. Nothing more expensive appears to be used than cardboard, poster paints and fishing line, the most valuable investment being in letting the cast size grow to four, the two faces new to **The Glee Club** on this occasion being **Catherine Kies** and **Ursula Lea**, who are entirely successful in identifying themselves with the company's always aimiable but straight-faced performance style.

Quite what material in the show was withheld or adapted for the children's version, **Young Cotton Mather ...**, I have no idea, as an essential feature of what **The Glee Club** seem to mean when they say that their theatre and music are "just right for *people*" is the deliberately child's-eye-view nature of what they represent.

This was most specific in this production in two of the few scenes in which words were used, when first **Mark Whitelaw** and later **Ursula Lea** came on with stereotypical black cone-hat, cloak and broom to tell tales of experiences in early childhood which made each of them 'know they were a witch.' Almost every stage image, however, set in front of the green poster paint of the hilly, cardboard, meadows, could easily have come out of a children's picture book. Certainly at least one seven-year-old who was present for the evening, adult, version was justifiably delighted throughout and in high spirits afterwards. **Ursula Lea's** tale did, indeed, have a gruesome conclusion but just of the kind children love and was very skilfully told, having us chuckling along with its evocation of happy experiences right up the point at which matters took a final turn of a different character.

I had wondered in advance how the performance was going to accomodate Cotton Mather, whose involvement in the late seventeenth-century witchcraft hysteria in Masssachussetts was part of something much nastier than the **Jill Murphy**-style witches, so popular in many children's books currently, and who proved to be the only type evoked in this play. We were told in the opening few words at the microphone with which **The Glee Club**, as usual, diffidently introduced themselves and the play, that all we needed to know about "that never-to-be-forgotten person" was that he was a Witch-Finder. If by any chance the delineation of the American

mid-west folk image, lovingly evoked by the production as a whole, is found accurate and appealing enough to enable **The Glee Club** to take their production across the Atlantic, as it well could, one hopes that they find audiences which either know no more or who can put aside any discordant additional information.

Mather is presumably the occupant of the coffin whose journey across the plains is one strand of the production. When he is finally buried the grave is well and truly danced upon, maybe just as a way of packing down the earth. Worms are shown carrying out parallel journeys to the human beings but if this is out of any interest in the corpse becoming available to them through interment, such an inference is not specifically confirmed. Their presence might be merely occasioned by their featuring in a brief quotation from an alleged memoir cited in the programme, "Angling With Zealots" by I V Burin, which both supplies several images developed in the production and sets it all in the context of aimiable fisherman's tales.

The jolly proceedings are also framed within the changing of the seasons and the recurrence of such annual communal activities as the town parade, – the four grey-suited performers managing to present this as an extended sequence of varigated humans and livestock, all marching past in due order to suitably jolly music. It is all very characterful but it never troubles itself with complexity or plot. The fact that one of the two pallbearers is far better provided for by way of rations and bedding on the journey is simply observed and accepted, as naturally as the passing sign-posts, scenery and rural population. The simply-levered and twine-drawn moving features all work perfectly efficiently but no effort is made to hide their mechanics or to deprive children of the pleasure of seeing the second actor, glimpsed from time to time as he moves the tail of the giant worm along the crest of the cardboard hills. The performance is entirely successful in evoking the wonder of its world whilst appearing to do nothing to make invisible the skill with which it was done.

11 MAY. MAKING LIGHT (88); BEANS (89); REPEAT HABITUAL DEFENDER (90); MINIMAL STORIES (50); Coliseum: Granada Studio.

Most of this evening of work by third-year students at the **Arden School of Theatre** was entirely of their own devising. The exception to this was the concluding selection of **Javier Tomeo's Minimal Stories**. This was greatly enjoyed by the audience and very skilfully performed but it seemed to me to have lost something of the distinctive atmosphere which the full performance had had when I saw it on 4 March. It now seemed more of an amusing collection of bizarre but less remarkable anecdotes. It may be that the performers were

constrained to hurry it along a bit, to fit in with other items on the programme, and reduced the spaces between what had originally seemed exceptionally sparse dialogue. The long ruminative periods between occasional utterances had originally been most successfully used to give the piece its most particular tone.

Compression did no harm whatsoever to the two preceding pieces, either side of the interval, both of them under ten minutes. They were both thoroughly enjoyable in their separate ways and most ably performed but lost nothing by not being extended beyond their modest length.

Repeat Habitual Offender, devised and performed by **Tara Daniels** and **Andrew Fillis,** proved to be mainly a movement piece and was thoroughly effective as such. Its subject was two co-habiting young people who had come to find each other's company thoroughly irritating. After an introductory series of well-turned cynical and somewhat surreal comments to us about their experiences, the relationship was silently danced out. At one stage it seemed as if, rather romantically, happy comradeship was about to be restored but it proved that this could not be sustained. The choreography was not all that original but it was thoroughly effective and most competently executed, forming a pointed but often witty vignette.

Lindi Glover's Beans, brief and amusing but, in its zany way, referring to a recognisable and

93

sadder reality, had the task of following on from the evening's most substantial piece. At first its more artificial way of suggesting domestic misfortune seemed a little out of place in that context but its brief humour proved to be quite a refreshing way to bring us to the interval. The nature of the character's unhappy childhood experiences were only partially sketched in. What we did learn was that they had left her so desperate to make a friend that she was unstoppable in pouring out her reflections to a new acquaintance. She was unable to assimilate the entreaties with which he repeatedly tried to interrupt her flow of words, that he could be a lot more attentive and sympathetic if he could first make use of her toilet. The main means she had adopted for trying to adjust to whatever disruptions had occured in her life was to interpret everything in terms of Country and Western. The Beans of the title were what this thought process had led her to think of as the most appropriate foodstuff for all occasions. The climax of the performance was an hilarious mime to an outlandish Country and Western ballad, which brought us all to the interval hooting with laughter.

This was not as inappropriate a way to follow **Joanne Curley's** vivid study of domestic violence in **Making Light** as one might think. It would not be proper to include among the meanings of the title any suggestion that her experiences were something of which she made light but the character was one of resilient spirit, who was borne up by some degree of hope and determination, even before her experiences began to take a turn for the better.

The forty-minute play had three scenes. In the first the young wife was picking herself up after a battering by her husband and we got to know something about her situation, the scene ending with her defying him by going out for an evening with the new friends who were beginning to develop her confidence, contrary to the threats he had made before departing for the pub. The second was sometime after he had been imprisoned for the attack he had made on her when she had returned from that expedition. She was experiencing the liberty this now brought her, in particular the freedom from her mother's belief, intensified by her having been a single parent, that she must above all hang onto her marriage for the sake of her son, this despite the fact that having a sometimes crying child about the house had proved to be something to which the young husband had been even less able to adjust than the basic problems of living decently with another person. In the third, briefer, final scene her modest dreams were beginning to come true, most notably the possible return of her child from foster care.

The play could have come to a satisfactory dramatic conclusion at the end of any of the three scenes. The second scene, however, enabled the development of the theme which linked her personal experiences with the interest she developed in **Amnesty International**, writing letters in support of whose prisoners of conscience she was effectively encouraged to take up by the better-educated friends whom she met through them coming to stack the same supermarket shelves as she did full-time, in order to supplement their student grants. Directing her concerns in that direction did successfully both relieve the pressure of her own problems and give her confidence that an "ordinary person" such as her could write to presidents and prison governors, even eventually send them faxes, and that this could have some influence.

This was done entirely persuasively, when it could easily have fallen into moralising artifice. We never saw her understand her own sufferings in terms of the elements of the Declaration of Human Rights with which she became so familiar. There were elements which seemed a little artificial, notably in the last scene when she not only got a helpful letter from Social Services about her son, but "a Christmas card from abroad", from the **Amnesty** prisoner she had been most industrious to support, something she had thought it would be "nice" to get but unrealistic to dream of, when she sat writing cards to prisoners some months before. This, combined with the somewhat "cavalry to the rescue" manner in which she was saved from what might have been her worse ever beating by her husband, made one a little conscious of the fiction in what was otherwise a very realistic

experience, both in form, as she sat chatting with us in her flat, and in substance. We felt we knew the characters we did not see and the complexities were evoked at some depth. Despite all she suffered from her husband she could see the sense in which he was "decent, really". When we met her again at the beginning of the second scene, after learning of the husband being removed, she responded to a sound as if it "might be him coming back. In a way I wish he would. I should have changed the locks, but there's the cost."

This speech in fact very successfully avoided getting an unwanted laugh for the explanation of the sound: "it's just the wind in the roof." The **Coliseum**'s new **Granada Studio**, hitherto only used as a rehearsal space, is right under the tiles, so the performance took place to a fair amount of authentic wuthering. Apparently this had been even more the case while the company had been preparing during the afternoon, so **Joanne Curley**, whose very impressive piece of work this was, had been forewarned that this was a hazard and simply and effectively avoided any emphasis which could have spoiled her well-sustained atmosphere. The whole tone, leaving no doubt as to the awfulness of her experience, whilst at same time showing how she sustained a perkiness and developed increased perception and optimism, painting a wide-ranging and perceptive portrait of our times as well as of a distinctive individual, was a most notable achievement, both in concept and performance.

18 MAY. ALFIE; Davenport. (92).

Alfie is without doubt a morality play and was intended as such. **Bill Naughton,** its author, wrote "You need harsh truth to carry any sort of message and from it you can also create the best entertainment. The deep undernote of **Alfie** has not been underlined ..." This comment follows his remarks on the use by Alfie and his mates of "'it' for any seductable female."

The very fine production at **Bolton** eighteen months ago certainly did not stint on this emphasis and in some ways I did not regret that I did not have time then to see the first visit of this touring production as this sort of terminology was, intentionally, unpleasant and also it seemed a possible fault in the play that Alfie's Use and Discard approach to such females was inevitably at odds with the sympathies of an audience which could become genuine interested in women characters who then vanished from the narrative.

This production, though very different, is of comparable quality and avoids something of these problems. May be it was different emphasis or just the chance to see more detail on a second experience of the play, but the degree to which his recollections of his son by Gilda lingers in Alfie's mind meant that her abrupt disappearance after Scene 2 did not leave such a sense for the audience of unfinished business. Whilst **Adam**

Faith stimulated a palpable enthusiasm amongst the female section of the audience, - a young lady in a United bonnet was staking out his bullet-grey Mercedes sports car behind the theatre in the hope of an autograph when I arrived to prop up my Honda 90 beside it -, he did not, to my mind make Alfie improperly sympathetic. What he did do effectively was to show a man trapped in his very fully conscious "You got to fink of yourself; don't get involved" philosophy. Because he was bright enough to work out clearly that these were his principles in life, he was less able to abandon them where their consequences hurt those decent instincts which he in fact possessed. **Bolton's** use of the film's refrain, "What's it all about, Alfie?", between scenes in fact took matters one step further than the play appeared to on this showing. I am not sure if the line does ever appear in the dialogue but although Alfie is very clear about his principles I am not so sure that he is so clear about the questions they can raise. I think his disquiet may not get beyond an experience of discordancy.

I do not know if this technique was so successful further back in the well-filled house but the way in which **Adam Faith** stood right on the edge of the stage and seemed to be conversing personally with those of us in the first few rows was certainly very effective from that position. A lot of credit must go to him as director for a production which contained many good performances and effectively and simply moved well through the many different scenes. This was no mega-star dominated production, even though he was on stage by far the greater part of the time. There was a nice company feeling and everybody got the chance with their very full characterisations to contribute significantly to a very entertaining play which has a lot of point and insight. One hopes they were rewarded by the sense of a large audience thoroughly enjoying themselves.

19 MAY. B-ROAD MOVIE; Coliseum. (96).

Coming out of the **Coliseum's Granada Studio** a couple of night's before, I found myself working my way through **B-Road**'s large First Night audience. Whilst the crowd was clearly in good humour, the individuals I spoke to seemed a little bit defensive: "They seem to have wanted to try something a bit different", "needs tightening up a bit", "Worth checking out; – some good stuff in the second half."

The second half is where one gets the closest interaction between stage and screen, characters rushing off one to appear immediately on the other. This is good fun but much of it is the same gags as in **An Experiment in Contraprojection** by **Forkbeard Fantasy**, whose "invaluable help and advice" **Lip Service** freely acknowledge. As the style of film of which they here make their pastiche is early 1930's costume romance and they have authentically tried to reproduce the rather grainy black-and-white which can seem

on television to have characterised such films, some impact is lost, as, when we are meant to be primarily interested in the screen, what we can see is often rather indistinct.

Lip Service have added some very fine gags of their own, however, notably the film's final duet becoming a four-part harmony, when, film characters and those in "real life" having become thoroughly mislocated, those on stage join in singing with those riding their camel off into the sunset. Whether this particular example of the popular series guyed throughout the show being called **Bound for Cairo** is an *homage* to **Woody Allen's Purple Rose** I would not know.

Like **Forkbeard**, **Lip Service** also make much skilful use of puns, in their own distinctive style and these no unfocussed camera can hide. One much enjoyed from the film was the Cad (played by **Sue Ryding**, short) explaining his malfeasance to the Hero (**Maggie Fox**, tall) by saying "Your family always looked down on us" and receiving the reply, with a brisk, Coward-like tremor, "That was inevitable." There was a good deal more of this in the first half, with its admixtures of small perceptions of the way we live now, such as the house rules of a Happy Eater or Holiday Inn, and straight-faced clowning, such as spelling out the ideograms of a message left in the window of a boarded-up Chinese Restuarant.

It all made a very jolly mix. This was a far more sumptuous production than anything **Lip Service** have previously staged,

skilful though the basic design
features of their previous work
have often been. Here they
have been able to draw on top-
drawer talent in every
department: Design, **Kate Burnett**,
Music, **Mark Vibrans**, Dance,
Nona Shepphard, Lighting, **Phil
Clarke**, Animation, **Cosgrove Hall**
... , all listed in a most amusing
and stylish pastiche Souvenir
Programme. Impressive though all
this is, however, the main fun
still comes from two distinctive
performers putting together their
own blend of facial and vocal
expression to bring out the
ludicrous in the everyday.

20 MAY. FUENTE OVEJUNA; Capitol. (93).

Until Notting Hill's **Gate Theatre**
brought their splendid production
of **La Fingido verdadero** (**The
Great Pretenders** in **David
Johnston**'s splendid translation) to
Abraham Moss Theatre in
November 1991, all I had known
of **Lope de Vega** was that he
had written a Believe It Or Not
number of plays - 1500 by his
own reckoning, several hundred
surviving to this day. I had
assumed that any talent spread
out this thinly could not have
produced works of any great
depth. Having been proved
conclusively wrong in this by the
Gate, I was delighted to have
the opportunity to see more of
de Vega's work in this production
at **Capitol.**

Instantly, in the first scene, as
the battle-hardened old warlord,
Fernando Gomez **(David Wotton)**,
comes to sound out and try to
manipulate his new seventeen-

year-old superior, the Grand
Master Rodriro Tellez Giron **Adam
Evans)**, I was reminded of the
subtlety of characterisation and
political manœuvring which had
contributed to the fascination of
The Great Pretenders. This is
not just a matter of intricate
deviousness but includes people in
high office who appear to be
much more open and conciliatory
than one might expect from their
exhalted status and potentially
fearsome authority.

The appearance of openness is
continued into the next scene
when the people of Fuente
Ovejuna welcome back their
feudal lord, Commander Gomes,
with apparently sincerely offered
gifts of produce, **Adrian Mitchell**
having most skilfully translated
the mayor's speech of welcome
into most aimiable doggerel. We
later learn that Gomes' crude
rapacity has already made him a
far from beloved leader. His
increasingly disrespectful abuse of
his authority climaxes in his using
his soldiery to abduct the mayor's
daughter from the public square
on her wedding day. He has
been inflamed particularly by her
and her intended being the only
two individuals who have resisted
his demands, rather than
submitting. This leads to the
central incident of the play, the
whole village eventually rising up
as one to destroy him, so that it
is literally true that "Fuente
Ovejuna killed the Commander."

This is the answer which all the
villagers agree amongst themselves
that they should give when their
action is investigated by the
Judge sent by the new national
monarchs, Ferdinand and Isabella.

As the founders of the newly united Spain in which **de Vega** wrote, it would have presumably have been as tricky for him to have suggested any serious criticism of their actions as it would have been for his contemporary, **Shakespeare**, to have said anything against their contemporary, Henry VII. Nevertheless, he shows them at least as party to decisions of some complexity. Although the Commander had been taking the lead in fighting against the spreading overlordship of Ferdinand and Isabella, they do not hesitate to order the investigation, through torture, and punishment of those responsible for his death. Admittedly this is based on a somewhat partial report of events but there can be no doubt that this action is based on a fundamental commitment to maintaining the principle of feudal authority. Nor is this contested by the villagers. Despite rhetoric at certain stages which would not have been out of place in **Edward Bond**'s Spanish Civil War play **Human Cannon**, performed at the **Capitol** a couple of years ago, what the villagers demand is *just* authority, not its abolition. The happy conclusion of the play is the recognition by Ferdinand and Isabella of the justice of their actions, after which the villagers assure the new rulers of their loyalty and there is no more to say.

The cast were highly successful in establishing both the diverse individual characters who made up the village community and their communal celebrations in song and dance. The acting area centred on a pale bordered rectangle in an open space, which could help to suggest the township's public square, in which the people should have been able to expect that their civic freedoms would be given some recognition, or the courts where their rulers from time to time held conference. Like the play, this had an apparent simplicity of concept but enabled the effective presentation of issues and a way of life of some considerable depth.

25 MAY. THE CANTERBURY TALES; Coliseum. (96).

Dramatising **Chaucer** in our day is tricky. He wrote very good tales but their real quality is in the language. If that is cut, either because it is feared that it will not be understood or simply because some adaptation is necessary to make the work into a play, with what can it be replaced to leave anything of remotely comparable quality?

The most widely performed current version, by **Michael Bogdanov**, does not bother itself with such considerations: it just hopes some primitive vulgarity, or the reputation of it, will be sufficient to find an audience. **Medieval Players**, Of Beloved Memory, had a brilliant version of **The Miller's Tale**, performed as at a fairground by glove puppets, with a huckster narrating a virtually complete original text as commentary. That was certainly fully comprehensible to even the most lightly educated modern youngster, several of whom were quite prostrate with mirth when this was brought to the **Library Theatre** seven years ago. **Salford University Theatre Company** drew on some of the same degree of stylisation by masking their actors and by comparable fabrication of the bared and branded buttocks. However, although **Conann Whelan**'s Miller effectively handled a fair amount of direct narration, the actors were involved in a full dramatisation.

Alive and Kicking, from Leeds, toured a much more similar and very successful perfomance of more or less the same selection of tales as **Salford's** in 1991. There the text had been modernised by **Martin Riley** but, as here, was often very close to the original. They used the rather bizarre format of the four young actors representing themselves as Medieval Italian alchemists, whose concoction of an Elixir of Eternal Youth had worked effectively on themselves but only minimally on Geoffrey Chaucer, whose body they had somehow acquired and had dragged round with them over the intervening centuries, hoping that their constant re-enactment of his tales would in some way penetrate his consciousness and revive him. This provided scope for a very vigorous performance style with *commedia del arte* elements, very direct contact with the audience and use of period music. **Salford** also made effective use of Medieval music and shared with **Alive and Kicking** their principal strength of not only keeping close to the original wording but respecting the original spirit and purpose of the

tales. They did not need such a contrived format, however. After making an initial suggestion of the Tabard at Southwalk where **Chaucer**'s pilgrims "by aventure yfalle in felaweshipe", by beginning with the four narrators used in the play gathered under an alemast, singing "Bring us in Good Ale", the production simply gets on with letting them tell us their stories.

Overall they do so very effectively. I think, however, that the production at this stage must be regarded as work in progress. Apart from incidentals such as the odd muffed lighting cue, there was a little under-emphasis generally, so that elements did not always get their full weight. For instance, after the very enjoyable representation on **The Nun's Priests Tale**, the first half of the performance could have been very effectively brought to its conclusion with the words appropriately selected from the original ending: "If you find this tale a folly,/As of a fox, or of a cock and hen,/Take the morality, good men./Take the wheat and let the chaff be still." With proper emphasis, this could have been a very good curtain line. At this stage of the performance's evolution, however, it was rather indistinct.

The Miller's Tale in its original has a tremendously dramatic ending, with the carpenter's tub crashing through the house and then all the rushing through the street as everyone comes to laugh at him lying shattered on the floor. Dropping an actor safely from such a height on stage obviously poses problems in a small scale production but, having taken the decision to end with the focus on him, rather than bring on the jeering multitude, some way to end his fall with a bigger bang or a sharper image of his humiliation or pitiableness seemed to me to need to be found. Again, the performance instead rather faded away.

Chaucer often does end his tales abruptly. " What nedeth it to sermone on it more?" cries the Pardoner when it has become obvious enough how his three ryotours are to meet Death. Like most occultation in **Chaucer**, this is far from meaning what it says and, as regards actual sermonising, the Pardoner is far from finished, going on for almost another hundred lines in the book. This aspect is well used in this production. The Pardoner launches into his moralising appeal to the audience, similar to that with which he began but, instead of being choked off by Host and Knight, the Wife of Bath siezes an opportunity to state her own morality and the production skilfully moves to her Tale by editing in the intervention which **Chaucer** gave the Pardoner in her Prologue: "Ye been a noble prechour in this cas./ I was aboute to wedde a wyf; allas!/ What sholde I bye it on my flessh so deere? ..."/ "Abyde!" quod she, "my tale is nate bigonne", and promptly gets on with it.

This was a good transition but the actual winding up of the Pardoner's Tale was again under-pointed. For whatever reason, perhaps just to ensure that the

trunk containing the fatal eight bushels of fine gold was got off stage, the actual stabbing and poisoning of the ryotours was not enacted. They just pottered off behind the tree with their box, leaving the Pardoner, who had most effectively been used to play all other parts in gleefully adopted disguising masks, to tell us what happened. Having said that the strength of **Chaucer** lies in the words, it would be perverse of me to claim that that could not have worked. As those particular words were not given much emphasis in this performance, however, it was another Tale which just rather faded out.

I do not think that this was a necessary fault in the conception of this production, merely a detail in this early stage of the evolution of its actual performance. In recording such details, which will probably have completely vanished by the time the production reaches further audiences, I do not wish them to obscure the virtues of a very enterprising and enjoyable piece of work. Nor, however, am I simple recording them because they seemed to be there. If they were transient they are unimportant. As this publication probably does not have the resources to include a later report, they are mentioned in case they are the only source of the "not quite yet" feel which took the edge off some of the evening or whether something more fundamental needs to be identified.

I began by asking how a modern dramatisation can compensate for the loss of **Chaucer**'s original language. Certainly this production contained many sharp and witty lines, as telling now as ever. Sometimes some of the rest seemed rather more ordinary, occasionally even a little like pantomime doggerel. The actors having more time to make all lines as effective as most might solve this but clearly other means to make it effective for the stage had been given serious attention. Heightening the style of physical movement might have been one dimension which could have been profitably developed far more but the two main fields which were looked to were medieval music and masks.

These both made a splendid contribution. One of the things some of the artists were discussing afterwards was the possibility of more music and songs. These will probably enhance the production greatly but the music is already a major element in the show's success. From the initial song to incidental contributions to various scenes or linking them, it does much to create the distinctive atmosphere and to add its own wit, as when recognisable phrases from a carol follow an impious episode.

The masks are an outstanding success. In a great variety of styles, full-face, half-face, simply adding to nose and cheeks or completely covering the whole head, as in the splendidly detailed and colourful creations for Chantecleer and Pertelote. These enabled their tale to get of to a vivid start, well maintained as **Ian Lashford** and **Lorraine Hackette** clucked,

crowed, strutted and showed what it means to rule the roost. Chantecleer's multitude of other wives were strikingly represented by a covey of colourful marionettes, operated by **Michael McKrell** whilst he told the tale, as the Nun's Priest. Sometimes the masques encouraged effective posing in tableaus reminicient of Renaissance records of such figures.

These were among the production's distinctive merits. The able performances will doubtless grow under **Bill Hopkinson**'s perceptive direction and give the whole a stature which will impress audiences even more fully than the substantial house, who so loudly enjoyed themselves watching the performance in Oldham.

28 MAY. MURDER IN THE CATHEDRAL; Cathedral. (94)

This was a splendidly vigorous, clear and always well-looking production. The cathedral space had been imaginatively and variously used and the style both combined constantly impressive stage images, so that almost every moment made an effective tableau, with great fluidity in moving from scene to scene. I am inclined to lay the blame for occasional inadequacies on the original script and, surprisingly, given the author, these, for the most part, seemed to be in the wording and verse.

The latest and least serious of

these was in the knights' final
apologias. This was meant to be
in contemporary style, as oppose
to the Historical or timeless form
of what was spoken elsewhere.
Doubtless it was an acceptable
stage representation of this when
the play was originally written
sixty years ago. Some of its
cadences are retained by a fair
number of our public figures
today, but their overall tone does
not readily include such phrasing
as "for my part I am awfully
sorry about it."

Even more than in the wording
has been the alteration in the
perception of our society. Most
of us may still value fairness but
a politician cannot now say to us
"You are Englishmen, and
therefore you believe in fair
play." Even the most primitive
in their perceptions have
assimilated that a general
audience contains women and that
it is not politic to ignore them.
Perceptions of sport are also
different. A leading footballer
can say without shame in public
that he regards a season involving
two sendings-off and several
cautions as "about average" and
politicians, while still as ready to
use the sportsfield as an analogue
for their activities, are often
willing to say openly "politics is a
dirty game." The anachronism in
all this was distracting but the
cast found as vigorous and
effective a way through it as
was possible. A last couple of
speeches, especially, had
considerable strength.

That this problem now exists in
that scene was no fault of the
author. The other two types of
problem with the script seemed

to me as if they probably were.
One difficulty was occasionally
stilted phrasing. Jo Burgess made
an extremely vigorous Messenger.
Dashing in excitedly with news of
the Archbishop's return was a
vivid and largely effective way to
play the scene. Taken at that
speed, however, such lines as "I
am here to inform you, without
circumlocution ..." and "You are
right to express a certain
incredulity" sounded awkward.
Would they have sounded right if
the character had been played as
an old bumbler? I am inclined
to think that some words would
still have sounded out of place
and that the advantages in
playing the scene fast greatly
outweighed any which there might
have been in playing it slow. In
general the production's variations
in tempo were well judged and
effective.

Because the verse-speaking was
in general so strong, whether in
allocating the lines of the chorus
to build up the sensation of
coalescing individual viewpoints or
in the mass panic after the
arrival of the knights in the
second act or, again, by the
more individual characters, I am
inclined to think that the reason
why the metre and sometimes the
rhymes were on occasion
distracting was because they were
not very apt, rather than because
they were mispoken. The
obtrusive stresses and imperfect
rhyme in "When men shall declare
that there was no mystery/About
this man who played a certain
part in history" may be a
deliberate means of trying to
convey the unease involved in a
Tempter trying to subvert the
beatification of a potential

Martyr. Given the stature of the poet who penned them it would be presumptuous to suggest otherwise. If such an explanation can excuse that particular couplet, however, lines with that many stressed and unstressed syllables did not always seem functional in some of the longer unrhymed speeches.

Noting such occasional distractions should not create the impression that that this was anything other than a well performed and well sounding evening. Apart from some not very distinct shouting in the middle of the second act, from where Thomas insists to the Knights that they make their charges "Now and Here" to when the nuns for the second time remove him from them by hustling him off to vespers, the clarity and character given to the lines was constantly impressive. The general ideas on the nature of martyrdom and on the legitimacy of the political desire to restore order in a country recently racked by civil war came across clearly, as did the continuing recognisability of such portrayals as "I see nothing quite conclusive in the art of temporal government,/But violence, duplicity and frequent malversation./King rules or barons rule:/The strong man strongly and the weakman by caprice./They have but one law, to seize the power and keep it,/And the steadfast can manipulate the greed and lust of others..." Although the lumbering syntax of the first line is, unfortunately, the initial thing to catch the attention, **Laura Wolfe** was able to handle the speech so that one was soon caught by the vividness

of the still all-too-accurate image.

The play's emphasis is first and foremost on its general ideas, Thomas being the only character who is clearly named, - such details as Fitz Urse or de Morville being clearly subsidiary to their being First or Second Knight -, but a great strength of this production was the clear characterisation which was built up by all members of the extensive chorus. There was, therefore, a powerful sense of individuals having to face the challenges of suffering and action as well the general picture they built up of a daily life which none would wish to see great events disrupt. Thomas, powefully and plausibly played by **John Draycott**, laying his hands in blessing on all individually as he arrived and, again, as his last act before his martyrdom, was a telling image, not only of all being united in a common sacrament but of each experiencing a personal blessing.

31 MAY. THE WONDERLAND OF ALICE; Heaton Park. (97).

This was great good fun. I was fortunate to be able to attend on a warm sunny evening during the school half-term holiday, so there was a good, congenial crowd, some of the children literate enough to be able to quote "What is the point of a book without pictures and without conversations?" to each other as we came up on Miss Prickett, the Governess, properly occupying herself with an improving volume, after we had passed Dodgson and Duckworth rowing Alice and Lorina on the lake. These then joined her and the conversation included useful fragments of Alice's formal education, so that we knew what was being distorted in Wonderland when the the Mock Turtle told of his lessons in reeling and writhing with the Old Tortoise and the Caterpillar recited his version of How Doth the Little Busy Bee.

As the warm sunshine reduced them to reverie and we followed Alice down the Rabbit Hole in pursuit of the White Rabbit, we passed the most fantastical and partly human artworks, which well conveyed the nature of the distorting Wonderland which we were entering, a grand-father clock and mantlepiece indicating that some elements were to be drawn from **Through the Looking Glass.**

I particularly liked the first half, in which the characterful and well-costumed actors enacted scenes with the Dodo, the Caterpillar, in the Duchess' kitchen, with a superbly condescending Cheshire Cat, and at the Mad Hatter's Tea Party, as these incorporated a great deal of chop-logic **Carroll** dialogue. The second half seemed to me to have rather more improvised lines, - including a highly amusing scene with the very camp Duchess -, and a bit less narrative drive but **City Life** particularly liked these scenes and certainly the settings, in the immediate purlieus on Heaton Hall, were especially apt and

picturesque. The croquet match, with its notably well-designed flamingoes and hedgehogs, was particularly vivid.

As often with **Midsommer** productions, events were particulaly well contrived to fit in with the waning daylight. The Gryphon placed a blanket round Alice's shoulders after their lively Lobster Quadrille and the Mock Turtle's lugubrious tones induced a somnolent atmosphere, so that Dodgson could re-appear after the concluding Trial of the Knave of Hearts, for which children in the audience were recruited as the jury, and carry Alice home to bed with wise reflections upon the wisdom of dreams.

1 JUNE. TOUCHED; Capitol. (105).

Excerpts from radio broadcasts are used effectively throughout this production, to pin-point the stages in national and international events which are taking place during the course of this tale of life in the back streets of Nottingham in the period between VE Day and VJ Day 1945. The first of these, from which we hear an extensive extract before any of the main action begins, proves to be one of the first reports after allied forces had reached Belsen. This is then completely forgotten, certainly on my part, as we meet the inhabitants of the street, taking in their washing and chatting about the rumour that the expected broadcast by Churchill at three o'clock is to announce the German surrender. We are then reminded of this opening right at the end, when part of the Belsen tape is replayed, speaking of the scattered bodies, amongst whom it is almost impossible to tell the living from the non-living. At first this seemed a very vivid key to what the play had come to be about. On later reflection I wondered if it was appropriate to use the enormity of Belsen as an image of the more diurnal lack of fulfilment in human lives, even if the latter may be indicated in such major texts as **St John's Gospel** as a central feature of the need for divine awareness in human existence.

For its first half **Touched** seems as if it could be understood simply as an Historical documentary, with a lot of its impact coming from reviving memories or telling a younger generation how things were. As such, both the detail of the writing and the skill of the playing in this production make it entirely effective. Then one has the perspective of hindsight. We know that the hopes many entertained of a Labour Government were only partially fulfilled and that returning Polish officers would not be able to resume their prosperous lives on landed estates. We know what the Nottingham people did not know when they thought the Japanese weak-spirited for surrendering after the dropping of one bomb, when they had survived a whole blitz.

There is more, however, to the play than either of these things. One of the central concerns of the main family whom we get to know is the pregnancy of one of its members and the expected strife and disgrace this will cause when the husband returns after recuperating from his time in a Japanese prisoner of war camp. After being put through the greater part of a gin-and-hot-bath abortion by her domineering sister, the expectant mother refuses to see her child disposed of in this way, in the same way as she refuses to continue the previous practices of minor pilfering from prosperous employers because of her belief that a society of entirely new standards is what will make the war worthwhile and what they must all strive to achieve. The fact that her pregnancy turns out to be an entirely false one, deluding her as well as her relatives, is not just a symbol of the emptiness of such hopes. The restrictive social attitudes, inter-twined with the family and neighbourly solidarity, do seem to be related to what is described in the indistinguishability of the living and non-living.

Whether this inadequacy is on the scale of Belsen is one question. Whether an image even remotely so dark deserves to be evoked in the context of a society and its constituent individuals who have been shown to have so many positive qualities is another. The child who has got herself thoroughly grubby, digging about in the wood while the family greet VJ Day by picnicing on the hillside, is forgiven on the grounds that it is a "once-in-a-lifetime experience", even though her grandmother cynically comments "It's the second time this year." The quietly vivid production by **Romy Baskerville** and the persuasiveness of all the acting sets an experience before us about which we can ponder whether to be forgiving or censorious, as we can of social reality to which the experience which they provide so closely relates.

2 JUNE. MOTI ROTI, PUTTLI CHUNNI; Dancehouse. (106).

What made this a great success was that the company not only had the skills but the resources to make this a really fine pastiche of Indian popular cinema. The setting was mostly contemporary London but the style was pure Bombay. Very stylish is was too. Where the musical numbers called for umpteen changes of glittering saris, these were to hand and the choreography, whether on stage or on film was impressive, – the best of this unfortunately all being in the first half, which thus undercut the second slightly.

Some undercutting was deliberate. When characters on stage suddenly burst into pre-recorded song there was a good laugh in the artifice of the artifice but this was never accompanied by anything less than performances of the highest skill. When the, ultimately reformable, villain sings winning smiles at the good woman, and shows us in asides the depth of his insincerity, this is all done with such impressive style that we can almost admire him for it, not surprisingly as it is performed by a noted superstar, **Nitish Bharadwaj**, who has performed Lord Krishna, no

less, in the immensely popular Indian television series dramatising the **Mahabharat.** Not every screen idol could be as impressive on stage, however.

As regards the expertise of the cast, we in Greater Manchester can take heart that three of the cast were either born here or have strong connections: **Shobna Gulati** was born in Oldham and last year played a leading rôle in **Peshkar**'s New Horizons, **Mina Anwar** has frequently performed with **M6**, most recently in **The Flood**, and with **Action Transport**, and **Kaleem Janjua** trained as a drama teacher at Manchester's then College of Higher Education. The expertise of **Moti Roti** shows the heights of quality to which our own developing Asian Theatre Groups can rise, although they will doubtless continue to pursue their own distinctive styles, such as **Aaj Kal**'s very penetrating exploration, notably in **Brothers**, of what it means to be Asian in Britain.

Moti Roti does not aspire to examine issues in that sort of depth but, in its very broad-brush, melodramatic terms, it does relate recognisably to certain aspects of Asian society here. It more seeks to affirm generally recognised virtues than to make any great development in their application. When **Monisha Bharadwaj**'s rich lady architect cries out "I shall do what I like and marry who I like," the reaction from the Asian element of the audience, including its young females, was of recognising a classic example of pride going before a fall, rather than any acclamation of social

FINETIME FONTAYNE as the devious Sidney, our guide through the world of Cotton Street in the BOLTON OCTAGON's outstanding World Premier staging of BILL NAUGHTON's DERBY DAY.

progressiveness. The piece also had a Dickensian style of Victorian values in that, while it was proper to show concern for the poor, the main focus of the plot was on enabling a few of them to join the super-rich by solving the Mystery of the Long-Lost Parent. Simple though the basic elements were, however, the fine skill with which they were all deployed, from **Ajay Chabra**'s exaggerated clown to the various cinema styles so faithfully re-captured, from the grand guilty nightmare on stage to the young love at the riverside on screen, all made this a most notable achievement, thoroughly enjoyable on many levels.

6 JUNE. DERBY DAY; Octagon. (98).

Lawrence Till has done a great good work in making this **Bill Naughton** radio play available for the stage. His adaptation is being published by **Samuel French** and will, without doubt, become regularly welcomed wherever Lancashire Theatre is known and loved.

The fact that many and various future productions, amateur and professional, can be anticipated of this very do-able play by all companies who can perform this Theatre well is not to belittle the excellence of the **Octagon's** World Premier, however. Both in conception and design and in all individual performances, the company do it proud.

Portraying events from dawn till dark in and around Cotton Street in Bolton on 1 June 1921, the play is another example that **Aristotle** was onto a good key to dramatic strength when he proclaimed the Unities of Time, Place and Theme. The unity of theme might seem a little open to question in a play which is predominantly one big laugh but which begins by clearly establishing itself in the context of a town impoverished by its miners being starved through a strike, to maintain the wages won during the recent war, and the other main employment, the mills, being on short time, through lack of coal to fire them. The Unity of Theme, however, is clearly to be found in the well-established tradition of Lancashire Comedy with Bottom.

It is not just the overtly serious references to the poverty, to the strike, to the war and to the physical toll of a miner's day which supply the Bottom. **Derby Day** seems to be a rendered down version of an earlier **Bill Naughton** radio play, **June Evening,** which used a cast of forty to re-create the whole life of a street. In **Derby Day** the larger whole is represented by just three young couples, having their first babies, two and a half rather older ones, - one is a war widow -, whose lads are now ten, and a grandmother whose sons would now all be adult if the war had not taken all but the married youngest, who still lives with her. Him

preventing his young wife from letting his mother be marginalised is one of the serious themes constantly being examined, even through the most hilarious scenes, as the young couples work out the ground rules of how they will live together and those more shaken down accomodate their wide social principles to their failings and to the need for some relaxation in their wearying lives. The audience can recognise, perhaps nostalgically, preconceptions now passed away, but, beneath these period details, we can also perceive enduring questions.

In some ways the tone is very romantic: those who deserve their come-uppance, get it; those who need to learn a lesson, do so; but, apart from Benny, all those thus corrected clearly have many virtues in addition to their noted faults and many characters are clearly good-hearted throughout, only needing the opportunity for their qualities to flourish or be recognised.

Concentrating on this bare dozen characters gives scope for all of them to be developed in sufficient detail for the main affirmation of the piece to come from the recognition of their full humanity and variety, communicated vividly through the performances of the cast. There is a romantic element to the perspective but this is entirely justified because one can perceive what is to be loved. The well-madeness of the play is noticable, so many details have their significance, and the production complements this by being entirely open about the fact that it is a

play we are watching: the
furnishings are minimal, a bed is
up-ended to become a door;
ladders are held parallel to
suggest a chase through the
ginnels, – two of the cast,
Christopher Penney and **Rosie
Cavaliero,** dashing to the piano
to supply **Mack Sennett**–style
chase-music; cast members
squeeze water through sponges
into basins to create the
atmosphere of a canal lock and
conclude the scene by launching
them in a barrage at the
Lothario whose display of prowess
to his fancied one, by walking
along the top of the gates, ends
disasterously with his falling into
the pound.

Despite such open elements of
stylisation, however, including
frequent acknowledgements of the
presence of the audience and the
cast bursting into period song
between scenes, picking up
trombones or a banjo to
accompany themselves or provide
sound effects, the main effect is
to create a persuasive reality.
The combination of artifice and
authenticity is well illustrated by
the cries of one couple's baby.
It is noticable, and indeed
acknowledged, that these come
from **Christopher Penney,** sitting
on a nearby step, but it is done
so realistically that it is not to
be noticed immediately and the
realism of the scene's spirit is
not diminished once it is.

Fine Time Fontayne, in the
splendid part of Sidney, is most
central to the style of
acknowledged artifice
accompanying authenticity,
combining a Chorus rôle with full
involvement in the plot. As the

former he has very few specific
lines after his initial brief
introduction but he is frequently
present in scenes where his
character is not and
communicates with us simply by
raising an eyebrow or showing us
his reaction to what is going on.
As a character he is foremost in
getting a deserved come-uppance
while still having serious
standards, despite his naughty
ways, which his wife
acknowledges by apologising for
disregarding them, whilst
justifiably upbraiding him for his
misconduct.

All parts are substantial, both in
themselves and in, thereby,
contributing to the play's
substance. **Kathryn Hunt**'s Amy
for quite some while seems to be
just "another neighbour" but,
before too long, emerges as
central to a significant sub-plot
and finally, in a notably well
received climactic scene, shows
herself to be of the same metal
as **Stanley Houghton**'s Fanny
Crawshaw, indeed could perfectly
well be Fanny, nine years on
from the events of **Hindle Wakes,**
– the metal, in this instance,
being manifested in her kitchen
poker. **Ann Rye**'s Sarah is a
character about whom we learn
increasing amounts throughout the
play, uncertain of her position
now that she has less domestic
responsibilities and aware that in
some respects she is beginning to
feel her age. Nevertheless she
visibly grows in stature in the
notable moment when she is
suddenly called upon to supervise
the birth of Polly's baby and
literally rises to to the occasion,
deploying all her old expertise to
take charge of the proceedings.

The realistic aspect of the play's production was here at its most vivid and for quite some while it seemed as if the actual birth was going to be presented centre stage, within feet of the two halves of the audience between which the street was recreated. Quite how those actual minutes were contrived, however, most of us did not notice, as our attention was drawn away to a conversation between **Christopher Penney**, as the young father whom the women have unceremoniously booted out of the house, and **Jack Smethurst**, as one of his older neighbours, giving him words of wisdom on how he should conduct himself once he is allowed to return.

The play is a constant source of joy and wisdom. Every detail tells and they all combine in a magnificent whole, which audiences will delight to see and actors to perform, in many halls, for as long as Lancashire Theatre flourishes.

8 & 9 JUNE 1994.
YOUNG PLAYWRIGHTS' FESTIVAL; Contact. (99– 104).

Unfortunately, one of the main sentiments with which I ended the first evening of this festival was a keen nostalgia for the days when one could see all six plays selected for production in the course of one evening of moderate length. I may be traducing those who gave professional help to the young finalists but it felt very much to me as though the principal form of encouragement had been in the form "You could develop that a bit more, you know." Every play contained interesting ideas and characters, in addition to well-turned lines, but each one seemed to me as if it would have benefitted from being more concise. This may have arisen from a genuine wish to recognise the stature of our young writers' talents, by helping them to develop beyond the confines of the fifteen-minute plays which were often so excellent in the past. This may have been encouraged by the wish to show the festival's new sponsors, **British Gas**, with what significant talents they have so helpfully identified themselves.

The services offered to the competition entrants are now substantial: twenty shortlisted plays get at least half a day's workshopping with professional actors; the six finalists get a residential week-end with professional helpers, as well as other guidance over half a year. The final production process has always been hectic, with half-a-dozen actors having to master all the parts in half-a-dozen still developing plays within a couple of weeks. This can be no easier now that each play has grown to a full one-act piece, producing two three-hour evenings, now with all the technical resources of a main house production. Naturally, in these circumstances, the second set of performances is likely to be tighter than the first but, having to see the first batch this year, I was not sure that this was the only reason why the skills of making a play shorter, just as important as those of making it longer, seemed to be one of the things which had had to be left out.

Often at the Festival, one would not be especially conscious of the youth of the writers. The first piece on this occasion was a patently juvenile satire on pacts with the Devil, **Friday the Halloweenth,** with schoolboys as its main protagonists. It contained much that was genuinely witty but was weighed down by a trend which has recently been noticable in some of our older Manchester writers: a tendency to overload a script with intended one-liners which are very hard to convert into fluent dialogue. Sometimes this is because the joke is meant to lie in describing some comparatively commonplace event in an elaborate and inappropriate collection of lengthy words, often linked by alliteration. More thought often seems to have been given to how amusing it might look on the page than to how it might be effectively spoken by an actor. **Debra Penny** sometimes resorted to flinging her arms wide and stamping out a "B-Boom" accompaniment or to curling her lip in open acknowledgement of the awfulness of the pun or the heaviness of the joke, to try to ease its passage. This was well within the spirit of the piece. In the second invocation of the devil, Regor was asked why he had paused and replied: "I was just waiting for Simon to interrupt me with another fatuous remark."

Despite all the skills of the actors, however, the material was just too clotted to be carried off. For the Demon, on one of his appearances, to have to explain his unusual costume by saying "I'm having to moonlight in Pantomime. It's the cut-backs, you know" could, on its own, have been quite an effective joke. To have to incorporate information about the television personalities who were his co-stars, the parts they were playing and the unusual location of their performance was just too much to handle wittily as a aside.

I thought for a moment that the play was going to end about fifteen minutes in, when the boys remet in the school playgound after their first night of necromancy. At that length it could have been an enjoyable little piece. Forty minutes later, too many possibly good jokes had either suffocated, been too much like each other or had been over-extended.

The next play, **Eliane Byrne's The New Arrival**, was both the shortest and best of the evening. Its situation, – the earth is about to be destroyed by a huge meteor –, might seem both too big, too extraordinary and too compact to develop into a serious and satisfactory one-act play. Its basic Three Little Pigs-type structure, of how each character tried to guard itself against the Big Bad Wolf, – This little piggie kept on working,/This little piggie stayed at home,/ This little piggie took some E-E-E/... And this one had a baby – might seem far too simple a way in which to handle The End of The World. In fact the simplicity, combined with the depth, style and plausibility, with which it handled the responses of a variety of characters and sketched in the social atmosphere around them, was part of the play's great strength.

The play began with a variety of characters, - a mechanic, a manager, a young girl chatting with her boyfriend, an expectant mother sitting at home -, going about their daily lives when they all simultaneously hear the first news on the radio. These diverse characters in fact all prove to be from the same family, or their boyfriends, and the context of the family life, in its rather fragmentary contemporary form, is the play's main focus. The baby, once born, is compared to the whole world in its final state, living but tiny and helpless, and its imminence has conditioned many of the family's responses. Emma, about fifteen, is fundamentally concerned that the baby will displace her in her parents' affections and this overwhelming preoccupation leads her to dismiss the arrival of the meteor as never going to happen. Her eventual acceptance of her new sister parallels the earth's final minutes, which she describes, of people behaving with various forms of individual dignity, going in the way that is right for them, as oppose to the frenetic behaviour of many during the preceding weeks. Her elder sister, Chloë, is the character we have seen most determined to spend the last two months having "fun", with such japes a department store hide-and-seek, separating herself from her boyfriend who finds it easier just

to carry on repairing motorcars, even for customers whom he knows will never return from their exotic overseas holidays. Her death of an overdose shows her parents how pre-occupied they had been with the significance of the new baby, which was to have been the one that would have benefitted from the experience they had gained in bringing up their first two daughters. The fact that Chloë had returned home after living out with her boyfriend had seemed just part of the incidental ebb and flow of modern living.

Keeping the focus in or near the relatively quiet family home and avoiding the frenetic city centre activities of the "fun" seekers, let alone a scream of fear at the beginning or a big bang at the end, helped to sketch in effectively the implications for ordinary people. The writing was very skilful in capturing the style both of occasional news items and of everyday speech and nothing was too much filled in, so that one's imagination could wander around the ably inwoven elements of people's lives which we did see, rather than having anything argued out in too much detail. There were able touches of humour, such as the smashed out Chloë murmuring, from the opposite side of the stage, in response to Emma's concerns about the new baby, "You mean, it will break up our close family relationship ..." but mostly it maintained an atmosphere of humane concern. The full house at **Contact** was held in rapt silence throughout.

The stature of the evening having

thus been so effectively restored, it seemed at first as if **Don't Cry Out Loud** by **Louise Anders** was going to raise it to even greater heights. Beginning with **Sally Sheridan** coming home as an apparent juvenile, wanting to join in the play other children were preparing on the verandah but concerned that Mummy would not want them to be late for supper, and then re-appearing as a mother, upbraiding her daughter for coming home at two in the morning, it was clearly going to be a play of more overtly sophisticated structure. This need not have been a bonus in itself but the characters seemed as if they were likely to be interesting.

Part of the interest was in quite who they were in relation to each other. The next scene was in an office where Stephen appeared to be intimate with Gillian, the **Sally Sheridan** character, but the talk was of Russel, who at that stage was mainly the absent boss but who later emerged as "in the rôle of a" husband to Gillian, but not the father of her daughter. When he finally appeared he was brilliantly performed by **Jim Byrne** as a genuinely tired businessman, probably not using his business trips for any particular infidelity, not unmindful of his domestic responsibilities but not able to be particularly pleasant either.

The central event proved to be the visit of Gillian's more famous actress sister, whom Gillian feels she could have emulated if she had not been excluded from their childhood theatricals and then caught by early motherhood,

whereas the sister, Isabelle, feels that Gillian, with a settled home, beautiful daughter and a responsible job, secured by her romantic liasons at work, has advantages which her high-profile television work and press attention can never bring her.

There were good scenes and character interest but somehow it all went on too long. There was what could have been a tremendously powerful final scene, of the two sisters having an extended conversation on a canal bank, recalling their childhoods and in some measure reconciling their jealousies, but with Gillian thereby failing to get a message to meet her daughter, who has been estranged by learning that Gillian blames her for preventing her becoming as famous as her Auntie Isabelle. This opportunity being missed before our eyes could have given the scene tremendous edge but as the information and insights that were coming from the dialogue were mostly what we had already sorted out, much of its drama was unfortunately doused by the sense of a long scene dragging out a comparatively long play, at what had become a rather late hour of night.

The overall standard of the second evening's plays was much more successful, although I still felt that a little trimming would have harmed none of them.

No Room 13 by **Ian Potter** began rather portentously with the lights going down on the set to dramatic music, then coming on one by one to highlight the various rooms into which it was divided, until the whole was illuminated and we were left for sometime looking at the set which we had already been able to see perfectly well since we had entered the auditorium. Then the lights went down and the actors took their places before the lights came up again.

The purpose of all this may have been to prepare us for the lighting cues which were intended to signal to us which character's thoughts we were hearing, as most of the words we heard were recorded. These clues were not in fact always desperately clear as a fairly high general overall level of lighting was maintained so that we could see what all characters were doing, with the result that the extra highlighting was not very great.

After this rather slow start, I was further discouraged to find that the events represented were taking place in a mental home, as I have often found that the interest which writers and actors seem to find in portraying such scenes exceeds that which they can provide for an audience. I also find that accepting such representations seriously is incompatible with accepting as a "joke" such behaviour, as here, as a character being unable to remember something he has only been told a minute earlier.

Nevertheless this was extremely well done, both in the writing and the performance, and increasingly gained my sympathy, interest and applause. The framework was provided by a young applicant coming for a post

as Care Worker, the emphasis of her thoughts being on how the three days on will still leave her with her evenings to herself and the opportunity to continue signing on in Stockport. When she eventually finds the Manager, brilliantly performed by **Martin Reeve,** the occasion is provided for the most extensive passages of direct dialogue in the play, splendidly written to provide both a vivid, world-weary character and a lot of contextual information for what we have already seen. His speeches both contain a lot of dry wit, at which we can laugh uninhibitedly, and what appears to be authentic professional information on the care of the mentally ill. This authenticity of dialogue, matched by the extended ravings of Alistair as he tries to type out a thesis co-ordinating ley lines with the behaviour of Jimmy Young on Radio 2, as well as by the more fragmentary utterances of other characters, is one of **Ian Potter's** great strengths as a playwright. The strength of the play as a whole is in setting its characters in the realistic context of our wider society. This connection is re-inforced towards the end by the discovery that one of the characters in the television room whose thoughts we have been overhearing, which, – apart from musings on the effectiveness of a ghost story told by one of the residents the previous evening, these have mainly been about getting out of the home and finding a low-stress job elsewhere –, is in fact one of the Care Workers, rather than another patient.

Kirree Seddon and **Helen**

Trafford, in **For the Good Times**, were outstandingly successful in creating the characters of two seventeen year old lads, from different backgrounds, who form a close friendship which is quickly ruined by one of them, desperate for money, borrowing the others car to do a dodgy driving job, which proves to be a drugs run, on which he is apprehended. His friend is thereby introduced to the rougher side of the police, who suspect him of involvement, and the six-month sentence on the driver co-incides with the death in Northern Ireland of the father whose dominating but intermittent home presence, we came to know, had so much to do with his leaving home.

Whether we also needed to know that this relationship had been specifically characterised by child abuse I am not so sure. We had already seen a totally convincing portrait of a natural friendship building up, its unpleasant disruption and the feelings of both the characters we saw and those we did not. This would have been entirely plausible without this extra detail, which seemed to me to sit rather awkwardly on top of a portrait which had seemed, in its way, complete without it, also adding a noticably unwelcome piece of extra length to what had been a nicely balanced piece. Nevertheless, with or without this scene, it was an impressive little tale, made all the more powerful by the splendid performances of **Jim Byrne** and **Michael Brent**.

You Used To is by no means **Matthew Dunster's** first play, which was his brilliant adaptation

seven years ago, while he was still at school, of **Clive Jermain's** television **Best Years of Your Life.** This is a very different piece. As the play opens, with an aged figure sitting on a sofa amidst piles of old junk, tearing up newspapers, it looks as if someone had expected to play Roderick Usher but had abruptly been required to play McCann from **The Birthday Party** on the set of **The Caretaker.** When, later, the bowler-hatted Mr Ballyrag **(Jim Byrne)** erupts from under the pile of street-rubbish upon which the elderly couple deposit themselves when they venture forth, its looks as if **Beckett's** Estragon has joined the proceedings. Many in the audience were raving enthusiatically about these vigorously presented events, long after the performance ended. **Matthew Dunster**, who will be in the cast of **Contact's** Christmas production this year, has been approached by both this theatre and **Radio 4** about future scripts. **Nigel E Higginson** has contributed the following appreciation:

YOU USED TO (104).

If ever a justification were needed for the **Young Playwrights Festival**, then 1994 proved to be the year. Taking place for the first time in the main house at **Contact**, the **Festival** contained the most exciting piece of new work to be presented at this theatre in the past five years. **Matthew Dunster's You Used To** was the desperate portrait of a blighted marriage, welded together by dependency, living out its last days under the siege of uncaring

Tory Britain. Both personal and political, this absurdist odyssey, from parlour to 'round the corner', was a shocking event, which, in one short hour, caressed and battered its audience with humour, deceit, compassion and devilry.

Provoked by an onslaught of bills from privatised Britain, a crabby old woman (**Debra Penny**) pushes and carries her disabled husband (**Stephen Ventura**) on a journey of protest. In between encounters with an array of misfits (**Jim Byrne, Michael Brent, Sally Sheridan, Carolyn Bazely**) flashback scenes unmask the past: romance, love, forced miscarriage, revenge, – brutal truths hidden by the battle to survive. Ultimately dreams die but the material substance of those hopes still remains in our own decaying physical presence.

You Used To brought an important new voice onto **Contact**'s stage. Credit must be given to director **Richard Gregory** and his young cast for presenting, in just four days, a unique and brilliant event.

NIGEL E HIGGINSON

15 JUNE.
CANDLESTICKS;
Manchester Jewish Museum. (120).

I was particularly glad of the chance to see this play after going to **Beau Jest** in Stockport a couple of months previously. That play had been an enjoyable light comedy of Goy meets Girl

but, as such, had not been able to explore too deeply into where this situation raises issues which good-heartedness alone cannot resolve. In particular, its brief reference to the possibility of the Gentile converting to Judaism had been far more flippant than its gentle good humour on other matters. **Candlesticks** addressed the question of convertion, in both directions, as a serious issue.

We first learn that Louise has been baptised as a Christian while at university. We learn that she considers this compatible with her Judaism, although her mother, Joanna, does not.

Interestingly the first and most profound objection which Joanna raises to Christianity is that it "makes foreignveness too easy," apparently in much the same sense as **Dietrich Bonhoeffer's** anathematising of "cheap Grace," a very radical criticism of a religion which, particulaly in the Pauline/Lutheran tradition from which **Bonhoeffer** came, sees Grace as the foremost divine quality revealed by the work of its Messiah. The only sense in which Joanna develops this, however, is with regard to Christians having done much for which they should not be too easily foreigven, notably in their treatment of the Jews, from the time of the Gospels onwards. Joanna does have the New Testament on her shelves and has given talks in the past on the nature of its religion.

Louise has developed a tendency to quote from this Testament over-freely, – "Cut the Godcrap," Ian, the boy next door, appositely tells her in an early scene. Nevertheless, we do not really get a clear picture of why Louise thought she was converting. She and we become aware later that her unconscious reason was a belief that it would enable her to marry Ian, who has been her friend and playfellow since infancy. Whether this could ever actually have helped, Ian's family background being "non-practicing Roman Catholic," is doubtful. The way they in fact miss each other is that Ian, probably with the same subconscious motives, converts to Judaism.

Probably they both somehow hoped they would "meet in the middle"; - instead, they become as "ships that pass in the night." Louise sees that, although Ian still professes his affection, he will come to want to marry "a good Jewish girl" and will no more accept that she is still truly Jewish than does her own mother.

The fact that Ian begins his journey towards conversion after he already knows that Louise has made hers makes his belief that conversion would bring him closer to her a little harder to credit. However, we do get a fuller picture of other factors which drew him to Judaism. Only ever having known one parent, his father in fact having been his mother's Jewish employer, although he does not know this, he found the happy family atmosphere of being in Louise' home as a child at such festivals as Pesach peculiarly attractive. Joanne accuses Mary, Ian's

mother, of contributing to Louise being seduced into Christianity by letting her attend midnight mass at Christmas with her and Ian as a child but, however attractive a service this might be, it is not apparent that this would have met a comparable personal need for Louise. Ian also found his months of living with an orthodox family, during his process of conversion, a particularly attractive experience. We learn nothing of the Christian circles which Louise experienced at university. When her mother asks her "What sort of a Christian are you?" she at first does not understand the question and then says "well, I was baptised at the Anglican chaplaincy, but it's ever so ecumenical," in tones which suggest that it was not of much importance to her. To be dismissive of denominationalism is perfectly plausible but to have known what did seem decisively important to her would have been useful.

Much of the focus of the play is on the two mothers. Apparently having lived as neighbours in the same block for over twenty years one wonders, in our increasingly economically segregated age, in just what corner of Greater Manchester they might be living. Joanna during the course of the play rises to a senior administrative position in the Social Services and her husband presumably has a significant professional income. Mary is constantly struggling to make ends meet by taking in extra cleaning jobs, although at the beginning of the play she is struggling to get an Open University degree, successfully, despite Joanna dismissing the possibility: "She can't spell." By the end of the play she has got a post on the staff of a women's refuge. They frequently argue, to the point of Joanna telling her never to come back to her home again, after Mary persists in remarks about Jewish treatment of Palestinians, but such separations clearly have no lasting effect: in the next scene, some time later, Mary is back at Joanna's without any explanation being necessary.

Despite their different economic and educational levels, however, they bear comparably burdens: Joanna having to undertake a debilitating round of cooking for each Jewish festival and Mary having to take on others' domestic duties as well as her own; both having untidy sons, Mary's frustration being with Ian's late teens discourtesy and lack of application to resat A Levels, her economic burdens being little eased by his intermittent work at McDonalds and his conversion to Judaism, while leading him to dress more neatly and tackle more domestic duties, also impelling him to make whispered comments to try and prevent her Gentile handling of Passover wine bottles in her friend's home. Joanna also has her daughter's apostasy to endure.

All this builds up a very persuasive and involving picture of many human issues of our age. I was less convinced with the divine aspect: just how it was that Louise came to be convinced that she had a decisively different perception of the nature and expectations of the Creator

God. I do not believe that the play was intending a purely secular interpretation: the conversions coming about more through human instincts than any detectable divine reality or of a Jewish community seeing itself as more defined by the persecutions of Hitler than by the actions of God through Moses. Its author specifically denies that the play is intended to provide answers but, without a little more information on the conversion experience, it runs the risk of being secularist by default, rather than simply leaving that interpretation open. As it is, however, it remains a play of substance, persuasively acted, and usefully touches those parts **Beau Jest** could not reach.

16 JUNE. HEART AND SOUL; Coliseum. (108).

Writing Community Drama can be tricky in many ways. One is that, needing to evoke something of signifance to a whole community and to provide scope for a large number of participants, its scale is likely to be so large and rambling that it loses dramatic focus and thereby impact. Another is that capturing everyday speech in written dialogue, either from today or from somewhere along the course of a community's heritage, is by no means easy.

Cheryl Martin, in what is almost certainly her best play to date, by a significant margin, triumphantly o'erleaps both these hurdles. Her dialogue, spoken by a largely inexperienced cast, always sounds entirely natural, whether coming from today's denizens of Tommyfield Market or from those whose lives found their focus there in earlier decades. Although there is a slight pile-up of conclusions at the end, hard to avoid in a work with many plot strands, not only does it succeed in integrating many elements into a complex but compelling structure, it is on occasion profoundly moving. This is most notably the case when evoking the significance of the destruction of the old market, towards the end of the first act.

After introducing us to many of the main characters in a scene of opening up on a present day morning, the first act then concentrates on showing us how things were in earlier years, through a narrative mainly centring on one particular family. Although in that act groups of characters several times entered to a vigorous musical accompaniment which made one expect that they would burst into song, at that stage they rarely did so. In the second act, which more builds up a collective portrait of life around the market today with images of various sub-groups, - the West Indians, the posse of young teenage girls, the young, often single, parents with their baby trolleys -, each of these has a song to sum up their perspective. Whether because I was too far forward to be in the line of the loudspeakers, although close to the actors, the edge was taken off lively and confidently delivered numbers by my not being able to hear the words. I could hear the chorus of the very well received, more traditional, ballad to the newly-

weds, "Farewell to Freedom/ Goodbye the Easy Life," but this may have been because it was slower, already partly familiar and repeated more often, rather than because the earlier singers had been performing less distinctly.

The production was dramatically highly successful, keeping constantly on the move, incorporating a wide variety of elements, from the humorous to the insightful, and capturing a unified swathe of historical and contemporary reality, without any of the limiting sense of artifice which can easily undermine such an attempt.

17 JUNE. THE ROVER; Ark. (109).

Certainly none of the current students at **Shena Simon** can be indicted for under-acting. If the effort they put into their performances was sometimes noticable, the basic approach of tackling everything with the utmost vigour was entirely successful. From the opening moment when the three sisters dashed on, proclaiming their determination to escape confinement and to secure husbands of their own choice, we were swept along by the energy of the production. The way in which it had been made "an edited version of the original play, (down to a bare ninety minutes), and some of the language ... updated to make it more accessible" had been most skilfully accomplished and was certainly entirely successful in achieving the adaptation's stated objective. Occasionally one heard a phrase not quite in period. "Why do you think our brother Pedro has gone thither? To lie with wenches!" would have been entirely comprehensible and as easy to say in its original form. "To have sex with women," as the alternative, sounded a little out of period but perhaps conveyed how blunt much of the original dialogue is. "Everybody has to go back to work" may sound a little humdrum but actually seemed to me to be a very good curtain line, losing more by Belvile and Florinda not quite being able to establish a suitable moment of quiet in which to say it, as everybody else dashed off back to the carnival, than through its being a less stylish line than "So now each one of you must back to's several occupations." Despite the universally acknowledged disaffection with our present government, it was probably wisest to pick on this simple truth with which to end than to try to doctor the original's aspirations for the Prince over the Water.

It was a little disappointing that in central Manchester, where so many resources exist to re-create the real thing, the stall at the back signifying that events were taking place during a Caribbean carnival looked more like a sideshow from a particularly unsuccessful village fête, despite the magnificently painted hillside and harbour on the backdrop, complemented in the night scenes by a skilfully superimposed giant sickle moon. Perhaps the full sound and colour of an authentic carnival would have overshadowed even the exeptionally vigorous

performances of the main actors. These included women, **Rachel Walter** and, particularly, **Sam Pope**, being entirely successful in representing two of the most dashing blades, Frederick and Willmore. Their companion Blunt is far from dashing, save in his own estimation, and was left in the male hands of **James Kinsella**, who won considerable affection, as well as constant laughter, from the audience in his increasingly disasterous attempts to demonstate his prowess.

Despite the considerable prominence that was being given to **Aphra Behn** as a Woman Writer some ten years ago, when the **Royal Shakespeare Company** actually came to stage **The Rover** at **The Swan** in 1986 it seemed to me a fairly standard piece of Restoration ribaldry which might have flowed from any pen, with no particularly female viewpoint. At **Shena Simon**, however, amidst the general merrymaking, it did seem as though the double standard was being identified particularly sharply, most specifically in Pedro, who in one action seeks to defend his sisters' virtue by locking them in and simultaneously dashing off to the carnival to indulge himself: "Shall Pedro frolic and leave us three mewed up?" It is the duplicity rather than the indulgence which is condemned. The response is not merely that "women should do as men do." A man whose doings more than earn him the name Willmore make him all the more attractive. Although Hellena makes sure that, much to his distaste, he actually marries her, vigour is seen to be as desirable as fidelity. There did seem to be this distinctive viewpoint behind all the romps which the cast played to the hilt. The piece seemed entirely fresh and contemporary, as much in such serious glimpses as the subjection of the whore Lucetta to her pimp Sancho as in the mainstream good humour. To reveal all this in a two-hundred-year-old play speaks well for the director, **Helen Larder**, who helped them find what was there and for the courage as well as the vigour of the cast in presenting it all so wholeheartedly.

18 JUNE. TIME AND THE ROOM; Capitol. (107).

It is obviously an entirely valid part of a Drama School student's training to tackle a major work of non-narrative theatre. This forms a significant element of the world in which he or she may find employment; witness, for example the current **New Stages** festival of work at the **Green Room** and **Contact**.

The only other **Botho Strauss** play which seems to have been performed in Manchester, **Great and Small**, which **Glenda Jackson** brought to the **Palace** in July 1983, was at least narrative theatre in overt structure, even if the amount of narrative in proportion to its length, as "Dotty Lotte" wandered hopefully from one group of acquaintances to another, seemed comparatively small. The narrative and its import was not particularly pelucid but it seemed then as if

this might have had something to do with the hours we got being allegedly a couple of hours less than **Strauss** had written.

Time and the Room fairly soon abandons any semblance of having a narrative in a conventional sense, although the proceedings for some time continue to provide explanations which would have their place in the logic of narrative cause and effect. The translator, **Tony Meech**, in a pre-performance seminar stressed how, just as the camera had freed Art from being representational, so Theatre had found that it could be freed from narrative. A door opening and someone entering was something which could have dramatic effect independent of its having anything to do with the development of a plot. In fact, although the first scene of the play consists largely of people who appear to be unknown to those already present making entrances, they all provide explanations of why they have done so in terms of their own narrative.

The first entrant has the most praeter-normal explanation, that she knows one of the room's occupants has just been talking about her, which is true, as he has been describing to his friend what he can see in the street. Her explanation of how she came to be there does not describe a procedure which many of us would follow but it is in tune with the outlooks of the room's occupants, who describe themselves as extreme sceptics who have given up trying to have any direction in their lives and who just accept whatever happens, as they do with equanimity as each new character makes their entrance.

We seem at this stage to be building up a sort of **N F Simpson, One Way Pendulum,** kind of logic. Arriving at the airport the first entrant, Marie Steuber, had found two-hundred-and-fifty identical suitcases coming round the luggage carousel and, rather than work out which was hers, had taken the first to hand. Heading for the Arrivals Gate, where she was meant to be met by Frank Arnold, she had serenely gone along with someone willing to answer to that name, although well aware it was not the man who was meant to meet her.

The next two entrants have more usual explanations for their intrusion. The first thinks he may have left his watch there, while at a party the previous night. The next is desperate to meet him again, after being smitten with him at the party. The fact that the room's occupants think there was no such party and the watchless man has no recollection of the woman could mean we are into **Harold-Pinter-Old-Times'**-Whose-Truth-Is-It-Anyway shenanigans or, more hopefully, that the identical patterns of rooms in mass-produced tower blocks in modern cities and of the forms of social recreation engaged in by their inhabaitants is going to lead to legitimate confusions, symbolic of uncertain identity, or some such.

The next entrant appears to be Frank Arnold, who threatens Marie with terrible consequences for failing to wait for him but then leaves, the first character to do so. The next two arrivals offer no explanation of themselves directly but we think we know who they are as they fit exactly a description Marie has just given of a man rescuing a deeply sleeping woman from a hotel fire across the street. After some discourse he carries her off towards the bedroom and Marie shortly lures off the watchless man in the same direction. When the originally comatose woman returns, now very much awake, and we have an **Old Times**-like discussion with Julius, one of the room's occupants as to whether he previously knew her. There is another entrant and a couple more departures but it looks basically as if what we are going to get is a) an accumulation of characters who will now interact with each other in various permutations for the rest of the evening and b) a situation in which such a pointless puzzle as to "what really happened" as might appear to present itself in a **Pinter** is not going to be seriously presented.

Neither of these assumptions is completely untrue but they are not pursued in an uninterrupted, here-they-all-are, now-what-will-be-done-with-them fashion. The next time the door is flung open, it is not another character that enters but, in a somewhat **Dumb Waiter**-like moment, two light suitcases are thrown in, followed by a blackout. The room is then re-arranged, the two suit cases are thrown in once more and followed by a much more diffident Frank Arnold and Marie, as though he had successfully met her at the airport. Here one seems to be on a what-if alternative strand. Other later scenes of Marie and others in various situations might conceivably be arranged into a narrative if one abandoned any idea of their possibly being in chronological order. I doubt if this is profitable line of reflection. I suspect one has something more like characters as a selection of playing cards dealt round in various fashions to see what patterns they make.

I have no basic objection to non-narrative Theatre. Presentation and performance can make certain material highly allusive or simply compelling. It can have stylish poetic language. It can be very funny. There was a certain amount of **Lewis Carrol**-like ludicrousness at various stages in the evening, which was enjoyable. Possibly intriguing strands emerged from time to time but not for very long. Such a piece can hold by sheer performance but that is a tall order. Apart from a feeling that one or two early characters spoke with excessive emotion, as if to convey that their words had significance, as well as to distinguish themselves from the extreme sceptics who accepted events more equably, the actors seemed to handle matters with a great deal of skill and plausibility but did not aspire to the hypnotic levels which would have carried the evening on their own. They may well have found it an interesting exercise but I am not convinced that **Strauss** had provided them with the material which could have made the whole evening interesting for the audience.

20 JUNE. BIG MOUNTAIN; Capitol. (110).

It is always a pleasure to see **M6** perform and their expertise with young audiences makes them a natural choice to provide a production specifically for the **City of Drama Passport to a World of Theatre** scheme, whose objective is to ensure that every school child in Manchester has an experience of live Theatre this year. In its way **Big Mountain** builds up to being an impressive hour of Theatre, with fine acting and a striking set, representing, through simple materials and lighting, the desert purlieus of The Grand Canyon in Arizona. hope it does well with its intended audience but I did rather wonder how great was its relevance.

Its primary achievement must be to give some taste of Navajo culture. The amount of this included, however, is comparatively small. Making us aware of a religion centred on Mother Earth and Father Sky is obviously valuable in our ecologically destructive culture and particularly apt as Manchester hosts the Global Forum Conference. Making the principal Navajo character one who is already beginning to lose some of the country craft he has only had a partial opportunity to inherit from his ancestors may be a good way of indicating how near to being lost such understandings are. It never becomes especially clear, however, in what particular way saving Big Mountain from the mineral excavators would assist such culture in being kept.

Some play is made of the misleading image most of us have gained of this culture through the traditional Western but the tale seems to rely on our prior knowledge of such stereotypes for its basic comprehensibility, for instance in assuming that we can assimilate the nature of a ruthless, presumably JR-like, off-stage mining tycoon, intent upon excavating Big Mountain, from comparatively little on stage reference to him. That he can call upon the resources of the state to gun down the Honest Injun may be a faithful image of how some parts of capitalism work but although this country may possibly sometimes exercise a shoot-to-kill policy, by and large we kill our citizens in other ways. That we do kill them in significant numbers is a sustainable thesis if one links agreed demographic patterns of health and mortality with low-wage policies, restraint of public spending, the preference for private cars over less asthma-inducing public transport, the closure of long-stay wards even if alternative means of keeping the very fragile alive are not to hand and the promotion of flexibility in the labour market, while freeing employers from red-tape and enabling high levels of reward for high levels of managerial achievement. The conflict of Navajo and Big Business interests is one particular outworking of such policies and setting it in a context other than

that most immediate to us and through comparatively simple detail, mediated through the experiences of a young white girl, may be an effective way to make some measure of it assimilable to an Upper Primary-aged audience.

However, **James Baldwin** happily spent his childhood years identifying with the cowboys at his local cinema, before he became aware than the society in which he lived cast him in the rôle of the Injun. The implications of this in the present context are two-fold. Although for many children in Rochdale and Manchester identifying with a white girl may take place effectively, it is not their most natural route into the material. More importantly, however, it is not a necessary route for their white colleagues. Very likely in this production a great deal of identification will build up with **Steve James'** persuasive representaion of several Navajo. Indeed, he is the principal narrator, leading us through the story. For me, however, I felt that I learnt a lot more of North American Indian culture and of the present plight of its people through **Adan Sanchez'** performance of **Matthew Witten's** **Sacred Journey** in the **New Mexico Rep** production which visited the **Green Room** and the **Nia Centre** last November and the **Bury Met** earlier this month. Particularly as it spent much time on the main character's youth and school days and because of its personal narrative style of performance, I would have thought it very accessible to a younger audience and its conclusion on the streets of the big city very recognisable here.

However, just because a visiting company has tackled one aspect of a theme well, does not mean that one of our best should not be free to tackle another. **M6** are far more expert than I in knowing what will strike home to our young audiences. Four years ago, I encouraged some Rochdale friends to take their young children to see their splendid production of **Neil Duffield's** version of **The Emperor's New Clothes.** Months later I found that the scene which still lived in their five-year-old's memory was that of the luminous butterflies, which I had found one of the less gripping but, in fact, had provided just the right level of simple fascination.

I hope that **Big Mountain** also proves to be pitched at just the right level, both to convey some of the significance of the issues raised and also, by the skill with which it is performed and presented, to draw its audience in to provide what usually seems to me **M6's** best claim upon its borough's Education Budget: irrespective of the often highly important themes which its plays tackle, it provides schools audiences with direct experience of excellence in art.
The basic story in **Big Mountain** is a comparatively simple drama which would once have fitted entirely naturally on children's television. Here the tale is told, and told well, in a distinctively Theatrical way and so should not only present young audiences with issues which will arouse their interest but a distinctive

experience which could well provide them with an enduring **Passport to the World of Theatre.**

23 JUNE; THE WOMEN; Green Room. (111).

This was a wonderful evening's Theatre.

In searching for a play appropriate for the disproportionately female make-up of their first graduating class, **Arden** have found not only a work suitable on that score but a very substantial piece, well worth reviving but one which few other than they could contemplate staging. There are 39 separate female characters, – no males –, and **Arden** is able to supply a cast of sixteen to cover them.

They do so splendidly. Eleven of them have substantial individual rôles but the other five, who sweep up the rest, also get a collection of wonderful opportunities, whether as individual characters or in the very fine group work which is a feature of this production.

One of the best received characters, in a comparatively short scene, was **Lindi Glover** as Lucy the Cook, spitting out curt, contemptuous comments, in a deep Bronx accent, on the maid's report of a major divisive argument between the master and mistress of the house, whilst messily ingesting the remains of a lemon meringue pie. Another fine piece of work was all five of what became in many respects the chorus, here in their rôles as

THE TWO MRS STEPHEN HAINES: The originally innocent Mary (HELEN STACEY, seated) developes the wiles to discomfort the heartless Crystal Allen (EMMA FERGUSON) who originally displaced her; – the climax of CLARE BOOTH LUCE'S notable THE WOMEN, finely performed by ARDEN SCHOOL OF THEATRE.

shop staff, pressing their ears to the (non-existent) partition of a changing room in a major department store, and showing their reactions to the almighty row inside between two of their affluent customers.

These two examples illustrate one of the ways in which this usually hilarious play has a very substantial content. **Clare Booth Luce** could perfectly well have dropped the article from her title and called it simply **Women.** One of its aims seems to be to present a very wide ranging panorama of the female sector of society. Its main focus is on super-rich New York Society Ladies, in 1936 but with many features enduring to this day, including some areas of Greater Manchester. The very different fortunes of those infinitely poorer persons who provide for them in their homes, shops, hospitals, health clubs, hotels, night clubs and solicitors offices are never forgotten, however. Both groups tend to make up what is lacking in their lives, either in respect of serious occupation or of income, by gossip about the rich, although those who actually belong to this group have the scope to use it as a tool to disrupt each other's lives deliberately. Tittle-tattle by a manicurist can also be as painful to a rich woman but here the harm done is likely to be less intentional.

The exclusively female cast also has a point to make about the substantial degree of social *apartheid* between the sexes. The two meet to some extent but for extensive periods of time the women are left to their own devices. There is no unnatural artifice involved in writing the play entirely through scenes in which no men are present.

Though in some measure being the objects of possibly genuine love and of passion, men gain no respect through their separate, but economically controlling, rôles. "A pity to waste it on a man" says one character, surveying the result of her expensive beautification treatment. "But what else is it for," her colleague replies with blunt realism.

The most destructive of the gossips might well not be so poisonous if they had something serious to do in life. Little Mary loves her mother but dreads growing up like her, with no task in society such as she sees being performed by men. Her mother's claim to have the "special job" of bringing up her children is clearly nonsense, as all the real work is done by servants and a governess.

Her mother's mother tells her daughter not to confront her husband with his infidelities: "It doesn't matter who he's with now; it's who he ends up with." She looks back to the days when divorce was nigh impossible and people 'had to make something of

it.' Nevertheless, when divorce has actually come to her daughter, she, being widowed, is able to try and console her by conceding that there are attractions to "being on one's own again." Men should be held onto for the security, not because there is necessarily anything very pleasant about them.

Eilis Hetherington is able to give considerable power to this older woman's brusque saws, beginning splendidly with her blunt divination of exactly the nature of the problem her daughter is too upset to be able to tell her about. **Helen Lacey**, however, is entirely convincing, amidst all this cynicism, as the daughter who cannot abandon the love of her husband, despite his infidelities, and his callousness in ringing her in Reno just to confirm that her divorce proceedings will be complete by noon the next day, in order that he can arrange his new wedding for that afternoon, about which he only tells her at that moment.

At first neither style nor substance seemed so promising. The first few cast members entered in black leotards and one wondered if so basic a performance manner was going to be appropriate to a play whose set, while fairly simply constructed, seemed to bespeak the need for a certain style. Then the wardrobe doors at the back, which came to serve as exits and entrances, flew open to reveal the whole of the rest of the cast, grouped in high, *art deco* style, with ankle length dresses, foot-long cigarette

128

holders, lengthy necklaces and varigated hats. They advanced to preen themselves in giant mirrors, presumed to be in the invisible fourth wall between them and the audience and then dispersed through the exits or to their places for the first scene.

In time one came to be able to notice that this stylish appearance was in fact achieved through the skilful addition of comparatively minor elements to black basic costumes, and through the consistently characterful performances of the persons wearing them, but achieved it certainly was, just as similar skills and additions enabled those who played a multitude of rôles to appear entirely convincing in what had at first seemed over-basic costumes.

The first scene showed the rich gathered at the bridge table and, although the wit in the tittle-tattle was well turned, one wondered if a whole evening of such back-biting and wise-cracks would add up to a very satisfactory play. As already shown, although the high wit continued throughout, the purview of the play grew naturally to become far more wide-ranging and substantial. It is extremely well-written, not only in having consistently interesting and amusing lines but in naturally developing the plot. The cast and production gave it all added interest and depth by developing matters far beyond the actual words spoken. That much of the plot was made up of avowedly much-used elements, of rivalry, inFidelity divorce, re-marriage was emphasised by the apt

selection from the romantic popular music of the period between scenes but, while the familiar words of the songs reminded us that the passions being felt by the characters were so oft-expressed as to be stereotypical, the way in which those still on stage were continuing to act and re-act added to the depth and distinctiveness which they had already established, so that although artifice was patently there, – the minor characters adjusting the set chorically advised us of the time and setting of the next scene –, we had much more human interest than in the mechanical elements of a traditional tale.

The character of Nancy Blake, for instance, has comparatively few scenes and lines. Like almost every rôle it had its distinctive place in the panorama, – here the never-married, independent woman, writing novels in New York and interspersing them with expeditions on her own to Africa and elsewhere. One might have wondered if her part, in the general disillusionment with men, might have been to develop the romance in a way that women alone can, but this is not an aspect of womanhood which **Clare Booth Luce** chooses to explore. Instead, Nancy's contributions to the plot are much more incidental, but because **Donna Alexander** plays the part so vividly, – reacting sympathetically to action in which she is not directly involved, or just professionally garnering detail for her next novel, (as did **Luce**, perhaps) –, she becomes one of the many characters in this

129

production in whom we become deeply interested, wanting to know more, and helping the whole play to became far more than the mechanical farce which many of its elements could enable it to be.

What is funny is very funny, such as **Joanna Curley's** constantly-begetting Edith, - "Are you Catholic or just careless" - explaining the odd look of her latest baby's nose whilst she is breast-feeding, "Oh, that's just a bit of ash", - as she is even less able than **Claire Dowie** to refrain from cigarettes in the maternity ward -, and seeking to blow it away with a great cloud of smoke. It is hilarious but accurate and perceptive satire, rather than just gags. It is a great play but needs, as well as deserves, this quality of acting and production to realise its stature as well as to exploit all its wit.

28-29 JUNE. THE COUNT OF MONTE CRISTO; Royal Exchange. '117).

Novels on Nineteenth-Century France seem currently to be the pre-eminent source of large scale popular theatrical entertainments. **Victor Hugo** achieved something of much greater stature in **Les Misérables** than **Boubil** and **Schönberg** could capture in their musical but very likely **Gaston Leroux** in his **Phantom of the Opera** only aspired to a popular entertainment of comparable quality to that created by **Andrew Lloyd Webber.**

The Count of Monte Cristo, as a novel, probably stands between the other two examples. Although the **Royal Exchange** fed **Plays and Players** the idea (April 1994 issue) that in France **Alexandre Dumas** is regarded as of comparable status to **Hugo**, it would seem likely that the author intended this work first and foremost as popular entertainment. Nevertheless it does have serious matter to explore about the nature of the instinct for revenge. The **Royal Exchange** production seems to be a very fair representation of that mix, containing much that is directly entertaining but the whole only making sense in the context of the more serious ideas behind it.

"If my enemies perish, that is their end, but my suffering can never end" claims Dantès, recalling the destruction of his mind during his fourteen years in the Château d'If, preying upon the villainy of those who had led him to be falsely imprisoned there on the eve of his wedding. There the Abbé Faria had enlightened him as to the dehumanising nature of the desire for revenge but after his escape he seeks out those who wronged him. He can claim "I have killed no one. They destroyed themselves through their own evil natures." Whether providing occasion for this to happen is any less guilty behaviour than leaving persons with known weaknesses with access to, say, alcohol or sharp instruments is doubtful and certainly he does come to be racked by increasing feelings of guilt.

The play begins with the scene concluded at its end, in which the captured Young Morrel cries out "I only want to die", echoing, as we later learn, Dantès' cries in the Chateau d'If. Although Dantès has by the end triumphed over all his enemies and is about to revive the son of his early benefactor by uniting him with the woman he loved and had thought dead, the words "I only want to die", though no longer on his lips, seem once more to have become his sentiments. The play ends with the slave Haydée, whose wrongs he has also avenged, seeking to win him back to love.

Although finding ingenious ways to seek out and exploit the weaknesses of those who betrayed him provides many dramatic episodes, the play also spends time establishing the intricate family details of the dynasties they have by then established in Paris. As a lengthy, Dickensian-style, weekly part-work, the original novel could use the introduction of numerous additional characters as the occasion for lively detail. Rendered down to fit even six hours' traffic of the stage, some of this establishing detail becomes less obviously dramatic. The interest in puzzling out how the details fit together can be annulled by the question of "where's all this leading?" By and large the production finds ways to keep itself moving, however. For those for whom period glitter and costume is not enough, there is the once more increasingly relevant portrayal of the expectations of social privilege expected by the super-rich and

of how the institutions of the law and the state can be conformed to them.

One of the best dramatic ideas is able to take its cue from the opening scene, with its masked desert-robed characters in North Africa. Similarly masked and Turkish-trousered scarlet "creatures" thereafter inhabit the rest of the play. These both act as the most athletic scene changers, – Motto: Never Walk If You Can Summersault –, as which they win frequent applause from the audience, and also increasingly hang imminent over scenes, from ledges and on top of carts and coffins, like devils around a scholar's cell in a Renaissance woodcut. These not only indicate the encroaching fate of the villains but high-light the humour in the ways each brings about his own doom.

Despite all the dramatic material the full effect is greater at sometimes than others. There has been much lively action and the introduction of interesting characters in the early stages of the play but it becomes infinitely more encrossing when **Colin Prockter**, as Abbé Faria, has popped up through the floor in his attempt to tunnel his way out of the Chateau d'If and we start to get some audience laughter. The first big laugh in fact came from **David Threllfall**'s desperate cry of "Because I never *thought* of it!" when the Abbé asks why, if he is so desperate to get out, he did not kill a guard and escape in his clothes. **Prockter** is able later, however, to combine the wit with the introduction of the play's serious issues, asking casually "Is there anything else you need to understand?" after resolving in an almost "elementary, my dear Watson" style the questions which have been destroying Dantès' mind for a decade, as he has puzzled over how he came to be imprisoned.

A similar degree of enhanced power came a comparable way into the second play when Mercédès, whom he had been about to marry when imprisoned, addresses the disguised Dantès as "Edmond", revealing that she had recognised him as soon as he appeared in Paris. He both comes to realise that she is not one of those responsible for his fate and there is the first sign of his faltering in their pursuit. Mercédès has come to him because her son has challenged him to a duel. Thus causing the son's death had probably been his plan for revenge upon her but, now convinced this is inappropriate, he assures her that though the duel will be fought, her son will not die, seeming to intend that it should be fatal for him instead.

Although this is moving deeper than in many scenes into the plays more profound explorations, these issues could be apprehended in part by many literate twelve year olds and I was surprised that these did not form a larger part of the audience, although I was pleased to see that some of those I noticed on the long first evening I was there had returned eagerly enough the next day. There was a Classics Illustrated feel to much of the evening, which may have been partly as a

result of having most of the cast speak in accented English. This seemed odd at first but there may have been a legitimacy in that characters and actions from many countries are involved, historically united by the seafaring routes of the Mediterranean and intensified in the play's own day by the burgeoning of international commerce. The play's early scenes are specifically in the Catalonian quarter of Marseilles and the world of Paris, in the same country, is culturally more foreign to this than much that is heard of or seen in Italy, Greece, Turkey and Morocco.

The ancient world of the Mediterranean trade routes, with whose matelots the play's events begin, is kept in mind as the soil from which the culture sprung by the sanded base upon which the performance takes place. High above, gilded dragons in the **Exchange's** roof suggest the remote world of the capitalist salons to which the plays most ruthless characters naturally gravitate. Those who come to reject its heartless nature, – Maximilien Morrel, Mercédès, her son Albert and Dantès himself –, return to the sands around the Mediterranean. This sandy substratum, especially with the scarlet creatures, as whom a large part of the cast take their turn, leaping and spinning on and above it, also gives the **Exchange's** circular stage something of the atmosphere of a circus ring. The enthusiasm various actors and directors express for the circus style often seems to me to lead to a laboured and uninteresting style of performance. Here, without over-conscious emphasis, it is most effectively deployed to give great immediacy to action taking place within a few feet of all of the audience.

This production was originally planned for the gilded grandeur of our **Palace** theatre, similar in style to that in which **Dumas'** own original dramatisation was staged and in which his prosperous Parisian characters sometimes foregather, taking more interest in their social acquaintances in the adjoining boxes than in the opera in performance on the stage. Back in Manchester's Metal O, the play's the thing. Not lost on a remote stage at one end of a giant hall, it is at the centre of our attentions, as in the ancient amphitheatres of the Mediterranean, from which our dramatic culture grew.

30 JUNE - 2 JULY. NORTH-WEST PLAYWRIGHTS SUMMER FESTIVAL; Contact. (112-116).

Beginning with two decidedly Scouse plays, very different in style although not unrelated in theme, this year's workshops for a time seemed as if they were to present us with a predominantly Liverpool Festival. All the other three plays were set very specifically in Manchester, however, and this shared specificity of locale did nothing to narrow their wider significance. This year, as an enhancement of the workshops assisted by the **City of Drama**,

playwights were invited from nine different European countries, from East and West, and, although they only contributed minimally to the public discussions following each performance, there seems little doubt that they fully recognised the issues addressed by our local playwrights.

As always, the workshops were characterised by the highest level of acting ability, ranging from those just graduated from our drama schools to those who have laboured in our vineyards with distinction for many decades. This mix in the first play, **Jan McVerry's Passive Smoking**, was notably exemplified by the two main parts being taken by **Joanne Sherry**, - working closely with her fellow recent graduate from the **Metropolitan University, Ann-Louise Grimshaw** -, and by **John Jardine.**

The large number of characters which, with proper costuming, might take even more than the eight actors used here to present in a full production of a play of under one hour, could be a problem in its being more widely staged. As lunch-time theatre seems at present to be in eclipse, but not the writing of good one-act plays, perhaps our theatres might consider the resurrection of double-bills, for which, among the other attractions, casts of the size manageable for full-length plays could be engaged.

The other problem, more commented on in discussion, involved in a full staging of this play was the large number of short scenes in different locations but there is little doubt that full production and a longer rehearsal period could turn what seemed to be a difficulty here into an apposite advantage. The brevity of many scenes was of their essence. We open with Linda "spending the night with Gary" but, after his principal exertions, he has nothing more to offer her than a brief "I love you" before "going for a slash."

This is very much a "searching for something more" play. When Linda is considering the application form to be a helper on an American Summer Camp, she asks Cathy, her fellow Care Assistant at the Rest Home where they both work, "Have we any Other Interests?" The reply is, "You mean, apart from drinking and shagging?"

The Passive Smoking of the title seems to be linked particularly to the way that, as an adjunct to such activities, Linda several times accepts the offer of a cigarette, even though she does not find smoking a pleasant experience. The passivity does not lie in the cigarette smoke coming from others' indulgence but in her drifting with the prevailing lifestyle, an activity she is coming to recognise as deadening in a much wider sense.

The standard reaction of both Linda and Cathy when meeting a new acquaintance at a party, bus stop or pub is to adopt a new name and more glamorous job description. This is perfectly possible in the anonymity of the big city but the fact that they do so indicates how little they feel to be of value in their actual selves or occupations. Although cleaning up deteriorating old people is often a far from pleasant occupation, Linda does it with a good spirit, not letting the cynicism of the surrounding social attitudes lead her into only a perfunctory execution of her duties and, thereby, missing the pleasures of genuine human contacts. She has an especial affection for John (**John Jardine**). His determination to "keep up standards" whilst surrounded by other residents far further gone, mentally and physically, than himself coincides with her feeling that she must seek something better for herself.

A notable feature of most of this year's plays was the skill of the dialogue, being both vivid, speakable and plausible. Chirpy Scouse has been exploited before as a stage resource but its use by **Jan McVerry's** is distinctive and it is not her only style. Apparently much of John's dialogue was written during the few days of rehearsals. Like the wittier exchanges between Linda and Cathy it was often extremely concise but in the skilled hands of **John Jardine** the lines provided material for the most affecting representation of an old man whose energies are ebbing away.

As another contemporary Scouse play, but of very different tone, **James McMartin's Bang on Top** could make a suitable second half to a double-bill with **Passive Smoking.** As a two-hander, however, it would not make much of a contribution to justifying the employment of a large cast.

If **Jan McVerry**'s Scouse, though
distinctive, had recognisable
connections with the wit of
Russell and **Bleasdale**, McMartin's
is a much more unrelieved howl
of rage, the first half consisting
of the two characters vulgarly
bellowing their fury at their
inaccessible neighbours.   He is in
a Newcastle prison for car theft,
where his sense of the injustice
at being taken so far from
Liverpool, rather than kept in
Walton, has prompted his violent
nature into acts which have led
to his being placed in solitary,
his feelings of outrage being
fuelled to even greater intensity
by his being placed on a wing
otherwised populated by the
despised sexual offenders.

She is similarly imprisoned, in a
Toxteth council flat, bellowing at
the neighbours for the din of
their radios, waking the child
with which he has left her,
although she and the child are
unable to sleep anyway, because
of painful rashes for which they
can get no appropriate NHS
treatement, and she is dependent
on the noisy neighbours for the
cigarettes for which she is
desperate.   Only able to subsist
by battling her way through the
demeaning DSS bureaucracy to
obtain Crisis Loans, she is none
the less determined, at this
stage, not to revert to the
indignities she suffered when
gaining her income from
prostitution.   Although Linda and
Cathy in **Passive Smoking** are
poorly paid for their unpleasant
work, we are here presented
with characters whose infinitely
greater economic and physical
deprivation almost justifies their
incandescent, vituperative rage.

All this information is conveyed
without noticable artifice as they
bellow through the cell doors or
mutter at the walls in the first
half of the play.   There is a
change of tone in the second, in
which some scenes showing how
the two met are intertwined with
others showing their fate a
couple of decades into the
future, him sitting hunched on a
park bench, sedated out of his
mind and hoping for the return
of a stray dog he had taken in,
her back on the corner, making
increasingly desperate offers to do
anything with any man who will
pay her but increasingly lacking
any feature which might attract
one.   This is a change of tone
from the irresistible white heat of
the sustained earlier eruptions but
these scenes are compelling
visions in their quieter way and
Tom Higgins and **Pauline Fleming**
rose entirely effectively to the
challenge of portraying the
characters convincingly at three
different stages in their lives.

The next play, **Wax**, a joint
work by **Sue Morris** and **Steve
Cochrane**, ended the Liverpool
setting of this year's productions,
even though it was essentially
produced by the now Liverpool-
based **Kaboodle** company, with
leading rôles once more taken by
recent recruits from the
**Manchester Metropolitan
University School of Theatre.** It
began in Manchester with two
visitors to the house of a
notorious mass murderer looking
round before the auction of
memorabilia.   The murderer
himself, **Stephen Banks**, then
materialised and jovially escorted
the better informed of the two

visitors, Louise, through the events of his earlier life. We saw no murders or even victims but only far more commonplace domestic and social events. The genial but sinister perspective of the guide gave them a fascination, however.

The second half of the play turned the focus onto Louise (**Sharon Muircroft**), through the question of why she was interested enough in the murderer to be writing a book about him. This had seemed to me to be scarcely worthy of remark, as I know from my work in council libraries that we cannot get enough books in the Dewey 364.1523, 'Orrible Murders, Section to satisfy reader demand and that the principal element in this demand comes from female borrowers. Books on the James Bulger case were ready to appear within a couple of weeks of the verdict and doubtless they are already being prepared to appear promptly as soon as anyone is sentenced in relation to the bodies found in the house of Mr and Mrs Frederick West. There's gold in that there gore and I saw no reason to assume that Louise was not just another writer out to dig it. The play had in fact been inspired by the authors reading a composite volume on such cases, obtained by one of their mothers to feed her interest in the subject.

It transpired, however, that Louise was interested because she was the natural mother of the murderer, who had been adopted at an early age and whom she had stopped visiting as his "auntie" when he was about six,

leaving a letter meant to be given to him "when he begins to ask about his real mother" but in fact read out to him by his adoptive father before she has made her final departure. The question in her mind was, therefore, was she in any way responsible for her son's later grisly activities.

The authors' intended answer to this was No: the number of adopted childred is so out of all proportion larger than the number of mass murders that no statistically significant link could possibly be made and that the conclusion of the play is Louise coming to appreciate this. As to the reasons for mass murder, they would not want to go beyond the response given by their character, John Ashton, "Fuck Knows", pronounced as one word and having a common assonance with "Footnotes."

This was not clear enough for many in the audience, some of whom felt that unwarranted aspersions were being cast at short-stay motherhood. I would have thought that the reason for this was not that the play's conclusions on the subject had not been underlined with a clarity which rewriting could introduce but that the play is not really geared to handling the question of causality at all. It does not handle the specifics of any case with enough precision to provide the basis for any such investigation. We more get a bizarre kaleidoscope of events from various aspects of daily life made up of images seen from the perspective of an unusual individual who happens to be a mass murderer. It is made dramatically effective by the vigorous and often rational way in which he conducts us through his world. Louise's story is less distinctive, though obviously having the potential to be emotionally gripping. The total performance may give scope for various kinds of social reflection but it is not geared to providing a prescriptive analysis of any of the problems of human conduct.

If the occasion of **Wax** was atypically sinister behaviour, so eventually was that of **Ian Karl Moore's Nowhere Man**, which ended with its main protagonist manically locking up in various rooms of his house all his relatives and acquaintances, so as to bring together "all the pieces of his jigsaw", to see what story they would produce. The captives include his pregnant cousin, the cries of whose child are one of the sounds poured into the play's final moments. Perhaps this related to the highly influential effect on the central character of the knowledge that his father had wished him to be aborted, so that his birth would not destroy the health of his beloved wife. The son's actual jigsaw does not have a picture which can tell a story, as all the pieces are black, but he associates its completion with the eventual death of his mother from the steadily intensifying calcium deficiency which his birth had initiated.

Whether, for its full effect, the play's conclusion should be absolutely terrifying I cannot be quite sure as, splendidly acted though it was, this atmosphere

was not fully realised, if it was intended, in the circumstances of a script-in-hand performance, rehearsed only for a few days. If it was, the trajectory would, intentionally, be from **Adrian Mole** to something of the character which I presume is in **Stephen King's Misery.**

Certainly the central character, who also acts as narrator, is a splendid part, brilliantly played by **Anthony Cairns.** He woos us in with his aimiable, **Mole**-like description of the apparently bizarre ménage in which he lives alone with his father and their interaction with his relatives. I say "apparently" as there is an intriguing ambiguity, which would be kept in a fully developed production, of how much of what we see is as we would perceive it ourselves and how much is as it appears in the very distinctive apprehension of Nigel Harris, the narrator. In this respect this element of the play is far superior to the stage version of **Adrian Mole,** which loses, through its cartoon-like representation, the book's ability to make us apprehend ordinary events behind the description of them by its very distinctive narrator. Here Nigel's father probably is a man of some eccentricity. So, possibly is Father Michael, although a supposedly randy priest whose depravity sinks no lower than a taste for sketching potential Altar Boys with their legs apart may well be more normal than those whose more advanced activities make the head-lines and lead bishops to set up emergency counselling teams. It is certainly a more interesting character to have on stage.

Also the variety of ways in which he is represented here seem to be a part of Nigel's deliberate plotting rather than of his probably distorted perceptions of some other matters. Otherwise the other characters are probably "really" quite everyday, although sometimes seeming not to be so because of the perceptions of the narrator.

Most of the piece was a joy to watch, both because of the fine way in which all characters were acted and because of the very considerable wit. What the total effect would be if the play became increasingly terrifying, I hope we may sometime get the opportunity to see in full production.

The only play in the festival in which some interest with regard to full production has already been shown appears to be **Owen Hagan's A Miniature Sprung Floor. The Library Theatre** apparently gave an earlier version some development time earlier this year.

It was by far the most traditionally structured work, set amongst an Irish family in Chorlton in the late 1950's. There was a present-day framework showing one of the main characters, Ronnie (**Jane Cox**), in a hospice, considering whether she should alter her will from leaving all to her criminal brother Sean, who made a fleeting visit from London in the 1950's sequence and has apparently not been seen since. Her Lancashire husband, **Steve Halliwell**, can think of relatives, and their own children, likely to

be far more deserving and able to benefit from the substantial sums she has accumulated from her chain of boutiques. It seems likely that she keeps to what is represented as an Irish tradition, to endow the nearest male blood relative, although the brief conclusion is far from clear. He says "Have you decided?", she says "Yes" and the play ends with him standing beside her in what was probably supportive resignation but could have been a relief which did not wish to wound by being over celebratory.

The instinct for this supposed tradition, however, would consummate what seemed to be the most consistent theme in a wide-ranging play: a denigration of Irish tradition in contrast with the English. It may just be that contrasts were raised and that audiences were trusted with evaluating them more evenly than the speakers, although the overt expression was always to the British advantage.

When Ronnie is considering the possibility of a new will at the beginning of the play and asks her Black, British-born, male nurse, "It is the law, isn't it?" he replies, with apparent deep sincerity, "You won't find another country in all the world with better laws." Whether all audiences in the 1990's can be relied on to have sufficient cynicism to downgrade such a comment, nothing is there in the actual script or performance to undercut it. The nurse himself is quietly assertive of his Britishness. When Ronnie responds to his comment on the laws by saying, "That's true, and it takes a

foriegner to see it" he gently
chides her, "Ay, ay; I was born
here, which is more than you
probably were" and confesses that
he often "cracks up, it sounds so
funny" when his dad and his
friends are talking about "the
homeland."

Ronnie, apart from earlier
rejecting the possibility of ever
returning to live in Ireland, is
incensed by the lack of hospital
treatment there which, if it had
been "like in England", she is
convinced would have saved her
pregnant sister Rona, after she
had been severely shaken in a
notably rough crossing on the
cattle ferry. Her characterisation
of the conditions on that ferry
through a supposed comment on
boarding, "Now which is the
Irish? Is it the four-footed
ones?", does not seem to be
attributed to English lips. The
words which do come from
English lips, her largely
affectionate husband's, are not
challenged: "I told her I was
ready to convert, but she said I
should wait till we were married.
When we were married, she said
I was just suggesting it to try
and win her round over
something. That's the way they
are, these Irish."

This is a quiet confidence, said
more in sorrow than in anger.
None of the lines quoted were
said with any especial emphasis.
It was just that in a wide-
ranging play, whose overall theme
may have been what it has
meant in that period to be Irish
in Britain, that was the viewpoint
which seemed most often to be
heard.

The household we see is that of
Bridi (**Judy Hawkins**), one of four
sisters from Donegal. She is
widowed and takes in an African
student lodger (**Joseph Jones**),
whom she is willing to allow to
stay without payment while he
re-sits his medical exams and the
family disputes over the money
from his recently deceased
father's estate are sorted out.
His presence arouses crudely
racist hostility in Irish neighbour,
Joe Devlin (**James Quinn**0, who
regards the student as "a fox in
the hen-run." Devlin's modest
proposal for establishing a
respectable male presence in the
household is to offer his own
services as a second husband for
Bridi. His ideal for her is that
he could support her in such a
way that "she need never set
foot outside her front door
again."

Perhaps partly with a view to
establishing a comparable pattern
of safety for her fifteen-year-old
daughter, Eileen, persuasively
played with great juvenile bounce
by **Lucy Sullivan**, Devlin has most
recently been demonstating his
concern to help the family by
making the Minature Sprung Floor
of the title, so that she can
develop her skills in Irish dancing
without wearing down the
carpets. Eileen has no great
proclivity for activities which
could arouse family concern.
Although she would far rather
stay to hear the news from a
long-awaited aunt, Sister Louise
(**Valerie Lilley**), a nun who has
been active in saving the
islanders of the South China Sea
from communism and in raising
funds for this purpose in the
United States, Eileen is compliant

enough in being dismissed to the kitchen to help her mother with preparing the food. Her two great enthusiasms are recalling the Munich Air Crash, "the best" of whose victims are perceived by her aunt Ronnie as having been both Irish and Catholic, and a newspaper photograph of an Alpine snowscape in which an airline pilot was convinced that he could see the features of Jesus delineated. The fact that the African lodger is ready to share in her penchant for offering this image her devotions intensifies Devlin's hostility, provoking him to initiate a physical attack on the student, in which he is joined by Bridi's gun-carrying twin brother Sean (**David Crellin**), making an unexpected visit from the London underworld, accompanied by his Cockney moll, for whom his care is limited and towards whom his violence is often extreme.

Whether this range of characters is meant to form a representative panorama of Irish in Britain at that period, I would not know but some such purpose would seem to be the most likely unifying principle behind the extensive number of characters and issues introduced. Some of those who left at the interval did so on the grounds that the play was a regrettable regression to the artifice of "Stage Irish" but most of the Irish involved in the production seemed to accept it happily as an authentic work. Of those who stayed for the discussion, some praised it for its authenticity, assuring the author he "must have known what it was like then." Others took a middle position, saying that they

had enjoyed reading the play but noticed that in performance the style seemed literary, rather than vernacular.

Up to the interval my own response was that if this was stage Irish, then it was of good quality. A good many turns of phrase were stylish and amusing, particularly as delivered by **Jane Cox**. Apart from her brisk response to her sister's enquiry as to whether all those killed at Munich were Catholic she gave considerable impact to such assertions as "some sins are too shameful to be in the commandments given to Moses." She also had vivid words to say on the virtues of Bridi's continued widowhood, "her children need never fear the heavy hand of a drunken father."

I was quite happy at that stage to see where events were going to lead but during the second half could feel the legitimacy in the perceptions of those who had left because the play seemed to be taking a long time to get nowhere in particular, partly by being repetitive. At that stage it was already noticable that Jim Devlin tended to say the same two things over again. As the part was in the highly able hands of **James Quinn**, it was felt that the fault must lie in a repetitious script rather than in its performance. I did wonder later, however, if the part might have made better sense if given to a repetitive old codger, a couple of decades senior to the woman he aspired to marry, who might not have felt up to initiating the physical attack on Ignatius Ali, the African student if he had not been joined by the more vigorous Sean. It was suggested in discussion that Sean's racist remarks against Ali were virtually carbon copies of those by Devlin and that this had contributed to the sense of *longueur*.

The dramaturg, **Bill Morrison**, conceded that the company had become aware of this sense that day, after they come had into the main house, following their few days of rehearsal in the intimacy of the **Brickhouse** studio. Perhaps it was because of this late apprehension of the problem that his technique of "Bracketing" had not been applied. This has been described in earlier years as placing brackets around substantial portions of a script with the comment "We'll decide what we're going to do about that later", "later" not being at a time arrived at before the public performance. The script as it stood, however, was defended on the grounds that a new author always feels that he "wants to put everything in" and that these Writers Workshops always specifically describe themselves as work in progress.

A good deal of the Second Act was devoted to Devlin's scheme of trying to advance his claims to Bridi's hand by trying to submit it to a formal democratic debate and vote by her assembled sisters. This did not strike me as overwhelmingly plausible but some of the speeches this involved were quite lively and well delivered.

I was not also particularly convinced by the plausibility of some of the lines given to the

African student but must confess that hearing **Wole Soyinka** on the radio a few days later, discussing the virtues of Yoruba religion in relation to his new novel **Ibadan**, part of which is set in England, where **Soyinka** was at the time of events presented in this play, I could hear the echo of similar sentiments to those I had thought a little stilted in this script. Certainly **Joseph Jones**, presenting both this part and that of the present day male nurse, showed the same ability to portray significantly different characters ably in one production as he did with very different parts in **Tom Sawyer** earlier in the year. Certainly his was a very valid character to include, even if, through no lack in its performance, it did not stand out so successfully as a highlighting contrast to the pervading adult Irishness as **Steve Halliwell**'s solid Lancashire good sense and **Lucy Sullivan**'s lively juvenile.

5, 9 & 15JULY; THE TIGER WITH GOLDEN CLAWS; Meech Street, Harding Street, Assheton Road and Dobson Court Mobile Libraries. (124).

It is said that those responsible for organising the contribution of **Manchester City Libraries** to the **City of Drama** were taken completely by surprise when the Director got up at the public announcement of their programme and declared that the year would see a dramatic event "in every library, *including all* the Mobiles." Abruptly faced with this challenge, however, they certainly came to the right people when they enlisted the **Manchester Actors Company** to make good the undertaking.

This energetic group, who are vastly experienced in presenting small scale works in almost any space, devised five up-dated **Arabian Nights** tales, varying in length from five to fifteen minutes, and well calculated to appeal to persons of any age group, including the very young and the very old, who are two of the main groups of people who value the mobile libraries.

The initiative had a mixed response. At one stop, a police car screeched up in mid-performance. Apparently a householder, seeing their turbans and hearing the word "Baghdad", had assumed that the avenue was being invaded by Iranian terrorists. Elsewhere some readers were alleged to have commented, "We don't want all this. We just want to be able to come and borrow books."

Although **Manchester Actors** can make a right old din when they have a mind to, all these pieces were much quieter essays in story telling and should not have disturbed anybody more than the general socialising for which the mobiles regularly provide occasion. At all the stops at which I was present, the performances were well received. At **Assheton Road** a reader, being told about the actors' expected arrival, went into an enthusiastic account of how, on a recent visit to Crewe, she had had the opportunity to experience the **Royal Exchange's**

touring production of **The Importance of Being Earnest.** She was just saying "It's something different when an actor appears from behind your elbow" as the first arrival from the **Golden Claws** team did just that. Nevertheless, as they began to perform outside on the pavement, many preferred to listen from inside the van or from their porches or windows, rather than look at the actors too directly. At this more discrete distance there was quite an amount of appreciation, as I discovered particularly at **Meech Street,** when I went over to the other side of the road to encourage people to come where they could see better. Most of them preferred to keep their distance but I was interested to see how many groups were intent upon the actors' activities.

At **Assheton Road** I wondered if the indelicacy of the first tale, **The Notorious Fart**, was the reason why readers studiously fixed their attentions on the shelves when the actors insinuated themselves and, squatting round in a circle on the floor, told each other the story of how over-indulgence at a wedding feast, including the consumption of a whole curried camel, led to a night that was to live in infamy. Many Mobile readers are not unrestrainedly modest, however, and that afternoon, at **Dobson Court,** all who were on the van, when the tale was retold, sat round and had a good giggle.

The actors then left the van to perform a further tale, their longest, a fifteen-minute **Ali Baba.** It sounded as though it

was all going good and strong
and I assumed their preparatory
leafleting of the nearby old
people's social centre had borne
fruit. When I was able to get
out to their concluding minutes,
however, I found them performing
vigorously, and with careful
detail, to no visible audience
whatsoever, although apparently a
few indelicate comments had
winged their way down from the
tower-block balconies inhabited by
young singles.

The uneven flow of readers to
these libraries meant that an
audience was not always
guaranteed. At **Meech Street,**
one of whose main functions is
as an after-school drop-in centre,
the children had been greatly
looking forward to the actors'
visit. Those who had organised
a holiday activity in the wake of
Jurassic Park the previous year
had been generally well received.
Although one studious seven-year-
old had dismissed the activity as
"just silly games", a younger lad
had managed to retain the
dinosaur transfer on his arm for
the next two weeks. On this
occasion, regretably, the tour
organisers had not been fully
conscious of the custom in this
country of keeping such persons
in preventive detention until after
three-thirty and brought the
actors along when the mobile
arrived an hour earlier, scheduled
to depart for another site before
the younger people could arrive.

One nine-year-old who had been
retained at home baby-sitting did
manage to attend with her
charge, however, and succeeded
in getting parts in two of the
episodes. She was praised by

the actors for her ability to
improvise, ending **The Invisble
Donkey** with a vigorous prance
across the area of park used as
a performance area, when
purchased at the market by the
foolish merchant who had been
persuaded by the thief who stole
his previous animal that he was
the mount who had been changed
into a donkey by Allah for the
mistreatment of his wife. Driven
off to market by his own wife
to buy a replacement, the
merchant, finding himself
confronted by his former creature
among the donkeys on offer,
abused him for returning to his
bad old ways and once more
being similarly punished, then
purchasing an alternative instead.
I thought **Hayley Cole**, the
preferred donkey, as much to be
commended for standing still
undistractingly when not so
prominent in the action, as a
supernumerary apparition in **The
Two Brothers** or as "my mate
be'ind that tree there" at an
earlier stage in **The Donkey**, as
for her final canter. Her
involvement, however, was a
particular tribute to the skills of
Manchester Actors, well able to
adapt to any development,
directing a line at a newly
arriving member of their
audience, moving in or out of
the van according to the vagaries
of the weather, adapting to the
resources of each site or leading
their whole audience to a new
performance area in mid-tale
when they found that a class of
primary school children, whom
they had settled on the grass,
had left them performing at
Harding Street with their backs
to impossibly noisy traffic.

143

The class had arrived because this was one of the occasions upon which the Library staff had rung up a local school to advise them of the attraction. The performance was equally enjoyed, however, by older people from the nearby retirement home and hostel, some of whom were particularly effusive in declaring what a good idea bringing the actors had been. While the tales and the style of performance were apparently in many ways very simple, they contained a lot of subtle detail which made them very suitable for all age groups and able to be appreciated on many levels. That particular perfomance, on one of the hottest days of this baking July and encouraged by the number present to include more episodes than usual, left the actors considerably dehydrated but at no stop did they stint the quality or energy of their proceedings.

6 JULY. THE MODERN HUSBAND; Arden. (118).

James White gets a deserved credit in the programme for "text transcribed from original manuscript" of this fine play by **Henry Fielding,** who seems to have written at least 25 works for the Theatre in his twenties, as against the half dozen novels for which he is now more famous. **Arden's** leadership deserves even greater credit for initiating the exhumation of this text, as do all involved in the production for bringing it so vividly to life.

Although written in the 1730's the play bears recognisable similarity in style to such a "Restoration" work, in fact "post-Glorious Revolution," as **Congreve's Way of the World,** although this, written in 1700, was in fact composed seven years before **Fielding** was even born.

The **Arden** manner of production makes the play seem significantly different in style from the way we usually see **Congreve** now, as our productions of him and his contemporaries usually seem to stress such stylisation as the painting of male faces and the seeking out of large venues, in which the wit is accentuated with grand gesture. Although the gentlemen here greet each other and depart with deep bows and exaggerated twirlings of the wrist, which might have looked even finer if more of them had had hats to doff, by staging the play in a small area, with the audience close to and on three sides of the action, the actors are able to perform far more initimately and thus bring out the genuinely human element in the events.

Some at the interval said the more formal style might have been abandoned because "it would not be understood now" but the garish face, in contemporary style, seems quite often to be used in new works, for instance by **Roar Material,** and also the one painted character in this production, **Andrew Pope** as **Captain Bellament,** drew a noticably warm response as soon as he appeared and, deservedly, maintained it through all his scenes. His theatrical

Journal

antecedence might have owed something to **Captain Brazen** of **The Recruiting Officer** (1706) but he was a much more successful wooer. Faced with a Millamant-like string of Conditions for independence within marriage by Lady Charlotte, he asserts how comparable they are to those he has already agreed with a lady rival whom he proposes to go off and marry directly, thus constraining Lady Charlotte to abandon all pretence of reticence and to bid desperately to secure his hand.

In them we have a pair who are goofy but willing and probably well suited. Lady Charlotte's being thus made unavailable means that Lord Richly can no longer constrain his nephew Gaywit to marry her, keeping her wealth within the family, thus losing his objection to Gaywit marrying Emilia. These two are apparently pure young lovers of high ideals, where most are untrue whether in public duty or domestically. Lord Richly is able to grant access to public office to those willing to provide him with either their coin or their women. He is content for it to be perfectly well known with how many others' wives he has been intimate, whereas others wish the image of respectability to be maintained.

Mr and Mrs Modern know very well of each other's infidelities. He appears even to have encouraged hers because of the revenue she can obtain from admirers, which he then appropriates. When this income begins to dry up before it reaches his hands, because of the

inconsistency of her skills at the gaming tables, he proposes to gain money instead by mulcting his wife's followers, through exposing them as her seducers. The most current of these is Mr Bellament, who cannot resist Mrs Modern's charms, despite being deeply attached to his wife. She is entirely virtuous and trusting and, when she does discover his infidelity, though initially deeply shocked, is able to adjust to a reconciliation. Her virtue has made her Lord Richly's next aspiration for seduction but also enables her to escape.

Lord Richly ends the play no better than he began, whereas Bellament probably does become more steadfast in virtue. Richly, however, is probably intended to attract some respect for the openness of his proclivities, the efficiency with which he conducts the veniality of his public responsibilities and cuts his losses when stymied in his moves for dynastic economy. Mr Modern probably attracts more serious opprobrium for the ruthlessness of his exploitation of his wife, albeit that much of what he encourages her to do very probably fits well enough with her tastes.

These permutations of virtue, fidelity and the lack or different forms of one or both of these provide a panorama which is probably meant to provide material for serious consideration on conduct in both public and private life, as well as providing for farcical good humour: "Must even the attendants of the attendants on the mighty be bribed?" cries Captain Merit desperately of **Andrew Fillis'**

145

smugly smiling porter, blocking his access to the house where Lord Richly is being received and whom he wishes to solicit for a military appointment. "That's one husband to many" exclaims Lord Richly, making a rapid exit, when his attentions to Mrs Bellament are interrupted by Mr Modern dragging in Mr Bellament to denounce him for his familiariy with Mrs Modern.

The cast, of students concluding their Second Year at the **Arden School of Theatre,** succeed in making all this very funny but it can be seen that these words are not the high "Wit" of much Restoration Comedy. It is very probable that the quieter, small scale style of the production is a faithful reflection of **Fielding** having written a more thoughtful piece than **Congreve,** serious though some of the latter's considerations probably were. The cast have taken dialogue which has been neglected for two and a half centuries and brought it to life as a clear and absorbing piece of enduring interest.

8 JULY. THE CLAYMAN; Upper Campfield Market. (119).

As we were ushered into the performance area, we at first stood in a confined section in which stood an old estate car, with a white-faced, white-clad woman lying on the roof rack. After we were all assembled, various other grotesque but formally dressed chracters approached and entered the car, which then drove off, the white-faced woman sitting up and looking at us in some puzzlement and perturbation as it did so.

It was then indicated that we should move to the left and as we did so, through a comparatively narrow aperture, we passed a bell, made from the top of an old gas cylinder, with a large bolt hanging from it, which was handed back by each member of the audience so that the next could strike a note on the bell when passing. We noticed that the car had left behind a character sitting in a deck-chair, eating sausage rolls.

We then found ourselves in a sanded area with clay domes upon it, from one of which crawled a man in a loincloth, with painted designs upon his arms, face and body, suggestive of a primitive culture. We then heard what was apparently the inspiring text of the piece:

"One night   a man has a dream
he dreams   of a clay figure
buried   deep in the earth.

In the morning   he sets off
with his spade   to find the place
where he must dig.

He digs until   the figure is
revealed
and brought to the surface,
where   the Clayman is fired in
a kiln
and released to the world."

As he set off, so did we in his wake, to find ourselves able to sit on chairs around a sandy mound, from the top of which could be seen protruding the crouched figure of a clay man and around which paraffin flames were being lighted. When this ignition was completed, as was our assemblage and Apeward, the man we had followed, stood over him looking bemused, the Clayman arose and walked off, taking no further direct part in the procedings, although he could be seen from time to time watching events from various platforms.

The white-robed woman whom we had seen being driven off on the roof of the car then came and lay in the hole left by the clay man, as in a grave, - his position, by contrast, having been at one point described as "foetal." Those who had been in the car now gathered round as mourners for her funeral and we began to identify their relationship to her, - Apeward, now having got some clothes, taking up the rôle of her youngest child. The man who had been left behind at the beginning, now attempted to join the party, still carrying his plate of sausage rolls. The reason for this seemed to be not that he loved woman less but that he loved sausage more. Rather, it asppeared that he had been her long-term lover before her marriage but that, being outside the family, his presence was not now welcomed by them. No such gross pun as "left without a rôle" was directly suggested but this was one of the strands which indicated a theme for the work and rescued it from being as pointless as I was beginning to fear it might be. "What's it all about, **Rikki?**" was a phrase which was beginning to come to mind.

It seems that a major element of the work is **Kevin Fegan** returning to the concept of Rites of Passage upon which he touched but did not develop in **Game Challenge - Level 7** last year. The excluded former lover was presumably in an analogous position to that often remarked on these days, for example by **Harvey Fienstein** in his **On Tidy Endings** and by **Jimmy Chinn** in his prefactory note on the origins of **Straight and Narrow:** of the surviving partner of a gay couple being given no recognised place when the family appear to take over the funeral arrangements.

The woman's shroud is as much suggestive of a wedding dress, as well as her grave being the Clayman's birthplace. All these times of Passage doubtless had their conventional Rites, even if they did not succeed in involving all those who would have benefitted from such ritual. The modern fracturing and restructuring of families and of marriages, however, lack rituals to help all parties to adjust to them. Other, longer established, times of passage now lack their ritual in our society to help both the individual and the community recognise changed status, even though other cultures have known how to mark them well enough. The infant Apeward reverts to climbing into his mother's bed because his sister says 'now that she's started wearing a bra' he can't climb into hers. Almost any African society knows how to mark this transition in a way that will leave all generations celebratory and none of them confused.

By contrast, the older sister is later involved in a ceremony with her peers for a new stage in social evolution: when a member of her set gets a new car they bring the keys to a welcoming ritual. Apeward is again excluded, not because there is no ceremony to give him access but because his tatty old near-wreck of an Escort is not considered a "car" in the sense the group understands the concept.

This suggestion of the need for unifying rituals in the here and now is linked to a sense of present society needing to understand its connections not only with the most distant origins of mankind but with those of the universe itself. Apeward's mother has worked at a research institute analoguos to Jodrell Bank. Listening by radio telescope for echoes of the Big Bang the rhythms detected seem similar to those beat out impressively through most of the performance to suggest the primitive context of the first, painted, Apeward and of the Clayman. The traditional Elements of Fire, Air, Earth and Water were prominent, which in their various combinations have been thought to provide the common raw material for living individuals and for the whole universe.

After the conclusion of activities at the mound we were invited to leave through a prolonged maze, marked out by sand and candles in narrow channels, along which we had to proceed in single file. Although the tendency was for people to move rapidly, it took at least five minutes to get

through. somehow the effect of people rushing past each other between the flames as the course wound to and fro seemed to make an appropriate and enlivening conclusion. In quite what way it was appropriate I am not too sure and if one did light upon a rationale it might be hard to specify it without it sounding ponderous. Whereas, earlier in the proceedings, I had been inclined to fear, during the second quarter, that the piece was in danger of becoming just a collection of stylised sounds and images with no particular burthen, but had felt that it had been rescued from pointlessness by a theme emerging, at the conclusion I was prepared to accept the happy effect of being part of the group going through the maze, without any particular concern for its significance. It just felt right. Maybe it was our Rite of Passage.

9 JULY. ANDY IN DIRE STRAIGHTS; Night and Day. (121).

That this is an "AIDS play" is indicated by the title in the style of its main character, an English lecturer living out his death sentence while the lively mind in his weakening body turns to much bitter wit but most frequently to a proclivity for turning any name or word upon which his attention can focus into anagrams or acronyms.

It is in many ways a well written and certainly well performed play. It is also the second production to open under the skilful direction of **Helen**

148

Parry within one week, the other being **The Modern Husband** **(118).** Nevertheless, I found it rather less satisfactory than other plays in this general category which I have seen. I tnink this was mainly because each other "AIDS play" I have encountered not only managed to gear itself into wider issues but to advance beyond the matters considered in the previous ones.

Larry Kramer's The Normal Heart, which I found very powerful in its **Bolton** manifestation in 1987, not only had the strength of a cry of rage and the zeal of a crusade to get the crisis recognised on its true scale. It was also a painful portrait in its own right of how those who might wish to unite in a desperate situation to reach a common goal, of whatever nature, can all too easily be drawn into fratricidal struggles with those with whom they wish to co-operate.

Andy Kirby's Compromised Immunity, brought to Manchester in the same year by **Gay Sweatshop,** not only had more to add through its English setting and being more up to date, so that while the need for adequate recognition and provision still needed to be advanced, it specifically addressed the issue of provision being retarded or being made in an inappropriate spirit or manner through homophobic prejudice against those those were regarded as having 'only themselves to blame.' Much of this was achieved through the main narrator figure being a straight male nurse who progressed from edgy dutifulness

to informed care but the play also had another dimension in the fine performance of **Peter Shorey** as the terminal patient, active in making good use of his final weeks of life, so far as he was able. This struggle was again strong in its own right, in significant measure independenly of the particular infection which had put him in this condition.

Those two plays were largely involved in campaigning for the recognition of AIDS as an issue and in spreading information about its nature. Work since then has felt able to take this as given. In **Andy In Dire Straights** whenever a sympton, aspect of medication or a Latinate term used to describe them is explained, the character addressed almost invariably responds "Yes, I know that", as if assuring the audience that it is not being treated as uninformed.

Perhaps the play's most distinctive feature is showing a fully organised "Buddy" system in operation, through which an able-bodied gay volunteer supports an AIDS patient by visiting him in his home to provide him with support and care. Several of the plays written in the intervening period, such as **Susan Sontag's The Way We Live Now** and **David Greenspan's Jake,** concentrated on the experience of patients' friends who tried to provide such care in the final months or, even, years. It is one of the things which makes Prior Walter's condition most painful for him in **Tony Kushner's Angels in America** that he sees himself as "the only Aids victim in New York who is not being

cared for by a friend or lover."
The onerousness of this task
which, in that play, made Louis
Ironson run off, fearing he would
be unable to cope, shows one
way in which the Buddy system
could come to be so desperately
needed. It is a great tribute to
the qualities of the Gay
community and its organisations
that **Andy In Dire Straights**
should be able to show this
demanding but deeply caring
system as an established and
recognised norm, needing no
elaboration.

Unfortunately, if one has seen
Angels in America, that play
greatly undercuts one's
appreciation of this one, as the
basic situation has been almost
entirely prefigured in it. Prior
Walter becomes Andy **(Martin
Gilbert)**, who even somewhat
resembles the **Kushner** character
when, like him, he wraps
himself in a long black scarf and
drags himself forth from his sick
room in order to confront his
absent lover. The bitter wit to
which he primarily resorts as a
response to his death sentence is
mostly directed against Max
(Andy Darbyshire), who,
paralleling Louis, rather than care
for him, absconds, apparently to
take up with another lover, when
Andy's deficiency reaches its
advanced stage. Nicky **(Joe
Simpson)**, the Buddy, takes up
functions played by Belize in
Kushner's play and Andy's
obsession with **Keats** mirrors Prior
Walter's growing interest in
Joseph Smith, the founder of the
Mormons.

Whereas, however, **Kushner** found
Smith's book "unmistakably

American" and has been able, in
his epic play, to work out
suggestive ideas about why the
Latter Day Saints have been "like
the United States itself," the
extensive quotations fron **Keats** in
Andy, with a repetition of the
longest of which the play ends,
do not succeed in establishing any
very clear wider resonance.

This play admittedly is a chamber
piece, the action always being
focused on Andy's one small
room, whereas **Kushner**'s is an
epic, concerned with the destiny
of his whole nation, and with
whether it is a nation. In
focusing entirely on one AIDS
sufferer and on two people
associated with him, **Michael
Harvey**, whilst in many ways
doing so very effectively, does
not seem to have anything to
add to insights and empathies
already covered on that level,
say, by **Kushner**, who covers so
much else as well. While there
was nothing very wrong with
deciding to write a much more
focused work, it would have
helped if **Michael Harvey**'s play
could have had some other
dimension, context or tone. It is
only a short piece, about one
hour, but even at that it did
feel a bit as though it was
rather a lot of the same thing,
fully deserving of serious
concentration though that was.
The acting and production were
powerful and persuasive in many
ways, the dialogue and structure
strong and fluent. The
reservations are because the play
did not seem to advance us very
far beyond what it seemed to
assume that we knew already.

RICHARD LINDOP, JAMES GRIFFITHS, JAMES READ, ADAM BAYLEY and ADRIAN MAWSON as the Public School Sixth Formers on the eve of the first Thatcher election victory. Whilst they are happy to follow the convention of discussing their political views in the terms of an Eighteenth Century Horticultaral Society's preference for "Good Husbandy", the louring presence in the foreground of ROB GIBBONS represents those ready to see such artifice "torn up by the roots." SANDBACH SCHOOL THEATRE's nationally acclaimed production of ROARING BOYS, specially commisioned from PHELIM ROWLAND.

22 JULY. **ROARING BOYS;** Green Room. **(123).**

The proclivities of Public Schoolboys have been used on more than one occasion to represent the ills of the nation. This play by **Phelim Rowland**, the only originally commissioned work

amongst the sixth finalists to be presented, by **Sandbach School,**

in the recent BT National Connections showcase at the **Royal National Theatre** of the best work by British Youth Theatres, uses this as part of a double analogy.

The lads concerned are Sixth-Formers in the habit of foregathering in the guise of an Eighteenth Century National Horticultural Society to discuss the affairs of the nation in rolling Augustan phrases, and elaborately embroidered waistcoats.   On this occasion their meeting is upon the evening of Thursday 3 May 1979, the polling day which ushered in the first Thatcher government.

They are in some excitation as they predict that the results of the poll will lead to the dispatch of those whom they term, in the argot of their Society, "the Levelling tendency" and the introduction of a government committed to the values summed up in their Society's motto: Property, Degree, Order and Firm Government. Another spring of action, however, is that some of the company are beginning to grow out of finding amusement in dressing up, talking in antique phrases and performing in Eighteenth Century Dance styles. They, therefore, initially suggest that their Chairman be replaced by a Lord of Misrule and then begin to disregard any authority but their own, declaring this to be part of their departure from living on the past, in favour of living in the present.

The Lord whom they initially seek to appoint is the retarded brother of a Fifth-Former who has been co-opted as "servant" for their proceedings. When he can make no utterance, the Fifth Former himself, who has no respect for their goings-on, to gain himself and his brother some respite, sends them off in search of "signs of the times," a task which the members perform with varying degrees of triviality or ruthlessness, according to their characters.

There is a degree of resonance with the style of government which was to fall upon this land,

brought in by a mixture of those who had some considerable respect for tradition and those who had none, the former being increasingly marginalised. I felt that as regarded the play's overall theme it would have been useful if some additional dimension could have emerged as, although apparently shortened since its original performance, now being under ninety minutes, in a single act, as regards deeper contents, one felt one had assimilated all there was sometime before the conclusion.

That aside, however, it was a most impressive evening. It was most suitable for its cast, allowing them to play boys of their own age in a context which was made plausible but which was far from conventional. The Augustan language was well sustained at a level which it was believable that intelligent and well-educated lads, if so minded, could improvise, indeed become so entrapped that they persist in it when they might have wished to have expressed themselves more directly. The Society Chairman (**James Read**) continues to use the style when he is expressing genuine shock that the Fifth Former, when driven off to find his own sign, should return with the War Memorial from the school chapel. On the other hand, when the retarded brother is being sent for as a Lord of Misrule, all the Society's members descend to a primitive chanting from their contemporary locker rooms: "Charlie Acker is a Mongol."

The standard of acting was very high. The cast produced very well-differentiated and plausible characters, from the most domineering to the most easily led, the latter sometimes going for extensive stretches without anything to say but still establishing their natures and their relationship to the group. There was particulary good acting by those outside the main focus at any particular time. We could see both the Society members centre-stage and their "servants" to one side and, as the audible dialogue passed between the two groups, one knew exactly what was transpiring in the one which was, for the time being, inaudible, because the nature of their argument or discussion was portrayed so well in visual terms.

Such transitions in the focus of attention were always most expertly handled and there was a great deal of drive throughout the production. The fights were very convincingly staged, being brief but vicious. Although the main action was notionally taking place in a cricket pavilion the effective set was in fact mainly made up of two very finely painted replicas of tabloid front pages, urging a Tory vote. Excellent Eighteenth Century costumes and apt contemporary ones had been procured and a very high level of commitment, as well as skill, was to be sensed in every aspect of the performance and its presentation.

23 JULY. ARDEN OF FEVERSHAM; Dukes 92. (122).

Castlefield now has several potentially excellent out-door theatre sites, from the epic scale of the fort itself to the more direct and involving platform area developed by **Dukes 92** on their forecourt. However, I feared when I saw **Dr Faustus** there last year that the kibosh might have put on this enterprise by the advent of **Metrolink**, so that performances did not only have to contend with the odd rumble from the railway arches but the considerable volume of a tramcar picking up speed at least every ten minutes. Happily, **Shakebag and Will Theatre Company** show in this production that, with the right actors and the right play, this venue can still be entirely viable, indeed highly appropriate.

Arden of Feversham tells, in the words of its prologue, how in 1551 Arden was "most wickedlye murdered, by means of his disloyal and wanton wyfe, who for the love she bore for one Mosbie, hyred two desperat ruffians, Black Will and Shakebag, to kill him." "Thus," say this company in their programme note, " a sensational murder ... was given to the public, first in popular ballads and pamphlets and then found its way onto the stage – the sort of play that would probably have been performed in a rough and ready way by Elizabethan actors and almost certainly became part of the popular repertoire on the open stage." An inn yard, which is essentially what **Dukes 92** has to offer, is therefore an ideal setting.

Although performers and audience would probably prefer fewer interventions from **Metrolink**, the actors are well prepared to act audibly and compellingly in the context of a far more constant background, from those who are only there for the beer. They manage to speak loudly without shouting, without loss of effect for the frequent well-turned lines and without making their volume seem inappropriate in what were quite often domestic, even secretive, activities.

In many ways the style was, indeed, "rough and ready" but not melodramatic. That might have seemed appropriate for what is essentially a **Maria Martin** of its day but the company, rightly and ably, decided to play it straight and sincerely. This was a much more sustainable tone for a full length play and also usefully kept characters in some touch with reality. On one level one could believe in Alice Arden **(Marion Bibby)** as possessed of a genuine passion for Mosby, plausibly dissembling to her husband, possibly even having a legitimate grounds for dissatisfaction in his frequent absences on business and, up to a point, believably desperate enough to have become determined to obtain her freedom through his murder. The way in which in the first half-hour she seeks to engage any man who enters as an assassin to this end is in its way ludicrous. Having heard the play described in advance as an "Elizabethan Whodunnit," I was reminded vigorously at this stage of the one **Agatha Christie** piece I have seen, in which absolutely every character was established as equally ready, willing and able to have done the deed. **Shakebag and Will** and the play's unknown

author(s?) manage to present something much more substantial than that cardboard nonsense.

This is not to say that there is not much that is intentionally ludicrous in the play. The most obvious element in which this is true is that it soon becomes apparent, although not made blatant from the first, that Black Will and Shakebag would be no more likely to be able to carry out a successful assassination than Nym and Bardolph would have been, or the Three Stooges, if they had been recruited for the task. "These villains will never do it!" cries Greene ((**David Reeves),** the dispossessed tenant whose grievance against Arden Alice had played upon to induce him to recruit the killers, who by this time have only made some three or four botched attempts. They have terribly commonplace misfortunes, such as standing in the wrong place in the London street where they first lie in wait for Arden, when a stall-holder comes to put up her shutters, knocking them over accidentally in the process, or creeping up at midnight to a door they have arranged to be left open and finding it locked.

These would be two great parts for a comedy duo who could avoid the trap of overplaying them. **David Kennedy** and **Letitia Thornton** certainly avoided that snare and played them with a good deal of character and energy, without losing a nice woebegone dimension which overtook them at certain times. I felt, however, that they did not quite have the natural comic touch which could have had an audience quietly shaking with laughter for prolonged episodes.

The audience when I saw the play was in fact comparatively quiet. The brief prologue, boldly spoken by **Fiona Brannigan**, drew some quite appropriate Hisses and Boos in its proclamation of Arden "wickedlye murdered" by the "disloyall" and the "desperat" but this style of response was not sustained. Mosby, for instance, drew a good laugh, particularly from a female swathe of the audience, when heseemed almost to have persuaded himself as well, after plausibly telling Arden that he had no continuing interest in his wife. He admittied that, naturally, as Arden had married such a beauty, he had initially been strongly impressed by her. Then he told Alice, the next time they were alone, "I have promised, I will no more solicit thee." She replied: "Thou needst not: I will solicit thee."

This laugh was earned, because the line was well inflected but spoken with apparent urgent sincerity, rather than pointed as a joke. If the audience was not always similarly loud in indicating its amusement, this was probably both because the tale was made genuinely absorbing and because much of the humour was appropriately of a quiet nature. The audience was not reluctant to laugh loudly when it took a joke broadly, as when the naked torsos of Arden and his friend Franklin popped up over the balcony when awakened from their slumbers at the London inn by their servant's nightmare, contemplating the outcome of his having left the door unlocked.

The existence of this balcony indicates the traditional element in the simple and effective design of this production, which enabled comparatively trouble free movement between the relatively few settings and also enabled the members of the small cast to disappear as one character and transfer themselves unobtusively to another point of entry, reappearing, after a simple but effective costume change, as another character. The show had been staged cheaply but the general look was plausibly in period and looked well. Carefully painted copies of contemporary maps of Kent and of London served as effective backdrops, distinguishing the two main settings in the play. Paintings based on woodcuts very likely used in the original pamphlet versions of the tale, appropriately showing an incredibly large number of separate characters holding daggers, made very suitable panels for the wings. – In the end pretty well every one takes a stab at Arden. "Give me the dagger!" cries Alice, delivering the first blow that stands any chance of being mortal, after Black Will and Shakebag have just about managed to knock Arden off his stool.

This was the one line I noticed which actually appears in a **Shakespeare** play, **Shakebag and Will** suggest "it is possible to view the play as a draft for the later writing of **Macbeth.**" Not by me it isn't, the level of language and imagination being so different. It is a very well constructed piece but tight plotting and concise narrative are not actually **Shakespeare's** principal virtues. This play has good, robust prose dialogue but it is not in the least poetic. When Blackwill and Shakebag, despite their conspicuous lack of success to date, end the first half, as performed here, by endeavouring to assert that they really are going to do a deed of fearful note, there are indeed 'echoes of lines found in other **Shakespeare** plays': they are quite like those of Pyramus' "Oh grim-look'd night! O night with hue so black!" We know **Shakespeare** wrote that but I do not think that we know of any work, however early, in which he was able to avoid writing real poetry as well.

Arden of Feversham is a very well written play of its kind, well worth performing, ably staged and well spoken as it is here, but it seems the work of a different **Will** and **Shake** from the one we know elsewhere. Perhaps that **Will** was in a bibulous group of writers and actors in 1592, who guffawed over the possibility of doing a London production of a melodrama some of them had been involved in out in the sticks, when someone had the sense to say: "It could be quite good, if we did it properly." **Shakebag and Will** have done so.

5 AUGUST. CITY OF LIES; RNCM. (162).

The sponsors of **Art in Schools** certainly got a splendid return on their investment in this notable production. The materials they made available had been converted into the most impressive masks and puppets of all descriptions by the secondary school pupils involved. Many of them, as well as members of the audience, could well be inspired to rush to the appropriate shops and buy supplies to continue or imitate their most professional achievements.

The performance area initially focused on a large screen. On the bottom half of this were half-a-dozen illustrations which, while in a bold, juvenile, poster-painted style, formed the same theme as the composite **Magritte** painting: "This is sponge" declared the lettering beside a picture of a pair of scissors. At the other end of the row of frames "This is an orange" accompanied the picture of a comb. In front of these was erected a huge tissue mask on an open wicker frame, presenting a face somewhat in the style of a Bini Bronze but having the colour of a wan moon. To the right lay the, rather sinister-looking, crumpled body of a sturdy marionette. On the left were ranged the gongs, drums and other instruments of the forty-piece **Manchester Gamelan** orchestra. As the lights went down, a single musician began reverberations from the largest gongs and the two narrators entered to stand over the marionette.

The tale they began had the same introductory phrase as most of the stories which were woven together to make up the whole programme: "Once upon a time, under distant skies ... ." In this instance it continued " ... there was an old man who lived in the desert." The marionette was then resurrected and began being walked, directly, without stings, across the area in front of the screen. "Who are you?" he asked, on encountering the giant mask. "My name is Truth" was the reply. "Why do you live out here in the desert, rather than in the city?" "I used to live there but, now it is so full of liars, there is no place for me."

At this point the other sixteen or so members of the cast entered from all directions, while the characters we had already met were removed behind the screen. They took their places at the gamelan instuments and, while playing one of the most developed pieces of their music in the performance, began singing their description of the City of Lies, where "Truth is false/And Yes is No;/Black is White/And Friend is Foe."

All this was punctuated with cries or whispers of "Liar! Liar!" At its conclusion Liar-Liar himself, the ruler of the city, swept on, in the form of a giant rod-puppet, needing three operators under his huge black cloak. This was surmounted by a large yellow face and hands, the principal feature of his grotesque facebeing an enormously long, perhaps **Pinocchio**-inspired, thin, curved nose. The citizens were summoned before him, one by one, and he roared with laugher as they each agreed with a minion who, holding up a large comb, pronounced variously, "This is an orange", "This is a smelly old sock." Interestingly enough, as I had arrived at work that

morning, in an unusually literary moment, my supervisor had jovially held up his hand before a colleague and asked, O'Brien-like, "How many fingers am I holding up?" He received the correctly Orwellian answer "Two! Two!"

In this performance, each citizen donned a disfiguring, half-face mask, on giving the required assent. The only one to insist that the object was a comb was promptly strangled. The masks were notably well made, each having a significantly different character and the cast were particularly good at this point in contorting themselves and moving in different styles, in keeping with their various masks.

In the next episode, – and the one, minor, fault with the evening was that, on occasion, it could be noticably episodic –, two characters had masks of a different style. These were like giant lollipops, with a face on each side: one with a polite smile, the other with a dismissive sneer. These were spun round as we heard what they said to each other and what they actually meant: "What have you been up to/ You prat?" – the unheard but truthful answer to this being "Trying to make some money and to avoid meeting you."

These masks were in a simpler, somewhat cartoon-like style. The complete-head masks in the next episode, illustrating the difference between those who had and had not been using ClearaSpot, were of a much more detailed type. The strikingly clear-featured one drew a wolf-whistle from the audience. He, despite the sales patter, was the one who had only been using soap and water.

The full company then assembled once again, in a circle, wearing their half-face masks and carrying small gongs from the orchestra, which they played manually. After a while they removed their masks with some relief and began to confide quietly with their neighbours until one proclaimed more loudly, "We've got to stop all this lieing. Remember the story of the Jackal," which was then duly told in most impressively cut out and manipulated Indonesian-style silhouette puppets, for which the back-ground screen was half illuminated. A very impressive Jackal was so convinced by the size of his own shadow, as he made his way home at the end of the day, that he thought he must be invincibly powerful and, therefore, to took no evasive action when confronted by a lion, by whose giant head we saw him being devoured, the red tongue in its jaws being the one departure from a purely black-and-white represention of this story. The moral was "Lies are dangerous, especially when you tell them to yourself."

The many styles of puppetry and masks had already shown that, although inspired by Indonesian forms, the company had confidently been able to use these alongside many others. The music heretofore, however, had been predominantly Indonesian in style, although a cheeky European da da-da da da had been used to round off one episode. At this point, however,

we had a distinctively Rap protest song, probably largely composed by the black member of the trio who sang it, while the rest accompanied on the Gamelan instruments. The refrain was "Liar-Liar/Your pants are on fire/Your nose is as long/As a telephone wire" and indeed the image of the long-nosed Liar-Liar, whom we had already seen at his full height, was shown as on a television screen, in a tissue representation. Television was presented as the source of the most distinctive mendacity, whether in the advertising of goods and what they would do for us or in the promises of politicians.

Two such, with large rosettes and characterful full-head masks, now presented themselves, eager to shake any hand in the front rows and to mouth their campaign rhetoric. They withdrew when a large, papier-mâché, flying pig on the end of a pole, came and flew over them.

The citizenry then regathered once one, similarly relieved themselves of their half-masks and conversed confidentially until publicly challenged, "We've got to act together, like the doves." The doves' story was told with the aid of little wooden figures, manipulated like children's toys. After being trapped in the hunter's net, the birds disputed as to what they should do until one cried out: "We must stop arguing: Remember the story of the Budum Bird."

Their own story was then suspended while this tale was told

by the Narrator and enacted by a puppeteer dancer, largely in black but with a splendidly painted circular blue and white chest design, to emphasise that the Budum Bird only had one belly, while having two heads, each of these being represented by two magnificently detailed glove-puppets, at the end of sinuous, green, flamingo-like necks, portrayed by the arms. One head, being jealous that the other refused to share a delicacy, vengefully drank poison, from the re-utilised ClearaSpot bottle, leading to both their deaths.

Enlightened by this tale, the doves co-ordinated their struggles beneath the net, so that they were able to lift it clear off the ground and capture the hunter in it on his return. Similarly inspired, the citizens began dashing about, tearing down the posters proclaiming "This is a sponge, This is an orange ..." and destroying the television image of Liar-Liar. The original giant puppet of Liar-Liar rushed to the scene but was defied by the citizens singing the protest Rap and finally destroyed by a giant turd, let fall by the flying pig. The mask of Truth returned to take up its central position and the final song confidently began "Once Upon a Time/Not Far from Here." It described the City of Truth where "Wrong is Wrong/And Right is Right;/Good is Good/And Light is Light."

The applause was deservedly strong. A good audience of all ages had been gathered. The appeal was as great to those who were barely five as to those eighty years their seniors, and to those at all points in between. It was a tremendous achievement for a group of teenagers to have been given the opportunity to create something of such universal quality and appeal.

They had clearly been given the most expert help by **Kevin Graal**, the storyteller, **Mike McManus**, from the **Obelon Art and Puppetry Company**, and **Maria Mendonça,** the main project worker on the musical side from the **Hallé Education Department.** These were all highly talented performers. Neverless they usually integrated themselves unobtrusively in the group work.

The expertise of this help, however, could not have been solely responsible over the ten working days of the project for the outstanding artistic quality of the masks and puppetry. These must have come in large measure from the personal talents of the sixteen young performers and the six Manchester schools from which they came, which have helped them develop these talents to such notable levels of achievement.

159

12 AUGUST. THE TEMPEST; Dunham Massey. (207).

"You've completely ruined my play." "I just thought it needed some poetry."

I agreed heartily with both these sentiments, hubristically expressed by an actor representing **William Shakespeare** and another who had just played Prospero, at the end of this **Oddsocks** production of **The Tempest.**

This is not to say that **Oddsocks** are a company without talent. Their warm-up material of juggling and of repartee with the audience, prior to the main performance, was most promising. This took place in front of an impressive large-scale model of a sailing ship, named The Golden Behind, which rocked to and fro most suitably during the opening storm scene and then opened out to represent Prosper's Cell as a plausible timber-framed cottage, suggesting he had made himself humbly quite at home in a distinctively English style.

In the ensuing scene doubts began to raise themselves, as Propero's explanation of the storm to Miranda, while containing some quite interesting points of characterisation and emphasis, very noticably lacked what that scene, and so many others in the play, contains so amply: real poetry.

There was time enough to be reflecting upon a common complaint by some, which I have not felt to be true in many

productions seen and produced in Greater Manchester, that "today's actors can't speak poetry", when **Nina Sosanya**'s splendid Ariel came leaping onto the stage and, not only by her lively and skilful movement but in her delightful handling of the verse, appeared to put that fear behind us.

Lamentably, this was a false dawn. Although **Nina Sosanya** did do well by any original lines on which she managed to keep hold, as well as giving a fully characterised airy spirit, dancing and cartwheeling, delighting in her tasks but looking forward with even greater enthusiasm to when she would be independent and free, most of the rest of the production made no endeavour to operate on the poetic level and was not equipped to do so.

The only occasion on which a substantial poetic section was played straight was Propero's great farewell to his art, beginning "Ye elves of hills, brooks, standing lakes and groves ..." The actor stressed the element of "I do forgive" heavily, then and when confronted with a not especially repentant Antonio, who took over the lines "If thou be'st Prospero,/Give us particulars of thy preservation" as a defiant challenge, before being faced down.

This was an interesting and acceptable adjustment of the text. What prevented it rising to any great heights was that this Prospero was quite unable to sound the Great Music of the initial speech. For his Epilogue, which gave rise to the exchange reported at the beginning of this report, the attempt to realise the poetry was not even made. It was delivered to deliberately distracting attempts to end the performance by the rest of the cast, in their personæ as supposedly, if deliberately anachronistic, Elizabethan actors settling a personal dispute, and concluded by the stage manager walking on to slap a custard pie in Prospero's face.

This was much more typical of the level of most of the performance, as if the whole play had been written in the spirit of its Stephano/Triculo scenes. **Oddsocks** "don't claim to recreate the Bard's company of players in any historically correct way but ... do attempt to encapture the spirit...: eye-catching, colourful, exciting and short." Although quoting **Shakespeare**'s references to "two hours' traffic" this performance exceeded two-and-a-half. A production consisting predominantly of broad, knock-about humour would have had to be of very high quality throughout to have sustained this length for any audience and the level here was much more variable.

The length worked significantly against the performance's suitability for children, towards whom the production's style was said to be especially directed. As is shown, however, by **Liz Lochead**'s one-hour adaptation, **The Magic Island**, the **Kazzum Arts Project**'s **Tempest**, which shared **Oddsocks'** enthusiasm for acrobats, stiltwalkers, jugglers and balancers, and also by the whole **City of Drama Manchester Schools' Shakespeare Project**,

there are countless ways in which to make this and many other **Shakespeare** plays fascinating for children *through* the poetry, rather than by abandoning it for slapstick humour.

Although **Oddsocks** cite in support of their general style the destruction of the original Globe Theatre by live cannon ammunition being fired, as a means of grabbing the audience's attention during a production of **Henry VIII**, a play probably at least as late as **The Tempest**, this is not really a play to attempt in the inn-yard style. It's spectacle, such as Ceres' masque, even its opening storm, was part of a work which could expect to receive the sophicated attention of the royal court, the first known production being at Whitehall, "before ye King's majestie." The **Oddsocks'** treatment would be better suited to an early work, such as **The Comedy of Errors**, but to tackle that or any other **Shakespeare** play still requires a company more than one of whose members can speak poetry.

17 AUGUST. **BRILLIANT WOMEN;** Manchester Town Hall. (250).

Usually when I hear it suggested of a new play that it might be better in some other medium, such as television, I am very jealous of the possibility of the stage being deprived of an interesting new work. On this occasion there might be much to recommend the proposal of **Willy Russell**'s Rita: "Do it on the Radio."

The cast, notably **Diane Brown's** Rose Hinchcliffe, did take advantage of the opportunity to address their words directly to a live audience, and the play could be developed into a tighter, more effective piece in its present medium. Tightening it does need, however. I suggest the radio as a possible form for doing this not only because it largely consists of narrative monologues, from three characters whose tales only gradually came together, in settings this production could do nothing to establish visually but which sound could do rather well. The author/director had also aspired to intertwine musical elements with his narrative in quite a complex way. In a fully developed modern theatre this could be done in a fluid manner but with the resources available to this very rudimentary small-scale touring production they quite often contributed to the lack of pace which frequently undermined the performance.

It was the staging, rather than integrating the music which proved to be cause of the cruellest example of this. After the play's rather slow start, **Diana Brown** had at last got some involvement and momentum going, both raising laughter with some vivid images of her husband's lack of personal hygiene, - "His black toenails crying out, ' You're mine! You're mine!'" as he sits slumped in front of the television -, and also an emotional account of how a sudden presentiment had enabled her to save her gay son from a suicide attempt, just as she was about to leave home.

She ended the scene with the declaration "I'll never forget the time I first met Bryony, outside Harrods." She marched off, leaving the impression that she was instantly to re-emerge to show us this encounter taking place. Instead we got a musical intermission so long and undramatic that one had time to think several time that it really must be an interval but that no one was stood-to to announce it or put the house-lights on. Eventually we got the scene we had been expecting. The reason for the prolonged intermission had clearly been to allow the actress to carry out a costume change. There would, of course be ways to achieve all this on the stage without such a deflating loss of pace but radio could handle it very naturally indeed.

Generally taking far too long to make a point was only one of the script's weaknesses. With male authorship, direction and administration if seemed to labour too hard to be assertively female and it seemed to involve a not-too-carefully-considered moral pattern of emotional response to follow the scene in which Kim tried to evoke the horror of her black lover, Bryony's adoptive sister, being knifed by prejudiced young lads in Brixton with Rose playing for jovial support for emptying a boiling chip-pan over her husband's genitals when she found him bedding her next-door neighbour. As the much admired Bryony, before she discovered that she preferred making love to herself, had made much of her affairs with other women's husbands, any consistency of commended principles seemed hard to detect.

The tag in the programme, "The only reason these characters are described as brilliant is simple (:) they're women!!!", seems a fair example of the lapses of thought and style in the script itself.

26 AUGUST. THE IDOL ON THE BRONZE HORSE; Contact. (251).

The great fascination of this production was to see the intermingling of the two completely different styles of the performers, from **Contact's** own **Youth Theatre** and from the **Theatre of Youth Creativity** in St Petersburg. This was manifested in the first two speeches, monologues from the two principal women characters. I at first took these to be the same words in the two different languages used in the performance, Russian and English. If they were not, the content was almost certainly closely parallel but the style was completely different. **Ekaterina Gorokhovskaya** (Elena) raised her eyes to the heavens and spoke with a bell-like and flowing poetic beauty. **Carla Henry** (Tamara) looked directly at the audience and told us in unstylish but effective everyday terms about the dream which she had had.

This seems to represent fairly the contrast between the youth theatres of the twinned cities: their principles, their leadership and their general membership.

When they arrived in St Petersburg for preliminary

discussions a year ago, "armed with proposed schedules and projected budgets, the English contingent were taken aback to find the Russians wanting to discuss art before administration." "The Theatre of Youth Creativity has become a place where its pupils not only train to be actors and experts of different theatrical professions but also a place where they can learn the main human treasures, such as friendship, love, justice and faith." "The underlying principle of **Contact's** community and education work is to encourage and enable young people to use the medium of theatre to express their interests and concerns."

When **Contact** members went to St Petersburg at Easter to begin the joint workshops on the project, the diary by **Phoebe Pallotti** which was published by **City Life** (20 April) focussed on such basic matters as getting out of bed and what they had to eat. When the Russians arrived here, the companion piece by **Dimitri Strelkov** (10 August) announced "I want to find out about the spirit of England, ... the country which gave the world **Marlowe, Shakespeare, Milton, Byron, Shelley ..."** The Mancunian in Russia was determinedly unelevated: "I went to see the Maly Ballet. ... It was beautiful but ballet is similar whichever country you are in, so this didn't exactly come top of the 'ultimate Russian experience' list." Some here do not speak too highly of what many regard as 'the ultimate Manchester experience' but it awakened the muse in **Dima Strelkov**: "We were walking by a lake on the

163

outskirts of Manchester. The sky
was very dark – it hung above
us like a big hat. Then the
water in the lake became heavy
and dark, and the trees
surrounding the lake looked like
people bowing their heads to
protect themselves from
something. A deep silence fell
for several moments and then
suddenly there was a huge roar
of thunder and a great flood of
water poured down on us. It
was my first swim of the
summer."

While in some ways the play
itself seemed a little obscure and
not having enough to say or
convey, in proportion to its
length, it was in fact very skilful
in providing opportunities for the
two cultures to display
themselves, first separately and
then in interaction.

The two prologues were delivered
in semi-darkness, from behind
gauze curtains halfway down the
stage, with the whole cast
ranged holding candles behind the
two speakers. Then they rushed
about far more actively on the
now lighted forestage, one of
them emerging as being borne
aloft by the others, – "Ah, the
bronze horseman" one thought.
This creature then came across
the prostrate figure of **Stuart
Bowden**, who was roused and
fled in fear before them, part of
the mass behind him separating
itself to form a giant slope,
down which he rolled, like
Lucifer falling from Heaven, and
found himself still desperate to
escape from mysterious forces at
the bottom.

At this stage one wondered if,

bi-lingualism having been found to
have its limitations, the movement
director was going to be the
presiding influence over the rest
of the evening. Although the
foregoing action had been very
well done, one wondered if it
could sustain a whole
performance. This was a
needless consideration, however.
Such elaborate movement work
was only one of the range of
theatre skills which the play gave
the cast the opportunity to
develop and deploy.

The mimed sequence had probably
been showing us something of
The Story So Far of the two
parallel communities which the
tale concerned, that represented
by the English-speaking group
having at some stage apparently
"come there" under the leadership
of Leo (**Guy Rhys**), the other
initially existing elsewhere,
perhaps even in a different
dimension, with Maxim (**Sergei
Nikolayev**, but perhaps
represented by **Stuart Bowden** in
the mime sequence) perhaps
having held a comparable position
to Leo within it.

Maxim now walked through the
gauze, from the back of the
stage to the front, carrying a
shoulder-bag, which we later
found to contain considerable
amounts of money. This
information was probably not
included in the remarks which he
then made in Russian, although
several of these were focussed on
the bag. After looking around
the few items standing on the
forestage, – a large candle-stand,
a few tool-boxes and a tall
tower –, he decided to secrete
himself at the top of the latter.

The English-speaking group then entered from the wings and set themselves to various tasks of shovelling, sawing, hammering, sweeping and construction. This was fairly low-intensity activity, apparently self-motivated in a reasonably happy atmosphere but without great evidence of high enthusiasm. As the craft workers included an oil painter at a canvas in the back-ground (**Michelle Calame**), this, with the leisurely pace, for a while suggested a rather **William Morris**, "News from Nowhere", style of society but this impression was undermined by the entrance of Leo, with a rolled-up plan in his hand, wandering round imposing unhelpful directions as to how the work should proceed. As the first of these included taking a broom from a girl to exchange it for a boy's hammer, one wondered if he was intent to create a society devoid of sexual stereotyping. Further intrusions lacked any such apparent purpose, however, and certainly had the effect of irritating everybody, who severally packed up. "Get real, Leo" was **Michelle Calame's** parting comment as she left him to an almost empty stage.

Tamara (**Carla Henry**) was the last to go, after Leo had tried to justify himself to her, saying he was only trying to get things done. Able to sense Maxim's presence at the top of the tower, but not to see him, Leo revealed that he was aware of his existence: "It's Maxim. I know he's here. I never used to be like this. He's out to get me."

Although this scene had contained such significant fragments of dialogue, much of it had been wordless. Some nice, and often quite amusing, points of character had emerged in the craftwork activity but by and large it was still looking as if dialogue was to be kept to a minimum. The next scene, however, was almost entirely verbal, as the Russian-speaking group reappeared behind the gauze and held a long and stylish conversation, probably on the topic of "Where's Maxim, and how are we going to manage without the money?", but there was nothing much to convey this to those who did not know Russian.

Maxim now descended from his tower and we saw the money he had in his bag as he laid it out in patterns and then tried to burn it. He was obviously still far enough into another dimension to be invisible to various of the English-speaking group who entered in a relaxed evening mood, expressing their dissatisfaction with Leo far more openly, showing the picture which had been being painted to portray him with a most unflatterring death's head, riding on a horse. Leo came in and sent them off, complaining "Am I really like that". The burning of the first note, however, enabled Leo to see it. This attention led Maxim to pack up the rest of the money but he was also invisible to Tamara, who now entered and whom Leo again failed to convince that he was acting for the good of the community. Tamara, left alone, then found, in what was later described as a dream, that she was able to communicate with Elena, speaking from behind the gauze, and asking "Where is Maxim?"

Although Maxim was still on stage, close to Tamara, she could only at that time answer? "I don't know. I haven't seen him." Obviously a night sleeping out on the ground in his new dimension did wonders for his visibility, however, for as **Stuart Bowden** came on, first on deck to start his next day's carpentry, most subtly and characterfully mimed, he became aware that he was not alone. The most amusing scene of the play then followed, in which **Stuart Bowden**, soon joined by **Abigail Pound** and, later, **Michelle Calame**, tried to communicate with Maxim across the language barrier.

This was at first done in a friendly spirit but, when they became intrigued by Maxim's bag and he refused to show them what was in it, they took advantage of his being distracted by the arrival of the rest of the group to grab hold of it, continuing to throw it about between them, even though it became evident that being forced into this involuntary game of pig-in-the-middle was causing Maxim considerable distress. Tamara entered and calmed them down. After her apologetic words to Maxim, however, he ran off with his bag and Tamara sent the others
back to work.

The Russian-speakers behind the gauze, now opened gaps in it and entered the dimension at the front of the stage, which they began to explore. Unlike Maxim,

they were perceivable from the first. They were encountered by Leo, who was hostile and tried to drive them off. Not being able to do this he called for Tamara to help him. When she proved welcoming to the strangers, Leo declared he was leaving. Some of the new arrivals having a few phrases of English, Tamara learnt that they wanted homes and food and undertook to let them stay. The act ended with her being introduced to Elena, it being said she knew her, with which she agreed, though neither at that point was too certain of the nature of their previous communication.

The second act began with the crafts group proceeding with their building, as if not much had changed. Tamara then came to announce that Leo had gone. Some wondered what they would do without him but others were confident: "We'll manage". When Tamara brought in the visitors, saying she had agreed that they could stay, they were greeted with only limited politeness but, while she went off to get food, the Russian-speakers began to introduce themselves and to help in various ways with the construction, with the result that closer and more friendly relations developed over the meal. The visitors asked what the group were doing and it was revealed that the tower was part of a church which they were converting into a theatre where "we're going to put on a play." Very interesting: "What play?" "We don't know. We'll sort it out."

Stuart Bowden then entered pushing a giant box, somewhat as he had pushed the dead pig a year ago during **Game Challenge – Level Seven,** when he had seemed to be half the size he is now. The box had been left behind by Leo, with a note saying "This was my latest idea," the contents proving to be the pieces for a rather ricketty wooden horse, which they constructed.

Good relations were then further developed by the visitors teaching the English-speakers lively Russian songs and dances. The spirited way in which everyone was drawn into these reminded we on the one time I was in Russia. En route to the 1957 World Youth Festival in Mosco, our train stooped at Minsk, where we were greeted by Cossack Dancers. The English did not have anything so spectacular with which to reciprocate but, providentially, I was with a Scottish group, from the Iona Community, and we proved to have a full pipe-band on the train, who paraded up the platform in appropriate costume. As the Cossack ran out of puff, a Scots dancer took over to his music and later the Cossack began dancing to the pipes, to the applause and enjoyment of all. **Contact** and St Petersburg recreated on stage the authentic way in which such music and dance can draw different peoples together.

In a more personal scene, once the new friends had dispersed, Tamara told Elena that Maxim, whom it had emerged had stolen the money, was around but they

no longer knew where he was. When Elena was alone, however, he re-appeared. The exact nature of their discussion in Russian, I would not know but Maxim, impressively played throughout by **Sergei Nikolayev,** perhaps somewhat Puck-like, was not presented as a villainous character. He clearly had his reasons for whatever he had done and offered Elena the money back, which she rejected, having perhaps once more highly valued his heart.

Tamara's heart was obviously beginning to be somewhat stirred by Mikhail (**Leonid Zibert**), the newcomer with the most phrases of English. He quoted her **Lermontov,** in Russian, which she found beautiful but incomprehensible. Their discussions, however, were interrupted by the return of Leo, to whom Tamara felt she had nothing to say but to whom Mikhail, – evidently a more honourable wooer than **Lermontov**'s Hero of Our Time –, insisted she must speak.

Any hoped for *rapprochement* did not get very far but, when she left, Leo found himself confronted with Maxim, whom he found that he could understand, despite their different languages. The nature of their symbiosis did not become desperately clear despite this and Leo demolished the wooden horse, apparently intending to replace it with a bronze one by using the money which he managed to steal, after observing where Maxim buried the bag.

Although, after observing the horse, the Russians had managed to give direction to the English-speakers' less-focussed aspirations by suggesting that this become the theme of their proposed play, the actual performance which probably represented this drama appeared to be more of a religious procession with candles, the accompanying words apparently being neither Russian nor English but Latin. Whether this was meant to indicate that the original purpose of the church building had been vindicated, I would not know. It certainly had both language groups, the older and newer members of the community, united as one. The only ones not to be involved were Maxim and Leo. Leo emerged from watching in the shadows and stood silent as Maxim descended once more from his church tower and, squatting, Leprechaun-like, on one of the cross bars, addressed various quizzical remarks to Leo in Russian.

It would have been nice to have known the burthen of these final comments and perhaps the play would have seemed to have amounted to a greater whole if one had been able to follow the dialogue in all scenes. Without this, it did seem from time to time a little short-weight. Whether or not that was true of the script, it can certainly not be said of the performances, and the script not only provided occasion for the display and combination of two very different acting styles: it gave scope for one to ponder upon the nature of the two cultures involved.

At one stage, when some of the English-speaking group of characters were adjusting to the presence of the newcomers in their midst, the perception was advanced: "They're just like us, really; - quite nice, actually." Even if on some levels the performers, as oppose to the characters, may have found this to be true in their weeks of working together, such reductionism would miss a lot. Whilst there is a great deal to be said for the basic honesty implied in the unstylish Manchester dialogue and diction, if the distorting artifices which one seeks to clear away by telling someone to "Get real" are indeed removed, the elevated poetry of the Russian may be one of the best tools with which to emphasise the human stature of what is then uncovered, rather than leaving everything to the non-prescriptive generalities of "We'll sort it out."

"When you've run away from the world, the past and everything you've known - where do you go?" is the question, possibly quoted from the Russian part of the script, which is printed in both languages on the cover of this play's programme. Both cultures can probably play a distinctive part in discovering the human treasures in answers that would meet the interests and concerns of young and old in both countries. It is hard to doubt that those from both Manchester and St Petersburg have both enjoyed and benefitted from working together on this project. It was certainly impressive to be able to experience the results of their co-operation.

1 SEPTEMBER.
RAVENHEART – THE
STORY OF CARMEN;
Alexandra Park, Oldham.
(252).

This was a splendidly stimulating performance. Almost completely wordless, it held by its involving action, its athleticism and extensive humour, its vivid colour and ceaseless, predominantly percussive music. Despite its stylisation and its clearly Mediterranean, principally Spanish, setting, its central character, especially, and her life were very recognisable. In spite of the flamboyance of much of the production, it clearly portrayed a society of urban impoverishment, surrounded by rural peasantry and attracting the constantly constraining attentions of the militia. Carmen was undoubtedly kin to the most sparky and assertive of our own low- or un-waged, who are determined that their lack of income and status, save in the camaraderie of their own associates, is not going to prevent them having "a good time." Their lack of respect for the authority which tries to constrain them is one of their most accessible forms of amusement.

We faced a bare circular stage, backed by colourful screens, with a musicians' shelter to one side. That shelter was probably needed the night before, not least for the limited amount of electrical amplification and the double-bass that was used, but this evening was a beautiful dry, clear night, the bright sunshine just beginning

fade as we started to hear the actors approaching. As we glimpsed then through the bushes, they appeared to have become a lot more colourful than the black-clad group we had been able to see exercising further along the path, off which we had turned to enter the performance area.

Taking very small steps in unison, not all of them forward but, at that stage, in very regular rhythm to the drum beats, their approach, as of a single entity, seemed almost mechanical. As they reached the top of the slope down which we had entered, brass intruments added their stain to the music and the action became more and more lively. A major element of the colour proved to be face masks, reminiscent of Indian deities or or devils from even further east, worn by all members of the company, except the Matador (**Tristan Sturrock**) whom they were accompanying. The main adornment of his, slightly whitened, features was the mascarara on his eyelashes and he clearly shared his companions' estimation of his heroic beauty as he posed and flirted with ladies in the front row while the rest of the company dashed about in increasingly wild excitement.

This preparation having reached its climax, most of the company ripped off their face-masks to become a more human audience for the bull-fight. The Bull, however, was represented by Carmen (**Bec Applebee**), holding a wooden mask, with the other main women performers acting as picadors. Once the bull had been slain, Carmen became herself, as the principal congratulator of the matador and celebrator of the dead bull's head. These festivities were terminated by the arrival of the militia who impounded the head and left the Corporal (**Giles King**) on guard over the box in which it was locked. He was distracted in his duties, first by the arrival of his peasant mother, searching for her long lost son, and then by the arrival of Carmen and the other women, intent on retrieving the bull's head. Their first ploy was for **Jo Kessell** and **Emma Rice** to carry out their laundry in the messiest possible way before him, drenching the stage, as well as a good bit of the audience, so the athletic, dancing, leaping, bull-fighting and stilt-walking which later took place can be no more hazardous for the cast on rainy nights than it was on this otherwise dry one.

Carmen then entered and sought to win over the Corporal with offers first of water melon and then of herself. A great deal of humour was generated in these entirely wordless scenes, not least by **Giles King**'s first seeking to remain dutiful but then becoming genuinely enamoured. Proceedings were interrupted, however, by the return of the Captain (**Jim Carey**) and the Guard. Once more the mime was side-splitting as he discovered that the Corporal's uniform was now decorated with the rose which Carmen had given him, she having originally received it from the Matador, **Tristan Sturrock** now acting as a fellow soldier who hilariously contrived to show

overwheening pride to us, at the same time as 'umble duty to his Captain, from whom he now received the stripes removed from the Corporal. The latter was, none the less, left with the task of escourting the arrested Carmen to the barracks, a process in which she was entirely unco-operative, making a complete fool of her demoted captor until entirely released from all contraints, when she agreed to walk there of her own accord.

Once arrived it became clear enough that the Captain's censure of the Corporal had been pure hypocrisy, as he now looked to receive similar favours from Carmen, which she was ready enough to grant, although the play she made of thereby having obtained the key to the trunk containing the bull's head does not seem to have led to anything as, several scenes later, it was still in the same place.

The former Corporal was further demeaned by being stood to to serve wine to the Captain and his guests, obedient if devastated to see the woman who had won his heart now seeming to offer hers to his Captain. All this was expertly played for laughs as was the ensuing scene in which, the next morning, the new Corporal exulted in detailing his predecessor to swab up with mop and bucket the residue of the revels of the previous night. Carmen entered, first of all to taunt him by throwing orange-peel onto the areas he had cleaned but then, once more, to draw him into her embraces. On this occasion, however, when they were interrupted by the

Captain, she remained loyal to the lower-ranked recipient of her favours, smote the Captain amidships as he tried to renew his advances and fled with the former Corporal.

All this having been so persistently comic, I had begun to wonder, in the odd moment as scenes changed, if this **Carmen** was related to one which I vaguely supposed to be, at least in part, tragic. The next scene did begin, however, to introduce a more sinister element, without suffering from any abrupt change of tone. A dance, in an apparently more rural setting, came to focus upon Carmen and her friends telling fortunes by casting bones. Not much liking the look of those she cast for herself, Carmen threw them for her friends. The imminent marriage of one and the three children to be expected by another were jovial mimed by a ring on the finger and by inverting the casting bowl over the belly. When she reverted to her own fortunes, however, the Matador, standing on a platform at the rear, raised a skull from behind his blood-red cape. When she was persuaded to try again, the same prediction was made.

Unsettled briefly, Carmen decided to dismiss the warning. As merry-making resumed, it was interrupted by the arrival of the militia, carrying the trunk in which the bull's head had been placed. There was much Laurel-and-Hardy-like humour as the Captain first delayed the order for his men to set down their heavy load and it them being put down on the toe of the new

Corporal, he agonising silently as his comrades were allowed to sit on the box while receiving further instructions from the Captain, whom he dared not interrupt.

The box was them opened and the bull's head removed, quite to what end I was not sure, but the proceedings were then interrupted by the arrival of the former Corporal, now in peasant costume. In a distressed state he sought to attack the militia with cutlasses, but was ineffective and was left in a collapsed state, in which he was discovered by his distraught mother.

The focus then shifted back to the town with another fiesta, in which the Matador, now on stilts entered with Carmen as his closest companion and the rest of the company once more in the colourful masks in which they had first entered. The bull on this occasion was a much more formidable creature and one wondered if the Matador might now have met his match. Its provocation now, rather than picadors, included the women leaping and rolling, Minoan-like, over its back.

The Matador's first major thrust did not prove fatal but as the crowd gathered to see the fight continued, the former Corporal entered, to have his affections spurned by Carmen. At first he seemed, sorrowfully, to accept this but, after further contemplation, he returned with a knife and cut her down. This caused him some distress, before running off, and, indeed, some to the crowd, when they discovered her body after the triumph of the matador. That triumph absorbed them even more, however, and her body had barely been carried away when her memory seemed to be completely obliterated by the entry of a giant flaming bull, stylishly designed in wrought iron, the heat of the parafin flames from the wadding twisted round it being palpable to the audience as it was borne aloft. The matador having despatched this too, he was fêted to the close with triumphant music and dance.

My only previous experience of the **Carmen** story was when I saw the last couple of minutes of the **Carmen Jones** film. I had entered a cinema, wishing to see the second half a a double-feature programme. Then the abrupt strangulation, followed immediately by the rolling of the credits, over a clearly artificially-burning torch, seemed fairly typical of the desicated style which I associated with the director, **Otto Preminger.** Here, the sudden disappearance of Carmen, not even to return prominently to take a bow, just, as the prolonged applause went on, unobtrusively coming on at the back to pick up a drum to join in the extended music session with which the company responded to the enthusiasm of the audience, did seem to have a certain point.

Her glory was in her life, not her memory. She loved widely if not well. Once destroyed by the rough world in which she took her chances with a spirited daring, she was gone with as

little trace as would the rest of the impoverished multitude among whom she lived, when their turn came to vanish without note.

A tale could be told which stressed the injustice of that society and the hope of a better one. That was not the point here. It simply showed a common enough world, in which many have had to live and many still live. In it, human humour and excellence shine forth in many vivid if tarnished ways but the light which inspires those who continue to struggle is the matador who is at present triumphant, rather than the lively comrade who is gone. Whatever is begotten lives and dies. This play showed some of the virtues possible within that framework, in a vivid if none too virtuous context. To question the context was not its first concern.

8 SEPTEMBER. A MIDSUMMER NIGHT'S DREAM; Manor Mill. (257)

It is not every mature actor who would wish to start the performance of a full-length play with a Hundred Yard Sprint. **Barrie Rutter** and **Ishia Bennison**, however, achieve this, without ending up noticably out of wind, when he, as Theseus, pursues her, as Hippolyta, down the full length of the **Manor Mill** upper loom room, in order to get this splendid production off to a vigorous start.

They were not in fact the first to enter. The action actually began with the Rude Mechanicals, sauntering down the same stretch in a much more leisurely fashion from works the canteen, in which we had seen them taking their break as we passed through on the way to our seats. Betaking themselves to their work-benches, their hammering, filing and snipping had formed an overture to the main action, to which our attention was then drawn by the precipitate entry of the queen and duke. The court having had its say, our attention was returned to the mechanicals, first by once more hearing the sound of their labours and then by realising that the sound of the factory hooter, which was leading them to down tools, was coming from the mouth of Peter Quince (**Roy North**), who, standing erect in his trim foreman's overalls, tea mug in hand, had materialised in the midst of the tight horseshoe of tiered seating, within which the main action of the play took place, thus summoning his company to prepare their interlude for the wedding of the Queen and Duke.

Such brisk, effective and appropriate transitions from scene to scene were one hallmark of this finely conceived production. The most advertised feature was that this company perform "In Real Northern Accents." There were a few moments in the early minutes when it seemed as if some cast members were using these as consciously as they complain that they are constrained to avoid them when performing with other companies in other regions. Soon, however, we were reaping the rewards of the actors' skill in using their own language, not only for bluntness, naturalness and comedy but for poetry. One of the first lines to be striking for its enhanced beauty was Hermia's reply to Lysander's "Why is your cheek so pale?/ How chance the roses there do fade so fast?" The long final syllable in **Helen Shael**'s tearful response, "Belike for want of rain," brought one very abruptly into the deep emotion of her feelings.

Not all the language is fully effective yet. Titania, perhaps to distiguish her speech from Hippolyta, is so strangulated with rage in her first scene that her deep concern for disordered nature was quite lost in her fury at Oberon. I was just wondering if, with her dark clothing and straggling hair, the concept was of the sort of spirit thought likely to arrive on a broom-stick when she climaxed on "knows not which is which", as the mazed world's response to how the seasons change their wonted liveries. I doubt if that was the point, however, but just a detail in what is for the most part a very fully realised production at the start of its tour.

Another speech at present a bit lost in a loud shout, rather than a more fully inflected expression of grief and fury, is Helena's protest at the way in which she believes the other three young Athenians have conspired to taunt her. Visually this scene was splendid, however, as she hollered at them furiously from one end of the acting area while they cowered in confusion at the other. **Ludmilla Vuli** is more than common tall and **Helen**

Sheals, as Hermia, was recently Little Voice herself in the recent production of Jim Cartwright's play at the Bristol Old Vic, so the scope for Helena to 'urge dwarfishness' could be well taken. As Vuli is a Daughter of Africa, although born and bred in South Yorkshire and thereby fully entitled to play for the county, her accusations of "Thou Ethiope" went. Theseus still had his lines on beauty in the brow of Egypt being only perceptible to the most besotted lover but, as the company's next production is to be Anthony and Cleopatra, the company well know that these were not Shakespeare's last words on the matter.

In the middle sections of the play its comic elements were allowed to dominate but these were never made too broad and, especially in the latter scenes, poetry and more profound considerations were allowed their proper place. The rude mechanicals were very funny but never turned into callow clowns. They were simple men but with a proper personal dignity, in accord with their skills and civic sense of duty.

John Branwell was ideally cast as Bottom, very fully characterised in his high opinion of himself but never being so outrageous in his attempts to prescribe how things should be done that one doubted how his friends could tolerate him. Both in his persuasive speaking of the lines, his well judged decisions on when to say them and in his reactions, or lack of them, to what was going on around him it was a contant joy to see the full detail of his performance. One particular

triumph was, when made an ass, his handling of his dialogue with the fairies. Often in performance these lines seem well beyond their sell-by date but they cannot be cut as there would then be nothing left of a major feature of the play. Just by speaking them simply, and using them to convey that, in a rather indolent way, nothing now so much interested him as hay, honey and a good scratch, the lines became a constantly intelligible source of quiet humour.

Much of the effectiveness of these scenes was ensured by the skilful group playing of those who doubled as both fairies and mechanicals. Francis Lee as Snug particularly won the hearts of the covey of female students occupying the head of the horseshoe seating, who started to go "Aah" at his every appearance and continued into a reminiscient laugh when Puck began the conclusion of the proceedings by announcing "Now the hungry lion roars."

Lee made no exaggerated attempts to attract this sympathy, however. He just sat quietly bemused as more assertive members of his company dominated preparations for their play and reacted with comparatively mild horror when some duty was abruptly thrust upon. The whole style of humour was infinitely more subtle than in the same company's very broad, but very successful, Merry Wives last year. The knock-on Lion laugh obtained by Puck was probably one of the few which Andrew Cryer in that part did

174

not play for, but that was because his particular characterisation was for all out merriment and attention-seeking, whether from us, Oberon or whoever. "I go, I go?" he cried when despatched on his latest mission but, as Oberon was turning his attention to anointing Demetrius, remained like a greyhound in this slips until he obtained regard for his fleet departure by demanding "Look how I go."

Music and dance were used very effectively in contributing to the general atmosphere, often unaccompanied or with a percussion beat out with any objects to hand but with folk instuments, such as fiddle, concertina, reed, guitar, drum, used on more elaborate occasions. The fairies attendant on Titania, who were appropriately dressed in Morris costume, sang "You spotted snakes with double tongue" to "On Ilkley Moor" and in their final reconciliation Oberon and Titania, with their company performed, a clog dance. As other actors left to transform themselves into their other characters, TC Howard, responsible for the dancing, performed a solo, which with its airborne pirouettes, might have looked more balletic but which I have seen Mori Men do in Sierra Leone, the one in the loading shed at Freetown Airport being called The Human Helicopter. "Moorish" is one of etymologies some give for Morris.

All these elements were most skilfully integrated into a delightful production. There was nothing elaborate, just a

constantly effective flow of simple ways to bring out the spirit of a happy and poetic text, which creates its own world but which was shown still to be part of ours.

14 SEPTEMBER. GYPSY; Players' Theatre, Delph. (258).

Avowedly inept acts for crummy children and tacky teenagers would not seem promising material for a full evening's theatre. **John Osborne's The Entertainer** takes the decline of British Variety into strip shows as an image of the degeneration of British Society, so the Theatre scenes can appropriately be irksome. **Gypsy**, however, clearly has a much more positive perception of the American society reflected through the latter days of Vaudeville, even during the Depression. When Baby June lisps to her audience that "all of us in the Theatre have someone we need to thank, – a mother, an uncle –, but today I would especially like to thank the uncle who belongs to us all: – Uncle Sam", as an introduction to one of her mother's ghastly dance routines, in which her juveniles can wave the Stars and Stripes, it is hard to doubt that, in large measure, the show's authors fundamentally agree.

Just as Archie Rice has always required a top quality actor to turn material scarcely able to engender "a burst of heavy breathing" into a major theatrical experience, so **Saddleworth Players** succeed in turning the elements of **Gypsy** into a thoroughly entertaining and celebratory evening, by the excellence of their performance and staging, in every department. The basic framework of the set, apparent brickwork covered with swirling pastel patterns from the whole colour spectrum, was a splendid image of those who spend most of their time in backstreets but continue to believe that they can fight their way to the end of the rainbow. **Anne Wright** as Rose powers her way through, driving her children and driven by the belief that she can make her daughter a star.

The second half very much emphasises the dark side of this, her insistence over the years that her children are still child artists clearly being linked to her inability to conceive of a situation in which they are not permanently in need of her direction. Insufferable though this in many ways becomes, the play ends with affirmation of the value in her ceaseless efforts and the recognition of this by her daughter Louise, who did became a star: Gypsy Rose Lee.

This second half relies increasingly on dialogue, with less music and dance. Much of this is not of a particularly sparkling nature and probably requires a certain style of American actor, in the small rôles as well as the large, to make it effective, but this is not to deny that there was a significant amount of quality acting going on, most notably by **Jo Anne Weetman**, who as Louise was throughout effective in conveying the evolution from the always interested, sympathetic

figure in the background, apparently without the performance skills to make her initially the main target of her mother's endeavours, but developing more and more positive elements in her background rôle and finally making the abrupt transition into becoming Gypsy Rose Lee entirely convincingly.

The first half was not only levened with more sparkling dialogue, – "Why have we got three daddies?", "'Cos you're lucky!"–, but much more musical material. The staged routines, supposedly devised by Rose for her infant troupe, were never made so slick as to belie the infant characters' criticisms of their quality as they grew older but they were made good entertainment both by being very witty pastiches of their genre and also because the children who performed them, notably **Alison Evans** as Baby June and the **Muldoon** brothers as her fellow performers, do have genuine talent, both as dancers and in handling their lines. They both made the acts enjoyable in themselves and showed that Rose was not building her dreams on nothing at all. They enlivened the proceedings right from the beginning, abetted by the quietly humorous performances of the adult characters amongst them: **John Kenworthy** as Uncle Jocko, the dubious promoter of a child talent contest, quietly muttering, "You should see her big sister's balloons" as he manouvered a favoured contestant, whose costume was largely coloured inflations, into the limelight; **Roger Boardman** as his assistant imperiously ordering a stage–hand to pick up his discarded cigarette butts. Their status was completely overthrown as Rose stormed in, her vivid emerald vanity coat blazing through the audience, left them to attend to her most compliant lapdog, **Dillan** as Chowsie, and set about reorganising things to her daughters' advantage.

Costumes were notably apt throughout, their variety complementing the constant, smooth transformations of the set, with striking small flats painted by **John Kenworthy**, whether of the Union Pacific surging across the country, - that action was "throughout the USA" was a major element of the theme -, or of dingy theatre ginnels or backstage premises. Subtle lighting enhanced these varied locales and the offstage band achieved a variety of tones from four instuments.

Apparently **Gipsy** was originally conceived as a "lavish history of American Musical Theatre." In presenting a "chamber version" in their comparatively small auditorium, **Saddleworth Players** were able to realise the play's theme of a great country enhanced by the struggles of its ordinary, yet extraordinary, people, their domestic conflicts being none the smaller for being such as are known to numerous households. The quality of performance and production actualised the virtues which the piece is designed to celebrate.

16 SEPTEMBER. THREE MEN IN A BOAT; Bury Met. (189).

As **Peter Cook**'s Casting Director might have advised Spiggott: "For **Three Men in a Boat**, three actors would normally be considered the minimal requirement." **Ridiculusmus**, however, are no normal company. They can do the job perfectly well with two.

This is not the only way in which their approach is distinctive. It was not only quite clear from any prior knowledge one might of the novel that they had set themselves to create something very different than the dark Irish pub atmosphere of **Flann O'Brien**'s **Third Policeman**, which the company brought to Bury exactly a year ago. Then members of the audience who had come by bicycle were offered a free pint of beer. On this occasion the offer was of post-performance tea and cucumber sandwiches to those who came suitably dressed, sufficiently well responded to for the appearance in the foyer of persons clad in boaters, blazers and white open-neck shirts, attended by flappers, to give the initial impression that the size of the cast might have been considerably enlarged, rather than halved.

Angus Barr and **Jon Darke**, however, needed no such supernumeraries to succeed once more in drawing us fully into a different world. Instead of the unusual dimensions of de Selby's Physics, as conceived by **Flann**

O'Brien, we entered the green fields of mid-Victorian England, as perceived by two domestically-incompetent male townies, quietly bumbling their way through it by water.

Two main means were used to achieve this. The first was to eschew the attempt, successfully made by **Riding Lights**, for example, in their stage adaptation, to render full dramatisations of **Jerome**'s anecdotes. Instead, single lines were plucked from his elaborately constructed essays and used as elements of fragmentary conversation or asides to the audience, as the couple endeavoured to row or camp. Instead, for instance, of a full reconstruction of J's experience with a medical dictionary, a few comments derived from it were used as banter when J tried to explain his rubbing of his shoulder, after his initial attempts to row, by saying that he was having trouble with his liver and Harris commented that this seemed to be most oddly located.

Whereas more conventional stage adaptations, understandably, seem desperate to avoid leaving out anything from the hilarious original, **Ridiculus**' bolder approach gave them the space to introduce considerable other matter, in the shape of music hall comic songs, most ably, if informally, rendered. As we entered, we discovered that the cast were not the costumed characters in our midst but two characters in off-white flannels, one at the piano, the other slouched in a chair and aimiably warbling in accompaniment. This was J (**Jon**

Darke), in fact awaiting his opportunity to interpolate "Leave that piano, Harris, or we'll miss our train." Having used his suitcase to fight off a man-eating dog, supposedly on the other side of the door by which we had just entered, the pair rushed away behind the seating and we could hear them shouting out the full list of paraphernalia with which they proposed to encumber themselves on their voyage. Harris (**Angus Barr**) re-emerged hauling out a long strip of paper which helped to suggest the Thames shore-line during the first half of the performance. Disappearing in pursuit of his toothbrush, he re-emerged as a railway employee who demonstrated, in his conversation with J, that lack of clear information as to when and whence trains will depart is not a degeneration brought about by nationalised industry but a full part of Victorian Values in the heyday of private enterprise.

Although **Barr** and **Darke** mainly kept to their personae as J and Harris, their brief representations of other persons encountered on their voyage were most skilfully and enjoyably carried out, as persuasive a part of the illusion as the rest of the world they created with scarcely any properties. Apart from a hamper and two cases to sit on, and a gaudy blazer representing George, the third man, much like his first appearance in the book, anything else that was visible was clearly made out of corrugated cardboard, including Montmorency, who appearance was greeted by a rendition of "Monty, the dog."

Such songs, sometimes ably accompanied by **Barr** on a minature banjo, did not need to be so specifically cued. The two could just start singing informally, as a natural alternative to their chat whilst taking their turn at the rowlocks, or arguing about why they should not. There are plenty of indications in the book that this would have been natural for the characters. Whether any cue was taken from Jerome's theatrical essays, **On Stage and Off**, I would not know.

Although the essay-style of the original had been abandoned, **Ridiculusmus** had in a way created their own essay, entirely faithful to the spirit of the original, mainly portraying its humour but also effectively incorporating the odd poetic line as well. Though the culture was mainly of people who knew "a splendid little place round the corner", this could be for fine wine, with an excellent meal costing only three-and-six, as well as for beer.

17 SEPTEMBER. THE NIGHT LARRY KRAMER KISSED ME; Library. (261).

David Drake is certainly an outstanding actor. The first five minutes of his performance of his own play were electrifying. When the stage lights went up on his Adonis-like figure, sitting right up to the front of the stage, I heard a gasp, apparently from female lips, although I would have guessed the straight element of the audience to have

been comparatively small, for this **It's Queer Up North** presentation.

The initial wide-eyed, sideways look, which may have helped to make his first appearance particularly striking, was in fact part of his representation of himself as a six-year old, or at least of his recollections of how on this birthday, 27 June 1969, whilst the Stonewall riots, which were later to become so significant for him in his pursuit of Gay Rights, were, unbeknownst to him, raging in the streets of New York, the New York streets which were before his amazed eyes were those represented in the dancing, dancing, dancing of **West Side Story.**

On his sixteenth birthday, the musical which amazed him was **Chorus Line.** He had thought that he had known this backwards from his long-playing record but this had given him only the music and lyrics, not the book. Now conscious of his orientation, he was reduced to tears by the Philippino's open description of his gay relationship. Driven back to his Baltimore home by "the older man", - aged 17, from the class above him -, the latter not only lent him his handkerchief, to dry his tears before going into the the the house, but gave him a good-night kiss, seen by his father and leading to an all-night shouting match with his parents, ending with the exchange, "If you were gay, - which you're NOT -, you know there's a place for people like that;" to which he replied, "Yes; New York."

Most of the rest of the play was about his experiences there, the first being his next significant birthday visit to the theatre, Larry Kramer's The Normal Heart, to which he apparently went, aged 22, mainly because he had heard that it contained a significant all-male kiss by Brad Davies, but by which he was then smitten, with all the power of a passionate kiss, by its crusading cry of rage, demanding an adequate response to the AIDS epidemic. Sometime later, it seems that he was literally kissed by Larry Kramer, after striking up a sympathetic conversation with a man he did not recognise, selling tee-shirts at a stall during a Stonewall anniversary rally.

All this was vividly and distinctively told, in stylish language and skilful visual and vocal emphasis. Thereafter, although the performance remaining highly vigorous, varied and talented and the script in many ways well-phrased, these were not enough to make the more familiar material which followed anything like so distinctive. Instead of leading on from his experience of Larry Kramer, the action first of all reverted to the character's infancy, his sexual character innocently being revealed in his choice of Christmas presents for his parents: a glass paperweight containing a beautiful purple butterfly for his eternally desk-bound father, and eschewing the jewellery he would have liked to buy for his mother, out of deference to her belief that gifts should be practical, and unable to get her another Supremes record,

to which he knew she liked to listen whilst cleaning, getting her one by Village People, whose music he enjoyed hearing at his barber's and whose costumes on the record sleeve, as Cowboys, Motorcyclists and the like, he found very exciting.

This was followed by sequences tracing the history of his gay life in New York, cruising at gym and club and, later, keeping vigil for AIDS victims, asking what happened to the lovers who just disappeared, as well as to those whom he had nursed. The two earlier sequences were essentially in the form of poems, That's Why I Go to the Gym and Twelve-Inch Single, and there were some memorable phrases elsewhere, an experience of love at first sight being described as "My eyes still wired to my heart... ." Despite the vivid and varied acting, skilfully conveying the character's different ages and attitudes over time, this was not enough to make the material seem other than rather familiar, if one had already seen some previous representations of the New York Gay Scene, although it may well have carried a significant homoerotic charge for those attuned to receive it. There did not even seem to be anything strikingly novel, or plausible, in the final sequence, set on the eve of the new millenium, the midnight movie about to be an all-male remake of The Way We Were and looking back to The AIDS War of 1996, in which apparently ACT-UP, in association with NOW, WHAM, WAC, TAG, P-FLAG, NAACP, ACLU and a dozen other acronyms, succeeded in the violent overthrow of the American Government, forcing the release of the cure for AIDS, - allegedly known for a year but held back by drug companies in the belief that they could make more money out of supposed palliatives -, the imprisonment of once leading figures in the Republican Party, the acceptance of gay marriage and freedom for gays to walk hand in hand, without fear, thoughout every state of the union. Though narrated with some pleasant wit, it did not succeed, for me, in becoming the inspiring vision, as which it was doubtless intended, despite the continuing exceptional dramatic skill with which it was performed.

18 SEPTEMBER 1994. THE DARK PERVERSITY OF CHAMELEONS; Dancehouse. (262).

I am not quite sure how this piece came to be the product of "experimental research." **Artaud**-inspired, non-realistic, primitive and ritualistic performances, on basic sets dominated by television screens, have been a regular part of the Theatre on offer in Manchester for over a decade, often with **Fiona Watson**, here making a welcome re-appearance, in the cast. One of the most enjoyable elements was her opening speech, rattling off suitable manifesto items for her alternative metaphysics Party. The concluding "Stop Italians from shooting migratory birds" was a fair specimen of the items of genuine social concern which, each having only a minority

following, sounded bizarre in concatenation.

The situation was of five neighbours, each with well-known but atypical proclivities, who put out the milk bottles, greet each other and do each other good turns like any other good citizens. Veronica **(Sara Bailes)** and Derek **(Steve Dixon)** are lovers but she wont pose for one of his paintings because he always murders his subjects. He explains his reasons for this in some detail to Sophia **(Fiona Watson)**, who attends his studio as a model and simply responds by saying "Bye, Bye. See you same time tomorrow." Veronica shares Sophia's possession of stigmata, though hers is in her navel, and tries to recruit Sophia to murder her brother Mike **(Paul Murphy)**, whose body-building concentration on developing his pectoral muscles is related to his preference for wearing his sister's dresses. She being flat-chested, however, he turns for supply to Rachel **(Sara Bailes)**, whose obsessive washing barely gives her time to put on more than her shift.

Most of these characteristics were supplemented on the television screens devoted to each character, from which one assimilated data additional to the live action. More or less everybody was conscripted to kill somebody else but they managed to attend each other's birthday parties and other social gatherings without further loss of life.

19 SEPTEMBER. MOON CHANT; Chinese Arts

Centre. (263).

This was a most delightful programme. Performed on the eve of the Chinese Mid-Autumn New Moon Festival, it wound the most ancient Chinese traditions together with the contemporary experiences of the modern Chinese for whom Manchester is only one of a myriad homes. After the singing of **Seung Yuet (Appreciating the Moon)** in virtual darkness, a single lateral beam illuminating the mother-of-pearl disks hung over the centre of the stage, the cast introduced themselves and the number of countries, from all continents in which they had lived was impressive. Few had lived in less than three, six or more was quite normal. Some definitely felt at home in Manchester, some did not. Many felt at home anywhere, simply because they liked people. Some spoke Cantonese or Mandarin but felt British, others could only speak English but felt Chinese.

The first major action was the original legend of the Moon Goddess. Peasants about their village labours came to find it oppressively hot and realised that this was because ten suns had risen. Providentially the greatest archer in the land was amongst them and undertook to destroy the suns with his ten arrows, although his virtuous wife, Seung Ngor, was wise enough to remove one arrow from his quiver and break it, so that one sun survived. The grateful villagers plied the archer with all manner of gifts in reward, one of which was eternal life. This had the

unfortunate effect of making him proud and cruel, so Seung Ngor realised that to save the world from his oppression she would have to discover where he had hidden this gift when he went out hunting and destroy it. Just as she found it, her husband returned and the only way she could prevent him reclaiming it was to swallow it. The only way she could escape from his fury was to go and live on the moon, where she remains to this day.

This tradition was found a useful key to making the particular Chinese heritage universal, the moon being visible everywhere and even visitable in the modern era. **Neil Armstrong's** words on landing came to sound as if they had been translated back from pictograms: "For me: small step; for Mankind: giant leap."

The astronaut came to be the agent for resolving a further legend interwoven with the performance, **The Dreaming Child**, represented by rod puppets, operated with extraordinary expressiveness by **Pauline Kam.** Looking for his mother, when he approached a modern teenager about to fly to Britain from Hong Kong, she helped him find her but she appeared entirely lifeless. When the child approached the astronaut, however, she was able to gather all humanity, whose unity was manifest from the moon, and their invocations, brought Seung Ngor to revive the child's mother.

Whether the taste of the modern British Chinese was "listening to the rain dripping off autumn leaves, under a crescent moon" or for the Big Dipper at a fairground, for the Cantonese Opera or a modern disco, the cast were able to represent all these experiences vividly in their performance and to realise the depth of a culture both local and universal, ancient and modern, accessible both to those who work in take-aways and to those in computer research, made available, through them, to all.

26 SEPTEMBER. THE GLASS MENAGERIE; Octagon. (138).

There is an intriguing degree of overlap between programming at the **Playhouse 2** in **Shaw** and the **Bolton Octagon.** Both have recently presented **Time and the Conways (84,** 3 May) and earlier this year **Crompton** hosted a visiting production of **The Glass Menagerie** by **3D Theatre Company (39,** 15 January). It is intended as no belittlement of the **Octagon,** though it is certainly a credit to **3D,** to treat the amateur and professional productions as worthy of comparison. The quality was certainly in many ways comparable. What was fascinating was the highly different emphases and interpretations found in these two plausible performances of the same score.

The difference was apparent from the very first moments. At **Shaw, Ean Burgeon's** Tom was a quiet, moody poet, **Nicholas Murchie's** far more brash and distinctively American. As he

came down the darkened fire escape, the lighting being barely noticably raised as he struck the match for his cigarette, he made full use of the "El Greco" lighting recommended by **Williams** to strike dramatic poses, to emphasise his speech.

The full, wrought-iron fire-escape platform surrounding the action, as well as the high gauze backcloth, through which could be seen, at appropriate times, not only the lights of the Paradise club but packing cases suggestive of Tom's warehouse, and on which could be projected both the portrait of Tom's father and the moon, was, of course, a much more sophisticated set than **3D** could afford. At first it did not seem likely that this was a resource of which the **Octagon** was going to make much play: as prescribed by **Williams,** the first meal was entirely in mime on a bare table, although as the "reality" which **Williams** associates with the Gentleman Caller approached, so the number of table dressings increased.

Rather going to town on its provision of food and cutlery was one of the things which had slowed down the scene changing in the **3D** production and achieving effective continuity of action was one respect in which the **Octagon** undoubtedly showed its greater professionalism to good purpose. If a prompt change was wanted it was made but often there would be effective punctuation between scenes, often emphasising Laura, as **Williams'** script suggests, polishing her menagerie or standing centre stage in horror after learning the identity of the imminent caller.

The more elaborate resources
were not always an advantage,
however. Tom's line on dropping
his doorkey, "One crack – and it
falls through", sounded less
appropriate when he was standing
on a metalwork grill. The giant
moon was very appropriate for
reinforcing the many related
images in the script but it looked
a lot more plausible full than
when, supposedly new, it was
meant to attract the wishes of
Amanda and Laura.

Apart from Tom's greater
brashness in this production, and
the emphasis on his indulgence in
the Kentucky Straight Bourbon he
got from assisting the magician at
the cinema stage show, rather
than just appreciating the magic
of the movies, suggested by the
Octagon programme cover and
seemingly the main interest of
the Tom created for **3D** by **Ean
Burgeon**, the most fundamental
difference was in the orientation
of his affections. **Ean Burgeon**
had painted a very effective
portrait of a young man who,
despite the wild outbursts into
which she provoked him, did love
his mother and regretted
everything which made their
relationship so difficult. **Nicholas
Murchie**, following the many
indications in the script and the
material quoted in the programme
by **Vicky Featherstone**, the highly
effective director, relating to the
relationship between **Tennessee
Williams** and his sister **Rose**, turns
his attentions far more towards
Laura: exchanging understanding
glances with her from the very
first scene whilst he is being
berated by his mother, freezing

in horror at the end of his
furious outburst in response to his
mother's refusal to believe that
he spends so long in the cinema,
– because he fears that his
violence has endangered the
precious glass cabinet –, sprinting
out of the house to her aid
when the cry from Laura suggests
that she has had a serious fall
on the fire escape, and
apostrophising her in the play's
final words.

Catherine Cusack's Laura was
alert enough to be a full partner
in this relationship. Unlike
Joanne Devlin's pronounced and
contorted limp, hers, as
prescribed, was indeed only a
slight, and usually barely
noticable, "defect." More
importantly, however, though
cowed by her mother, away from
that influence she shows genuine
vigour in those moments of
independence, responding quite
firmly, "Yes. But let her tell it,"
– modifying Tom's behaviour from
half way across the room when
he complains "I know what's
coming," on detecting the signs
that his mother is once more to
recall the gentleman callers of
her youth. She is deeply
entranced by her menagerie and,
more distinctively, although
promptly removing the "gay
deceivers" which her mother has
thrust down the front of her
dress, as soon as she has an
opportunity, she does begin to
look at herself in the glass and
begin to anticipate the possibility
of a visitor with some pleasure
until completely shattered by
learning it is to be Jim
O'Connor.

Although, when they do meet,

she struggles for long enough to prevent him seeing her face, she seems to have used her time in collapse upon the couch, while the rest were at supper, to gather her forces in some measure. She asks "Mr O'Connor, have you kept up with your singing?" quite strongly, as if she had determined that this was the route by which she had decided that she would dare to make him aware of their previous acquaintance.

Raymond Coultham's Jim presented himself with such studied "social poise" from his very first entry that it was hard to predict his being drawn into any genuine emotional contact. Certainly, he not only made himself so stylish that Amanda was clearly struck from first sight with the belief that her prayers for her daughter's happiness had been answered but his artificial politeness ideally meshed with hers, he knowing the correct response to every phrase she gushed forth from her long unused arsenal of polite conversation. The artifice was so intense that it placed a very effective satiric interpretation upon the description of him in the prologue as "an emissary from the world of reality." His clean-cut good looks and sharp suit contrasted splendidly with the crumpled and surly Tom.

"Stumble John" did not come as such a natural piece of self-accusation to this supremely disciplined Jim as it does in a more gauche representation of this enthusiast for the new American age but certainly the emotion which led him to utter it

was telling: Laura's simple naturalness having moved him to abandon his clearly mapped out social intentions and kiss her, his recollection of Betty then abruptly hauling him back to his previously prescribed path.

"Plans and provisions – The future we've mapped out for ourselves" is the talisman of Amanda Wingfield's approach. Her resilience in ever seeking new ways to get her daughter back to the style of life she had envisaged for herself, from a base of dingy poverty that she could never have dreamed of in her youth, shows remarkable strength. **Mary Cunningham**, whilst making clear the awfulness of the experience that this often imposes on her children, nevertheless presents a woman, who is not just making another self-pitying and brow-beating complaint when she says "My devotion has made me a witch and so I make myself hateful to my children." She is not entirely purblind and does know that they need love as well the better economic niche that she fights to win for them, especially for Laura. She does manage to draw closer and to put her arm round each of them in the intervals between tirades.

3D somehow had use of a script which emphasised Amanda's lack of awareness: Tom having the line "It's already come, mother" when she praised Jim's choice of Night School classes, "Radio engineering! A thing for the future," and her discovering at the end of her second sales pitch for renewed subscriptions to The Home-Maker's Companion that it is early morning by the standards of the lady whom she is ringing and who is, therefore, still in bed.

These are not in the most generally available published text and they have no place in the **Octagon** production. Amanda has more awareness, both emotionally and practically, the most critical element on the borders her conscious and unconscious being the need for money. Among the variety of emotions which strike her, both when she learns that Laura has not been attending her typing classes and when she realises that Jim is not eligible, are the cost, the money that has gone for nothing: "Fifty dollars tuition, ... - just gone up the spout," "The expense! ... All for what?" Without over-emphasis, **Mary Cunningham**, made this wounding and increasing impoverishment stand out clearly. Although she says "I'm old and don't matter" when urging Tom to stay until Laura is provided for, the truer emphasis is "So what are we going to do for the rest of our lives," which she exclaims after learning the truth about Laura's abandoning the means to a "business career." That or marriage would not only rescue Laura from being eternally "stuck away in some little mousetrap of a room" but would enable Amanda to escape it too.

The Glass Menagie is gem of a play, brilliant in stucture, profound in its perceptions. This **Octagon** production was most impressive in revealing yet more patterns in which light can be refracted through its text.

Contributed by LYNDA BELSHAW

5 OCTOBER. JULIUS CAESAR, Royal Exchange, (287) & HENRY VI, Upper Campfield Market (286).

Two **Shakespeare** plays in one day: - would I be able to cope with this overdose of culture? I need not have worried. **Robert Delamere's** Julius Caesar proved to be as critically taxing as an episode of **Eastenders**, despite a brave effort by **Patrick O'Kane** as Brutus to lift the performance above the mundane. During its three-hour performance, **Shakespeare's** Roman tragedy failed to stir the senses. **Denys Hawthorne** was a puzzling choice for the key rôle of Caesar, who succeeded only in making the audience wonder just what took Brutus so long, - a view echoed by the lady who sighed with relief as Caesar uttered the immortal line "Et tu, Brutē," adding that she had been going to kill him herself if no-one else did. However, on the bright side, the burning tree in the second half of the performance brought a little light into the otherwise gloomy setting and ensured that at least some of the audience were awake when the play finished.

There was no danger of anyone falling asleep in **Katie Mitchell's** **Henry VI** at **Campfield Market**. The old building shook with vitality as a brilliant cast thundered its way through one of **Shakespeare's** less popular history plays. **Jonathan Firth** was superb as the sensitive head that wears the crown, albeit on a somewhat intermittent basis, and **Ruth Mitchell** as his queen was impeccable in her performance, as she slipped from the rôle of mother to Amazon with seeming ease. But for me, the one performance that made the play was **Tom Smith**'s Richard, even if his accent alternated somewhat between Essex-boy and Eddie Grundy. **Smith** made me keen to see the sequel, quite an achievement after such a long day, as he and the rest of the cast injected life and humour into a play that was in danger of needing it. The only bad performance came from the tree, which, unlike its cousin at the **Exchange**, failed to ignite, but then, again, no-one needed waking up at this performance.

LYNDA BELSHAW

Section 2

PRODUCTION
NUMBERS

2. PRODUCTION NUMBERS

195

197

213

217

Section 3

PROGRAMME DETAILS

ABBREVIATIONS

.

ACCESS

D: Regular Described Performances by Headphone, for Blind/ Partially Sighted.

G: Provision for Guide Dogs.

H: Hearing Loop Installed.

S: Regular Sign Language Interpreted Performances.

W: Wheelchair Access and Adapted Toilet.

MAP REFERENCES

AZ: AZ Manchester Street Atlas, published by Geographer's A–Z Map Co Ltd.

XAZ: Extended Edition of **AZ Manchester Street Atlas.**

16,C2: Page 16, Square C2 in these atlases.

PRESS

A: The Advertiser (Prestwich–Whitefield edition); Group Offices: 30 Church Street, ECCLES, M30 0DF; 061– 789 5015.

ANT: Area News Today, 232 Claremont Road, RUSHOLME, M14 4TS; 061–227 9377.

AR: Ashton Reporter, Park House, Acres Lane, STALEYBRIDGE, SK15 2JR; 061–303 1910/0005

AS: Amatuer Stage, 83 George Street, LONDON W1H 5PL; 071–486 1732

BEN: Bolton Evening News, 54 Bridge Sreeet, BOLTON BL1 2EG; 0204 26686

.

BI: The Big Issue, (Manchester Edition), 10 Swan Street, MANCHESTER, M4 5JN; 061–832 4846

BT: Bury Times, PO Box 1, Marklet Street, BURY,

BL9 0PF; 061-764 9421

CH: Cheshire Life,

CL: City Life, 164
Deansgate, MANCHESTER,
M60 2RD; 061-839 1310

DR: Droylesden Reporter,
Park House, Acres Lane,
STALYBRIDGE, SK15 2JR;
061-333 1910/0005

EMR: East Manchester
Reporter, Park House,
Acres Lane,
STALEYBRIDGE, SK15
2JR; 061-303 1910/0005

F: Flexi, Unit 6, Moss
Side Enterprise Estate,
Denhill Road, M15 5NR;
061-232 0876

G: The Guardian, 164
Deansgate, MANCHESTER
M60 2RD; 061-832 7200

MEN: Manchester Evening
News, 164 Deansgate,
MANCHESTER M60 2RD;
061-832 9191

MM: Manchester Metro
News, 2 Blantyre Street,
MANCHESTER M15 4LF;
061-834 9677

MME: Moston, Middleton,
Blackley and Crumpsall
Express, 061-205 8031

MNG: Middleton and North
Manchester Gaurdian, 24a
Fountain Street,
MIDDLETON, M24 1AH;
061-643 3615.

MR: Mossley Reporter,
Park House, Acres Lane,
STALEYBRIDGE, SK15
2JR; 061-303 1910/0005

NCH: North Cheshire
Herald, Park House, Acres
Lane, STALEYBRIDGE,
SK15 2JR; 061-303
1910/0005

OC: Oldham Evening
Chronicle, 172 Union
Steet, OLDHAM, OL1
1EQ; 061-633 2121

PP: Plays and Players, 18
Friern Park, LONDON,
NI2 9DA; 081-446 2282

RO: Rochdale Obsever,
82-86 Drake Street,
ROCHDALE OL16 1PH;
0706 354321/55333

S: The Stage: 47

Bermondsey Street, LONDON; SE1 3XT; 071-403 1818

SAM: Sale and Altrincham Messenger, 7 The Downs, ALTRINCHAM, WA14 2QD; 061-928 5759

SEA: Stockport Express and Advertiser, Wood Street, Holywood, STOCKPORT SK3 0AB; 061-448 4600/6601

SCR: Salford City Reporter, 496 Liverpool Street, SALFORD M6 5QZ; 061-736 7815

SDR: Stalybridge and Dukinfield Reporter, Park House, Acres Lane, STALEYBRIDGE, SK15 2JR; 061-303 1910/0005

SME: South Manchester Express and Advertiser, Wood Street, Hollywood, STOCKPORT, SK3 0AB; 061-480 4491

T: The Times, I Rennington Street, LONDON E1 9XW; 061-228 0210

TES: Times Educational Supplesment, Priory House,

St John's Lane, LONDON EC1M 4BX; 061-228 0210

THES, Times Higher Educational Supplement, Priory House, St John's Lane, LONDON EC1M 4BX; 061-228 0210

TLS: Times Literary Supplement, Priory House, LONDON EC1M 4BX; 061-228 0210

WO: Wigan Observer, PO Box 59, Woods Street, WIGAN WN 4ES; 0942 228000

YP: Yorkshire Post, Wellington Street, LEEDS, LS1 1RF; 0532 432701

BOLTON

NEITHER PENNINE NOR PYRENEES but drawing on the strengths of both: CLIVE MOOR as The Bridegroom and VALERIE LILLEY as his Mother set the tone at the opening of the BOLTON OCTAGON's impressive production of HENRY LIVINGS' new translation of LORCA's BLOOD WEDDING (71) (Photo: Previous Page)

THE ALBERT HALLS,
Victoria Square, BL1 1RU; 0204 364333; AZ: 16, C2; XAZ: 24, BG. G, H, W

579. SNOW WHITE AND THE SEVEN DWARFS; *1i* December 1993 - 8 January 1994. Wicked Queen: *Maxine Spencer.*
Press: BEN: 13&21/12/94

149. MR MEN IN NURSERYLAND, based on the books by Roger Hargreaves; PHIL DERRICK for CHILDREN'S SHOWTIME; *10 April 1994.*

130. KING'S RHAPSODY; Devised, written and composed by Ivor Novello; Lyrics by Christopher Hassall; FARNWORTH AMATEUR OPERATIC AND DRATIC SOCIETY; *18-23 April 1994.*

153. THANK YOU, MR GERSHWIN; *30 April 1994.* Elaine Delmar.

158. THAT'LL BE THE DAY; *20 May 1994.*

272. LIFE'S A PANTOMIME; original revue, devised and produced by Bernard Smith for

FARNWORTH AODS; *24-25 September 1994.*

601. CINDERELLA; FACTORY FAME PRODUCTIONS; *3 December 1994 - 7 January 1995.*

THE ARTS CENTRE;
Bolton School, Chorley New Road, BOLTON BLI 4PA; 0204 849474; AZ: 16, B1; XAZ: 23, F6. G, W

586. ROMEO AND JULIET by William Shakespeare; BOLTON SCHOOL; *15-19 March 1994.*

ARTS THEATRE;
Westshoughton High School, Bolton Road (A58), WESTHOUGHTON, BL5, 3B2; 0942 814122.

129. GROUNDED by Eileen Murphy; M6 THEATRE COMPANY; *2 & 3 March 1994.*

599. AN EVENING OF DRAMA; compilation by WESTHOUGHTON HIGH SCHOOL; *15 November 1994.*

BARLOW INSTITUTE,

Bolton Road,
EDGEWORTH; 0204
852583.

585. ALADDIN; ST ANNE'S
CHURCH, TURTON, YOUTH
THEATRE; *February 1994.*

**BOLTON LITTLE
THEATRE:** Hanover Street,
BOLTON BL1 4TG; **0204
24469; AZ:** 16, C2;
XAZ: 24, A6.
G, H

133. SHAKESPEARE
COUNTRY by Peter Whelan;
16-23 October 1993. W Billy
Shake: *Adam Berlyne;* Webbo:
Jenny Hancock. Director/Design:
Geoff Bennett; Music: *Peter
Lewis, Ian Smith.*
Press: AS: December 1993.

134. GREAT EXPECTATIONS
by Charles Dickens, adapted for
the stage; *20-27 November
1993.*

135. A CHILD'S CHRISTMAS
IN WALES by Dylan Thomas,
Jeremy Brooks and Adrian
Mitchell; *11-18 December 1993.*

137. SISTERLY FEELINGS by
Alan Ayckbourne; *5-12 February
1993.*

136. YOUR HOME IN THE
WEST by Rod Wooden; *12-19
March 1994*

132. PRIVATE LIVES by Noël

Coward; *23-30 April & 25-29
August 1994.*

276. LAST TANGO IN
WHITBY by Mike Harding; *24
September - 1 October 1994.*

271. EQUUS by Peter
Shaffer; *29 October - 5
November 1994.*

275. THE WIZ by William F
Brown and Charlie Smalls; *3-10
December 1994.*

BOLTON MOAT HOUSE,
1 Higher Bridge Street,
BOLTON, BL1 2HA; **0204
3833338; AZ:** 17, D1;
XAZ: 24, 5B.
G, W

152. PERKINS' PROMOTION
by Liz Lees; GREEN LIGHT
THEATRE COMPANY; *22 April
1994.* Cast: *Liz Lees, Janine
Bardsley, Martin Buchan, Richard
Howell-Jones, Angela Morrison.*
Director: *Stanley Sutton.*
Press: AR: 28/10/93

**CHORLEY OLD ROAD
METHODIST CHURCH;**
BL1 3AA; **0204
840824/491886; AZ:** 16,
C1; **XAZ:** 23, H5.
G, W

583. THE CAINE MUTINY
COURTMARTIAL; MARCO
PLAYERS; *23-26 February
1994.*

225

159. CHASE ME, COMRADE
by Ray Cooney; MARCO
PLAYERS; 8-11 June 1994.

591. WHEN WE ARE
MARRIED by J B Priestley;
MARCO PLAYERS; 5-8 October
1994.

THE DEANE SCHOOL,
New York, BL3 4NG;
0204 64521; XAZ: 37,
D3.

129. GROUNDED by Eileen
Murphy; M6 THEATRE
COMPANY; 4, 11 & 23 March
1994.

ESKRICK STREET, BL1
3BJ.

277. ON THE STREET;
BOLTON COMMUNITY DRAMA,
WELFARE STATE
INTERNATIONAL, BL1 ARTS
CO-OP; 28 August 1994.

FARNWORTH LITTLE
THEATRE, Cross Street,
BL4 7AG; 0204 74864;
AZ: 26,C1; XAZ: 39,F6.
G, W

144. THE STRANGE CASE
OF DR JEKYLL AND MR HYDE
by David Edgar, based on the
story by Robert Louis Stevenson;
13, 17-20 November 1993.
Gabriel John Utterson: Henry
Mason; Richard Enfield/A Parson:
Stephen Stubbs; Katherine
Urquart: Rene Barlow; Lucy:
Claire Whitehouse; Charles: Omar
Grundy; Annie Loder: Tracy
Oxtoby; Dr Henry Jekyll FRS:
Andrew Close; Poole: David
Stirzacker; Dr Hastie Lanyon/Sir
Danvers Carew MP: Eric Smith;
Mr Hyde: John Howarth; A
Matchgirl/A Maid: Danielle
Wooton. Director: Eric Bromby;
Stage Manager: Dave Eyre;
Stage Crew: Paul Wallwork,
Omar Grundy; Lighting: Phil
Brookes; Sound: Chris Norris;
Costumes: Val Armstrong, Elaine
Gawthorpe; Music: Shelley
Aldred; Props: Doreen Bromby,
Elaine Tyler; Prompt: Mona
Smioth; Portraits: Sarah Hassall;
Set Design: Eric Bromby; Set
Construction: Cyril Armsrong, Eric
Bromby, Norman Pickles.

145. QUEST FOR A
GOLDEN KEY by Geoffrey
Thornber; 15, 19-22 January
1994. Sybil, The Witch: Elaine
Taylor; Little Monster: Adam
Marsh; Blot: Terry Willis;
Sadsack: Siobhan Partington: Tea
Boy: Paul Wallwork; The
Professor: Clarke McWilliam;
Pippa: Pamela Higson; Tommy:
Matthew Littler; Precious
Twinkle/Marigold: Tracy Oxtoby;
Tatterwork: Stuart McKay;
Fibula: Danielle Wooton; Queen:
Annaliese Edwards; Peregrine:
Jonathan Bradley; A Visitor:
Omar Grundy. Producers and
Directors: Jason Tyler, Clarke
McWilliam; Stage Manager: Glen
Nixon; Assistant Stage Manager:
Omar Grundy; Lighting: Phil
Brookes; Lighting: Chris Norris;
Costumes: Val Armstrong, Cyril
Armstrong; Backcloth and Flats

Painting: *Sara Hassall;* Set Design and Construction: *Youth Theatre Workshop;* Prompt: *Pat Stirzaker;* Props: *Elaine Gawthorpe.*

146. RING AROUND THE MOON by Jean Anouilh; adapted and translated by Christopher Fry; *12, 16-19 March 1994.* Joshua: *Harold Smith;* Hugo/ Frederick: *Stephen Stubbs;* Diana Messerschmann: *Stephanie Bradley;* Lady India: *Heliene Gogging;* Patrice Bombelles: *Steve Benson*, Madame Desmortes: *Jean Smith;* Capulet: *Helen Hamilton;* Messerschmann: *Michael Hope;* Romaineville: *John Howarth;* Isabelle: *Sara Harrison;* Isabelle's Mother: *Rita Mayoh;* Footman: *Glenn Nixon.* Director: *Andrew Close;* Stage Manager: *Glenn Nixon;* Lighting: *Phil Brookes;* Sound: *Chris Norris;* Prompt: *Kate Partington;* Set Design: *Norman Pickles.*

147. SECOND FROM LAST IN THE SACK RACE, adapted by Michael Birch from David Nobbs' novel "The Life and Times of Henry Pratt"; *14, 18-22 May 1994.* Ezra/Billy/Mr Quell Geoffrey Porringer/A Club Compere/The Amazing Illingworth/ Mr Hargreaves/Tosser Pilkington-Brick/The Sergeant Major: *Michael Tonge;* A Parrot/Uncle Teddy/Eric Lugg/Mr Gibbons/ Liam O'Reilly/A Tram Conductor/ Paul Hargreaves/Lampo Davey: *Richard Hannant;* Cousin Hilda/ Ada Pratt/Miss Forest/Daphne Porringer/Mrs Hargreaves/The Tadcaster Thrush: *Elaine Tyler;* Norah/Aunty Doris/Lorna Arrow/Miss Candy/Mabel Billington/Diana Hargreaves: *Carol*

Butler; Henry Pratt: *Dave Eyre;* The Paradise Lane Gang: *Terry Willis, Jonathan Broadley, Stuart McKay;* Voice on Wireless: *Harry Mason.* Director: *Harry Smith;* Stage Manager: *Keith Wensley;* Sound: *Chris Norris;* Lighting: *Phil Brooks, Chris Norris;* Slide Operators: *Eric Smith, Dave Fowler;* Costume: *Val Armstrong and Cast;* Props: *Elaine Gawthorpe, Lesley Norris;* Set: *Norman Pickles, Cyril Armstrong;* Music Compilation: *Erioc Smith, Harold Smith;* Prompt: *Kate Partington;* Parrot Maker: *Karen Smith;* Stage Assistants: *Stuart McKay, Omar Grundy, Paul Wallwork.*

273. DANGEROUS OBSESSION by N J Crisp; *14-17 September 1994.* Sally Driscoll: *Rita Mayoh;* John Barrett: *Norman Pickles;* Mark Driscoll: *Keith Wensley;* Lady Visitor: *Hilda Pickles.* Director and Producer: *John Price.* Stage Manager: *Dave Eyre;* Sound: *Chris Norris;* Lighting: *Phil Brookes, Chris Norris;* Costume: *Val Armstrong;* Properties: *Mona Smith, Eric Smith;* Set Design and Construction: *Eric Bromby, Cyril Armstrong;* Prompt: *Hilda Plckles;* Set and Backcloth Artist: *Sara Hassall.*

274. SEASON'S GREETINGS by Alan Ayckbourn; *15-19 November 1994.*

EAGLE MALL: Bolton Institute, College Way, BOLTON, BL3 5AE; **0204 28851.**

GIRLS DRAMA THEATRE;
Bolton School, Chorley New Road, BOLTON BLI 4PA; 0204 849474; **AZ:** 16, B1; **XAZ:** 23, F6.

593. STAGES by irene Lizzie Jones; WILLPOWER THEATRE WORKSHOPS; *22 October 1994.*

HALLIWELL ROAD METHODIST CHURCH,
Harvey Street, HALLIWELL BL1 8BH; **AZ:** 6, B3; **XAZ:** 23, H2. **G, W**

590. CAT'S CRADLE by Leslie Sands; HALLIWELL ROAD METHODIST DRAMA GROUP; *17-19 March 1994.*

600. AN INSPECTOR CALLS by J B Priestley; HALLIWELL ROAD METHODIST DRAMA GROUP; *17-19 November 1994.*

HARPER GREEN SCHOOL; Harper Green Road, FARNWORTH BL4 0DH; 0204 77451; **AZ:** 26, B1; **XAZ:** 38, D6.

592. OKLAHOMA! by Richard Rodgers and Oscar Hammrstein II; ST CATHERINE'S AMATEUR MUSIC SOCIETY; *10-15 October 1994.*

HAYWARD SCHOOL;
Lever Edge Lane, Morris Green, BL3 3HH; 0204 62605; **XAZ:** 37, 5G.

129. GROUNDED by Eileen Murphy; M6 THEATRE COMPANY; *25 February 1994.*

HIGH STREET COMMUNITY CENTRE;
BL3 6TA; 0204 399315; **AZ:** 16, C3; **XAZ:** 38, A3.

154. KALA KAPRA (Black Cotton); BAHAR PRODUCTIONS; *May 1994.*

NEW BURY COMMUNITY CENTRE, Buckley Lane, FARNWORTH, BL4 9PQ; **AZ:** 26, 3B; **XAZ:** 55, E2.

148. Scenes from ROAD by Jim Cartright; PATHWAY THEATRE COMPANY; *18 February 1994.* Cast: *Lee Oldfield, Elaine Goodman, Stella Blackburn, Paul Murphy.* Director: *Kevin Bates.*

228

OCTAGON: Howell Croft
South, BOLTON BL1 1SB;
0204 20661. AZ: 16,
C2; XAZ: 24,B6.
D,G,H,S,W

125. POSSESSION by Paul
Abbott; *6-30 October 1993.*
Liz: *Mary Cunningham;* Lorraine:
Sharon Muircroft; John: *Tom
Higgins.* Director: *Lawrence Till;*
Design: *Craig Hewittt;* Music:
Mark Vibrans; Lighting: *Jeremy
Newman-Roberts;* Sound: *Fiona
Lewry;* Sigh Language
Performance Interpreter: *Byron
Campbell;* Assisstant Stage
Manager on the Book: *Juliet
Michaels;* Production Manager:
Jim Niblett; Scenic Artist/Props
Maker: *Graeme McHugh;* Stage
Manager: *Katie Vine;* Deputy
Stage Managers: *Sasha Savage,
Nick Chesterfield;* Assistant Stage
Manager: *Tara Beard;* Stage
Technician: *Sean Curran;* Theatre
Carpenter: *Lee Pearson;* Assistant
Carpenter: *John Winward;*
Wardrobe Supervisor: *Mary
Horan;* Assistant Wardrobe
Supervisors: *Andrea Smith,*

126. BILLY LIAR by Keith
Waterhouse and Willis Hall; *4-27
November 1993.* Florence
Boothroyd: *Veda Warwick;* Alice
Fisher: *Maureen Flynn;* Geoffrey
Fisher: *Robert Whelan;* Billy
Fisher: *Nick Conway;* Arthur
Crabtree: *Nick Cottle;* Barbara:
Victoria Finney; Rita: *Jane
Hazlegrove;* Liz: *Henrietta
Whitsun-Jones.* Director: *Peter
Rowe;* Design: *Richard Foxton;*
Lighting: *Fiona Lewry;* Sound:
Jeremy Newman-Roberts; Sign
Language Performance Interpreter:

Byron Campbell; Deputy Stage
Manager on the Book: *Glynis
Ainsworth;* Production Manager:
Jim Niblett; Scenic Artist/Props
Maker: *Graeme McHugh;* Stage
Manager: *Katie Vine;* Deputy
Stage Managers: *Sasha Savage,
Nick Chesterfield;* Assistant Stage
Manager: *Juliet Michaels;* Stage
Technician: *Sean Curran;* Theatre
Carpenter: *Lee Pearson;* Assistant
Carpenter: *John Winward;*
Wardrobe Supervisor: *Mary
Horan;* Assistant Wardrobe
Supervisors: *Andrea Smith,*
Press: MEN: 6/11/93

127. A CHRISTMAS CAROL
by Charles Dickens, adapted by
David Holman; *2 December
1993 - 8 January 1994.* Jacob
Marley/Mr Fezziwig/Stockboker:
Nicholas Blane; Bob Cratchit/
Dick Wilkins/Stockbroker: *Nick
Conway;* Fred Scrooge/Charlie/
Stockbroker: *Matthew Cottle;*
Mrs Fezziwig/Mrs Fred Scrooge/
Mrs Delaney: *Victoria Finney;*
Teenage Scrooge/Tupper/
Christmas Future: *Tony Forsyth;*
Belle/Florence/Mrs Cratchit/May:
Jane Hazlegrove; Scrooge: *Robert
Pickavance;* Christmas Past/
Martha Cratchit/Second
Philanthropist: *Greta Stoddart;*
First Philanthropist/Christmas
Present/Elsie/Mrs Maggs:
Henrietta Whitsun-Jones; Tiny
Tim/Little Charlie: *Jonathan
Barnes* or *Craig Mellet;* Young
Scrooge/Boy/Ignorance: *Martin
Dempsey* or *Adam Johnson;*
Belinda Cratchit/Need: *Jennie
Atkinson* or *Nicola Evans.*
Director: *Vicky Featherstone;*
Design: *Richard Foxton;* Lighting:
Jeremy Newman-Roberts; Sound:
Fiona Lewry; Musical Director:
Chris Monks; Musician: *Tony*

Trundle; Dance: *Lorelie Lynn;*
Sign Language Performance
Interpreter: *Byron Campbell;*
Deputy Stage Manager on the
Book: *Nick Chesterfield;*
Production Manager: *Jim Niblett;*
Scenic Artist/Props Maker:
Graeme McHugh; Stage Manager:
Katie Vine; Deputy Stage
Managers: *Sasha Savage,*
Assistant Stage Manager: *Juliet
Michaels;* Stage Technician: *Sean
Curran;* Theatre Carpenter: *Lee
Pearson;* Assistant Carpenter: *John
Winward;* Wardrobe Supervisor:
Mary Horan; Assistant Wardrobe
Supervisors: *Andrea Smith,*
Wardrobe Assistants: *Andrew
Culliver, Vanessa Pickford, Mary
Rudkin, Joanne Vickers.*

128. SLEUTH by Anthony
Shaffer; *13 January - 12
February 1994.* Andrew Wyke:
Jonathan Burn; Milo Tindle: *Julian
Protheroe.* Director: *Ian Forrest;*
Design: *Craig Hewitt;* Lighting:
Jeremy Newman–Roberts; Sound:
Fiona Lewry; Sign Language
Performance Interpreter: *Byron
Campbell;* Production Manager:
Jim Niblett; Scenic Artist/Props
Maker: *Graeme McHugh;* Stage
Manager: *Katie Vine;* Deputy
Stage Managers: *Nick
Chesterfield;* Assistant Stage
Managers: *Juliet Michaels, Glynis
Ainsworth;* Stage Technician:
Sean Curran; Theatre Carpenter:
Lee Pearson; Assistant Carpenter:
John Winward; Wardrobe
Supervisor: *Mary Horan;* Assistant
Wardrobe Supervisors: *Andrea
Smith,*
Press: G: 20/1/94; **MEN:**
15/1/94

**70. MY MOTHER SAID I
NEVER SHOULD** by Charlotte

Keatley; *17 February - 12
March 1994.* Rosie Metcalfe:
Rosie Cavaliero; Jackie Metcalfe:
Jane Hazlegrove; Margaret
Bradley: *Judy Holt;* Doris
Partington: *Valerie Lilley.*
Director: *Vicky Featherstone;*
Design: *Richard Foxton;* Lighting:
Jeremy Newman–Roberts; Sound:
Fiona Lewry; Sign Language
Performance Interpreter: *Byron
Campbell;* Assistant Stage
Manager on the book: *Juliet
Michaels;* Production Manager:
Jim Niblett; Scenic Artist/Props
Maker: *Graeme McHugh;* Design
Student on Placement: *Dinah
Wilson;* Stage Manager: *Katie
Vine;* Deputy Stage Managers:
Sasha Savage; Student Stage
Manager on Placement: *Clare
Lewis;* Stage Technician: *Sean
Curran;* Theatre Carpenter: *Lee
Pearson;* Assistant Carpenter: *John
Winward;* Wardrobe Supervisor:
Mary Horan.
Press: G: 8/2/94; **MEN:** 18 &
22/2/94

71. BLOOD WEDDING by
Federico Garcia Lorca, translated
by Henry Livings; *17 March–9
April 1994.* The Groom: *Clive
Moore;* The Mother: *Valerie
Lilley;* A Neighbour/Beggarwoman,
as Death: *Judy Holt;* Leonardo's
Mother in Law: *Rita May;*
Leonardo's Wife: *Jane Hazlegrove;*
Leonardo: *Antony Byrne;* The
Maid/A Neighbour: *Pauline
Jefferson;* The Bride: *Angela
Clarke;* A Girl: *Rosie Cavaliero;*
The Father: *Richard Mayes;* The
Foresters: *Tom Higgins, Tony
Forsyth* (as the Moon), *Gregory
Campbell;* Villagers: *Karen
Bowden, Steve Durbin, Carole
Edwards, Margaret Mather,
George Penny, Juliet Ranger;*

Children: *Jordan Barry/Stephen McCutcheon, Charlotte Mallion/ Donna Morrison, Sally O'Donnell/ Miriam Willan;* Musicians: *Tim Laycock, Tony Trundell, Robert A White.* Director: *Lawrence Till;* Assistant Director: *Jake Lushington;* Design: *Richard Foxton;* Music: *Terry Davies;* Movement: *Lorelei Lynn;* Dialect Coach: *Penny Dyer;* Lighting: *Fiona Lewry;* Sound: *Jeremy Newman-Roberts;* Deputy Stage Manager on Book: *Sasha Savage;* Sign Language Performance Interpreter: *Byron Campbell;* Production Manager: *Jim Niblett;* Scenic Artist/Props Maker: *Graeme McHugh;* Design, Student Placements: *Lisa Lillywhite, Robina Wilkinson;* Stage Manager: *Katie Vine;* Deputy Stage Managers: *Juliet Michaels, Glynis Ainsworth;* Stage Management, Student Placements: *Matt Dixon, Andrew Keir;* Stage Technician: *Sean Curran;* Theatre Carpenter: *Lee Pearson;* Assistant Carpenter: *John Winward;* Wardrobe Supervisor: *Mary Horan;* Deputy Wardrobe Supervisors: *Andrea Smith, Anita Bateson;* Tailoring/ Costume Maker: *Phil Smith;* Wardrobe Maintenance/ Dresser: *Joanne Vickers;* Wardrobe Assistant: *Mary Rudkin.*
Journal: 5/4/94
Press: CL: 23/3/94; **G:** 21/3/94; **MEN:** 3, 17 & 19/3/94

84. TIME AND THE CONWAYS by J B Priestley; *14 April – 14 May 1994.* Mrs Conway: *Christine Cox;* Alan: *Clive Moore;* Madge: *Judy Holt;* Robin: *Christopher Penney;* Hazel: *Kathryn Hunt;* Kay: *Janet Hazlegrove;* Carol: *Rosie*

Caveliero; Joan Helford: *Angela Clarke;* Ernest Beevers: *Tom Higgins;* Gerald Thornton: *Antony Byrne.* Director: *Lawrence Till;* Design: *Patrick Connellan;* Music: *Terry Davis;* Lighting: *Jeremy Newman-Roberts;* Sound: *Fiona Lewry;* Deputy Stage Manager on the Book: *Juliet Michaels;* Sign Language Performance Interpreter: *Byron Campbell;* Production Manager: *Jim Niblett;* Scenic Artist/Props Maker: *Graeme McHugh;* Stage Manager: *Katie Vine;* Deputy Stage Managers: *Sasha Savage, Glynis Ainsworth;* Stage Management, Student Placements: *Matt Dixon, Andrew Keir;* Stage Technician: *Sean Curran;* Theatre Carpenter: *Lee Pearson;* Assistant Carpenter: *John Winward;* Wardrobe Supervisor: *Mary Horan;* Deputy Wardrobe Supervisor: *Anita Bateson;* Tailoring/Costume Maker: *Phil Smith;* Wardrobe Maintenance/ Dresser: *Joanne Vickers;* Wardrobe Assistant: *Mary Rudkin.*
Journal: 3/5/94
Press: CL: 20/4/94; **MEN:** 7,15/4/94

98. DERBY DAY by Bill Naughton, adapted for the stage by Lawrence Till; *19 May – 18 June 1994.* Sidney: *Fine Time Fontayne;* Ned: *Jack Smethurst;* Maggie: *Eileen O'Brien;* Beatty: *Rosie Cavaliero;* Albert: *Clive Moore;* Sarah: *Ann Rye;* Fanny: *Christine Cox;* Benny: *Ken Bradshaw;* Jack: *Christopher Penney;* Polly: *Deborah McAndrew;* Amy: *Kathryn Hunt;* Lizzie: *Vanessa Rosenthal;* Boys: *Simon Lee Fielding, Oliver Lancaster, James Pope, Daniel Russell;* Musicians (both Clarinet and Saxophone): *John Rebbeck,*

Catherine Shrubshall. Director: *Lawrence Till;* Assistant Director: *Tom Higgins;* Design: *Richard Foxton:* Music: *Terry Davies;* Movement: *Lorelei Lynn;* Lighting: *Jeremy Newman-Roberts;* Sound: *Fiona Lewry;* Deputy Stage Manager on the Book: *Sasha Savage;* Sign Language Performance Interpreter: *Wendy Ebsworth;* Audio Describer: *Anne Hornsby;* Production Manager: *Jim Niblett;* Scenic Artist/Props Maker: *Graeme McHugh;* Stage Manager: *Katie Vine;* Deputy Stage Managers: *Juliet Michaels, Glynis Ainsworth;* Stage Management, Student Placements: *Michelle Derby, Alan Shaw;* Stage Technician: *Sean Curran;* Theatre Carpenter: *Lee Pearson;* Assistant Carpenter: *John Winward;* Wardrobe Supervisor: *Mary Horan;* Deputy Wardrobe Supervisor: *Anita Bateson;* Tailoring/Costume Maker: *Phil Smith;* Costume Maker: *Mary Rudkin.*
Journal: 6/6/94
Press: CL: 1/6/94; **G:** 28/5/94; **MEN:** 26 & 28/5/94

138. THE GLASS MENAGERIE by Tennessee Williams; *8 September - 1 October 1994.* Amanda: *Mary Cunningham;* Tom: *Nicholas Murchie;* Laura: *Catherine Cusack;* Jim: *Raymond Coulthard.* Director: *Vicky Featherstone;* Design: *Richard Foxton;* Costumes: *Mary Horan;* Lighting: *Jeremy Newman-Roberts;* Sound: *Fiona Lewry;* Deputy Stage Manager on the Book: *Juliet Michaels;* Sign Language Performance Interpreter: *Byron Campbell;* Audio Describer: *Anne Hornsby;* Dialest Coach: *Catherine Charlton;* Production

Manager: *Jim Niblett;* Scenic Artist/Props Maker: *Graeme McHugh;* Stage Manager: *Katie Vine;* Deputy Stage Manager: *Sasha Savage;* Assistant Stage Manager: *Clare Lewis;* Stage Technician: *Sean Curran;* Theatre Carpenter: *Lee Pearson;* Assistant Carpenter: *John Winward;* Deputy Wardrobe Supervisor: *Anita Bateson;* Dresser and Wardrobe Maintenance: *Joanne Vickers.*
Journal: 26/9/94
Press: CL: 21/9/94; **G:** 12/9/96; **MEN:** 1 & 10/9/94; **RO:** 20/8/94, 17/9/94

267. DISHONOURABLE LADIES; anthology compiled and performed by Honor Blackman; *23 October 1994.* Musical Director and accompanist: *William Blezzard.*

139. THE SUICIDE by Nikolai Erdman, translated by Peter Tegel; *6-29 October 1994.* Semyon Semyonovich Podssekalnikov: *Bob Mason;* Maria Lukianovna: *Sharoan Muircroft;* Serafima Ilinchna: *Mary Cunningham;* Alexander Petrovich Kalabushkin: *James Quinn;* Margarita Ivanovna Peryesvetova: *Fenella Norman;* Aristarch Dominikovich Golashchapov: *Billy Clarke;* Cleopatra Maximovna: *Rosie Cavaliero;* Egor Timovyevich: *Matthew Vaughan;* Nikifor Arsenyevich Pugachov: *Phillip King;* Viktor Viktorovich: *Raymond Coulthard;* Father Elpidi: *James Tomlinson;* Raissa Filipovna: *sally Ann Matthews;* Waiter/Suspicious Looking Characters/Boys/Undertakers/Old Ladies: *Gregory Campbell, James Nickerson;* Boys: *Alistair Laverty,*

Robert Thoday. Director: *Lawrence Till;* Design: *Penny Titt;* Movement: *Lorelei Lynn;* Lighting: *Jeremy Newman-Roberts;* Deputy Stage Manager on the Book: *Sasha Savage;* British Sign Language Performance Interpreter: *Byron Campbell;* Audio Describer: *Anne Hornsby;* Production Manager: *Jim Niblett;* Scenic Artist/Props Maker: *Graeme McHugh;* Stage Manager: *Katie Vine;* Deputy Stage Manager: *Juliet Michaels;* Assistant Stage Manager: *Clare Lewis;* Stage Technician: *Sean Curran;* Theatre Carpenter: *Lee Pearson;* Assistant Carpenter: *John Winward;* Deputy Chief Electrician: *Fiona Lewry;* Deputy Wardrobe Supervisor: *Anita Bateson;* Dresser and Wardrobe Maintenance: *Joanne Vickers.* **Press: MEN:** 8/10/94

140. THE ACCRINGTON PALS by Peter Whelan; *3-26 November.* Director: *Sue Sutton Mayo;* Design: *Chris Kinman.*

141. MOWGLI'S JUNGLE; adapted from Rudyard Kipling by Adrian Mitchell; *1 December 1994 - 14 January 1995.* Mowgli: *Callum Dixon;* Baloo: *Peter Rylands;* Bagheera: *Sharon Muircroft;* Sheer Khan: *James Quinn;* Also: *Rachel Gleaves, Matthew Vaughan, Rosie Cavaliero.* Director: *Ian Forrest;* Design: *Richard Foxton;* Choreographer: *Lorelei Lynn.*

Octagon Studio

24. PLAYHOUSE CREATURES by April de Angelis;

THE SPHINX; *26 October 1993.*

131. WILD THINGS by Anna Reynolds; PAINES PLOUGH in association with SALISBURY PLAYHOUSE; *3 February 1994.* Director: *Deborah Paige;* Design: *Geraldine Pilgrim.* **Press: MEN:** 27/1/94.

BILL NAUGHTON THEATRE, at the Octagon.

142. BRIMSTONE AND TREACLE by Dennis Potter; *7-29 October 1994.* Mr Bates: *John Joyce;* Mrs Bates: *Di Langford;* Martin Taylor: *Nicholas Murchie;* Pattie: *Rachel Gleaves;* Director: *Jake Lushington;* Design: *Richard Foxton;* Lighting: *Kevin Fitz-Simons;* Sound: *Fiona Lewry;* Deputy Stage Manager on Book: *Mike Shinks;* British Sign Language Performance Interpreter: *Byron Campbell;* Audio Describer: *Anne Hornsby;* Production Manager: *Jim Niblett;* Scenic Artist/Props Maker: *Graeme McHugh;* Stage Manager: *Katie Vine;* Deputy Stage Manager: *Juliet Michaels;* Assistant Stage Manager: *Clare Lewis;* Stage Technician: *Sean Curran;* Theatre Carpenter: *Lee Pearson;* Assistant Carpenter: *John Winward;* Deputy Chief Electrician: *Fiona Lewry;* Deputy Wardrobe Supervisor: *Anita Bateson;* Dresser and Wardrobe Maintenance: *Joanne Vickers.* **Press: MEN:** 30/9/94; 7/10/94

233

143. THE FASTEST CLOCK IN THE UNIVERSE by Philip Ridley; *2-26 November 1994.* Sherbet Gravel: *Rosie Cavaliero;* Captain Tock: *James Quinn.* Cougar Glass: *Matthew Vaughan.* Director: *Lawrence Till;* Design: *Richard Roxton;* Costumes: *Mary Horan.*

OUR LADY OF LOURDES SOCIAL CENTRE, Plodder Lane, FARNWORTH, BL4 0BR; 0204 73728; AZ: 26, A2; XAZ: 54, B1. W

155. THE BOYFRIEND by Sandy Wilson; OUR LADY OF LOURDES AMATEUR OPERATIC AND DRAMA SOCIETY; *3-7 May 1994.*

ST JOSEPH'S SCHOOL, Chorley New Road, HORWICH BL6 7QB; 0204 697456.

581. BILLY LIAR by Willis Hall and Keith Waterhouse; SJ JOSEPH'S SCHOOL; *3-5 February 1994.*

ST OSMUND'S SCHOOL, Blenheim Road, BOLTON, BL2 6EL; 0204 32866; AZ: 18, A1; XAZ: 25, G6. G

157. INTIMATE EXCHANGES - AFFAIRS IN A TENT by Alan Ayckbourn; ST OSMUND'S

AMATEUR PRODUCTIONS; *17-19 May 1994.*

595. VERONICA'S ROOM by Ira Levin; ST OSMUND'S AMATEUR PRODUCTIONS; *27-29 October 1994.*

ST PETER'S METHODIST CHURCH HALL, St Helens Road, BOLTON, BL3 3SE; 0204 302560; AZ: 16, A4; XAZ: 37, 5E.

580. QUEEN OF HEARTS by Wilfred Miller; ST PETER'S METHODIST CHURCH AMATEUR DRAMATIC SOCIETY; *2-5vFebruary 1994.* Knave of Hearts: *Paul Cohen;* Queen of Hearts: *Stan Porter;* Tilly Flop: *Louise Hatton;* Alice: *Joanne Eccleshare;* White Rabbit: *Nicola Jones.* Producer: *Tony Bowden.* **Press: BEN:** 2/11/93.

150. SPIDER'S WEB by Agatha Christie; ST PETER'S METHODIST CHURCH AMATEUR DRAMATIC SOCIETY; *14-16 April 1994.*

ST PHILIP'S PAROCHIAL HALL, Bridgeman Street, BOLTON BL3 6TH; 0204 59586; AZ: 16, C3; XAZ: 38, A3. G

584. HELLO DOLLY by Michael Stenart, based on *The Matchmaker* by Thornton Wilder; ST PHILIP'S AODS; *28 February - 5 March 1994.* Dolly: *Eileen Powell;* Horace Vandergeldar: *Don Howcroft;* Others: *Graham*

234

Cohen, Kristian Worsley, Julioe Holmes, Susie Riley, Robin Thompson, Jan Ashton, Marion Henrys, Kevin Worseley. Direction and Design: Nora Howcroft; Set Construction: Andrew Henrys and team; Set Painter: Sylvia Woods; Lighting: Michael Rogers; Props: Connie Rorrison and team; Costumes: Jean Foley; Musical Director: David Wilson; Choreographer: Barbara Grant.
Press: BEN: 1/3/94

ST SIMON & ST JUDE'S PRIMARY SCHOOL;
Newport Road, GREAT LEVER BL3 2DT; 0204 26165; AZ: 17, 4D; XAZ: 38, 4C. G

602. DICK WHITTINGTON;
ST SIMON & ST JUDE'S ADS; 27-30 December 1994.

SHARPLES SCHOOL THEATRE, Hill Cot Road BL1 8SN; 0204 308421; AZ: 7, D2; XAZ: 11, E6. G, H, W.

589. LITTLE SHOP OF HORRORS; Music by Alan Menken, Book and Lyrics by Howard Ashman; SHARPLES SCHOOL; 16-19 March 1994.
Press: BEN: 7/3/94

SMITHILLS SCHOOL,
Smithills Dean Road, BL1 6JS; 0204 842382; XAZ: 6, B3; XAZ: 23, 1G,

129. GROUNDED by Eileen Murphy; M6 THEATRE COMPANY; 28 February, 11 & 21 March 1994.

THEATRE CHURCH,
Seymour Road, Astley Bridge, BOLTON, BLI 8PU; 0204 304332. G, W

582. OLIVER by Lionel Bart; ST PAUL'S (ASTLEY BRIDGE) AOS; 14-19 February 1994.
Oliver: Edward Millington alternating with Kathy Langham; Fagin: Graham Yardley; Nancy: Julie Johnson; The Artful Dodger: Hilary Brownson.
Press: BEN: 8 & 15/2/94

61. TEMPTATIONS – THE DRAMA by Michael J Austin; PALAVER PRODUCTIONS; 29-30 March, 15 July 1994.
Jesus: Peter Moreton. Director: Colin Bean; Lighting Adviser: Roni Wood; Set: David Aspinall, Roy Parkinson; Costume: Olwyn Ranoe.
Journal: 30/3/94
Press: BEN: 30/3/94

151. OKLAHOMA!; Music by Richard Rogers, Book and Lyrics by Oscar Hammerstein II, based on Green Grow the Lilacs by Lynn Rigg; BOLTON CATHOLIC MUSICAL AND CHORAL SOCIETY JUNIOR WORKSHOP; 21-23 April 1994.

160. OUR DAY OUT by Willie Russell; Songs and Music by Bob Eaton, Chris Mellor, Willie Russell; YOUNG THEATRE CHURCH WORKSHOP; 9-11

June 1994.

THORNLEIGH SALESIAN COLLEGE, Sharples Park, BL1 6PQ; 0204 301351; AZ: 6, C2; XAZ: 23, H1. G

740. GUYS AND DOLLS; Music and Lyrics by Frank Loesser; Book by Joe Swerling and Abe Burrows, from the stories of Damon Runyon; BOLTON CATHOLIC MUSICAL & CHORAL SOCIETY; *25-30 October 1993.* Nathan Detroit: *Neville Moss;* Miss Adelaide: *Judith Stanford;* Sarah Brown: *Susie Riley;* Sky Masterson: *Chris Oldham;* Nicely-Nicely Johnson: *Adrian Pollitt;* Producer: *Judith Stanford;* Choreographer: *Barbara Grant.*
Press: BEN: *26/10/93, 25/10/94.*

587. THE KING AND I; Music by Richard Rodgers; Lyrics by Oscar Hammerstein II; THORNLEIGH SALESIAN COLLEGE; *16-19 March 1994.*

594. WEST SIDE STORY; Book by Arthur Laurents, Music by Leonard Bernstein, Lyrics by Stephen Sondheim; BOLTON CATHOLIC MUSICAL AND CHORAL SOCIETY; *24-29 October 1994.*

TRINITY CHURCH HALL, Market Street, FARNWORTH BL4 8EZ; 0204 73594/793172; AZ:

26, C1; **XAZ:** 39, 6F. G

596. MIST OVER THE MISTLETOE by Dan Sutherland; *2-5 November 1994.*

UNITED REFORMED CHURCH HALL, Chorley Old Road, BOLTON BLI 3BE; 0204 27692; AZ: 6, B2; XAZ: 23, G4; G

588. SEE HOW THEY RUN by Philip King; PHOENIX THEATRE COMPANY; *16-19 March 1994.* Cast included: *Rick Sykes, Jacky Gill.*
Press: BEN: *22/2/94*

598. WUTHERING HEIGHTS, from Emily Bronte; PHOENIX THEATRE COMPANY; *8-12 November 1994.*

UNITED REFORMED CHURCH, Park Road, WESTHOUGHTON, BL5 3H; XAZ: 36, A6

270. A FUNNY THING HAPPENED ON THE WAY TO THE FORUM, by Stephen Sondheim, out of Plautus; BETHEL CROWD AMATEUR DRAMATIC SOCIETY; *19-24 September 1994.*

WALMESLEY PARISH HALL, Blackburn Road, EGERTON, BL7 9RZ; 0204 20334; XAZ: 10, B1. G, W

831. **ROBERT AND ELIZABETH;** Book and Lyrics by Ronald Millar, Music by Ron Grainer, from an original idea by Fred G Morrit, based on *The Barretts of Wimpole Street* by Rudolph Besier; WALMSLEY CHURCH AODS; *8-13 November 1993.* Robert Browning: *Graham Edgington;* Elizabeth Barrett: *Irene Bowers.* **Press: BEN:** 26/10/93

156. **HOW TO SUCCEED IN BUSINESS WITHOUT REALLY TRYING** by Abe Burrows, Jack Weinstock and Willie Gilbert; Music and Lyrics by Frank Loesser; based on the book by Shepherd Mead; WALMSLEY CHURCH AMATEUR OPERATIC AND DRAMA SOCIETY; *9-14 May 1994.*

161. **WEDDING OF THE YEAR** by Norman Robbins; WALMSLEY CHURCH AMATEUR OPERATIC AND DRAMA SOCIETY; *9-11 June 1994.*

597. **SHOWBOAT** by Jerome Kern and Oscar Hammerstein II; WALMSLEY CHURCH AMATEUR OPERATIC AND DRAMA SOCIETY; *7-12 November 1994.*

WESTHOUGHTON HIGH SCHOOL, - see **ARTS THEATRE.**

WITHINS SCHOOL, Newby Road, BL2 5JB; 0204 26519; **AZ:** 8, A4; **XAZ:** 25, H3.

129. **GROUNDED** by Eileen Murphy; M6 THEATRE COMPANY; *16 & 17March 1994.*

WOODSIDE SENIOR SCHOOL; 425 Chorley New Road, BL1 5DH; 0204 843637; **XAZ:** 22, C6.

129. **GROUNDED** by Eileen Murphy; M6 THEATRE COMPANY; *23 March 1994.*

237

B U R Y

TREVOR GARE, in THE KING'S PLAYER (91), faces up to the problems of a vagabond minstrel who arrives in Elsinore just after an abrupt and suspect change of government and finds himself conscripted for a Royal Command performance. His hilarious experiences can be seen again at the BURY MET on 27 January 1995

BROAD OAK HIGH SCHOOL, Hazel Avenue, BL9 7QT; **061-797 6543. AZ:** 11, 3D; **XAZ:** 29, 3F.

129. GROUNDED by Eileen Murphy; M6 THEATRE COMPANY; *25 March 1994.*

205. ARTFUL DODGER.

CASTLEBROOK HIGH

SCHOOL, Parr Lane, BL9 8EL; 061-796 9820; **AZ:** 21, E4; **XAZ:** 43, G4.

CLOSE PARK, Dumers Lane; RADCLIFFE, BL9 9PQ.

ELM BANK SCHOOL, Ripon Avenue, Whitefield, M45 8PJ; 061-766 1597; **AZ:** 20, 4C; **XAZ:** 43, 5E.

129. GROUNDED by Eileen Murphy; M6 THEATRE COMPANY; *8 March 1994.*

ELTON HIGH SCHOOL, Walshaw Road, BURY, BL8 1RN; 061-763 1434; **AZ:** 9, F3; **XAZ:** 27, G1.

201. THE WIZARD OF OZ; adapted from the book by L Frank Baum; *Spring 1994.*

EMMANUEL HOLCOLME CE PRIMARY SCHOOL, Helmshore Road, Holcolme, RAMSBOTTOM, BL8 4PA; 0706 823498; **XAZ:** 4, C3.

199. MEREDITH THE CAMEL; *December 1993.*

HOLY CROSS COLLEGE,

Manchester Road, BURY BL9 9BB; 061-763 1290; **AZ:** 20, B1; **XAZ:** 28, C5.

198. METAMORPHOSIS by Franz Kafka, dramatised by Stephen Berkoff; HOLY CROSS COLLEGE; *December 1993.*

203. FIDDLER ON THE ROOF; Book by Joseph Stein; Music by Jerry Bock; Lyrics by Sheldon Harnick; HOLY CROSS COLLEGE; *Spring 1994.*

THE MET ARTS CENTRE, Market Street, FREEPOST BL 5162F, BURY, BL9 0YZ; 061-761 2216. **AZ:** 10,3; **XAZ:** 28: C3. **W**

180. HEAD OF STEEL; QUONDAM; *10 November 1993.*

176. HABEUS CORPUS by Alan Bennett; GLORYBUTTS THEATRE GROUP; *18-20 November 1993.*

177. LIFE AND JEFF: A MATTER OF ... by Barry Shannon; POP-UP THEATRE COMPANY; *19 November 1993*

178. DERBY DAY; YORKSHIRE THEATRE COMPANY; *24 November 1994.*

163. THE PITY OF WAR;
devised and performed from the
poetry and letters of Wilfred
Owen by Peter Florence; PETER
FLORENCE PROJECTS; *1
December 1993.*

**165. IN THE BLEAK
MIDWINTER** by Charles Way;
HIJINX THEATRE CO-
OPERATIVE; *3-4 December
1993.* Zac: *Richard Berry;*
Miriam: *Fuirenza Guidi;* Gill:
Helen Gwyn; Mak: *David
Murray.* Director: *Rosamunde
Hutt;* Stage Manager/Lighting
Designer/Set Construcion: *Ian
Buchanan;* Designer: *Richard
Aylwin;* Musical Director/
Composer: *Paula Gardiner;*
Costume Supervisor: *Claire-Louise
Hardie;* Technical Consultant: *Ian
Hill;* Set Construction: *Chris
Kelly;* Director's Assistant: *Robert
Lane.*

179. BONAVENTURE by
Charlotte Hastings; DERBY
PLAYERS; *9-11 December
1993.*

164. FLICKERING LOVES;
devised by BURY ACTORS
COMPANY; *4 February 1994.*
Michelle: *Gwen Bishop;* Joe:
Martin Badham; Steve: *Irshad
Ashraf;* Terri: *Danielle Kay;*
Lecturer: *Leanne McGonagle;*
Hannah: *Helen Hill;* Gran: *Sara
Catherine Lang;* Billy: *Zena
Barrie;* Michelle's Dad: *Chris
McMullen;* Michelle's Mum:
Samantha Reid; Steve's Dad:
James Delargy; Vinnie: *Neil C
Blackshaw;* Dylan: *Chris J Lord;*
Karen: *Claire Quick;* Yvonne/
Waiter: *Emm Airey;* Chorus:

*James Delargy, Leanne
McGonagle, Zena Barrie, Claire
Quick, Emm Airey.* Director:
Sue Reddish; Technical Support:
Simon Baxter, Lee Burgoyne;
Film: *James Delargy, Philip
Jackson.*

129. GROUNDED by Eileen
Murphy; M6 THEATRE
COMPANY; *8 February 1994.*
Barry: *Michael Atkinson;* Adam:
Chris Cooke; Joanne: *Alison
Darling;* Lisa/Karen/Doctor:
Katherine Hart; Mary: *Maggie
Tagney.* Director: *Joe Sumsion;*
Design: *Caroline Wilson;* Stage
Manager: *Anna Howarth;*
Costumes and Set: *Caroline
Wilson.*
Journal: 8/2/94

181. ANDY CAPP; Book by
Trevor Peacock; Music by Alan
Price; Lyrics by Trevor Peacock
and Alan Price; PADOS (Youth
Section); *8-11 February 1994.*

**183. THE SOUND
COLLECTOR** by Roger McGough;
QUICKSILVER THEATRE FOR
CHILDREN; *12 February 12
February 1994.*

166. THE KAOS HAMLET;
William Shakespeare, dilated,
opened out and exploded by
KAOS THEATRE; *3 March
1994.* Rosencrantz/Bernado/
Player 1: *Fernanda Amaral;*
Laertes/Guildenstern: *Laura
Bridgeman;* Hamlet: *Richard
Crawford;* Ophelia: *Jacquelyn
Hynes;* Claudius: *Chris Lailey;*
Polonius/Marcellus/Clown: *Xavier
Leret;* Horatio: *Phil Morle;*
Gertrude: *Sharon Schaffer.*

240

Director: *Phil Morle;* Assistant
Director: *Xavier Leret;* Company
Manager: *Richard Williams;* Body
Preparation: *Fernanda Amaral;*
Music Score: *Elizabeth Purnell
and the group;* Ophelia's Music:
Jacquelyne Hynes.

183. MERLIN; LAMBETH
CHILDREN'S THEATRE
COMPANY; *4 March 1994.*

**168. THE END OF TEDDY
HEDGES** by Alastair Goolden;
THE NATURAL THEATRE
COMPANY, in association with
the BRITOL OLD VIC; *9 March
1994.* Robby McIldowie: *Eric
MacLennan;* Kenneth Tynan: *Jason
Morell;* Esme Dunn/Daphne
Wickham/Mrs Mazzini: *Joanna
Phillips-Lane;* Alec Innes/Sidney
Stratford/Harry Parker/Arthur
Pendleton: *Andrew Pollard;* Teddy
Hedges: *Brian Popay.* Director:
Faynia Williams; Design: *Katy
McPhee;* Production Manager:
Pavel Douglas; Stage Manager/
Technician: *James Hyde;* Assistant
Stage Manager: *Rose Popay;*
Lighting Design: *Tim Streader;*
Costume Makers: *Olive Pike,
Jacqui Popay;* Crown made by:
Richard Cooper; Set Building:
Bristol Old Vic Workshops;
Technical Director: *David Miller.*

167. ACCRINGTON PALS by
Peter Whelan; DERBY PLAYERS;
10-12 March 1994. Sarah
Harding: *susan Simms;* Annie
Boggis: *Sonja Wilson;* May
Hassall: *Jayne Kelly;* Tom
Hackford: *Michael Roscoe;*
Diane Byrne; Siobhan Byrne.
Director: *John O'Connell.*
Press: BT: 4 & 18/3/94

184. THE MAGIC FINGER by
Roald Dahl; OPEN HAND
THEATRE COMPANY; *26 March
1994.*

185. PANCHATANTRA;
CHITRALEKA AND COMPANY;
8 April 1994. Chitraleka Bolar.

**186. GRANNY KETTLE'S
CAKE;** EDINBURGH PUPPET
COMPANY; *9 April 1994.*

76. ROXANA by Daniel
Defoe, adapted by Peter
McGarry for EYEWITNESS
THEATRE COMPANY; *15 April
1994.* Roxana: *Clare Barry;*
Gentleman/Prince: *Roger Cook;*
Amy: *Kirstie Maginn;* Young Man/
Merchant: *John Ryder;* Young
Man/Susan: *Jane Sheraton.*
Incidental Music: *Richard Strauss;*
Choreography: *Peter McGarry,
Clare Barry;* Costumes: *Helen
Corrin.*
Journal: 15/4/94

79. TO CATCH A WHALE
by Chris Webb; THE COMPANY;
20-21 April 1994. Pauline:
Jane Lancaster; Trish: *Sharon
Power;* Carol: *Kerrie Thomas.*
Director: *Sue Sutton Mayo;*
Design: *Sue Pearce;* Lighting:
Bev Pearson; Stage Manager:
Dean Clarkin.
Journal: 21/4/94
Press: CL: 20/4/94

91. THE KING'S PLAYER,
devised and performed by Trevor
Gare; *22 April 1994.* Director:
Joanna Weir; Costume: *Louise
Jacobs.*
Journal: 22/4/94

241

80. DREAM TIME devised by the 12-13 year-old group of BURY THEATRE WORKS; *28-29 April 1994.* The Dreamer: *Paul McMahon;* Angela: *Linden Ratcliffe;* Devillia: *Madeleina Solazzo;* Hayley: *Rachel Ponka;* Hayley's Mum: *Ian Buchan;* Colin: *Matthew Littler;* Tina: *Nickey Ruzza;* Tina's Gang: - Kathy: *Michelle Longden;* Miz: *Miriam Smith;* DB: *Samantha Todd -;* Susan: *Lora D Jones;* Mrs Brown: *Helen Currie;* Dan: *Dean Hudson;* Tracey: *Emma Riley;* Dan's Dad: *David Mulholland;* Mrs McKennie: *Nina Martyn* or *Lee-Ann Johnston;* Judy: *Carrie Paterson;* Judy's So-called Friends: - Joanne: *Claire Kirkham;* Mandy: *Zena Martyn;* Carol: *Michelle Lee - ;* Sarah: *Claire Casey;* Sarah's Mum: *Kate Ridley;* Helen: *Nicola Beswick;* Sammy: *Sarah Shivnam;* Jane: *Lee-Ann Johnson;* Dreamtime Chorus: *Charlene Leydon, Maria McKenna, Nicola Casey.* Drama Worker: *Sue Reddish;* Trainees: *Shilsan Lee, Matthew Badham;* Technical Support: *Lee Burgoyne.*
Journal: 29/4/94

81. UNITY; devised by 14-16 year-old group of BURY THEATRE WORKS, in collaboration with THIRD ESTATE; *28-29 April 1994.* Cast: *Pam Bailey, Karen Bell, John Clayton, Alan Dawson, Christopher Eccles, Collette Leyden, Colin MacKay, Andrew MacKay, Claire McMullen, Sarah Platt, Joanna Fagbadagon, Jasmin Smith, Joanne Todd, Lucy Whelan.* Drama Worker: *Ed Oxley;* Assistant Drama Worker: *Gill Pemberton;* Technical

Support: *Lee Burgoyne*
Journal: 29/4/94

171. TALES FROM A TREEHOUSE; FREEHAND THEATRE; *14 May 1994.*

169. THE LATE EDWINA BLACK by William Dinner and William Morum; MIDDLE GROUND THEATRE COMPANY; *14 May 1994.*

172. DEADLY VIRAGO by Peter Smith; HATS; *19-21 May 1994.*

170. AND THE SHIP SAILED ON; devised and performed by Nola Rae and Sally Owen; LONDON MIME COMPANY; *25 May 1994.* Director: *Carlos Trafic;* Design: *Matthew Ridout;* Music: *Peter West.*

18. SACRED JOURNEY by Matthew Witten; NEW MEXICO REP; *4 June 1994.*

174. WHOSE SHOES by Mike Kenny; M6 THEATRE COMPANY; *18 June 1994*

206. THE BEST DAYS OF OUR LIVES, partly based on poems by Allen Ahlberg; BURY THEATRE WORKS; *23-24 June 1994.* Cast: *Andrew Alexander, Roger Beale, Sarah Beswick, Kate Billington, Dave Bygrave, Natalie Daly, Alex DeMartiis, Ann Marie Edwards, Kathryn Hickman, Rebeca Jones, Laura Kenyon, Heather Kerr, Victoria Maxwell, Arif Andrew Mollai, Rachel Morris, Elizabeth Noonan, Philip Price, Sarah Proffit, Katie*

Reed, Hayley Roberts, Daniel Solazzo, Adele Straccia, Charlotte Thompson. Directors: Sue Reddish, Matthew Badham.

175. LIFE IN A BUN, WITH RELISH, PLEASE; WHITEFIELD THEATRE WORKSHOP; 30 June & 2 July 1994.

36. PEACOCK; DOO COT; 15 July 1994.

187. THE WIZARD OF CASTLE MAGIC; MAGIC CARPET THEATRE COMPANY; 5 August 1994.

188. THE CHILD OF HALE by Sue Gerrard and Chris Roach; COWLEY SCHOOL, ST HELENS; 20 August 1994. John Middleton: *Neil Hurst;* Smithy Senior: *Gareth Twist;* Squire: Janis Crabbe; Mrs Smith: *Phil Foley;* Sarah: *Nicola Topping;* Artist Gerhart: *Dean Houghton;* Devil/Ventriloquist: *Andrew Briggs;* King James: *Chris Conqueror;* Caller: *Anthony Burns;* Mrs Middleton/Queen: *Kristy Geraghty;* Gypsy Red: *Fleur Geraghty;* Catherine: *Lyndsy Farnworth;* Dummy: *Gareth Pawson;* Young Smithy: *Chris Peddie;* Musicians: *Andrew Briggs, Ian Penketh, Ian Abbott.* Director: *O;* Lights: *Dobromir Harrison, John Bonnry, Gary Ashdown.*

189. THREE MEN IN A BOAT by Jerome K Jerome, play devised by RIDICULUSMUS from an adaptation by Jon Haynes and Angus Barr; 16 September 1994. Harris: *Angus Barr;* J: *Jon Darke.* Assistance from *Rob Ballard* of

the *Performance Theatre Company.* Journal: 16/9/94

85. COTTON MATHER'S WONDERS OF THE INVISIBLE WORLD; THE GLEE CLUB; 23 September 1994.

86. YOUNG COTTON MATHER'S WONDERS OF THE INVISIBLE WORLD; THE GLEE CLUB; 24 September 1994.

190. SINK OR SWIM by Mike Kenny; QUICKSILVER THEATRE with MACLENNON DANCE AND COMPANY; 14 October 1994

191. THE MAYOR OF CASTERBRIDGE by Thomas Hardy; SNAP THEATRE COMPANY; 15 October 1994.

192. GIMPEL THE FOOL by Isaac Bashevis Singer, translated by Saul Bellow; Performed by David Schonman; 20 October 1994.

193. THE LAST DEMON by Isaac Bashevis Singer, translated by Saul Bellow; Performed by David Schonman; 20 October 1994.

194. LOVE AT A LOSS by Catharine Trotter; WILD IRIS; 27 October 1994.

195. MAD MASH ONE; BODGER AND BADGER; 28 October 1994. Simon Bodger.

641. THE PLOT; MIND THE ... GAP; 3 November 1994

196. SKELETONS IN THE CUPBOARD by Lemn Sissay; BURY ACTORS COMPANY; 9-12 November 1994. Director: Sue Reddish. Design: Marcus Rapley. **Press: BT:** 17/12/93

792. MOVE OVER, MRS MARKHAM by Ray Cooney and John Chaopman; HATS; 17-19 November 1994.

676. doors; OPEN DOOR THEATRE COMPANY; 24 November 1994.

197. THE SNOW QUEEN by Hans Christian Anderson, dramatised by Neil Duffield; M6 THEATRE COMPANY; 25 November 1994 - 14 January 1995.

PADOS HOUSE, St Mary's Road, PRESTWICH, M25 5AQ; 061-795 9163; AZ: 30, 4A; **XAZ:** 59, 5F.

266. WOLFSBANE by Georgina Reid; PADOS; 14-20 November 1993. Joan Meredith: Gail Lees; Luke Meredith: Jason Dunk; Howard Meredith: Charles Service: Gran: Stella Hall; Sarah Bond: Emma Lacey; Mrs Bond: Jenni Lomax. Director: Maureen Service; Sound: Allen Meachin; Lighting: Ray Halstead, Michael Hall; Stage Manager: Rick Hartree; Workshop: Tony Hannnaby, John Fort, Jack Richardson; Wardrobe: Audrey Meachin; Make-Up: Joan Tomlinson; Props: Maureen

Thomas; Prompt: Doreen Robinson. **Press: BT:** 12/11/93

260. THE HEIRESS, adapted by R & A Goetz from WASHINGTON SQUARE by Henry James; PADOS; 13-19 March 1994. Maria: Jane Hoolachan; Dr Austin Sloper: Chris Ainsworth; Mrs Lavinia Penniman: Maureen Thomas; Catherine: Katie Haydock; Mrs Elizabeth Almond: Carole Bernstein; Marion Almond: Jane Murphy; Arthur Townsend: Jason Dunk; Morris Townsend: Chris Elks; Mrs Montgomery: Jennie Lomax. Director: Garyk Barnett; Stage Manager: Rick Hartree; Workshop: Rick Hartree, Jack Richardson, Tony Hannanby; Lighting: Ray Halstead, Mike Hall; Sound: Allan Meachin; Wardrobe: Audrey Meachin; Hair and Make-up: Joan Tomlinson; Props: Pat Hill, Sarah Barnett; Prompt: Doreen Robinson, Stella Hall.

265. THE MURDER OF MARIA MARTEN or THE RED BARN by Brian J Burton; PADOS; 9-14 May 1994. Thomas Marten: Chris Ainsworth; JohnnY Badger: Peter Nunn; Tim Bobbin: Cliff Burton; Anne Marten: Diane Hoolachan; Meg Bobbin/Alice Rumble: Diana Sronson (AKA Sandra O'Nions); Nell Hatfield: Joan Tomlinson; Willam Corder: Ian Howarth; Mrs Marten: Lesley Nunn; Petra: Maureen Thomas; Rosa: Pat Cassidy; Pharos Lee: Penn Turner. Director: Brian Seymour; Choreographer: Janet Gorton; Musical Director: Sarah Barnett; Pianist: Pat Greenwood;

244

Stage and Workshop Manager:
Rick Hartree; Workshop: *Jack
Richardson, Tony Hannaby, John
Forte;* Sound: *Allen Meachin;*
Lighting: *Ray Halstead, Mike
Hall;* Wardrobe: *Audrey Meachin;*
Make-Up: *Joan Tomlinson;*
Properties: *Maureen Thomas, Pat
Cassidy, Sandra O'Nions;*
Continuity: *Doreen Robinson,
Eveline Seymour.*

PEEL CENTRE, Parliament Street, BL9 OTE; O61-763 1505, 761 2216. AZ: 10,B4; XAZ: 28,C4.

298. **SHAKESPEARE'S
GREATEST HITS;** MANCHESTER
ACTORS COMPANY; *14
February 1994.*

791. **FRANKENSTEIN'S
MOTHERS;** Foursight Theatre;
17 November.

RADCLIFFE HIGH SCHOOL, Abden Street, Radcliffe, M26 3AT; 061-723 3110; AZ: 19, 4F; XAZ: 41, 4G.

129. **GROUNDED** by Eileen
Murphy; M6 THEATRE
COMPANY; *10 February 1994.*

ST MONICA' RC HIGH SCHOOL; Bury Old Road, PRESTWICH, M25 OFG; 061-773 6436; AZ: 39, E1; XAZ: 59, G6.

200. **MARIA MARETN AND
THE MURDER IN THE RED
BARN;** *December 1993.*

202. **THE MERCHANT OF
VENICE** by William Shakespeare;
Spring 1993.

THEATRE ROYAL, Smithy Street, RAMSBOTTOM, BLO 9AT; O61-797 0180. XAZ: 5,E3.

528. **SKI WHIZZ** by Richard
Ingham; SUMMERSEAT
PLAYERS; *2-9 October 1993.*
Ernest Edelbaum: *Peter Larkin;*
Leslie Bookett: *Stephen Larkin;*
Philip Butler: *Daniel Clynes;*
Jenny Lorrimer: *Eileen Hamilton;*
Helen: *Karen Kennedy;* Cecily
Lacock: *Jean Taylor.* Director:
Geoffrey B Sword; Set Design:
Mike Heaps, Lynn Snowden;
Stage Manager: *Paul Farmer;*
Prompt: *Graham Humphreys;*
Wardrobe: *Sue Royle, Elise
Brack;* Properties: *Rosemary
Wilde, Val Whittall;* Lighting:
Roger Salin, Jeff Demain; Sound:
Walter Hamilton; Set
Construction: *Mike Heaps, Allen
McGuiness, Barry Atkinson, Brian
Cummings, Jill Hunt, Karen
Stowell, Viv Broadbent.*
Press: BT: 1&15/10/93

529. **SHADOWLANDS** by
William Nicholson; SUMMERSEAT
PLAYERS; *20-27 November
1994.* CS Lewis: *Malcolm
Ashton;* Major WH Lewis: *Geoff
Sword;* Professor Christopher
Riley: *Stuart Birtwell;* Rev
"Harry" Harrington: *Ron Decent;*
Dr Alan Gregg/Doctor: *Laurie*

Lancashire; Waiter in
Tearoom/Priest: *Carl Hamilton;*
Joy Gresham: *Clodagh O'Flynn;*
Douglas: *Joel Moore/Alex
Wheeler;* Registrar: *Helen
Humphreys;* Nurse: *Helen
Goldstraw;* Waiter in Hotel: *Paul
Farmer.* Director: *Graham
Humphreys;* Set Design: *Mike
Heaps;* Stage Manager: *Paul
Farmer;* Prompt: *Kay Sword;*
Wardrobe: *Sue Royle, Elise
Brack;* Properties: *Helen
Humphreys, Margaret Heaps,
Maureen Sutton, Zoë Booth;*
Lighting: *Roger Salin, Jeff
Demain;* Sound: *Walter Hamilton,
David Royle;* Set Construction:
*Mike Heaps, Allen McGuiness,
Barry Atkinson, Brian Cummings,
Jill Hunt, Karen Stowell, Alan
Rogers, Roland Moss.*
Press: BT: 19&26/11/93

530. LOOT by Joe Orton;
SUMMERSEAT PLAYERS; *22-29
January 1994.* McLeavy: *Laurie
Lancashire;* Fay: *lindsay Eavis;*
Hal: *Andy Greenwood;* Dennis:
Paul Farmer; Truscott: *Brian
Hunt;* Meadows: *John Garvey.*
Director: *Brian Seymour;* Set
Design: *Mike Heaps;* Stage
Manager: *Malcolm Ashton;*
Prompt: *Jean Taylor;* Wardrobe:
*Sue Royle, Elise Brack, Miranda
Crompton;* Properties: *Rosemary
Wild, Jack Palmer, Barbara
Palmer;* Lighting: *Roger Salin;*
Sound: *Walter Hamilton, David
Royle;* Set Construction: *Mike
Heaps, Allen McGuiness, Barry
Atkinson, Brian Cummings, Jill
Hunt, Geoff Sword, Alan Rogers,
Jeff Demain, Stephen Phillips.*
Press: BT: 21&29/1/94

**531. THE ACCRINGTON
PALS** by Peter Whelan;

SUMMERSEAT PLAYERS; *12-19
March.* May: *Karen Kennedy;*
Tom: *Mark Labrow;* Ralph:
Richard Blease; Eva: *Miranda
Bevin;* Sarah: *Helen Goldstraw;*
Bertha: *Lydia Marsh;* Annie:
Paddy Harrison; Arthur: *Steve
Phillips;* Reggie: *Darriel Graham;*
CSM Rivers: *Malcolm McQuoid.*
Director: *Peter Larkin;* Set: *Mike
Heaps;* Stage Manager: *Brian
Cummings;* Prompt: *Jean Taylor;*
Production Assistant: *John Garvey;*
Wardrobe: *Sue Royle, Elise
Brack;* Properties: *Rosemary Wild,
Jack Palmer, Barbara Palmer,
Margaret Heaps;* Lighting: *Roger
Salin;* Sound: *Walter Hamilton,
David Royle;* Set Construction:
*Mike Heaps, Barry Atkinson,
Brian Cummings, Viv Broadbent,
Roland Moss, Steve Phillips, Rita
Newsholme, Sue Joseph;* Piano:
Pam Larkin, Cobbler's Items: *Bill
Allpress;* Trolley and Last: *Earnest
Hutchinson.*

532. STEEL MAGNOLIAS by
Robert Harling; SUMMERSEAT
PLAYERS; *7-14 May 1994.*
Truvy: *Lindsay Eavis;* Annelle:
Heather Rothwell; Clairee: *Carol
Taylor;* Shelby: *Heather
Goldstraw;* M'Lynn: *Carol
Berlynne;* Ouisser: *Margaret
Ingham.* Director: *Garyk
Barnett;* Set Design: *Mike Heaps;*
Stage Managers: *Brian Cummings,
Barry Atkinson;* Prompt: *Jill Hunt;*
Wardrobe & Properties: *Jack
Palmer, Barbara Palmer, Rita
Newsholme, Elise Brack, Miranda
Crompton;* Lighting: *Roger Sallin;*
Sound: *David Royle;* Set
Construction: *Mike Heaps, Barry
Atkinson, Brian Cummings, Viv
Broadbent, Roland Moss, Steve
OPhillips, Sue Joseph.*

208-244: GREATER MANCHESTER DRAMA FEDERATION THIRTY-FOURTH ANNUAL ONE-ACT PLAY FESTIVAL:

208. DREAMJOBS by Graham Jones; FORTUNE YOUTH WORKSHOP; *22 May 1994.* Angela: *Anne-Marie Maxwell;* Joan: *Deborah Hazledean;* Mandy: *Claire Mason;* Beverly: *Beverly Hancock;* Fiona: *Lucie Dobbing.* Director: *David Tolcher.*

209. THE CINDERELLA STORY by Kenneth Lillington; HEALD GREEN THEATRE CLUB; *22 May 1994.* Presswoman: *Jodie Kempster;* The Queen's Secretary: *Angela Hammond;* Lavinia: *Vicky-Jane Worsley;* Honoria: *Kate Goulden;* Cinderella: *Jo Schilling;* The Godmother: *Emma Johnston;* Baroness: *Francesca Lever;* The Prince: *Simon Mills.* Directors: *Dianne Jenkins, Barbara Ritchie.*

210. TRUTH GAMES by Malcolm King; LIVING ROOM THEATRE; *22 May 1994.* Mike: *Chris Burton;* Liz: *Carolyn Hooper;* Ann: *Eleonor Metcalfe;* Mary: *Nuala O'Rouke;* Paul: *Tony Brown;* Maggie: *Gilly Winstanley.* Director: *Malcolm King.*

211. SIT DOWN AND BEHAVE YOURSELF by Barry Massey; BRADSHAW DRAMA GROUP; *23 May 1994.* Emily: *Julie Crowder;* Lee: *Mitch Massey;* Doreen: *Heather Colley;* Malcolm: *Brian Chadwick;* Annie: *Margaret Knott;* Tommy: *Bill Mason;* Nurse: *Nichola Hunt;* Doctor: *Albert Roberts.* Director: *Philip Taylor.*

212. RATS by Alan Gardner; BOLLINGTON JUNIOR FESTIVAL PLAYERS; *23 May 1994.* Teacher: *Tom Petty;* BD: *Tom Butterworth;* Emma: *Lorna Needham;* Simon: *Daniel Owen;* Rat 3: *Timothy Gee;* Rat 4: *Jenny Auton;* Rat 5: *Helen Hadfield;* Rat 1: *Ruth Auton;* Rachel: *Liz Youles;* Martin: *Robin Owen;* Rosemary: *Jenny Lee;* Sarah: *Emma Backhouse;* Carol: *Molly Butterworth;* Anne: *Joanne Lee;* Jane: *Sarah Hodgson;* Lyndsey: *Carly Pearson;* Chris: *Matthew Gee;* Jackie: *Katie Mills;* Father: *Bradley Vearncombe;* Mother: *Melissa Cann.* Director: *Liz Bratt.*

213. FACING THE WALL by Andrea Greenwood and Sue Waddington; BEACON DRAMA; *23 May 1994.* Cast: *Janet Ash, Andrea Greenwood, Linda Jones, John Tse, Sue Waddington.* Director: *Linda Jones.*

214. SOMEBODY FOR DINNER by Ted Sharpe; ST JOSEPH'S PLAYERS; *24 May 1994.* Ralph: *Earnest Earlam;* Helen: *Maureen Service;* Dad: *Norman Hardman;* Zoë: *Helen Dawson;* Garth: *Simon Wilkes.* Director: *Betty Hardman.*

215. THE HAPPY MAN by H Adams; SUMMERSEAT YOUTH THEATRE; *24 May 1994.* Lord Chamberlain: *Natalie Lobel;* Maid:

Helen Bowe; King: *Fleur Bremner;* Queen: *Emma White;* Dr Stout: *Katie Bremner;* Dr Lankey: *Ruth White;* Pages: *Nichola Mather, Melanie Jaworska, Elizabeth Curry, Suzanne Beech;* Peasants: *Kim Smith, Catherine Mather;* Villagers: *Rachel Mather, Julia Hayes, Katie Greaves, Laura Duffy, Helen Keely, Carla Robb;* Vagabond: *Louise Isherwood;* Sentinels: *Matthew Ashworth, Alex Duncan,;* Cooks: *Sarah Cooper, Laura Jazwinska, Karen Platt.* Director: *Peter Larkin.*

216. HENRY HEREAFTER by Hal D Stewart; BOLLINGTON FESTIVAL PLAYERS; *24 May 1994.* Seraph: *Bradley Vearncomb;* Catherine of Aragon: *Barbara Northwood;* Ann Boleyn: *Alison Ross;* Jane Seymour: *Lorna Needham;* Catherine Howard: *Melissa Cann;* Henry VIII: *Peter Mannion;* Catherine Parr: *Jacqui Wood;* Ann of Cleves: *Helen Valentine.* Director: *Doreen Young.*

217. LETTER FROM AMERICA by Philip Stagg; ARENA THEATRE COMPANY; *25 May 1994.* Gwen Devine: *Pat Matthews;* Alec: *Philip Stagg;* Estelle: *Joanne Puddephatt;* Walter Pascoe: *Mike Hall;* Brad: *Ken Ward;* Frank: *Stuart Puddephatt;* Ginny: *Heather Hall;* Eric Babbington: *Mitch Law;* Abby Thiering: *Emma Stagg.* Director: *Mitch Law.*

218. ERNIE'S INCREDIBLE ILLUCINATIONS by Alan Ayckbourn; SUMMERSEAT METHODIST PRIMARY SCHOOL; *25 May 1994.*

Ernie: *Thomas Allen;* Mum: *Caroline Ellis;* Dad: *Dean Clegg;* Doctor: *Paul Hopton;* Officer: *Oliver Hawley;* Auntie May: *Charlene Stanley;* Referee: *Luke Jackson;* Attendant: *Jon Wilsdon.* Director: *Stuart Birtwell.*

219. LAST TANGO IN LITTLE GRIMLEY by David Tristram; PLAYERS DRAMATIC SOCIETY; *25 May 1994.* Gordon: *Jeff Wilson;* Bernard: *Carl Birkenhead;* Joyce: *Ena Wint;* Margaret: *Anna Davies.* Director: *Rhoda Hills.*

220. AFTERMATH by Rae Terence; PARKLAND PLAYERS; *26 May 1994.* Vicar: *Kevin Lyons;* John Ferris: *Steve Graham;* Ellie: *Janet Taylor;* Regional Controller Evans: *Steve Jacobs;* Captain Martin: *James S Kinsella;* Doctor Henderson: *Olivia Smyth.* Director: *John L Byron.*

221. THE ONION SELLER by Jessica Fraser; HEALD GREEN THEATRE CLUB; *26 May 1994.* Storytellers: *Sarah Armstrong, Saloni Shah;* Wei Ku: *Craig Biezke;* Wei Li: *Thomas Reynolds;* Wei Lu: *Clare Halfpenny;* Wei Pi: *Christopher Ridehalgh;* Wei Pu: *Jennifer Ridehalgh;* Yueh Lao Yen: *Gemma Pritchard;* Lo Chung: *Jodie Kempster;* Lu Tung Pin: *Christopher Biezke;* The Scribe: *Anna Brett;* Wang Hong: *Lisa Williams;* Ah Chang: *Clare Ridehalgh;* Lo Sung: *Sara Williams;* Kuan Yin: *Alicia Montrose;* Servants/Passers By: *Sarah Lee, Samantha Gabriel, Jennifer Gabriel.* Director: *Brenda Stranger.*

222. GOSFORTH'S FÊTE by

Alan Ayckbourn; 3D THEATRE COMPANY; *26 May 1994.* Milly: *Annette Slater;* Mrs Pearce: *Mal Fidler;* Gosforth: *Rod Fitton;* Vicar: *Neil Sampson;* Stewart: *Colin Gibson.* Director: *Andrew Fidler.*

223. MIRAGE by Dilys Gater; WOODFORD COMMUNITY PLAYERS; *27 May 1994.* Carruthers: *Malcolm Gregory;* Hughes: *Bill Dooton;* Blanche: *Janine Schultz.* Director: *Jessie Monaghan.*

224. THE SAXON WIVES OF ELLANDUNE by L Du Garde Peach; HULME HALL SCHOOL; *27 May 1994.* Winfreth: *Amanda Latimer;* Freda: *Abigail Moxon;* Editha: *Ruth Summerly-Barron;* Emma: *Amargit Sagar;* Judith: *Emma Lane;* Bertha: *Wendy Craven;* A Dane: *Robert Flynn.* Director: *C Ridout.*

225. PICKING BONES by Stephen Keyworth; INCREASINGLY IMPORTANT THEATRE COMPANY; *27 May 1994.* Cast: *Stephen Keyworth, Caroline Chick, Toby Hadoke, Greg Macklin.* Director: *Colin Snell.*

226. HOW HE LIED TO HER HUSBAND by Bernard Shaw; HEALD GREEN THEATRE CLUB; *28 May 1994.* Henry Apjohn: *Paul Mizen;* Aurora Bompass: *Dianne Jenkins;* Teddy Bompass: *Peter Womby.* Director: *Julie Ward.*

227. CECILY by Gillian Plowman; THE RIVERSIDE PLAYERS; *28 May 1994.* Cecily: *Anna Blizzard;* Sheila: *Jeanette Arnold;* Ellen: *Janet Blizzard.* Director: *Bryan Evans.*

228. THE ACTOR'S NIGHTMARE by Christopher Durang; MACCLESFIELD AMATEUR DRAMATIC SOCIETY; *28 May 1994.* George Spelvin: *Steven Johnson;* Meg: *Kirsty Thraves;* Sarah Siddons: *Jan Hart;* Dame Ellen Terry: *Debi Lidbetter;* Henry Irving: *Andrew Smith.* Director: *Francesca Dykes.*

229. STAGES by Jerome McDonough; PADOS; *30 May 1994.* Director: *Chris Ainsworth;* Figure: *Peter Nunn;* Assistant Director: *Marchia Ogden;* Stage Manager: *Cliff Burton;* Corrie: *Diane Hoolachan;* Kim: *Helena Sims;* Laura: *Jennie Lomax;* Ted: *Keith Lomax;* Ty: *Jason Dunk;* Kurt: *John Ford;* Willie: *Sheila Ward;* Chorus: *Pat Cassidy, Sandra Onions.* Director: *Lynda Burton.*

230. ONE FAITH by Alec Freedman; ROSSENDALE YOUTH THEATRE; *30 May 1994.* Narrator 1: *Katie Senior;* Narrator 2: *Joanne Swale;* Faith: *Clair Harris;* Mother: *Clair Harris;* Mother: *Joanne Howard;* Father: *Ben Hyde;* Brother: *Matthew Swale;* Teacher 1: *Shelley Tattersall;* Teacher 2: *Daniel Crowley;* Youth 1: *Lucy Howary;* Youth 2: *Saoirse Cowley;* Instructor 1: *Rebecca Berry;* Instructor 2: *Cassie Smith;* Worker 1: *Charlotte Hudson, Clair Howard;* Worker 2: *Kirsten Greaves, Caroline Quinn;* Police 1:

Francesca Gittins; Police 2:
Matthew Crowley; Harry:
Dominic Branningan. Directors:
D Finnigan, A Heslop.

231. ALBERT by Richard
Harris; MOSSLEY AODS; *30
May 1994.* Karin: *Lisa Kay;*
Nico: *Malcolm Nield;* Albert:
Byrom McGuinness. Director:
Denise Shawcross.

232. JUVIE by Jerome
McDonough; PADOS; *31 May
1994.* Jean: *Michelle Hills;*
Sunny: *Russell Greenhalgh;* Skip:
David Yorke Robinson; Carey:
Helen Halstead; Andrew: *David
Livesey;* Ann: *Helena Sims;*
Pinky: *Richard Livesey;* Jane:
Claire Neilson; Gaurd 1: *Sara
Yates;* Gaurd 2: *Philip Buckley;*
Gaurd 3: *Hayley Doherty.*
Director: *Lynda Burton.*

**233. LAST TANGO IN LITTLE
GRIMLEY** by David Tristram;
SLYNE WITH HEST DRAMA
GROUP; *31 May 1994.*
Gordon: *Peter Brooks;* Bernard:
Derek Garside; Joyce: *Barbara
Woodland;* Margaret: *Elizabeth
Brewster.* Director: *Julia
Brotherton.*

234. A BITE OF THE APPLE
by David Shutte; WIRRAL
HOSPITAL PLAYERS; *31 May
1994.* Christian: *Cathy
Marland;* Agnosticus: *Peter
Muncer;* Atheos: *Michael Hunter;*
God: *Celia Edwards;* Adam:
Michael Davidson; Eve: *Lyndsey
Gorman.* Director: *Liane
Gannon.*

235. THE VALIANT by
Holworthy Hall and Robert

Middlemass; FARNWORTH LITTLE
THEATRE; *1 June 1994.*
Warden Holt: *Jonathan Broadley;*
Father Daly: *Paul Wallwork;*
James Dyke: *Stuart McKay;*
Josephine Paris: *Pamela Higson;*
Dan: *Adam Marsh;* An Attendant:
Siobhan Partington. Directors:
Jason Tyler, Clarke McWilliam.

236. THE ORCHESTRA by
Jean Anouilh, translated by
Miriam John; CELESTA
PLAYERS; *1 June 1994.*
Patricia: *Doreen Richards;*
Pamela: *Krys Rodda;* Madame
Hortense: *Rosemary Blayds;*
Suzanne Délicias: *Halla Cousins;*
Emmeline: *Mary Dunger;* Léona:
Sue Keyworth; Monsieur Léon:
Eddy Bell; Monsieur Lebonze:
Geoff Richards; Waiter: *Keith
Smitheman.* Director: *Mary
Dunger.*

237. BETWEEN MOUTHFULS
by Alan Ayckbourn; UPPERMILL
STAGE SOCIETY; *1 June 1994.*
Waiter: *Jonathan Simm;* Pearce:
Des Powell; Mrs Pearce: *Joan
Bradbury;* Martin: *John Molyneux;*
Polly: *Sandra Simm.* Director:
Alan Whitham.

238. MURDER PLAY by Brian
J Burton; BROOKDALE
DRAMATIC SOCIETY; *2 June
1994.* Peter Darrell: *Paul
Hazelby;* Robyn Darrell: *Sue
McEwen;* Jane Valentine: *Ann
Seymour;* David Valentine: *Rodney
Bracewell.* Director: *John
Woodruff.*

239. OTHER SIDE STORY by
Brendan Quinn; TAMESIDE
YOUTH DRAMA GROUP; *2
June 1994.* Satan: *Brendan*

Quinn; St Peter: *Mark Hilton;*
Samantha Birtles: *Vicky Clayton;*
L S Lowry: *Kerrie Rushton;* Jane
Whitworth: *Stephanie Austin;*
Christine Belmont: *Emma Wilcox;*
God: *Darren Nightingale;* Lucy
Fer: *Karen Ellery;* Thaddeus:
Andrew Marshall; Joan Benny:
Nicola Turner; Alice: *Katie
McDonald;* Beryl: *Julioa Maden;*
Lost Soul: *Kerrie Rushton.*
Directors: *Mark Hilton, Brendan
Quinn.*

240. LUCY by John F Banks;
WILMSLOW GUILD PLAYERS; *2
June 1994.* Lucy: *Jean
Drinkwater;* Kiwi: *Dai Richards;*
Norman: *David Carlile;* Dancers:
Lucille Connolly, Alan Lucas;
Eric: *Gordon Livingston;* Whiplash:
Nancy Richards. Director: *John F
Banks.*

241. AN ENGLISHMAN
ABROAD by Alan Bennett;
CHADS THEATRE COMPANY; *3
June 1994.* Coral Browne:
Chris Bullimore; Guy Burgess:
Michael Bullimore; Tolya/Shop
Assistant: *Bill Nolan;* Tailor: *Nigel
Westbrook.* Director: *Nigel
Westbrook.*

242. MAGIC by Richard
Harris; SADDLEWORTH
PLAYERS; *3 June 1994.* May:
Jean Bintley; Arthur: *John
Kenworthy;* Sandra: *Jacqueline
Colton;* Brenda: *Eileen Southard;*
Ron: *Tony Stallard;* Joan: *Edwina
Rigby.* Director: *Roger T
Holland.*

243. THE MALEDICTION by
Carolyn Hooper; MANCHESTER
UNIVERSITY STAGE SOCIETY;
3 June 1994. Franks: *Ian*

Newton; Martin: *Chris Burton;*
Jess: *Nuala O'Rourke;* Heather:
Ella Burton; Steven: *Tony Brown;*
1st Man: *Malcolm King;* 2nd
Man: *Michael Elphick.* Director:
Carolyn Hooper.

244. THE LONG CHRISTMAS
DINNER by Thornton Wilder;
SUMMERSEAT PLAYERS; *4 June
1994.* Lucia: *Clodagh O'Flynn;*
Roderick: *John Garvey;* Mother
Bayard: *Margaret Heaps;* Cousin
Brandon: *Stuart Birtwell;* Charles:
Steve Philllips; Genevieve: *Debbie
Woods;* Leonora Banning: *Lindsey
Eavis;* Ermengarde: *Kay Sword;*
Lucia: *Lydia Marsh;* Sam: *Paul
Farmer;* Roderick: *Carl Hamilton.*
Director: *Geoff Sword.*

533. ON GOLDEN POND by
Ernest Thompson; SUMMERSEAT
PLAYERS; *1-8 October 1994.*
Norman Thayer Jr: *Barrie Miller;*
Ethel Thayer: *Jean Taylor;*
Charlie Martin: *Franco Paolucci;*
Chelsea Thayer Wayne: *Kathleen
Booth;* Billy Ray: *Daniel Graham;*
Bill Ray: *John Garvey.* Director:
Geoff Higginbotham; Design: *Mike
Heaps;* Stage Manager: *Brian
Cummings;* Prompt: *Jean Ward,
Rita Newsholme;* Wardrobe: *Sue
Royle, Elise Brack, Miranda
Crompton;* Properties: *Jack
Palmer, Barbara Palmer, Sue
Joseph;* Lighting: *Roger Sallin,
Walter Hamilton, Jeff Demain;*
Sound: *David Royle;* Set
Construction: *Mike Heaps, Barry
Atkinson, Viv Broadbent, Margaret
Heaps, Mary Baynes, Alan
Rogers, Paddy Harrison, Alan
McGuiness, Jill Hunt, Geoff
Sword.*

534. A SMALL FAMILY
BUSINESS by Alan Ayckbourn;

251

SUMMERSEAT PLAYERS; *26 November - 3 December 1994.*

TOTTINGTON HIGH SCHOOL, Laurel Street, TOTTINGTON, BL8 3LY; 0204 882327/885913. AZ: 9,E1; XAZ: 13,H5.

129. GROUNDED by Eileen Murphy; M6 THEATRE COMPANY; *11 February 1994.*

99. THE NEW ARRIVAL by Eliane Byrne; CONTACT THEATRE COMPANY; *June 1994.*

WOODHEY HIGH SCHOOL, Bolton Road West, RAMSBOTTOM, BL0 9QZ; 0706 825215; XAZ: 4, C6.

298. SHAKESPEARE'S GREATEST HITS; MANCHESTER ACTORS COMPANY; *7 February 1994.*

204. SEVENSIDED DICE; *Spring 1994.*

MANCHESTER

ABBEY HEY MOBILE LIBRARY, Abbey Hey Lane, M18; **AZ**: 52, B1; **XAZ**: 103, 1G.

124. THE TIGER WITH GOLDEN CLAWS; MANCHESTER ACTORS COMPANY; *20 July 1994.*

ABRAHAM MOSS CENTRE THEATRE, Crescent Road, CRUMPSALL, M8 6UF; 061–795 4186. AZ: 40, B3; XAZ: 74: C3. G,H,W

282. HAPPY JACK by John Godber; HULL TRUCK THEATRE COMPANY; *1-2 October 1993.*

283. WONDERLAND by Mick Martin; MAJOR ROAD THEATRE COMPANY; *15-16 October 1993.*

284. TWELFTH NIGHT by William Shakespeare; SHOW OF HANDS THEATRE; *3 November 1993.*

278. A STRANGE AND UNEXPECTED EVENT; A celebration inspired by Jose G Posada; HORSE AND BAMBOO THEATRE; *5 November 1993.* Writer and Director: *Bob Frith;* Tour Director and Performer: *Jo King;* Performers: *Jill Penny, Ursula Burns;* Maker and Performer: *Sarah Frangleton;* Musical Director: *Stu Barker;* Musician: *Claire Ingleheart;*

Performer and Musician: *Mary Keith;* Lighting and Musical Support: *Neville Cann;* Makers: *Anne Barber, Mafalda da Camara, Brad Harley.*

12. LEAR by Edward Bond; EGG ROCK THEATRE; *15-17 November 1993.*

279. LOVE AND EXILE, devised by EEIc THEATRE COMPANY; *26-28 January 1994.* Cast: *Sheila Culleton, Julie Duffy, Craig Evans, Peter Stankard, Marcela Hervia, Mandy Hobson, Adam Jones, Janet Leach, Tom McCourt, Frances McKeown, Michael Robinson, Lily Murray, Rob Owen, Tony Palin, Julieann Quinlan, Lynn Roden, Lesley Skelly, Carl Smith, Janet Spooner, Alexis Tuttle, Tim Wesley.* Directors: *Gerri Moriaty, Lynn Roden, Michael McKrell;* Stage Management: *Sheila Culleton, Mandy Hobson, Danny Hurst, Peter Green, Terry Cowley;* Design Team: *Julie Duffy, Craig Evans, Peter Green, Francis McKeown, Daevid Crawley, Lynn Roden.*

280. GREEK by Stephen Berkoff; RAW DEAL THEATRE COMPANY; *8-9 April 1994.* Eddy/The Fortune Teller: *Michael McKrell;* Wife/Doreen/Waitress 1: *Lily Murray;* Dad/Manager of Café: *Tony O'Leary;* Mum/Sphinx /Waitress 2: *Lesley Skelly.* Direction: *Irving Czechowicz and cast;* Production: *Irving Czechowicz;* Lighting: *Peter Green;* Costumes: *Lesley Skelly.*

281. A CLOCKWORK ORANGE by Anthony Burgess;

FOUNDATION THEATRE
COMPANY; *23-26 March 1994.*
Director: *Bogdan Pilecki;* Musical
Director: *Richard Pallister;*
Choreographer: *Sarah Taylor;*
Design: *Susan Norris.*

285. **ANIMAL FARM** BY
George Orwell; RAW DEAL
THEATRE COMPANY; *29-30
September 1994.* Napoleon:
I nda Cleary; Snowball/Pilkington/
Dog: *Lily Murray;* Squealer: *Nick
Carroll;* Hens: *Sonia Morris,
Lesley Skelly;* Benjamin: *Fran
McKeown;* Boxer/Dog: *Glen
Edwards;* Moses/Jones/Clover:
Tony O'Leary; Voices: *Dave
Brace, Michael McKrell.*
Director: *Michael McKrell;*
Producer: *Irving Czechowicz;*
Original Music: *Dave Brace;*
Masks: *Eleanor Baxter, Pete
Freeman, Phil Rudder, John
Taylor;* Stage Manager: *Sue
Norris;* Lighting: *Matt Smith,
John Harten;* Sound: *Irving
Czechowicz;* Technical Assistance:
Terry Cowley, Matt Smith;
Crew: *Sheila Culleton, Mandy
Hobson, Cêllan Scott, Martin
Drew, Samantha MacWilliam,
Donna Kelly.*

288. **DEREK THE DEALER;**
ONE WAY PRODUCTIONS; *14
October 1994. Kay Bee, The
Bygraves and Moston Youth
Centre.*

299. **TORY! TORY! TORY!;**
MANCHESTER ACTORS
COMPANY; *October 1994.*

289. **SHIRLEY VALENTINE** by
Willy Russell; PARKLAND
PLAYERS; *11-12 November
1994.*

290. **SWEENEY TODD;**
FOUNDATION THEATRE
COMPANY; *30 November - 3
December 1994.*

APOLLO THEATRE,
Stockport Road, ARDWICK,
M12 6AP; 061-273
6921; (Cards: 061-242
2560/9; Fee: £1); AZ:
102,C2; XAZ: 167,F4.

ARDEN COLLEGE, Sale
Road, NORTHENDEN,
M23 0DD; 061-957
1719. AZ: 81,E1; XAZ:
128,A2. W

5. **THE LOVE OF THE
NIGHTINGALE** by Timberlake
Wertenbaker; ARDEN SCHOOL
OF THEATRE; *28-29 October
1993.* Philomele: *Tracy Shaw;*
Procne: *Donna Alexander;* Tereus:
Chris Rogers; Niobe/Theseus:
Rachel Gleaves; King Pandion/
Captain: *John Draycott;* Chorus/
Soldier: *Andrew Fillis;* Chorus
Soldier: *Graham Proctor;* Itys/
Echo: *Beki Whitney;* Queen/Iris:
Zoë Ginster; Phædra/Hero: *Nicola
Barnfield;* Aphrodite/June/Nurse:
Susan Sands. Director: *Maggie
Ford;* Design: *Sue Condie;*
Lighting: *Vince Herbert;* Stage
Manager: *RIchard Gee;* Production
Manager: *Helen Maguire.*

6. **WHALE MUSIC** by
Anthony Minghella; ARDEN
SCHOOL OF THEATRE; *28 &
30 October 1993.* Caroline:

255

Linda Glover; Stella: *Emma Ferguson;* Fran: *Jo Curley;* Kate: *Laura Wolfe;* D: *Sarah McAdam;* Sheelagh O'Brien/Waitress: *Janet Stanley;* Nurse/Staff Nurse/Veronica: *Fiona Macdonald.* Director: *Gregory Hersov;* Design: *Sue Condie;* Lighting: *Vince Herbert;* Sound: *Paul Clifford;* Production Manager: *Helen Maguire;* Stage Manager: *Jak Kearney;* Assistant Stage Managers: *Anthony Dickinson, Paul Lane;* Lighting Board Operator: *Dean Poskitt;* Saxophonist: *Barbara Thompson.*

7. THE BEGGAR'S OPERA 2000: John Gay adapted by Chris Monks; ARDEN SCHOOL OF THEATRE; *29-30 October 1993.* Derek Cheatham: *Peter Machen;* Claimant, Frank Heather: *Steve Hillman;* Claimant/Mrs Bet Cheatham/Penny Tenchery/Wife: *Tara Daniels;* Claimant/Charley Cheatham: *Vicki Stevens;* Claimant/Governor Pat Locke: *Yasmin Mackowska;* Claimant/Officer Lorraine Locke: *Emma Steele;* Claimant/Ann Cuff/Mrs Jenny Daliah: *Eliza Hetherington;* Claimant/Jelly Ben/Honor Back/Dr Emma Rage: *Michelle Carr;* Claimant/Miss Crookes/Boy Ted/Joy Rider: *Rebecca Fortune;* The Beggar/Mat The Mugger/Tanya Hyde: *Helen Lacey;* The Actress/Smackhead/Juanella Valet: *Rachel France;* Nicki Hall/Boring Brian/Sheila Blyge/Wife: *Jo Burgess;* MUSICIANS: Keyboards: *Akintayo Akinbode;* Guitar: *Pete Owen;* Bass: *Rob McGuire;* Flute: *Ali Russel.* Director: *Chris Monks;* Design: *Sue Condie;* Musical Director: *Akintayo Akinbode;* Choreographer: *Carey*

Hnederson; Lighting: *Vince Herbert;* Production Manager: *Helen Maguire;* Stage Manager: *Michael Tompkins;* Asssistant Stage Managers: *Simon Patterson, Chris Ramage;* Video Camera Work: *Graham Proctor;* Technician/Board Operator: *Dean Poskitt.*

292. RESTORATION COMEDY; Selection by ARDEN SCHOOL OF THEATRE; *2&5 February 1994.* **The Country Wife** by William Wycherley (Act IV, Scene III): Horner: *Peter Machen;* Quack: *Steven Hillman;* Lady Fidget: *Emma Ferguson;* Sir Jasper: *Andrew Fillis;* Lady Squeamish: *Lindi Glover;* Old Lady Squeamish: *Joanne Curley.* **The Plain Dealer** by William Wycherley (Act II, Scene I): Olivia: *Donna Alexander;* Eliza: *Sarah McAdam;* Lettice: *Fiona Macdonald;* Novel: *Andrew Fillis;* Plausible: *Peter Machen;* Boy: *David Brown.* **The Man of Mode** by George Etherege: Mrs Loveit: *Laura Wolfe;* Pert: *Lindi Glover;* Belinda: *Helen Lacey;* Dorimant: *Steven Hillman;* Page: *David Brown.* **The Relapse** by John Vanbrugh: Loveless: *Andrew Fillis;* Amanda: *Sue Sands;* Berinthia: *Zoë Ginster;* Worthy: *Stephen Hillman;* Foppington: *Peter Machen;* Servant: *David Brown.* Scenes from **The Provoked Wife** by John Vanbrugh: Sir John: *Steven Hillman;* Lady Brute: *Vicki Stevens;* Bellinda: *Fiona Macdonald;* Lady Fancyfull: *Rebecca Fortune;* Mademoiselle: *Joanne Curley;* Cornet: *Emma Ferguson;* Pipe: *Lindi Glover;* Heartfree: *Andrew Fillis.* Director: *Chris White;* Design: *Liane Sommers, Camilla Winter;*

Lighting: *Paul Moorhouse;*
Production Manager: *Helen Maguire;* Stage Manager: *Karen Smith;* Resident Technician: *Tom Weir.*
Press: ANT: 3/2/94

291. **Extracts from MOLIÉRE, MARIVAUX and GOLDONI;** ARDEN SCHOOL OF THEATRE; *3-4 February 1994.* The Learned Ladies by Molière: Amanda: *Carla Steele;* Henrietta: *Jo Burgess;* Clitandre: *Chris Rogers;* Bélise: *Rachel France;* Chrysale: *John Draycott;* Martine: *Michelle Carr;* Philaminte: *Rachel Gleaves;* Trissotin: *Graham Proctor.* **Harlequin's Lesson in Love** by Pierre Marivaux: Fairy: *Nicci Barnfield;* Trivelin: *Chris Rogers;* Harlequin: *John Draycott;* Silvia: *Janet Stanley;* Pepito the Shepherd: *Graham Proctor.* **Il Camiello** by Carlos Goldoni: Zorzetto: *Chris Rogers;* Lucietta: *Beki Whitney;* Gnese: *Yasmin Mackowska;* Orsola: *Michelle Carr;* Gasparina: *Tracy Shaw;* Pasqua: *Tara Daniels;* Katherina: *Eliza Hetherington;* Count: *Graham Proctor;* Anzolletto: *John Draycott.* Director: *Romy Baskerville;* Design: *Liane Sommers, Camilla Winter;* Lighting: *Paul Moorhouse;* Production Manager: *Helen Maguire;* Stage Manager: *Pam Vision;* Resident Technician: *Tom Weir.*
Press: ANT: 3/2/94

298. **SHAKESPEARE'S GREATEST HITS;** MANCHESTER ACTORS COMPANY; *8 February 1994.*

50. **MINIMALIST STORIES** by Javier Tomeo, translated by Isabel

Alves; ARDEN SCHOOL OF THEATRE; *4-5 March.* Company: *Rebecca Fortune, Zoë Ginster, Lindi Glover, Eliza Hetherington, Yasmin Karlinska, Sarah McAdam, Tracy Shaw, Leah Stanley, Beki Whitney, Steven Hillman, Graham Proctor.* Director: *Antonio Capelo;* Design: *Catherine Howell;* Lighting: *Bill Yendle;* Stage Management: *Chris Williams;* Board Operator: *Thomas Weir;* Set Construction: *Carl Richardson;* Scenic Painter: *Jenny Freeman;* Production Manager: *Helen Maguire.*
Journal: 4/3/94

55. **ALL CATS ARE GRAY IN THE DARK** by Chris Monks (Book, Score and Lyrics): ARDEN SCHOOL OF THEATRE; *11-12 March 1994.* Sophie: *Rachel Gleaves;* Eugenie: *Laura Wolfe;* Vivette: *Nicola Barnfield;* Camille: *Michelle Myers;* Louise: *Vicki Stevens;* Roxane: *Tara Daniels;* Captain D'Artagnan: *John Draycott;* Raoul de Bragellone: *Chris Rogers;* Paul du Vallon de Bracieux de Pierrfonds: *Andrew Fillis;* René d'Herblay: *Donna Alexander.* Director: *Chris Monks;* Musical Director & Keyboards: *Akintayo Akinbode;* Flute: *Ali Russell;* Guitar: *Pete Owen;* Design: *Elizabeth Lynch;* Lighting: *David Winpenny;* Fight Director: *Renny Krupinski;* Production Manager: *Helen Maguire;* Stage Manager: *Karen Smith;* Technician: *Tom Weir.*
Journal: 11/3/94

293. **THE GOOD PERSON OF SICHUAN** by Berholt Brecht, translated by Michael Hofman; ARDEN SCHOOL OF THEATRE; *30 June - 2 July 1994.* Wang:

Christopher Rogers; First God/ Boy/Ni Tzu: *Sarah McAdam;* Second God/Niece: *Michelle Myers;* Third God/Grandfather/ Old Prostitute: *Yasmin Karlinska;* Shen Te/Shui Ta: *Nicola Barnfield:* Mrs Shin/Sister in Law: *Vicki Stevens;* The Wife/ Mrs Mi Tzu/Mrs Yang: *Beki Whitney;* The Husband/Priest: *John Draycott;* Nephew/Yang Sun: *Graham Proctor;* Unemployed Man/Brother/Shu Fu: *Lawrence Gough;* Lin To/ Policeman/Waiter: *Andrew Fillis.* Director: *Stephen Whitehouse;* Design: *Paul Brown;* Production Manager: *Helen Maguire;* Lighting: *Christine Knibbs, Thomas Weir;* Stage Manager: *Christine Knibbs;* Technician: *Tom Weir;* Additional Scenic Artist: *Jason Redgrave.*

294. OFF THE ROAD;
devised and performed by ARDEN BTEC PERFORMING ARTS COURSE; *30 June - 1 July 1994.*

118. THE MODERN HUSBAND by Henry Fielding; ARDEN SCHOOL OF THEATRE; *6 & 9 July 1994.* Lord Richly: *Mr (Marc) Goodall;* Mr Bellamant: *Mr (Shaun) Dooley;* Captain Bellament: *Mr (Andrew) Pope;* Mr Gaywit: *Mr (Noel) Wilson;* Mr Modern: *Mr (Lawrence) Gough;* Lady Charlotte Gaywit: *Mrs (Zoë) Lucker;* Mrs Bellamant: *Mrs (Dawn) Williams;* Mrs Modern: *Mrs (Emma) Kanis;* Emilia: *Mrs (Louise) Nulty;* Lately: *Mrs (Susan) Macleod;* Lord Lazy: *Mr (Gavin) Morris;* Colonel Courtly: *Mr (Gary) Williams;* Mr Woodall: *Mr (David) Brown;* Captain Merit: *Mr*

(Martin) Hill; Captain Bravemore/John: *Mr (Ralph) Casson;* Porter: *Mr (Andrew) Fillis;* Servants: *Mrs (Jennifer) Farley, Mrs (Julie) Calvert, Mrs (Stephanie) Tabner.* Director: *Helen Parry;* Set: *Shaun Dooley;* Text transcribed from original manuscript: *James White;* Lighting Board: *Tom Weir;* Sound: *Lawtrence Gough;* Sound Operator: *Uki Amaechi.*
Journal: *6/7/94*

299. TORY! TORY! TORY!;
MANCHESTER ACTORS COMPANY; *October 1994*
ARK THEATRE, Shena Simon College, Whitworth Street, M1 3HB; 061–236 3418. AZ: 102, A5; 166, B1.

295. WAITING FOR LIFE;
Book and Lyrics by Shane Cullinan; Music by Gary Nuttall; V1 THEATRE GROUP; *27 February 1994.* Young Susan: *Clare Feely;* Caroline/Mother: *Lorna Curran;* Patricia Clancy: *Gemma Feely;* Susan Stables: *Elizabeth Barret;* Angel: *Claire O'Brien;* Devil: *Wole Sawyerr;* Bobby (Aged 10)/Young Phillip: *Stefano Girolami;* Andrew (Aged 10): *Marc Withington;* Simon (Aged 10): *Jordan Dudley;* Bobby (Aged 15)/Milkman: *Simon Connelly;* Andrew (Aged 15): *Daniel Wright;* Simon (Aged 15): *Jack Murphy;* Bobby Stables: *Shane Cullinan;* Andrew Stables: *Michael Pender;* Simon Stables: *Mark Heywood;* Mrs Balreave-Jones: *Sarah Regan;* Liyla: *Jayne Banks;* Didi: *Laure Carter;* Phillip Stanley: *Yoshio Tazaki;* Hilary

Pinter/Grandma: *Claire Walsh;* Devil Girls: *Eliozabeth Byrne, Catrionas McKeeva;* Young Angel: *Patricia Keville.* MUSICIANS: Piano: *Gary Nuttall;* Keyboards: *Matthew Steele;* Electric/Acoustic Guitars: *Neil Anderson;* Saxophone: *Magda Kokocinska;* Bass Guitar: *Ann Phillips;* Percussion: *Collum Coss.* Director: *Shane Cullinan;* Producers: *Shane Cullinan & Ann Phillips;* Musical Director: *Gary Nuttall;* Stage Manager: *Ann Phillips, Louise Dalton;* Lighting: *Richard Clarke, Paul Muskat;* Sound: *Gareth Knight.*

296. RITES OF PASSAGE; CITY OF DRAMA project, involving students from BURNAGE, NEWALL GREEN, OAKWOOD & TRINITY HIGH SCHOOLS, SHENA SIMON COLLEGE & MANCHESTER METROPOLITAN UNIVERSITY SCHOOL OF THEATRE; *May 1994.* Cast includes: *Kate Hambleton, Lesley Ayres, Samantha Pope.* See also **544** and **545**, part of the project.

109. THE ROVER by Aphra Behn; SHENA SIMON THEATRE STUDIES; *15-17 June 1994.* Florinda: *Kate Hambleton;* Hellena: *Alexandra Morris;* Valeria: *Nichola Wren;* Callis: *Susan Worthy;* Pedro: *Graham Bell;* Frederick: *Rachel Walter;* Belvile: *Gavin Eaton;* Blunt: *James Kinsella;* Willmore: *Sam Pope;* Sancho: *Lee Fisher;* Lucetta: *Sam Brandolani;* Angellica: *Lisa Rudge;* Moretta: *Rosalie Carew;* Antonio: *Lesley Ayres.* Director: *Helen Larder;* Set: *Francis Fitzgerald, Susun Worthy, Lee Fisher;* Lighting: *Tim*

Benson, Rory McGregor, James Leigh, Kye Edwards, Steve Parkinson, Malcolm Cooper; Sound: *Nathan Brooks, Andrew Long;* Costumes: *Rachel Walter, Nicola Wren, Lisa Rudge, Alex Morris.* **Journal:** *17 June 1994*

ASSHETON ROAD MOBILE LIBRARY, Newton Heath, M40; **AZ:** 52, 1A; **XAZ:** 89 1F.

124. THE TIGER WITH GOLDEN CLAWS, c) & d); MANCHESTER ACTORS COMPANY; *15 July 1994*

BAGULEY MOBILE LIBRARY, Floatshall Road, M23; **AZ:** 81, D3; **XAZ:** 127, 5H.

124. THE TIGER WITH GOLDEN CLAWS; MANCHESTER ACTORS COMPANY; *12 July 1994.*

BARLOW MOOR LIBRARY; 21 Merseybank Avenue, M21 2NW; 061– 446 2061; **AZ:** 71, 3E; **XAZ:** 116, 5B.

432. CHATTERBOX PUPPETS; *17 August 1994.* John Piper.

301. BIG BAD WOLF; MANCHESTER ACTORS COMPANY; *December 1994.*

BESWICK LIBRARY; Grey
Mare Lane, M11 3AZ;
061-223 9614; **AZ**: 51,
4E; **XAZ**: 88, 5C.

429. EVERYONE KNOWS
WHAT A DRAGON LOOKS
LIKE; ACE PUPPETS; *1 August
1994.*

301. BIG BAD WOLF;
MANCHESTER ACTORS
COMPANY; *December 1994.*

**BLACK RESOURCE
CENTRE,** The Old Library,
Cheetham Hill Road, M8
7JW; **061-740 7575.**
AZ: 40,A3; **XAZ**: 74,B3.

**BODDINGTON'S CREAM
TENT;** forecourt of British
Council Headquarters,
Medlock Street, M15 4AA;
AZ: 105, 1F; **XAZ**: 165,
3G

297. THE FABULOUS
LYPSINKA SHOW; created and
performed by John Epperson;
SANDPIPER PRODUCTIONS;
10-11 September 1994.
Director: *Kevin Malony;* Lighting
Design: *Douglas Kuhrt;* Lighting
Plot: *Doug Pete Porras;*
Soundtrack Engineer: *Alex Noyes;*
Costume Design: *Anthony Wong,
Mark Happel;* Costume Execution:
Mark Happel; Wig Design: *Mathu
Anderson;* Backdrop Illustration:
Robert Anderson; Company and

Stage Managers: *Mig Kimpton,
Douglas Kuhrt.*
Press: T: *29/4/94.*

390. HEADLINE CABARET;
14 & 22 September 1994.
Performers: *Dave Gorman, Roger
Monkhouse, Hovis Presley, Ian
Baskeville, Matt Seber, Claire
Mooney, Tim Woodhouse, Janine
Campbell, Johny Dangerously;*
Comère: *Tara Newley.*

BRITON'S PROTECTION,
50 Great Bridgewater
Street, M1 5LE; 061-236
5869.

300. THE MAIDS by Jean
Genet, translated by Bernard
Frechtman; MANCHESTER
ACTORS COMPANY; *5, 8, 12
June 1994.* Claire: *Nigel
Capper;* Solange: *Steve Tabner;*
Madame: *Michael McKrell.*
Direction & Design: *Stephen
Boyes.*
Press: CL: *1/6/94;* **MEN:**
10/6/94.

**BLACKLEY MOBILE
LIBRARY;** Kendrew Walk,
M9 4AJ. **AZ**: 41, D2;
XAZ: 75, G2.

124. THE TIGER WITH
GOLDEN CLAWS;
MANCHESTER ACTORS
COMPANY; *22 July 1994.*

BROOKLANDS LIBRARY;
4 Maple Road, M23 9HJ;
061-973 7996; **AZ**: 80,

A1; **XAZ:** 126, C3.

301. BIG BAD WOLF;
MANCHESTER ACTORS
COMPANY; *December 1994.*

BURLINGTON ROOMS,
The University of
Manchester, M13 9PL.

527. THE COMMUNICATION
CHORD; *8-11 March 1994.*

48. GIMME SHELTER by
Barrie Keeffe; MACATASHNIK
THEATRE COMPANY; *13 March
1994.*

522. LOVERS by Brian Friel;
STICKS AND STONES
THEATRE COMPANY; *15-17
March 1994.* Director: *Caoimhe
McAvinchey.*

523. THE ZOO STORY by
Edward Albee; STICKS AND
STONES THEATRE COMPANY;
15-17 March 1994.

BURNAGE LIBRARY;
Burnage Lane, M19 1EW;
061-442 9036; **AZ:** 73,
E2; **XAZ:** 118, B3.

301. BIG BAD WOLF;
MANCHESTER ACTORS
COMPANY; *December 1994.*

BURNAGE VILLAGE HALL,
West Avenue, MI9, 2NY;
061-224 1584; **AZ:** 73,

D1; **XAZ:** 118, B2. G

303. THE CONSTANT WIFE
by W Somerset Maugham;
BURNAGE GARDEN VILLAGE
PLAYERS; *8-13 November
1993.* Mrs Culver: *Barbara
Williamson;* Bentley: *Nina
Westley;* Martha Culver: *Carmel
Vernon;* Barbara Fawcett:
Elizabeth Vernon; Constance
Middleton: *Diane Owen;* Marie-
Louise Durham: *Elaine Hughes;*
John Middleton FRCS: *Malcolm
Cooper;* Bernard Kersal: *Stuart
Cammack;* Mortimer Durham:
Tony Hughes. Producer: *Harold
Onions;* Stage Manager: *Geoff
Goulding;* Stage, Set Erection,
Décor: *Geoff Goulding, Tony
Hughes, Robert Owen, Hughes
Owen Thornborough Williamson;*
Sound: *Robert Owen;* Wardrobe:
Pat Cammack; Properties: *Jean
Short;* Prompt: *Barbara Goulding.*

302. TOM, DICKON, HARRY
by Christopher Denys; BURNAGE
GARDEN VILLAGE PLAYERS;
14-19 February 1994. Tom:
Stuart Cammack; Dickon:
Malcolm Cooper; Joan: *Kath
Hindle;* Old Joan: *Mavis
Kennersley;* Henry: *Chris Stenson;*
Caxton: *Tony Hughes;* Margaret:
Pat Cammack; Godfrey: *Steve
Millns.* Producer: *Harold Onions;*
Stage Manager: *Geoff Goulding;*
Set Design: *Robert Owen;* Set
Construction: *Geoff Goulding,
Tony Hughes, Robert Owen,
Hughes Owen Thornborough
Williamson;* Sound: *Robert Owen;*
Wardrobe Co-ordination: *Pat
Cammack;* *Barbara Goulding,
Elizabeth Vernon, Barbara
Williamson;* Properties: *Jean
Short;* Prompt: *Barbara Goulding,,*

261

Elizabeth Vernon.

305. LADIES IN RETIREMENT by Edward Percy and Reginald Denham; BURNAGE GARDEN VILLAGE PLAYERS; *25-30 April 1994.* Lucy Gilham: *Kath Hindle;* Leonora Fiske: *Mabe McKee;* Ellen Creed: *Barbara Williamson;* Albert Feather: *Chris Stenson;* Louisa Creed: *Elizabeth Vernon;* Emily Creed: *Mavis Kennersley;* Sister Theresa: *Margaret Millns.* Producer: *Harold Onions;* Stage Manager: *Geoff Goulding;* Set Design, Construction & Lighting: *Geoff Goulding, Tony Hughes, Robert Owen, Thornborough Williamson;* Sound: *Tony Hughes;* Wardrobe: *Elsie Clarke;* Properties: *Jean Short;* Prompt: *Barbara Goulding*

306. BIG BAD MOUSE by Philip King and Falkland Cary; BURNAGE GARDEN VILLAGE PLAYERS; *7-12 November 1994.*

BUTLER STREET MOBILE LIBRARY; Miles Platting, M4; **AZ:** 102, C3; **XAZ:** 163, G3.

124. THE TIGER WITH GOLDEN CLAWS; MANCHESTER ACTORS COMPANY; *15 July 1994.*

CAPITOL, School Lane, DIDSBURY, M20 0HT; **061-448 1845. AZ:** 72, C4; **XAZ:** 117, G6.

307. TWELFTH NIGHT by William Shakespeare; MANCHESTER METROPOLITAN UNIVERSITY SCHOOL OF THEATRE; *26-30 October 1993.* Sir Andrew Aguecheek: *Adam Cockerton;* Orsino: *Steve Durbin;* Fabian/Curio: *Adam Evans;* Maria: *Ann Marie Frater;* Ferdinand/1st Officer/Captain: *Dennis Herdman;* Sir Toby Belch: *Ben Hull;* Sebastian: *Joel Lawrence;* Olivia: *Collette Murray;* Priest: *James Nickerson;* Viola: *Kati Spencer;* Antonio/Valentine: *Alex Whetham;* Malvolio: *Steve Wright;* Feste: *David Wotton.* Director: *Alexander Clements;* Musical Arrangement: *Judy Kent;* Additional Music: *Ben Hull;* Set Design & Construction: *Bill Connor;* Lighting and Sound: *Mark Thurston;* Wardrobe Supervisor: *Sheila Payne;* Stage Management: *Jennie Lamont.*

308. THE WOMEN OF TROY by Euripides; MANCHESTER METROPOLITAN UNIVERSITY SCHOOL OF THEATRE; *10-13 November 1993.* Hecuba: *Jane Bellamy;* Chorus: *Sarah Jane Field, Anne Louise Grimshaw, Clare Jarvis, Victoria Morris, Juliet Ranger;* Cassandra/Chorus: *Sarah Kirkman;* Poseidon/Menelaus/Chorus: *James Nickerson;* Andromache/Chorus: *Laura Richmond;* Helen/Chorus: *Joanne Riding;* Talthybius: *Richard Stevens;* Athene/Chorus: *Kerrie Thomas.* Director: *Peter Lichtenfels;* Design & Construction: *Bill Connor;* Lighting and Sound: *Mark Thurston;* Wardrobe Supervisor: *Sheila Payne;* Stage Management: *Jennie Lamont;* Work Experience

Student: *Loretta Rodgers.*

309. WHO CARES?, compiled from various Medieval cycles of Mystery Plays; MANCHESTER METROLPOLITAN UNIVERSITY SCHOOL OF THEATRE; *15-18 December 1993.* Cherubim/ Mothers Chorus/Camel: *Jane Bellamy;* Isaac/Devil's Chorus: *Adam Cockerton;* Noah/Devil/ Soldier/Shepherd: *Steve Durbin;* Abel/King: *Adam Evans;* Cherubim: *Sarah Jane Field;* Herod/Sheep/Devil's Chorus/ Mothers Chorus: *Anne Marie Frater;* Herod/Mothers Chorus: *Ann Louise Grimshaw;* Adam/ King/Soldier: *Dennis Herdman;* Abraham/Soldier/Shepherd: *Ben Hull;* Mak's Wife/Devil's Chorus: *Clare Jarvis;* Mary/Angel: *Sarah Kirkman;* Jesus/Angel/King: *Joel Lawrence;* Angel/Singer/Mothers Chorus: *Collette Murray;* Devil's Chorus/Mothers Chorus: *Victoria Morris;* Joseph/Devil's Chorus: *James Nickerson;* Angel Gabriel: *Laura Richmond;* Mrs Noah/Angel/ Mothers Chorus: *Joanne Riding;* Death: *Juliet Ranger;* Eve: *Kati Spencer;* Cain/Soldier/Devil: *Richard Stevens;* Mothers Chorus/ Devil's Chorus: *Kerrie Thomas;* Herod's Councillor/God's Assistant: *Alex Whetham;* God: *David Wotton;* Lucifer/Mak: *Stephen Wright.* Director: *Lee Beagley;* Design & Construction: *Bill Connor;* Lighting and Sound: *Mark Thurston;* Wardrobe Supervisor: *Sheila Payne;* Stage Management: *Jennie Lamont;* Additional Designs: *Martin Butler, Mike Griggs, Jane Hammit.*

310. KING LEAR by William Shakespeare; KABOODLE; *20-24 October 1992.* Gloucester:

Steven Rayworth; Kent: *Nick Birkinshaw;* Edmund: *Steven Book;* Edgar: *Russ Edwards;* Lear: *Lee Beagley;* Fool: *Paula Simms;* Goneril: *Esther Wilson;* Regan: *Laura Richmond;* Cordelia: *Kati Spencer;* Cornwall: *Matt Mason;* Albany: *Stepohen Chapman;* Burgundy: *Steve Givnan;* France: *Russ Edwards;* Oswald: *Steve Givnan;* Chorus (Knights and Beggars): *Steven Book, Steve Givnan, Matt Mason, Kati Spencer, Russ Edwards, Stephen Chapman;* Music: *Eleanor Knight, George Ricci.* Directors: *Lee Beagley & Josette Bushell-Mingo;* Music Direction & Composition: *Andy Frizell;* Production Management: *Spencer Hazel;* Tripod Design: *Mark Hill;* Costume Design & Stage Management: *Amanda Bracegirdle;* Costume Assistant: *Fabienne Pym;* Lighting Design: *Steve Curtis.* **Press: BI:** 28/2/94; **G:** 1/3/94; **P:** Feb 1994

49. YERMA by Federico García Lorca, translated by David Johnson; MANCHESTER METROPOLITAN SCHOOL OF THEATRE; *23-26 February 1994.* Storyteller: *Adam Cockerton;* Boy: *Sam Donaldson;* Shepherd, Mask: *Steve Durbin;* Maria: *Sarah-Jane Field;* Dolores, Washer Woman: *Ann Marie Frater;* Washer Woman, Old Woman: *Ann Louise Grimshaw;* Victor: *Ben Hull;* Girl: *Clare Jarvis;* Sister in Law, Girl, Mask: *Victoria Morris,* Sister in Law, Woman: *Juliet Ranger;* Pagan Woman: *Joanne Sherry;* Yerma: *Kerrie Thomas;* Juan: *Stephen Wright;* Musicians, Peasants: *Jan Linnik, Maike Mullenders, David Slater, Terence Chapman.*

263

Directors: *Bill Hopkinson, Patricia Roy;* Design & Construction: *Bill Connor;* Lighting and Sound: *Mark Thurston;* Wardrobe Supervisor: *Sheila Payne;* Stage Management: *Jennie Lamont;* Music: *Carol Donaldson;* Choreography: *Iseult de Graal;* Mask Makers: *Lorraine Hackett, David Mason.*
Journal: *23/2/94*

311. TARTUFFE by Molière; MANCHESTER METROPOLITAN SCHOOL OF THEATRE; *9-12 March 1994.* Dorine: *Jane Bellamy;* Police Officer/Filipote: *Adam Evans;* Valere: *Dennis Herdman;* Elmire: *Sarah Kirkman;* M. Loyal: *Joel Lawrence;* Mdm Pernelle: *Collette Murray;* Orgon: *James Nickerson;* Mariane: *Pauline Shanahan;* Tartuffe: *Richard Stevens;* Damis: *Alex Whetham;* Cleante: *David Wotton.* Director: *Peter Lichtenfels;* Design & Construction: *Bill Connor;* Lighting and Sound: *Mark Thurston;* Wardrobe Supervisor: *Sheila Payne;* Stage Management: *Jennie Lamont;* Design Assistant: *Sheryl Robertson.*

312. BOUNDARY; devised by Sheila Hill and IOU THEATRE COMPANY; *24-27 March 1994.* Performers: *Kazuko Hohki, Stephanie Jalland, Caroline England, Jag Plah, Nabil Shaban;* Maker/Performers: *Tony Newman, Andy Platt, Jane Revitt, Chris Squire, Suzy Thomas, Bryan Tweddle;* Composer/Musicians: *Clive Bell, David Humpage;* Words and Lyrics/Maker: *Louise Oliver.* Director/Maker: *David Wheeler;* Lighting Design: *John Cumming;* Lighting Operator: *Tim*

Haunton.
Press: MEN: *25/3/94;* SAM: *10/3/94*

313. A VIEW FROM THE BRIDGE by Arthur Miller; KABOODLE; *19-23 April 1993.* Alfieri: *Stephen Steven Rayworth;* Marco: *Stephen Book;* Rudolpho: *Russ Edwards;* Eddie Carboni: *Lee Beagley;* Beatrice: *Laura Richmond;* Catherine: *Kati Spencer;* Mike: *Steve Chapman;* Louis: *Steve Givnan;* Music: *George Ricci.* Directors: *Lee Beagley, Paula Simms;* Costume, Production and Tour Management: *Amanda Bracebridge;* Music Direction and Composition: *Andy Frizzell;* Lighting Design: *Spencer Haze;* Lighting Technician: *Alasdair Graebner;* Language Tutor: *Claudio Filocamo.*
Press: BI: *5/5/94;* G: *28/3/94;* MM: *22/4/94;* OC: *12/5/94;* S: *19/5/94*

93. FUENTE OVEJUNA by Lope de Vega, translated by Adrian Mitchell; MANCHESTER METROPOLITAN UNIVERSITY SCHOOL OF THEATRE; *18-21 May 1994.* Don Manrique/Barrildo: *Adam Cockerton;* Cimbranos/Alonso: *Steve Durbin;* Grand Master Rodrigo Tellez Giron: *Adam Evans;* Laurentia: *Ann Marie Frater;* Mengo: *Ann Louise Grimshaw;* Frondoso/Leonelo: *Dennis Herdman;* Sergeant Ortuna: *Ben Hull;* Pascuala: *Clare Jarvis;* Alderman/Father Oliver: *Joel Lawrence;* Jacinta: *Victoria Morris;* King Ferdinand/Juan Rojo: *James Nickerson;* Queen Isabella of Castile: *Juliet*

GABRIEL GAWIN (Director, right), with RICHARD STEVENS (Julius) and KERRIE THOMAS (The Woman [who was] Asleep), as they explore BOTHO STRAUS' dialogue in TIME AND THE ROOM (107)

Ranger; Commander Fernando Gomez: *Alex Whetham,* Esteban: *David Wotton;* Captain Flores: *Stephen Wright.* Director: *Andrew Farrell;* Assistant Director: *Victoria Morris;* Design & Construction: *Bill Connor;* Lighting & Sound: *Mark Thurston;* Wardrobe Supervisor: *Sheila Payne;* Stage Management: *Jennie Lamont;* Music: *Ben Hull, Steve Durbin,* other members of cast. **Journal:** 20/5/94

105. TOUCHED by Stephen Lowe; MANCHESTER METROPOLITAN UNIVERSITY SCHOOL OF THEATRE; *1 June 1994.* Betty: *Jane Bellamy;* Bridie: *Sarah Jane Ellis;* Sandra: *Sarah Kirkman;* Johnny: *Joel Lawrence;* Mary: *Victoria Morris;* Pauline: *Maike Mullanders;* Joan:

Collette Murray; Mother: *Juliet Ranger;* Harry: *Mark Walker;* Keith: *David Wotton.* Director: *Romy Baskerville;* Design & Construction: *Bill Connor;* Lighting and Sound: *Mark Thurston;* Wardrobe Supervisor: *Sheila Payne;* Stage Management: *Jennie Lamont.* **Journal:** 1/6/94

107. TIME AND THE ROOM by Botho Strauss, Translated by Tony Meech; MANCHESTER METROPOLITAN SCHOOL OF THEATRE; *15-18 June 1994.* Julius: *Richard Stevens;* Steve Durbin: *Olaf;* Marie Steuber: *Joanne Sherry;* Man With No Watch: *James Nickerson;* The Impatient Woman: *Sarah Jane Field;* Frank Arnold: *Adam Evans;* The Woman Asleep: *Kerrie Thomas;* Man in a Winter Coat:

Adam Cockerton; The Completely Unknown Man: Alex Whatham; The Column: David Wotton. Director: Gabriel Gawin; Rehearsal Dramateur: Thomas Kraus; Design and Construction: Bill Connor; Lighting and Sound: Mark Thurston; Wardrobe Supervisor: Sheila Payne; Stage Management: Jennie Lamont.
Journal: 18/6/94

110. BIG MOUNTAIN by John Wood; M6 THEATRE COMPANY; 20-24 June 1994. Ruth: Carole Copeland; Amy: Alison Darling; Ishi/Narrator/Servant: Steve James; Dominique/Policeman: Yomi Michaels. Director: Joe Sumsion; Music: Julian Ronnie; Design: Jon Carnall; Lighting: Jenny Kagan; Stage Manager: Anna Howarth; Technical Stage Manager: Paul Towson; Set Construction: Steve Kirk; Stage Crew: Simon Knowles, Edward Armitage, Steve Chambers.
Journal: 20/6/94
Press: MM: 9/9/94; **RO:** 26/6/94

314. THE TEA LADY by Tony Broughton; STRINES THEATRE; 5-8 October 1994. Annie Horniman/Theatre Goer/et al: June Broughton; Guide/Flanagan/Irishman/et al: Tony Broughton; Music/Men in Street/et al: John Spooner. Director: Colin Stevens; Gown: Charles Alty; Design: June Broughton; Velvet Tabs: Brenda Holton; Lighting: Bill Connor; Set Construction: Derek Cochrane; Choreography: Caroline Clegg; Sound: Stan Bannister.
Press: MEN: 30/9/94, 6/10/94

315. PYGMALION by Bernard Shaw; MANCHESTER METROPOLITAN UNIVERSITY SCHOOL OF THEATRE; 26-29 October 1994. Director: Dominic Cooke.

316. RICHARD III by William Shakespeare; MANCHESTER METROPOLITAN UNIVERSITY SCHOOL OF THEATRE; 9-12 November 1994. Director: Peter Lichtenfels.

317. MR PUNTILA AND HIS MAN MATTI by Bertold Brecht; MANCHESTER METROPOLITAN SCHOOL OF THEATRE; 14-17 December 1994. Director: Annie Castledine; Movement: Monika Pagneux.

CASTLEFIELD ART GALLERY; 5 Campfield Avenue; DEANSGATE; M60 3DQ; 061- 832 8034; AZ: 105, E1; XAZ: 165, F2.

436. THE MAIDS by Jean Genet; BPF; 5 July 1994.

CATHEDRAL, M3 1SX. AZ: 101,F3; XAZ: 161,H3.

94. MURDER IN THE CATHEDRAL by T S Eliot; THE ARDEN SCHOOL OF THEATRE; 26-28 May 1994. Thomas: John Draycott; 1st Nun: Vicki Stevens; 2nd Nun: Rachel Gleaves; 3rd Nun: Laura Wolf; Messenger: Jo Burgess; 1st

Tempter: *Tara Daniels*; 2nd
Tempter/2nd Knight: *Andrew
Fillis*; 3rd Tempter/1st Knight:
Steven Hillman; 4th Tempter:
Donna Alexander and *Yasmin
Karlinska*; 3rd Knight: *Graham
Proctor*; 4th Knight: *Chris
Rogers*; Women of Canterbury:
*Eilis Hetherington, Zoë Ginster,
Joanne Curley, Tracy Shaw,
Michelle Myers, Fiona Macdonald,
Susan Sands, Emma Ferguson,
Helen Lacey, Lindi Glover, Leah
Stanley, Beki Whitney, Sarah
ZMcAdam, Carla Steele, Nicola
Barnfield*; Child of Canterbury:
Amy Warhurst; Choir: *Eilidh
Alexander, Sophie Bates,
Katherine Berryman, Matthew
Bryon; Robert Curbishley, Kerry
Gannon, Dawn Finnerty, Terence
Hughes, Mandy Hunter, Kathleen
Johnson, Men Yee Lai, Paul
Lomax, Ian Maher, Robert Munro,
Christian Newton, Kathryn
Pemberton, Richard Raduechel,
Alice Selwyn, Rachel Shore,
Elizabeth Taylor, Helen
Warburton, ZMohammed Wasim,
Fiona Wass, Karen West, Susan
Womersley, Mark Wood.*
Director: *Peter Oyston*; Lighting:
Paul Colley; Production Manager:
Helen Maguire; Stage Manager:
Karen Smith; Technician: *Tom
Weir*; Set Construction: *Carl
Richardson, Jan Callaghan*;
Composer/Organist: *Chris Rogers*;
Flautist: *Sam Kynaston.*
Journal: 28/5/94

THE CELLAR, Union
Building, Manchester
University M13 9PL; 061–
275 2930; **AZ:** 103, A4;
XAZ: 101, F2.

515. HANDMAIDS by Juliet

Raynsford, based on *The
Handmaid's Tale* by Margaret
Atwood; *8 March.* Director:
Juliet Raynsford.

519. THE VIRTUOUS BURLAR
by Dario Fo; THE ACTIVE
PERFORMANCE SOCIETY; *14–
15 March 1994.*

520. RIDERS TO THE SEA
by J M Synge; THE ACTIVE
PERFORMANCE SOCIETY; *14–
15 March.*

CENTRAL LIBRARY; St
Peter's Square, M2 5PD;
234 1974; **AZ:** 101, F5;
XAZ: 165, H1.

298. SHAKESPEARE'S
GREATEST HITS; devised by
Stephen Boyes; MANCHESTER
ACTORS COMPANY; *3 February
1994.* Juliet/Calpurnia/Lady
MacBeth/TV Reporter/Julie:
Stephanie Pearce; Julius Caesar/
MacBeth/First Fairy/Julie's Mum:
Nigel Capper; Romeo/Oberon/
Servant/Political Correspondent/
Ronnie: *Ian Lingard*; Mark
Anthony/Puck/Decius Brutus/
American Tourist: *Steve Tabner.*
Director: *Stephen Boyes*; Design:
Kate Jowatt

435. PLAYED BACK;
EXPERIENCE PLAY BACK
THEATRE; *22 June 1994.*

428. DREAMS' WINTER;
FORCED ENTERTAINMENT; *15–
20 July 1994.* Performers:
*Robin Arthur, Richard Lowdon,
Claire Marshall, Cathy Naden,
Terry O'Connor, Sue Marshall,
Paulette Terry Brien, Kath Cook,*

Jamie McAffer, Kit McCudden, Michelle Stanbridge, Ellen Mills, Alex Bliss, Fleur Soper, Ian Greenall, Tim Hall, Juliet Sebley, Susan Scott, Susie Dick, Nicola J Bertram, Steve King, Alex Kelly, Rachel Walton, Nicky Beaumont, Steve Jackson, Liz Tomlin. Director: Tim Etchells; Design and Lighting: Richard Lowdon; Text: Tim Etchells and the Company; Administration: Deborah Chadbourn; Soundtrack: John Avery; Sound Assistant: Emma Leslie; Producer: Stella Hall.
Press: CL: 13/7/94; **MEN:** 11&14/7/94; **MM:** 15/7/94; **S:** 18/8/94

301. BIG BAD WOLF; MANCHESTER ACTORS COMPANY; December 1994.

CHARLESTOWN ROAD MOBILE LIBRARY,
Charlestown, M9; **AZ:** 41, E1; **XAZ:** 62, 6A.

124. THE TIGER WITH GOLDEN CLAWS; MANCHESTER ACTORS COMPANY; 4 July 1994.

CHEETHAM HILL MOBILE LIBRARY, Heywood Street, M8; **AZ:** 40, 4A; **XAZ:** 74, C5.

124. THE TIGER WITH GOLDEN CLAWS; MANCHESTER ACTORS COMPANY; 5 July 1994.

CHINESE ARTS CENTRE,

36 Charlotte Street, M1 4FD; 061–236 9251; **AZ:** 101, G5; **XAZ:** 162, B6.

263. MOON CHANT by Local British Chinese; 19 September 1994. Participants: Graham Chan; Fay Cherje, Pauline Kam, Kwong Lee, Kim Leung, Peter Leung, Florence Li, Rosa Lo, Christina Pau, Tai Lai Kwan. Directors and Facilitators: Veronica Needa, David Tse.
Jounal: 19/9/94

CHORLTON LIBRARY;
Manchester Road, M21 1PN; 061–881 3179; **AZ:** 59, D4; **XAZ:** 99, H6. W.

299. TORY! TORY! TORY! Written and Performed by Stephen Boyes; MANCHESTER ACTORS COMPANY; 11 April 1994. Design: Nick Hyam Edwards.

432. CHATTERBOX PUPPETS; 23 August. John Piper.

301. BIG BAD WOLF; MANCHESTER ACTORS COMPANY; December 1994.

CLAYTON LIBRARY; 2
Clayton Street, M11 4HR; 061– 223 2065; **AZ:** 52, F2; **XAZ:** 89, D3.

301. BIG BAD WOLF; MANCHESTER ACTORS COMPANY; December 1994.

COLLIERS, 4 Dale Street, M1 1JW; 061-236 5141; AZ: 102, A4; **XAZ:** 162, B5.

318. MISSIS MOSES by John D Slater; BIJOU THEATRE PRODUCTIONS; *27-30 October 1994.* Missis Moses: *Denise Baglow.* Director: *Colin Bean*

CONTACT, Oxford Road, M15 6JA; **061-274 4400 / 4747.** AZ: 60, B1 & 106, A4; XAZ: 101, F2. G, H, S, W.

31. DRACULA by Liz Lochhead, from the novel by Bram Stoker; *28 October-20 November 1993.* Mina Westerman: *Alison Fielding;* Lucy Westerman: *Jane Hollowood;* Florrie Hathersage: *Joy Blakeman;* Renfield: *Nicholas Blane;* Arthur Seward: *Simeon Andrews;* Nurse Nisbett/Nurse Grice: *Jill Graham;* Jonathan Harker: *Dominic Taylor;* Dracula: *Paul Brightwell;* Van Helsing: *Paul Humpoletz;* Orderly: *Mark Walker;* Children: *Phillip Williams, Luke Critchley, Josie Carhill, Ellen Tickle.* Director: *Brigid Larmour;* Design: *Simon Banham;* Movement: *Sue McLennan;* Music: *Mark Vibrans;* Lighting: *Chris Brockhouse;* Deputy Stage Manager on Book: *Stephen Sumner;* Assistant Director: *Victoria Moss;* Sign Language Interpreter: *Caroline Taylor;* Assistant Designer: *Andrew Wood;* Design Assistants: *Katie Mundy, Emma Tonge, Kerry Strong;* Design Student: *Stephie Seding;* Production Manager:

Hilary Russell; Chief Electrician: *Chris Brockhouse;* Deputy Electrician: *John Owen;* Master Carpenter: *Colin Honeyman;* Deputy Carpenter: *Jo Topping;* Construction: *Jez Horrox;* Stage Manager: *Sam Fraser;* Deputy: *Scott McDonald;* Assistant Stage Manager: *Jacqueline Bell;* Wardrobe Supervisor: *Kevin Pollard;* Deputy Supervisor: *Nicky Isaac;* Wardrobe Assistant: *Emma Harden.*

33. THE ADVENTURES OF TOM SAWYER by Mark Twain, adapted by Bryan elsley; Music by Julian Ronnie; *30 November 1993 - 15 January 1994.* Tom Sawyer: *Mark Niven;* Huckleberry Finn/Becky Thatcher: *Rachel Ogilvie;* Joe Harper/Dr Robinson/ Judge Thatcher: *Joseph Jones;* Aunt Polly/School Mistress/Muff Potter: *Yolande Bastide;* Sidney/ Injun Joe: *Michael Nardone;* MUSICIANS: Violin: *Simon Swarbrick;* Percussion: *Colin Seddon;* Keyboards: *Dave Whittleworth;* Guitars & Banjo: *James Muir Morrison.* Director: *Bryan Elsley;* Co-Director/ Choreographer: *Gregory Nash;* Musical Director: *Julian Ronnie;* Design: *Simon Banham;* Costume: *Kevin Pollard;* Aerial; Advisor: *Andy Gill;* Lighting: *Chris Brockhouse;* Sound: *John Owen;* Deputy Stage Manager on Book: *Scott McDonald;* Assistant Director: *Victoria Moss;* Assistant Designer: *Andrew Wood;* Design Student: *Helen Davies;* Production Manager: *Hilary Russell;* Chief Electrician: *Chris Brockhouse;* Deputy Electrician: *John Owen;* Master Carpenter: *Colin Honeyman;* Deputy Carpenter: *Jo Topping;* Construction: *Jez*

TOM SAWYER's resistance to Aunt Polly's recipes for good, clean living got the year off to a lively start at CONTACT; MARK NIVEN and YOLANDE BASTIDE in BRYAN ELSLEY's adaptatation of MARK TWAIN.

Horrox; Stage Manager: *Sam Fraser;* Deputy: *Scott McDonald;* Assistant Stage Manager: *Jacqueline Bell;* Wardrobe Supervisor: *Kevin Pollard;* Deputy Supervisor: *Nicky Isaac;* Wardrobe Assistant: *Emma Harden.* **Press: CL:** 8/12/93; **G:** 21/12/93 **MEN:** 2&16/12/93

32. ANGELS IN AMERICA by Tony Kushner; ROYAL NATIONAL THEATRE; *20-29 January 1993.* **Part One: THE MILLENIUM APPROACHES:** Rabbi Isidor Chemelwitz/Henry/Martin Heller/ Prior 1: *Harry Towb;* Roy M Cohn/Prior 2: *David Schofield;* Joseph Porter Pitt/Eskimo: *Daniel Craig;* Harper Amity Pitt: *Clare Holman;* Mr Lies/Belize: *Joseph Mydell;* Louis Ironson: *Jason Isaacs;* Prior Walter/Man in the Park: *Stephen Dillane;* The Voice/Emily/Sister Ella Chapter/ Woman in the South Bronx: *Nancy Crane;* Hannah Porter Pitt /Ethel Rosenberg: *Susan Engel;* Funeral Cantor: *Henry Goodman.* **Part Two: PERESTROIKA:** Rabbi Isidor Chemelwitz/Henry/Aleksii Antedilluvianovich Prelapsarianov: *Harry Towb;* Roy M Cohn: *David Schofield;* Joseph Porter Pitt/ Mormon Father/Europa: *Daniel Craig;* Harper Amity Pitt/ Africanii: *Clare Holman;* Mr Lies/Belize/Caleb/ Oceania: *Joseph Mydell;* Louis Ironson/ Australia/Sarah Ironson: *Jason Isaacs;* Prior Walter/ *Stephen Dillane;* The Angel/ Emily/Voice at the Mormon Visitors' Centre/ Mormon Mother/Orrin: *Nancy Crane;* Hannah Porter Pitt /Ethel Rosenberg/Asiatica: *Susan Engel;* Recorded Newsreader: *Robin Houston.* **Both Parts:** Director: *Declan Donnellan;*

MUSICIANS: Keyboards: *Duncan Chave;* Saxophone: *David Roach;* Design: *Nick Ormerod;* Original Lighting: *Mick Hughes;* Lighting Recreated: *Ian Williams;* Music: *Paddy Cunneen;* Director of Movement: *Joan Washington;* Company Voice Work: *Patsy Rodenburg;* Staff Directors: *Kenneth Mackintosh, Fiona Laird;* Production Manager: *Jason Barnes;* Company & Stage Manager: *David Milling;* Deputy Stage Manager: *Liz Ryder;* Assistant Stage Managers: *Andrew Eastcott, Garth Kelly;* Sound: *Freya Edwards;* Music Programming Consultants: *Duncan Chave, Freya Edwards;* Assistant Production Manager: *Miles King;* Costume Supervisor: *Angie Burns;* Design Assistant: *Laura Hibbs;* Technical Manager: *Harold Bowerman;* Operational Assisant: *Stuart Smith;* Rigger: *Lenny Thomas;* Stage Technicians: *Danny Boyle, Dave Malaley, Dessie Powell;* Chief Lighting Technician: *Ian Williams;* Senior Lighting Technicians: *Tim Bray, Mike Atkinson;* Sound Operator: *Sue Patrick;* Production Sound Engineer: *John Owens;* Wardrobe Supervisor: *Kathy Gordon;* Wig Mistress: *Beatrix Archer;* Wig Master: *Peter Grice;* Wig Assistant: *Hanne Bewernick.*
Press: G: 25/1/94; **MEN:** 21 & 24/1/94; **MM:** 28/1/94; **PP:** December 1993.

319. STRANGE ATTRACTORS
by Kevin Fegan; CONTACT THEATRE COMPANY; *10-26 February 1994.* Three: *Nicholas Murchie;* Nine: *Jane Hollowood;* Eight: *Kulvinder Ghir;* Hypnotist: *Yolande Bastide;* Jade: *Joy Blakeman;* Amber: *Alison Swann;*

Slatey: *Stephen Ventura;* Basalt: *Phillip King.* Directors: *Brigid Larmour, Richard Gregory;* Design: *Angela Davies;* Sign Interpreter: *Caroline Taylor;* Movement: *Sue McLennan;* Music: *Graeme Miller;* Fight Director: *Renny Krupinski;* Lighting: *Chris Brockhouse;* Sound: *John Owen;* Deputy Stage Manager on the book: *Stephen Sumner;* Design Assistants: *Katie Mundy, Totie Smith, Elaine Starks;* Design Student: *Natalie Tuckwell;* Production Manager: *Hilary Russell;* Chief Electrician: *Chris Brockhouse;* Deputy Electrician: *John Owen;* Master Carpenter: *Colin Honeyman;* Deputy Carpenter: *Jo Topping;* Construction: *Jez Horrox;* Stage Manager: *Sam Fraser;* Deputy: *Scott McDonald;* Assistant Stage Manager: *Jacqueline Bell;* Wardrobe Supervisor: *Kevin Pollard;* Deputy Supervisor: *Nicky Isaac;* Wardrobe Assistant: *Emma Harden;;* GRANADA TELEVISION PRODUCTION TEAM: Producer: *Gareth Morgan;* Graphic Designer/Animator: *David Jeffries;* Graphics Consultant: *Matt Howarth;* Editor: *Steve Seddon;* Camera: *Andy Hibbert;* Sound: *Ian Hills;* Sound Editor: *John Rotherham;* Make-Up: *Sally Hughes.*
Press: BI: 22/2/94; **MEN:** 11/2/94; **I:** 12/2/94; **O:** 13/2/94; **OC:** 11/2/94; **SAM:** 24/2/94.

320. DER BESUCH DER ALTEN DAME
by Friedrich Dürrenmatt; UNIVERSITY OF MANCHESTER GERMAN SOCIETY; *2-4 March 1994.* Clare Zachanassian: *Fiona Bingham;* Ihre Gatten: *Adrian*

Millward-Sadler; Der Butler:
Daryll Ezekiel; Toby: Ian Gordon;
Roby: Ed Palmer; Koby: Margitta
Kahrs; Loby: Ingrid-Marie Sauer;
Ill: Peter Davies; Frau Ill:
Mariane Arnot; Die Tochter:
Fiona Cragg; Der Sohn:
Johnathon Dinkeldein; Der
Bürgermeister: Simon Green; Der
Pfarrer: Michael Parsons; Die
Lehrerin: Catherine Schofield; Der
Artz: Richard Corcoran; Polizist:
Lydia Penke; Die Bürger:
Christine Mercer, Heater Moyes,
Sören Anders, Jim Siddle; Der
Maler: Richard Rouse; Die Frau:
Rebecca Jones; Fräulein Luise:
Fiona Cragg; Zugführer: Carolyn
Walker; Der Turner: Martin
Sinclair; Pfändungsbeamter:
Jonathan Dinkeldeein; Kamerafrau:
Clare Coombes; Radioreporterin:
Carolyn Walker. Directors:
Hannah Rees, Martin Sinclair;
Stage Manager: Mark Pollard;
Wardrobe: Christine Mercer;
Props: Mark Pollard, Claire
Collingworth, Ruth Kendall, Nic
Schofield, Victoria McMurruck;
SOund: Kay Billingham; Make-up:
Rachel Felix-Davies; Lights: Mark
Pollard, Martin Sinclair, Jo;
Language Consultants: Thomas
Kraus, Thomas Despositos; Special
Assistance: Alexandra Guski;
Incidental Music: Ed Palmer;
Music: John Sttephen.

324.   HUIS CLOS by Jean-
Paul Sartre; MANCHESTER
UNIVERSITY FRENCH
DEPARTMENT; 9-11 March
1994.

325.   IL FAUT QU'UNE
PORTE SOIT OUVERTE OU
FERMÉE by Alfred de Musset;
MANCHESTER UNIVERSITY
FRENCH DEPARTMENT; 9-11

March 1994.

343.   RAW CHUNKS; selections
of new work by MANCHESTER
UNIVERSITY DRAMA
DEPARTMENT; 12 March 1994.

60.   THE MAN WHO; Peter
Brook, with the collaboration of
Marie-Hélène Estienne and of the
performers, inspired by THE MAN
WHO MISTOOK HIS WIFE FOR
A HAT by Oliver Sachs;
tranlated from the French by
Peter Brook; Contributions to the
French language production:
Maurice Bénuchon; Poem LIVING
DEATH from book PRIDE AND
THE DAILY MARATHON by
Jonathon Coe; 16-26 March
1994. Performers: David
Bennent, Sotigui Kouyate, Bruce
Myers, Yoshi Oida; Music:
Mahmoud Tabrizi-Zadeh.
Director: Peter Brook; Literary
Adviser: Jean-Claude Carrière;
Video Images: Jean Claude
Lubtchansky; Technical Direction:
Jean-Guy Lcat; Stage
Management and Lighting: Philippe
Vialatte; Props and Costumes:
Mustapha El Amri; Producers:
William Wilkinson, Micheline
Rozan.
Journal: 26/3/94
Press: CL: 9/3/94; MEN: 10 &
18/3/94

75.   THE THREEPENNY
OPERA by Bertolt Brecht,
translated by Robert David
MacDonald; 13 April - 7 May
1994. Narrator: Michael
Vaughan; Jenny: Tessa Burbridge;
Mr Peachum: Robert Pickavance;
Filch/Matt the Mint: Stefan
Karsberg; Mrs Peachum: Elizabeth
Mansfield; MacHeath: Bernard
Lloyd; Polly Peachum: Josette

Bushell-Mingo; Tiger Brown: *Andrew Bolton;* Lucy: *Charlotte Barker;* Pianist: *Sally Bradnam;* Sign Interpreter: *Caroline Taylor.* Director: *Annie Castledine;* Design: *Simon Banham;* Movement: *Josette Bushell-Mingo;* Musical Director: *Tony Castro;* Lighting: *Nick Beadle;* Sound: *John Owen;* Deputy Stage Manager on Book: *Stephen Sumner;* Assistant Director: *Victoria Moss;* Assistant Designer: *Andrew Wood;* Design Assistants: *Katie Mundy, Michael Snodgrass, Kerry Strong;* Production Manager: *Hilary Russell;* Chief Electrician: *Chris Brockhouse;* Deputy Electrician: *John Owen;* Master Carpenter: *Colin Honeyman;* Deputy Carpenter: *Jo Topping;* Construction: *Jez Horrox;* Stage Manager: *Sam Fraser;* Deputy: *Scott McDonald;* Assistant Stage Manager: *Jacqueline Bell;* Wardrobe Supervisor: *Kevin Pollard;* Deputy Supervisor: *Nicky Isaac;* Wardrobe Assistant: *Emma Harden.*
Journal: 26/4/94
Press: CL: 20/4/94; **MEN:** 15/4/94; **MM:** 22/4/94; **SAM:** 7/4/94

321. THE FALL OF THE HOUSE OF USHER by Edgar Allan Poe, adapted by Steven Berkoff; CONTACT THEATRE COMPANY; *12 May – 4 June 1994.* Roderick Usher: *Kevin Walton;* Madeline Usher: *Orla Brady;* Edgar/Friend: *Stuart Bowman;* Musician: *Jane MacFarlane.* Director: *Bryan Elsley;* Signed Language Interpretor: *Caroline Taylor;* Movement Director: *Frank McConnell;* Design: *Simon Banham;* Music: *Jane MacFarlane;*

Lighting: *Chris Brockhouse;* Sound: *John Owen;* Deputy Stage Manager on the Book: *Scott McDonald;* Assistant Designer: *Andrew Wood;* Design Assistant: *Kerry Strong;* Production Manager: *Hilary Russell;* Chief Electrician: *Chris Brockhouse;* Deputy Electrician: *John Owen;* Master Carpenter: *Colin Honeyman;* Deputy Carpenter: *Jo Topping;* Construction: *Lee Pearson;* Stage Manager: *Sam Fraser;* Deputy: *Stephen Sumner;* Assistant Stage Manager: *Jacqueline Bell;* Wardrobe Supervisor: *Kevin Pollard;* Deputy Supervisor: *Nicky Isaac;* Wardrobe Assistant: *Emma Harden*
Press: MEN: 5 & 14/5/94; OC: 16/5/94.

CONTACT YOUNG PLAYWRIGHTS' FESTIVAL:

100. FRIDAY THE HALLOWEENTH by Richard Parkin; *8 & 10 June 1994.* Simon: *Stephen Ventura;* Robert: *Jim Byrne;* Regor/Roger: *Michael Brent;* Demon: *Debra Penny;* Teacher: *Sally Sheridan;* Becky: *Carolyn Bazely.* Director: *Jacqui Home;* Director's Assistant: *Nigel Higginson.*

99. THE NEW ARRIVAL by Eliane Byrne; *8 & 10 June 1994.* Emma: *Debra Penny;* Chris: *Jim Byrne;* Chloë: *Carolyn Bazely;* Mark: *Michael Brent;* James: *Stephen Ventura;* Carol: *Sally Sheridan.* Director: *Renny O'Shea.*

101. DON'T CRY OUT LOUD by Louise Anders; *8 & 10 June 1994.* Gillian: *Sally*

273

Sheridan; Isabelle: *Debra Penny;*
Stacie: *Carolyn Bazely;* Russel:
Jim Byrne; Graham: *Stephen
Ventura;* Alison: *Carolyn Bazely;*
Waiter/Young Neighbour: *Michael
Brent.* Director: *Jacqui Home;*
Director's Assistant: *Nigel
Higginson.*

102. NO ROOM 13 by Ian
Potter; *9 & 11 June.* Gail:
Carolyn Bazely; Ron: *Martin
Reeve;* Trevor: *Stephen Ventura;*
Brian: *Jim Byrne;* Rita: *Debra
Penny;* Alistair: *Michael Brent;*
Patsy: *Sally Sheridan.* Director:
Richard Gregory.

**103. FOR THE GOOD
TIMES** by Kirree Seddon and
Helen Trafford; *9 & 11 June
1994.* John: *Michael Brent;*
Chris: *Jim Byrne.* Director:
Renny O'Shea.

104. YOU USED TO by
Matthew Dunster; *9 & 11 June
1994.* Jean Patchett: *Debra
Penny;* Harry Patchett: *Stephen
Ventura;* Ballyrag: *Jim Byrne;* The
Man: *Michael Brent;* The Woman:
Sally Sheridan; WPC Pommel:
Carolyn Bazely. Director:
Richard Gregory.

99–100. Writer in Residence,
as Dramaturg: *Julie Wilkinson;*
Design: *Andrew Wood;* Lighting:
Chris Brockhurst, Andrew Wood;
Sound: *John Owen;* Deputy Stage
Managers on the Book: *Jackie
Bell, Jo Topping;* Design
Assistants: *Katie Mundy, Kerry
Strong;* Production Manager:
Hilary Russell; Master Carpenter:
Colin Honeyman; Construction:
Jez Horrox; Stage Manager: *Sam
Fraser;* Deputy: *Stephen Sumner,*

Scott *McDonald;* Wardrobe
Supervisor: *Kevin Pollard;* Deputy
Supervisor: *Nicky Isaac;* Wardrobe
Assistant: *Emma Harden.*
Journal: 8 & 9/6/94
Press: BT: 25/2/95; **MEN:**
2/6/94

**322. TANTAMOUNT
ESPERANCE** by ROSE
ENGLISH, BARCLAYS NEW
STAGES; *23-25 June 1994.*
Tantamount Esperance: *Rose
English;* Espiritu La Verdad:
Helene Patarot; Imogen Grave:
Jan Pearson; Epitome Plaisir:
Alison Swann; Vanitas Splendid:
George Yiasoumi; El Alma:
Christine Denniston; Magicians:
Paul Kieve, Fluke; Aerialist:
Jeremy Robins; Violin: *Simon
Christopher;* Double Bass: *Enrique
Guerra;* Accordion: *Ian Hill.*
Director: *Rose English;* Design:
Simon Vincenzi; Composer: *Ian
Hill;* Lighting: *Chahine Yavroyan;*
Flying Consultant: *Jonathan
Graham;* Illusions Consultant:
O*Paul Kieve;* Magic Consultant:
Ann Pownall; Tango Consultant:
Christine Dennison; Assistant
Director/Research Assistant: *Jeanie
O'Hare;* Production Manager:
Jonathan Bartlett; Stage Manager:
Helen Bond; Flying Apparatus:
Set Makers: *Streeter & Jessell;*
Curtains: *Gerriets;* Flying
Operator/Specialist Harness/
Flying Research: *Jonathan
Graham;* Flying Assistants: *Patrick
Kavenga, Simon Peril;* Design
Student Placement: *Abigail
Davies;* Wardrobe Supervisor:
Anna Watkins; Costumes: *Jude
Ward;* Fabric Printer: *Eley
Kishimoto;* Jewelery Maker: *Simon
Costin;* Wigs and Beards: *Brian
Peters;* Stools and Espiritu's
Shoes: *Robert Bryce-Muir.*

Press: CL: 15/6/94; MEN: 24/6/94; T: 30/5/94

112-116. NORTH-WEST PLAYWRIGHTS SUMMER FESTIVAL.

112. PASSIVE SMOKING by Jan McVerry. *30 June 1994.* Linda: *Joanne Sherry;* Cathy: *Ann-Louise Grimshaw;* Jim/Market Trader/Man Outside Chippy: *Claude Close;* John/Man Outside Chippy: *John Jardine;* Ged/Neil/ Mark: *Ravin J Ganatra;* Bea/ Maureen: *Mary Cunningham;* Dolly/Gloria: *Ann Rye;* Gary/Pub Crawler: *Mark Chatterton.* Dramaturg: *Val Windsor;* Sue Sutton Mayo. **Journal:** 30/6/94 Press: MEN: 23, 24/6/94; 1/7/94

113. BANG ON TOP by James McMartin; *1 July 1994.* Shark: *Tom Higgins;* Bird: *Pauline Fleming.* **Dramaturg:** *Jim Burke;* Director: *Bryan Elsley.* **Journal:** 1/7/94

114. WAX by Sue Morris and Steve Cochrane; *1 July 1994.* John Ashton: *Stephen Banks;* Louise: *Sharon Muircroft;* Mike/ Pete/Graham: *Steve Book;* Banks/Simon/Frank: *Steve Chapman;* Olive/Jennifer: *Laura Richmond;* Helen/Joanne/Julie: *Kati Spencer.* Dramaturg: *Bill Hopkinson;* Director: *Lee Beagley.* **Journal:** 1/7/94

115. NOWHERE MAN by Ian Karl Moore; *2 July 1994.* Nigel Harris: *Anthony Cairns;* Brian Harris: *Chris Wilkinson;* Frank

Harris: *Martin Reeve;* Anne (Valerie) Harris: *Jane Hollowood;* Father Michael: *Robert Calvert;* Ira Harris: *Jane Hazlegrove;* Steve "Joker" Jones: *Howard Gay.* Dramaturg: *Diane Whitley;* Director: *Peter Rowe.* **Journal:** 2/7/94

116. A MINIATURE SPRUNG FLOOR by Owen Hagan; *2 July 1994.* Bridi Wilson: *Judy Hawkins;* Eileen Wilson: *Lucy Sullivan;* Jim Devlin: *James Quinn;* Ignatius Ali/Anthony: *Joseph Jones;* Ronnie: *Jane Cox;* Duggie: *Steve Halliwell;* Sister Louise: *Valerie Lillley;* Brona/ Rita: *Louise Yates;* Sean: *David Crellin.* Dramaturg: *Bill Morrison;* Director: *Eileen Murphy;* Music: *David Crellin.* **Journal:** 2/7/94

251. THE IDOL ON THE BRONZE HORSE by James Poyser; CONTACT YOUTH THEATRE and THE THEATRE OF YOUTH CREATIVITY, ST PETERSBURG; *25-27 August 1994.* Leo: *Guy Rhys;* Maxim: *Sergei Nikolayev;* Tamara: *Carla Henry;* Elena: *Ekaterina Gorokhovskaya;* Mikhail: *Leonid Zibert;* Maggie: *Michelle Calame;* Lyonya: *Yuri Yelagin;* James: *Stuart Bowden;* Katerina: *Katerina Medvedeva;* Louise: *Chanje Kunda;* Lyuba: *Anna Skakalskaya;* Jude: *Marcelle Holt;* Boris: *Georgi Kobiashvili;* Jenny: *Claire Bleasdale;* Kiril: *Dmitri Strelkov;* Ivan: *Andrei Makhov;* Doris: *Abigail Pound;* Catherine: *Beth McHugh;* Andrei: *Dmitri Lebedev;* John: *Darren Pritchard;* Sonya: *Ekaterina Lisovaya;* Kate: *Hannah McHugh;* Lucy: *Phoebe Palloti;* Dmitri: *Gleb Abayev.* Directors:

Richard Gregory, Alice Ivanova, Renny O'Shea, Yevgeny Sazonov; Set Design: Simon Banham; Assistant Set Designer: Andrew Wood; Costume Design: Lyubov Ribkina, Tatyana Vasilyeva; Composer: Alexander Soynikov; Movement Director: Kathy Crick; Lighting Designer: Alexai Vasilyev; Deputy Stage Manager on the Book: Jacqueline Bell; Technical Director, in St Petersburg: Alexei Udaltsov; Wardrobe Supervisor: Nicky Isaac; Project Co-ordinators: Vladimir Ivanov, Caroline Redmond; Interpreters: Inna Landman, Laura Thompson; Translator: Alice Ivanova; Production Manager: Hilary Russell; Acting Electrician: Paul Colley; Deputy Electrian: John Owen; Master Carpenter: Colin Honeyman; Construction: John Ashworth, Jez Horrox; Stage Manager: Sam Fraser; Deputy: Stephen Sumner, Scott McDonald; Wardrobe Supervisor: Nicky Isaac; Wardrobe Assistant: Emma Harden; Wardrobe Student on Placement: Lesley Race; Project Patrons: Peter Brook, Lev Dodin.
Journal: 26/8/94
Press: CL: 20/4/94, 10 & 24/8/94; MEN: 26/8/94

323. DIARY OF A NEW YORK by William Barber, adapted by Neil Wallace; TRULY FIERCE PRODUCTIONS; 9-10 September 1994. Cast: Harold Finley.

95. B-ROAD MOVIE; LIP SERVICE; 12-17 September 1994.

326. LYSISTRATA by Aristophanes, Translated and Adapted by Kenneth McLeish; CONTACT THEATRE COMPANY; 29 September - 22 October 1994. His Honour: Jonathan Coyne; Lysistrata: Doña Croll; Kinesias: Steve Evets; Lampito: Su Douglas; Kalonike: Valerie Lilley; His Excellency: Ron Meadows; Myrrhine: Julie Riley; Eudemon: Jim Whelan. Director: Noreen Kershaw; Design: Simon Banham; Lighting: Jimmy Simmons; Choreographer: Sheila Carter; Music: Akintayo Akinbode; Assistant Designer: Andrew Wood; Design Assistant: Julie Nelson; Production Manager: Hilary Russell; Chief Electrician: Simon Mills; Deputy Electrian: John Owen; Master Carpenter: Colin Honeyman; Construction: Jez Horrox, Carl Richardson; Stage Manager: Sam Fraser; Deputy: Stephen Sumner, Scott McDonald; Assistant Stage Manager: Jacqueline Bell; Wardrobe Supervisor: Jackie Davies; Deputy Supervisor: Nicky Isaac; Wardrobe Assistant: Emma Harden..

327. THE PICTURE OF DORIAN GRAY by Oscar Wilde, adapted by Neil Bartlett, with original score by Nicolas Bloomfield; GLORIA, LYRIC HAMMERSMITH & NOTTINGHAM PLAYHOUSE; 25-29 October. Cast: Maria Aitken, Benedick Bates, Bette Bourne, Tim Piggott-Smith, Joanna Riding, Paul Shaw. Directors: Neil Bartlett, Leah Hausman; Design: Ian MacNeil; Lighting: Rick Fisher.
Press: G: 14/9/94; S: 22/9/94

328. THE IDIOT, adapted from Fyodor Dostoyevsky, into

Hebrew; GESHER THEATRE COMPANY; *31 October - 5 November 1994*. Director: *Yevgeny Arye*. **Press: S:** 11/8/94

329. GAMES IN THE BACKYARD by Edna Mazya; MUNICIPAL THEATRE OF HAIFA; *8-12 November 1994*. Director: *Oded Kotler*. **Press: S:** 11/8/94

330. CINDERELLA - THE PLAY by Stuart Paterson; CONTACT THEATRE COMPANY; *30 November 1994 - 14 January 1995*. Director: *Benjamin Twist*.

THE BRICKHOUSE – Contact Theatre Studio.

30. FRANKENSTEIN, adapted by CONTACT YOUTH THEATRE from the novel by Mary Shelley; *10-13 November 1993*. Cast: *Kay Boggett, Stuart Bowden, Eliane Byrne, Celia Forbes, Chanje Kunda, Ruth Lister, Hannah McHugh, Phoebe Pallotti, Abigail Pound, Sally Roe, Guy Rhys, Julia Roy-Williams*. Director: *Renny O'Shea;* Choreographer: *Tom Roden;* Design: *Becky Hawkins;* Composer /Musical Director/Sound Operator :*Rupert Brewer;* Lighting: *Chris Brockhouse;* Stage Manager on the Book: *Cheryl Hickman;* Assistant Stage Manager: *Katie Nicholls;* Lighting Operator: *Jack Lloyd;* Sound Technician: *John Owen;* Wardrobe Supervisor: *Nicky Isaac;* Wardrobe Assistants: *Emma Harden, Ann Heffernan;* Dressers: *Michelle Calame, Carla*

Henry; Set Construction: *Jo Topping, Becky Hawkins, Andrew Wood;* Scenic Artist: *Helen Davies;* Musicians: *Rupert Brewer, Ruth Lister, Hannah McHugh, Phoebe Pallotti;* Production Manager: *Hilary Russell*.

331. DÆMON; developed from Mary Shelley's FRANKENSTEIN by CONTACT YOUTH THEATRE; *2-5 March 1994*. Cast: *Aimée Asbury, Angela Blayds, Kay Boggett, Mark Burnett; Eliane Byrne, Luke Critchely, Eva Crompton, Shelly Dewhurst, Celia Forbes, Shelley Halstead, John-Paul Reily, Katherine Shenton, Annoush Sookasian, Ellen Tickle, Sally Roe*. Director: *Zoë Higgins;* Sign Interpreter: *Clare Marsden;* Composer/Musical Director: *Olly Fox;* Design: *Andrew Wood;* Design Assistants: *Celia Forbes, Annoush Sookasian, Fadima Zubairu;* Choreographer: *Sally-Ann Barker;* Lighting: *Jack Lloyd;* Stage Managers: *Cheryl Hickman, Katie Nicholls;* Wardrobe Assistant: *Emma Harden;* Dressers: *Beth McHugh, Julia Roy-Williams;* Construction: *Colin Honeyman, Jo Topping;* Production Manager: *Hilary Russell*.

343. RAW CHUNKS: Selections from new plays by the UNIVERSITY OF MANCHESTER DRAMA DEPARTMENT; *10-11 March 1994*.

NEW WORK '94: DESIRE:

332. THE CURTAINS by Deborah Freeman; *24 June 1994*. Cur: *Michael O'Hara;* Tans : *Richard Howell-Jones;* Lady

Partycastle: *Georgina Lamb.*
Director: *Maggie Willett.*

333. LACRIMA by Derek
Martin; *24 June 1994.* Fiona:
Gina May. Director: *Jess
Tyrrell.*

334. ELEPHANT by Michael
Harvey; *24 June 1994.* Joel:
Richard Howell-Jones; Arjun: *Guy
Rhys;* Waitress: *Martine Brown.*
Director: *Pete Walker;*
Dramaturg: *Richard McCann.*

335. LOVE RENEWED by
Daniel Williams; *24 June 1994.*
Angel: *Georgina Lamb;* Beatrice:
Martine lamb; Virgil: *Charles
Richards;* Dante: *Rick Forest.*
Director: *Jess Tyrrell.*

336. LEAVING HOME by
Russell Tennant; *24 June 1994.*
Irvin: *Simon Norbury;* Kara:
Virginia Clay; Milo: *Andrew
Whitehead.* Director: *Maggie
Willett.*

337. DESIRE by John Turley;
24 June 1994. Darren: *Rick
Forest.* Director: *Jenny Eastop;*
Dramaturg: *Richard McCann.*

338. VELVET SWAMP by Rose
Hughes; *25 June 1994.*
Woman: *Martine Brown.*
Director: *Ian Karl Moore.*

339. IN TRANSIT by Bernard
Padden; *25 June 1994.*
Woman: *Pauline Jefferson;* Man:
Pete O'Connor; Conductor:
Michael O'Hara. Director: *Jenny
Eastop.*

340. TILL ROCKS MELT by

Steen Agro; *25 June 1994.*
Joe: *Simon Norbury;* Eddie:
Andrew Whitehead. Director:
Jess Tyrrell; Dramaturg: *Richard
McCsnn.*

**341. THE SWEETS DADDY
GAVE US** by Elizabeth Baines;
25 June 1994. Trish: *Andrew
Whitehead;* Carol: *Celln Scott;*
Jane: *John Henshaw.* Director:
Ian Karl Moore.

342. AFTER THE FIRE by
Richard McCann; *25 June 1994.*
Faust: *Simon Norbury.* Director:
Pete Walker.

332-342: Stage Manager:
Rachel Coles; Design: *Andrew
Locke;* Sound: *Michael Elphick;*
Lights: *Steve Bryan;* Producers:
Richard McCann, Jess Tyrrell;
Script Selection: *Richard
McCann, Jess Tyrell, Bill Taylor.*

CRUMPSALL LIBRARY;
Abraham Moss Centre,
Crescent Road, M8 6UF;
061-721 4555; AZ: 40,
B3; XAZ: 74, C3.

**430. PAT BRENNAN
PUPPETS;** *3 August 1994.*

301. BIG BAD WOLF;
MANCHESTER ACTORS
COMPANY; *December 1994.*

LILO BAUR as Lucie Cabrol, in her Third Life – beyond the grave –, returns to haunt Jean (SIMON McBURNEY), the man whom she had twice tried to draw into marriage.

DAM HEAD MOBILE LIBRARY; Dam Head Drive, Charlestown, M9; **AZ:** 41, D1; **XAZ:** 61, G6.

124. THE TIGER WITH GOLDEN CLAWS; MANCHESTER ACTORS COMPANY; *6 July 1994.*

DANCEHOUSE THEATRE, 10 Oxford Road, M1 5AQ; 061–242 2555 (5% Booking Fee). **AZ:** 105, G2; **XAZ:** 166, A3 **G, W.**

35. THE THREE LIVES OF LUCIE CABROL, adapted by Simon McBurney and Mark Wheatley from the short story by John Berger, devised by THEATRE DE COMPLICITE; *12–15 January 1994.* Lucie Cabrol: *Lilo Baur;* Jean: *Simon McBurney;* Marius Cabrol: *Hannes Flaschberger;* Mélanie Cabrol: *Hélène Patarot;* Emile Cabrol/St Just: *Stefan Metz;* Henri Cabrol: *Tim McMullan;* Edmund Cabrol/ André Masson: *Mick Barnfather;* The Land/Animals/Children/ Villagers/The Dead: *Members of the Cast.* Director: *Simon MvBurney;* Assistant Director: *Mark Wheatley;* Design: *Tim Hatley;* Lighting: *Paule Constable;* Sound: *Christopher Shutt;*

279

Producer: *Catherine Reiser;* Associate Collaborators: *Annabel Arden, Annie Castledine;* Production Manager: *Alison Ritchie;* Company Stage Manager: *Anita Ashwick;* Costume Supervisor: *Johanna Coe;* Sound Operator: *John Mackinnon;* Production Electrician: *Ian Beswick;* Technical Stage Manager: *Ian Richards;* Student Assistant Stage Manager: *Cath Binks;* Design Assistants: *Lotte Collet, Cathy Wren;* Stage Technician: *Chris Sleath.*
Press: M: 20/1/94; **MM:** 14/1/94

51. BEAUTIFUL THING by Jonathan Harvey; BUSH THEATRE; *21-26 February 1994.* Jamie: *Mark Letheren;* Leah: *Sophie Stanton;* Sandra: *Amelda Brown;* Ste: *Shaun Dingwall;* Tony/Ronnie: *Richard Bonneville.* Director: *Hettie Macdonald;* Design: *Robin Don;* Lighting: *Johanna Town;* Sound: *Paul Bull;* Production Manager: *Padraig O'Neill;* Stage Managers: *Tim Fletcher, Alexandra Owen;* Assistant Director: *Stephen Wright;* Associate Lighting Designer: *Jenny Kagan;* Costume Supervisor: *Rachel Turner.*
Journal: 22/2/94
Press: BI: 22/2/94; **CI:** 23/2/94; **MM:** 25/2/94

345. HELL, HULL AND HUDDERSFAX by Gary Brown; ASPECTS THEATRE COMPANY; *1 March 1994.* Nick Taylor: *Adam Riches;* Helen Fraser: *Joanne Arber;* Rob Baker: *Paul Fox;* Rita Baker: *Louise Carter;* Les Winters: *Tony Brown;* Jonathan Brand: *Benjamin Frain;* Jack Johnson: *Jonathan Smallman;*

Dagbeesha: *Phil Marley;* Darren Murray: *Rob Hamer;* Skinhead/ Mugger: *Chris Balmer;* Worshipper: *Jo-Anne Walker.* Director: *Lloyd Peters;* Assistant Director: *Carl Walker;* Stage Manager: *Jo-anne Walker;* Costume: *Nicola Emmett, Andrea Fishley;* Production Manager: *Ian Currie;* Production Technician: *Gordon Isaacs;* Company Manager: *Lisa Duncan.*

52. BITTER 'N' TWISTED by Michael Ellis; BLACK THEATRE CO-OPERATIVE; *4-5 March 1994.* Courtney: *Wayne Buchannan;* Natasha/Peggy: *Llewella Gideon;* Daniel: *Anthony Ofoegbu;* Bibby: *Angela Wynter;* God Voice-Over: *Glenna Forster-Jones.* Director: *Joan-Ann Maynard;* Set & Costumes: *Janey Gardiner;* Lighting & Sound: *Richard de Cordova;* Production Manager: *Sharon Ricketts;* Technical Stage Manager: *Yahw McCalla;* Company Stage Manager: *Debra Tidd;* Set Painter: *Jenny Espley;* Assistant Painter: *Christine Russell;* Wardrobe Assistant: *Jane Cruddas.*
Journal: 5/3/94

344. HATED NIGHTFALL by Howard Barker; THE WRESTLING SCHOOL; *9-12 March 1994.* Disbanner: *Philip Barnes;* Helen: *Rebecca Charles;* Denadir: *James Clyde;* Christophe: *Paul Gonshaw;* Romanoff: *Nicholas Jones;* Dancer: *Ian McDermid;* Arrant: *Keith Osborn;* Caroline: *Anna Patrick;* Albeit: *Claire Rushbrook;* Fitch: *Raymond Sawyer;* Griselda: *Nicola Walker;* Jane: *Jane Wood.* Director: *Howard Barker;* Design: *Johan Engels;* Composer: *Matthew*

Scott; Lighting: *Ace McCarron;*
Company Manager: *Chris Corner;*
Stage Manager: *Michael Tomkins;*
Deputy Stage Manager: *Kate
Meredith;* Assistant Stage
Manager/Sound Operator: *Sara
Carlick;* Wardrobe Supervisor:
Frances Roe; Assistant Directors:
Roxana Silbert, Andrew Cooper;
Costumes: *Bermans Angets Lts;*
Floor: *PL Parsons Ltd;* Additional
Prop Work: *Steve Fin McLay;*
Richard Palmer-Romero.
Press: G: 14/3/94, 9 &
16/4/94 **I:** 15/3/94, 13/4/94;
INS: 17/4/94; **MEN:** 10/3/94;
O: 17/4/94; **S:** 5/5/94; **T:**
13/4/94

67. E D R **(Earliest Date of
Release)** by BLACK MIME
THEATRE; *22-24 March 1994.*
Ensemble: *Tracey Anderson,
Michael Mannash-Daniels, Carol
Moses, Cassi Pool, Benji Reid.*
Director: *Denise Wong;* Musical
Director: *Errollyn Wallen;* Musical
Tuition: *Tracey Anderson;*
Choreographer: *Susan Lewis;*
Design: *Ann Hubbard;* Lighting:
Richard Jenkins; Stage Managers:
Hugh Wong, Joanna Rawlinson;
Research: *Nikki Batten, Rose
Newman.*
Journal: 24/3/94
Press: G: 4/11/94; **MEN:**
23/3/94

346. RICHARD III by William
Shakespeare, in a Romanian
version by Mihai Maniutiu;
ODEON THEATRE OF
BUCHAREST; *10-14 May 1994.*
King Edward IV: *Serban Ionescu;*
Richard III: *Marcel Iures;*
Clarence: *Florin Zamfirescu;*
Buckingham: *Radu Amzulescu;*
Hastings: *Virgil Andriescu:*
Stanley: *Mircea N Cretu;* Rivers:

Florin Dobrovici; Grey: *Mugur
Arvunescu;* Brackenbury: *Dan
Badarau;* Lord Mayor: *Mirceau
Constantinescu;* Morton/Ely:
Nicolae Ivanescu; Ratclif: *Marian
Ghenea;* Catesby: *Gelu Nitu;*
Tyrell: *Constantine Cojocaru;*
Lovel: *Ionel Mihailescu;*
Messenger: *Laurentiu Lazar;*
Citizens: *Niculae Urs, Radu
Panamarenco;* The Fool (Dog):
Marius Stanescu; Lady Anne:
Camelia Maxim; Elizabeth: *Oana
Stefanescu;* Margaret: *Irina
Mazanitis;* Duchess of York:
Virginia Rogin; Guards: *Mircea
Gherghiu, Drabos Stamate, Andrei
Duban, Felex Totolici, Daniel
Badale, Adrian Ancuta, Radu
Baitan, Mihai Danu, Bogdan
Voicu, Carol Becher, Tudor
Smoleanu, Dan Iacob.* Director:
Mihai Maniutiu; Costumes: *Doina
Levintza;* Design: *Constantine
Ciubotariu;* Choreographer: *Sergiu
Anghel;* Music: *Marius Popp.*
Press: G: 14/5/94; **MEN:** 5 &
11/5/94; **S:** 2/6/94.

347. MANIFESTO; Karl Marx
and Friedrich Engels, adapted by
VOLCANO THEATRE
COMPANY; *16-18 May 1994.*
Performers: *Juan Carracoso, Paul
Davies, Denise Evens, Steven
Hoggett, Fern Smith, Simon
Thorp.* Director: *Nigel
Charnock;* Design: *Andrew Jones;*
Set Construction: *Paul Emmanuel;*
Sound: *Spencer Hazel;* Original
Music: *Stuart Lucas;* Based on an
original production directed by
Janek Alexander.

348. EVERYDAY LIFE IN ...;
ROAR MATERIAL; *19-21 May
1994.* **Hollywood:** Make-up
Girl: *Rachel Bull;* Freda Fopper:
Phillippa Coslett; Karina

Cruikshank: *Karen Crook;* The
Producer: *Phil Dennison;* The
Agent: *Richard Gallagher;* Lola
Locket: *Lorraine Hackett;* The
Typist: *Ian Lashford;* The
Bodyguard: *Phil Marks.* **The
Japanese Empire:** Ξ: Rachel Bull;
Ω: *Philippa Coslett;* Crocus Bulb:
Cloud; Lotus Blossom: *Karen
Crook;* The Bridegroom: *Phil
Dennison;* Jasmin: *Lorraine
Hackett;* Shino: *Sam Kristie:*
Wokhead: *Phil Marks.* **Paris,
Rome, Munich:** Martha: *Rachel
Bull;* Theda von Mayerling:
Philippa Coslett; Karina: *Karen
Crook;* Preston: *Phil Dennison;*
Voice-Over: *Cecilia D'Eque;* Sam
Valance: *Richard Gallagher;*
Lottie: *Lorraine Hackett;*
Chambermaid: *Sam Kristie;*
Gustave: *Ian Lashford;* Willie: *Phil
Marks.* **Berlin:** Voice of Berlin:
Philippa Coslett; Karina: *Karen
Crook;* Helmut: *Phil Dennison;*
Taxi: *Lorraine Hackett;* Cesare:
Ian Lashford; The Director:
Camden McDonald. Musical
Director/Keyboards: *Carol
Donaldson;* Percussion: *Phil
Marks;* Saxophones: *Richard
Scott.* Director: *Camden
McDonald;* Costumes: *Jackie
Haynes;* Settings: *Niola Bowden,
Sarah Richman, Stephen Iles;*
Lighting: *Steve Curtis;*
Technicians: *Phil Ellams, Giles
Clarke, Oliver Driver;* Video
Work: *Tony Ryan-Carter, Camden
McDonald.*
Press: MEN: 22/3/94,
20/5/94.

**106. MOTI ROTI, PUTTLI
CHUNNI (Thick Bread, Thin
Veils)** by Diane Esguerra, from
an original idea by Keith Khan;
Script Consultant: Ali Zaidi;
MOTI ROTI COMPANY and

THEATRE ROYAL, STRATFORD
EAST; *1-4 June 1994.* Vijay
'Bhai' Kumar: *Kaleema Janjua;*
Chandani Kumar: *Jamila Massey;*
A J Kumar: *Nitish Bharadwaj;*
Sunny Kumar: *Pravesh Kumar;*
Solicitor/Servant/Dancer/Policeman
: *Karim Karim;* Policewoman/
Secretary/ Dancer: *Shobna
Gulati;* Bunty Saleem: *Ajay
Chhabra;* Zeenat Saleem: *Monisha
Bharadwaj;* Priya Mohun: *Mina
Anwar;* Laxmi Mohun: *Laila Khan;*
Vikram Mohun: *Nirjay Mahindru.*
ADDITIONAL FILM CAST: Young
Laxmi: *Derekshan Najamessani;*
Vikram: *Zeshan Arsalan;* Dancer:
Monisha Patil Bharadwaj;
Homeless Person: *Jonathan
Dawes;* Café Owner: *Mohamed
Faiz Khan;* Café Youths: *Munir
Khardin, Wahid Khan, Thusani
Weerasaki;* Video Shop Man: *Abi.*
Direction and Design: Keith Khan
with *Ali Zaidi;* Choreographer:
Monisha Patil-Bharadwaj; Lighting:
Stephen Watson; Music: *Gavin
O'Shea, Pete Harman,* Production
Manager: *Paul O'Leary;* Company
Stage Manager: *Scott Howarth;*
Technical Assistant Stage
Manager: *Anne Howarth;* Deputy
Stage Manager, Production
Electrician and Re-Lights: *Nigel
Baker;* Wardrobe Supervisor:
Mandy Hooper; Costumes: *Athar
Hafiz;* Additional Costumes:
*Bushra Hafiz, Joanna Rice,
Spencer Horne.* FILM CREW:
Directors: *Keith Khan, Ali Zaidi;*
Assistant Director: *Shad Ali;*
Editors: *Zikethiwe Ngcobo, Saquib
Asghar;* Assistant Editor: *Swantee
Toocaram;* Art Director: *Gavin
O'Shea;* Camera: *Ali Zaidi;*
Camera Assistant: *Darrel Butlin;*
Lighting: *Nigel Baker;* Sound:
Chinna Boapeah; Musical
Directors: *Gavin O'Shea, Pete
Harmon;* Production Manager:

Paul O'Leary; Make-up: Helen
Hunte; Costume: Jo Anderson,
Terry King, Spencer Horne.
Journal: 2/6/94
Press: MEN: 31/5/94

**349. TIMON OF ATHENS/
TIMON DE ATENAS** by William
Shakespeare; MANCHESTER
METROPOLITAN UNIVERSITY
CREWE AND ALSAGER
FACULTY in collaboration with
FORUM EUROPEO DEL LAS
ARTES TEATRO Y JUVENTUD,
BENIDORM '94; EL TEATRO
ESPAÑOL DE LA JUVENTUD at
the FUNDACION SHAKESPEARE
DE ESPAÑA, VALENCIA; 5-6
July 1994. Prologue/Amazons:
Julie Baldwin, Alex Bliss, Cath
Cooke, Sonia Friend, Karen
Gillingham, Georgina Lamb, Kit
McCudden, Ellen Mills, Fleur
Soper, Michelle Stanbridge, Sarah
Watts; Timon: Arturo Muñoz,
Duncan Ryall; Ventidius: David
Slater; Alcibiades: Oscar
Martinez, James Nickerson;
Painter: Fleur Soper; Flaminius:
Oscar Martinez; Phrynia: Cath
Cooke; Lords: Jose Alberto
Herrero, Oscar Martinez, Andy
Newman; Sepronius/Apemantus:
Peter Glover; Poet: Andrew
Newman; Flavius: James Haydon,
Oscar Mira Alabau; An Old
Athenian: James Nickerson;
Timandra: Alex Bliss; Certain
Senators: David Slater, James
Haydon, Jose Alberto Herrero,
Oscar Martinez, Fleur Soper.
Directors: Vicente Genoves, David
)'Shes; Choreographer/Deviser of
Womens Movement Score/Prologue
Director: Nancy Reilly-McVittie;
Assistant to Ms Reilly-McVittie:
Juliet Sebley; Lighting: Pele
Duart; Assistant Lighting
Technician: Fiona Henderson;

Music: David Slater; Stage
Manager: Matthew Harbour;
Assistant Stage Managers: Lee
Danby, Joanne Stapleton;
Company Manager (Spain):
Christina Pitarch; Company
Manager (England): Amanda Jane
Lees

255. ROMEO AND JULIET by
William Shakespeare;
MANCHESTER YOUTH
THEATRE; 2-10 September
1994. Capulet: Paul Murphy;
Lady Capulet: Phiippa Murphy;
Juliet: Amanda Jones; Nurse: Lisa
May; Tybalt: Sam Clarke; Peter:
Simon Trinder; Sampson: Denis
Adshead; Gregory: Michael
Plunkett; A Servant: Stuart
Holden; Montague: Jason Tynan;
Lady Montague: Melanie Levy;
Romeo: Michael Wareing;
Benvolio: Ben Pain; Abraham:
Amanda Beswick; Balthasar:
Simon Connolly; Escalus: Andrew
Batty; Mercutio: Aidan Crowley;
Paris: Craig Stevens; Page to
Paris: Kathryn Bailey; Friar
Laurence: Martin Paling; Friar
John: Paul Glew; Apothecary:
Steve Walsh; The Watch:
Elizabeth Hill, Stephanie Ridings,
+ almost everyone else from time
to time. Director: Maria
Mescki; Design: Alison Hefferman;
Lighting: Paul Colley;
Choreography: Kathryn Beverley;
Fights: Paul Jaynes; Director's
Assistant: Philip Brennan; Stage
Manager: Rosie Robinson; Deputy
Stage Manager: Natalie Hall;
Assistant Stage Managers: Joanne
Greenwood, Louisa Smalley;
Technical Assistants: Gemma
Francis, Clare Hyland, Gareth
Tomlinson; Design Assistants:
Leanne Mankowski, Russell Miller;
Wardrobe Assistants: Emma

Farley, Gillian Summers,
Technical Manager: Martin Doran;
Wardrobe Supervisor: Alison
Humphrey; Company Stage
Manager: Marcus Wilson; Deputy
Company Stage Manager: Vivien
Routledge; Senior Design
Assistant: Kate Hind; Assistant
Wardrobe Supervisor: Amanda
Morris; Tutors: Lynna Barlow,
Pamela Davies, Rachel
Katzenellenbogen.
Press: MEN: 3/9/94

36. PEACOCK; DOO COT;
17 Seoptember 1994.

**262. THE DARK PERVERSITY
OF CHAMELEONS;** devised by
the cast; ARTAUD'S BLUEPRINT;
18 September 1994. Rachel:
Sara Bailes; Derek: Steve Dixon;
Mike: Paul Murphy; Veronica:
Wendy Reed; Sophia: Fiona
Watson. Director/Video
Photography and Editing: Steve
Dixon; Composer: John
Durrant; Music Engineer: Stephen
Parker; Technical Manager: Ian
Currie; Stills/Sound: Lawrence
Murphy; Production Technician:
Tim Chisholm; Additional Viseo
Photography: Paul Murphy; Final
Video Sequence Editing: Lloyd
Peters.
Journal: 18/9/94

**350. THE BOURGEOIS
GENTILHOMME** by Molière,
adapted by TARA ARTS; 22-24
September 1994. Thirru Kaka
Deen: Vincent Ebrahim; Amma
Kaka Deen/Dorimene: Josephine
Welcome; Lori/Jane/Pandit:
Kumiko Mendl; Kalia/Rik/Sun
King: Ravin J Ganatra; Karapandi
/Music Teacher/Tailor: Yogesh
Bhatt; Nila/Dance Teacher:
Cuckoo Parameswaran;

Edupadi/Dorante: Richard Santhiri;
Musician: Joji Hirota. Director:
Jatinder Verma; Assistant
Director: Iqbal Husain; Design:
Magdalen Rubalcava; Lighting/
Production Tour Manager: Paul
O'Leary; Choreographic
Consultant: Shobana Jeyasingh;
18th Century French Dance:
Stephen Preston, Sarah Cremer;
Puppetry Consultant: Sue
Buckmaster; Tamil Language
Consultant: M Yogeshwaran;
Company Manager: Scott
Howarth; Stage Manager:
Stephanie Trickett; Costume
Maker: Victoria Baker; Dyeing:
Gabrielle Firth; Consruction
Drawings: Miles King; Set
Painter: Billy Jones; Set Builders:
Harris Bros; Research: Rosaleen
O'Donnell.
Press: MEN: 16/9/94

351. AS YOU LIKE IT by
William Shakespeare; CHEEK BY
JOWL; 27 September - 1
October 1994. Orlando: Scott
Handy; Oliver: Jonathan
Chesterman; Jacques de Boys/Le
Beau: Sean Francis; Adam/
Audrey: Richard Cant; Dennis/Sir
Oliver: Steve Watts; Duke
Frederick/Banished Duke: David
Hobbs; Celia: Simon Coates;
Rosalind: Adrian Lester;
Touchstone: Peter Needham;
Charles/Corin: Paul Kissaun;
Jaques: Michael Gardiner; Amiens/
William: Rhashan Stone; Silvius:
Gavin Abbott; Phebe: Wayne
Cater. Director: Declan
Donnellan; Design: Nick Ormerod;
Composer/Musical Director: Paddy
Cunneen; Movement Director:
Sue Lefton; Lighting: Judith
Greewood; Assistant Director:
Fiona Laird; Fight Director: John
Waller; Company Stage Manager:

Marcus Bray; Production
Manager: *Jon Howes;* Wardrobe
Manager: *Rachel Dickson;* Deputy
Stage Manager: *Paula Spinks;*
Wardrobe Supervisor: *Angie Burns,*
Press: CL: 21/9/94; **MEN:**
28/9/94

352. THE PLAYBOY OF THE
WESTERN WORLD by J M
Synge; COMMUNICADO; *11–15
October 1994.* Christy Mahon:
Mark Aiken; Pegeen Margaret:
Cara Kelly. Director: *Gerry
Mulgrew.*
Press: CL: 5/10/94 **S:** 22/9/94

353. CLAIR DE LUZ;
conceived by Pete Brooks;
Devised by INSOMNIC
PRODUCTIONS in association
with PHYSICAL STATE
INTERNATIONAL; *17–20
October 1994.* Cast: *Tony
Guilfoyle, Amanda Hadingue,
Caroline Pegg, Craig Stephes.*
Director: *Pete Brooks.*

355. RAATER RODE **(Night's
Sunlight)** by Ketaki Kushari
Dyson; SANGBARTA GROUP
THEATRE OF CALCUTTA; *21–
22 October 1994.* Director:
Sunil Das.

354. IF WE SHADOWS;
conceived by Pete Brooks and
devised from William
Shakespeare's **Midsummer Night's
Dream** by INSOMNIAC
PRODUCTIONS in association
with PHYSICAL STATE
INTENATIONAL; *21–26
November 1994.* Director: *Pete
Brooks;* Design: *Laura Hopkins;*
Lighting: *Nigel Edwards;*
Soundtrack: *Towering Inferno;*
Producer: *Di Rbson.*

**DEBDALE PARK MOBILE
LIBRARY; AZ:** 62, B2;
XAZ: 103, H3.

124. THE TIGER WITH
GOLDEN CLAWS;
MANCHESTER ACTORS
COMPANY; *21 July 1994.*

**DENISON ROAD MOBILE
LIBRARY,** Victoria Park,
M14; **AZ:** 60, C3;
XAZ: 101, G4.

124. THE TIGER WITH
GOLDEN CLAWS;
MANCHESTER ACTORS
COMPANY; *7July 1994.*

DIDSBURY LIBRARY; 692
Wilmslow Road, M20
0DN; 061–445 3220; **AZ:**
60, B4; **XAZ:** 117, F6.

432. CHATTERBOX
PUPPETS; *24 August 1994.*
John Piper.

301. BIG BAD WOLF;
MANCHESTER ACTORS
COMPANY; *December 1994.*

DOBSON COURT,
Newton Heath, M40; **AZ:**
51, F1; **XAZ:** 89, E1.

124. THE TIGER WITH
GOLDEN CLAWS, d) **The
Notorious Fart; e) Ali Baba and
the Forty Thieves;**
MANCHESTER ACTORS

285

COMPANY; *15 July 1994.* Evil Magician/Donkey /Ali Baba/Fisherman/Wife: *Stephen Boyes;* Morgiana/ Shehrezade/Apparition/Old Crone/ Soldier/The Roc: *Viv Warentz;* Beggar Caliph/Baba Mustapha/ Cobbler/Robber Captain/Flatulent Man: *Steve Tabner.*
Journal: 5, 9 & 15/7/94

DUKE'S '92, Castle Street, Castlefield, M3 4LZ; **061-839 8646; AZ:** 105, D1; **XAZ:** 165, E2.

122. ARDEN OF FEVERSHAM by Anon; SHAKEBAG & WILL THEATRE COMPANY; *19-23 July 1994.* Arden/Mayor of Feversham: *Scott Whitehead;* Franklin/Clarke/Black Will: *David Kennedy;* Alice/Lord Cheiny: *Marion Bibbyl;* Michael/A Ferryman: *Fiona Brannigan;* Mosby/Greene: *David Reeves;* Susan/Shakebag: *Letitia Thornton.* Director: *Niall Whitehead;* Lighting: *Alan Balmer;* Costumes: *David Kennedy;* Settings: *Bob Cunning, Derek James.*
Journal: 23/7/94
Press: MEN: 21/7/94

EAST DIDSBURY METHODIST HALL, Parrs Wood Road, M20 0QQ; **061-437 2441, 061-445 3199.**

356. PANIC STATIONS by Derek Benfield; CELESTA

PLAYERS; *16, 22 & 23 October 1993.*

357. HOBSON'S CHOICE by Harold Brighouse; CELESTA PLAYERS; *15, 21, 22 October 1994.*

FAIRY LANE MOBILE LIBRARY; Chetham Hill, M8; **AZ:** 39, F4; **XAZ:** 74, A6

124. THE TIGER WITH GOLDEN CLAWS; MANCHESTER ACTORS COMPANY; *22 July 1994.*

FALLOWFIELD LIBRARY; Platt Lane, M14 7FB; **061-224 4153; AZ:** 60, 4A; **XAZ:** 101, E6.

430. PAT BRENNAN PUPPETS; *10 August 1994.*

301. BIG BAD WOLF; MANCHESTER ACTORS COMPANY; *December 1994.*

FORUM THEATRE, Civic Centre, Leningrad Square, WYTHENSHAWE, M22 5RT; **061-437 9663. AZ:** 91,E1; **XAZ:** 140: A2. **H, W.**

8. THE JUNGLE BOOK, adapted from Rudyard Kipling by Neil Duffield, with music by Roger Haines; additional music by

Charles Miller; LIBRARY THEATRE COMPANY; 26 November 1993 - 22 January 1994. Mowgli: Karl Seth; Baloo: Mel Taylor; Bagheera: Norma Atallah; Shere Khan: Royce Hounsell; Messua/Raksha: Yasmin Wilde; Buldeo/Akela: Tim Lambert; Father Wolf/Fire Dancer: Felix Medina; Queen of the Cobras/Chil: Carolyn Bazely; Wolf/Monkey/Villager: Zeki Hilmi. Director: Roger Haines; Design: Judith Croft; Lighting: Robert Bryan; Musical Director & Piano: Charles Miller; Keyboards II: Carol Donaldson; Percussion: Craig Vear; Choreography: Norma Attalah; Animal Movement Consultant: Niamh Dowling; Assistant Director: Paul Jaynes; Fight Director: Renny Krupinski; Sound: Ian Dickinson; On the Book: Jak Kearney; Sign Language Performance Interpreter: Byron Campbell; Production Manager: Michael Williams; Assistant Production Manager: Jeanette Aldcroft; Scenic Artist: Colin Piggott; Technical & Safety Manager: Tim Stott; Head of Lighting and Sound: Gail Leah Wroth; Deputy Lighting: Lee J Threlfall; Deputy Sound: Matthew Tompsett; Production Electrician: Chris McLean; Wardrobe Supervisor: Cathy Alger; Deputy Wardrobe Supervisor: Liz Horrigan; Cutter: Gill Chapman; Construction Manager: Derek Jones; Deputy Construction Manager: Gary Armstrong; Property Maker: Timothy Wylie; Construction Assistant: David Doyle; Stage Manager: Dean Clarkin; Assistant Stage Manager: Katherine Mahony.
Journal: 30/12 /93
Press: BI: 4/1/94; **CL:** 8/12/93; **MEN:** 25/11/93,

1/12/93; **MM:** 3/12/93

358. HAPPY FAMILIES by John Godber; LIBRARY THEATRE COMPANY; 4-26 March 1994. John: Derren Litten; Dot: Joanna Bacon; Vic: Ron Meadows; Liz: Margaret Ashcroft; Jack: John Jardine; Aunty Doris: Nickie Goldie; Aunty Edna: Christine Cox; Rebecca/Lyn Sutton: Julie-Ann Gillitt. Director: Sue Sutton Mayo; Design: Judith Croft; Lighting: Paul Colley; Sound: Ian Dickinson; On the Book: Jak Kearney; Sign Language Performance Interpreter: Mary Connell; Production Manager: Michael Williams; Assistant Production Manager: Jeanette Aldcroft; Scenic Artist: Colin Piggott; Technical & Safety Manager: Tim Stott; Head of Lighting and Sound: Gail Leah Wroth; Sound Operator: Gary Rhodes; Wardrobe Supervisor: Cathy Alger; Deputy Wardrobe Supervisor: Liz Horrigan; Cutter: Gill Chapman; Construction Manager: Derek Jones; Deputy Construction Manager: Gary Armstrong; Property Maker: Timothy Wylie; Construction Assistant: David Doyle; Stage Manager: Dean Clarkin; Assistant Stage Manager: Katherine Mahony.
Press: BI: 22/3/94; **CL:** 9/3/94; **G:** 15/3/94; **MEN:** 3&9/3/94; **S:** 28/4/94; **SAM:** 17/3/94

77. BROTHERS AND SISTERS; Part One: MEETINGS AND PARTINGS; Part Two: ROADS AND CROSSROADS; dramatised from the novels of Fyodor Abramov by Lev Dodin, Sergei Bekhterev and Arkady

Katsman; MALY DRAMA
THEATRE COMPANY OF ST
PETERSBURG; *20, 21, 24 April
1994.* Anfisa Petrovna Minina:
Tatiana Shestakova; Denis
Kharitonovich Persin: *Mikhail
Samochko;* Ivan Dmitrievich
Lukashin: *Nikolai Lavrov;* Gavrila
Andreevich Ganichev: *Sergei
Bekhterev;* Mikhail Priaslin: *Piotr
Semak;* Anna: *Nina Semenova;*
Lisaveta: *Natalia Akrimova;*
Tatianka: *Alla Afanaseva;* Petka:
Alesha Bazarova; Grishka: *Iura
Ivanov;* Yegorsha: *Sergei Vlasov;*
Varvara Iniakhina: *Natalia
Fomenko;* Grogori Minin: *Vladimir
Artemov;* Piotr Zhitov: *Igor
Ivanov;* Olena: *Alla Semeneshina;*
Ilya Maksimovich Netesov: *Anatoli
Kolibianov;* Maria: *Galina
Filimonova;* Valentina: *Tatiana
Popova;* Trofim Lobanov: *Feliks
Raevsky;* Pelageya: *Lidia
Gorianova;* Avdotia: *Marina
Gridasova;* Tatiana: *Svetlana
Gaitan;* Grandchildren: *Misha
Kasapov, Vova Mikhailov, Natasha
Barkhatova;* Timofei Lobanov:
Vladimir Zakharev; Anisia: *Elena
Vasileva;* Alexandra Durynina:
Nelli Babicheva; Raechka
Klevakina: *Lia Kuzmina;* Daria
Kropotova: *Bronislava Proskurnina;*
Marfa Repishnaia: *Svetlana
Grigoreva;* Pavla Tugoluvkova:
Evgenia Barkan; Polina Chugaeva:
Irina Nikulina; Anattoli Chugaev:
Vladimir Artemov; Filia-Petukh:
Mikhail Samochko; Ignat Baev:
Sergei Muchenikov; Sofron-Mudri:
Sergei Kozreyev; Mitenka-
Malyshnia: *Vladimir Semichev;*
Yura: *Igor Sklira;* Father: *Sergei
Kozyrev.* Director: *Lev Dodin;*
Design: *Eduard Kochergin;*
Costumes: *Inna Gabai;* Coach:
Valarie Galendeev; Stage
Mechanics: *Roman Gerasimov,
KonstantinBelodubrovsky, Piotr*

Razuvaev, Alexander Pulinets;
Lighting: *Oleg Kozlov, Ekaterina
Dorofeeva, Vitali Skorodumov;*
Sound: *Alla Tikomirova, Evgeni
Kagan;* Properties: *Iulia Zverlina,
Vera Epifanova;* Dressmakers:
Maria Fomina, Marina Khozhina,
Makeup: *Galina Varukhina;* Stage
Managers: *Olga Dazidenko,
Natalia Sologub, Tamara
Satretinova.*
Journal: 20,23,24/4/94
Press: G: 11,26/4/94; **MEN:**
21,22/4/94

**78. STARS IN THE
MORNING SKY** by Alexander
Galin; MALY DRAMA THEATRE
OF ST PETERSBURG; *22-23
April 1994.* Maria: *Anzhelika
Nevolina;* Anna: *Tatianna
Shestakova;* Lora: *Tatiana
Rasskozova;* Klara: *Marina
Gridasova;* Alexander: *Sergei
Bekhterev;* Valentina: *Galina
Filimonova;* Nikolai: *Sergei
Kozyrev* or *Igor Ivanov.*
Director: *Lev Dodin;* Co-Director:
Tatiana Shestakova; Design:
Alexei Porai Koshits; Stage
Mechanics: *Roman Gerasimov,
Konstantine Belodudrovski,
Alexander Pulinets, Piotr Razuaev;*
Light: *Oleg Kozlov, Vitali
Skorodumov;* Properties: *Iulia
Zverlina;* Sound: *Alla Tikhomiroa;*
Dressmaker: *Maria Fomina;*
Makeup: *Galina Varukhina.*
Journal: 20, 23, 24/4/94

359. GIANT by Bruno Stori;
TEATRO DELLE BRICIOLI; *10-
14 May 1994.* Performer:
Monica Morini; Giant's Voice:
Alberto Branca; Animators: *Paolo
Romanini.* Director: *Maurizio
Bercini;* Collaboration: *Marina
Allegri;* Music: *Alessandro Nidi;*
Costumes: *Evelina Barilli.*

Press: MEN: 12/5/94; S:
30/6/94.

360. teechers by John Godber;
HULL TRUCK COMPANY; *17–
22 October 1994.* Director:
John Godber.

362. A MIDSUMMER NIGHT'S
DREAM by William Shakespeare;
COMPASS THEATRE; *8–12
November 1994.*

363. ALADDIN AND THE
MAGIC LAMP by Neil Duffield;
LIBRARY THEATRE COMPANY;
*24 November 1994 – 14
January 1995.* Director: *Eileen
Murphy.*

FREE TRADE HALL; Peter
Street, M2 3NQ; **AZ:**
101, F5; **XAZ:** 165, G1.

361. BURNING QUESTIONS:
THE *ON FIRE* REVUE by Paul
Field and Stephen Deal; ROBERT
FROST PRESENTATIONS; *12
February 1994.* Team: *Julian
Carr, Polly Louise Deal, Paul
Field, Annie McCaig, John
Talbot, Karen C Williams,
Stephen Deal, Rob Frost,
Humphry Jaeger, Kate Strafford.*

GORTON LIBRARY;
Garratt Way, M18 8HE;
061–205 2637; **AZ:** 62,
A1; **XAZ:** 103, F2. **W**

433. PUPPET CABARET;
PRESTO PUPPETS; *19
august 1994.*

301. BIG BAD WOLF;

MANCHESTER ACTORS
COMPANY; *December 1994.*

**GORTON WEST MOBILE
LIBRARY,** Bennett Street,
M12; **AZ:** 107, F3;
XAZ: 88, B6.

124. THE TIGER WITH
GOLDEN CLAWS;
MANCHESTER ACTORS
COMPANY; *7 July 1994.*

GREEN ROOM, 54/56
Whitworth Street West,
MANCHESTER M1 5WW;
061–236 1677. **AZ:**
105, G1; **XAZ:** 166, A3.
G, H, W

26. THE DANCING
PRINCESSES; Jakob and Wilhelm
Grimm adapted by EDINBURGH
PUPPET COMPANY and
THEATRE ARLEKIN; *17
November 1993.*

10. THE PLUMMETING OLD
WOMAN, devised by SLEEPING
GIANT from stories by Oscar
Wilde and Daniil Kharms,
translated by Joseph Ryan and
Peter Davies; Original Music by
Chris Selden; *18–19 October
1994.* Actors: *Stephen
Keyworth, Chris Solomon, Annabel
Walker;* Caretakers: *Shaji
Revindran, Emily Stones;*
Musicians: *Beverly Mizon, Chris
Shelden.* Director: *Caroline
Chick;* Lighting: *Colette
Cunningham;* Design: *Catherine
Alexander;* Producer & Company
Director: *Stephen Keyworth.*

11. KABARETT VALENTIN; devised by David Lavender and Colin Granger from the following songs, sketches and comic monologues by Karl Valentin: **Zwangvorstellungen** *(Compulsory Theatre)*, **Tingeltangel** *(Whatsisname/The Train Dream)*, **Lichtbildreklamen** *(Small Ads)*, **Die Vier Jahreszeiten** *(Song of the Seasons)*, **Spracht und Wirklichkeit** *(Language and Reality)*, **Das Hunderl** *(The Dog)*, **Tingeltangel** *(Coincidence)*, **Die Uhr von Loew** *(Loewe's Watch)*, **Kragenknopf und Uhrenzeiger** *(From Studs and Watchhands)*, **Die Raubritter vor München** *(Duckdream)*, **Das Aquarium** *(The Aquarium)*, **Das Lied vom Sonntag** *(Song of Sunday)*, **Beim Arzt** *(At the Doctor's)*, translated by Eva Schiffer, Karin Lynton and Marina Kobler; Music and Additional Material by Michael Mann; UMBRELLA THEATRE; *22-23 October 1993.* Karl Valentin: *Michael Mann;* Liesl Karlstadt: *Christine Furness.* Director: *David Lavender;* Stage Manager: *Marina Kobler;* Costumes and Properties: *Marina Kobler, Melanie Fowkes;* Lighting Operator: *Jason Wingrove.*

22. THE CARETAKER by Harold Pinter; SHORT AND STOCKY THEATRE COMPANY; *28-30 November 1994.* Cast: *Mark Attwood, Stephen Swift, Nigel Capper.* Director: *Alan Pattison.*
Press: CL: 27/10/93

278. A STRANGE AND UNEXPECTED EVENT; HORSE AND BAMBOO THEATRE; *31 October 1993.*

23. NIGHT AFTER NIGHT PART ONE, written and performed by Neil Bartlett, with live music by Nicolas Bloomfield; GLORIA; *2 November 1994.*

24. PLAYHOUSE CREATURES by April de Angelis; THE SPHINX; *3 November 1993.* Doll Common: *Jean Marlow;* Nell Gwyn: *Fleur Bennett;* Elizabeth Farley: *Nicola Grier:* Mary Betterton: *Frances Cuka;* Rebecca Marshall: *Geraldine Fitzgerald.* Director: *Sue Parrish;* Design: *Annabel Lee;* Resident Composer: *Claire van Kampen;* Lighting Design: *Di Stedman;* Movement Director: *Linda Dobell;* Assistant Director: *Jane Wolfson;* Fight Director: *Philip Croskin;* Production Manager: *Sarah Rowe;* Stage Manager: *Kim Wiltshire;* Soprano: *Susannah Waters;* Set BuildinG: *Terry Taylor, Dave Peltier;* Costume Supervisor: *Heather Joiner-Tucker;* Scene Painter: *Julian Adams.*
Press: I: 2/1/94; T: 17/12/93

18. SACRED JOURNEY by Mark Witten; THE NEW MEXICO REP, presented by FIFTH AMENDMENT LTD; *8 November 1993.* Performer: *Adan Sanchez.* Director: *William Partlan;* Design: *Steve Light-Orr;* Costume: *Jim Alford;* Lighting: *Lynn Janick;* UK Design Supervision: *Patrick Joseph;* Technical and Company Manager: *Adam Quinn.*

13. LECTIA / THE LESSON by Eugene Ionesco, translated into Romanian by Elena Vianu;

NATIONAL THEATRE OF CLUJ, ROMANIA; *9-11 November 1993.* The Teacher: *Anton Tauf;* The Pupil: *Anda Chirpelean;* The Servant: *Viorica Michelea.* Director: *Mihai Maniuti;* Stage Design: *Mihai Ciupe;* Electrician: *Ioan Vuscan;* Props: *Giovanni Mateescu.* **Press:** G: 23/11/93

25. CLUB OF NO REGRETS by FORCED ENTERTAINMENT with music by John Avery; *12-13 November 1993.*

27. THE TEMPEST; William Shakespeare adapted for 7-12 year olds by KAZZUM ARTS PROJECT; *14 November 1993.*

362. DEF CABARET; *14 November 1994.* Martin Adams, Fiona Clarke, Adrian Cook, Ed First, Barbara Getliffe, Dave Gorman, Steve Hignett, Simon Kent, Peter Kerry, Noreen Kershaw, Alison Lyon, Bill McCoid, Nick Marston, Claire Mooney, Franchine Mulrooney, Hovis Presley, Joe Puller, James H Reeve, Julie Rutterford, Mat Seber, Rade Serbedzije, Joe Simpson, Dave Spikey, Trevor Suthers, Julie Westwood, Bronwen Williams; Compère: *James H Reeve;* Director: *Noreen Kershaw;* Producers: *Trevor Suthers, Robin Thornber.*

14. ALL HE FEARS by Howard Barker; Music by Matthew Scott; MOVING STAGE MARIONETTE COMPANY; *15/16 November 1993.* Operators: *Cheryl Asterly, Anna Ingleby, Rachel Riggs, Juliet Middleton, Gren Middleton;*

Voices: Botius: *Ian McDiarmid;* Opina: *Harriet Walter;* The Rat/The Mother: *Stephie Fayerman;* The Man/Agent of the Police/Hooligan: *Bill Stewart;* Prostitute: *Louise Middleton;* Taxi/Hooligan/The Horse: *David Schaal.* Director: *Mike Pearce;* Producer: *Gren Middleton;* Puppets and Costumes: *Juliet Middleton, Gren Middleton;* Wire Figures: *Colleen Magennis;* Scrims and Landscapes: *Annabel Keatley;* Aluminium Stage: *Jolyon Havinden;* Sound Recording: *Graham Harper;* Lighting: *Gren Middleton.*

29. BIKINI CLAD AND TIGHT TRUNKS; TINSELTOWN THEATRE; *17 November 1993.*

12. LEAR by Edward Bond; EGG ROCK THEATRE COMPANY, with MANCHESTER UNIVERSITY ENGLISH SOCIETY; *18 November 1993.* Cornwall/Foreman/Soldier: *Rupert Blackstone;* Lear: *George Cockerill;* Cordelia/Soldier: *Rebecca Downey;* Ben/Dying Rebel/Sergeant: *Deborah Galloway;* Commandant: *Shelley Gordon;* Bodice/Stranger: *Rebecca Harker;* Judge/Officer/Old Orderley: *Lucille Howe;* Bishop/Clerk/Pete/Thomas: *Tim Hyam;* Lewis/Spy/Susan/Soldier: *Caroline Jester;* Dead Worker/Ghost: *Gregory Macklin;* Councillor/Soldier: *Caoimhe McAuinchey;* Aide/Officer/Prison Doctor: *Juliet McMyn;* Engineer/John/North: *Mark Paterson;* Carpenter/Soldier: *Paul Smith;* Fontanelle/Stranger: *Ella Tong;* Warrington/Spy/Stranger: *Carl White.* Director: *John Myatt;* Producer: *Kate Mayne;* Costume Design: *Chloé Thompson;* Lighting Design: *Chris*

Lindsay; Make-up and Effects: *H Tamen/C Harris;* Music: *Christopher Seldon;* Properties: *Helen Bush;* Set Construction: *Robert Booth;* Sound: *Tom Glastonbury;* Technical Assistant: *Whizz Biddlecombe;* Wardrobe: *Natasha Rotte.*

28. STUPID CUPID by John Binnie with lyrics by Phil Willmott; GAY SWEATSHOP; *19-20 November 1993.* Cast: *Andy Spiegel, Nicholas Rylance, Karen Parker, Juley McCann, Simon Ashmore.*
Press: I: 4/11/94; **MEN:** 20/11/93; **T:** 4/1/94

20. TWO by Jim Cartwright; WOT NO BOOTS! THEATRE COMPANY; *25-26 November 1993.* Landlord/Moth/Old Man/Mr Iger/Roy/Fred/Boy: *Jamie Greer;* Landlady/Old Woman/Maudie/Mrs Iger/Lesley/Alice/Woman: *Sharon Marsden;* Musicians: *Gary Heatherinton, Andi Cooper, Geraldine Martin.* Director: *Louise Barry;* Stage Manager: *Pam Devine;* Song Writer: *Gary Heatherington;* Lighting: *Sam Fear;* Sound: *Andi Cooper;* Mime Advisor: *Russ Lane.*

15. EVA PERÓN by Copi, translated by Annie Lee Taylor, adapted by Camden McDonald; ROAR MATERIAL; *8-10 December 1993.* Eva "Evita" Perón: *Philippa Coslett;* Isabellita: *Karen Crook;* Perón: *Phil Dennison;* The Nurse: *Lorraine Hacket;* The Mother: *Sam Kristie.*
with

16. THE FOUR TWINS by

Copi, translated by Annie Lee Taylor; ROAR MATERIAL; *8-10 December 1993.* Leila: *Rachel Bull;* Josephine: *Karen Crook;* Maria: *Phil Dennison;* Fougerre: *Ian Lashford.*
For **15 & 16:** Frocks: *Jackie Haynes;* Settings: *Nicola Bowden, Michelle Mellor;* Lighting Design/Deputy Stage Manager: *Tamsin Drury;* Director: *Camden McDonald.*

17. THE SUPER-INCREDIBLE INVISIBLE MAN SHOW, devised and performed by THE GLEE CLUB PERFORMANCE COMPANY, in conjunction with the GREEN ROOM with music by Steve Mead; *1-24 December 1993.* Performers: *Eddie Aylward, Martin Gent, Bea Pemberton, Mark Whitelaw;* Trumpet/Percussion: *Bob Dinn;* Clarinet/Bassoon: *Caroline Gee;* Drums: *Ray Hughes;* Tenor Saxophone: *Paul Smyth;* Other Instruments: *Steve Mead.* Lighting: *Paul Towson, Kath Geraghty.*

9. FRAGMENTS by Philip Lightfoot; LAST RESORT THEATRE COMPANY; *16-17 January 1994.* Andrew Rose: *James Higginson;* Libby Rose: *Nicola Jenkinson;* Roy Goodman: *Graham Simmonds;* Pam Knowles: *Christine Dalby;* Cathy Trust: *Julia Swindells.* Director: *Stephen C Buckwald;* Lighting: *Gaynor Cowle;* Stage Management: *Ian Micklewright.*

19. NOT LIKE JIMMY WHITE by Keith Sturgess; RED ROSE THEATRE COMPANY; *19 January 1994.* Jessie Blythe:

Margaret Eddershaw. Director:
Keith Sturgess; Sound: *Steve
Sims.*

21. HEARTSTRINGS, devised
by TALKING PICTURES; *21-22
January 1994.* Performers:
*Clarissa Malheiros, Joy Merriman,
Analia Perego, Jonny Potter,
Mladen Vasary.* Director: *Sandra
Mladenovitch;* Light and Sound:
Stuart Low.
Press: CL: 12/1/94; **MEN:**
22/1/94

389. DECADENCE by Stephen
Berkoff; HATS AND TEA
THEATRE COMPANY; *23-24
January 1994.*

**388. SOOKI AND THE
KOZZIBIMWEH;** GREEN CANDLE
DANCE COMPANY; *30 January
1994.*

36. PEACOCK by DOO
COT; *1 February 1994.*
Artistic Director/Puppeteer:
Nenagh Watson; Chief
Scenographer: *Rachael Field;*
Musical Director/Composer: *Sylvia
Hallett;* Musician/Composer: *Jamie
McCarthy;* Musician: *Jez Dolan;*
Lighting: *Richard Jenkins;*
Company Stage Manager: *Tania
Peach;* Technical Stage Manager:
Cathy Johansen; Set Construction:
Dave Chadwick; Costume:
*Rachael Field, Sue Auty, Clone
Zone, Wig Wam, Evelyn & Derek
Field, Vintage Clothing, Art Deco
Ceramics.*
Journal: 1/2/94
Press: CL: 26/1/94; **M:**
14/2/94; **MEN:** 27/1/94,
3/2/94; **S:** 16/6/94

37. TOP GIRLS by Caryl

Churchill; MANCHESTER
METROPOLITAN UNIVERSITY
DRAMA SOCIETY; *2 February
1994.* Marlene: *Virginia Clay;*
Isabella/Joyce/Mrs Kidd: *Helen
Win;* Lady Nijo/Win: *Kirsty
Harling;* Dull Gret/Angie: *Claire
Quinn;* Pope Joan/Louise: *Yvonne
Way;* Patient Griselda/Nell/Jeanine
: *Catherine Maunder;* Waitress/Kit
/Shona: *Hayley Rawson.*
Director: *Emma Reed;* Stage
Manager: *Catherine Skelton;* Set:
Andrew Lock; Lighting: *Julia
Baker;* Sound: *John Allen;*
Costume: *Louise Lock, Jane
O'Donnell;* Props: *Rushna Avari;*
Stage Hands: *Rushnas Avari, Bret
Adsly.*
Journal: 2/2/94

**38. EVERYTHING IN THE
GARDEN,** written and performed
by Heather Phoenix, as Marie
Lloyd. *5 February & 9 July
1994.* Director: *Nadia Molinari;*
Pianist: *Peter England;* Lighting:
*Spot the Dog Lighting and
Sound.*
Press: ANT: 3/2/94; **MM:**
4/2/94

363. THE CHAIRS by Eugene
Ionesco, translated by Donald
Watson; THEATRE FACTORY;
9-10 February & 23 May 1994.
An Old Man: *David Caird;* An
Old Woman: *Tracey Meredith;*
The Emperor: *John Henshaw;* The
Orator: *Judy Hawkins.* Director:
Nigel E Higginson; Lighting:
James Callm; Production
Manager/Sound: *Rachel Coles.*
Press: MEN: 10/2/94.

364. EFFIE'S BURNING BY
Valerie Windsor; SLEEPING
GIANT; *11 February 1994.*
Effie Palmer: *ALexandra Lilley;*

Ruth Kovacs: *Catherine Alexander.* Director: *Caroline Chick;* Lighting: *Simon Maunders, Collette Cunningham.*

225. PICKING BONES;
Written and Performed by Stephen Keyworth; SLEEPING GIANT; *11 February, 7 March 1994.* Director: *Colin Snell.* Lighting: *Will Varley.* Press: CL: 23/2/93

182. THE SOUND
COLLECTOR by Roger McGough; QUICK SILVER THEATRE; *13 February 1994.*

46. STALINLAND by David
Grieg; RUMBLE THEATRE COMPANY; *19 February 1994.* Joseph: *Jim Burke;* Helena: *Sarah Stow;* Karin: *Charlotte Somers;* Lydia: *Helen Blackhurst;* Alex: *Nick Bodger.* Director: *Helen Blackhurst;* Lighting Design: *Simon Maunder;* Lighting Operator/Set Design: *Mike Patterson;* Sound: *Louise Mason.*
Journal: 19/2/94
Press: M: 10/2/94

48. GIMME SHELTER
(incorporating GEM, GOTCHA and GETAWAY) by Barrie Keeffe; THE MACATASHNIK THEATRE COMPANY; *21-22 February 1994.* Kev: *Greg Macklin;* Gary: *John Myatt;* Janet: *Camilla MacDonald;* Bill: *Rob Gurner;* Ton: *George Cockerill;* Lynne: *Anna McGarry;* Kid: *Mark Paterson;* Head: *Blake Woodhouse.* Directors and Producers: *Mark Paterson, Greg Macklin;* Stage Manager: *Galya Goodman;* Set Design: *Sarah Webster;* Lighting: *Scot Pryor;*

Sound: *Sarah Webster;* Assistant Stage Managers: *Lucy Hovland, Emily Craig, Katherine Cairns.*
Journal: 21/2/94

366. STORM READING; based
on the writings of Neil Marcus; adapted for the stage by Roger Marcus, Rod Latham and Neil Marcus; ACCESS THEATRE OF SANTA BARBARA; *23-25 February 1994.* Performers: *Neil Marcus, Matthew Ingersoll, Kathryn Voice.* Producer and Director: *Rod Latham;* Design: *Theodore Michael Dolas;* Sound: *Thomas W Rollerson;* Set Construction: *Gerald Brady;* Costume: *Janis Martin;* Costume Assistant: *Sue Kennedy;* Photography: *Roger Marcus, Rod Latham, Susan Jorenson, Christopher Gardner, Michael Hughes;* Slide Paintings: *Grace Hodgson;* Brush Calligraphy: *Kathy Lathim;* Audio Description: *Daniel Girard.*
Press: G: 2/3/94; MEN: 24/2/94; SAM: 4/3/94

365. LEAKING FROM EVERY
ORIFICE; Written and performed by Claire Dowie; *26 February 1994.*

373. 1984, dramatised from
George Orwell's novel by Max Rubin & Toby Hadoke; CHARLATAN THEATRE; *27-28 February.* Winston Smith: *Max Rubin;* O'Brien: *Toby Hadoke;* Julia: *Alexandra Lilley;* Exercise Woman/Barmaid/Thought Criminal/ Chorus: *Rosie Collins;* Goldstein/ Parsons/ Waiter/Chorus: *Asa Goldschmied;* Mrs Parsons/ Prostitute/Conductress/Chorus: *Louise Bolton;* Winston's Mother/ Old Woman/Anna/Chorus: *Anna*

Ratcliffe; Syme/Charrington/Guard /Chorus: Simon Letherman. Director: Toby Hadoke; Producers : Max Rubin, Toby Hadoke; Stage Manager: Annabel Walker; Lighting: Scott Pryor; Sound Engineer: Tom Glastonbury; Assistant Director: George Cockerill; Masks and Movement: Max Rubin; Composer and Musician: Steve LeDoguer

419. SHAKEN; EGG ROCK THEATRE COMPANY; 7 March 1994.

392. THIS IS ALL I HAVE TO SAY; SuAndi; 8 March 1994

393. WALKING TALL; Susan Lewis; 8 March 1994.

56. FULL OF NOISES, an adaptation by Christopher Newell of THE TEMPEST by William Shakespeare; 11–12 March 1994. Cast: Susan Sands, Joanna Curley, Carla Steele, Rachel France, Fiona Macdonald, Jo Burgess, Emma Ferguson, Helen Lacey, Peter Machen. Director: Chris Newell; Musical Director: Paul Barker; Design: Stephen Wilkins; Assistant Director/Lighting Design/Sound Operator: Pam Vision; Production Manager: Helen Maguire; Sound Engineer: John Delf; Lighting Design/Operation: Chris Williams. Journal: 12/3/94

57. SNIFF OUR CoDPIECE – The CoD Wars Cabaret; 13 March 1994. Contributors: Martin Adams, Ian Baskerville, Claire Beck, Allan Beswick, Holly

Burton, Fiona Clarke, Adrian Cook, Barbara Getliffe, Steve Hignett, Alison Lyon, Nick Marston, Bill McCoid, Claire Mooney, Hovis Presley, Dave Puller, Mat Seber, Joe Simpson, Dave Spikey, Trevor Suthers, Kenneth Alan Taylor, Julie Westwood, Bronwen Williams. **Press:** CL: 10/3/94

394. LITTLE RED RIDING HOOD AND FRIENDS; BOOSTER CUSHION THEATRE; 13 March 1994.

368. AFTER THE TONE by David Christy; MAIDEN THEATRE COMPANY; 14–15 March 1994. Daniel: Scott Kentrell; Sheelagh: Christine Brennan; Mother: Caroline Woodruff; Graham: Lee Wolstenholme; Agent: Steve Evets; Dancers: Christine Brennan, Philip Brennan. Director: David Christy; Production Manager: Meryl Bruen; Stage Manager: Joanne Flannery; Zoey Wade. **Press:** CL: 9/3/94

369. SONG OF THE WHORE by Julie Jones; MAIDEN THEATRE COMPANY; 14–15 March 1994. MARIE: Hilly Barber; Tony: Steve Evets; Amelia: Christine Brennan; Mother: Caroline Woodruff; Priest: Philip Brennan; Man Client/Rapist: Scott Kentrell. Director: David Christy; Production Manager: Meryl Bruen; Stage Manager: Joanne Flannery; Zoey Wade. **Press:** CL: 9/3/94

One Emphasis of the CITY OF DRAMA has enabled us to see a much wider variety of Disability Theatre. This chance for comparison has helped us to see that our own NEW BREED company are, with GRAEAE, well ahead of many others in their interest to a general audience. Similarly, the CITY OF DRAMA, in arranging for the NEW STAGES Festival of innovation in Independent Theatre to be held in Manchester, revealed the two local companies selected, NEW BREED and THE GLEE CLUB, to be presenting infinitely more accessible and immediately enjoyable work than that by companies from elsewhere.

NEW BREED's offering, GRIMM (372), portrayed here in the portrait of one of its participants, MIKE PARKER, was a much darker piece than the lightness of this picture suggests, despite its significant amount of humour. Described as "the story famous brothers dared not write", it was in fact a collection of tales in a dark forest set, created by a border of long, sliced, pitch-coated pendant logs, – practical for the performers as it swung aside for wheel-chairs and proving bearings for the unsighted –, and atmospheric for the audience.

The most Grimm of the tales told was of woodcutter who, meeting the Devil in the forest, sold him his daughter, his wife then taking the most ruthless steps to keep her from the Devil's power. NEW BREED's gruesome taste was best illustrated by their tale of how, "when Our Lord and St Peter walked the earth," they were petitioned by a crippled begger, whom they assisted by straightening him out on the blacksmith's anvil. The former cripple's family were much impressed and resolved to use the same methods upon his sister-in-law but, "lacking the divine touch," made rather a mess of things. NEW BREED have got well beyond making disbility the open theme of their work but can give such topics as religious healing wry side-glances.

370. FOREVER NINETEEN by David Christy; MAIDEN THEATRE COMPANY; *16-17 March 1994*. Madame/ Mildred: *Caroline Woodruff;* Jenny Slattery: *Christine Brennan;* Ameil'e: *Hilly Barber,* William: *Phillip Brennan;* Captain Johny Holbrook: *Scott Kentell;* Ted: *Lee Wolstenholme.* Director: *David Christy;* Production Manager: *Meryl Bruen;* Stage Manager: *Joanne Flannery; Zoey Wade.* **Press: CL:** 31/3/93; **MEN:** 1/9/93.

371. THE POST CARD by David Christy; MAIDEN THEATRE COMPANY; *18-19 March 1994*. Patrick: *Philip Brennan;* Mary: *Christine Brennan;* Liam: *Lee Wolstenholme;* Bridie: *Caroline Woodruff;* Seaun: *Scott Kentell;* Rosie: *Hilly Barber;* Aidan/O'Flaherty: *Steve Evets;* Auctioneer: *David Christy.* Director: *David Christy;* Production Manager: *Meryl Bruen;* Stage Manager: *Joanne Flannery; Zoey Wade.* **Press: CL:** 8/4/92

184. MAGIC FINGER by Roald Dahl; OPEN HAND THEATRE COMPANY; *20-21 March 1994*.

395. THE HARLOT'S CURSE; TAMESIDE COLLEGE BTEC PERFORMING ARTS; *24-26 March 1994*.

396. WIND IN THE WILLOWS by Kenneth Graham, dramatised by COMPASS THEATRE; *27 March 1994*.

372. GRIMM; NEW BREED THEATRE COMPANY; *31 March*

& 15-16 June 1994. Performers: *Keith Barlow, Alex Dubrowski, Mike Parker, Norma Pearson, Margaret Shaw, John Travis, Garry Robson.* Director: *Gabriel Gawin;* Assistant Director: *Garry Robson;* Sign Language Interpreter: *Derrick Robinson;* Collaborators/ Researchers: *Mickey Fellowes, Brenda Hall, Elsie Kirk;* Design: *Paul Kondras;* Lighting: *Sara Domville;* Stage Managers: *Dave Turner, Mike Bowden;* Technician: *Geoff Farmer;* Performers' Assistants: *Richard Lofthouse, Siobhan Carmichael.* **Press: CL:** 23/3/94 **MEN:** 31/3/94; **OC:** 16/5/94

74. BOY by Shaun Duggan; ALTERED STATES THEATRE COMPANY; *7-8 April 1994*. Boy: *Micky Poppins;* Boy: *Derek Hicks;* Boy: *Sean McKee;* Girl/ Mother/Teacher/Girl2: *Ayse Owens;* Man/Friend/Man2: *John Brobbey;* Bully/Friend2/Man3: *James McMartin.* Director: *Kate Rowland;* Designer: *Hannah Mayall;* Lighting: *Paul Russell;* Sound: *Paul Cargill;* Production Manager: *Michael White;* Costume: *Liz Hanna;* Set Building: *Hamish Darlington.* **Journal:** 8/4/94 **Press: TES:** 11/3/94

397. RITA, SUE AND BOB TOO by Andrea Dunbar; SHORT AND STOCKY; *11-14 April 1994*. Bob: *Mark Attwood;* Sue: *Michelle Radcliffe;* Rita: *Alison Clark;* Father: *Stephen Swift;* Mother: *Grace Allen;* Michelle: *Heather Phoenix.* Director: *Alan Pattison.* **Press: BI: CL:** 6/4/94

**374. BALLAD OF LUCY
JORDAN** Hilary Jones and
Christopher Wright; THE
HONEYMOON KILLERS; *19
April & 4 November 1994.* Lucy
Jordan: *Hilary Jones.* Director:
Christopher Wright.

375. STRAWMAN DANCE;
written and performed by Tyrone
Henderson; Music: David Louis
Bindman; *22 April 1994.*

376. QUACK FM!; Robert
Fraser-Munro; *23 April & 18
October 1994.*

79. TO CATCH A WHALE
by Chris Webb; THE COMPANY;
24-25 April 1994.

377. SKIN by Sara Mason;
ALLÉGRESSE; *27-28 April
1994.* Jean-Marc: *Ricco Ross;*
Suzanna: *SAra Mason;* Marty:
Corinna Richards; Frank: *Mark
Carlisle.* Director: *Fiona
Branson;* Design: *Julie Harris;*
Choreographer: *Sara Brignall;*
Percussion: *Tim Watson, Barnaby
Green;* Company Manager: *Bryan
Hands;* Stage Manager and
Lighting Design: *Shaz McGhee,
Harvey Webb;* Co-Producer:
Andrew Bancroft; Directorial
Assistance: *Stuart Trotter.*
Press: MEN: *28/4/94*

**382. CONQUEST OF THE
SOUTH POLE** by Manfred
Karge, translated by Tinch Minter
and Anthony Vivas; THEATRE
FACTORY; *11-15 May 1994.*
Slupianek: *Scott Kentrell;*
Buscher: *Peter O'Conner;*
Seiffert: *David Caird;*
Braukmann: *Richard Oldham;* La
Braukmann: *Christine Brennan;*

Frankieboy: *Fiona Clarke;* Rudi:
Philip Prennan; Rosi: *Suzy
Yannis.* Director: *Nigel E
Higginson;* Design: *Andrew Wood;*
Lighting: *Martin Adams.*

378. THYESTES by Lucius
ANNAeus Seneca, translated by
Caryl Churchill; ROYAL COURT
THEATRE; *1-4 June 1994.*
Young Tantalus/The Fury:
Sebastian Harcombe; Chorus:
Rhys ifans; Minister: *James
Kennedy;* Atreus: *Kevin
McMonagle;* Thyestes: *Ewan
Stewart.* Director: *James
MacDonald;* Design: *Jeremy
Herbert;* Costume Design: *Jennifer
Cook;* Lighting: *Jon Linstrum;*
Sound: *Paul Arditti;* Stage
Management: *Cal Hawes, Paul
Hennessy;* Student Assistant Stage
Manager: *Kate Lawson;* Assistant
Director: *Jeremy Herrin;* Voice
Coach: *Helen Strange;* Costume
Supervisor: *Glenda Nash.*
MEN: *3/6/94;* **O:** *12/6/94;* **S:**
7/7/94

379. HOPE; DESPERATE
OPTIMISTS; *7-9 June 1994.*
Performers: *Joe Lawlor, Christine
Molloy, Kaffe Matthews, Laurence
Lane.* Technician: *Cath Brittan;*
Assistant Technicians: *Kevin
Weaver, Kirsten Lavers;* Stage
Management: *James Molly, Helen
Lawlor.*
Press: CL: *1/6/94*

**380. SCENES FROM A
MEN'S CHANGING ROOM;**
EDWARD LAM COMPANY; *10-
11 June 1994.* Performers:
*Michael Chorney, Peter Duffin,
Andrew Hammerson, Igor Jocic,
Ka-Che Kwok, Mern Morrison,
Richard Riddle, Dick Wong.*
Director/Choreographer/Décor:

Edward Lam; Costumes: *Thomas Chan;* Soundtrack: *Steven Hall;* Lighting: *Tina Mshugh;* Dramaturg: *Felix Schneider-Henniger;* Technical Director: *Steven Rolf;* Project Co-ordinator: *Michael Chorney.*
Press: CL: 1/6/94

381. THE LIGHTS ARE ON BUT NOBODY'S AT HOME by Huw Chadbourn; SEMBLANCE; *13-14 June 1994.* Performers: *Frank Bock; Tamzin Griffin, Sophie Vaughan, Will Waghorn.* Director: *Huw Chadbourn;* Music: *Conor Kelly, Sam Park;* Lighting: *Luke Sapsed;* Production Manager: *Justin O'Shaughnessy;* Set: *Huw Chadbourn.*
Press: BI: 21/6/94; **MEN:** 14/6/94

85. COTTON MATHER'S WONDERS OF THE INVISIBLE WORLD; THE GLEE CLUB; *17-18 June & 23 October 1994.*

86. YOUNG COTTON MATHER'S WONDERS OF THE INVISIBLE WORLD; THE GLEE CLUB; *19 June & 23 October 1994.*

111. THE WOMEN by Clare Booth Luce; ARDEN SCHOOL OF THEATRE; *23-25 June 1994.* Nancy: *Donna Alexander;* Miriam Aarons: *Jo Burgess;* Edith: *Joanne Curley;* Jane: *Tara Daniels;* Crystal Allen: *Emma Ferguson;* A Pedicurist/A Saleswoman/Maggie/Sadie: *Zoë Ginster;* Sylvia: *Rachel Gleaves;* A Hairdresser/Saleswoman/Miss Trimmerback/Lucy/A Society Lady /A Cutie/A Debutant: *Lindi Glover;* Mors Morehead: *Eilis*

Hetherington; Mary: *Helen Lacey;* Olga/A Model/Princess Tamara/ Helene/A Girl in Distress: *Fiona Macdonald;* Euphie/Miss Fordyce/ A Saleswoman/AN Exercise Intructress/A Cigarette Girl: *Susan Sands;* Peggy: *Tracy Shaw;* A Hairdresser/A Salesgirl/ Miss Watts/A Nurse/A Society Woman/A Cutie/A Dowager: *Leah Stanley;* Little Mary: *Carla Steele;* Countess Delarg: *Laura Wolfe.* Director: *Ian Forrest;* Production Manager: *Helen Maguire;* Stage Manager: *Clare Smout;* Assistant Stage Manager: *Matt Twist;* Technician: *Tom Weir;* Set Construction: *Carl Richardson;* Costume and Set Design: *Kasia Szostak-Walker;* Help with Costumes: *Sonia Zajdel.*
Journal: 23/6/93

123. ROARING BOYS by Phelim Rowland; SANDBACH SCHOOL THEATRE; *22 July 1994.* Mr Walton: *James Read;* Mr Hassett: *Rob Gibbons;* Mr Bentham: *James Griffiths;* Mr Scammell: *Richard Lindop;* Mr White: *Adam Bayley;* Mr Luce: *Peter Garratt;* Willy: *Neil Gibbons;* Charlie Acker: *Carl Bevin.* Director & Design: *John Lonsdale;* Stage Management: *Richard Leese, Danny Howell-Jones, Mick Peirson;* Props: *James Griffiths, Karen Powell, Lynn Tomlinson;* Hairdressing: *Joan Owen;* Lighting: *Richard Lindop, Rob Gibbons, Adrian Mawson;* Soundtrack: *Chris Thompson, John Owen;* Political Research: *Jane Lonsdale, Jill Cobb.*
Journal: 22/7/94

256. THE LOVE OF THE NIGHTINGALE by Timberlake

Wertenbaker; MANCHESER
YOUTH THEATRE; *5-15
September 1994.* Philomele:
Clare Calbraith; Procne: *Ellen
Chadwick;* Niobe: *Cherry
Bartlett;* Queen: *Carys Lamb;*
Hero: *Katie Cross;* Iris: *Joanne
Haworth;* June: *Kerry Bratt;*
Echo: *Kate Webster;* Helen:
Victoria Gillmon; Aphrodite:
Venesha Browne; Phaedra:
Gemma Evans; Servant: *Sam
Houldsworth;* Female Chorus:
Greta Ghiro; Tereus: *James
McLaren;* Captain: *Wole Sawyerr;*
1st Soldier: *Gavin Ladle;* 2nd
Soldier: *Stephen Carroll;* 3rd
Soldier: *Steven Garry;* 4th
Soldier: *Stefan Gudjonsson;*
Hippolytus: *Alexander Clare;*
Theseus: *Kenneth Goodison;* Itys:
Alexander MacKintosh; Pandion:
Ben Redmond; Male Chorus:
Sajad Bobby, Stewart Pile.
Director: *Jennie Darnell;* Design:
Alison Heffernan; Lighting:
Andrew Pygott; Director's
Assistant: *Robert Wolstenholme;*
Stage Manager: *Alison Morris;*
Deputy Stage Manager: *Alison
Morris;* Assistant Stage Manager:
James O'Donovan; Senior
Technical Assistant: *Chris Ingold;*
Design Assistant: *Vicky Valdes,
Jason Woods;* Wardrobe Assistants:
Rosita Sweeney, Emma Walker;
Production Manager: *Tim Wyllie;*
Technical Manager: *Martin Doran;*
Wardrobe Supervisor: *Alison
Humphrey;* Company Stage
Manager: *Marcus Wilson;* Deputy
Company Stage Manager: *Vivien
Routledge;* Senior Design
Assistant: *Kate Hind;* Wardrobe
Assistant Supervisor: *Amanda
Morris;* Tutors: *Lynne Barlow,
Pamela Davies, Rachel
Katzenellenbogen.*
Press: BI: 13/9/94; **MEN:**
6/9/94

384. POETRY SLAM;
CULTURAL INDUSTRY LTD; *10
September 1994;* **NuYorican
Poets:** *Tracie Morris, Willie
Perdomo, Edwin Torres, Dael
Orlandersmith, Mike Tyler.*
SLAM: *Victoria McKenzie* (22),
Sancher (20), *Stephanie Tongue*
(25), *Carol Boateng* (25,9);
Lemn Sissay (29.4), *Johny
Ogundange:* "We Are Terribly
Polite in Manchester" (27.98),
Fritz (29.4). - Figures show
scores, obtained from average of
median three of five subjectively-
marking, non-poet judges, co-
opted impromptu from the
audience. **Fritz** was winner as
Lemn Sissay refused to contest
against his admired mentor in a
tie-break run off. These names
and marks are an incomplete
record of three-minute pieces
from ten local contestants, jotted
down on scrap in the hectic and
informal atmosphere.

**418. TANDARICA PUPPET
THEATRE, BUCHAREST,** *17-18
September 1994.* Puppet Master
: *Biendusa Zaita Silvestru.*

386. BLOODSTREAM by
Andrew Buckland;
MOUTHPEACE; *19-20
September 1994.* Performers:
Andrew Buckland, Lionel Newton.
Director: *Janet Buckland,*
Lighting: *Wesley France;*
Production Manager: *Lisa Audouin.*
Press: MEN: 20/9/94

383. HIGH RISK; APPLES
AND SNAKES; *21 September
1994.* Performance Poetry from
Sapphire and *Patience Agbabi.*

387. RAISIN IN THE SUN by Lorraine Hansberry; BLACK ARTS DEVELOPMENT PROJECT; *25-30 September 1994.* Ruth Younger: *Jacqueline Kington;* Travis Younger: *Aaron Stapleton;* Walter Younger: *Andy Burke;* Lena Younger: *Nicola Gardner;* Joseph Asagai: *Oswald McCarthy;* George Murchison: *Kevin MCCurdy;* Karl Linder: *Michael O'Hara.* Director: *Helen Parry;* Assistant Director/Stage Manager: *Alison Benefield;* Design: *Kim Parker;* Lighting: *Michael Elphick.* **Press: MEN:** 28/9/94.

385. WE KNOW WE DON'T KNOW WHAT WE'RE DOING; THE GLEE CLUB & PETER ZEGVELD; *3 October & 5-24 December 1994.*

399. ASSIMILATION; written and performed by Shishir Kurup; THE RAVEN GROUP; *4-5 October 1994.* **Press: MEN:** 5/10/94.

400. BLACK SON - NO FATHER: Lynel Gardner; *4-5 October 1994.* **Press: MEN:** 23/9/94, 5/10/94

401. FULL OF FRENCH; OPEN ZIP COMPANY; *8 October 1994.*

402. STORY OF M; SuAndi; *13-14 October.*

403. INTERNATIONAL STORYTELLERS; WORD OF MOUTH; *15 October 1994.* Paul Middlljin, Abbi Patrix.

404. FEVER PITCH by Nick Hornby, adapted for the stage by Paul Hodson; BRIGHTON THEATRE EVENTS; *19-20 October 1994.* Nick Hornby: *Steve North.* Director: *Paul Hodson.* **Press: CL:** 5/10/94; **MEN:** 7/10/94; **OC:** 19/9/94

405. I NEVER MADE IT AS A SEX KITTEN by Lisa Watts; *21 October 1994.*

406. BACK TO MY PLACE by Anne Seagrave; *21 October 1994.*

407. NOTES ON NOISE II by Oscar MacLennan; *21 October 1994.*

405. MUCH ADO ABOUT NOTHING by William Shakespeare; ASTIR PLAYERS; *22 October 1994.*

408. MOTHER F; F MULTI MEDIA; *24 October.*

409. NEGERANGST; SUVER NUVER; *25-26 October 1994.*

411. T.V.O.D. *29 October 1994,.*

412. EARNEST, based on Oscar wilde by STAN; *1-2 November 1994.*

413. MANUEL THE CREATOR: HET ALIBI; *5-6 November 1994.*

414. WAITING FOR GODOT by Samuel Becket; MUNICIPAL THEATRE OF HAIFA; *8-10*

November 1994.
Press: S: *28/4/94*

415. PARASITE; RECKLESS
SLEEPERS; *11 November 1994.*

**416. SUZY WRONG -
HUMAN CANNON** by Anna
Chen; MU LAU THEATRE
COMPANY; *17-18 November
1994.*

190. SINK OR SWIM; QUICK
SILVER THEATRE &
MACLENNAN DANCE
COMPANY; *20 November 1994.*

417. UBU by Alfred Jarry;
GRAEAE; *24-25 November
1994.*

**HARDING STREET
MOBILE LIBRARY,**
Ancoats, M4; **AZ:** 103,
D5; **XAZ:** 163, G5.

**124. THE TIGER WITH
GOLDEN CLAWS** a, c & e;
MANCHESTER ACTORS
COMPANY; *9 July 1994.*

HARPURHEY LIBRARY;
Park View, Rochdale Road,
M9 1TF; 061-205 2637;
AZ: 40, C4; **XAZ:** 75,
F5.

432. CHATTERBOX PUPPETS
16 August. John Piper.

301. BIG BAD WOLF;
MANCHESTER ACTORS
COMPANY; *December 1994.*

HEATON PARK, Prestwich,
M25 5SW; **061-773 1085
/6500/8044. AZ:** 30, C3;
XAZ: 60,A4. **G**

**97. THE WONDERLAND
ADVENTURES OF ALICE,**
adapted from Lewis Carroll by
Simon Corble; LIBRARY
THEATRE COMPANY with
MIDSOMMER ACTORS; *18 May
- 4 June 1994.* Door/Hare/
Five of Spades/Gryphon: *Robert
Alexander,* replaced at Haigh and
Dunham by *Phillip King;* Miss
Prickett/Mouse/The Cook/Queen
of Hearts: *Cathy Bass;* Dodgson/
Dodo/Ugly Duchess/Executioner:
Patrick Brimm; Monkey/Fish
Footman/Mad Hatter/Seven of
Spades/Executioner: *Peter
Clifford;* Lorina/Lory/Cheshire Cat
/Knave: *Ruth Dawes;* Alice:
Catriona Martin; Duckworth/Duck
/Frog Footman/Dormouse/Two of
Spades/Mock Turtle: *Robin
Samson;* White Rabbit: *Trevor
Baskerville;* Caterpillar/King of
Hearts: *Colin Stevens.* Director:
Simon Corble; Designer: *Judith
Croft;* Assistant Design: *Celia
Perkins;* Composer and Musical
Director: *Patrick Bridgman;*
Movement Director: *Caroline
Clegg;* Deputy Stage Manager on
the Book: *Katherine Mahony;*
Production Manager: *Michael
Williams;* Assistant Production
Administrator: *Jeanette Aldcroft;*
Scenic Artist: *Colin Piggott;*
Technical & Safety Manager: *Tim
Stott;* Head of Lighting and
Sound: *Gail Leah Wroth;* Sound
Engineer: *Ian Dickinson;*
Electrician: *Chris McLean;* Crew:

Nick Devaney, Rupert Griffiths,
Caroline Gee, Neil Kelly;
Wardrobe Supervisor: Cathy
Alger; Deputy Wardrobe
Supervisor: Liz Horrigan; Cutter:
Gill Chapman; Construction
Manager: Derek Jones; Deputy
Construction Manager: Gary
Armstrong; Property Maker:
Timothy Wylie; Construction
Assistant: David Doyle;
Construction Asssistant: David
Doyle; Stage Manager: Dean
Clarkin; Assistant Stage Manager:
Claire Watts. **Tour**: Tour/Stage
Manager: Rachèle Howard;
Deputy Stage Manager: Beckie
May; Assistant Stage Managers:
Geoff Aquatias, Paul Hemmings;
Assistant Director: Pam Vision.
Journal: 31/5/94
Press: CL: 1/6/94; G: 2/6/94;
MEN: 12/5/94

**HIGHER BLACKLEY
LIBRARY;** Victoria Avenue,
M9 3RA; 061-740 1534;
AZ: 31, F4; **XAZ**: 61,
E4.

**432. CHATTERBOX
PUPPETS;** 24 August 1994.
John Piper.

301. BIG BAD WOLF;
MANCHESTER ACTORS
COMPANY; December 1994.

HOP AND GRAPE; Union
Building, Manchester
University, Oxford Road
M13 9PL; 061-275 2930;
AZ: 106, A4; **XAZ**: 101,
F2.

**521. THE STRANGE
BROTHERS;** Mid March 1994.

HULME LIBRARY; Hulme
Walk, M15 5FQ; 061-
226 1005; **AZ**: 105, E3;
XAZ: 165, F6.

**432. CHATTERBOX
PUPPETS;** 12 August 1994.
John Piper.

301. BIG BAD WOLF;
MANCHESTER ACTORS
COMPANY; December 1994.

**IRISH ASSOCIATION
SOCIAL CLUB;** 17 High
Lane, CHORLTON-CUM-
HARDY M21 1DJ; 061-
881 2898; **AZ**: 71, D1;
XAZ: 115, H1.

459. WIDOWS' PARADISE by
Sam Cree; MANCHESTER IRISH
PLAYERS; May 1994.

J W JOHNSON'S; 78
Deansgate, M3 2FW;
061-831 7772; **AZ**:
101, F4; **XAZ**: 161, G5.

390. HEADLINE CABARET;
22 June: Performers: Tony Sides,
Adrian Cook, Ian Baskeville, Holly
Burton, Dave Puller, Mat Seber;
Compère: Antony H Wilson; 29
June: Performers: Kevin Seisay,
Adrian Cook, Ian Baskeville, Tony
Burgess, Raisa Hall; Compère:

Mike Harding; 6 July:
:Performers: *Frank Sidebottom, Dave Gorman, Brendan Riley, Matt Seber, Helen Lake;* Compère: *Phil Korbel; 13 July:* Performers: *Suzy Yannis, Sue Chlopiki, Dave Spikey, David Rothnie, Nick Smith, Holly Burton, Julie Rutterford, Cheryl Martin, Dave Pulley;* Comère: *Tara Newley; 20 July:* Performers: *Claire Mooney, Tony Sides, Dave Gorman, Peter Kerry, Tim Woodhouse, Claire Beck;* Chair: *Mike Kiddey;* Director: *Lawrence Till; 27 July:* With: *Henry Normal, Johhny Dangerously, Lemn Sissay, Julie Westwood, Andy Robinson;* Compère: *Alan Beswick;* Director: *Gary Hersov; 3 August:* Performers: *Holly Burton, Ian Baskeville, Phil Davey;* Compère: *Eamonn O'Neal; 10 August:* Performers: *Dave Gorman, Hovis Presley, Adrian Cook, Matt Seber;* Comère: *Louise Randall;* Director: *Braham Murray; 17 August:* Performers: *Hovis Presley, Ian Baskeville;* Compère: *Dave Spikey; 24 August:* Performers: *Claire Mooney, Helen Lake, Raisa Hall, Mary Ann Coburn, Ben Treacher, Steve Hignett, Fiona Clarke, Janine Campbell, Matt Seber;* Compère: *Alan Beswick; 31 August:* Performers: *Steve Hignett, Sue Chlopicki, Adrian Cook, Joe Simpson, Nick Marston, Fiona Clarke, Janine Campbell, Mary Ann Coburn, Matt Seber;* Compère: *Phil Korbel.* Producers: *Trevor Suthers, Robin Thornber.* **Press: CL:** 15/6/94, 10/8/94; **MEN:** 10&28/6/94, 16&28/7/94; **MM:** 26/8/96

KWIK SAVE MOBILE LIBRARY, Ashton Old Road, Openshaw, M11; **AZ:** 53, 4A; **XAZ:** 89, G6.

124. THE TIGER WITH GOLDEN CLAWS; MANCHESTER ACTORS COMPANY; *14 July 1994.*

LEVENSHULME LIBRARY; Cromwell Grove, M19 2QE; 061–224 2775; **AZ:** 61, F4; **XAZ:** 102, D6. W

434. GIRDLE AND HOSE; *27 May 1994.* Reminiscience-based performance.

432. CHATTERBOX PUPPETS *16 August.* John Piper

301. BIG BAD WOLF; MANCHESTER ACTORS COMPANY; *December 1994.*

LIBRARY THEATRE, St Peter's Square, M2 5PD; 061–236 7110. **AZ:** 101, F5; **XAZ:** 165: H1. G, H, W

1. A MIDSUMMER NIGHT'S DREAM by William Shakespeare; *4 November – 4 December 1993.* Hippolyta/Titania: *Nimmy March;* Theseus/Oberon: *Christopher Wright;* Philostrate/Puck: *Ray Emmet Brown;* Egeus/

Peter Quince: *Robert Calvert;*
Hermia: *Suzanne Packer;*
Demetrius: *Fidel Nanton;*
Lysander: *Chris Garner;* Helena:
Kathryn Hunt; Nick Bottom:
David Fleeshman; Francis Flute/
Pease Blossom: *Anthony Cairns;*
Tom Snout/Cobweb: *Josh Moran;*
Snug/Moth: *Andy Burke;* Robin
Starveling/Mustard Seed: *David
Brett.* Director: *Chris Honer;*
Designer: *Michael Pavelka;*
Composer and Musical Director:
Chris Jordan; Movement Director:
Gil Graystone; Lighting Designer:
Paul Colley; Assistant Director:
Simon Corble; Sound: *Matthew
Tompsett;* Deputy Stage Manager
On the Book: *Porl Cooper;* Sign
Language Performance Interpreter:
Byron Campbell; Production
Manager: *Michael Williams;*
Assistant Production Administrator:
Jeanette Aldcroft; Scenic Artist:
Colin Piggott; Technical & Safety
Manager: *Tim Stott;* Head of
Lighting and Sound: *Gail Leah
Wroth;* Deputy Lighting: *Lee
Threlfall;* Follow Spots: *Richard
Cunningham, Paul Moorhouse;*
Dresser: *Julia Wade;* Wardrobe
Supervisor: *Cathy Alger;* Deputy
Wardrobe Supervisor: *Liz
Horrigan;* Cutter: *Gill Chapman;*
Construction Manager: *Derek
Jones;* Deputy Construction
Manager: *Gary Armstrong;*
Property Maker: *Timothy Wylie;*
Construction Assistant: *David
Doyle;* Stage Manager: *Sharon
Stoneham;* Deputy Stage
Manager: *Phillippa Smith;*
Assistant Stage Manager:
Charlotte Aiken.
Press: CL: 10/11/93; G:
16/11/93

62. THE SNOW QUEEN by
Hans Christian Andersen, written

for the stage by Nick Stafford;
Music by David Roper; *9
December 1993 - 22 January
1994.* Narrator: *Joe Vera;*
Gerda: *Alexandra Sumner;* Kai:
Ray Emmet Brown; Snow Queen:
Penelope McGhie; Little Robber
Girl, Little Troll One, Butterfly,
Daisy, Crow Two: *Penny Layden;*
Prince, Big Troll, Tiger Lily,
Reindeer: *Chris Garner;* Princess,
Little Trool Two, Swallow,
Buttercup, Wood Pigeon Two,
Finnish Woman: *Julia Winwood;*
Grandmother, Old Lady, Crow,
Old Robber Woman, Old Lapp
Woman: *Carol Noakes* or *Kathryn
Hunt;* Voice of Rose, Wood
Pigeon One: *Penelope McGhie.*
Director: *Sue Sutton Mayo;*
Design: *Jessica Tyrwhitt;* Musical
Director and Musician: *Akintayo
Akinbode;* Lighting: *Gail Leah
Wroth;* Choreographer: *Francesca
Jaynes;* Sound: *Matthed Tompsett;*
On the Book: *Porl Cooper;*
Signed Performances: *Mary
Connell.*
Press: CL: 22/12/93; G:
30/12/93

44. RACING DEMON by
David Hare; *27 January - 26
February 1993.* The Revd
Lionel Espy: *Darryl Forbes–
Dawson;* The Right Revd Charlie
Allen: *Richard Mayes;* The Revd
Tony Ferris: *Stephen Mapes;* The
Revd Donald 'Streaky' Bacon:
Stephen Tindall; The Revd Harry
Henderson: *Alan Rothwell;* The Rt
Revd Gilbert Heffernan: *Malcolm
Raeburn;* Frances Parnell: *Kathryn
Hunt;* Stella Marr: *Jacqueline
Kington;* Heather Espy: *Ann Aris;*
Ewan Gilmour: *Ian Michie;*
Tommy Adair/Head Waiter/Server:
Robert Garrett; Waiter/Server:
Patrick Bridgman; Server: *Mary*

RICHARD MAYES' Bishop turns incandescent when confronted by DARYL FORBES-DAWSON's leader of a slum Team Ministry; Servers ROBERT GARRETT and PATRICK BRIDGMAN, with MALCOLM RAEBURN's Suffragan feel the heat; one of the most powerful scenes in the LIBRARY THEATRE production of DAVID HARE's RACING DEMON (44)

Connell. Director: *Chris Honer;* Design: *Paul Kondras;* Lighting: *Gail Leah Wroth;* Sound: *Matthew Tompsett;* On The Book: *Charlotte Aiken;* Production Manager: *Michael Williams;* Assistant Production Administrator: *Jeanette Aldcroft;* Scenic Artist: *Colin Piggott;* Technical & Safety Manager: *Tim Stott;* Head of Lighting and Sound: *Gail Leah Wroth;* Deputy Lighting: *Lee Threlfall;* Crew: *Nick Devaney, Caroline Gee;* Wardrobe Supervisor: *Cathy Alger;* Deputy Wardrobe Supervisor: *Liz*

Horrigan; Cutter: *Gill Chapman;* Construction Manager: *Derek*

Jones; Deputy Construction Manager: *Gary Armstrong;* Property Maker: *Timothy Wylie;* Construction Assistant: *David Doyle;* Stage Manager: *Sharon Stoneham;* Deputy Stage Manager: *Porl Stothers;* Assistant Stage Manager: *Julia Wade.*
Journal: 7/2/94
Press: CL: 9/2/94; **G:** 9/2/94;
MEN: 27/1/94

63.   DEBORAH'S DAUGHTER
by Pam Gems; *3-26 March 1994.* Deborah Pedersen: *Anna Carteret;* Rhoda, Lady Wiggins: *Jane Freeman;* Stephanie Pedersen: *Mia Fothergill;* Hassan Sa'id Ibn Said: *Raad Rawi;* Eric

Bellairs: *Peter Yapp;* David Delavigne: *Philip Darling;* Ali Madur: *Nasser Memarzia;* Soldier/ Yusuf: *Royce Hounsell.* Director: *Sue Dunderdale;* Design: *Shimon Castiel;* Lighting: *Jim Simmons;* Sound: *Ian Dickinson;* On the Book: *Porl Strothers;* British Sign Language Interpreter: *Byron Campbell;* Production Manager: *Michael Williams;* Assistant Production Administrator: *Jeanette Aldcroft;* Scenic Artist: *Colin Piggott;* Technical & Safety Manager: *Tim Stott;* Head of Lighting and Sound: *Gail Leah Wroth;* Deputy Lighting: *Chris McLean;* Assistant Electrician: *David Clare;* Crew: *Nick Devaney, Caroline Gee, Rupert Griffiths, Bev Pearson;* Wardrobe Supervisor: *Cathy Alger;* Deputy Wardrobe Supervisor: *Liz Horrigan;* Cutter: *Gill Chapman;* Construction Manager: *Derek Jones;* Deputy Construction Manager: *Gary Armstrong;* Property Maker: *Timothy Wylie;* Construction Assistant: *David Doyle;* Stage Manager: *Sharon Stoneham;* Deputy Stage Manager: *Charlotte Aiken;* Assistant Stage Manager: *Julia Wade.*
Journal: 22/3/94
Press: CL: 23/2/94 & 9/3/94; **G:** 7/3/94; **M:** 10/3/94; **MEN:** 24/2/94, 3 & 5/3/94; **MM:** 11/3/94; **SAM:** 24/2/94

423. STRIPPED by Julie Rutterford; ATLAS THEATRE COMPANY; *17–26 March 1994.* Liberty Belle: *Julie Riley.* Director: *Noreen Kershaw.*
Press: CL: 23/3/94 **SAM:** 4/3/94; **T:** 7/12/93

420. FRANK PIG SAYS

HELLO by Pat McCabe; CO-MOTION THEATRE COMPANY; *29–31 March 1994.* Piglet: *David Gorry;* Frank: *Sean Rocks.* Director: *Joe O'Byrne;* Design: *Ian McNicholl;* Lighting: *Rupert Murray;* Production Manager: *David Butler;* Tour Manager: *Kate Bowe;* Stage Manager: *Audrey Hession;* Scenic Artist: *Barbara Dempsey;* Lighting Technician: *Mark Waldron.*
Press: G: 31/3/94; **MEN:** 30/3/94

72. LADY WINDERMERE'S FAN by Oscar Wilde; ROUGH MAGIC THEATRE COMPANY; *5–9 April 1994.* Lady Windermere: *Ali White;* Parker/Mr Hopper/Lady Plymdale: *Mal Whyte;* Lord Darlington: *Martin Murphy;* Lady Agatha Carlisle/Mr Cecil Graham: *Miche Doherty;* Lord Windermere: *Paul Hickey;* Mr Dumby/Lady Jedburgh: *Darragh Kelly;* Lord Augustus Lorton/ Duchess of Berwick: *Sean Kearns;* Mrs Erlynne: *Helene Montague.* Pianist: *Andrew Synnott;* Violinist: *Aingeala de Burca.* Director: *Lynne Parker;* Set Design: *Barbara Bradshaw;* Costume Design: *Kathy Strachan;* Lighting Design: *Stephen McManus;* Musical Director: *Helene Montague;* Production Manager: *Padraig O'Neill;* Production Co-Ordinator: *Kate Hyland;* Stage Manager: *Annette Murphy;* Props/Wardrobe: *Suzanne O'Halloran;* Costume Construction: *Monica Ennis;* Set Construction: *Pat Byrne, Shay Byrne, Stephen Morris, Annabel Konig;* Set Painter: *Stephen Rynn;* Hair: *Shane Boyd (The Natural Cut);* Producer: *Siobhan Bourke.*
Journal: 7/4/94

Press: G: 20/4/94; **MEN:**
31/3/94, 6/4/94; **MM:** 8/4/94
S: 26/5/94; **TLS:** 13/5/94

421. LOST IN YONKERS by

Neil Simon; LIBRARY THEATRE
cOMPANY; *14 April - 14 May
1994.* Jay: *Ross McCall;* Arty:
Mohammed Mukhlis; Eddie: *Neale
Goodrum;* Bella: *REgina Reagan;*
Grandma Kurnitz: *Margaret
Robertson;* Louie: *David
Fleeshman;* Gert: *Nancy Gair.*
Director: *Roger Haines;* Design:
Chris Kinman; Lighting: *Nick
Richings;* Deputy Stage Manager
on the Book: *Charlotte Aiken;*
British Sign Language Interpreter:
Mary Connell; Production
Manager: *Michael Williams;*
Assistant Production Administrator:
Jeanette Aldcroft; Scenic Artist:
Colin Piggott; Technical & Safety
Manager: *TIm Stott;* Head of
Lighting and Sound: *Gail Leah
Wroth;* Sound Engineer: *Gary
Rhodes;* Assistant Electrician:
David Clare; Crew: *Katherine
Mahony, Bev Pearson;* Wardrobe
Supervisor: *Cathy Alger;* Deputy
Wardrobe Supervisor: *Liz
Horrigan;* Cutter: *Gill Chapman;*
Construction Manager: *Derek
Jones;* Deputy Construction
Manager: *Gary Armstrong;*
Property Maker: *Timothy Wylie;*
Construction Assistant: *David
Doyle;* Stage Manager: *Sharon
Stoneham;* Deputy Stage
Manager: *Porl Strothers;* Assistant
Stage Manager: *Julia Wade.*
Press: CL: 20/4/94; **MEN:** 9
& 19/4/94; **MM:** 15/4/94

422. DEATH AND THE

MAIDEN by Ariel Dorfman;
LIBRARY THEATRE COMPANY;
26 May - 18 June 1994.
Paulina Salas: *Amanda Boxer;*

Gerardo Escobar: *Will Knightley;*
Roberto: *Stephen Tindall;* Usher:
Paula J Horton. Director: *Chris
Honer;* Design: *Paul Kondras;*
Lighting: *Gail Leah Wroth;* Sound:
Ian Dickinson; Deputy Stage
Manager on the Book: *Porl
Stothers;* Production Manager:
Michael Williams; Assistant
Production Administrator: *Jeanette
Aldcroft;* Scenic Artist: *Colin
Piggott;* Technical & Safety
Manager: *TIm Stott;* Electrician:
Chris McLean; Crew: *Beverley
Pearson;* Wardrobe Supervisor:
Cathy Alger; Deputy Wardrobe
Supervisor: *Liz Horrigan;*
Wardrobe Maintenance: *Debbie
Newton;* Cutter: *Gill Chapman;*
Construction Manager: *Derek
Jones;* Deputy Construction
Manager: *Gary Armstrong;*
Property Maker: *Timothy Wylie;*
Construction Assistant: *David
Doyle;* Stage Manager: *Sharon
Stoneham;* Deputy Stage
Manager: *Charlotte Aiken;*
Assistant Stage Manager: *Julia
Wade.*
Press: CL: 1/6/94; **G:**
2&8/6/94; **MEN:** 26&28/5/94,
10/6/94; **MM:** 17/6/94

397. RITA, SUE AND BOB

TOO by Andrea Dunbar; SHORT
AND STOCKY THEATRE
COMPANY; *19-24 July 1994.*
Here: Sue: *Georgina Lamb.*

254. MANCHESTER NIGHTS by Alan Williams; MANCHESTER YOUTH THEATRE; 6–10 September 1994. Marx/Scally 1: Rob Davidson; Engels/Scally 2: John Smethurst; Jimmy Hart/ Iolo: Barry Jones: Man 1/Stan: Tom Wright; Man 2/Levenshulme Lovething: David Rogers; Man 3/ Oggie: Neil Flavell; Man 4/ Derek: Mathew Czornekyi; Man 5/Roger: Tom Walker; Man 6/ Librarian/Vic: David Walker; Man 7/Gibbo: Clegg/Billy: James Moore; Drunkard/Martin: Mick Dacks; Parson/Russell: James Hall Morhouse; Barman/Ian: Antony Bradley; Young Tom/Crusty Rose: Vicky Ellis; Chorus/Siobhan: Liz Heslip; Chorus/Lulu: Yvonne Sweeney; Irish Susie/Animal: Lindsey Fawcett; Chorus/Sharon: Julia Jolly; Janet Clegg/Julie: Anna Simpson; Mrs Clegg/Emmy: Laura Hayes; Irish Kathleen/ Cassie: Sarah Shaw; Chorus/ Belinda: Joanne Jones; Flower Girl/Janet: Lucy Bellingham; Chorus/Joy: Pam Bailey; Irish Maggie/Jules: Lucy Stirzacker; Barmaid/Stage Manager: Victoria McGlynn; Chorus/Marina: Anna Chambers. Director/Lighting: Bill Hopkinson; Design: Jon Carnall; Musical Director: Carol Donaldson; Stage Manager: Liz Needham; Deputy Stage Manager: Vanessa Jackson; Assistant Stage Manager: Cara Boardman, Jennifer; Desigh Assistants: Nazeera Atcha, Angeli Sweeney; Wardrobe Assistants: Sarah Brameld, Margaret Chamberlain, Emma-Claire Kershaw; Technicians: Richardf Kennedy, Robert Jackson; Choreographer: Kathryn Beverley; Production Manager: Tim Wylie; Technical Manager: Martin Doran; Wardrobe Supervisor: Alison Humphrey; Company Stage Manager: Marcus Wilson; Deputy Company Stage Manager: Vivien Routledge; Senior Design Assistant: Kate Hind; Assistant Wardrobe Supervisor: Amanda Morris; Directors' Assistants: Philip Brennan, David Harrison, Robert Wolstenholme; Tutors: Lynne Barlow, Pamela Davies, Rachel Katzenellenbogen. Press: MEN: 7/9/94.

424. ANORAK OF FIRE by Stephen Dinsdale; G&J PRODUCTIONS; 12–14 September 1994. Gus Gascoigne: James Holmes. Director: Sarah Frankcom. Press: CL: 7/9/94; DT: 15/9/94; DM: 27/8/93; MEN: 13/9/94; ST: 22/8/93.

261. THE NIGHT LARRY KRAMER KISSED ME; written and performed by David Drake; SANDPIPER PRODUCTIONS; 15–17 September 1994. Director: Chuck Brown; Lighting Design and Company Stage Manager: Douglas Kuhrt; Original Sound Design: Ray Schilke; Original Music for '12-Inch Single': Steven Sandberg; Producer: Harold Sanditen. Journal: 17/9/94 Press: G: 31/8/94

425. SMALL CRAFT WARNINGS by Tennessee Williams; LIBRARY THEATRE COMPANY; 22 September – 15 October 1994. Leona: Rosemary McHale; Violet: Melanie Hudson; Doc: John Levitt; Monk: William Roberts; Bill: John Sharian; Steve: Richard Purro; Quentin: Michael Packer; Bobby: Michael Magee; Tony: Anthony Hannan.

Director: *Roger Haines;* Design: *Judith Croft;* Lighting: *Nick Richings;* Sound: *Ian Dickinson;* Assistant Director: *Nigel Higginson;* Dialect Coach: *Judith Windsor;* Deputy Stage Manager on the Book: *Katherine Mahony;* Production Manager: *Michael Williams;* Assistant Production Administrator: *Jeanette Aldcroft;* Scenic Artist: *Colin Piggott;* Technical and Safety Manager: *Tim Stott;* Head of Lighting and Sound: *Chris McLean;* Deputy Head of Lighting and Sound: *Stephen Sinclair;* Sound Engineer: *Ian Dickinson;* Follow Spot Operator: *David Clare;* Wardrobe Supervisor: *Cathy Alger;* Deputy Wardrobe Supervisor: *Liz Horrigan;* Wardrobe Maintenance: *Debbie Newton;* Wardrobe AssistantL *Sharon Heald;* Construction Manager: *Derek Jones;* Deputy Construction Manager: *Gary Armstrong;* Property Maker: *Timothy Wylie;* Connstruction Assistant: *David Doyle;* Stage Manager: *Sharon Stoneham;* Deputy Stage Manager: *Port Stothers;* Assistant Stage Managers: *Julia Wade, Christine Sinclair.*
Press: CL: 5/10/94; **MEN:** 23 & 27/9/94

426. TEIBELE AND HER DEMON by Isaac Bashevis Singer and Eve Friedman; LIBRARY THEATRE COMPANY; *28 October - 19 November 1994.* Director: *Grigorii Dityatkovsky;* Design: *Emil Kapilusch:-* Both of MALY THEATRE).

427. THE SECRET GARDEN br Frances Hodgson Burnett, dramatised by Dave Simpson; Music by Roger Haines; LIBRARY

THEATRE COMPANY; *2 Dcember 1994 - 14 January 1995.* Director: *Roger Haines.*

LONGSIGHT LIBRARY; 519 Stockport Road, M12 4NE; 061-224 1411; AZ: 61, D2; XAZ: 102, B3. W

298. SHAKESPEARE'S GREATEST HITS; MANCHESTER ACTORS COMPANY; *17 January 1994.*

430. PAT BRENNAN PUPPETS; *9 August 1994*

301. BIG BAD WOLF; MANCHESTER ACTORS COMPANY; *December 1994.* Red Riding Hood/Beauty/Gretel/Wolf: *Nicola Barnfield;* Jack Frost /The Woman/Wolf: *Stephen Boyes;* Soldier/Cackle/Scuttle/Wolf: *Nigel Capper;* Hansel/Grandmama/Wildcat/Wolf: *Viv Warentz.* MUSICIANS: Violin: *John Wilson;* Flute: *Nicola Barnfield.* Design: *Stephen Boyes.*

MAINSTAGE; Liverpool Road, Castlefield, M3 4JN; AZ: 104, D1; XAZ: 164, D1.

250. BEAUTIFUL WOMEN by Paul Fox; WILD PINK TURKEYS; *14 August 1994.*

MANCHESTER DANCE CENTRE; Shena Simon

310

College, Whitworth Street, M1 3HB; 061–236 3095; **AZ:** 102, A5; **XAZ:** 166, B1.

436. THE MAIDS by Jean Genet, adapted by BPF; *11 July 1994.* Madame: *Janet Spooner;* Claire: *Margaret Robertson;* Solange: *Mureen Lynch;* Shadow/ Vocal Accompaniment: *Helen Lake.* Acting Director: *Phil Dennison;* Musical Director: *Phil Dennison;* Choreography: *Maureen Lynch;* Production & Stage Manager: *Gaynor Rawsterne;* Art Work: *Jonathan Ingham;* Costumes: *Gina Akinyemi;* Producer: *Margaret Robertson;* Assistant Producer: *Maureen Lynch.*
Press: MEN: 29/6/94

MANCHESTER GAY CENTRE; Sidney Street, M60 1LP; 061–274 3814; **AZ:** 105, 2G; **XAZ:** 166, 4B.

121. ANDY IN DIRE STRAIGHTS by Michael Harvey; REALLIFE THEATRE COMPANY; *8 July 1994.*

MANCHESTER JEWISH MUSEUM, 190 Cheetham Hill, M8 8LW; 061–624 2829. **AZ:** 50, A1 **XAZ:** 87, E1.

120. CANDLESTICKS by Deborah Freeman; TWO TRIANGLES THEATRE

COMPANY; *13–15 June 1994.* Louise: *Angela Morrisom;* Joanna: *Eliozabeth Holt;* Mary: *Terza Aspen;* Ian: *Patrick Bridgman.* Director: *Chris Bridgman;* Technician: *Kal Ross;* Cantor: *David Apfel,* recorded by *Max Sound (Leeds) Ltd;* Stage Management: *Gideon D Freeman, Simon Taylor.*
Journal: 15/6/94

MANCHESTER TOWN HALL, Albert Square, M60 2LA; 061–234 3039; **AZ:** 101, F5; **XAZ:** 161, H6.

438. LA CASA DE BERNADA ALBA by Federico Garcia Lorca; TELON THEATRE COMPANY; *15–16 April 1994.*

437. RICHARD III by William Shakespeare; EMPIRE THEATRE COMPANY; *14–16 April 1994.* King Edward: *T Michael Kelly,* Bishop of Ely: *Philip Lindsay;* Prince of Wales: *Eva Louise Kelly;* Clarence/Buckingham/ Richmond: *Ian Britten-Hull;* Richard: *Gino Brandolani;* Catesby: *Samantha Brandolani;* Lord Stanley: *Nicola Jeffery-Sykes;* Queen Elizabeth: *Rebecca Bridle;* Rivers: *Robbie McWhinnie;* Lord Hastings: *Andy Clarke;* Lady Anne: *Abigail Rhodes;* Brakonbury: *Hardy;* Tyrrell: *Rupert Steerforth;* Mistress Shore: *Sam Pope.* Stage Management: *Kevin Potts;* Battle Costume: *Barbara Brandolini;* Peace Costume: *Philip Lindsay;* Lights: *Ann Morton.*

311

250. BEAUTIFUL WOMEN by Paul Fox; WILD PINK TURKEYS; *16-17 August 1994.* Beautiful Bryony: *Joanne Boyle;* Rose Hinchcliffe: *Diana Brown;* Kim: *Juliet Redelsperger.* Director: *Paul Fox;* Music Technician: *Gayle Coates.*
Journal: 17/8/94

MEAD HILL CENTRE,
Middleton Road,
CRUMPSALL, M8 6NB;
061-795 8445; **AZ:** 39,
F2; **XAZ:** 74, B2.

129. GROUNDED by Eileen Murphy; M6 THEATRE COMPANY; *1 March 1994.*

MECHANICS INSTITUTE;
Princess Street, M1 6DD;
061-228 7212; **AZ:** 101,
G5; **XAZ:** 166, A1.

439. BRANDY OF THE DAMNED by Maggie Willet; SALFORD OPEN THEATRE; *13-16 December 1994.* Archie Street: *Michael Matthews;* Polymnia/Leader of the Choosing: *Anna Welsh;* Calliope/Kate Williams: *Iris Kennedy;* Clio/The Talking Teapot: *Kathryn Bailey;* Thalia/Roger's Cello: *Jane Flynn;* Melpomene/Sal: *Jan Barrett;* Urania/Auntie: *Angela Elphick;* Erato/Marie Lloyd: *Andrea Liptrot;* Euterpe/Record Shop Girl: *Vicki McHugh;* Terpsichore/Young Ivy Benson: *Julie Bailey;* Joe Williams: *John McElhatton;* Roger Bricoux/Bailiff/ John Morton: *Conan Whelan;* Little Joe/Pavarotti/Monty/

Dinosaur Prey: *Gregg Baines;* Composer/Songman/Ship's Officer/ C.O./Sal's Beau: *Dave Gorvett;* Music Hall Chairman/Drunk: *Daniel Norris;* The Jazz Singer/Ship's Captain/Cinema Manager/Porter: *Ernie Kearney;* Mother in Queue: *Maureen Reid;* Child in Queue/Bartender: *Lyndsey Reid;* Newsvendors: *Louise Norris, Kate McHugh, Lyndsey Reid, Leanne McHugh, Robert McLanachlan;* Passengers/ Customers/Reporters ...: *Sheila Mahon, Kate Barrett, Laura Reid ...,* "Musicians": *Marc Lyth, Robert McLanachlan, Dave Gorvett, Conan Whelan, John McElhatton, Ernie Kearney.*
MUSICIANS: Musical Director/ Bass Guitar/Banjo/Mandolin: *Paul Mitchell Davidson;* Flute/Clarinet/ Alto Sax: *Munch Manship;* French Horn/Synthesiser: *Jim Ledger;* Tuba/Sousaphone: *Helen Minshall;* Keyboards: *Robin Joiner;* Percussion: *Dave Hassell.*
Director: *Maggie Willett;* Co-ordinator: *Terry Doyle;* Lighting/Sound: *Michael Elphick;* Design & Props: *Robina Wilkinson, Marianne Price, Rebekah Shaw;* Set Builder: *Peter Green;* Costume: *Jan Barrett, Kate Barrett, Wendy Bailey;* Props: *Wendy Bailey;* Stage Management: *Wendy Bailey, Diane Lee;* Sound Recording: *Richard Willett;* Projectionist: *Sue Harrison.*

METHODIST CENTRAL HALL; Oldham Street, M1 1JN; **AZ:** 102, A4; **XAZ:** 162, B5.

440. DOWN AND OUT, adapted from Maxim Gorki's **THE LOWER DEPTHS** by John Barlow; ASPECTS THEATRE COMPANY; *4 June 1994.* Michael Contantine: *Neil Owen;* Lisa Constantine: *Paula Combe;* Nikki Preston: *Sarah Cottham;* John David Kennedy: *Andy Bennett;* Keith: *Anthony Bryan;* Anna: *Deborah Birch;* Phil: *Greg Barnett;* Tanya: *Julie Ward;* Kristina: *Glenda Hill;* Marquis: *James Carr;* Ace: *Jonathan Benn;* Actress: *Amanda Edwards;* Mama Roux: *Susan Dick;* Ziggy: *Emma Baron;* Zarena: *Nicole Mundle.* Director: *John Barlow;* Assistant Director/Stage Manager: *Glenda Hill;* Production Technician: *Gordon Isaacs;* Production Manager: *Ian Currie.*

MEECH STREET MOBILE LIBRARY, Openshaw, M11; **AZ:** 51, F3; **XAZ:** 89, E5.

124. THE TIGER WITH GOLDEN CLAWS; a) The Festival of Fibs; b) The Dream of the Two Brothers; c) The Invisible Donkey; MANCHESTER ACTORS COMPANY; *5 July 1994.* Devised and Performed by *Stephen Boyes, Viv Warentz and Steve Tabner.* **Journal:** 5/7/94.

MILES PLATTING LIBRARY; Varley Street, M10 8EE; 061-205 8956; **AZ:** 103, D1; **XAZ:** 163, H1.

432. CHATTERBOX PUPPETS *23 August 1994.* John Piper.

301. BIG BAD WOLF; MANCHESTER ACTORS COMPANY; *December 1994*

MOSTON LIBRARY; Moston Lane, M10 9NB; 061-205 1064; **AZ:** 41, E2; **XAZ:** 76, A3.

430. PAT BRENNAN PUPPETS; *19 August 1994.*

301. BIG BAD WOLF; MANCHESTER ACTORS COMPANY; *December 1994.*

NELL LANE MOBILE LIBRARY, Chorlton-cum-Hardy, M21; **AZ:** 71, E1; **XAZ:** 116, B2.

124. THE TIGER WITH GOLDEN CLAWS; MANCHESTER ACTORS COMPANY; *7 July 1994.*

NEWALL GREEN MOBILE LIBRARY, Wastdale Road, M23; 82, D4; 139, G1.

124. THE TIGER WITH GOLDEN CLAWS; MANCHESTER ACTORS COMPANY; *13 July 1994*

NEW MOSTON LIBRARY; Nuthurst Road, M10 6JB;

313

061–688 6291; **AZ:** 42, A2; **XAZ:** 77, E2. **W**

429. EVERYONE KNOWS WHAT A DRAGON LOOKS LIKE; ACE PUPPETS *10 August 1994.*

301. BIG BAD WOLF; MANCHESTER ACTORS COMPANY; *December 1994.*

NEWTON HEATH LIBRARY; Old Church Street, M10 6JB; 061–688 8513; **AZ:** 41, F4; **XAZ:** 76, B5. **W**

430. PAT BRENNAN PUPPETS; *8 August 1994.*

301. BIG BAD WOLF; MANCHESTER ACTORS COMPANY; *December 1994.*

NIA CENTRE, Chichester Road, M15 5EU; 061–227 9254.

18. SACRED JOURNEY by Matthew Witten; THE NEW MEXICO REP; *7 November 1993.*

45. SONG OF AN HONORARY SOULMAN by Randhi McWilliams; SMILIN' MONGOOSE THEATRE COMPANY; *3-12 February 1994.* Frenchie: *Trevor H Laird;* Claxton: *Ryan Romain;* Joy : *Maxine Burth;* Mrs Willis: *Joan*

Carol Williams; Sweetboy: *Craig Kelly;* Denzil: *Michael Rochester;* Erica: *Kerry Angus.* Director: *Roger Watkins;* Design: *Simon D Beresford;* Music: *Akintayo Akinbode;* Lighting: *Jim Simmonds;* Sound: *Simon Thomas;* Production Manager: *David Evans;* Deputy Stage Manager: *Angela Fagg;* Assistant Stage Manager: *Madeleine Willis;* Technical Asssistant Stage Manager: *Steve Bryan;* Costume Co-ordinator: *Dr Elizabeth Wells.*
Journal: 16/2/94
Press: MEN: 3 & 5/2/94; **MM:** 11/2/94

69. BLOOD, SWEAT AND FEARS by Marie Oshodi; ONE STEP THEATRE COMPANY; *17-19 February 1994.* Ben Stranelle: *Guy Rhys;* Ashley: *Beverly Scarlet;* Curtis/Kid: *Brian Morgan;* Hayes/Doctors: *Peter Kerr;* Peggy/Nurses: *Karen Crook;* Tessa: *Janet Spooner.* Stage Manager: *Marcus Hercules;* Lighting/Sound: *Stuart Myles;* Design: *Joe Purcell.*
Journal: 18/2/94
Press: MEN: 18/2/94

441. MOUNTAINTOP by David Simon; BEAT THEATRE COMPANY; *20 February 1994.* Selma: *Irma Inniss;* Wilson: *Len Trusty;* Armstrong: *Shryo Chung;* Mrs J/Little Selma: *Stephanie Sibliss;* MacKintosh: *Earth G.* Producer: *David Simon;* Design: *Dotte Cole;* Technical & Tour Manager: *Paul Hatton;* Stage Manager: *Heather Trail;* Music: *Linda Conboy, Keith Aubrey;* Choreographer: *Allison White.*

68. KING LEAR by William Shakespeare; TALAWA; *24-26*

314

February 1994. Kent: *David Webber;* Gloucester: *David Fielder;* Edmund: *David Harewood;* Lear: *Ben Thomas;* Goneril: *Lolita Chakrabarti;* Regan: *Cathy Tyson;* Cordelia: *Diane Parish;* Burgundy/Oswald: *Karl Collins;* France/Doctor: *Evroy Deer;* The Fool: *Mona Hammond;* Cornwall: *Jeff Diamond;* Albany: *David Prescott.* Director: *Yvonne Brewster;* Design: *Ellen Cairns;* Lighting: *Ace McCarron;* Choreography: *Greta Mendez;* Music: *Matthew Rooke;* Voice Workshops: *Cicely Berry;* Production Manager: *Dennis Charles;* Company and Stage Manager: *Em Parkinson;* Deputy Stage Manager: *Rupert Horder;* Assistant Stage Manager: *Fiona McCann;* Wardrobe Supervisor: *Hilary Lewis;* Additional Costumes: *Judith Ward;* Wardrobe Maintenance: *Wendy Olver;* Set Construction: *Robert Batchelor (Scenery) Ltd;* Set Painter: *Tony Fleming;* Throne Construction: *Nick Redgrave;* Production Carpenter: *Nick Bache;* Student Director: *Matthew Brewster.*
Journal: 24/2/93
Press: CL: 23/2/94; **G:** 21/3/94; **SAM:** 4/3/94

443. THE BIBI CREW – ON A lEVEL; *11-12 March 1994.* Joanne Campbell, Judith Jacob, Suzette Llewellyn, Josephine Melville, Beverley Michaels, Suzanne Packer.
Press: F: March 94; **MEN:** 12/3/94

447. DEAR PASTOR ... WHA DIS?; ANTHEA HALL THEATRE COMPANY; *24-27 March 1994.*

448. LAMENT FOR RASTAFARI; *24 April.* Brian Morgan, Felix Dexter.

442. REET PETITE by Julia Davis; OPEN DOOR THEATRE COMPANY; *5-7 May 1994.* Jackie Wilson: *Arby Sonny Preston;* James Brown/Michael Jackson/B Womack: *C P Lacey;* Diana Ross/Dinah Washington/ Berry Gordy's Secretary/Actress: *Toni Devonish;* Berry Gordy: *Denny ffrench;* Paul Brown/DJ: *Hubert Moses;* Fan/Paul Brown's Secretary/Other Woman: *Sue Pollitt;* Sam Cooke: *Eugene Paul;* Elvis Presley/Manager/Singing Teacher: *David Beeler.* BAND: Musical Director & Bass: *Joseph Ross;* Guitar: *Paul Reid;* Keyboards: *Lisa Cook;* Drums: *Shaun Brown.* Director: *JUnior Douglas;* Design: *Rodney Ford;* Assistant Designer: *Liz Ashcroft;* Lighting: *Brian Harris;* Sound: *Richard York, Saul V Mud;* Costume: *Alison Ashton;* Choreographers: *Junior Douglas, CP Lacey, Sonny Preston;* Stage Manager: *Derek Scriminger;* Deputy Stage Manager: *Catherine Palmer;* Assistant Stage Manager: *Bruce Anderson;* Techniv cal Co-ordinator: *Graham lister;* Production Carpenter: *Pat Ayling;* Sound Operator: *Keith Brake;* Production Electricians: *Kevin Fitzsimons, Rob Halliday.*
Press: March 94; **G:** 19/5/94; **MEN:** 5/5/94; **MM:** 6/5/94; **S:** 30/6/94, 7/7/94; **T:** 19/5/94

444. FULL HOUSE by Oliver Samuels; BLUE MOUNTAIN THEATRE; *8 May 1994.* Cast: *Oliver Samuels, Volier Maffie Johnson, Audrey Reid.* Director:

Oliver Samuels.

445. TWO CAN PLAY by Trevor Rhone; UMOJA THEATRE COMPANY; *12-14 May 1994.* Gloria: *Laverne Archer;* Jim: *Jason Rose.* Director: *Anton Phillips;* Production Manager: *Witty Forde;* Stage Manager: *Aaron Mapp;* Assistant Stage Manager: *Neil Johnson;* Design: *Clary Salandy;* Lighting: *Larry Coke.* Press: **MEN:** 13/5/94

446. HALLEY'S COMET by John Amos; *25-28 May 1994.* Performed by *John Amos.* Director: *John Harris;* Executive Producer: *Theodore Rawlins;* Production Stage Manager: *Chad Spies;* Assistant to John Amos: *Shannon Amos.* Press: **ANT:** 26/5/94; **CL:** 18/5/94; **F:** May 94; **MEN:** 19/5/94; **OC:** 19/4/94, 26/5/94; **S:** 30/6/94

384. POETRY SLAM; NUYORICAN POETS; *9 September 1994.*

449. BATTY RIDERby Devon Morgan; *8 October 1994.*

410. SURVIVAL OF CULTURAL TRADITIONS; URBAN BUSH WOMEN; *27-28 October 1994.*

450. DANCING ON BLACKWATER by Bonnie Greer; BLACK THEATRE CO-OPERATIVE; *20 November 1994.* Cast: *Jacqui Gorrdon-Lawrence, Sandra James-Young, Pauline Miller, Jacqueline de Peza.* Director: *Joan-Ann*

Mynard;* Design: *Juliet Green;* Lighting: *Dee Kyne.*

451. LEADBELLY - BALLING THE BLUES by John Chambers; ONE STEP THEATRE; *24-26 November 1994.* Producer: *Brian Morgan.*

NIGHT AND DAY, Oldham Street, M1 1JR; 061-236 4957; AZ: 102, A4; XAZ: 162, B5.

452. TO by Jim Cartwright; EDIBLE THEATRE COMPANY; *27 January 1994.* Landlord, Moth, Old Man, Mr Iger, Roy, Fred, Little Boy: *Lee Oldfield;* Landlady, Old Woman, Maudie, Mrs Iger, Lesley, Alice, Woman: *Stella Blackburn.* Director: *Elaine Goodman;* Sound and Lighting: *Kevin Bates.*

453. LOUTS by Trevor Suthers; REAL LIFE THEATRE COMPANY; *3-5 February 1994.* Cast: *Peter O'Connor, Graham Galloway, Joe Simpson.* Director: *Jenny Eastop;* Stage Manager: *Martin Adams.* Press: **MEN:** 3&4/2/94

454. TURN by Trevor Suthers; REAL LIFE THEATRE COMPANY; *3-5 February 1994.* Cast: *Maria Meski.* Director: *Jenny Eastop;* Stage Manager: *Martin Adams.*

522. LOVERS by Brian Friel; STICKS AND STONES THEATRE COMPANY; *23-24 February 1994.*

455. AN INNOCENT ABROAD by Trevor Suthers; REALLIFE THEATRE COMPANY; *24-26 March 1994.* Cast: *Fiona Clarke, Suzi Yanis, Pete O'Connor.* Director: *Nigel E Higginson.*

66. SHEER MURDER: Four 1930's melodramas, combined into a single evening's entertainment by NORTHERN EDGE; *31 March - 2 April 1994.* The Moonlight Glissandos: *Jim Peacock, Gaby Asher;* Whistling Harry Tuppelow: *Jim Burke.* **THE WAITER** by Sydney Box: Waiter: *Neil Edmund;* Customers: *Juliette Bott, Justin Edwards, Jim Burke, Jim Peacock;* Manager: *Gareth Beazley;* Minion: *Jim Eldred;* **THE SECOND GUEST** by Hugh Beresford and C S St Brelade Seale: Host: *Gareth Beazley;* Owens: *Justin Edwards;* **THE SPELL** by Mary Kelly: Farmsteaders: *Juliette Bott, Alison Clarke;* **A NIGHT AT THE INN** by Lord Dunsany: Toff: *Justin Edwards;* Skittles: *Neil Edmunds;* Fellow Sailor: *Jim Eldred;* Intruders: *Juliette Bott, Alison Clarke.* Director: *Gareth Beazley;* Production Manager, Light, Sound: *Simon Maunder;* Design: *Henry Matthews.* [Incomplete reconstruction of unpublished programme]. Journal: 2/4/94

NIGHT AND DAY saw two productions within a couple of weeks in July of JEAN GENET's THE MAIDS. That by BPF (436) explored what dance could add to the interpretation. That by MANCHESTER ACTORS (300) kept to GENET's intention that the parts should be played by men. Here: MICHAEL McKRELL as Madame.

456. TWIST by Trevor Suthers; REAL LIFE THEATRE COMPANY; *26-28 May 1994.* Cast: *Joe Simpson.* Director: *Alan Simpson.*

457. FALL by Trevor Suthers; REAL LIFE THEATRE

COMPANY; *26-28 May 1994.*
Buddy Windrush: *Alan Simpson.*
Director: *Joe Simpson.*
Press: CL: 18/5/94.

300. THE MAIDS by Jean
Genet, translated by Bernard
Frechtman; MANCHESTER
ACTORS COMPANY; *2-4 & 9-
11 June 1994.* Claire: *Nigel
Capper;* Solange: *Steve Tabner;*
Madame: *Michael McKrell.*
Direction & Design: *Stephen
Boyes.*

436. THE MAIDS by Jean
Genet, adapted by BPF; *6-8
July 1994.* Madame: *Janet
Spooner;* Claire: *Margaret
Robertson;* Solange: *Mureen
Lynch;* Shadow/ Vocal
Accompaniment: *Helen Lake.*
Acting Director: *Phil Dennison;*
Musical Director: *Phil Dennison;*
Choreography: *Maureen Lynch;*
Production & Stage Manager:
Gaynor Rawsterne; Art Work:
Jonathan Ingham; Costumes: *Gina
Akinyemi;* Producer: *Margaret
Robertson;* Assistant Producer:
Maureen Lynch.

121. ANDY IN DIRE
STRAIGHTS by Michael Harvey;
REALLIFE THEATRE COMPANY;
9 July 1994. Andy: *Martin
Gilbert;* Max: *Andy Darbyshire;*
Nicky: *Joe Simpson.* Director:
Helen Parry; Stage Manager:
Ged Mulherrin.
Journal: 9/7/94

501. SEXUAL PERVERSITY IN
CHICAGO by David Mamet;
THEATRE FACTORY; *28-30
October 1994.* Bernie: *Scott
Kentrell;* Danny: *Joe Simpson;*
Dedra: *Christine Brennan;* Joan:

Fiona Clarke. Director: *Nigel E
Higginson.*

301. BIG, BAD WOLF;
MANCHESTER ACTORS
COMPANY; *1-3 December
1994.*

NORTHENDEN LIBRARY;
Church Road, M22 4WL;
061-998 3023; **AZ:** 81,
F1; **XAZ:** 128, B2.

301. BIG BAD WOLF;
MANCHESTER ACTORS
COMPANY; *December 1994.*

**OLD HALL LANE MOBILE
LIBRARY,** Rusholme, M13;
AZ: 61, 4D; **XAZ:** 102,
B5.

124. THE TIGER WITH
GOLDEN CLAWS;
MANCHESTER ACTORS
COMPANY; *13 July 1994.*

OPERA HOUSE, Quay
Street, M3 3JT; 061-834
1787 (Cards: 061-242
2509; Fee £1); **AZ:** 101,
E5; **XAZ:** 161, F6.

458. THE PHANTOM OF
THE OPERA by Richard Stilgoe
and Andrew Lloyd-Webber, based
on the novel by Gaston Leroux;
Music by Andrew Lloyd-Webber;
Lyrics by Charles Hart and
Richard Stilgoe; CAMERON
MACKINTOSH and THE REALLY
USEFUL THEATRE COMPANY;
From 19 October 1993. The

UNQUESTIONABLY THE MOST POPULAR PRODUCTION in the CITY OF DRAMA, THE PHANTOM had been running for three months when the yesr began and there was no sign of its ceasing to draw packed houses indefinitely when it closed. Its insignia adorned the Town Hall and the lamp posts to mark the opening of the Year of Drama. Even the GLEE CLUB were co-opted to teach school children how to make masks like that worn here by DAVE WILLETTS, embracing LISA HULL, as Christine.

Phantom: *Dave Willets;* Christine Daae: *Lisa Hull* (or *Josie Walker);* Raoul: *Mike Sterling;* Monsieyr Firmin: *Alan Rice;* Monsieur André: *Simon Green;* Carlotta Giudicelli: *Valda Aviks;* Madame Giry: *Veronica Page;* Ubaldo Piangi: *Geoffrey Pogson;* Monsieur Reyer: *Joshua Cohen;* Passarino: *Bryan Kesselman;* Meg Giry: *Lucy Potter;* Monsieur Lefèvre: *Allan Fredricks;* Auctioneer/Don Attilio: *Tim Morgan;* Joseph Buquet: *Howard Totty;* Lionman: *Clinton Brown;* Slavemaster: *Ben Tyrrell;* Porter/Policeman in Pit: *Garth Bardsley;* Page: *Janet Cowley;* Fireman/Innkeeper: *Russell Hibberd;* Princess: *Josie Walker;* Page: *Emma Cooper;* Porter/Fireman: *Paul; Monaghan;* Wardrobe Mistress/Confidante: *Avril Gray;* Madame Firmin: *Anna Bernadin;* Innkeeper's Wife: *Claire Louise Hammacott;* Ballet Chorus: *Lucy Cook, Julie Carlton, Linda Foster, Deborah Radin, Holly Rook, Denise Whiteman*(Captain)*;* Swings: *Helen Astrid, David Fortune,. Arwel Price, Sarah Ryan;* Ballet Swing: *Katie Gibson.* ORCHESTRA: Leader/Violin: *Julian Jackson;* Violins: *William Davies, Amanda Britton, Michael Kahan, Julia Parsons, Peter Leighton-Jones, Nigel Evans;* Violas: *Jacqueline Anthony, Anne Morrison;* Cellos: *Jeremy Lamburn, Rebecca Maunder;* Double Bass: *James Manson;* Harp: *Philippa Tunnell;* Flute/Piccolo: *Sarah Harrison;* Flute Clarinet: *Munch Manship;* Oboe/Cor Anglais: *Judith Allen;* Clarinet/Bass Clarinet/EÞ Clarinet: *Nick Foster;* Bassoon: *Vicky Chandler;* Trumpets: *Ian Lynch, John Blackshaw;* Bass Trombone: *Barry Dakin;* Horns: *James Moore,*

319

Clare Holliday, Simon Twigge; Percussion: Liz Gilliver; Keyboards: Paul Slater; Keyboards/Assistant Musical Director: Robin McEwan; Orchestra Manager: Stephen Hill. Director: Harold Prince; Design: Maria Bjornson; Lighting: Andrew Bridge; Sound: Martin Levan; Musical Director: Julian Bigg; Musical Supervision: Anthony Inglis; Orchestration: David Cullen, Andrew Lloyd Webber; Musical Staging/Choreography: Gillian Lynne; Associate Director: Arthur Masella; Associate Designer: Jonathan Allen; Associate Costume Designer: Irene Bohan; Associate Lighting Designers: Howard Eaton, Mike Odam; Associate Sound Designer: Richard Sharratt; Associate Choreographer: Patricia Merrin; UK Resident Director: Geoffrey Ferris; Company Manager: Anthony Pinhorn; Stage Manager: Graham Coffey; Deputy Stage Manager: Suzanne Berry; Assistant Stage Managers: Craig Becker, Penelope Foxley; Resident Director: Larry Oaks; Sound Operator: Neil McNally; Deputy Sound Operator: John Asher; Assistant Sound: Alison Bailey; Number 1 Automation Operator: Mike Sharp;; Assistant Console Operator: Peter Watt; Creation and Design of Phantom Make-Up: Christopher Tucker; Magic Consultant: Paul Daniels; Production Administrator: Trevor Jackson; Production Manager: Kevin Eld; Production Stage Manager: Alan Hatton; Production Carpenter: Glyn Cook; Touring Carpenter: Russell Goold; Production Electrician: Alistair Grant; Touring Electrician: Alistair Grant; 1st Assistant to Sound Designer: Paul Spedding; 2nd

Assistant to Sound Designer: Midge; Production Sound Engineer: Andy Brown; Synthesizer Consultant and Programmer: Mike Stanley; Properties Supervisor: Simon Crawford; Assistant Costume Supervisor: Lucy Gaiger; Wardrobe Mistress: Anne Marie Winstanley; Painting and Dying: Jane Clive, Penny Hadrill; Hats: Jenny Adey, Lil Scott; Wigs: Pam Foster, Sarah Weatherburn, Wendy Farrier, London New York Wig Company; Shoes: Gamba. Press: BEN: 1&20/10/93; BT: 31/12/93; CL: 27/10/93; MEN: 5/2/93, 4/5/93, 3/6/93, 3/8/93, 4,7,19 /10/93, 2/12/93, 5/5/94;MM: 28/5/93, 11/3/94, 22/4/94, 6/5/94; OC: 5/7/93, 10/8/94; RO: 23/10/93; S: 12/5/94, 17/6/94; SCA: 13/5/93.

OWENS PARK, 293 Wilmslow Road, M14 6HD; 061–225 5555; **AZ:** 60, C4; **XAZ:** 101, H6.

518. SAVE THE LAST DANCE FOR ME, a musical by Corin Child; 12-15 March 1994. Director: Claire; Choreographer: Chris Appleby.

PALACE SOCIAL CLUB, Farmside Place, LEVENSHULME M19 3AD; 061–257 3538; **AZ:** 61, 4E; **XAZ:** 102, C6.

459. WIDOWS' PARADISE by Sam Cree; MANCHESTER IRISH

PLAYERS; *26 April 1994.* Ruby Dempsey: *Eileen M O'Boye;* Lucy McGarry: *Anna Brogan;* Rachel Cathcart *Margaret Cowan;* Vanessa Burton: *Rose Mellett;* Sylvia Dempsey: *Nuala Horan;* Harry Bradshaw: *Liam Bradshaw;* Ernest Gillespie: *Geoffrey Hannam;* Alan Bradshaw: *Paul Collins;* Wilfred McNeilly: *Andrew Woods;* John McGonigle: *Paul Collins.* Director: *Eileen M O'Boye;* Stage Manager: *Kathy Cunnibgham,* Backstage: *Hayley Blackmore, Michelle Brennan, Siobhan Whelan, Kevin Kenny;* Props and Costumes: *Nuala Horan, Bernadette Cooke, Evelyn Gallagher;* Lighting: *Declan O'Boyle.*

PALACE THEATRE,
Oxford Street, MI 6FT; 061-242 8503; (Cards: 061-242 2503; Fee: £1); AZ: 105, G1; XAZ: 166,A2.

460. SCROOGE; Book, Music and Lyrics by Leslie Bricusse, adapted from Charles Dickens; GARRY MULVEIN, in association with THE ALEXANDRA THEATRE, BIRMINGHAM and CHURCHILL THEATRE, BROMLEY; *9-13 November 1993 and 10 December 1994 - 4 February 1995.* Ebenezer Scrooge: *Anthony Newley;* Bob Cratchit: *Paul Downing;* Harry/ Young Scrooge: *Richard Elfyn;* Bess/Mrs Fezziwig: *Paula Margetson;* Wine Merchant/ Phantom 1/Dick Wilkins: *Chris Talman;* Mr Pringle/Phantom 3:

Ian Caddick; Jocelyn Jollygoode: *Harry Dickman;* Hugo Hearty/ Fezziwig: *David Oakley;* Bissett/ Phantom 4/Ghost of Christmas Yet to Come: *John Clay;* Mrs Dilber: *Nanette Ryder;* Miss Dilber/Mary: *Lorinda King;* Beggar Woman/Mrs Pringle: *Angie Smith;* Punch 'n' Judy Man/Phantom 2/ Topper: *Philip Hazelby;* Tom Jenkins/School Teacher: *Sean Kinsley;* Chestnut Seller: *Sarah Jane King;* Jacob Marley: *Barry Howard;* Ghost of Christmas Past: *Susanne McMendrick;* Isabel /Helen: *Gemma Page;* Ghost of Christmas Present: *Stratford Johns;* Ghost of Christmas Present: *Stratford Johns;* Jack-in-the-Box: *Alex Campbell;* Raggedy -Anne *Jo Leigh Williams;* Mrs Ethel Cratchit: *Elaine George;* Children, *from The Elliott Clarke School.* ORCHESTRA: Musical Director: *Stuart POedlar;* Assistant Musical Director/ Conductor: *Barry Todd;* 1st Keyboards: *David Beer;* Keyboards: *Neil Sunderland;* Percussion: *Catherine Newell;* Double Bass: *Bernard Herrmann;* French Horn: *Sian Fergusson;* Trumpet/Flugel Horn: *Nick Baker;* Trumpet/Piccolo Trumpet: *David Wood;* Trombone: *Nick Smith;* Flute/Clarinet/Piccolo: *Pat Kyle;* Flute/Alto Flute/ Clarinet: *John Graham;* Flute/Clarinet/Bass Clarinet: *Patricia Walker;* Musical Arrangements: *Gordon Langford, Ian MacPherson;* Synthesisers Programmer: *Kelvin Thompson.* Director: *Bob Tomson;* Choreographer: *Tudor Davies;* Design: *Paul Farnsworth;* Lighting: *Hugh Vanstone;* Sound: *Kevin Swain;* Illusions: *Paul Kieve;* Flying by Foy; Assistant Director: *Madeleine Loftin;* Assistant Choreographer: *Domini Winter;*

321

Company Manager: *Peta Stratford Johns;* Stage Manager: *Karen Szameit;* Assistant Stage Managers: *Michael Sherwin, Michael Smith;* Production Manager: *Iain Gillie;* Dance Captain: *Lorinda King;* OProduction Electrician: *Paul Siequien;* Wig Mistress: *Sandria G Reeses;* Wig Assistant: *Barbara Alderson;* Wardrobe Mistress: *Jemimah Tomlinson;* Wardrobe Assistant: *Jackie Kennedy;* Second Wardrobe Assistant: *Shelby Newley;* Sound Operator: *Tim Stephens;* Assistant Sound: *Tony Algar;* Production Carpenter: *Ken Milligan;* Flying Supervisor: *Ben Haynes;* Associate Lighting Designer: *Mike Sobotnicki;* Scenery Painters: *Christine Nash, Sue Dunlop;* Metalwork: *Jim Sullivan;* Costumes: *Angels Bermans, Wendy Harrison, Sian Harris, John Sheward, Sue Bradley, Jackie Bitton, Mary Tryfonos, Naomi Kritcher, Joy Duffet, Alan Selzer.*
Press: OC: 9&10/11/93

461. DICK WHITTINGTON, devised by Malcolm Goddard; BARRY CLAYMAN CONCERTS and APOLLO LEISURE, by arrangement with KEN DODD; *11 December 1993 - 6 February 1994.* King Rat: *Howard Sykes;* Fairy: *Sybie Jones;* Alice Fitzwarren: *Diana Lee-Carol;* Alderman Fitzwarren: *Glyn Owen;* Mate: *Bunny Jay;* Bosun: *Gordon Jay;* Blodwyn the Cook: *Wyn Calvin;* Idle Jack: *Ken Dodd;* Dick Whittington: *Susan Maughan;* Tommy the Cat: *Mark Howard;* Sultana of Morocco: *Jennifer Stanton;* The Ray Cornell Dancers: *Sue Bailey, Hugh Bernard, Scott Beswick,*

Linda Doyle, Joanne Gaskin, Kathryn Harlow, Amanda Jones, Paul Judge, Marc Lawlor, Julie Ann Philips; The Diddy Men: *Sarah Battle, Jennifer Calpin, Katherine Cherry, Emma Coghlan, Tracie Couper, Jennifer Crook, Lucy Hulse, Natalie Kelly, Caroline Lavelle, Gemma McFarlane, Kerry McKee, Danielle Mallia, Emma Mallie, Ann-Marie Robinson, Hayley Tierney, Stacey Waterhouse;* The Diddy Kids: *Jodie Jayes, Emma Calpin, Jade Davies, Laura Hesford, Hayley Holuj, Sarah Lawrence, Terri Lucas, Emma McIllvenny, Catherine Mannion, Jodie Mannion, Emma Martin-Henry, Carla Mining, Natalie Sergeant, Faye Tierney, Natalie Webster, Natalie White.*
ORCHESTRA: Musical Director: *Peter Whitfield;* Trumpet: *Simon Barnes;* Trombone: *Laurie Cooper;* Woodwind: *Phil Chapman;* Bass Guitar: *Pete Windle;* Guitar: *Martin Bleasdale;* Keyboards: *Kevin Speight;* Drums: *Irven Tidswell;* Orchestra Contractor: *Arthur Dakin.* Director: *Malcolm Goddard;* Choreographer: *Annie Livesey;* Executive Producer: *Barrie C Stead;* Lighting: *John Holding;* Company Manager: *Keith Woolfenden;* Deputy Stage Manager: *Amy Louise O'Connor;* Assistant Stage Manager: *Hugh McInally;* Sound: *Wigwam;* Production Carpenter: *John Ashworth;* Wardrobe Mistress/ Supervisor: *Sharon Howarth;* Wardrobe Assistant: *Julie Burke.*
Press: CL: 22/12/93; **BEN:** 13/10/93; **G:** 21/12/94; **MEN:** 12&21/4/93; **OC:** 13/12/93 **SEA:** 28/4/93; **SME:** 29/4/93

462. WHERE'S THE BIRDIE:-

SESAME STREET LIVE; STREET PROMOTIONS; *1-4 March 1994*. Press: **MEN:** 2/3/94

463. WHEN DID YOU LAST SEE YOUR TROUSERS? by Ray Galton and John Antrobus, based on a story by Ray Galton and Alan Simpson; LIVE WIRE THEATRE PRODUCTIONS; *21-26 March 1994. Linda Lusardi, Arthur Bostrom, Hilary Minster, John D Collins, Anna Karen, Glen Davies, Carol Carey, Howard Nightingale, Kieran McGivern.* Director: *Roger Smith;* Design: *Simon Kimmel;* Lighting: *David Kidd;* Producer: *Richard Haddon;* Associate Producer: *James Tapp.* Press: **MEN:** 22&23/3/94; **MM:** 25/3/94; **OC:** 22/3/94; **RO:** 26/3/94; **S:** 24/3/94

59. PEER GYNT by Henrik Ibsen, in a version by Frank McGuiness, from a literal translation by Anne Bamborough; THELMA HOLT, by arrangement with the ROYAL SHAKESPEARE COMPANY & POINT TOKYO COMPANY; *17-19 March 1994.* Peer Gynt: *Michael Sheen (18 March:* Graham Ingle*);* Ase: *Paola Dionisotti;* Kari/Mountain Girl/ Fellah: *Julie Byrne;* Aslak/ Eberkopf/Huhu: *Vincent Regan;* Master of Ceremonies/Eberkopf/ Overseer/Gaurd/Bosun: *Graham Ingle;* Young Girl: *Mandy Cheshire;* Youth/Look-Out: *Jonathan Butterell;* Mads Moen/ Cotton/Hussein/Cook: *Ronan Vibert;* Groom's Father/Brat/ Trumpeterstrale/Gaurd/Priest: *Christopher Brand;* Solveig's Father/Ballon/Receiver/Ship's Captain/ Parish Sheriff: *Peter Holmes;* Solveig: *Catherine White;*

Groom's Mother/Anitra: *Miriam Kelly;* Helga: *Anna Niland;* Solveig's Mother/Slave: *Sybil Allen;* Ingrid's Father/Troll King: *Espen Skjønberg;* Ingrid/Green Woman/ Overseer: *Bronagh Gallagher;* Mountain Girls: *Louise Francis, Kate Fenwick;* Thief/ Guard/Ship's Mate: *Dickon Tyrell;* Begriffenfeldt/Traveller: *Michael Fitzgerald;* Buttonmoulder: *Haruhiko Joh;* Other Parts: *Cast & Michael Barber, Clair Bryan, Ben de Wynter, Jacqui Dubois, Paul Gooding, Rupert Mason, Julie Nunn, Claire Storey.* Director: *Yukio Ninagawa;* Choreographer: *Matthew Bourne;* Assistant Choreographer: *Scott Ambler;* Japanese Dance Consultant: *Suketaro Hanayagi;* Design: *Tsukasa Nakagoshi;* Costumes: *Lily Kominel;* Costumes Assistant: *Kazuko Numata;* Costume Superviser: *Claire Mitchell;* Assistant Costume Supervisor: *Lindsay Pugh;* Wardrobe Mistress: *Maria Kirby;* Wardrobe Asssistant: *Sarah Leese;* Wigs Mistress: *Barbara Alderson;* Lighting: *Tamotsu Harada;* Sound: *Akira Homma;* Music: *Ryudo Uzaki;* Music Arrangers: *Takayuki Inoue, Akira Sekiya;* Company Stage Manager: *Jeremy Adams;* Deputy Stage Manager: *Lorraine Tozer;* Assistant Stage Managers: *Kate Forrester, Michael Sherwin;* Palace Stage Manager: *Jamie Grouse;* Sound Operator: *John Owens;* Sound Assistant: *Mika Morishita;* Technical Directors: *Michael Cass Jones, Jun Mano;* Assistant to Technical Director: *Iain Gillie;* Palace Technical Manager: *Pat O'Leary;* Production Assistant: *Yuriko Akishima;* Props Design: *Hiromi Tokumasu;* Props Supervisor: *Jane Slattery;* Production Carpenter: *Robert*

Knight; Production Electrician:
Nick Jones; Palace Chief
Electrician: *David Moore;*
Starlight Operators: *Satoshi
Fujimaki, Jason Harvey;* Computer
Graphics Design: *Noriyoshi Asano;*
Graphics Assistants: *Yumiko
Suzuki, Kentano Tatsube.*
Journal: 18/3/94
Press: G: 5/3/94; **MEN:**
18/3/94

**464. THE OFFICIAL TRIBUTE
TO THE BLUES BROTHERS;**
DAVID PUGH LTD; *28 March –
2 April 1994.* Elwood: *Simon
John Foster;* Jake: *Mark White;*
Bluettes: *Yvonne Newman, Joe
Speare, David Danna.* BAND:
Lead Guitar: *Paul Gendler;*
Trrumpet: *Lindsay Bennett;*
Drums: *Chris Buck;* Saxophone:
Tony McCormick; Bass Guitar:
Pat Davey; Keyboards: *Jeff
Wraight.* Director: *David Leland;*
Musical Supervision: *Tony
McCormick;* Design: *Caroline
Amies;* Lighting: *Patrick
Woodroffe;* Musical Staging:
Carole Todd.
Press: MEN: 29/3/94; **RO:**
2/4/94; **S:** 29/9/94

83. COPACABANA; Music by
Barry Manilow, orchestrated with
Andy Rumble, sometimes based on
original orchestrations by Artie
Butler, Larry Hochman, Eddie
Arkin and Lee Shapiro; Lyrics by
Bruce Sussman and Jack Feldman;
Book by Barry Manilow, Jack
Feldman and Bruce Sussman;
APOLLO LEISURE GROUP and
BARRY CLAYMAN CONCERTS
LTD, in association with GARRY
C KIEF and JOHN ASHBY, by
arrangement with THEATRE
ROYAL, PLYMOUTH; *7 April –
14 May 1994.* Tony/Stephen:

Gary Wilmot; Lola: *Nicola;* Rico:
Richard Lyndon; Conchita: *Anna
Nicholas;* Sam: *Howard Attfield;*
Gladys: *Jenny Logan;* McManus/
Mr Brill/Pirate Captain: *Duncan
Smith;* Young Man Auditioning/
Copacabana Doorman/Louis: *John
Derekson;* Mr Schwartz/Willy/
Carlos: *Jon Emmanuel;*
Impressionist: *Martin Ryan;*
Audition Pianist 1/Copacabana
Doorman: *David Olton;* Audition
Pianist 2/Bus Boy: *Adam Richard
Jones;* Audition Pianist 3:
Jonathan Craig; Jingle Singers/
Mermaids: *Petrina Johnson, Nicola
Smythe;* Maitre D: *Douglas
Franklin;* Bolero Dancers: *Gina
Lee Lincoln, Natalie Holtom,
Rebecca Parker, Sergio Covino,
Warren Carlyle, Bryn Walters;*
Fernando: *Laurence Stark;*
Mermaids: *Melanie Stace, Tracy
Darnell;* Ensemble: *Sarah Bayliss,
Warren Carlyle, Sergio Covino,
Jonathan Craig, Tracy Darnell,
Kerry Dawkins, John Derekson,
Jon Emmanuel, Douglas Franklin,
Rebekka Gibbs, Natalie Holtom,
Petrina Johnson, Adam Richard
Jones, Gina Lee Lincoln, David
Olton, Rebecca Parker, Trudi
Rees, Martin Ryan, Nicola
Smythe, Melanie Stace, Laurence
Stark, Eli Stalhand, Andy Tyler,
Bryn Walters, Rachel Woolrich.*
ORCHESTRA: Musical Director/
Keyboards: *Andy Rumble;*
Keyboards 2/Assistant Musical
Director: *Phil Hawkes;* Keyboards
3: *Paul Moran;* Basses: *Lewis
Evans;* Guitars: *Andy Holdsworth;*
Drums: *Mike Grigg;* Percussion:
Kevin Campbell; Trumpet 1/
Flugelhorn: *Dave Plews;* Trumpet
2/Flugelhorn: *Mark Cumberland;*
Trombone: *Pat Hartley;* Reed1:
Bob McKay; Reed 2: *Adrian
Bullers;* Orchestral Management:
Bill Occleshaw; Assistant

Orchestral Manager: *Arthur Dakin.* Director: *Roger Redfarn;* Choreographer: *Dorian Sanchez;* Assistant Choreographer: *Adrian Allsopp;* Lighting Design: *Hugh Vanstone;* Sound Design: *John Del Nero;* Design Concept: *Gary Withers, of Imagination;* Projection Design: *Chris Slingsby, Jon Turner;* Scenic Design: *Martin Grant;* Costumes: *Hugh Durrant;* Executive Producer: *Adrian Leggett;* Company Manager: *Frank Lee-White;* Stage Manager: *Gregg Shimmin;* Deputy Stage Manager: *Natalie Langer;* Assistant Stage Managers: *Mark Berry, Clare Whitfield;* Wardrobe Mistress: *Patricia McCauley;* Wardrobe Assistants: *Darren Linaker, Caroline Waterhouse;* Wig Master: *Mark Pilcher;* Wigs Assistant: *Maria Moore;* Sound Operator: *Tom Button;* Sound Assistant: *Jill Rowley;* Projection Operator: *Karen Morid;* Automatioon Operator: *Adam Strallen;* Projection/Automation No 2: *Rob Hayden;* Touring Production Electricians 1&2: *Tim Stevens, Alistair Mullen;* Vari*Lite Operator: *Ros Evans;* Technical Manager: *Graham Lister;* Assistant Lighting Designer: *Alistair Grant;* Assistant Sound Designer: *Mike Furness;* Director's Assistant: *Paul Luke;* Costume Desing Assistant: *Helen Skillicorn;* Vari*Lite Design: *Richard Knight;* Dance Captain: *Andy Tyler;* Keyboard Technician: *Michael S Murray;* Fight Arranger: *Jonathan Howell;* Dialect Coach: *Sally Grace;* Rehearsal Pianist: *Tim Cumper;* Production Electricians: *Jim Hepplethwaite, Paul Cook, Tim Stephens, Ben Jeffery;* Production Sound: *CHris Full, Nigk Gilpin;* Production Projection: *Dave Herd, Martyn Elliot;* Projection

Programmer: *Allstair Haig;* Production Automation: *John Hastie, Ted Moore;* Production Carpenters: *Andy Chelton, Colin Ligandel;* Production Rigger: *Tim Roberts;* Props Buyer: *Katie Spencer;* R&R Advisor: *Tom Pearce;* Digital Production in Los Angeles: *David Denson, Ran Ballard, for Hydra Tech;* Wardrobe Supervisor: *Dina Hall;* Costume Makers: *B&J Costumes, Sue Bradley, Claire Christie, Alison O'Brian, Trevor Collins, Jane Gonin, Rupert Gordon, Stephen Gregory, Sian Harris, Wendy Harris, Michael Kennedy, Nathasha Kornilof, Angela Mizner, Carol Molyneux, Della Rebours, Alan Selzer, John Sheward;* Hats and Headress Makers: *Sean Barrett, Jack Britton, Simon Dawes, Catherine Delaney, Sue Hole, Sandra Kierans, Mark Wheeler;* Beading: *Daphne Randle;* Fabric Painting: *Frances Esen;* Accessories: *Naomi Critcher;* Gloves: *Cornelia James;* Shoes: *Anello and Davide;* Feathers: *Miss Ruhle;* Wigs: *Danute Barszczewska, Bodyline.*
Journal: 18/4/94
Press: CL: 22/4/94; **MEN:** 17/12/93, 24,31/3/94, 8,9/4/94; **O:** 26/6/94; **OC:** 15/11/93; **PP:** July/August 1994; **RO:** 16/4/94

468. PATSY CLINE, devised by Mervyn Conn; THEATRE MANAGEMENT CONSULTANTS; *16-21 May 1994.* Cast includes: *Sandy Kelly, George Hamilton IV.* Director: *Johnny Worthy;* Musical Director: *David Beer.*

465. THE ROCKY HORROR SHOW by Richard O'Brien;

THEATRE ROYAL PLYMOUTH; *24-28 May 1994.* Magenta/ Usherette: *Patricia Quinn;* Janet: *Sophie Lawrence;* Brad: *Paul Collis;* The Narrator: *Windsor Davies;* Riff Raff: *Kraig Thornber;* Columbia: *Joanne Redman;* Frank 'n' Furter: *Jonathon Morris;* Rocky: *David Ingram;* Eddie/Dr Scott: *Peter Gallagher;* Phantoms: *Joanne Cameron, Michael Dalton, Simon Gillespie, Mary Savva;* BAND: Musical Director/Keyboards: *Dave Brown;* Synthesiser/Assistant Musical Director: *Chris Parren;* Tenor Saxophone: *Geoff Driscoll;* Drums: *Clem Cattini;* Electric Guitar/Acoustic Guitar: *Derek Griffiths.* Director: *Christopher Malcolm;* Design: *Robin Don;* Musical Arrangements: *Richard Hartley;* Costumes: *Sue Blane;* Lighting: *Michael Odam;* Sound: *Paul Farrah;* Assistant Choreographer: *Stacey Haynes;* Company and Stage Manager: *Teg Davies;* Deputy Stage Manager: *Jo Miles;* Assistant Stage Managers: *Jenny Dezille, Mary O'Leary;* Sound Engineers: *Graham Chrimes, Gary Kenyon;* Wardrobe: *Helen Parris;* Wig Mistress: *Nathalie Branch;* Touring Electrician: *Paul Maloney;* Production Manager: *Matt Britton;* Production Electricians: *John Bishop, Claire Self;* Touring Carpenter: *Simon Blackmore;* Props: *Acme, Naomi Jeffries, Richard Sinclair;* Men's Tailoring: *Alan Selzer;* Costumes: *Kim Witcher;* Hats: *Jenny Adey;* Wigs: *Michael Ward, Showbiz Wigs;* Dyeing and Printing: *Penny Hadrill.*
Press: MEN: 19&25/5/94; OC: 23&25/5/94; S: 24/3/94

466. THE BFG by Roald Dahl, adapted by David Wood; CLARION PRODUCTIONS; *7-11 June.* Dad/The BFG: *Anthoney Pedley;* Sophie: *Ruby Evans;* Mum/The Childchewer/Miss Plumridge/The Queen of England: *Marcia King;* Guy/The Bonecruncher/The Headmaster/Mr Tibbs: *Oliver Gray;* Daniel/The Fleshlumpeater/Classmate/Simpkins /The Head of the Army: *Andy Couchman;* Sam/The Bloodbottler/ Sam Simpkins/The Head of the Airforce: *TRistan Middleton;* Katherine/The Meatdripper/ Classmate/Mary: *Mary Waters;* Rebecca/The Gizzardgulper/ Dreamer/Undermaid/The Queen of Sweden: *Katie Purslow;* Chef: *Chris Langrish;* Maid: *Emma Bown.* Director: *David Wood;* Musical Director/Keyboards: *Torquil Munro;* Composer: *Peter Pontzen;* Design: *Susie Caulcutt;* Lighting: *Simon Courtney-Taylor;* Company Manager: *Kevin Chadderton;* Stage Manager: *Gilda Frost;* Technical Assistant Stage Manager: *Martin Drew;* Assistant Stage Managers/ Understudies: *Chris Langrish, Emma Bown;* Sound Engineer: *Keith Hutchinson;* Wardrobe Mistresses: *Rachel Coreroy, Helen Paris;* Assistant Director: *Adam Stafford;* Sound: *Mike Furness;* Production Manager: *Simon Robertson;* Costume Supervisors: *Val Kirkman, Adrian Gwillym.*
Press: MEN: 8/6/94; **OC:** 25/11/93, 6/6/94; **TESS:** 11/3/94.

467. RETURN TO THE FORBIDDEN PLANET by Bob Carlton; POLA JONES with THEATRE ROYAL, PLYMOUTH. *10-22 May 1993.* Captain

Tempest: *Stuart Nurse;* Dr Prospero: *Peter Alexander;* Ariel: *Frido Ruth;* Cookie: *Marcos D'Cruze;* Science Officer: *Rebecca Wright;* Bosun Arras: *Simon Jessup;* Navigation Officer: *Clive Fishlock;* Miranda: *Sarah Whittuck;* Chorus: *Patrick Moore;* The Infant Miranda: *Rebecca Ptaszynski;* Heidi High: *Yngvil Vatten;* Ensign Nora Carrott: *Jill Myers;* Tex Ako: *Tim Parker;* Hugo Sthair: *Mark Crossland.* Director: *Bob Carlton;* Production Musical Director: *Kate Edgar;* Set Design: *Rodney Ford;* Associate Director: *Peter Rowe;* Costumes: *Sally Lesser;* Ariel Costume: *Adrian Rees;* Musical Staging: *Carole Todd;* Special Effects: *Gerry Anderson;* Lighting: *Benny Ball;* Sound: *Bobby Aitken;* Company Stage Manager: *Lloyd Martin;* Deputy Stage Manager: *Rosie Gilbert;* Assistant Stage Manager: *Eamonn Byrne;* Second Production Electrician and Board Operator: *Tom Goode;* Sound Operators: *David Ogilvy, Elio Di Risio;* Wardrobe Mistress: *Kathy Powell;* Instrument Technician: *Derek Byrne;* Video Technician: *Anthony Stephenson;* Tour Production Manager: *Ted Irwin;* Associate Lighting Designer and Production Electrician: *Chris Jaeger;* Production Sound Engineers: *Ian Stevenson, Alan Mathieson;* Wardrobe Consultant: *Karen Marsh.*
Press: MEN: 9/6/94; **MM:** 17/6/94; **OC:** 13/6/94; **RO:** 18/6/94

469. NODDY by Enid Blyton, adapted by David Wood; CLARION PRODUCTIONS; 5-9 July 1994. Noddy: *Karen Briffett;* Big Ears: *Eric Potts.*

Director: *David Wood;* Design: *SUsie Caulcutt;* Lighting: *Simon Opie;* Music: *Peter Pontzen;* Sound: *Mike Furness.*
Press: MEN: 30/6/94, 6/7/94; **OC:** 5/7/94; **T:** 28/12/93

470. ME AND MY GIRL by L Arthur Rose & Douglas Furber, revised by Stephen Fry and Mike Ockrent; Music by Noel Gay; POLA JONES/FARWORLDS LTD/THE RICHARD ARMITAGE - NOEL GAY ORGANISATION; 7 September-16 October 1993. Bill Snibson: *Andrew O'Connor;* Sally Smith: *Rebecca Thornhill;* Maria, Duchess of Dene: *Clare Welch;* Sir John Tremayne: *Gary Lyons;* Lady Jacqueline Carstone: *Claire Massie;* The Hon Gerald Bolingbroke: *Nigel Leach;* Herbert Parchester: *Derek Beard;* Sir Jasper Tring: *Jim Wiggins;* Charles, The Butler: *Peter Schofield;* Lord Battersby: *Peter Honri;* Lady Battersby: *Audrey Palmer;* Mrs Brown/Mrs Worthington-Worthington: *Audrey Leybourne;* Bob Barking: *Stuart Liddle;* Sophia Stainsley-Asherton: *Rosalind McCutcheon;* Constable: *Richard Shilling;* Pearly King: *Martin Johnson;* Major Domo: *Michael Morgan;* Lady Brighton: *Joyce Blane;* Miss Miles: *Rachel Stanley;* Pearly Queen: *Maria Holley;* Thomas de Hareford/Hall Footman: *Christopher Coleman;* Lord French: *Alan Mack;* Richard Hareford: *Chris Hornby;* Simon de Hareford: *Richard Twyman;* Telegraph Boy: *Tony Lucken;* Cockney Tart: *Maria Holley;* Hall Footman: *James Horne;* Farmers: *Richard Shilling, Alan Mack;* Pub Pianist: *Robert Tapsfield;* Maids/ Footmen/Guests/Cockneys: *Joyce Blane, Emma Buckle, Maria*

327

Holley, Susaannah Jupp, Sarah
Keeton, Rachel Stanley, Laura
Whittard, Philiip Aiden,
Christopher Coleman, James
Doubtfire, Chris Hornby, James
Horne, Martin Johnston, Stuart
Liddle, Tony Lucken, Alan Mack,
Michael Morgan, Richard Shilling,
Richard Twyman, Ian Waller.
Orchestra: Musical Director: Rob
Mitchell; Woodwind: Chris
Caldwell, Geoff Young, Andy
Lovell, Katheryn Seabrook;
Trumpets: Bill Pettigrew, Don
Morgan; Trombone: Phil Judge;
Horn: Gillian Jones; Piano/
Assistant Musical Director: Robert
Tapsfield; Bass: Brian Wiltshire;
Drums: Jim Matthews;
Guitar/Banjo: Alex Coburn;
Percusssion: Lee Adams; Violins:
Ian Berridge, Kirsteen Scott,
Susan Blathorn; Harp: Anna
Christensen. Director: Mike
Ockrent; Choreographer: Gillian
Gregory; Costume Designer: Ann
Curtis; Set Design: Martin Johns;
Lighting: Chris Ellis; Production
Musical Director and
Orchestrations: Chris Walker;
Sound: Rick Clarke; Associate
Director: Nigel West; Dance
Captain: Stuart McLeod;
Production Manager: Ted Irwin;
Costume Supervisor: Adrian
Gwillym; Wig Supervisor: Pam
Foster; Assistant to Costume
Designer & Supervisor: Val
Kirkman; Props Supervisor: Jane
Slattery; Company Manager:
Michael Hyatt; Stage Manager:
Neil Andrew White; Deputy Stage
Manager: Sarah Khasgalian;
Assistant Stage Managers:
Christopher Alderton, Valerie
Nash; Wardrobe Mistress: Tracey
Drake; Wardrobe Assistant: Lisa
Preston; Wig Mistress: Sarah
Packham; Wig Assistant: Pamela
Humpage; Sound Operators: Rob

Summers, Tracy Campbell;
Touring Electrician: Andrew
Younger; Touring Carpenter: Jem
Nicholson; Scenery Painter:
Frances Waddington, Paddy
Hamilton; Prop Makers: Sue
Dunlop, Russell Beck, Richard
Pocock, Diz Marsh, Howard
Munford, Chesterfields of London,
Jenny Heap, Rolf Driver, Vicky
Heron.
Press: CL: 27/7/94; **MEN:** 14
& 20/7/94; **OC:** 18&20/7/94;
S: 17/3/94

**471. JOSEPH AND THE
AMAZING TECHNICOLOR
DREAMCOAT** by Tim Rice and
Andrew Lloyd Webber; REALLY
USEFUL THEATRE COMPANY;
17 August – 22 October 1994.
Joseph: *Darren Day;* Narrator:
Lisa Pearce: Jacob/Potiphar/Guru:
Malcolm Rennie; Pharaoh/Levi:
David J Higgins; Butler/Gad:
Miles Western; Baker/Issachar:
Martin Callaghan; Mrs Potiphar/
Naphtali's Wife: *Sarah MacDuff;*
Apache Dancer/Zebulun: *Warren
Grant;* Apache Dancer/Issachar's
Wife: *Charlotte Peck;* Reuben:
Anthony Lyn; Reuben's Wife:
Siobhan Coebly; Simeon: *Graham
Hoadly;* Simeon's Wife: *Nicola
Bolton;* Levi's Wife: *Jane Housley;*
Naphtali: *Ray Strachan;* Asher:
Paul Manuel; Asher's Wife:
Elizabeth Kate Hamilton; Dan:
Vas Constnti; Dan's Wife: *Maria
O'Brien;* Zebulun's Wife: *Joanne
Henry;* Gad's Wife: *Julie Barnes;*
Benjamin: *James Gillan;* Benjamin's
Wife: *Louise Dominy;* Judah:
Dilim Andrew Esiaka; Judah's
Wife: *Michelle Chilton;* Swings:
*Adrian Edmeades, Martin Eyre,
Nina French, Kenny Linden, Chris
Moppett, Sue O'Brian;* Chorus:
From St Anne's RC High School

- *Stockport, Thorp County Primary School, St Peter's High School - Orrell; North Cheshire Theatre School;* ORCHESTRA: Leader: *Ann Morfee;* Violin 2: *Juliet Leighton-Jones;* Viola: *Niamh Nichanainn;* Cello: *Elizabeth Parker;* Oboe/Cor Anglais: *Deborah Boyes;* Flute/Clarinet/Alto Saxophone: *Scott Povey;* Horn: *Phil Woods;* Synthesisers/Assistant Musical Directors: *Martin Leberman, Stuart Calvert;* Drum Kit: *Tim Goodyer;* Keyboards: *Marcus Tilt;* Electric Guitar/Acoustic Guitar: *Lewis Osborne;* Guitar: *Graeme Taylor;* Bass Guitar: *Steve Richardson;* Percussion: *Keith Fairbairn.* Director: *Steven Pimlott;* Associate DirectorL *Nichola Treherne;* Design: *Mark THompson;* Choreography: *Anthony van Laast;* Musical Supervision: *Michael Reed;* Musical Director: *Robert Purvis;* Orchestration: *John Cameron;* Lighting: *Andrew Bridge;* Sound: *Martin Levan;* Resident Director: *Wayne Fowkes;* Children's Director: *John Ramster;* Company Manager: *Michael Townsend;* Stage Manager: *Chris Walters;* Deputy Stage Manager: *Helen bHighwater;* Assistant Stage Managers: *Victoria Brown, Michael Connock, Niall Franchi, Andy Stirrat;* Dance Captain: *Chris Moppett;* Vari*Lite Operators: *Stuart Porter, Tony Shea;* Touring Production Electricians: *Matt Barker, Simon Evans;* Touring Production Technician: *John Ginley;* Sound Operator: *Steve Brierley;* Assistant Sound Operator: *Janet Moorhouse;* Sound Operator Number 3: *Sarah Sendell;* Wardrobe Mistress: *Sheila Toner;* Deputy Wardrobe Mistress: *Moira Bromley-Wiggins;* Walker

Assistants: *Jo Walker, Ruth Webb;* Wig Mistress: *Carole Hancock;* Deputy Wig Master: *Matthew George;* Wig Assistant: *TAmsin Dorling;* Mr Day's Costumes: *Henrietta Webb;* Mr Day's Armour: *Ivo Coveney;* Mr Day's Potiphar Jacket: *John Sheward;* Miss Peace's Costumes and The Dreamcoat: *Kim Witcher;* Jacob's Costumes: *Judith Darracott;* Brothers' Costumes: *Kay Coveney;* Naphtali's Cardigan: *Marie McCloughlin;* Brothers's Hats: *Jaquie Bitten;* Wive's Costumes/Boys' and Butler's skirts: *Debbie Marchant;* Hoe-down Hata and Veils: *Louise McDonald;* Swing Costumes: *John Sheward;* Beading: *Roger Bremble, Janet Timms, Ella Kidd;* Mrs Potiphar's Dress: *MBA, Anna Houghton;* Potiphar's & Mr Day's Headresses: *Sean Barrett;* Boys' Jackets: *Alan Selzer;* Pharaoh's Costumes, Male Fat Cows: *Sue Long;* Female Thin Cows, Princesses' Dresses: *Stephan Harrington;* Gold Rope Dresses: *Sue Nicholson;* Egyptian Collar, Belts, Jewellery: *Martin Adams;* Pharaoh Head-Dress: *Simon Dawes;* Gadget Hats, Cow-heads, Helmets, Jewels: *Dominic Murray;* Other Hats: *Ella Kidd, Jenny Adey;* Dyeing and Printing: *Shultz & Wiremu;* Shoes: *Gamba;* Wigs: *Michael Ward;* Beards: *Sarah Weatherburn;* Gloves: *Cornelia James.*
Press: AR: 25/8/94; **BT:** 19/8/94; **CL:** 24/8/94; **MEN:** 18&25/8/94; **OC:** 29/4/94, 15/8/94; **RO:** 20/8/94.

472. FASCINATING AIDA; HIGHFIELD PRODUCTIONS; *18 September 1994.* Dillie Keane, Adèle Anderson, Issy Van

Randwyck. Director: *Nica Burns.*
Press: S: 12/5/94; **T:** 28/3/94

**473. FIDDLER ON THE
ROOF;** Book by Joseph Stein,
Music by Jerry Bock, Lyrics by
Sheldon Harnick, based on
Sholem Aleichem Stories; BARRY
CLAYMAN; *15-26 November
1994.* Tevye: *Topol;* Golde:
Sara Kestleman; Tzeital:
Jacqueline Yorke; Hodel: *Jo John;*
Chava: *Marsha Ward;* Bielke:
Alicia Davies; Yente: *Margaret
Robertson;* Motel: *Neil
Rutherford;* Perchik: *Peter
Darling;* Fyedka: *Kieran McIlroy;*
Lazar Wolf: *David Bacon;*
Constable: *Bruce Montague;* The
Fiddler: *Tim Flannigan;* Grandma
Tzeitel: *Marsha Ward;* Fruma-
Sarah: *Karen Davies;* Villagers:
*George Little, Jon Rumney,
Anthony Styles, Peter Johnson,
Tim Willis, Millie Kieve, John
Stacey, Alex James Campbell,
Lee Ives, Ian McLarnon, Steven
Harris, Mason Taylor, Peter
Edbrook, Hugh Rathbone, Michael
SAnds, Jon Osbaldston, Nick
Tcherniak, Alastair Bull, Karen
Lynne, Su Goodacre, Joyce
Teevan, Felicity Duncan, Susan
Paule.* Director and
Choreographer: *Sammy Dallas
Bayes,* reproducing the original by
Jerome Robbins; Musical Director:
Nick Barnard; Lighting: *Nick
Richings;* Sound: *Grey Pink.*
Press: G: 30/6/94; **MEN:**
30/6/94; **PP:** July/August 1994

**PLANTHILL HIGH
SCHOOL,** Planthill Road,
BLACKLEY; **M9 0WQ;
061-740 1831; AZ:** 31,
F4; XAZ: 61, E5.

129. GROUNDED by Eileen
Murphy; M6 THEATRE
COMPANY; *24 February 1994.*

**PRESTWICH HIGH
SCHOOL;** Heys Road,
M25 1JZ; 061-773 2052;
AZ: 30, 4A; **XAZ:** 59,
4E.

**298. SHAKESPEARE'S
GREATEST HITS;** MANCHESTER
ACTORS COMPANY; *19 January
1994.*

**PRINCESS PRIMARY
SCHOOL MOBILE
LIBRARY,** Alexandra Park
Estate, MOSS SIDE, M16;
AZ: 59, F2; **XAZ:** 100,
C3.

**124. THE TIGER WITH
GOLDEN CLAWS;**
MANCHESTER ACTORS
COMPANY; *8 July 1994.*

THE PUMP HOUSE; Left
Bank, off Bridge Street,
M3; 061-228 7212; **AZ:**
101, E4; **XAZ:** 161, F5.

475. DIRTY OLD TOWN;
devised by ASPECTS THEATRE
COMPANY; *1-4 June 1994.*
Rachael Bennett, Marc Careswell,
Dave Fendick, Lucy Page,
Richard Palmer, Lynn Richards,
Rebecca Shoosmith, Sheena
Spinks, Andrea Turner, Sharon

Williams, Fiona Wilmot, Richard Whitmore. Direction: *Mark Bishop, Sue Scott;* Choreographer : *Jools Beech;* Sound & Lighting: *Ian Currie, Gordon Isaacs;* Stage Manager: *Sue Scott.*
Press: CL: 18/5/94

474. OUT OF THE RED by Anne Caldwell; CARTWHEEL COMMUNITY ARTS; *9–11 June 1994.* Dora Whittington: *Louise Brown;* Jennufer Whittington: *Tina Merrick;* Saleswoman 1/Neighbour 2/Shark: *Anji Robinson;* Saleswoman 2/Neighbour 1/Shark: *Anne Phelan;* Salesman 3/ Magician: *Richard Pickup;* Debt Collector/Shark: *Christine Dearden;* Elsie Ramsbottom: *Alana Decourcey;* Mrs Worthing/Fairy Godmother: *Lynne Brosnan.* Director: *Anne Caldwell;* Stage Manager: *Ray Williams.*

502. JACK by David Greenspan; ASPECTS THEATRE COMPANY; *13–14 October 1994.*

RACKHOUSE LIBRARY, 103 Sale Road, M23 0BQ; 061–998 2043; AZ: 81, D1; XAZ: 127, H2.

301. BIG BAD WOLF; MANCHESTER ACTORS COMPANY; *December 1994.*

THE REMBRANT HOTEL, Sackville Street, M1 3LZ; 061–236 1311. AZ: 101, G5; XAZ: 166, B1.

121. ANDY IN DIRE STRAIGHTS by Michael Harvey; REALLIFE THEATRE COMPANY; *7 July 1994.*

RENOLDS THEATRE, UMIST, MI 7HS; 061–236 3311; AZ: 106, A1; XAZ: 166, C2.

517. THE TAMING OF THE SHREW by William Shakespeare; REYNOLDS THEATRE COMPANY; *9–11 March 1994.* Director: *Nicola Fogg.*

ROYAL EXCHANGE, St Ann's Square, M2 7DH; 061–833 9333. AZ: 101, F4; XAZ: 161, H5. H, W, + Braille & Large Print Programmes.

3. HEDDA GABLER by Henrik Ibsen, translated by Nicholas Rudall, from a literal translation by Kari Dickson; *14 October–13 November 1993.* Miss Tesman: *Marlene Sidaway;* Berte: *Pauline Jefferson;* Jorgen Tesman: *Phillip Joseph;* Hedda Gabler: *Geraldine James;* Mrs Elvsted: *Cecily Hobbs;* Judge Brack: *Dave Hill;* Eilert Lovberg: *Hilton McRae.* Director: *Joseph Blatchley;* Designer: *Michael Vale;* Lighting: *Chahine Yavroyan;* Sound: *Philip Clifford;* Music: *Stephen Warbeck;* Musicians: *Biff Harrison, Kevin Walton, Julie Gelson;* Stage Manager: *Laura Deards;* Deputy Stage Manager: *Lucy Barter;* Assistant Stage Manager: *Amy Richardson;* Lighting Operator: *Andy Whipp;*

Sound Operator: *Colin Renwick;*
Deputy Head of Props and
Settings: *Robert Kirkpatrick;* Set
& Props: *Ged Mayo, Alan Fell,*
Fiona Randall, Samantha Hanks,
Martin Mallorie, Nicola Bowden,
Lerz Plper; Assistant Costume
Supervisor: *Sophie Doncaster;*
Men's Tailor and Cutter: *Robert*
Rainsford; Cutters: *Debbie Attle,*
Marie Dunaway; Costume
Assistants: *Rose Calderbank,*
Jeanette Foster, Andrew Gilliver,
Jacqueline Parkinson; Vanessa
Pickford, Marianne Ruby, Janet
Wilson; Additional Costumes: *Sally*
Payne, Alan Seltzer; Wig &
Make-up Assistant: *Jo Schofield,*
Vicky Peters; Wigs: *Ray Marston;*
Maintenance Wardrobe Mistress:
Sarah L Brown; Maintenance
Wardrobe Assistant: *Helen*
Johnson; Head Dresser: *Enid*
Geldard; Dresser: *Amanda*
Sawdon; First Technician: *Alan*
Catz Carradus; Stage
Technicians: *Stuart Leon, Andy*
Smith.
Press: CL: 27/10/93; **MEN:**
14/10/93

3. SMOKE by Roy Wooden;
18 November-11 December
1993. Several: *Rade Serbedzija;*
Symond: *Rhys Jeans;* Wilse:
Sorcha Cusack; Ysod: *Steven*
Hartley; Agnes: *Margaret*
Robertson: Greta: *Beaux Bryant;*
Jig: *David Fishley;* Wyand/
Yaxley, Clock: *Simon Tyrell;*
Yallop/ The Gaoler/ Howling/
The King's Messenger: *Peter*
Rutherford; Starling/ The Leper:
Emma Dewhurst; Mow/ The
Hooded Man/ The Prince of
Masturbators: *Jonathan Coyne;*
Kittle/ Jacker/ Huck: *Ruth*
Mitchell; Musicians: *Chris Monks,*
Adam Ryan-Carter. Director:

Braham Murray; Designer: *David*
Short; Music: *Chris Monks;*
Words and music for songs: *Roy*
Wooden; Movement: *Fergus Early;*
Llghting: *Ace McCarron;* Sound:
Philip Clifford; Assistant Director:
Jacob Murray; Stage Manager:
Catherine Lill; Deputy Stage
Manager: *Suzi Blakey;* Assistant
Stage Manager: *Sylda O'Brien;*
Lighting Operator: *Beverley*
Pearson; Sound Operator:
Rebecca Watts; Deputy Head of
Props and Settings: *Robert*
Kirkpatrick; Set and Props: *Ged*
Mayo, Alan Fell, Samantha
Hanks, Martin Mallorie, Steve
Bedford, Leigh Carey, Ian
Goodwin, Jez Horrox, Totie
Smith; Assistant Costume
Supervisor: *Sophie Doncaster;*
Men's Tailor and Cutter: *Robert*
Rainsford; Cutters: *Debbie Attle,*
Marie Dunaway; Costume
Asssistants: *Rose Calderbank,*
Jeanette Foster, Andrew Gilliver,
Jacqueline Parkinson, Vanessa
Pickford, Marianne Ruby;
Costume Props: *Johanna Bryant,*
Nicola Bryant; Additional
Costumes: *Juliet Hardiker;* Wig
and Make-up Assistant: *Jo*
Schofield, Vicky Peters; Wigs:
Ray Marston; Facial Hair: *Sarah*
Phillips; Maintenance Wardrobe
Mistress: *Sarah L Brown;*
Maintenance Wardrobe Assistant:
Helen Johnson; Head Dresser:
Enid Geldard; Dresser: *Amanda*
Sawdon; First Technician: *Alan*
Catz Carradus; Stage
Technicians: *Stuart Leon, Andy*
Smith, Paul Moorhouse; Students
on Attachment: *Sally Anderson,*
Paul Brown, David Russell.
Press: CL: 24/11/93 **G:**
22/11/93; **MEN:** 18/11/93

4. THE IMPORTANCE OF

BEING EARNEST by Oscar Wilde; *16 December 1993 - 29 January 1994.* Lane/Merriman: *James Masters;* Algernon Moncrieff: *Samuel West;* John Worthing JP: *Neil Dudgeon;* Lady Bracknell: *Avril Elgar;* Hon Gwendolen Fairfax: *Zara Turner;* Cecily Cardew: *Melanie Ramsay;* Miss Prism: *Marcia Warren;* Rev Canon Chasuble DD: *John Branwell.* Director: *James Maxwell;* Designer: *Tom Rand;* Lighting: *Robert Bryan;* Sound: *Pete Goodwin;* Choreographer: *Nigel Nicholson;* Assistant Director: *Jacob Murray;* Stage Manager: *Laura Deards;* Deputy Stage Manager: *Adrian Pagan;* Assistant Stage Manager: *Jane Smailes;* Lighting Operator: *Andy Whipp;* Sound Operator: *Colin Renwick;* Deputy Head of Props and Settings: *Robert Kirkpatrick;* Set & Props: *Ged Mayo, Alan Fell, Samantha Hanks, Martin Mallorie, Imogen Peers, Jimmy Ragg, Susan Ross, Mathilde Sandberg, David Whetton;* Assistant Costume Supervisor: *Sophie Doncaster;* Men's Tailor and Cutter: *Robert Rainsford;* Cutters: *Debbie Attle, Marie Dunaway;* Costume Assistants: *Rose Calderbank, Jeanette Foster, Andrew Gilliver, Jacqueline Parkinson, Vanessa Pickford, Marianne Ruby;* Additional Costumes: *Naomi Isaacs, Alan Seltzer;* Milliner: *Louise Macdonald;* Student on Attachment: *Gemma Smith;* Wig and Make-up Assistants: *Jo Schofield, Vicky Peters;* Wigs: *Ray Marston;* Facial Hair: *Sarah Phillips;* Maintenance Wardrobe Mistress: *Nicola Meredith;* Maintenance Wardrobe Assistants: *Helen Johnson, Amanda Sawdon;* Head Dresser: *Enid Geldard;* First

Technician: *Alan Catz Carradus;* Stage Technicians: *Stuart Leon, Andy Smith.* **Journal:** 1/1/94 **Press:** MEN: 16,17/12/93; OC: 17/12/93

47. THE LODGER by Simon Burke; ROYAL EXCHANGE; *3-26 February 1994.* Wise: *Philip Jackson;* Lois: *Julia Ford;* Reed: *Matthew Marsh;* Pollock: *Mark Womack;* Miss Cheesman: *Liz Stooke;* Tom: *Robert Calvert.* Director: *Richard Wilson;* Design: *Julian McGowan;* Lighting: *Johanna Town;* Sound: *Alastair Goolden;* Music: *Howard Davidson;* Fight Director: *Malcolm Ranson,* Stage Manager: *Catherine Lill;* Deputy Stage Manager: *Suzi Blakey;* Assistant Stage Manager: *Laura Deards;* Lighting Operator: *Beverley Pearson;* Sound Operator: *Rebecca Watts;* Deputy Head of Props and Settings: *Robert Kirkpatrick;* Set and Props: *Ged Mayo, Samantha Hanks, Martin Mallorie, Susan Ross, Julioa Heskin, Jimmy Ragg, Nixon Tod,* Assistant Costume Supervisor: *Sophie Doncaster;* Men's Tailor and Cutter: *Robert Rainsford;* Cutters: *Debbie Attle, Marie Dunaway;* Costume Asssistants: *Rose Calderbank, Jeanette Foster, Andrew Gilliver, Jacqueline Parkinson, Vanessa Pickford, Marianne Ruby;* Wig Supervisor: *Barbara Taylor;* Wig and Make-up Assistant: *Jo Schofield,* Maintenance Wardrobe Mistress: *Sarah L Brown;* Maintenance Wardrobe Assistant: *Helen Johnson;* Head Dresser: *Enid Geldard;* Dresser: *Amanda Sawdon;* First Technician: *Alan Catz Carradus;* Stage

333

Technicians: *Stuart Leon, Andy Smith.*
Journal: 15/2/94
Press: CL: 26/1/94, 9/2/94;
MEN: 3,4/2/94

58. VENICE PRESERVED by
Thomas Otway; *3 March-2 April
1994.* Priuli: *David Gant;*
Jaffeir: *Jonathan Cullen;* Pierre:
George Anton; Belvidera: *Helen
McCrory;* Aquilina: *Diana Kent;*
Renault: *Sylvester Morand;*
Spinosa: *Michael Healy;* Eliot:
Charles Foster; Brainveil: *Ian
Peck;* Durand/Officer/Secretary
to the Council: *Stephen
Mackenna;* Brabe/Priuli's Man:
Ken Bradshaw; Bedamore/Duke of
Venice/Priest: *David Fleshman;*
Aquiliona's Maid/Belvidera's Nurse:
Sue McCormick; Antonio: *David
Ryall.* Director: *Gregory Hersov;*
Design: *David Short;* Lighting:
Kevin Sleep; Sound: *John
Leonard;* Fight Director: *Nicholas
Hall;* Composer: *Mia Soteriou;*
Violins: *Julie Hanson, Rebecca
Thompson;* Stage Manager: *Liz
Ellis;* Deputy Stage Manager:
Andrea Storey; Assistant Stage
Manager: *Amy Richardson;* Sound
Operator: *Colin Renwick;* Set
and Props: *Ged Mayo, Samantha
Hanks, Martin Mallorie, Susan
Ross, Julie Heskin, Jimmy Ragg,
Loren Hickson, Jez Horrox, Kathy
Stewart, Rob Stirling, Nixon
Todd;* Deputy Costume
Supervisor: *Sophie Doncaster;*
Men's Tailor and Cutter: *Robert
Rainsford;* Cutters: *Debbie Attle,
Marie Dunaway;* Costume
Assistants: *Rose Calderbank,
Jeanette Foster, Andrew Gilliver,
Jacqueline Parkinson, Vanessa
Pickford, Marianne Ruby;*
Costume Props: *Nicola Meredith;*
Wig Supervisor: *Barbara Taylor;*

Wig and Make-up Assistants: *Jo
Schofield, Jessica Martin;* Wigs:
Joanne Taylor; Maintenance
Wardrobe Mistress: *Sarah L
Brown;* Maintenance Wardrobe
Assistant: *Helen Johnson;* Head
Dresser: *Enid Geldard;* Dressers:
Karen Dooley, Toby Stevens;
Student on Attachment to
Wardrobe: *Anna O'Doherty;* First
Technician: *Alan Catz Carradus;*
Stage Technicians: *Stuart Leon,
Ivan Seymour, David Gregory,
Mark Ashford.*
Journal: 16/3/94
Press: CL: 9/3/94; **G:**
11/3/94; **MEN:** 24/2/94,
4/3/94

476. PROSPERO'S ISLAND,
culmination of the CITY OF
DRAMA and MANCHESTER
SCHOOLS **SHAKESPEARE
PROJECT;** *20 March 1994.*
Set in the context of **THE
TEMPEST (495),** performed by
THE TEACHERS' GROUP: *Peter
Wilkinson, Dud Newell, Mike
Cockett, Mya Freeman, Judi
Challiner, Christina McAlpine,
Tess McDermott, Jane Howarth,
Tom Wells, Bryan McGuiness,
David Carlile, Sue Moulson;*
based on the conceit that as he
wrote his last play, scenes from
earlier work would have come to
Shakespeare's mind, the
programme included the following
scenes: *(Initial Scene Numbers
indicate the parts of* The
Tempest *to which they were
related)* Act I, Scene ii, 55,:
**THE WNITER'S TALE (486) Act
II, Sc 1:** ST CLEMENT'S
PRIMARY SCHOOL; **A
MIDSUMMER NIGHT'S DREAM
(493) Act II, Sc 1:** ELLEN
WILKINSON HIGH SCHOOL;
THE WINTER'S TALE (478) Act

V, Sc 1: MEDLOCK PRIMARY
SCHOOL; Act II, Sc iii, 25:
KING LEAR (481) Act I, Sc i:
PARRS WOOD HIGH SCHOOL;
Act I, Sc ii, 321: A
MIDSUMMER NIGHT'S DREAM
(487) Act III, Sc i, 131:
WHALLEY RANGE GIRLS HIGH
SCHOOL; Act 1, Sc ii, 405:
ROMEO AND JULIET (484) Act
II, Sc 4: BURNAGE HIGH
SCHOOL; Act I, Sc ii, 437: A
MIDSUMMER NIGHT'S DREAM
(489) Act III, Sc ii, 448:
ABRAHAM MOSS HIGH
SCHOOL; Act I, Sc ii, 473:
ROMEO AND JULIET (494) Act
III, Sc v, 150: NORTH
MANCHESTER HIGH SCHOOL
FOR GIRLS; Act II, Sc i, 130:
THE WINTER'S TALE (480) Act
I, Sc ii, 164: POUNDSWICK
JUNIOR SCHOOL; Act II, Sc ii,
216: MACBETH (477),Act II,
Sc v, 40: TRINITY HIGH
SCHOOL; Act II, Sc i, 275:
MACBETH (490), Act II, Sc vi:
MANCHESTER GRAMMAR
SCHOOL; Act II, Sc ii: HENRY
V (491), Act IV, Sc i: WRIGHT
ROBINSON HIGH SCHOOL; Act
III, Sc i: TROILUS AND
CRESSIDA (483), Act III, Sc ii:
ST PAUL'S HIGH SCHOOL; Act
III, Sc iii: THE WINTER'S TALE
(488), Act II, Sc ii: HAVELEY
HEY JUNIOR SCHOOL; Act IV,
Sc i, 20: A MIDSUMMER
NIGHT'S DREAM (485), Act II,
Sc I, 60: BARLOW RC HIGH
SCHOOL; Act IV, Sc i, 55:
ROMEO AND JULIET (479),
Act II, Sc vi: LEVENSHULME
HIGH SCHOOL; Act IV, Sc i,
95: A MIDSUMMER NIGHT'S
DREAM (487), Act III, Sc ii:
WHALLEY RANGE HIGH
SCHOOL FOR GIRLS; Act V,
Sc i, 130: MERCHANT OF
VENICE (492), Act I, Sc iii,

42: OAKWOOD HIGH
SCHOOL; Act V, Sc i, 200: A
WINTER'S TALE (480), Act V,
Sc iii, 120: POUNDSWICK
JUNIOR SCHOOL. Contributions
throughout from MANCHESTER
YOUTH DANCE THEATRE,
directed by *Sue Moulson*. Music:
Mark Goggins (St Vincent de
Paul RC High School), *Lucy
Tasker* (Abraham Moss High
School), *David Holdridge & Roger
Child* (Manchester Music Service)
Press: AR: 17/3/94

**82. WHAT THE BUTLER
SAW** by Joe Orton; 7 April - 7
May 1994. Doctor Prentice:
David Horovitch; Geraldine
Barclay: *Kate Winslet;* Mrs
Prentice: *Deborah Norton;*
Nicholas Beckett: *Neil Stuke;* Dr
Rance: *Trevor Baxter;* Sergeant
Match: *Billy Hartman.* Director:
Robert Delamere; Designer:
Ashley Martin-Davis; Sound:
Robert Tice; Lighting: *Mick
Hughes;* Stage Manager: *Suzi
Blakey;* Deputy Stage Manager:
Linda Fitzpatrick; Assistant Stage
Manager: *Harry Teale;* Lighting
Operator: *Jon Langley;* Sound
Operator: *Colin Renwick;* Set
and Props: *Ged Mayo, Samantha
Hanks, Martin Mallorie, Susan
Ross, Julie Heskin, Jimmy Ragg,
Jez Horrox, Bill Martin, Carl
Richardson, Nixon Todd;* Deputy
Costume Supervisor: *Sophie
Doncaster;* Men's Tailor and
Cutter: *Robert Rainsford;* Cutters:
*Debbie Attle, Marie Dunaway,
Marianne Ruby;* Additional
Costumes: *Sally Payne, Rose
Calderbank,* Men's Suits: *Andrew
Tryfon;* Wig and Make-up
Assistant: *Jo Schofield;*
Maintenance Wardrobe Mistress:
Sarah L Brown; Maintenance

Wardrobe Assistant: *Helen Johnson;* Head Dresser: *Enid Geldard;* Dresser: *Joanne Richardson;* Students on Attachment to Wardrobe: *Virginie Alberico, Cecile Nouveau, Emmanuelle Voineau;* First Technician: *Alan Catz Carradus;* Stage Technicians: *Stuart Leon, Ivan Seymour;* Student on Attachment to Stage Management: *Katy de Main.* **Journal:** 2/5/94 **Press:** G: 13/4/94; **MEN:** 31/3/94, 7,8/4/94; **SAM:** 7/4/94

496. THE BEST OF TIMES; devised and performed by Denis Quilley; *24 April 1994.* Director: *Stella Chapman;* Piano: *Carol Wells.*

117. THE COUNT OF MONTE CRISTO by Alexandre Dumas, adapted for the stage by James Maxwell and Jonathan Hackett; *18 May - 6 August 1994.* Edmond Dantès: *David Threlfall;* Gérard de Villefort: *Simon Tyrell;* Danglars: *James Saxon;* Fernand Mondego: *Malcolm Jamieson;* Gaspard Caderousse/Doctor d'Avrigny/ President of the Assizes: *John Cording;* Abbé Faria/Marquis de Saint-Meran: *Colin Prockter;* Vicomte Albert de Moncerf/ Peppino: *Ian Pepperell;* Maximilien Morrel: *Daniel Tobias;* Andrea Cavalcanti: *Jonathan Weir;* M Lucien Debray/Luigi Vampa/Comte de Salvieux/Prison Doctor: *Michael Gould;* M Beauchamp/ Old M Morrel/M de Boville: *Terry Taplin;* Ali: *Clive Llewellyn;* Old Cavalcanti/Old Dantés/ President of Peers: *Ray Llewellyn;* Bertuccio/Comte de

Château-Renaud/Fencing Instructor /Speaking Peer: *John Langford;* Creatures: *Liam McKenna, John Killoran, Liam Steel;* Mercédès: *Brana Bajic;* Mademoiselle Valentine/Mademoiselle Renée de Saint-Méran: *Sandra Reinton;* Mademoiselle Eugènie Danglars: *Katy Carmichael;* Baronne Hermine Danglars: *Naomi Buch;* Haydée: *Natscha McElhone;* Marquise de Saint-Méran/ Cornélie: *Marie Collett;* Héloise/ La Carconte: *Geraldine Alexander;* Edouard de Villefort: *Jonathan Bethell* or *Edward Blum* or *Michaek Moore.* Director: *Braham Murray;* Design: *Simon Higlett;* Lighting: *Vince Herbert;* Sound: *Philip Clifford;* Composer: *Chris Monks;* Choreographer: *Fergus Early;* Aerial & Tumbling Specialist: *Emil Wolk;* Dialect Coach: *Penny Dyer;* Fight Director: *Malcolm Ransom;* Assistant Director: *Katherine Bond;* Movement Associate: *Liam Steel;* Musical Director + Jembe, Keyboards, Double Bass, Guitar, Flutes: *Akintayo Akinbode;* Oboe, Shenai: *Heather Cross;* Guitar, Mandolin, Cheng, Keyboards: *James Muir Morrison;* Lyra, Viola: *Carolyn Tregaskis;* Stage Managers: *Jerry Knight Smith, Cath Lill;* Deputy Stage Manager: *Paula Spinks;* Assistant Stage Manager: *Sylda O'Brien;* Lighting Operators: *Dexter Tullett, Andy Whipp;* Sound Operators: *Colin Renwick, Rebecca Watts;* Set and Props: *Ged Mayo, Samantha Hanks, Martin Mallorie, Susan Ross, Julie Heskin, Jimmy Ragg, Ian Callaghan, Jez Horrox, Bill Martin, Carl Richardson, Rob Stirling, Philip Swindells, Nixon Todd, Julia Walker;* Properties Buyer: *Kim Ford;* Deputy Costume Supervisor: *Sophie*

DAVID THRELFALL, as Edmund Dantès, discovers the Treasure that will enable him to become THE COUNT OF MONTE CRISTO.

Doncaster; Men's Tailor & Cutter: *Robert Rainsford;* Cutters: *Debbie Attle, Marie Dunaway, Marianne Ruby;* Costume Assistants: *Jeanette Foster, Andrew Gilliver, Rachael Jones, Jacqueline Parkinson, Vanessa Pickford;* Additional Costumes: *Wallace & McMurray, Rose Calderbank, Kay Coveney, Lucy Nye, Kit Reading, Alan Seltzer;* Haty: *Johanna Bryant;* Jewellery: *David Short;* Costume Production Buyer: *Nicola Meredith;* Wig and Make-up Supervisor: *Barbara Taylor;* Wig and Make-up Assistants: *Jo Schofield, Vicky Peters, Jessica Taylor;* Wigs: *London New York Wig Company;* Maintenance Wardrobe Mistress: *Sarah L Brown;* Maintenance Wardrobe Assistant: *Helen Johnson;* Head Dresser: *Enid Geldard;* Dressers: *Kaeran Dooley, Anne Dwyer, Niall Mills, Jane Ransome, Joanne Richardson,*

Amanda Sawdon; First Technician: *Alan Catz Carradus;* Stage Technicians: *Stuart Leon, Andy Smith, Ivan Seymour;* Students on Attachment to Wardrobe: *Virginie Alberico, Cecile Nouveau, Emmanuelle Voineau;* 1 Students on Attachment to Stage Management: *Helen Bunkall, Katy de Main.*
Journal: 28-29/6/94
Press: CL: 1/6/94; G: 21/5/94; OC: 20/12/93, 16, 19/5/94; MEN: 23/12/93, 19/5/94, 5/7/94; PP: April 94

497. OUT THERE; conceived by Campbell Graham, written by Simon Black, compositions by DJANGO BATES, with improvisations by all member of HUMAN CHAIN; FIFTH FLOOR; 12 June 1994. Zoë: *Karen Ascoe;* Saxophones, Steve, Fred: *Iain Bellamy;* Keyboards, E-Flat

Peck Horn, Hooter, God, Lou: *Django Bates;* Clare, Lisa, Stewardess, Freda, Pain: *Sarah D'Arcy;* Cliff: *Robert Horwell;* Drums, Percussion, Billy, Marco, Louise: Bass Guitar, Penny, Daphne, Samantha: *Michael Mondesir;* Harold, Nigel, Sam: *Trevor Stuart.* Director: *Campbell Graham;* Lighting: *Simon Corder, Steve Wald;* Sound: *Jeremy Farnell;* Stage Manager: *Jo Keating;* Cabinet & Crucifix: *Guy Driscoll.*
Press: G: 14/6/94; **S:** 9/6/94

287. JULIUS CAESAR by William Shakespeare; *8 September - 15 October 1994.* Julius Caesar: *Denys Hawthorne;* Calpurnia: *Amanda Boxer;* Marcus Brutus: *Patrick O'Kane;* Caius Cassius: *Robert Gwilym;* Casca/ Lucilius: *Leo Wringer;* Trebonius/ Claudius/A Cobbler/2nd Soldier: *James Bannon;* Decius Brutus/ Titinius: *Trevor Cooper;* Metellus Cimber/Marullus/Messala: *Mark Healy;* Cinna/Pindarus/1st Soldier: *Nicholas Bailey;* Caius Ligarius/ Strato/Servant of Marcus Antonius: *James Allen;* Portia: *Catherine White;* Octavius Caesar/Popilius Lena/Servant of Caesar: *Matthew Flynn;* Marcus Antonius: *Danny Sapani;* Lepidus, Flavius/Dardanius: *Adrian Bower;* Cicero/Artemidorus/A Poet: *Richard Evans;* Publius/Clitus/ Cinna the Poet/A Carpenter: *Ian Blower;* Young Cato/Lucius: *Alan Westaway;* Volumnius/Varo/A Soothsayer/Sevant of Octavius: *Tim Crouch;* Director: *Robert Delamere;* Design: *Rob Howell;* Lighting: *David Lawrence;* Sound: *Philip Clifford;* Composer: *Gary Yershon;* Fights: *Terry King;* Stage Manager: *Cath Lill;* Deputy

Stage Manager: *Andrea Storey;* Assistant Stage Manager: *Katy de Main;* Lighting Operator: *Andy Whipp;* Sound Operators: *Colin Renwick;* Set and Props: *Ged Mayo, Alan Fell, Samantha Hanks, Martin Mallorie, Susan Ross, Julieann Heskin, John Ashworth, Nicola Bowden, Rick Kent;* Deputy Costume Supervisor: *Sophie Doncaster;* Men's Tailor and Cutter: *Robert Rainsford;* Cutters: *Debbie Attle, Marie Dunaway, Marianne Ruby;* Costume Assistants: *Jeanette Foster, Andrew Gilliver, Jacqueline Parkinson, Vanessa Pickford;* Additional Costumes: *Kit Reading, David Short;* Costume Production Buyer: *Nicola Meredith;* Wig and Make-up Supervisor: *Rowena Dean;* Wig and Make-up Assistants: *Jo Schofield;* Maintenance Wardrobe Mistress: *Sarah L Brown;* Maintenance Wardrobe Assistant: *Helen Johnson;* Head Dresser: *Enid Geldard;* Dressers: *Anne Dwyer, Niall Mills,* Stage Technicians: *Stuart Leon, Andy Smith,* Student on Attachment to Wardrobe: *Janet Weston.*
Journal: 5/10/94
Press: CL: 21/9/94; **G:** 17/9/94; **MEN:** 27/8/94, 8&9/9/94; **MM:** 26/8/94; **S:** 29/9/94; **RO:** 17/9/94.

498. STEADY EDDY – QUANTUM LIMP; *16 September 1994.*
Press: CL: 7/9/94; **MEN:** 17/9/94; **MM:** 9/9/94; **S:** 8/9/94

499. ABSURD PERSON SINGULAR by Alan Ayckbourn; *20 October - 3 December 1994.* Sidney Hopcroft: *Trevor*

Cooper; Jane Hopcroft: *Margot Gunn;* Eva Jackson: *Catherine White;* Geoff Jackson: *Patrick O'Kane;* Ronald Brewster-Wright: *Denys Hawthorne;* Marion Brewster-Wright: *Amanda Boxer.* Director: *James Maxwell;* Design: *David Millard;* Lighting: *Taras Kochan;* Sound: *Frank Bradley;* Choreographer: *Nigel Nicholson.* **Press: MEN:** 20/6/94; **OC:** 14/7/94

500. CHARLEY'S AUNT by Brandon Thomas; *8 December 1994 - 21 January 1995.* Director: *Emil Wolk.*

ROYAL NORTHERN COLLEGE OF MUSIC, 124 Oxford Road, M13 9RD; 061-273 4504 / 5534.

34. LES PIEDS DANS L'EAU by Jerome Deschamps and Macha Makeieff, with the collaboration of Françoise Darne and Raymond Sarti; Music by Philippe Roueche; COMPAGNIE JEROME DESCHAMPS; *27-29 January 1994.* Cast: *Jean-Marc Bihour, Fabienne Chaudat, Bruno Lochet, Yolande Moreau, Francois Morel, Olivier Saladin;* Accordion: *Philippe Roueche.* Lighting: *Dominique Brugiere;* Costumes: *Macha Makeieff;* Technical Director: *Baptiste Chapelot;* Technicians: *Olivier Girard, Sophie Gonthier-Maurin;* Production Co-ordinator: *Billie Klinger;* Technical Manager: *Jack Thompson;* Master Carpenter: *Mark Abrahams.* **Press: CL:** 26/1/94; **MEN:** 28/1/94

"THIS IS AN ORANGE": KEVIN GRAAL, who did much to develop the project, here portrays one of the citizens under the tyrannous rule of Liar-Liar in THE CITY OF LIES (162)

339

XAZ: 127, F4.

734. GUYS AND DOLLS;
Music and Lyrics by Frank
Loesser, Book by Joe Swerling
and Abe Burrow, based on
Damon Runyon; EAST CHESHIRE
AMATEUR OPERATIC SOCIETY;
18-24 April 1994.

505. THE KING AND I; Music
by Richard Rodgers; Book and
Lyrics by Oscar Hammerstein II,
based on *Anna and The King of
Siam* by Margaret Landon;
NORTH MANCHESTER AODS;
18-21 May 1994,

162. THE CITY OF LIES;
developed by the cast from
Æsop, with the help of Kevin
Graal, Mike McManus and Maria
Mendonça; THE HALLÉ
EDUCATION DEPARTMENT/
MANCHESTER GAMELAN; *5
August 1994.* Makers and
Performers: *Timothy Brookes, Kati
Donelan, Lee Gibbons, Marc
Greaves, Philip Harold, John
Kenehan, Megan Lumsdaine, Marie
Royle, Catherine Staniforth,
Darren Anthony Smith, Ian
Tabbron, Kevin Graal, Mike
McManus, Maria Mendonça.*
Journal: 5/8/94

506. EMILY by S Robertson-
Brown; ALCHEMY THEATRE
COMPANY; *24 October 1994.*

**ROYAL OAK MOBILE
LIBRARY,** Altrincham Road,
M23; **AZ:** 81, D2;

**124. THE TIGER WITH
GOLDEN CLAWS;**
MANCHESTER ACTORS
COMPANY; *11 July 1994.*

**ST BRENDAN'S
CATHOLIC IRISH
CENTRE;** City Road M15
4DE; 061-872 1976; **AZ:**
104, C3; **XAZ:** 164, C6.

459. WIDOWS' PARADISE by
Sam Cree; MANCHESTER IRISH
PLAYERS; *June 1994.*

ST PETER'S HOUSE,
University Precinct Centre,
Oxford Road, M13 9NR;
061-273 1465. AZ:
106,A3; **XAZ:** 106,C5.

516. TWELFTH NIGHT by
William Shakespeare;
MANCHESTER UNIVERSITY
DRAMA SOCIETY and THE
THEATRE OF FALLOWFIELD;
9-11 March 1994. Director:
Toffael Rashid.

**CITY OF DRAMA /
MANCHESTER SCHOOLS
SHAKESPEARE PROJECT
FESTIVAL;** 14 -25 June
1994.

(The following productions were
all pupil-performed, to a very
high standard, but it was only
the members of staff involved

who managed to get their names into the Festival programme.)

477. MACBETH; TRINITY HIGH SCHOOL; *14 June 1994.* Staff Involved: *Tom Wells, A Bardesley, S Lewis.*

478. THE WINTER'S TALE; MEDLOCK PRIMARY SCHOOL; *14 June 1994.* Staff Involved: *Jayne Kennedy, Dave Hulson, Wynn Moran, Stuart Herrington, Joan Hanlon + students from Xaverian College.*

479. ROMEO AND JULIET; LEVENSHULME HIGH SCHOOL; *15 June 1994.* Staff Involved: *Jules Gibb, Julie Bradwell.*

480. THE WINTER'S TALE; POUNDSWICK JUNIOR SCHOOL; *15 June 1994.* Staff Involved: *Mya Freeman.* The School also worked with the staff and students from Manchester University engaged on production **503.**

481. KING LEAR; PARRS WOOD HIGH SCHOOL; *16 June 1994.* Staff Involved: *Stephen Waters, Lucy Huntbach.*

482. A MIDSUMMER NIGHT'S DREAM; ST VINCENT DE PAUL RC HIGH SCHOOL; *16 June 1994.* Staff Involved: *Mark Goggins.*

483. TROILUS AND CRESSIDA; ST PAUL'S RC HIGH SCHOOL, WYTHENSHAWE; *17 June 1994.* Staff Involved: *Alicia Bardsley, Rachel Britton, John Dever, Clare*

Cowell,

484. ROMEO AND JULIET; BURNAGE HIGH SCHOOL; *17 June 1994.* Staff Involved: *Christine McAlpine, Tess McDermott, Pauliner Partington.*

485. A MIDSUMMER NIGHT'S DREAM; THE BARLOW RC HIGH SCHOOL; *18 June 1994.*

486. THE WINTER'S TALE; ST CLEMENT'S CHURCH OF ENGLAND PRIMARY SCHOOL; *18 June 1994.* Staff Involved: *Janet Foley, Gillian MacNeill, Mike Cockett, Roger Wright.*

487. A MKIDSUMMER NIGHT'S DREAM; WHALLEY RANGE HIGH SCHOOL FOR GIRLS; *21 June 1994.* Staff Member Involved: *Martyn Taylor.*

488. THE WINTER'S TALE; HAVELEY HIGH JUNIOR SCHOOL; *21 June 1994.* Staff Involved: *Judi Challiner, Madeleine Jones, Julie Moore, Liz Mulholland* and help with singing from *Jules Gibb* of Levenshulme High School.

489. A MIDSUMMER NIGHT'S DREAM; ABRAHAM MOSS HIGH SCHOOL; *22 June 1994.* Staff Involved: *Jane Howarth, Sheene MacGowran, Lucy Tasker.*

490. MACBETH; MANCHESTER GRAMMAR SCHOOL; *22 June 1994.* Staff Involved: *Kim Simpson, Miguel Jackson.*

491. HENRY V; WRIGHT

341

ROBINSON HIGH SCHOOL; *23 June 1994.*

492. THE MERCHANT OF VENICE; OAKWOOD HIGH SCHOOL; *23 June 1994.*
Staff Involved: *Marj Baggaley, Christine Greenhalgh, Jude Cooper, Sarah Angress.*

494. A MIDSUMMER NIGHT'S DREAM; ELLEN WILKINSON HIGH SCHOOL; *24 June 1994.*
Staff Involved: *P Carroll, A Bostock, J Clough.*

495. THE TEMPEST; MANCHESTER TEACHER'S GROUP; *25 June 1994.*

ST WERBURGH'S HALL, St Werburgh's Road, CHORLTON-CUM-HARDY, M21 IUE; 061-445 5829. AZ: 59, E4; XAZ: 100, A6

507. THE UNEXPECTED GUEST by Agatha Christie; ATHENÆUM DRAMATIC SOCIETY; *25-27 November 1993.* Richard Warwick: *A N Other;* Laura Warwick: *Mary Morlet-Mower;* Michael Starwedder: *Jim Woodward;* Miss Bennett: *Marion Datson;* Jan Warwick: *Ian Hawthorne;* Mrs Warwick: *Nora Jackson;* Henry Angell: *Johnson Trueman;* Sergeant Cadwallader: *Chris Stenson;* Inspector Thomas: *Colin Backhouse;* Julian Farrar: *Ian Darke.* Director: *Sue Maher;* Stage Manager: *Veronica Tipton;* Assistant Stage Manager: *Veronica Martin;* Lighting: *Andrew Hewitt;*

Sound: *Sarah Forth;* Properties: *Pamela Darke, Rosalind Hard;* Wardrobe Supervisor: *Ina Jones.*

508. THE SACRED FLAME by Somerset Maugham; THE ATHENÆUM DRAMATIC SOCIETY; *24-26 February 1994.* Maurice Tabret: *Mark Quinn;* Dr Harvester: *Simon Thorp;* Mrs Tabret: *Veronica Martin;* Nurse Weyland: *Pauline White;* Alice: *Jean Ashbourne;* Major Linconda: *Anthony Martin;* Stella Tabret: *Barbara Jervis;* Colin Tabret: *David Hooton.* Director: *Bob Pearson;* Stage Manager: *Derek Tipton;* Assistant Stage Manager: *Jean Nicholson;* Lighting and Sound: *Andrew Hewitt;* Properties: *Rosalind Hard, Grace Abbott;* Wardrobe Supervisor: *Ina Jones.*

509. THE LATE MRS EARLY by Norman Robbins; ATHENÆUM DRAMATIC SOCIETY; *28-30 April 1994.* Terry Early: *Tom Burney;* Susan Rickworth: *Kathryn Worthington;* Mabel Sutton: *Betty Blackwell;* Sam Early: *Jim Woodward;* Alice Louise Early: *Sue Maher;* Joe Gittings: *Ian Hawthorne;* Rueben Rickworth: *Mark Cavill;* Lucy Rickworth: *Angela Brooker.* Director: *Ian Darke;* Stage Manager: *Derek Tipton;* Assistant Stage Manager: *Grace Abbott;* Set Builders: *Derek Tipton, Mark Abbott;* Lighting & and Sound: *Lynne Owen;* Properties: *Pamela Darke;* Wardrobe Supervisor: *Ina Jones.*

510. OLIVER! by Lionel Bart; CHORLTON YOUTH THEATRE; *15-18 June 1994.* Cast and Crew: *William Haigh, Paul Owen, Rachel Owen, Nick*

Jackson; Matthew Nolan, Rosalyn
Norbury, Michael Eades, Simon
Renwick, Danielle Barnes, Rachel
Whalley, Danny Newton, Tessa
Hutton, Robert Sutton, Robert
Nix, Verity Sommerley-Baron,
Cathy Daldwin, Sally McGrath,
Anna Gibbard, Anna Hutton,
Laura Smith, Rosie Giles, Emily
Robertson, Molly Jones, Alison
Norbury, Luke Woolfson, Jams
Nolan, Jessica Suarez, Eleanor
Sherwood, Jenny Hargreaves,
Cathy Murphy, Amy Sherwood,
Nikhil Gomes, Peter McSweeney,
Clare Leach, Paul Madden, Jack
Newton, Mori Finni, Danny
Summers, Keziah Warburton, Jenni
Dyson, Rebekah Moseley, Katja
Lannon, Pilar Lannon, Diana
James, Serena James, Andrew
Lomas, Phillipa Stevens, Shahinda
Yassin, Laura McGrath, Dahlia
Francis, Louise Mansoor, Rachel
Statham, Vicky Martin, Rosie
Roberson, Vicky Mannion, Lauren
Baroli, Billie Walbank, Gemma
Slater, Luke Abraham, Brendan
O'Shea, Simon Pickering,
Francesca Nolan, Bethany
Warburton, Gemma Feasey.
Director: Alison Chaplin; Assistant
Director: Irving Czechowicz;
Musical Director: Alastair
Chadwick; Stage Manager: Tim
Kay; Costumes: Jane Jones; Band:
Margaret Whalley, Bekky Apps,
Jon Monument.

525. DAISY PULLS IT OFF
by Denise Deegan; ATHENÆUM
DRAMATIC SOCIETY; 26-28
November 1994.

**SHIRLEY ROAD MOBILE
LIBRARY,** Cheetham Hill,
M8; **AZ:** 40, 3A; **XAZ:**
74, CA.

124. THE TIGER WITH
GOLDEN CLAWS;
MANCHESTER ACTORS
COMPANY; 5 July 1994.

**SIMPSON MEMORIAL
HALL,** Moston Lane,
MOSTON M40 9PA;
061-682 1517. **AZ:** 41,
E2; **XAZ:** 76, A3.

511. CINDERELLA by David
Antrobus; NORTH MANCHESTER
AODS; 7-11 December 1993.
Fairy Godmother: Joan Littlefair;
Mrs Mop: Christine Sewell;
Buttons: Alastair Chadwick; Dame
Agatha Allcock: Bob Townsend;
Dodo: John Jackson; Dede:
Harold Mafia; Cinderella: Una
O'Connell; Dandini: Debra
Finnigan; Prince Charming:
Phillipa Rigby; Baron Hardup: Ron
Stanway; Princess Regent: Doreen
Byrne; Lady Amozel: Joanne
Simpson; Footman: Peter
Bretherton; DANCERS: Louise
Gorton, Mary Harrison, Eunice
Hamnett, Toni Openshaw,
Vanessa Randall, Karen Smith,
Anita Stuttard; LADIES'
CHORUS: Muriel Boardman,
Helen Dennerley, Margaret
Gledhill, Hilda Jones, Victoria
Parry; MEN'S CHORUS: Harry
Blease, Graham Birch, Peter
Bretherton, Peter Clough, Norman
Davies, John Gee, Bryn Gilbert,
Phil Tepper; CHILDREN'S
DANCING CHORUS: L Anderson,
R Barnard, S Baxendale, J
Caine, H Corcoran, S Davies, N
Diggle, L Dunn, N Gately, R
Hardman, L Jamieson, J Leese, S
Lowe, L McLaughlin, C Maggs,
D Maffia, C Moulkd, L

343

Radcliffe, K Rhodes, G Robinson, F Rodgers, E Sharples, K Stubbs, N Toon, V Whiteman; MICE: L Anderson, S Applebey, S Bancroft, S Beedle, K Boss, D Boyle, R Brobbin, H Butterworth, L Byrne, C Caine, S Carrington, C Chadwick, R Couser, S Farnell, S Fildes, J Ford, J Green, N Greenhalkgh, H Hardman, L Kay, N Kornyk, S Kornyk, J Latimer, M McLaughlin, R Marchant, N Ricketts, A Robinson, L Robinson, D Rostron, E Salkeld, H Stidolph, A Thorp, S Tomlinson. Producer: David Garside; Musical Director: Colin Trickett; Choreographer: Stage Manager: Bob Morrissey; Stage Staff: Barry Stuttart, Brian Amis, Christine Amis, Melanie Rigney; Lighting: Len Ross; Sound: Alan Boardman; Scenic Design: Ian Orry; Wardrobe: Margaret McEwen; Props: Christine Sewell; Prompt: Marjorie Lyons.

STANCLIFFE ROAD MOBILE LIBRARY,

Sharston, M22; AZ: 81, F3; XAZ: 128, C6.

124. THE TIGER WITH GOLDEN CLAWS; MANCHESTER ACTORS COMPANY; 7 July 1994.

STAR & GARTER; 18-20

Fairfield Street M1 2QF; 061-273 6726; AZ: 106, B1; XAZ: 166, D2.

512. MOURNING TV by Bill McCoid; ARTY PARTY THEATRE COMPANY; 22-24 September 1994. Jeremy Jipp: Tim Clark;

Diane Collymore: Maureen Evans; PA/Joyrider: Alison Clark; All Guests: Nick Naff, Walter, Claude, Maureen McMahon: Mark Attwood; Roger/Pilice Officer: Charles Waples. Director & Producer: Bill McCoid; Stage Manager: Ged McCormick; Makeup: Anita Rudyj.

513. THE DUMB WAITER by Harold Pinter; SPRINGBOARD THEATRE COMPANY; 27 September 1994.

STAVERTON CLOSE MOBILE LIBRARY,

Brunswick, M13; AZ: 106, B2; XAZ: 167, E4.

124. THE TIGER WITH GOLDEN CLAWS; MANCHESTER ACTORS COMPANY; 14 July 1994.

STEPHEN JOSEPH STUDIO, Manchester

University Campus, Lime Grove, MI3 9PL; 061-275 3347. AZ: 106:A4; XAZ: 101, F2.

514. POCOHONTAS devised, with Gregory Doran and Steve Elm by THE MANCHESTER UNIVERSITY DRAMA DEPARTMENT; 2-4 December 1993. Mr William Pyecroft: Ribert Tinley; Mrs Magnolia: Charlotte Somers; Evening Standard Reporter: Sarah Webster; The Beggar: Megan Jacobs; The Spanish Spy: Juliet Rainsford; Pocohontas: Claudia

Sermbezis; Uttamatamakin: *Raza Jaffrey;* Reverend Whittaker: *Rosie Collins;* John Rolfe: *Seamus Hayes;* Wingfield: *Camilla Schneideman;* Percy: *Alexandra Lilley;* Isabel de la Warre: *Deborah Galloway;* Cecilia de la Warre: *Annabel Walker;* Queen Anne: *Caoimhe McAvinchey;* Kawasha: *Deborah Newbold;* John Smith: *James Myers.* Director: *Gregory Doran;* Lighting: *Simon Maunder;* Board Operator: *Simon Carter;* Music Composer: *Amy Finch;* Set: *Annabel Walker, Deborah Newbold, Raza Jaffrey, Camilla Schneideman, Sarah Webster;* Costume: *Rosie Collins, Claudia Sermbezis, Alexandra Lilley, Caoimhe McAvinchey;* Properties: *Megan Jacob, Deborah Galloway;* Sound: *Juliet Raynsford;* Production Manager: *Robert Tinley;* Project Co-ordinator: *Claudette Williams;*

503. THE WINTER'S TALE by George Taylor; MANCHESTER UNIVERSITY DRAMA DEPARTMENT; *17 March 1994.* Emelia/Cleomenes/Time/Dorcas: *Sofia F Ahsan;* Autolycus/Lord: *Catherine Alexander;* Clown: *Peter Bhari;* Perdita/Officer: *Louise Bolton;* Leontes: *Craig Byrne;* Old Shepherd/Lady/Messenger: *Caroline Chick;* Polixenes: *Justin Edwards;* Florizel/Antigonus: *Asa Goldschmied;* Paulina: *Rebecca Harker;* Camillo/Gaoler/Mariner: *Mark Patterson;* Mamillius: *Christopher Seymour,* Hermione/Mopsa: *Emily Stones.* Director: *George Taylor;* Lighting/Stage Management: *Cornelia Geidel;* Music: *Amy Finch;* Voice Coach.

TATTON ARMS MOBILE

LIBRARY, Ringway Road West, M22; **AZ:** 91, F3; **XAZ:** 141, C6.

124. THE TIGER WITH GOLDEN CLAWS; MANCHESTER ACTORS COMPANY; *13 July 1994.*

UNISON SOCIAL CLUB; 5 Peter St, M2 5QR; 061–839 5247; **AZ:** 101, E5; **XAZ:** 161, F6.

526. LADIES AND GENTLEMEN by Trevor Suthers; REAL LIFE THEATRE COMPANY; *28–30 April 1994.* April: *Fiona Clarke;* June: *Hilly Barber;* Carl: *Joe Simpson;* Brian: *Graham Galloway;* Andy: *Peter O'Connor.* Director: *Helen Parry;* Stage Manager: *Martin Adams.*

UPPER CAMPFIELD MARKET, Liverpool Road, M3 4JG; 061–242 2555. AZ: 105, E1; XAZ: 165, F2. G, W

119. CLAYMAN by Kevin Fegan, inspired by Sculptor Ray Brooks; EL INOCENTE; *7–9 July 1993.* Grandmother: *Myriam Acharki;* Mother: *Jane Belshaw;* Voice: *Kevin Fegan;* Beau: *Tony Keirle;* Apeward: *Simon Startin;* Clayman: *Allen Stnoe;* Sister: *Sarah Jane Strachan;* Guide: *Rikki Tarascas.* Director: *Rikki Tarascas;* Artist/Maker: *Roger Bloomfield;* Lighting: *Chris Lucas;*

Percussion: *Trevor Davies, Tony Watt;* Production Manager: *Lee Dawkins;* Production Assistant: *Rachel Dickinson;* Producers: *Rikki Tarascas, Kevin Fegan;* Costumes: *Rachel Hird;* DJ: *Steve Moran.*
Journal: 8/7/94
Press: MEN: 8/7/94; **MM:** 15/7/94

253. THE HISTORY OF TOM JONES by Henry Fielding, adapted by Andrew Weekes; MANCHESTER YOUTH THEATRE; *1-10 September 1994.* Mr Allworthy: *Stephen Lewis;* Bridgit Allworthy: *Jo March;* Captain Blifil: *Anthony Hickling;* William Blifil: *Edward Donnelly;* Thomas Jones: *Richard Ellis;* Mrs Wilkins/Second Thug: *Kerri Manning;* Mr Thwackum: *Lawrence Moran;* Dowling/Ensign Northerton: *Andrew Losowsky;* Squire Western: *Colin Ravey;*Aunt Western: *Rachel Hick;* Sophia Western: *Rachael Wooding;* Honour: *Jennie Rowlandson;* Mr Fitzpatrick: *Gareth Hockenhull;* Molly Seagrim: *Jacqui Evans;* Mr Partridge/A Priest: *Daniel Nickson;* Mrs Partridge: *Sharon Cross;* Jenny Jones: *Joanne Gardner;* A Surgeon/A Guide: *Karl Heaver;* A Fellow: *Stephen Pritchard;* Sergeant Medley/A Footpad: *Scott Andrew;* Lady Booby: *Kelly Palin;* The Coachman: *Andrew Thompson;* Her Footman: *Phillip Sutcliffe;* The Landlady: *Dawn-Marie Leonard;* Mrs Fitzpatrick: *Laura Haughy;* Lady Bellaston: *Sarah Driver;* Lord Fellamar: *James White;* Mrs Miller: *Georgina Tattersall;* Hangman: *Elisabeth McLeilan;* First Thug: *Michelle East.* Director: *Joe Sumsion;* Design: *Jon Carnall, Sarah*

Taylor, Kate Warner, Kate Hind; Lighting: *Paul Colley;* Assistant Director: *Jilly Turnbull;* Wardrobe: *Sarah Niven, Zarina Tily, Rosie Westhead;* Technicians: *Tom Boucher, Simon Copper, Chris Dale, Julia Heyhoe;* Music: *Pamela Davies;* Director's Assistant: *David Harrison;* Choreographer: *Kathryn Beverley;* Production Manager: *Tim Wylie;* Technical Manager: *Martin Doran;* Wardrobe Supervisor: *Alison Humphrey;* Company Stage Manager: *Marcus Wilson;* Deputy Company Stage Manager: *Vivien Routledge;* Assistant Wardrobe Supervisor: *Amanda Morris;* Tutots: *Lynne Barlow, Pamela Davies, Rachel Katzenellenbogen.*
Press: MEN: 2/9/94; **MM:** 9/9/94

264. THE PETERLOO MASSACRE by Mike Harris; CITY OF DRAMA & BODDINGTONS MANCHESTER FESTIVAL; *19-24 March 1994.* Princess Caroline: *Margaret Mary Carrol;* Prince Regent: *Kim Walsh;* Princess Charlotte/Bather: *Elianne Byrne;* Rachel Carlile: *Lyn Poole;* John Lees: *Peter Morris;* Sarah Lees: *Barbara Quinn;* Viscount Sidmouth: *Ian Butterfield;* Richard Carlile: *Bernard Burke;* Henry Hunt: *Paul Marshall;* Jack Bagguley: *Don Moore;* Rev Mrs Norris JP: *Gwen Crawford;* Nadin: *Richard Catmore;* Sam Harding/Journalist/Yeoman/ Secret Service: *Marc Foster;* Aunt Augusta/Steward: *Olwyn O'Connor;* Aunt Sophia: *Di Byrne;* Aunt Mary/Steward/Singer : *Susi Madron;* Old Queen/YeomanFemale Reformer/Secret Service: *Alison Kelly;* Lady de

Clifford/Gaoler 3: *Vicki Harker;* Jane Carlile: *Hilary Slater;* Mary-Anne Carlile: *Angela Moriati;* Susan Wright: *Leslie-Ann Keefe;* Tom Watson/Lord Byron: *Michael Crowley;* Bed Bradley: *Steve Hilton;* Grandma Lees/Steward: *Grace Bushell;* Archbishop of Canterbury/Billy Wright/Drilling Weaver: *Chris Littler;* Labourer/ Journalist/Turner/Gaoler 1/Bather/ Drilling Weaver/Gaurd 1: *Ivan Holdsworth;* Maid/Mrs Harding: *Karen Prescott;* Maid/School Child: *Kelly Hilton;* Maid/ Journalist/School Child/Bather: *Eleanor Livesey;* Maid/Journalist/ Bather 1/Gaoler 2/Waitress: *Kate Spivey;* Maid: *Sarah Hill;* Maid/ Yeoman/School Child: *Christina Hill;* Maid/Steward/School Child: *Michelle Webster;* Maid/School Child/ Caddy: *Martha Kelly;* Maid/ School Child/Bather: *Jennifer Appleby;* Secretary: *Clare Becket;* Officer/Pergami/ Yeoman/Oliver/ Drilling Weaver: *Mark Griffin;* Hannah Lees: *Clare Ollerhead;* Lees Child 1/School Child: *James Wild;* Lees Child 2: *Janine Moroe;* Monitor 1/Bather: *Tamara Albachari;* Monitor 2/Journalist: *Ellen Kelly;* Journalist: *Yvonne Rayner;* Journalist/Civil Servant/ Jill: *Kate Piercy;* Journalist/Jane Rowbotham/Secret Service: *Jane Gallagher;* Journalist: *Pam Whittaker;* Police/Secret Service/ Yeoman/Bather: *Yasmin Gheith;* Mann/Drilling Weaver: *Dominic Keefe;* Ludlum/Yeoman: *Andrew Withers;* Prince of Orange/ Judge/Yeoman/Drilling Weaver: *Leonard Casey;* Fiona: *Clare Becket;* Female Reformer: *Joanne Cullen;* Female Reformer/School Child/Bather: *Mariam Varachia;* Stewards: *Lesley Keefe, Clare Hibbert;* Steward/School Child:

Anne *Breuilly;* Steward/School Child: *Sarah Kavanagh;* Yeoman/ Secret Service: *Caroline Price;* Yeoman: *Yvonne Brooks;* School Children: *Jade Connor, Sarah Howarth;* School Child/ Caddy: *Naomi Curley;* Cameraman: *Andrew Lock;* Caddy: *Patrick Cunningham;* Singer: *Pauline Bennet;* Official: *Ian Butterworth;* Musicians: *Joanne Cullen, Marc Foster, Ellen Kelly, Martha Kelly, Marco Paoula;* News Reader: *Bob Greaves.* Director: *Mike Harris;* Production and Design: *Dave Moutrey;* Music: *Katherine Wren;* Assistant Director: *Dave Jones;* Assistant Producer: *Frances Hunt;* Video Sequence Filming: *Tim Hopwell, Colin Bell, John Piper,* of Granada Television; Stage Management: *Fiona Flynn, Phil Hadget, Pamela Topham, Sally Frost, Clair Hibbert, Sheila McAnulty;* Properties: *Fiona Flynn, Phil Hadget, Pamela Topham, Saly Frost, Ivan Holdsworth, Chris Littler, Michael Crowley;* Costumes: *Pauline Bennett, Clare Becket, Grace Bushell, Caroline Price, Karen Prescott, Angela Moriati;* Lighting Operator: *Elaine Beaumont;* Follow Spots: *Amer Salam, Den Body, Steven May, Ben Pugh;* Sound and Video Operator: *DAve Cullen;* Video Technician: *Andrew Locke;* Technical Manager: *Jack Thompson;* Assistant Technical Manager: *Jon Keely;* Production Electrician: *Ken Coker.*
Press: AR: 17 & 31/3/94; **DT:** 21/9/94; **MEN:** 21/9/94

286. HENRY VI – The Battle for the Throne by William Shakespeare; ROYAL SHAKESPEARE COMPANY; *4-8 October 1994.* Earl of

347

Warwick: *John Keegan;* Montagu/ Rutland's Tutor/A Yorkist Father: *Declan Conlon;* Richard, Duke of York/Mayor of York/ Lewis XI: *Stephen Simms;* Edward IV: *Colin Tierney;* Richard, Duke of Gloucester: *Tom Smith;* George, Duke of Clarence: *Jo Stone-Fewings;* Rutland/Jack Vyner/ Lieutenant of the Tower: *Tam Williams;* Northumberland: *Dugald Bruce-Lockhart;* Clifford/Hastings: *Jamie Hinde;* Exeter/Sinklo: *Chris Garner;* Henry VI: *Jonathen Firth;* Queen Margaret: *Ruth Mitchell;* Edward, Prince of Wales: *Tom Walker;* Gabriel Thorpe: *Nick Bagnall;* Lady Elizabeth Grey: *Liz Kettle.* Director: *Katie Mitchell;* Design: *Rae Smith;* Lighting: *Tina McHugh;* Music: *Helen Chadwick;* Movement: *Paul Allain;* Fights: *Malcolm Ranson;* Sound: *Andrea Cox;* Assistant Director: *Wils Wilson;* Stage Manager: *Martyn Sergent;* Deputy Stage Manager: *Flip Tanner;* Deputy Stage Manager: *Suzi Blakey;* Musicians (Shawms, Percussion, Bagpipes): *William Lyons, Nicholas Perry, Belinda Sykes, Keith Thompson;* Tour Manager: *Jasper Gilbert;* Electricians: *Chris Jordan, Ian Watson;* Sound: *Martin Slavin;* Stage Carpenters: *John Bluck, David Samuels;* Wardrobe: *Kay Fox, Andrew Hunt.*
Journal: 5/10/94
Press: MEN: 30/9/94, 5/10/94

THE WEST INDIAN CENTRE, Carmoor Road, CHORLTON-ON-MEDLOCK; M16 0FB; O61-257 2092. AZ: 106, C5; XAZ: 101, H3.

WITHINGTON LIBRARY; 410 Wilmslow Road, M20 9BN; 061-445 1991; AZ: 72, B1; XAZ: 117, G2. W

301. BIG BAD WOLF; MANCHESTER ACTORS COMPANY; *December 1994.*

WRIGHT ROBINSON HIGH SCHOOL; Falmer Close, ABBEY HEY; M18 8XJ; 061-370 6542; AZ: 62, B1; XAZ: 103, H1.

491. HENRY V by William Shakespeare; *30 November - 2 December 1993.* Cast: *Jaime Douglas (*Katherine's Maid), *Jane Halpin* (Katherine, Scroop, et al), *Howard Livesey, David O'Neil, Lee Haughton, Michelle Simmonett, Jordana Ceterer, Wesley Wilson, Michael Singleton, Kirsty Orgen, Lyndsey Worthington, Emma Westerman, Darren Heaney, Alani Dutton, Marianne Goodier, Alison Ankers, Daniel Lam, Paul Sparrow* (Henry V)*,Jay Downend, John Kilgariff, Gareth Philipson, Richard Morris, Cherie Cairns.* Costumes: *Pamela Hunt,* Set Design: *Ola Mokliak;* Props: *John Fielden & CDT Department;* Set Design & Painting: *Charlotte Fagan, Tracey Ireland, Karen Garrard, Jerry Dodoo, Austen Aggrey, Lyndsey Wong, Lesley Robinson, Paul Fitton, Claire Turner, Alison Ankers, Andrea Hewlitt, Alani Dutton and Art Department;* Other Staff Involved: *John Jones, Susan Pope, Martyn Potts, Helen Spencer, John Whitehead, Ian*

Peters; Music Composer: *David Holdridge* (Schools Music Service); Dance: *Lynn Jordan* (Manchester Dance Centre).
Press: MEN: 1/12/93

WYTHENSHAWE LIBRARY;
The Forum, M21 5RT;
061–437 8211; **AZ:** 91,
E1; **XAZ:** 140, A2. W

431. LIZ GAMLIN PUPPETS;
19 August 1994.

301. BIG BAD WOLF;
MANCHESTER ACTORS
COMPANY; *December 1994.*

OLDHAM

OLDHAM COLISEUM brings JIMMY CHINN's STRAIGHT AND NARROW (54) back where it belongs: PAULA TILBROOK as the tyrannous Mum, KAREN HENTHORN as her most resilient daughter and ERIC HULME as the son-in-law best able to remain calm under fire.

ALEXANDRA PARK, Kings Road, OL8 2BJ; 061-911 4072; AZ: 34, C4; XAZ: 64, D4. W

252. RAVENHEART - THE STORY OR CARMEN, based on Prosper Merimée by KNEEHIGH THEATRE and INNER SENSE; *31 August - 1 September 1994.* Carmen: *Bec Applebee;* Mercedes: *Jo Kessell;* Michaela: *Emma Rice;* Matador: *Tristan Sturrock;* Captain: *Jim Carey;* Corporal:

Giles King; Bull: *Alan Drake; * Other Characters: *The Above + Chris Davies, Ian Holmes Lewis, Ravin Jayasuriya, Jon Thorne, Eddie Sherwood, Sue Ferner, Colin Seddon, Tracy James, Wayne Mansell.* Director: *Bill Mitchell;* Assistant Director: *Mike Shepherd;* Musical Director: *Jim Carey;* Associate Musical Directors: *Chris Davies, Raz Jayasuriya, Colin Seddon;* Designer: *Sue Hill;* Technical Co-ordinators: *Allan Drake, Wayne Mansell;* Words: *Anna Maria Murphy;* Choreographer: *Nicola*

Rosewarne; Production Manager: *Allan Drake;* Costume: *Sean Donohoe;* Set Construction: *John Voogd;* Makers: *Trelawney Mead, Sky Crossingham, Adam Hebb,* Training: *Sarah Dekker, Edson Bispo.*
Journal: 1/9/94
Press: MEN: 1&9/9/94; OC: 18/8/94, 1/9/94

BLUECOAT SCHOOL,
Egerton Road, OL1 3SQ; 061-624 1484; **AZ:** 34, C2; **XAZ:** 64, D2.

298. SHAKESPEARE'S GREATEST HITS; MANCHESTER ACTORS COMPANY; *1&9 February 1994*

COLISEUM, Fairbottom Street, OLDHAM OL1 3SW; 061-624 2829. AZ-34,C2; XAZ-64,D2. H, W.

40. ROMEO AND JULIET by William Shakespeare; *7-30 October 1993.* Musician/Servant to Capulet/Apothecary/2nd Watch /Peter: *Jonathan Aris;* Chorus/Escalus/Friar John: *John Spooner;* Servant to Montague/Paris: *Ian Aspinall;* Servant to Capulet/Friar Laurence : *Timothy Kightley;* Benvolio: *Oliver Jones;* Tybalt/1st Watch: *Andrew Grainger;* Lord Capulet: *Renny Krupinski;* Lady Capulet: *Lynette Edwards;* Lord Montague/Old Cousin Capulet: *Tony Broughton;* Lady Montague: *Penny Leatherbarrow;* Romeo: *Nicholas Murchie;* Page to Paris/Mercutio: *Keith Woodason;* Nurse:

Mary Sheen; Juliet: *Caroline Milmoe.* Director: *Warren Hooper;* Fight Director: *Renny Krupinski;* Choreographer: *Marjorie Nield;* Design: *Jacqueline Trousdale;* Lighting: *Shauan Woodhouse;* Sound: *Sharon Nokes;* Music Arranged and Adapted: *Jonathan Aris, Warren Hooper;* Production Manager: *Phil Clarke;* Switchboard Operator/Production Secretary: *Catherine Seabright;* Production Trainee: *Dave McKinnon;* Assistant Electrician: *Joanne Moss;* Trainee Electrician: *Andy Walker;* Construction Manager: *Danny Marsden;* Assistant Construction Manager: *Carl Richardson;* Design Assistant: *Celia Perkins;* Assistant Painter: *Mathew Jones;* Wardrobe Supervisor: *Louise Borland;* Deputy Wardrobe Supervisor/ Cutter: *Fiona Atkinson;* Wardrobe Assistants: *Angela Wellwood/Judith Lamb;* Mask Maker: *Sonia DiGennaro;* Stage Manager: *Richard Pattison;* Deputy Stage Manager: *Sharon Speirs;* Assistant Stage Managers: *Tara Beard, Neil Hughes, Trish McClenaghan, Anthony Dorsett.*
Press: CL: 13/10/93; OC: 5&8/10/93; RO: 13/10/93

41. SEASON'S GREETINGS by Alan Ayckbourn; *4-27 November 1993.* Harvey: *Keith Clifford;* Bernard : *Timothy Kightley;* Belinda: *Lynette Edwards;* Pattie: *Caroline Milmoe;* Neville: *Renny Krupinski;* Eddie: *Steven Pimder;* Rachel: *Anna Barnes;* Phyllis: *Penny Leatherbarrow;* Clive: *Nicholas Murchie.* Director: *Warren Hooper;* Design: *Keith Orton;* Lighting: *Phil Clarke;* Sound: *Sharon Nokes;* Production

Manager: *Phil Clarke;* Switchboard Operator/Production Secretary: *Catherine Seabright;* Production Trainee: *Dave McKinnon;* Chief Electrician: *Shaun Woodhouse;* Assistant Electrician: *Joanne Moss;* Trainee Electrician: *Andy Walker;* Construction Manager: *Danny Marsden;* Assistant Construction Manager: *Carl Richardson;* Design Assistant: *Celia Perkins;* Assistant Painter: *Mathew Jones;* Wardrobe Supervisor: *Louise Borland;* Deputy Wardrobe Supervisor/ Cutter: *Fiona Atkinson;* Wardrobe Assistants: *Angela Wellwood;* Wigs: *Chris Bullimore;* Mask Maker: *Sonia DiGennaro;* Stage Manager: *Richard Pattison;* Deputy Stage Manager: *Sharon Speirs;* Assistant Stage Managers: *Neil Hughes, Trish McClenaghan, Anthony Dorsett.* **Press: CL:** 10/11/93 **MEN:** 5/11/93; **OC:** 3/11/93

42. ROBINSON CRUSOE by Warren Hooper; *2 December 1993 - 15 January 1994.* Sarah the Cook: *Earl Grey;* Robinsom Crusoe: *Ian Kelsey;* Cap'n Hogwash: *Michael Atkinson;* Jolly Roger: *Wayne Cater;* Girl Friday: *Sara West;* THE FABULOUS SEYCHELLES: Rock-On: *Jacki Perkins;* Roll-On: *Sarah Ingram;* Mor-On: *Stephen Reynolds;* A Pathetic Castaway: *Mark Lawrence;* YOUNG COMPANY: Red Team: *Marc Gibson, Katie McCarthy, Kaye Meakin, Laura Meakin, Matthew Richardson, Christopher Simms, Jorden Sinckler, Nicola Skeldon, Sophie Skeldon, Jenny Walsh;* Blue Team: *Jennifer Chadwick, Robert Dermody, Kirsten Hampson, Leanne Hampson, reeve*

Howarth, Vicki Henderson, Daniel Hopper, Elizabeth Lane, David Ward, Hilary Williamson; THE BAND: Keyboards: *Dave Bintley;* Bass: *Aidan Lawrence;* Drums: *Aidrian Rea.* Director: *Warren Hooper;* Musical Director: *Dave Bintley;* Choreographer: *Marjorie Nield;* Design: *Jacqueline Trousdale;* Lighting: *Phil Clarke;* Sound: *Sharon Nokes;* Production Manager: *Phil Clarke;* Switchboard Operator/Production Secretary: *Catherine Seabright;* Production Trainee: *Dave McKinnon;* Assistant Electrician: *Joanne Moss;* Trainee Electrician: *Andy Walker;* Construction Manager: *Danny Marsden;* Assistant Construction Manager: *Carl Richardson;* Carpenter: *Foz;* Design Assistant: *Celia Perkins;* Assistant Painter: *Mathew Jones;* Wardrobe Supervisor: *Louise Borland;* Deputy Wardrobe Supervisor/ Cutter: *Fiona Atkinson;* Wardrobe Assistants: *Angela Wellwood, Judith Lamb, Carol Bamforth, Emma Jordan;* Wigs: *Chris Bullimore;* Mask Maker: *Sonia DiGennaro;* Stage Manager: *Richard Pattison;* Deputy Stage Manager: *Sharon Speirs;* Assistant Stage Managers: *Neil Hughes, Trish McClenaghan,* **Press: CL:** 8/12/93 **MEN:** 3/12/93; **OC:** 6/12/93; **S:** 13/1/94

535. AND MOTHER MAKES THREE by David Dale; *9 January 1994.* Cast: *David Dale, Rebecca Clow, Matthew Gould.* Music: *Neil Carter.* **Press: OC:** 5&21/1/94, 7/2/94

53. MY MAD GRANDAD by Mike Stott; *20 January - 12 February 1994.* Gil: *Graham*

352

Gill; Dad/Kenny: *Stephen Reynolds;* Mum: *Sherry Ormerod;* Grandad: *Gordon Warmby;* Sammy: *Mark Charnock;* Arnold Butler-Cockcroft JP/Dr Kershaw: *David Ericsson;* Muffin: *Eric Hulme;* Lesley Holroyd: *Karen Henthorn/Jacqueline Turnbull;* Production Manager: *Phil Clarke;* Switchboard Operator/Production Secretary: *Catherine Seabright;* Production Trainee: *Dave McKinnon;* Assistant Electrician: *Joanne Moss;* Trainee Electrician: *Andy Walker;* Construction Manager: *Danny Marsden;* Assistant Construction Manager: *Carl Richardson;* Carpenter: *Foz;* Design Assistant: *Celia Perkins;* Assistant Painter: *Mathew Jones;* Wardrobe Supervisor: *Louise Borland;* Deputy Wardrobe Supervisor/ Cutter: *Fiona Atkinson;* Wardrobe Assistant/ Cutter: *Janet Wilson;* Wardrobe Assistant: *Angela Wellwood;* Stage Manager: *Richard Pattison;* Deputy Stage Manager: *Sharon Speirs;* Assistant Stage Managers: *Neil Hughes, Trish McClenaghan,* Trainee Stage Manager: *Anthony Dorsett.*
Journal: 9/2/94
Press: CL: 26/1/94 G: 3/2/94

54. STRAIGHT AND NARROW by Jimmie Chinn; *17 February-12 March 1994.* Bob: *Graham Gill;* Jeff: *Paul McCleary;* Nona: *Sherry Ormerod;* Lois: *Karen Henthorn,* Vera: *Paula Tilbrook;* Bill: *Eric Hulme;* Arthur: *David Ericsson.* Director: *Warren Hooper;* Design: *Celia Perkins;* Lighting: *Phil Clarke, Richard Muirhead;* Sound: *Sharon Nokes;* Production Manager: *Phil Clarke;* Switchboard Operator/Production

Secretary: *Catherine Seabright;* Production Trainee: *Dave McKinnon;* Assistant Electrician: *Joanne Moss;* Trainee Electrician: *Andy Walker;* Construction Manager: *Danny Marsden;* Assistant Construction Manager: *Steve Kirk;* Assistant Painter: *Mathew Jones;* Wardrobe Supervisor: *Louise Borland;* Deputy Wardrobe Supervisor/ Cutter: *Fiona Atkinson;* Wardrobe Assistant/ Cutter: *Janet Wilson;* Wardrobe Assistant: *Angela Wellwood;* Stage Manager: *Richard Pattison;* Deputy Stage Manager: *Sharon Speirs;* Assistant Stage Managers: *Neil Hughes, Trish McClenaghan,* Trainee Stage Manager: *Anthony Dorsett.*
Journal: 8/3/94
Press: CL: 23/2/94; **MEN:** 17 & 19/2/94

72. LA RONDE by Arthur Schnitzler, translated by Mike Alfred; *17 March – 9 April 1994.* The Prostitute/The Housemaid/The 'Sweet Girl': *Joy Blakeman;* The Son of the House/The Writer: *Stefan Escreet;* The Young Wife/ The Actress: *Kate Paul;* The Soldier/The Husband/The Count: *Bev Willis.* Director: *Ian Forrest;* Set and Costumes: *Jacquelune Trousdale;* Lighting: *Richard Muirhead;* Sound: *Sharon Nokes;* Production Manager: *Phil Clarke;* Switchboard Operator/ Production Secretary: *Catherine Seabright;* Assistant Electrician: *Joanne Moss;* Trainee Electrician: *Andy Walker, Dave McKinnon;* Construction Manager: *Danny Marsden;* Assistant Construction Manager: *Steve Kirk;* Design Assistant: *Celia Perkins;* Wardrobe Supervisor: *Louise Borland;*

Deputy Wardrobe Supervisor/
Cutter: *Fiona Atkinson;* Wardrobe
Assistant/ Cutter: *Janet Wilson;*
Wardrobe Assistant: *Angela
Wellwood;* Stage Manager:
Richard Pattison; Deputy Stage
Manager: *Sharon Speirs;* Assistant
Stage Managers: *Neil Hughes,
Trish McClenaghan,* Trainee Stage
Manager: *Anthony Dorsett.*
Journal: 6/4/94
Press: CL: 6/4/94; **MEN:**
19/3/94; **OC:** 14&18/3/94;
RO: 26/3/94 **S:** 12/5/94

536. ROCKULA by Christopher
Lillicrap; *14 April – 7 May
1994.* Priest/Villager: *Mark
Carroll;* Nun/Villager/Zola:
Amanda Noar; Nun/Villager/Nola:
Jennifer Ness; Doctor Von
Helsinc: *Roger Leach;* Helga Von
Helsinc: *Joanne Rowden;* Rudy
Von Hassellblat: *Dan Milne;* Ivan:
Tony Whittle; Lola: *Claire
Callaghan;* Dracula: *Bogdan
Kominowski.* BAND: Keyboards:
Dave Bintley; Guitar: *Steve
Beharrell;* Bass: *Aidan Lawrence;*
Drums: *Adrian Rea;* Director:
Warren Hooper; Choreographer:
Lindsay Dolan; Musical Director:
Dave Bintley; Musical
Arrangements: *Dave Bintley, Andy
Davidson;* Illusions: *Paul Kieve;*
Magic Tricks: *Jonathon Thompson;*
Set: *Jacquelune Trousdale;*
Costumes: *India Smith;* Lighting:
Richard Muirhead; Sound: *Sharon
Nokes;* Production Manager: *Phil
Clarke;* Switchboard Operator/
Production Secretary: *Catherine
Seabright;* Assistant Electrician:
Joanne Moss; Trainee Electrician:
Andy Walker, Dave McKinnon;
Construction Manager: *Danny
Marsden;* Assistant Construction
Manager: *Steve Kirk;* Design
Assistant: *Celia Perkins;* Wardrobe

Supervisor: *Louise Borland;*
Deputy Wardrobe Supervisor/
Cutter: *Fiona Atkinson;* Wardrobe
Assistant/ Cutter: *Janet Wilson;*
Wardrobe Assistant: *Carol
Bamforth, Judith Lamb;* Stage
Manager: *Richard Pattison;*
Deputy Stage Manager: *Sharon
Speirs;* Assistant Stage Managers:
Neil Hughes, Trish McClenaghan,
Trainee Stage Manager: *Anthony
Dorsett;* Millinery: *Ella Kidd;*
Wigs: *Chris Bullimore.*
Press: CL: 20/4/94; **MEN:**
15/4/94; **OC:** 15&21/4/94,
3/5/94; **RO:** 23/4/94; **S:**
12/5/94

**313. A VIEW FROM THE
BRIDGE** by Arthur Miller;
KABOODLE; *11–12 May 1994.*

537. ALIENS; devised and
performed by Dominique
Grandmougin and Ezra
Hjalmarsson; TALKING
PICTURES; *13 May 1994.*
Director: *Babette Masson;* Set,
Props, Costumes: *Marie
Desforges;* Mask Reproduction:
Martin Rezard; Light and Sound:
Stuart Low; Music: *Johasn
Soderberg.*

372. GRIMM; NEW BREED;
14 May 1994.

95. B-ROAD MOVIE by
Maggie Fox and Sue Ryding; LIP
SERVICE; *17–21 May 1994.*
STAGE: Tina: *Sue Ryding;*
Yvonne: *Maggie Fox;* Voice
Overs: *Peter Kerry, Malcolm
Raeburn;* SCREEN: Cliff
Montgomery: *Maggie Fox;* Margo
Miers: *Sue Ryding;* The Mummy:
John Capps; Singers: Soprano:
Amanda Crawley; Tenor: *Claude*

Close; Baritone: *Malcolm Raeburn.* Director: *Gwenda Hughes;* Design: *Kate Burnett;* Music: *Mark Vibrans;* Lyrics: *Malcolm Raeburn;* Dances: *Nona Shepphard; Jean Jeanette Charles;* Help in Finding Yvonne and Tina: *Linda Bassett;* Lighting: *Phil Clarke;* Musical Director/ Keyboards: *Stephen Owens;* Guitar: *Paul Mitchell-Davidson;* Production Manager: *Jim Niblett;* Company Stage Manager: *Louise Tischler;* Sound Technician: *Kate Purkis;* Lighting Technician: *Neil Hughes;* FILM: Producer: *Tony Bulley;* Editor: *Bryce Clayton;* Camera: *Tony Coldwell;* Sound: *John Curtis;* Dubbing Mixer: *Terry Cavigan;* Spark: *Eric Flowers;* Technical Advice: *Daf Hobson;* Wigs and Make-up: *Kim Freeland;* Costume Maker: *Janet Rogers;* Mummy Maker: *Emma Yates;* Printing: *Rank Film Labs (Leeds and Denham);* Filmed entirely on location; ANIMATION (Cosgrove Hall): Producer/ Director: *Jackie Cockle;* Editor: *Jane Hicks;* Background Artist: *Beverley Bush;* Xerox: *Anthony McAlees;* Title Artwork: *Roy Huckerby;* Sound: *John Wood;* Keyteam Animation: *Dan Whitworth, John Offord;* Paint and Trace: *Colour Crew;* Rostrum Camera: *Peter Kidd.*
Journal: 19/5/94
Press: CL: 7/9/94; **MEN:** 12 & 18/5/94 **OC:** 17/5/94

538. A LOAD OF OLD TRIPE; Lancahire folk and humour from Edith Ralphs, Cheapside, Mike Riley, Phil Harding; *23 May 1994.*

539. ROMANY – "THE SAINT" by John Chambers and Keith Clifford; SCANDALOUS PRODUCTIONS; *24 May 1994.* Romany (& others): *Keith Clifford.*

540. FRANK RANDALL – "THE SINNER" by Keith Clifford and John Chambers; SCANDALOUS PRODUCTIONS; *24 May 1994.*

96. THE CANTERBURY TALES (The Miller's Tale, The Nun's Priest's Tale, The Pardoner's Tale, The Wife of Bath's Tale) by Geoffrey Chaucer, adapted by Bill Hopkinson; SALFORD UNIVERSITY THEATRE COMPANY; *25 May 1994.* Alison/Pertelote/Ryotour/The Wife of Bath/Guinevere/Crone: *Lorraine Hackett;* Absalom/Chantecleer/The Pardoner: *Ian Lashford;* The Scholar/The Priest/Ryotour/The Knight: *Michael McKrell;* The Miller/The Carpenter/The Smith/ The Fox/Ryotour: *Conann Whelan.* Director: *Bill Hopkinson;* Producer: *Guy Holloway;* Design: *Alex Russell;* Masks: *(David) Mason & (Lorraine) Hackett;* Original and Period Music: *Dave Praties, Carol Donaldson;* Technical Direction: *Phil Ellams, Giles Clarke;* Lighting: *Giles Clarke;* Sound: *Mat Jones.*
Journal: 25/5/94
Press: ANT: 30/9/94; **MEN:** 7/10/94.

93. FUENTE OVEHUNA by Lope de Vega, translated by Adrain Mitchell; MANCHESTER METROPOLITAN UNIVERSITY SCHOOL OF THEATRE; *26 May 1994*

108. HEART AND SOUL by Cheryl Martin, with original music by Tim Browne; lyrics by Mark Babych, with aditional lyrics by Tim Browne and Julie Corrigan; COLISEUM COMMUNITY COMPANY; *4-18 June 1994.* Dot: *Molly Eastham;* Julia: *Julia Mills;* Susan/Dot (20's): *Mimi Rogers;* Danny/Jerry (20's): *Steve Ingram;* Catherine: *Grace Lewis;* Judith: *Caroline Roach;* Mavis: *Diane Roach;* Winnie: *Muriel Agard;* Lewis: *Nigel Stewart;* Casuals: *Janice Webb, Lynn Neil, Joyce Newman, Steve Power, Julie Ann Quinlan, Clair Abbott, Susan Sale, Helen Clegg, Joanne Kilcourse, Dorothy Kilcourse, Brenda Dillon, Gary Thomas, Mike Hall;* Inspector/Mr Developer: *Martin Heyhoe;* Inspector's Assistant/Colin: *Keir Hardie;* Jerry: *John Hankin;* Young Dot: *Leanne Buckley;* Young Cissy: *Rachel Jones;* Friends: *Angela Jones, Katrina Roman, Cathy Boardman;* Mum/ Sadie Buckley: *Mary Thomas;* Dad: *Gary Thomas;* Flo: *Susan Sale;* Miss Mottram: *Linda Clegg;* Princes and Kings: *Steve Roman, Kyra Byron, Robert Hardman;* Paul (20's)/Tony: *Steve Power;* Cissy (20's): *Claire Abbott;* Irate Shopper: *Lynn Neil;* Narrator: *Steve Titley;* Traders: *Joanne Kilcourse, Dorothy Kilcourse, Brenda Dillon, Linda Clegg, Lynn Neil, Susan Sale, Helen Clegg, Mike Hall;* St John Buckley: *Bryn Taylor;* Winnie's Friends: *Violet Drummond, Aileen Gittens, Cynthia Lovell, Eulene Roach, May Thomas;* Gladys: *Julie Ann Quinlan;* Pram Pushers: *Gary Thomas, Susan Sale, Claire Abbott, Janice Webb;* The Posse: *Bev Lynch, Tricia Goodridge, Katrina Roman, Cathy Boardman, Rachel Jones, Angela Jones, Leanne Buckley;* Linda: *Joyce Newman;* BAND: Bass/Whistle/ Vocals: *Nick Laurel;* Drums/Percussion/Vocals: *Colin Wonder;* Guitar/Keyboards/Vocals: *John Evans;* Guitar/Keyboards/ Vocals: *Tim Browne;* Vocals: *Cheryl Martin.* Director: *Mark Babych;* Design: *Keith Orton;* Musical Director: *Tim Browne;* Assistant Director: *Julie Corrigan;* Movement: *Katy Dymoke;* Lighting: *Richard Muirhead;* Sound: *Sharon Nokes;* Production Manager: *Phil Clarke;* Switchboard Operator/Production Secretary: *Catherine Seabright;* Assistant Electrician: *Joanne Moss;* Trainee Electrician: *Andy Walker, Dave McKinnon;* Construction Manager: *Danny Marsden;* Assistant Construction Manager: *Steve Kirk;* Design Assistant: *Celia Perkins;* Wardrobe Supervisor: *Louise Borland;* Deputy Wardrobe Supervisor/ Cutter: *Fiona Atkinson;* Wardrobe Assistant/ Cutter: *Janet Wilson;* Wardrobe Assistant: *Angela Wellwood;* Stage Manager: *Richard Pattison;* Assistant Stage Managers: *Neil Hughes, Trish McClenaghan,* Trainee Stage Manager: *Anthony Dorsett.* **Journal:** 16/6/94 **Press:** CL: 15/6/94; G: 9/6/94; MEN: 2 & 8/6/94; OC: 31/5/94, 8/6/94; RO: 11/6/94

546. BARNUM; Music by Cy Coleman; Lyric by Michael Stewart; Book by Mark Bramble; THE CONGRESS PLAYERS; *22 June - 2 July 1994.* Phineas Taylor Barnum: *Howard G Raw;*

Charity Barnum: *Shirley Simm;* Ring Master/Julius Goldschmidt/ James A Bailey: *Bill Nicholson;* Joice Heth/Blues Singer: *Brenda Phillips;* Chester Lyman/Tom Thumb/Edgar Templton: *Craig Wright;* Amos Scudder: *Don Munro;* First Woman: *Liz Bradbury;* Second Woman: *Alison Bell;* Sherwood Stratton: *Duncan Anderson;* Mrs Sherwood Stratton: *Rosalind Styles;* Jenny Lind: *Suzanne Matherl* Concert Master: *Paul Firth;* Wilton: *Stephen Simm;* Hunbert Morrissey: *Shaun Booth;* Highwire: *Wendy Jack;* Trapeze: *Julie Profitt;* Stilt Walkers: *David Clay, Simon Crompton;* White-Faced Clown: *Phil Cooper;* Juggler: *Clifford Cowling;* Shoe Dancer: *Emma Williams;* Dancer: *Jacci Nicholson;* Acrobat: *Alan Ball.* Director: *Peter R Wakefield;* Musical Director: *Paul Firth;* Choreographer: *Kay Lilley;* Stage Manager: *Andy Maloney;* Lighting: *Richard Muirhead;* Sound: *Glenn Knight;* Book: *Paul Osbaldson;* Stage Team: *Paul Shiel, Derek Hyde, Victor Swinson, Bill Radburn, Greg Radburn, Wendy Tomlinson, Wendy Schofield, Phil Nichols, Dave Ferguson, Peter Stigwood,* Flys: *Tony Rhodes, Neil Hughes;* Follow Spots: *Steve Young, Adrian Parker;* Wardrobe Mistresses: *Gail Smith, Terri Parker;* Wigs & Hair: *Betty Sheard;* Make-Up: *Hillary Steele;* Dressers: *Tony Glennon, Carole Bardsley, Rita Whyatt, Alison Kay, Jean Oldham, Mary Lees;* Props: *Joy Orton, Ken Orton, Diane Burrington, Carolyn Sturdy, Jean Fleming, Lisa Clayton, Darren Hill, Aln Johnson, Steve Clarkson,;* Rehearsal Pianists: *Jackie Dawber, Christine Grinrod, Sylvia Hoare;* Circus Training:

Clifford Cowling; Trapeze & Choreography: *Cath Peel;* Rigging and Props: *Howarth Wrightsons;* Scenery: *Proscenium.*
Press: OC: 15/3/94, 28/6/94

547. BILLY; musical based on *Billy Liar* by Keith Waterhouse and Willis Hall; BLACK HORSE PRODUCTIONS, INCREASINGLY IMPORTANT THEATRE COMPANY, C'EST TOUS DANCE COMPANY; *5–9 July 1994.* Directors: *Colin Snell and Chris Appleby;* Choreographer: *Chris Appleby;* Musical Director: *Adele Camty;* Lighting: *Phil Ellams, Giles Claire;* Sound: *Olive Driver.*

548. WOMEN BEHIND BARS by Tom Eyen; TARTS ON TOUR; *25–30 July 1994.* The Matron: *David Dale;* Louise: *Dee Robillard;* Blanche: *Cressida Carre;* Jo-Jo: *Noma Dumezweni;* Cheri: *Lacey Bond;* Granny/ Warden: *Linda Clark;* Gloria: *Stacey Charlesworth;* Ada: *Elizabeth Charbonneau;* Guadalupe: *Amanda Russell;* Mary-Eleanor: *Nicole Salinger;* The Man: *Mark Montgomerie.* Director: *Rae Coates;* Producer: *David Minns;* Production Stage Manager: *Sarah Yelland;* Set: *Jean Frsncois Drigout;* Lighting: *Sharon N Riley.*
Press: MEN: 23/6/94, 21 & 26/7/94; **OC:** 22&26/7/94 **S:** 21/7/94

549. ONCE A CATHOLIC by Mary O'Malley; *8 September – 1 October 1994.* Mary Mooney: *Fiona Christie;* Mary McGinty: *Susan McArdle;* Mary Gallagher: *Jennifer Hennesey;* Mary O'Grady: *Helen Lacey;*

357

Mother Peter: *Leda Hodgson;*
Mother Basil: *Madeleine Moffatt;*
Mother Thomas Aquinas: *June
Brougton;* Mr Emmanuelli:
Stephen Hancock; Father
Mullarkey: *Desmond Jordan;*
Cuthbert: *Mark Charnock;* Derek:
Clive Moore. Director: *Warren
Hooper;* Musical Supervisor:
Stephen Hancock; Design:
Jacqueline Trousdale; Costume:
Celioa Jones; Lighting: *Richard
Muirhead;* Sound: *Sharon Nokes;*
Production Manager: *Phil Clarke;*
Stage Technician: *Neil Hughes;*
Assistant Electrician: *Joanne Moss;*
Trainee Electricians: *Philip
Nicholls, Paul Knott;* Construction
Team: *Steve Kirk, Jimmy Ragg;*
Freelance Scenic Artist: *Matthew
Jones;* Wardrobe Supervisor: *Alison
Heyes;* Deputy Wardrobe
Supoervisor/Cutter: *Janet Wilson;*
Wardrobe Assistant/Cutter: *Scott
Langridge;* Wardrobe Assistant:
Angela Wellwood; Stage Manager:
Richard Pattison; Deputy Stage
Manager: *Kim Wiltshire;* Assistant
Stage Manager: *Donna Dawson,
Trish McClenaghan;* Trainee
Assistant Stage Manager: *Rebecca
Merry.*
Press: CL: 21/9/94; MEN:
1&9/9/94; OC: 29/8/94,
8/9/94 RO: 17/9/94 S:
29/9/95

550. BARE by Renny
Krupinski; *9-22 October 1994.*
Arden: *Brian Croucher;*
Skinner:*Ross Boatman;* Blythe/
Chrissie/Val: *Melanie Ramsay;*
Chesney/Reeve: *Roy Heather;*
Ratcliffe/Dave/Lazarus: *Stephen
Banks;* Pickering–Jay/Davies/
Marco: *Paul Aves;* Bergen/
Curzon: *George Sweeney;* Spikey
Joe/Leon/PC: *Joe Speare.*
Director & Fights: *Renny*

Krupinski; Design: *Keith Orton;*
Lighting: *Phil Clarke;* Sound:
Sharon Nokers; Deputy Stage
Manager On the Book: *Kim
Wiltshire;* Production Manager:
Phil Clarke; Stage Technician:
Neil Hughes; Chief Electrician:
Richard Muirhead; Assistant
Electrician: *Joanne Moss;* Trainee
Electricians: *Philip Nicholls, Paul
Knott;* Construction Team: *Steve
Kirk, Jimmy Ragg;* Design
Assistant: *Celia Perkins;* Freelance
Scenic Artist: *Matthew Jones;*
Wardrobe Supervisor: *Alison
Heyes;* Deputy Wardrobe
Supoervisor/Cutter: *Janet Wilson;*
Wardrobe Assistant/Cutter: *Scott
Langridge;* Wardrobe Assistant:
Angela Wellwood; Stage Manager:
Richard Pattison; Assistant Stage
Manager: *Donna Dawson, Trish
McClenaghan;* Trainee Assistant
Stage Manager: *Rebecca Merry.*
Press: CL: 19/9/94; MEN:
7/10/94; OC: 28/9/94,
7/10/94

551. EDUCATING RITA by
Willy Russell; *3-26 November
1994.* Rita: *Deborah
McAndrew.*
Press: OC: 23/6/94

552. SINDAD THE SAILOR by
Warren Hooper; *2 December
1994 - 14 January 1995.*
Press: OC: 27/9/94

Granada Studio Theatre, at the COLISEUM.

541. TALES AND VOICES
FROM THE HILL; devised by
Claire Mooney and performed by
users of the Fitton Hill centre;
advice from Bill McCoid. **9**

May 1994 Cast of 30+, including: *Carl Henderson, Hannah Drummond, Selina Hetherington, Alison Cooper, Nadine Hetherington, Anna Hetherington, Andy Peacock, Leanne Trelfoy.* Director: *Sue Reddish.* **Press:** OC: 29/9/94.

88. MAKING LIGHT, devised and performed by Joanne Curley;

89. BEANS, devised and performed by Lindi Glover, with Christopher Roger;

90. REPEAT HABITUAL OFFENDER, devised and performed by Tara Daniels and Andrew Fillis;

50. MINIMAL STORIES by Antonio Capelo, performed here by *Lindi Glover, Elis Hetherington, Yasmin Karlinska, Sarah McAdam, Tracy Shaw, Leah Stanley, Beki Whitney;* ARDEN SCHOOL OF THEATRE; *11 May 1994.* **Journal:** 11/5/94

542. TABOO; devised by GREAVES STREET PLAYERS, in conjunction with students from Huddersfield University Department of Drama; *14 May 1994.*

544. WOLF; written and directed by the cast from MANCHESTER METROPOLITAN SCHOOL OF THEATRE; *17 May 1994,* Emir Tika: *Valur Freyr Einarsson;* Mr Obidiah: *Terence Chapman;* Hannah Obidiah: *Catherine Green;* Victor Petrowski: *Greg Scott;* Jim: *Shane McCory;* Ena: *Maike Mullenders;*

545. FRANKIE SAYS REVIVE; written and directed by the cast from MANCHESTER METROPOLITAN UNIVERSITY SCHOOL OF THEATRE; *17 May.* Mr Stain: *David Slater;* Miss Glaze: *Lenny McEwan;* Rock: *Roz Thomas;* Frank: *Jan Linnick;* Governor Tape: *Mathew Cureton.* Music composed and Performed: *David Slater.*

543. SUNDAY AT SIX; devised and researched by YER-WAT-SAY THEATRE COMPANY; *18 May 1994*

81. UNITY; BURY YOUTH THEATRE; *24 May 1994.*

225. PICKING BONES by Stephen Keyworth; INCREASINGLY IMPORTANT THEATRE COMPANY; *25 May 1994.*

CROMPTON HOUSE SCHOOL, Rochdale Road, Shaw, OL2 7HF; 0706 847451; **AZ:** 25, F1; **XAZ:** 35, E6.

298. SHAKESPEARE'S GREATEST HITS; MANCHESTER ACTORS COMPANY; *31 January 1994.*

129. GROUNDED by Eileen Murphy; M6 THEATRE COMPANY; *2-3 February 1994.*

DAISY NOOK VISITOR CENTRE, Stannybrook Road, FAILSWORTH M35

9WJ; 061-308 3909; **AZ:**
43, 4E; **XAZ:** 78, B5.
G, W

644. SHADOW OF THE
PAST; MEDLOCK VALLEY
WARDENS SHADOW PUPPETS;
21 August 1994.

**FAILSWORTH
COMPREHENSIVE
SCHOOL,** Brierley
Avenue, M35 9HA; 061-
681 3763; **AZ:** 42, C3;
XAZ: 77,G4

298. SHAKESPEARE'S
GREATEST HITS; MANCHESTER
ACTORS COMPANY; *24 January
1994*

**FITTON HILL YOUTH
CENTRE,** Fir Tree Avenue,
OL8 2SW; 061-624
1775; **AZ:** 43, 1F; **XAZ:**
79, E1

541. TALES FROM THE
HILL; *29-30 May 1994.*

GRANGE ARTS CENTRE,
Rochdale Road, OLDHAM
OL9 6EA; 061-624 8013.
AZ: 34, B2; **XAZ:** 64,
C2. **W, H**

558. RASHOMON by Fay and
Michael Kanin, based on the
stories of Ryunosuke Akutagawa;
OLDHAM COLLEGE
PERFORMING ARTS; *20-23*

October 1994. Priest: *Katrina
Heath;* Woodcutter: *Kelly
Llorenna;* Wigmaker: *Jill Moore;*
Deputy: *David Hollingdale;*
Bandit: *Mark Hilton;* Husband:
Phil Hopwood; Wife: *Zoë*
Kulezycki alternating with *Joan
Potter;* Mother: *Emma Dawson;*
Medium: *Nina Rosling.* Direction
& Design: *Colin E Crowther;*
Co-ordinator: *Nina Rosling;*
Fights: *Mark Hilton;* Props: *Jill
Moore;* Costume Research:
Katrina Heath; Music/Sound
Research: *Phil Hopwood;* Make-up
Research: *Kelly Llorenna;* Japanese
Language Research: *David
Hollingdale;* Technician: *Gordon
Salt;* Set: *Jolyon Coombs;*
Lighting: *David Evans;* Sound:
Tim Harrison; Production
Manager: *Meic Watkins;* Stage
Manager: *Jane Jones;* Deputy
Stage Manager: *Claire Smith;*
Assistant Stage Managers: *Brian
Lees, Alan Lancelott, Richard
Clough;* Master Carpenter: *Garry
Mann;* Wardrobe Supervisor:
Deena Kearney; Lighting Board
Operators: *Andrew Watt, Alan
Henstock;* Stage Electrician:
David Plant; Sound Operator:
Andrea Fitton.

559. JESUS CHRIST
SUPERSTAR Tim Rice and
Andrew Lloyd Webber; OLDHAM
COLLEGE PERFORMING ARTS;
7-11 December 1993. Jesus
Christ: *David Noble;* Judas
Iscariot: *Matthew Storey;* Mary
Magdalene: *Sarah MacDonnell;*
Caiaphas: *Anthony Bailey;* Annas:
Chris Claydon; Pontius Pilate:
Anthony James; King Herod:
Philip Wood; Simon, The Zealot:
Mark Hilton; Peter: *Phil
Hopwood;* Priests: *Michael Eyres,
Simon Carter;* Apostles/Apostle

Women/The Mob/Soldiers:
Natasha Aiken, Tracie Baker,
Simon Carter, Michael Eyres,
Katrina Heath, Samantha Higgs,
David Hollingdale, Machala
Rennie, Lisa Thompson, Mark
Whittenbury, Mark Irvine, Lisa
Kirton, Gillian Landregan, Aaron
Lee, Kelly Lorrenna, Janet
Parkinson, Karin Reed, Jamie
Shaw, Amanda Tyrrell, Anthony
Bailey, Chris Claydon, Anthony
James, Philip Wood, Mark Hilton,
Philip Hopwood. THE BAND:
Electric Rhythm Guitar/Acoustic
Guitar: Malik Green; Keyboards/
Percussion: Francis Grixti;
Electric Bass Guitar: Simon
Houghton; Keyboards/Synthesisers/
Pianos: Mark Swift, Paul Scott;
Drum Kit/Percussion: Riccardo
Toniolo; Lead Guitar/Acoustic
Guitar: Anthony Minshull; Sound
Liason Officer: Paul Riley.
Director & Choeographer: Joan
Illingworth; Musical Director:
David Golightly; Production
Manager: Scott Palmer; Design:
Jolyon Coombes; Costume: Deena
Kearney; Assistant Costume: Alex
Steele; Lighting: Richard Blomley;
Sound: Richard Gibson; Sound
Assistant: Ranil Sonnandara;
Assistant Directors: Anthony
James, Janet Parkinson; Assistant
Choreographer: Tracie Baker;
Production Assistants: Philip
Hopwood, Janet Parkinson, Aaron
Lee, Michael Eyres; Stage
Manager: Rebekah Watts; Deputy
Stage Manager: Steven Bailey;
Assistant Stage Managers: Cathy
Mangan, Gus Shaw, Glen
Thompson, Alan Lancelott;
Camera Operator: Rick Lane;
Master Carpenter: Craig Price;
Deputy Carpenter: Garry Mann;
Flyman: Craig Dennis; Lighting
Board Operators: Michael Oates,
Keith Ashton; Follow Spot

Operators: Chris Kerr, Steve
Ackley, Marc Graneek, Mayur
Patel, Adam Beaumont, David
Renfrew, Carl Rhymes, Christian
Smith; Sound Opearators: Richard
Ayres, Simon Harrison, Dan
Hartley, Matt Hewitt, Alan
Hodkin, Davod Williams; Technical
& Stage Management Crew:
Victoria Campbell, Alison Hilton,
Lisa Entwhistle, Rick Lane, Greg
Radburn, Steve Scott, David
Smith, Peter Clark, Suzanne
Peary, Kevin Taylor; Lighting
Crew: Phil Masrjoram, David
Plant, John Forster, Andrew
Moores, Gareth Richie, Phil
Rudder; Technician: Gordon Salt.

560. RUMPELSTILTSKIN, from
Jakob and Wilhelm Grimm; NEW
MUSIC; 13-15 January 1994.
Cast: Ruth Brown, Russell
Learmont. Director: Peter
Entwhistle.

561. SALT OF THE EARTH
by John Godber; INCREASINGLY
IMPORTANT THEATRE
COMPANY; 11-15 September
1993. May: Connie Walker;
Annie: Catherine Pemberton; Roy/
Paul: Carl Morgan; Harry:
Howard Carter; Kay/Mrs Potter/
Mrs Gillespie/Cherry: Rachel
Powell; Tosh/Mr Poole: Neil Bell.
Director: Colin Snell; Sound:
George Lee; Lighting/Slides:
Alasdair Graebner; Set: Kim
Morrow; Props: Melissa Wells;
Stage Manager: Craig Price;
Costumes: Matthew Harrmer for
Charles Alty.
Press: OC: 18/1/94

**565. THE COMEDY OF
ERRORS** by William Shakespeare;
OLDHAM COLLEGE; 16-19
February 1994. PART ONE:

Egeon: *Dave Snelling;* Gaoler:
Sean Cernow; Duke of Ephesus:
Andrew Husband; 1st Merchant:
Louise Harney; Antipholus of
Syracuse: *Mark Hilton;* Dromio of
Syracuse: *Simon Carter;* Dromio
of Ephesus: *Anthony Bailey;*
Adriana: *Elizabeth Burgoyne;*
Luciana: *Katrina Heath;* Angelo:
Clare Davies; Antipholus of
Ephesus: *Paul Hughes;* Balthasar:
Jason Dickson; Nell: *Catherine
Kelly;* PART TWO: 2nd
Merchant: *Samantha Joyce:*
Angelo: *Paula Derrig;* Officer:
Nicola Faal; Antipholus of
Ephesus: *Matthew Storey;* Dromio
of Syracuse: *Allan Leach;*
Adriana: *Sarah MacDonnell;*
Luciana: *SAmantha Higgs;*
Antipholus of Syracuse: *Derek
Owens;* Courtesan: *Kelly
Llorenna;* Dromio of Ephesus:
Andrew Murphy; Pich: *David
Hollingdale;* Abbess: *Joan Potter;*
Egeon: *Chris Judge;* Duke of
Ephesus: *Jamie Shaw;* Messenger:
Vicky Walsh. Director: *Steve
Hobson;* Production Assistants:
Caroline Haigh, Sean Cernow;
Voice Coach: *Joyce Kirkman;*
Assistant Director: *Michael Eyres;*
Technician: *Gordon Salt;* Set:
Jolyon Coombs; Lighting: *Mark
Lilley;* Sound: *Caroline Burrell;*
Production Manager: *Meic
Watkins;* Stage Manager: *Glen
Thompson;* Deputy Stage
Manager: *Jane Jones;* Assistant
Stage Manager: *Ben Lawrence;*
Wardrobe Master: *Alexandra
Steele;* Lighting Board Operator:
Andrea Fitton; Chief Electrician:
Craig Dennis; Sound Operator:
Keith Ashton; Assistant Lighting
Designer: *Tim Harrison.*

566. LIFTING THE LIMITS;
OLDHAM COLLEGE

PERFORMING ARTS; *9-12
March 1994.*

567. CHRISTIE IN LOVE by
Howard Brenton; OLDHAM
COLLEGE PERFORMING ARTS;
27 Arril 1994. Christie: *Phil
Hopwood;* Inspector: *Jill Bowen;*
Constable: *Mark Hilton;* Voice
Over 1: *Derek Owens;* Voice
Over of Girls: *Cath E Kelly,
Donna Sharrod, Joan Potter.*
Director: *Joan Potter;* Set/Master
Carpenter: *Garry Mann;*
Production Manager: *Scott
Palmer;* Stage Manager: *Claire
Smith;* Deputy Stage Manager:
Jane Jones; Wardrobe Consultant:
Alexandra Steele; Lighting: *Andrea
Fitton;* Sound: *Craig Dennis;*
Production Assistant: *David
Hollingdale.*

568. SUMMER SONG by
Eric Maschwicz and Hy Kraft;
Lyrics by *Eric Maschwicz;* Music
by Bernard Grun, from themes by
Anton Dvorák; NEW MUSIC; *3-
7 May 1994.* Abe: *Norman
Hill;* Milli: *Alison Kay;* Blodek:
Julian Taylor; Karolka Novak:
Carole Moody; Uncle Marek:
John Hoyland; Ma Flannagan:
Suzanne Nixon; Mr Gilmore: *Lee
Fitzpatrick;* Shaun Flannaghan:
Mike Riley; Tomas Tomashek:
peter Entwistle; Dr Anton
Dvorák: *Feeney; Ian Gardner;* Joe
Gianello: *Russ Learmont;* Jake:
Gavin WIthey; Barstow: *SAm
Molineaux;* Attendant: *Richard
Brown;* Jeff/First Reporter:
Norman Lee; Priest: *Len
Gooseman;* Second Reporter: *Rob
McKoy;* Chorus: *Bernie Wood,
Catarine Airey, Jayne Seville,
Richard Brown, Lynsey Seville,
Lesley Bradley, Leigh Hardy,
Stephen Fitzpatrick, Len*

Gooseman, Jean Molineux, Marian
Ford, Susan Power, David
Ferguson, Lyndsay Henderson, Sue
Brogan, Janet Longbottom,
Malcolm Entwistle, Norman Lee,
Wain Fletcher, Lesley Hodges,
Lynn Bialowas. Joe Warburton,
Robert McCoy, Hayley Hilton,
Helen Whalley, Lee Fitzpatrick,
Paul Nicholls, Darren Shaw;
Adult Dancers: Ruth Brown, Abi
Sheard, Leanne Tunner, Alison
Kay, Julie Meredith, Carol
McKenzie, Steve Fitzpatrick,
Simon Hodgson; Young Dancers:
Julie Shaw, Jane Swallow, Sarah
Crewe, Leanne Ingle, Hayley
Robinson, Ben Moody, Emma
Booth, Caroline Rhodes, Samara
Saied, Jacqueline Bett, Rachael
Nealis, Bethasn Nealis, Melanie
Semple, Katie Pennington,
Rebecca Semple, Helen Wood,
Helen Jackson. Producer: Peter
Entwistle; PA to Producer/
Properties: Helen Stack;
Choreography: Nicola Edwards;
Musical Director: Harry
Butterworth; Stage Manager: Jim
Nixon; Wardrobe: Margaret
Chadwick; Assistant Stage
Manager: Tony Novotny;
Dressers: Emily Crompton, Edith
Blackey; Hairdressing: Betty
Sheard; Make-Up: Wilfred Miller;
Contruction: Tony Novotny, Peter
Gore, Jim Nixon; Stage Crew:
Peter Chadwick, Julian Taylor,
Martin Bradley, Phil Hopkins,
Gavin Withey, Peter Dixon, Mike
Kennedy.
Press: OC: 3/5/94

569. CAROUSEL; Music by
Richard Rodgers; Lyrics by Oscar
Hammerstein; OLDHAM
METROPOLITANB AMATEUR
OPERATIC SOCIETY; 10-14
May 1995.

570. OUR COUNBTRY'S
GOOD by Timberlake
Wertembaker; OLDHAM
COLLEGE PERFORMING ARTS;
9-11 June 1994

572. AND A NIGHTINGALE
SANG by C P Taylor; NEW
MUSIC; 14-16 July 1994.
Helen Stott: Suzanne Nixon;
Joyce: Suzanne Sinfield; George:
Bill Holland; Peggy: Sandra
Birchall; Andie: Peter Entwistle;
Eric: Chris Morris; Norman: Russ
Learmont. Producer: John
Dewsnap; Stage Manager: Jim
Nixon; Lighting: Peter Freeman;
Sound: Gordon Salt; Continuity:
Mark Entwistle; Properties: Alison
Kay; Costumes: Chrles Alty
Costume Hire.
Press: OC: 13/7/94

571. DREAMS AND SOUP by
Damien O'Connor; CREDIBILITY
THEATRE COMPANY; 20-22
July 1994. Syd: Sydney Rowe;
Man: Stephen Gartside; Mother:
Margaret Baron; Stephen: Paul
Greenwood; Bill: Phil Hopwood;
Alice: Sarah Brame; Roger: Eddie
Mullany; Ian: Richard Morrow;
Judy: Sarah Richards; Amy:
Gemma O'Connor; Geoff: Leslie
Taylor; Jack: Dougie Price; Jo:
Hardcastle. Director: Margaret
Baron; Set: John Cooke; Sound:
Eddie Mullany; Sound OPerator:
Craig; Lighting: Gordon Salt.
Press: MEN: 22/7/94; OC:
28/6/94, 20/7/94

573. BENT by Martin
Sherman; INCREASINGLY
IMPORTANT THEATRE
COMPANY; 27 September - 1
October 1994. Max: Howard

Carter; Horst: *Paul Phillips;*
William Ash, John Wood.
Director: *Colin Snell.*
Press: OC: 27/9/94

574. A MIDSUMMER NIGHT'S
DREAM by William Shakespeare;
OLDHAM COLLEGE
PERFORMING ARTS; *18-22*
October 1994.

575. CHAPATI AND CHIPS,
by Maggie Willett, based on the
novel by Almas Khan; PESHKAR
THEATRE COMPANY; *4-5*
November 1994.

576. CAMELOT by Alan J
Lerner and Frederick Loewe; THE
PLAYERS GROUP; *15-19*
November 1994.

577. PETER PAN; J M
Barrie; OLDHAM COLLEGE
PERFORMING ARTS; *1-10*
December 1994.

578. DICK WHITTINGTON by
Jeff Longmore; JEFF
LONGMORE PRODUCTIONS;
21 December 1994 - 5 January
1995. Sarah: *Jeff Longmore.*

HARRISON CENTRE;
Rochdale Road, OLDHAM
OL9 6EA; 061-624 8013.
AZ: 34, B2; XAZ: 64,
C2.

563. THE WASTELAND by T
S Eliot; OLDHAM COLLEGE
PERFORMING ARTS; *13-14*
February 1994.

564. THE CAUCASIAN

CHALK CIRCLE by Bertholt
Brecht; OLDHAM COLLEGE
PERFORMING ARTS; *9-11*
March 1994

**HIGGINSHAW VILLAGE
PROMENADE
PERFORMANCE,** starting
from The White horse Inn,
Top O'the Edge, Henshaw
Street and following
Ringway Paths on top of
Oldham Edge.

634. ROOT AND BRANCH,
devised by local school, residents
and Higginshaw Rangers;
HIGGINSHAW ARTS PROJECT &
ACTION SPACE MOBILE; *5-7*
May 1994.

LYCEUM, Union Street,
OL1 1QG; 061-633
1860; AZ: 34, C3; XAZ:
64, D3.

603 LAST TANGO IN
WHITBY by Mike Harding;
LYCEUM PLAYERS; *26*
November - 4 December 1993.
Jimmy: *Rod Fitton;* Henry: *Terry*
Biltcliffe; Kathleen: *Nell*
Hardwood; Joan: *Pat Lowe;*
Maureen: *Olwen Newton;* Jessie:
Joan Duffin; Pat: *Jackie*
Mathews; Phil: *Rod Cadd;* Edna:
Jessie Wright; Mrs Mingham:
Jenny Swinbourne; Clare:
Stephanie Waugh; Debbie: *Sara*
Thulis; Coach Driver: *Steve Lee;*
Sid/Jet Shop Man: *Norman Lee;*
Alice: *Barbara Rowley;* Edie:
Kath Cannon; Gino/Honeymooner:
Gavin Withey; Sally: *Sue Garlick;*

John: *Ray Morton;* Tea-Lady: *Ellen Mulligan;* Bell-Boy: *George Perks.* Director: *Phil McCarthy;* Stage Manager: *Anne-Marie Hurley;* Deputy Stage Manager: *Matthew Allen;* Stage Crew: *Andrea Walsh, Andrew Nicholls;* Costumes: *Maureen Hurley, Sheila Hall;* Choreography: *H S Walsh, Dave Lewis, Rodney Cadd;* Technical Director: *Steve Lee;* Lighting: *Lee Stephens;* Sound: *Alan Spencer;* Set Construction: *Derek Berryman, Peter Corr, Peter Tucker, Dave Chadwick, Nigel Marland, Ronnie Calvert, Mike Russell.*

604. **A DAY IN THE DEATH OF JOE EGG** by Peter Nichols; LYCEUM PLAYERS; *28 January - 5 February 1994.* Bri: *Colin Smith;* Sheila: *Margaret Blaszczok;* Joe: *Carrie Alker;* Freddie: *Richard Griffiths;* Pam: *Amanda Hooley;* Grace: *Jean Bintley.* Director: *Jessie Wright;* Stage Director: *Derek Berryman;* Stage Manager: *Peter Tucker;* Technical Director: *Steve Lee;* Set Construction: *Derek Berryman, Ronnie Calvert, David Chadwick, Peter Corr, Bob Critchley, Nigel Marland, Mike Russell, Peter Tucker, Janet Berryman;* Deputy Stage Managers: *Sue Garlick, Gavin Withey;* Lighting: *Jenny Swinbourne, David Allen, Bob Critchley, Tony Rhodes;* Sound: *Matthew Allen, Alan Spencer.* **Press: OC:** *25/1/94*

605. **CONFUSIONS** by Alan Ayckbourn; LYCEUM PLAYERS; *15-23 April 1994.* **a) Mother Figure:** Lucy: *Clare Corcoran;* Rosemary: *Pat Lowe;* Terry: *Roger Boardman;* **b) Drinking**

Companions: Harry: *Colin Smith;* Paula: *Rosalind Styles;* Bernice: *Clare Corcoran;* Waiter: *Russ Learmont;* **c) Between Mouthfuls:** Waiter: *Peter Cadman;* Pearce: *John Fletcher;* Mrs Pearce: *Marion Datsun;* Martin: *Colin Smith;* Polly: *Sue Garlick;* **d) Gosforth's Fête:** Mrs Pearce: *Marion Datsun;* Milly: *Pat Lowe;* Gosforth: *Peter Cadman;* Vicar: *John Fletcher;* Stewart: *Colin Smith;* **e) A Talk in the Park:** Arthur: *Peter Cadman;* Beryl: *Sue Garlick;* Charles: *Roger Boardman;* Doreen: *Marion Datsun;* Earnest: *Russ Learmont.* Director: *Nigel Marland;* Assistant to Director: *Concepta Walker;* Stage Manager: *Janet Berryman;* Deputy Stage Manager: *Ann-Marie Hurley;* Stage Crew: *Amada Hooley;* Set Design: *Brian Howard, Nigel Marland;* Technical Design: *Tony Rhodes;* Technical Team: *Jenny Swinbourne, Phil Nicholls;* Set Construction: *Derek Berryman, Janet Berryman, Peter Corr, Bob Critchley, Connie Walker, David Wright, Dave Chadwick, Nigel Marland, Ronnie Calvert, Mike Russell.* **Press: OC:** *12&18/4/94*

606. **RUN FOR YOUR WIFE** by Ray Cooney; LYCEUM PLAYERS; *17-25 June 1994.* Mary Smith: *Margaret Blazczok;* Barbara Smith: *Lois Hawcroft;* John Smith: *Richard Griffiths;* Detective Sergeant Troughton: *Matthew Allen;* Stanley Gardener: *Nigel Marland;* Newspaper Reporter: *Alan Maley;* Detective Sergeant Porterhouse: *Derek Lewis;* Bobby Franklyn: *John Fletcher.* Direction and Design: *Brian Howard;* Stage Manager: *Jessie Wright;* Deputy Stage

365

Manager: *Alan Maley;* Assistant Stage Manager: *Joanne Bell;* Technical Design: *Steve Lee;* Lighting and Sound: *Steve Lee, Phil Nicholls;* Set Construction: *Derek Berryman, Janet Berryman, Peter Corr, Bob Critchley, David Wright, Dave Chadwick, Nigel Marland, Ronnie Calvert, Mike Russell.*

607. PUTTING IT TOGETHER; LYCEUM PLAYERS benefit for Connie Walker; *22-24 July 1994.* Featuring: *Sean Wilson, Tony Marshall, Jeff Longmore, Jenny Luckcraft, Sherry Ormerod.* Artistic Co-ordinator: *Brian Howard.* **Press:** OC: 1/8/94

608. THE CURIOUS SAVAGE by John Patrick; LYCEUM PLAYERS; *23 September - 1 October 1994*

609. ROPE by Patrick Hamilton; LYCEUM PLAYERS; *25 November - 3 December 1994.*

MANOR MILL, Victoria Street, CHADDERTON, OL9 OHQ; 061-678 4072; AZ: 34, A1; XAZ: 64: A1.

257. A MIDSUMMER NIGHT'S DREAM by William Shakespeare; NORTHERN BROADSIDES; *7-11 September 1994.* Theseus/ Oberon: *Barrie Rutter;* Hippolyta/ Titania: *Ishia Bennison;* Egeus/ Quince: *Roy North;* Lysander: *Dickon Tyrell;* Demetrius: *Conrad*

Nelson; Helena: *Ludmilla Vuli;* Hermia: *Helen Sheals;* Bottom: *John Branwell;* Flute/Fairy: *Andrew Whitehead;* Starveling/ Fairy: *Owain Swain;* Snout/Fairy: *Paul McCrick;* Snug/Fairy: *Francis Lee;* Puck/Philostrate: *Andrew Cryer;* Fairy: *TC Howard.* Director: *Barrie Rutter;* Design: *Jessica Worrall;* Dance: *TC Howard;* Music: *Conrad Nelson;* Company Stage Manager: *Maria Gibbons;* Technical Stage Manager: *Fraser Marlow;* Deputy Stage Manager: *Lizzie Chapman;* Wardrobe Supervisor: *Annette Allen;* The Wall: *Ken Weatherley.* **Journal:** 8/9/94 **Press:** CL: 7/8/94; MEN: 25/8/94, 8/9/94

MILLGATE CENTRE, now PLAYERS' THEATRE **OLDHAM THEATRE WORKSHOP,** Harrison Street OL1 1PX; 061-624 0170; **AZ:** 34, 3C; **XAZ:**64, 3D.

626. LORD OF THE FLIES, adapted from William Golding; OLDHAM THEATRE WORKSHOP; *7-12 February 1994,*

633. CHARLEY IS MY DARLING; OLDHAM THEATRE WORKSHOP; *18-23 April 1994,*

PAKISTAN COMMUNITY CENTRE, Olive Street OL8; 061-628 4800; **AZ:** 34, A3; **XAZ:** 64, 3B.

G, W

640. THE GATEKEEPER'S
WIFE; ALARMIST THEATRE
COMPANY; *23 October 1994.*

PLAYERS' THEATRE
Millgate, DELPH, OL3
5JG; 0457–874644; **XAZ:**
51,H3; **H**

610. BRIGHTON BEACH
MEMOIRS by Neil Simon;
SADDLEWORTH PLAYERS; *20–
27 November 1993.* Eugene:
Richard Tamworth; Blanche:
Pauline Walsh; Kate: *JUne
Holmes;* Laurie: *Sophie Powell;*
Nora: *Marion Kneale;* Stanley:
Ric Norton; Jack: *Kevin Grocock.*
Director: *Ken Wright;* Design:
Debbie Hill, Lisa Robins; Crew
Boss: *Mike Sarson;* Set
Construction: *Ed Blincoe, Richard
Henderson, Norman Hayes, Ken
Deighton, Ken Wright, Lisa
Robins, Debbie Hill;* Lighting:
Nick Royle, David Houle; Sound:
Joy Wrigglesworth; Stage
Manager: *Cathy Varley;* Props:
Linda Pemberton, Claire Bordas;
Wardrobe: *Jean Sykes, Cathy
Varley;* Prompt: *Anne Wright.*

611. ALICE THROUGH THE
LOOKING GLASS, adapted from
Lewis Carroll by Roger T
Holland; *15–22 January 1994.*
Alice: *Sarah Bimpson;* Pieces and
Pawns: *Edward Blincoe, Kate
Boardman, Roger Boardman,
Jacqueline Colton, Ian Gardner,
John Kenworthy, Derek Lewis,
Eileen Southard, Kate Southard,
Mike Watson.* Director: *Eileen*

Southard; Design: *Sally McKee;*
Set Construction: *Richard
Thackray, Norman Hayes, Richard
Henderson;* Crew Boss: *Richard
Thackray;* Stage Manager/Props:
Mike Watson; Lighting: *Herbert
Mallalieu;* Sound: *Paul Hilton;*
Wardrobe: *Jean Sykes, Pat
Caldwell, John Kenworthy, Roger
T Holland.*

612. AN INSPECTOR CALLS
by J B Priestley;
SADDLEWORTH PLAYERS; *26
February – 5 March 1994.*
Inspector Goole: *Bob Atkins;*
Arthur Birling: *Derek H Lewis;*
Sybil Birling: *Anne Wright;* Sheila
Birling: *Jo Weetman;* Eric Birlng:
Stephen Bennett; Gerald Croft:
Ric Norton; Edna: *Doreen
Cooper.* Director: *Philip
Weetman;* Design & Crew Boss:
John Gillespie; Construction: *Paul
Bradbury, Les Burdekin, Norman
Hayes, Richard Henderson,* Stage
Manager: *Mike Watson;* Lighting:
Herbert Mallalieu; Sound: *PAul
Hilton;* Wardrobe: *Jean Sykes,
Dorothy Green;* Props: *Anne
Tunnicliffe, Mike Watson;* Prompt:
Pauline Walsh.
Press: OC: *22/2/94*

613. QUARTERMAINE'S
TERMS by Simon Gray;
SADDLEWORTH PLAYERS; *16–
23 April 1994.* St John
Quartermaine: *John Tanner;*
Henry Windscape: *Ian Perks;*
Anita: *Claire Bordas;* Eddy
Loomis: *John Gillespie;* Derek
Meadle: *KIt Thorne;* Melanie:
Eileen Southard; Mark Sackling:
Mike Sarson. Director: *Derek H
Lewis;* Design: *Peter Carsberg;*
Construction: *Peter Carsberg, Ed
Blincoe, Norman Hayes, Rebecca
Norton, Ric Norton, Ken Wright;*

367

Lighting: *Brian Hilton;* Sound: *Joy Wrigglesworth;* Stage Manager: *Jacqueline Coulton;* Wardrobe: *Jean Sykes;* Props: *Jacqueline Coulton, Kate Southard, Katey Rochford;* Prompt: *Doreen Cooper;* P A: *Pat Woolfe.*
Press: AR: 14/4/94; **OC:** 12/4/94

614. STEPPING OUT by Richard Harris; SADDLEWORTH PLAYERS; *4-11 June 1994.* Mavis: *Elaine Wilson;* Mrs Fraser: *Pauline Walsh;* Lynne: *Deborah Hill;* Dorothy: *Kathleen Hodgson;* Maxine: *Pat Lowe;* Andy: *Margaret Hauxwell;* Geoffrey: *Vince Kelly;* Sylvia: *Eunice Hamnett;* Rose: *Opal Danvers;* Vera: *Denise Shawcross;* Other Parts: *Roger Boardman, Abigail Rhodes, Anne Wright, Ken Wright.* Director: *Nita Bennett;* Choreographer: *Marjorie Nield;* Design & Sound: *Ken Wright;* Construction: *Ken Wright, Norman Hayes, Peter Carsberg, Ric Norton, Linda Lewis;* Lighting: *Brian Hilton, David Houle;* Wardrobe: *Jean Sykes, Abigail Rhodes;* Props: *June Holmes, Rebecca Towe;* Stage Manager: *Roger Boardman;* P A/Prompt: *Anne Wright.*
Press: AR: 10/2/94; **OC:** 6/6/94

258. GYPSY, adapted from the memoirs of Gypsy Rose Lee by Arthur Laurents; Music by Julie Styne; Lyrics by Stephen Sondheim; SADDLEWORTH PLAYERS; *10-17 September 1994.* Uncle Jocko/Kringelein/Bourgeron-Cochon: *John Kenworthy;* George/Weber/Mr Goldstone/Phil: *Roger Boardman;* Clarence/Newsboy: *Matthew*

Muldoon; Baloon Girl: *Danielle Peel;* Baby Louise: *Hannah Saxon;* Baby June: *Alison Evans;* Rose: *Anne Wright;* Pop/Cigar: *Wayne Baxter;* Newsboys: *Daniel Muldoon/ James Muldoon;* Herbie: *Derek Lewis;* Louise: *Jo Anne Weetman;* June: *Catherine Schofield;* Tulsa/Farmboy: *Iain Lapsley;* Yonkers/Farmboy: *Matthew Richardson;* Angie/Farmboy: *Mark Fielding;* LA/Farmboy: *Ben Richardson;* Miss Cratchitt/Mazeppa: *Pat Lowe;* Hollywood Blondes: *Claire Bamford, Sarah Bimpson, Julia Green, Kay Millward, Catherine Schofield, Olivia Wood;* Pastey: *Ric Norton;* Tessie Tura: *Carole Moody;* Electra: *Karen Smith;* Maid: *Sarah Bimpson;* Cow: *Claire Bamforth, Kaymilward;* Chowsie: *Dillan;* BAND: Keyboards: *Paul Fletcher, Mark Goggins;* Percussion: *Andrew Bold;* Bass: *Tony Anderson.* Director: *Brian Howard;* Musical Director: *Paul Fletcher;* Choreographer: *Bernadette Heys;* Director's Personal Assistant: *Eileen Southard;* Set Design: *Brian Howard, David Allen;* Stage Manager: *Rebecca Tow;* Deputy Stage Manager/Set Construction: *Ken Wright;* Scenic Artists: *John Kenworthy, Abigail Rhodes, David Allen;* Lighting Design: *Roger T Holland, Herbert Mallallieu;* Sound: *Ian Shepherd;* Wardrobe: *Patricia Redshaw, Sarah Bimpson, Penelope Burns, Jean Sykes;* Properties: *Jacqueline Colton, Kate Southard, Katie Rochford;* Prompt: *Claire Bordas.*
Journal: 14/9/94

615. DEATH OF A SALESMAN by Arthur Miller; SADDLEWORTH PLAYERS; *29*

October - 5 November 1994.
Director: *John Gillespie.*

259. **PLASTER** by Richard
Harris; SADDLEWORTH
PLAYERS; *3-5 November 1994.*

260. **MAGIC** by Richard
Harris; SADDLEWORTH
PLAYERS; *3-5 November 1994.*

616. **THE LION IN WINTER**
by James Goldman;
SADDLEWORTH PLAYERS; *10-
17 December 1994.*

PLAYHOUSE 2, Newtown
Street, SHAW, OL2 8NX;
0706 846671; **XAZ:** 49,
1F.

43. **THE ENTERTAINER** by
John Osborne; CROMPTON
STAGE SOCIETY; *October
1993.* Archie Rice: *Charles
Foster;* Billy Rice: *John Gillespie;*
Phoebe Rice: *Joanne Bramall;*
Jean Rice: *Jill Bromley.*
Press: OC: *12/10/93*

554. **THE FIFTEEN STREETS**
by Catherine Cookson, adapted
by Rob Bettinson; CROMPTON
STAGE SOCIETY; *11-18
December 1993.*

39. **THE GLASS MENAGERIE**
by Tennessee Williams; 3D
THEATRE COMPANY; *14-16
January 1994.* Amanda
Wingfield: *Sybil Murray;* Lan
Burgon: *Tom Wingfield;* Laura
Wingfield: *Joanne Devlin;* Jim
O'Connor. Directors: *Dilys
Kershaw, Martine Brown;* Stage
Managers: *Philip M Park, Annette*

Slater; Lighting: *Andrew Fidler;*
Sound: *David Walker;* Properties:
*Anita Clegg, David Clegg,
Rebecca Slater;* Costume: *Mal
Fidler;* Continuity: *Barbara Flynn.*
Press: RO: 15/1293, 5/1/94,
6/7/94.

555. **WHEN DID YOU LAST
SEE YOUR TROUSERS** by Ray
Galton and John Antrobus;
CROMPTON STAGE SOCIETY;
19-26 February 1994. Cast:
*Barrie Cottam, Lesley Abbott, Ian
Perks, Greg Sherrington, Bill
Robertson, Jason Sharp, Gillian
Hulme, Ian Gardner, Sue
Edwards.* Director: *Gwyneth
Jones.*
Press: OC: 15/2/94; **RO:** 9 &
19/2/94.

556. **MY MOTHER SAID I
NEVER SHOULD** by Charlotte
Keatley; CROMPTON STAGE
SOCIETY; *16-23 April 1994.*
Cast: *Vivienne Ashworth, Ann
Cottam, Gwyneth Jones, Amanda
Peacock.* Director: *Joanne
Brammall.*
Press: OC: 12/4/94; **RO:**
6&27/4/94

557. **YOU NEVER CAN TELL**
by George Bernard Shaw;
CROMPTON STAGE SOCIETY;
11-18 June 1994. Mrs
Clandon: *Olwen Newton;* Dolly
Clandon: *Jane Dawson;* Philip
Clandon: *Michael Turner;*
Crampton: *Eric Walton;* Harold:
Phillip Weetman; Gloria: *Jo Ann
Weetman;* Bohun: *Ian Perks;*
Steve Bennett. Director: *Charles
Foster.*
Press: OC: 13/6/94

QUEEN ELIZABETH HALL,

West Street, OL1 1UT;
061-678 4072; **AZ:** 34,
B2; **XAZ:** 64, C2. **G, H,
W**

631. THE MICHAEL FARADAY
ALL-ELECTRIC ROAD SHOW by
Johnny Ball; *15 March 1994.*

632. STORIES FROM SOUTH
ASIA; SINGH THEATRE
COMPANY; *27 March 1994.*
Rani Singh.

641. THE PLOT; MIND THE
GAP; *2 November 1994.*

**ROYTON ASSEMBLY
HALL,** Market Square, OL2
5QD; 061-620 3505;
AZ: 25, E3; **XAZ:** 48,
B3. **G, W**

182. THE SOUND
COLLECTOR by Roger McGough;
QUICKSILVER THEATRE; *11
February 1994*

630. BRETEVSKI STREET by
Lin Coghlan; THEATRE CENTRE;
16 March.

638, THE ADVENTURES OF
MALIC; LA FANFARRA; *20 May
1994.*

SADDLEWORTH SCHOOL
High Street, UPPERMILL
OL3 6BU; 04577 6986;
XAZ: 52, B6.

617. A STING IN THE TALE
by Brian Clemens and Dennis

Spooner; UPPERMILL STAGE
SOCIETY; *18-20 November
1993.* Nigel Forbes: *Vince
Kenny;* Max Goodman: *Jonathan
Simm;* Jill Prentice: *Sandra
Simm;* Ann Forbes: *Joan
Bradbury;* Detective Inspector
Berry: *Des Powell.* Producer:
Allan Whitham; Set Design and
Construction: *Ken Richardson,
Peter Mallalieu, Joyce Mallalieu;*
Lighting and Sound: *Andrew
Sinfield, John Molyneux, Colin
Watt, Stephen Wrigley;*
Properties: *Linda Sanderson,
Maureen Poulter;* Continuity:
Marjorie Simm.

618. SOUTH PACIFIC; Music
by Richard Rodgers; Lyrics by
Oscar Hammerstein II; Book by
Oscar Hammerstein II and Joshua
Logan; UPPERMILL STAGE
SOCIETY; *15-19 February
1994.*

**ST HERBERT'S PARISH
CHURCH,** Broadway,
CHADDERTON OL9 0JY;
061-633 9059; **AZ:** 33,
F2; **XAZ:** 63, G1. **W**

635. OLD KING COLE;
SHADES; *1-5 February 1994.*
King Cole: *Len Kelly;* Dame:
Terry Matthews; Cow: *Angela
Hatch, Paul Nicholls;* Queen of
Hearts: *Suzanne Nixon;* Wee
Willie Winkie: *Alex Nixon;* Also:
Claire Perkins.
Press: OC: 1/2/94

643. A BASINFUL OF THE
BRINY by Leslie Sands; SHADES;
11-21 May 1994.

ST MARK'S PARISH HALL;

370

Waterloo Street,
GLODWICK; OL4 1ER;
061-652 3546; **AZ:** 35,
D3; **XAZ:** 65, F4.

636. HELLO DOLLY by
Michael Stenart, based on *The Matchmaker* by Thornton Wilder; ST MARK'S STAGE SOCIETY; *19-23 April 1994.*

SALEM MORAVIAN CHURCH HALL; Lees Road, OLDHAM OL4 3AJ; 061-626 3908; **AZ:** 35, E3; **XAZ:** 65, H3.

619. CINDERELLA; SALEM COMMUNITY THEATRE; *30 November - 4 December 1993 and 14-15 January 1994.* Fairy: *Sharon Igo;* Sybil: *Lyndsey Ashworth;* Lavidia: *Martin Bell;* Cinderella: *Claire Mellor;* Prince Charming: *Pat Braodbent;* Buttons: *Mark Dickinson;* Baron Stoneybroke: *Harold Brierley;* Baroness: *Lynda Clegg;* Candy: *Beryl Binns;* Floss: *Joyce Brierley;* Prince's Secretary: *Stephen Greaves;* Dandini: *Lee D'Souza;* Small Man: *Keith Broadbent;* DWARFS: Doc: *Sarah-Jane Igo;* Grumpy: *Sean White;* Happy: *Richard Clegg;* Sneezy: *Alexis Ashworth;* Sleepy: *Simon Clegg;* Cana: *Gary Kendrick;* Ewart: *Katie-Louise Igo;* Dopey: *Curtis Ashworth;* Bashful: *Martin Mellor;* Chicken: *Pat Broadbent;* Footmen: *Shaun White, Curtis Ashworth, Simon Clegg, Richard Clegg;* Mirror: *Natalie Sarsfield;* Women and Fairies: *Natalie Sarsfield, Sarah Jane Igo, Alexis*

Ashworth, Katie-Louise Igo. Producer: *John Slinger;* Assistant Producer: *Stuart Brierley;* Pianist: *Michael O'Neill;* Stage Management: *Anne Broadbent;* Lighting: *Michael Dearden;* Costumes: *Sharon Igo, Claire Mellor;* Set: *Beryl Binns, Lyndsey Ashworth + other members of the cast.*

620. PIECE OF GREASE; SALEM COMMUNITY THEATRE; *22-24 April 1994.* Sandy: *Laura Taylor;* Rizzo: *Natalie Sarsfield;* Marty: *Sarah Igo;* Frenchie: *Charlene Fogarty;* Jan: *Victoria Harrison;* Patty Simcocks: *Katie Igo;* Betty: *Katie Taylor;* Cha Cha: *Yvette Fogarty;* Danny: *Carl West;* Kenicke: *Lee d'Souza;* Putzie: *Stephen Greaves;* Sonny: *Gary Kendrick;* Doody: *Michael Dearden;* Eugene: *Martyn Mellor;* Tom Scorpion: *Mark Bamford;* Cameraman Scorpion: *Richard Chamberlain;* Vince Fontain: *Mark Dickinson;* Chorus: *SAmantha Grisdale, Carla Boohroyd, Rachael Harrison, Rachael Dearden.* Producers: *Sharon Igo, Mark Dickinson;* Prompt: *Claire Mellor;* Lights and Sound: *Stacey Charlton;* Costumes: *Charles Alty, Sharon Igo;* Set: *Sharon Igo, Mark Duickinson, + other members of cast.*

621. SIX OF THE BEST; SALEM COMMUNITY THEATRE; *17-21 May 1994.* Katie Lawrence: *Claire Mellor;* Jack Lawrence: *Stuart Brierley;* Mrs Best: *Lesley Hodges;* Annie Featherstone: *Joyce Brierley;* Ada Heep: *Beryl Binns;* Louise Monk: *PAt Broadbent;* Aubrey Phelps: *Ken Thompson;* Sam Handwich:

Martin Bell; Henry Lush: *Harold Brierley;* The Reverend Rodney Honeychurch/Cecil Honeychurch: *John Slinger;* Dr Gertrude Bludgeon: *Anne Broadbent;* Big Boy: *Ben.* Producer: *Jeff Lenton;* Prompt: *Marjorie Bottomley;* Set: *David Wilson, Keith Broiadbent, Anne Broadbent, Jeff Lenton;* Props: *Sharon Igo;* Lights and Sound: *Mark Dickinson.*

622. THE UNEXPECTED GUEST by Agatha Christie; SALEM COMMUNITY THEATRE; *20-24 September 1994.* Richard Warwick: *Lynda Cklegg;* Laura Warwick: *Janet Hall;* Michael Starwedder: *John Slinger;* Miss Bennett: *Joyce Brierley;* Jan Warwick: *Neal Hey;* Mrs Warwick: *Beryl Binns;* Henry Angell: *Martin Bell;* Inspector Thomas: *Harold Brierley;* Sergeant Cadwallader: *Pat Broadbent;* Julian Farrar: *Stuart Brierley.* Producer: *Stuart Brierley;* Prompt: *Marjorie Bottonley;* Set: *beryl Binns, Pat Broadbent, Gareth Robishaw.* Stage Help: *Tony Moogan;* Lights and Sound: *Alan Porgezelec.*

SIXTH FORM COLLEGE;
Union Street West, OL8 1XU; 061–628 8000; AZ: 34, B3; XAZ: 64, C3. W

628. ŒDIPUS by Sophocles; FIN DE SIÈCLE; *8 March 1994.*

629. THE HAUNTED HOUSE; FIN DE SIÈCLE; *8 March*

1994.

637. NOTRE DAME DE PARIS (The Hunchback of Notre Dame, in French) by Victor Hugo; THÉÂTRE SANS FRONTIÈRES; *4 May 1994.*

639. BEBE VILAEYAT WICH (Mother in England) by PS Sindra; ASIAN FOLK BALLET ENSEMBLE; *20 May 1994.*

623. DEAD FISH by Gordon Steel; HULL TRUCK THEATRE COMPANY; *19 October 1994.* Dad: *Colin MacLachlan;* Youngest Son: *Marin Garner.* Director: *Gordon Steel.* **Press: CL:** 5/10/94; **OC:** 6/10/94

624. DANCE OF WHITE DARKNESS; conceived by Bob Firth; HORSE AND BAMBOO THEATRE in collaboration with LUDUS DANCE COMPANY; *16 November 1994.* Director: *Bob Firth.*

625. A SHAFT OF SUNLIGHT by Abhijat Joshi; TAMASHA THEATRE COMPANY; *6 December 1994.* Cast: *Sudha Bhucha.*

SOUTH CHADDERTON SCHOOL, Butterworth Lane, OL9 8EA; 061–681 4851; AZ: 42, B1; XAZ: 63, 6E.

129. GROUNDED by Eileen Murphy; M6 THEATRE

COMPANY; *23 February 1994.*

642. ABSOLUTELY POSITIVE;
FLYING GEESE PRODUCTIONS;
October 1994. Jeff Longmore.

ROCHDALE

The opinion has been attributed to C S Lewis that if a book is not worth reading when one is 60, it is probably not worth reading when one is 6. In terms of Drama, the M6 production of MIKE KENNY's WHOSE SHOES (174) passed this test with flying colours. Its premier followed the performance of JOHN CHAMBERS' INSIDE OUT (173), comissioned for the M6 YOUTH THEATRE, whose teenage members then became a large part of the audience for this play, intended for 4-6 year-olds. MAGGIE TAGNEY, however, abetted by Musician CHRIS WEAVER, held all fascinated with her variety of tales, centred around the subsequent history of Cinderella's slippers. The pair of them have a running argument as to which of them it was that was left to guide Prince Charming back to his love, the girl in whose father's cobbler's shop the slippers had come to be on display having an even more extensive voyage of discovery.

CASTLETON COMMUNITY CENTRE: 0706 860599.

GRACIE FIELDS THEATRE, Oulder Hill Community School, Hudsons Walk, ROCHDALE OL11 5EF; 0706 341 527. AZ:

4,A4; XAZ: 18, 4D.

129. GROUNDED by Eileen Murphy, M6 THEATRE COMPANY; *10 March 1994.*

110. BIG MOUNTAIN by John Wood; M6 THEATRE COMPANY; *27 June - 1 July, 4-8 July 1994*

374

FALINGE PARK HIGH SCHOOL, OL12 6LD; 0706 31246; AZ: 5, B3; XAZ: 19, F2

648. MAP OF THE HEART
by William Nicholson; 3D
THEATRE COMPANY; *22-24
September 1994.* Ruth
Steadman: *Annette Slater;* Albie
Steadman: *Ean Burgon;* Sally
Steadman: *Sara Cunliffe;* Bernard
Fisher: *David Lee;* Angus Ross:
Jason Sharpe; Mary Hanlon:
Joanne Devlin; Smithy: *Rod
Fitton;* Andrew Rainer: *Colin
Gibson;* June Armitage: *Karen
Knox;* Studio AFM: *John
Ramsden.* Director: *Mal Fidler;*
Character Workshops: *Martine
Brown;* Set Construction: *Philip
M Park;* Lighting: *Andrew Fidler;*
Sound: *Stephen Lord;* Organ
Music: *Brian Pickup;* Properties:
*Anita Clegg, Dilys Kershaw,
Rebecca Slater;* Costume: *Cheryl
Mills;* Continuity: *Barbara Flynn.*
Press: RO: 24/8/94

HEYWOOD CIVIC HALL, Wood Street, OL10 1LW; 0706 624104 / 368130. AZ: 12,C3; XAZ: 31:F3.

646. OLIVER by Lionel Bart;
HEY KIDS; *20-23 October
1993.* Mr Bumble: *Ian Stott;*
Widow Corney: *Jane Clarke;*
Oliver Twist: *Jonathon Dawson;*
Mr Sowerberry: *Simon Pickup;*
Mrs Sowerberry: *Victoria
Schofield;* Charlotte: *Katrina
Mullen;* Noah Claypole: *Paul
McKeown;* The Artful Dodger:
Andrew Weir; Fagin: *Anthony
Howarth;* Nancy: *Jill Thomas;*

Bet: *Hazel Goodison;* Mr
Brownlow: *Dominic Beaver;* Bill
Sykes: *Kenneth Goodison;* Mrs
Bedwin: *Natalie Wyatt;* Dr
Grimwig: *Simon Pickup;*
CHORUS: *Gabrielle Barnes,
Rachel Beaver, Gemma Beirne,
Fiona Boland, Elizabeth Bullock,
Helen Bond, Shelley Byrne, Blaze
Caffrey, Elizabeth Caffrey, Adam
Cooney, Marie Coulton, Jascqui
Danvers, Andrea Day, Nicola
Geddes, Sally Geddes, Lesley
Goodison, Gemma Heyes, Naomi
Ingham, Jamie Kelly, Joanne
Kemp, Marc Kemp, Lauren
Kenyon, Charlotte Law, Kevin
McNeive, Sheyanne McNeive,
Anna McKeown, Laura Miller,
Samantha Moss, Gavin Pickup,
Angela Power, Joanne Power,
Michelle Power, Oliver Redman,
Emily Richardson, Lucy
Richardson, Charlotte Schofield,
Samuel Smith, Jenny Taylor,
Emma Thompson, Donna
Warburton, Katherine Weir,
Catherine Wicker, Claire Wicker,
Juliette Wicker, Sarah Woods;
Steven Woods.* ORCHESTRA:
Piano: *Alan Turnbull;* Bass Guitar:
Charlie Peacock; Percussion:
Michael Galloway; Synthesizer:
Steve Gooding. Producer: *Irene
Miller;* Choreographer: *Jill
McIntosh;* Musical Director:
Francis Kenyon; Wardrobe
Mistresses: *M Schofield, L Byrne;*
Make-Up Mistress: *Mrs C
Downham-Clarke;* Prompt: *Joanne
Simpson;* Properties: *M Frain, M
Simpson;* Stage Manager: *H
Downham-Clarke;* Lighting and
Sound: *Adrian Montgomery;*
Continuity: *Helen Rudman,
Catherine Schofield.*

649. SHOWBOAT by Jerome
Kern and Oscar Hammerstein II;

HEYWOOD AODS; *7-12 March 1994.*

HEYWOOD COMMUNITY SCHOOL, Sutherland Road; OL10 3PD; 0706 360466; AZ: 11, 4F; XAZ: 30, 4A.

646. NOWHERE TO RUN by David Holman; M6; *29 November 1993.*

129. GROUNDED by Eileen Murphy, M6 THEATRE COMPANY; *21 February 1994.*

HOLLINGWORTH HIGH SCHOOL, Cornfield Street, MILNROW, OL16 3DR; 0706 41541; AZ: 15, F1; XAZ: 21, G5.

298. SHAKESPEARE'S GREATEST HITS; MANCHESTER ACTORS COMPANY; *25 January 1994.*

HOPWOOD HALL TERTIARY COLLEGE, Rochdale Campus, St Mary's Gate, OL12 6RY; 0706 345346; AZ: 4, C4; XAZ: 19, G4.

298. SHAKESPEARE'S GREATEST HITS; MANCHESTER ACTORS COMPANY; *25 January 1994.*

LITTLEBOROUGH COMMUNITY SCHOOL,

Calderbrook Road, OL15 9JQ; 0706 377475.

M6 THEATRE, Hamer CP School, Albert Royds Street, ROCHDALE OL16 2SU; 0706 355898; AZ: 5, E2; XAZ: 20, B1.

646. NOWHERE TO RUN by David Holman; M6 THEATRE COMPANY; *28 September 1993.* Paul James: *Jim Byrne;* Garry Higgins/Mr James: *Jack Randle;* Tony Bell: *Peter Farrah;* Mrs Summers/Mrs Bell: *Fiona Farley.* Director: *Romy Baskeville;* Design: *Caroline Wilson;* Stage Manager: *Hassina Khan;* Costumes and Set: *Caroline Wilson;* Carpenter: *Steve Kirk.*

129. GROUNDED by Eileen Murphy, M6 THEATRE COMPANY; *1 February 1994.*

173. INSIDE OUT; written with and for M6 YOUTH THEATRE by John Chambers; *24 May 1994.* Cast: *Sidrah Arif, Sarah Armstrong, Rebecca Bannon, Alice Bewick, Laura Booth, Sam O'Brien, Sarah Butterworth, Katie Chicot, Sarah Clarke, Peter Clough, Lorraine Cockram, Lindsey Cooper, Nicola Crawley, Carrie Dawson, Helen Dennerly, Paul Devine, Szonya Durant, Kathy Forsyth, Gemma Hancock, Karmel Khela, Claire Morgan, Rebecca Schofield, Anna Simpson, Gemma Taylor, Ryan Taylor, Nichola Wheatley.* Directors: *Sue Reddish, Dot Wood;* Design: *Jack Wright;*

376

Music: *Brendan Murphy;* Dance/ Movement Assistant: *David McCormick;* Costumes: *Jessica Kippen;* Students on Work Experience Placement: *Jayne Dunphy, Carl McIntyre.* Press: BT: 13/5/94

174. WHOSE SHOES? by Mike Kenny; M6 THEATRE COMPANY; *24 May 1994.* Imelda: *Maggie Tagney;* Musician: *Chris Weaver.* Director: *Gll Graystone;* Design: *Caroline Wilson;* Cart: *Steve Kirk.*

651. HERO by Neil Duffield; M6 THEATRE COMPANY; *12 September 1994.* Bunjy: *Pete Farrah;* Mrs Styles/Frankie: *Maureen Sheerin;* Jase: *Paul Wallis.* Director: *Mike Kay;* Design & Costumes: *Caroline Wilson;* Stage Manager: *Chris Knibbs;* Set Construction: *John Ashworth, Lee Pearson.*

MIDDLETON CIVIC HALL, Fountain Street, M24 1AF; 061–643 2389. AZ: 32,B2; XAZ: 62,A1.

650. KIDS' PRAISE; *9 October 1994.* Stage Manager: *Peter Leigh.*

NORTON GRANGE HOTEL, Manchester Road, Castleton, OL11 2XZ; 0706 755085; AZ: 23, F1; XAZ: 33, G6.

129. GROUNDED by Eileen Murphy, M6 THEATRE COMPANY; *4 February 1994.*

QUEEN ELIZABETH HIGH SCHOOL, Boardman Fold Road, ALKRINGTON, Middleton, M24 1PR; 061–643 2643; AZ: 32, B3; XAZ: 62, A4.

298. SHAKESPEARE'S GREATEST HITS; MANCHESTER ACTORS COMPANY; *17 January 1994.*

ST CLEMENT'S PARISH CHURCH, Willbutts Lane; ROCHDALE; OL11 5BE; 0706 31353 / 351190. AZ: 4,A4; XAZ: 19,E3.

ST CLEMENT'S PAROCHIAL HALL, Sandy Lane, ROCHDALE OL11 5DR; 0706 31353 / 351190.

647. THE GLASS MENAGERIE by Tennessee Williams; ST CLEMENT'S AD&MS; *19–23 October 1993.* Amanda: *Sybil Murray;* Tom: *Ean Burgon;* Laura: *Joanne Devlin;* Jim: *David Lee.* Producer: *Dilys Kershaw;* Production Assistant: *Martine Brown;* Stage Manager: *Philip M Park;* Set Consruction & Design: *Andrew Fidler, Colin Gibson, Martin Gollop, Bob Roberts, Annette Slater, Derek Smith;* Lighting & Sound: *Derek Ellis, David Walker, Phil Twynam;* Wardrober: *Mal Fidler;* Continuity: *Barbara Flynn.*

ST CUTHBERT'S R C
SCHOOL; Shaw Road,
OL16 4SH; 0706 47761;
AZ: 15, 4C; XAZ: 33,
H4.

129. GROUNDED by Eileen
Murphy, M6 THEATRE
COMPANY; *14-15 March 1994.*

WHITWORTH HIGH
SCHOOL, Hall Fold,
OL12 8TS; 0706 343218;
XAZ: 6, C1.

129. GROUNDED by Eileen
Murphy, M6 THEATRE
COMPANY; *9 March 1994.*

378

SALFORD

ADELPHI STUDIO THEATRE, University College Salford, Peru Street, SALFORD M3 6EQ; 061-834 6633. AZ: 100, C3; XAZ: 160, C3

661. THE BACCHAE by Euripides; ASPECTS THEATRE COMPANY; *5-8 November 1993.*

662. THE TINDERBOX; ASPECTS THEATRE COMPANY; *13-18 December 1993.*

658. VINEGAR TOM by Caryl Churchill; ASPECTS THEATRE COMPANY; *4-5 February 1994.*

345. HELL, HULL AND HUDDERSFAX by Gary Brown; ASPECTS THEATRE COMPANY; *18-19 February 1994.*

659. LE MISANTHROPE by Molière; THÉÂTRE DU CROISSANT; *21-25 February 1994.*

660. THE RAFT OF THE MEDUSA by George Kaiser; ASPECTS THEATRE COMPANY; *25-26 March 1994.*

652. VOLPONE by Ben Johnson; ASPECTS THEATRE COMPANY; *14-16 April 1994.* Castrone: *Kenan Ali;* Corvino: *Christopher Brennan;* Volpone:

LORRAINE HACKETT as one of the three ryotours in CHAUCER's PARDONER'S TALE, counting the gold found underneath the tree and wearing one of the masks she herself made, which contributed so much to the quality of BILL HOPKINSON's production of THE CANTERBURY TALES (96) at the CHAPMAN THEATRE and in OLDHAM.

379

Dominic Fowler; Peregrine: *Claire Gallagher;* Voltore: *Justin Gregg;* Bonario: *Stuart Green;* Celia: *SAlly Jensen;* Policeman/Merchant: *Caroline Jones;* Sir Politic Wouldbe: *Richard Jones;* Policeman/Merchant: *Miselo Kunda;* Lady Wouldbe: *Nicola Maxfield;* Notary/Woman: *Angela Merriman;* 1st Magistrate: *Anthony Mernal;* Corbaccio: *Maria Ratcliffe;* Androgeno: *Ellen Rogers;* 3rd Magistrate: *Natalie Sanders;* Nano: *Andrew Shepherd;* Mosca: *Katy Swarbrick;* 2nd Magistrate: *Leon Toutounzakis.* Director: *Jackie Smart;* Director's Assistant: *Richard Jones;* Stage Manager: *Catherine Cooke;* Costume Design: *Caroline Jones, Miselo Kunda;* Choreography: *Jools Beech;* Vocal Score: *Sue Heggie;* Costume: *Nicola Emmet, Andrea Fishley;* Production Technician: *Gordon Isaacs;* Production Manager: *Ian Currie.*

ARMITAGE COMMUNITY PLAYING FIELDS, Little Hulton; AZ: 26, A4; XAZ: 54, C5.

669. A BIT OF MAGIC; CHOL THEATRE, with local children; *March 1994.*

CHAPMAN THEATRE, University of Salford, University Road, M5 4WT; 061-745 5000, ex 3248. AZ: 100, A2; XAZ: 85, H2. G, H, W

96. THE PARDONER'S

TALE, Geoffrey Chaucer; SALFORD UNIVERSITY THEATRE COMPANY; *3 November 1993.* **Press:** MEN: 23/11/93

653. A TASTE OF HONEY by Shelagh Delaney; ENGLISH TOURING THEATRE; *23-24 November 1993.* Jo: *Nichola Buckingham;* Helen: *Joanna Bacon.* Director: *Polly Teale;* Design: *Idit Nathan.* **Press: CL:** 9/11/94; **MEN:** 24/11/94

65. THE ALCHEMIST by Ben Jonson; SALFORD UNIVERSITY THEATRE COMPANY; *6-11 December 1993.* Subtle: *Steve Chapman;* Face: *Mike McKrell;* Dol Common: *Laura Ainley;* Dapper: *Max Barrett;* Drugger: *Steve Tabner;* Sir Epicure Mammon: *Anthony Collier;* Surly: *Rowland Jobson;* Tribulation: *Willem Groenewegen;* Ananias: *Jennifer Ohsowski;* Kastril: *Louis Martin;* Dame Pliant: *Catherine O'Dea;* Lovewit: *Tom Evans;* Neighbours: *Emma Kiwanuka, Dawn Bradley, Paul Marshal.* Director: *Bill Hopkinson;* Design: *Sophie Tyrell;* Producer: *Guy Holloway;* Technical Director: *Phil Elams;* Lighting: *Giles Clarke, Oliver Driver;* Sound: *Charles Pestell;* Set: *Dave Charnock, Mark Nemo;* Consultant Voice Coach: *Patricia Roy.*

654. 0898, devised by IMPULSE THEATRE COMPANY; *13-14 January 1994.* Linda: *Liz Frewer;* Alex: *Vanessa Lee Walker;* Burt/Man: *Gerard Bellew;* Murial: *Danny Hurst;* Janine: *Sarah Cooper;*

Gary/Marco: *Stuart A Green.*
Director: *Craig Harris;* Stage
Crew: *Neil Mills, Sue Scott,*
Rebecca Snoo Smith

64. ANTHONY AND
CLEOPATRA by William
Shakespeare; SALFORD
UNIVERSITY THEATRE
COMPANY; *14-25 March 1994.*
Mark Antony: *Anthony Collier;*
Octavius Caesar: *Michael*
McKrell; Lepidus/Canidius/Seleucus
: *Douglas Keyte;* Domitius
Enobarbus: *John Still;* Eros:
Connan Whelan; Canidius/Menas:
Max Barrett; Decetas/Sextus
Pompey: *Dean Sumner;* Philo/
Proculeius: *Dave Charnock;*
Demetrius: *Steve Potts;*
Maecenas: *Gerry Dodd;* Dolabella:
Guy Holloway; Thidias/Gallus/
Alexas: *Mark Maguire;*
Menecrates/Boy: *Paul Jackson;*
Soothsayer/Ambassador/Clown:
Dave Slack; Cleopatra: *Caroline*
Black; Charmian: *Emma*
Kiwanuka; Iras: *Dawn Bradley;*
Mardian: *MArc Lyth;* Diomedes:
Willem Groenewegen; Messenger:
Cellan Scott; Octavia: *Catherine*
O'dea. Directors: *Guy Holloway,*
Tim Weaver; Producer/Design:
Alex Russell; Original Music:
Dave Praites; Choreography:
Fiona Rowe; Video: *Matt Smith;*
Costumes: *Rachel Ward, Back T*
Front; Graphic Design: *Alex*
Russell, Wendy Pennington; Stage
Management: *Phil Ellams, Giles*
Clarke; Lighting: *Oliver Driver;*
Sound: *Charles Pestell, Sharon*
Lord; Technical Crew: *Andrew*
Mitchell, Mark Billington, Mar
Jones, Mark Evans, Steve Turner.
Journal: 21/3/94
Press: CL: 23/3/94

655. PAIN WITHOUT,

POWER WITHIN, conceived and
devised by STRATHCONA
THEATRE COMPANY; *26-27*
May 1994. David/Father
Fitzpatrick: *Pius Hickey;* Mary/
Mother's Friend: *Liz Rock;*
Samuel/Mark/Peter's Father:
Sheldon Antoine; David's
Mother/Rachael: *Nicola Smith;*
Peter: *Ian Willis;* Father Gerrard:
Paul Wakelin. Directors and
Choreographers: *Ann Cleary, Ian*
McCurragh; Design: *Katrina*
Lindsay; Music: *Adrian Johnson;*
Lighting: *Ace McCarron;* Vocals:
Melanie Pappenheim; Stage
Manager: *Suzie Kirklewski;*
Costume Maker: *Rosamund*
Calthorp; Set Builder: *Robert*
Batchelor; Costume Care: *Edna*
Smith.

440. DOWN AND OUT,
adapted from Maxim Gorki's **THE**
LOWER DEPTHS; ASPECTS
THEATRE COMPANY; *31 May-*
3 June 1994.

663. ŒDIPUS by Sophocles,
adapted by Ted Hughes;
ASPECTS THEATRE COMPANY;
16-18 June 1994.

674. TWO by Jim Cartwright;
SALFORD UNIVERSITY
THEATRE COMPANY; *3-4 July*
1994, Man: *Anthony Collier;*
Woman: *Sue Womersley.*
Producer/Designer/Director: *Guy*
Holloway; Lighting Design: *Phil*
Ellams; Sound: *Charles Pestell;*
Lighting Crew: *Giles Clarke;* Set:
Fitzroy Godfrey.

675. BROTHER JACQUES;
book and lyrics by Nick Stimson;
music by Cris Williams; IMPULSE
THEATRE COMPANY; *23-27*

September 1994.

96. THE CANTERBURY
TALES; SALFORD UNIVERSITY
THEATRE COMPANY; *10-15
October 1994.*

656. WAX by Lavinia Murrayl
PAINES PLOUGH; *24-25
October 1994.* Cast: *Shona
Morris, Alan Aldridge.* Director
& DesignerL *Anna Furse;* Music:
Stephen Warbeck; Lighting: *Ace
McCarron.*

664. THE GANG SHOW by
Andrew Williams; YORKSHIRE
THEATRE COMPANY; *16
November 1994.*

677. OUR COUNTRY'S
GOOD by Timberlake
Wertenbaker; SALFORD
UNIVERSITY THEATRE
COMPANY; *5-10 December
1994.*

**ECCLES RECREATION
GROUND,** Oxford Street,
M30 OFW. **061-736
9448.**

HULTON HIGH SCHOOL,
Longshaw Drive,
WORSLEY, M28 6AZ;
061-790 4214.

M/S FITZCARRALDO,
SALFORD QUAYS,
Ordsall, M5 2SQ.

**LADYWELL COMMUNITY
CENTRE;** Eccles New Road

M5 2AH; 061-434 8666;
AZ: 47, F3; XAZ: 84,
B3; G, H, S, W

676. doors; OPEN DOOR
THEATRE COMPANY; *25
November 1993.*

**LANCASTRIAN HALL
THEATRE,** Chorley Road,
SWINTON, M27 2AE;
061-794 7466. AZ:
37,E3; XAZ: 71,F3. G,
S, W

665. SNOW WHITE AND
THE SEVEN DWARFS; *10-15
January 1994.*

668. PACK OF LIES by Hugh
Whitemore; SPADES; *24-26
February 1994.*

670. A NIGHT OF COARSE
ACTING by Michael Green;
SPADES & BARTON PLAYERS;
*29 September - 1 October
1994.*

**METHODIST CHURCH
HALL,** Worsley Road,
SWINTON, M27 5SF;
061-794 8266; AZ: 37,
D4; XAZ: 70, D5. G

672. ONE FOR THE POT by
Ray Cooney and Tony Tilton;
THE PRIESTLEY PLAYERS; *27-
30 1993.* Amy Hardcastle: *Sue
Lane;* Cynthia Hardcastle: *Sue
Lane;* Jugg: *Eric Lucas;* Jonathan

Hardcastle: *Roger Partington;*
Clifton Weaver: *John Nunn;*
Arnold Piper: *Steve Boresbey;*
Charlie Barnet: *Anthony Robinson;*
Hickory Wood: *Anthony Monaghan;* Winnie: *Clare White;*
Guests: *Sandra Partington, Jeff Clarke, Nigel Smith, Neil Dixon.*
Producer: *Nigel Anderson;* Stage Manager: *Jeff Clarke;* Design: *Nigel Anderson;* Lighting and Sound Design: *Roger Partington;* Lighting and Sound Operator: *Sandra Partington;* Sound Effects: *Carol Newby et al;* Make-Up: *Arthur Barrett;* Hairstyles: *Sue Lane.*

667. THE LATE MR LARRINGTON by Mary Wheeler; THE PRIESTLEY PLAYERS; *26-29 January 1994.*

673. CELEBRATION by Keith Waterhouse and Willis Hall; THE PRIESTLEY PLAYERS; *20-23 April 1994.*

671. THE UNEXPECTED GUEST by Agatha Christie; THE PRIESTLEY PLAYERS; *26-29 October 1994.*

PEEL GREEN COMMUNITY CENTRE;
061-793 8859.

666. AFTER THREE by Elsine McCann and Dean Sumner; BARTON THEATRE COMPANY; *11-15 January 1994.*

POPE JOHN PAUL II HIGH SCHOOL; Britannia St, PENDLETON M6 6FX;

061-736 4074.

646. NOWHERE TO RUN by David Holman; M6 THEATRE COMPANY; *1 December 1993.*

SALFORD QUAYS.

678. THE BIG SPLASH by Julie Rutterford; THE SALFORD COMMUNITY PLAY, involving SALFORD OPEN THEATRE, ORDSALL COMMUNITY ARTS and WALK THE PLANK; *21-25 September 1994.* Sean Maguire: *Ben Ashdown;* Broughton Banshees: *Julie Bailey, Cathy Bailey, Emma Kennedy, Vicki McHugh, Leanne McHugh, Kate McHugh, Kate Waring;* Dot 2: *Wendy Bailey, Angela Elphick;* Witches: *Jan Barrett, Margaret Jones;* Dave: *Tryston Blyth;* Workers/Mourners: *Rachel Brockway, Michelle Davies, Adele Fowles, Emma Fidler, Kate Gardiner, Heather Green, Claire Hudson, Michelle Jones, David Milne, Maureen Stirpe;* Workers/Headless Monks: *Rebecca Collier, Hannah Entwhistle;* Worker/Mourner/Witch: *Margaret Dawes;* Mourner: *Elizabeth Edge;* The Girl: *Jane Flynn;* Jack Hughes: *Roy Greenhalgh;* Caitlin Maguire: *Julie Hobbs;* Lenny the Liar: *Ernie Kearney;* Renee: *Jean Kearney;* Midnight Mary: *Iris Kennedy;* Arthur Nelson: *Marc Lyth;* Worker: *Kevin Maguire;* Acid Bath Malone: *Bradley Mulligan;* Dangerous Albert: *John McElhatton;* Speaker/Dot 1: *Lorraine McHugh;*Nelly: *Sheila Mahon;* Headless Monk: *Dominic Norton;* Caitlin's Daughter/ Mourner: *Rachel Norton;* Kev:

Michael Oliver; Frank: Phillip
Payne; Dot 1: Marian Redmond;
Danny: Daniel Roche; Keeper of
the Memory: Leon Smith;
Pavement Monster: Bob
Wainwright; Emily: Anna Welsh;
Kylie: Joanne Welsh. STRING
QUARTET: Violin & Oboe: Tim
Conibear; Violin & Director:
Vivienne Green; Viola: Ben
Hanson; Cello: Elinor Smith;
MUSICIANS: Guitar: Ben
Ashdown; Keyboards: Pete Ball,
Lee Kearney; Percussion: Malcolm
Craven, Elizabeth Edge, Heather
Green, Kevin Maguire, Lee
Millington; Bassoons: Caroline
Plum, Heidi Nunn; Drums and
Percussion: Stephen Fidler, Craig
Winterburn; Piano/Saxophone:
Olly Fox; Trumpet and String
Arrangements: Ben Haughton;
Percussion/Mouth Organ: Sammy
Marques; Violin: Helen Norton;
Piano/String Arrangements: Philip
Payne; Mandolin/Bass Guitar/
Percussion: Mark Stanley;
Melodeon: Dave Wynn; INTERVAL
BAND: Kamikazi Ceilidh Band.
Director: Andy Farrell; Co-
ordinator: Sandra Blue; Design:
Mandy Dike; Musical Director:
Olly Fox; Production Manager:
John Burgess; Design Assistants:
Hilly McManus, John Goodwin,
John Preston; Lighting and Sound:
Stuart Myles, Charles Poulet;
Stage Management: Aileen
Robertson, Jenny Lamont;
Costume: Sheila Payne; Project
Management: Liz Pugh, John
Wassell, Nancy Barrett; Design
and Backstage Team: kevin
Maguire, David Milne, Peter
Green, Tryston Blyth, Christine
Howard, Barbara Abraham, Mrs
Entwistle, Craig Winterburn,
Bradley's Grandmother.
Press: MEN: 22/9/94

WENTWORTH HIGH
SCHOOL, Wentworth
Road, ECCLES, M30 6BP;
061-789 4565; AZ: 47,
1F; XAZ: 83, 1H.

298. SHAKESPEARE'S
GREATEST HITS; MANCHESTER
ACTORS COMPANY; 11
February 1994.

STOCKPORT

CARVER THEATRE,
Church Lane, MARPLE,
SK6 7AW; **SK6 7AW.**
AZ: 87,D3; XAZ:
134,D6.

679. I'LL BE BACK BEFORE
MIDNIGHT by Peter Colley; *24
September 1994.* George
Sanderson: *Michael Ross;* Jan
Sanderson: *Kate Millward;* George
Willowby: *Geoff Harrison;* Laura
Sanderson: *Heather Baguley.*
Director: *Shirley Molloy;* Prompt:
Val Metcalfe; Stage Manager:
Dave Davies; Assistant Stage
Manager: *Mike Coleman;* Lighting
Design: *Rik Whittaker;* Lighting:
Alan Jackson, Andy Tinsey;
Sound: *John Sims;* Wardrobe:
Serena Botterman; Make-up:
Lesley Whittle; Properties: *Debbie
Healey, Ruth Harrison, Elizabeth
Galloway, Heather Smith, Doreen
Bolton;* Set Construction: *Brian
Bircher, Brian Swann, Brian
Bolton, Alan Jackson, Ken Wood.*

680. CELEBRATION by Keith
Waterhouse and Willis Hall; *12–
20 November 1993.* Christine
Lucas: *Carol Wood;* Rhoda Lucas:
Ann Wood; Edgar Lucas: *Terry
Lee;* Jack Lucas: *Steve Johnson;*
Irene Howes: *Alice Kennett;* Lilian
Howes: *Janice Bolland;* Frank
Broadbent: *David Lodge;* Arthur
Broadbent: *Eric Millward;* Stan
Dyson: *Adrian Smith;* Bernard
Fuller: *Neill Drennan;* Edna
Fuller: *Doreen Bolton;* Alice
Fuller: *Sam Kristie;* Lionel Fuller:
Paul Molloy; Margot Fuller:
Helen Carter; May Beckett:

ALFIE the character expected
women to wait upon him hand
and foot but ADAM FAITH as
Director, as well as star, made
his production (92), visiting the
DAVENPORT, a clearly effective
team effort; here with CATIE
GOODWRIGHT as Gilda

Beryl Swann; Sergeant-Major
Tommy Lodge: *Ian Rice.*
Producer: *Heather Baguley;*
Prompt: *Shirley Molloy;* Stage
Manager: *Mike Colemann;*
Assistant Stage Manager: *Heather
Smith;* Lighting Design: *Andy
Tinsley;* Lighting: *Paul
Hargreaves;* Sound: *Brian Bircher;*
Wardrobe: *Serena Botterman;*
Make-up: *Jenny Robinson, Barbara*

Scholles, Tonia Williams;
Properties: Pat Bircher, Val
Metcalfe, Joyce Tattersall; Set
Construction: Brian Bircher, Bryan
Bolton, Dave Davies, Heather
Smith, Stan Bannister, Vera
Coleman, Andy Griffin, Alan
Jackson, Ken Wood.

681. TWO MONTHS IN
ARLES by Mark Denny; OUR
THEATRE COMPANY; 26-27
November 1993. Vincent Van
Gogh: Mark Denny; Paul
Gaughin: Adam Sunderland.
Music: Mark Denny, Steve
Grihault; Stage Management,
Lighting & Sound: Jennie Lamont.
Press: MEN: 19/11/93

684. PINOCCHIO by David
Swan; 7-15 January 1994.
Jimmy Crankit: Christine
Millington; Grazia: Ruth Harrison;
Signor Verruca: Ken Smith;
Geppetto: Ian Rice; Charlie: Paul
Hargreaves; Semolina: Jo Rourke;
Confetti: Natalie Hunt; Rambino:
Steve Johnson; Baby Dimples:
Carol Wood; Mama Scrumpi: Alan
Jackson; Fungus: Rosie Wilson;
Maggot: DEbbie Healey;
Sapphire: Joyce Tattersall;
Pinocchio: James Wild; Gondoliers:
Andrew Howard, Richard
Howarth; Tannoy: Susannah
Pitcher. Director: Bernice Yates;
Choreographer: Kathryn Proctor;
Assistant Director & Prompt:
Doreen Bolton; Stage Manager:
Vic Morton; Assistant Stage
Manager: Dave Davies; Set &
Scenic Design: Brian Hargreaves;
Sound Design: Andy Tinsley;
Lighting Design: Gary Fielding;
Sound Operator: Mike Coleman;
Lighting Operator: John Mills;
Wardrobe Mistress: Serena

Botterman; Wardrobe: Janet
Barnes, Heather Bagulaey, Elaine
Jubb; Make-up: Pat Hammersley,
Mandy Mandal, Jil Reeder, Beryl
Swann, Sylvia Walton, Leslie
Whittle, Jenny Robinson, Barbara
southworth, Properties: Pat
Bircher, Viv Bath, Barbara
Scholes; Accompanist: Enid Hall;
Percussion: Stephen Harrison; Set
Construction: Brian Bolton, Dave
Davies, Stan Bannister, Mike
Coleman, Brian Hargreaves, Brian
Swann, Spencer Rogers, Ken
Wood,, Set Décor: Dave Catlow,
Brian Hargreaves.

682. HARD TIMES by Charles
Dickens, adapted by Steophen
Jefferys; 25 February - 5 March
1994. Mr Gradgrind: Trevor
Jones; Mrs Gradgrind: Paddy
Manson; Louisa Gradgrind: Rachel
Hague; Tom Gradgrind: Bjorn
Dockree; Mr Bounderby: Geoff
Harrison; Mrs Sparsit: SHirley
Molloy; Stephen Blackpool: Andy
Griffin; Rachael: Liz Galloway;
Mrs Pegler: Pat Bircher; Bitzer:
Paul Hargreaves; Sissy Jupe: Ruth
Harrison; Mr Sleary: Spencer
Rogers; Mr Harthouse: Alan
Jackson; Mary Stokes: Barbar
Scholes. Director & Design:
David Lodge; Prompt: Heather
Baguley, Leslie Whittle; Stage
Manager: Brian Birch; Lighting &
Sound Design: Andy Tinsley;
Fielding; Sound Operator: Mike
Coleman; Lighting Operator: John
Mills; Wardrobe Serena
Botterman; Heather Bagulaey,
Make-up: Leslie Whittle, Jenny
Robinson, Properties: Jil Reeder,
Dorothy Ardern; Set Construction:
Bryan Bolton, Dave Davies, Stan
Bannister, Steve Mason, Ken
Wood

386

683. BEDROOM FARCE by Alan Ayckbourn; *13-21 May 1994.* Ernest: *Eric Milward;* Delia: *Beryl Swann;* Nick: *PAul Hargreaves;* Jan: *Sandra Clarke;* Malcolm: *John Mills;* Kate: *debbie Healey;* Trevor: *Barrie Darby;* Susannah: *Christine Millington.* Producer: *Peter Darby;* Prompts: *Brenda Holton, Susan Jones;* Stage Manager: *Dave Davies;* Lighting & Sound Design: *Gary Fielding;* Sound Operator: *Heather Smith;* Lighting Operator: *Alan Jackson;* Wardrobe *Serena Botterman;* Make-up: *Leslie Whittle;* Properties: *Barbara Hambleton, Susan Sheasby, Janice Bolland, Ruth Harrison;* Set Construction: *Bryan Bolton, Stan Bannister, Brian Bircher, Caroline Bowler, Sara Jackson, Nudrat Smoult, Ken Wood.*

CHADS THEATRE, Mellor Road, CHEADLE HULME, SK8 5AU; 061-486 1788. AZ: 93, F2; XAZ: 142,4D.

685. ABSURD PERSON SINGULAR by Alan Ayckbourn; *27 November - 4 December 1993.*

245. A VIEW FROM THE BRIDGE by Arthur Miller; *15-22 January 1994.*

687. THE CHALK GARDEN by Enid Bagnold; *19-26 March 1994.*

688. TWELFTH NIGHT by William Shakespeare; *14-21 March 1994.*

245-249: CITY OF DRAMA CELEBRATION:

245. A VIEW FROM THE BRIDGE by Arthur Miller; CHADS THEATRE COMPANY; *11 July 1994.*

246. SALT OF THE EARTH by John Godber; MOSSLEY AMATEUR OPERATIC AND DRAMATIC SOCIETY; *12 July 1994.* May: *Dorothy Hynes;* Annie: *Jenny Swinbourne;* Roy: *John Fletcher;* Harry: *John Meredith;* Paul: *Andrew Ryder;* Tosh/Mr Poole: *Stuart Redfearn;* Kay: *Amanda Hooley;* Cherry: *Amanda Buckley;* Mrs Potter/Mrs Gillespie: *Stella McDevitt.* Director: *Byron McGuiness;* Stage Manager: *Robert Godfrey;* Assistant Stage Manager: *Frank Webster;* Stage Assistants: *Barry Rushton, Ian Maden, Richard Ryder, Brian Whittacker, John Buckley, Gary Wright, Ross McLarnon;* Scenic Design & Production Secretary: *John Buckley;* Lighting: *Martin Ogden, Stuart Redfearn;* Properties: *Linda Sanderson, Tricia Furness;* Wardrobe: *Malcolm Neild;* Make-up: *Jean Sheridan.*

247. BLOOD FEUDS by Mike Harris; GUIDE BRIDGE THEATRE; *13 July 1994*

248. MY FRIEND MISS FLINT by Donald Churchill; BROOKDALE DRAMATIC SOCIETY; *14 July 1994.*

217. LETTER FROM AMERICA by Philip Stagg;

ARENA THEATRE COMPANY;
15 July 1994.

249. RUN FOR YOUR WIFE
by Ray Cooney; HEALD GREEN
THEATRE CLUB; *16 July 1994*

DAVENPORT THEATRE,
Buxton Road, Stockport
SK2 7AH; 061–483 0683
(Card: 061–242 2506,
Fee: £1); AZ:84,C3;
XAZ: 132,A5. W

689. CAMELOT by Alan Jay
Lerner and Frederick Loewe;
STOCKPORT AMATEUR
OPERATIC SOCIETY; *18–23
October 1993*

690. SNOW WHITE AND
THE SEVEN DWARFS; *17
December 1993 – 22 January
1994.* Snow White: *Letitia
Dean;* Fairy Kindheart: *Jakki
Denver;* Jason: *Martin Ball;*
Prince: *Stephen Dean;* Freddie
Garrity, Junior Dancers: *Vale
School of Dance*
Press: CL: 22/12/93; MEN:
18/12/93; OC: 20/12/93 S:
20/1/94

691. MR MEN IN TOYLAND,
based on the books by Roger
Hargeaves; PHIL DERRICH for
CHILDREN'S SHOWTIME; *5
March 1994.*

631. THE MICHAEL FARADAY
ALL–ELECTRIC ROADSHOW;
Written and produced by Johnny
Ball; *14 March 1994.*

692. BARNUM: Music by Cy

Coleman, Lyrics by Michael
Stewart, Book by Mark Bramble;
ROMILEY OPERATIC SOCIETY;
21–26 March 1994

87. BEAU JEST by James
Sherman; BIRMINGHAM STAGE
COMPANY in association with
the ALMOST PERFECT
PRODUCTION COMPANY; *10–
14 April 1994.* Sarah Goldman:
Lucy Scott; Chris (Her
Boyfriend): *Tim Wallers;* Bob
(Her Escort): *Eric Loren;* Joel
(Her Brother): *Neal Foster;*
Miriam (Her Mother): *Libby
Morris;* Abe (Her Father): *Brian
Greene.* Director: *Graeme
Messer;* Design: *Jamie Vartan;*
Lightning Designer: *Ian Scott;*
Production Manager: *Simon
Robertson;* Company and Stage
Manager: *Mark Brattle;* Deputy
Stage Manager: *Tamsin Ford;*
Assistant Stage Manager: *Jeff
McDonald;* Set Building: *Adrian
Snell Production Services;* Set
Painter: *Erin Sorensen;* Costume
Buyer: *Gaynor Rhine.*
Journal: 13/4/94
Press: G: 25/4/94

92. ALFIE by Bill Naughton;
ALAN FIELD for CORNER
TABLE PRODUCTIONS; *16–21
May 1994.* Alfie Elkins: *Adam
Faith;* Siddie/Doctor/Annie: *Sara
Richardson;* Gilda: *Katie
Goodwright;* Humphrey/Perc:
Marco Capozzoli; Carla/Flo:
Annie Grimes; Harry Clamacraft:
Sean Jackson; Joe/Mr Smith:
Leonard Fenton; Lily Clamacraft:
Joanne Allen; Sharpey: *John
Hoye;* Ruby: *Ava Healy.*
Director: *Adam Faith;* Company
and Production Stage Manager:
Paul Bryan; Set: *Shelagh Keegan;*
Costumes/Wardrobe: *Maggie*

Scobbie; Adam Faith's Tailoring: *Gerry Freedman;* Wardrobe: *Sophie Haysom;* Lighting Design, Production Electrician and Sound Operator: *Nigel Catmuir;* Assistant Stage Managers: *Christopher Alderton, Marco Capozzoli, Annie Grimes, John Hoye, Helena Sykes;* Production Carpenter: *Christopher Alderton;* Director's Assistant: *Emma Legge.* **Journal:** 18/5/94 **Press:** BEN: 7/11/92; MEN: 12/5/94; OC: 30/11/92

693. PINOCCHIO, based on Carlo Collodi; PLAYTIME PRODUCTIONS; *18 September 1994.*

694. HIGH SOCIETY, Cole Porter; STOCKPORT OPERATIC SOCIETY; *17-22 October 1994.*

695. TALES FROM THE JUNGLE BOOK; *23 October 1994.* Features: Pan Puppets.

696. SNOW WHITE AND THE SEVEN DWARFS: "World's Longest Running Touring Pantomime"; *26 October 1994.*

697. THE CARE BEARS; *29 October 1994.*

698. GODSPELL; Stephen Schwartz; CHARLES VANCE; *7-12 November 1994.* Jesus: *George Alex Livings.* Director: *Ed Wilson.*

699. MOTHER GOOSE by Bill Roberton; BCC, APOLLO LEISURE, ALBERMARLE; *17 December 1994 - 29 January*

1994. Mother Goose: *John Inman;* Squire: *Christopher Farries;* Jill: *Jo-Anne Sale;* Mike: *Hope;* Alby: *Keen;* Sammy: *Andy Greaves & Lewis;* Fairy: *Gayle Thomas;* Priscilla: *Barbara Newman;* Colin: *Claire Jayne Sweeney;* Poison Ivy: *Lynne Perrie;* The Ray Cornell Dancers; The Vale School Dancing. Director: *Bill Roberton;* Musical Director: *Duncan Waugh;* Executive Producer: *Barrie C Stead;* Choreographer: *Fran Young.*

GARRICK THEATRE, Exchange Street, Wellington Road South, STOCKPORT, SK3 0EJ; 061-480 5866. AZ: 84,B1; XAZ: 131,G2.

733. FIFTH OF JULY by Langford Wilson; *19-26 February 1994.*

736. PLAYING WITH TRAINS by Steven Poliakoff; *19-26 March 1994.*

737. LADY WINDERMERE'S FAN by Oscar Wilde; *7-14 May 1994.*

738. BOLD GIRLS by Rona Munro; *8-11 June 1994.*

INTERNATIONAL AMATEUR DRAMA FESTIVAL 13-25 JUNE 1994

700. SHEINDALE by Amnon Levi and Rami Danon; TACT GROUP & ENGLISH DRAMA

LEAGUE IN ISRAEL; *13-14 June*. Sheindale: *Dawn Nadel*. Director: *Helen Eleasari*.

701. TWO by Jim Cartwright; *15 June 1994*. Man: *John Smeathers;* Woman: *Jean Simpson*.

241. AN ENGLISHMAN ABROAD by Alan Bennett; CHADS THEATRE COMPANY; *22-23 June 1994*.

702. BILLY BALL by Ross Daniels, from sundry plays by William Shakespeare; ACT; *22-23 June*.

KINGSWAY SCHOOL, Foxland Road, GATLEY SK8 4QA; **061-428 7706; AZ:** 82, B4; **XAZ:** 141, G1.

129. GROUNDED by Eileen Murphy; M6 THEATRE COMPANY; *24 February 1994*.

739. CAUCASIAN CHALK CIRCLE by Bertold Brecht; THE KINGSWAY SCHOOL; *16-18 March 1994*.

THE NEW THEATRE, Cheadle Royal, North Drive,SK8 3DG; **061-437 3383;** AZ: 92,C1; XAZ: 141,G3.

703. RING AROUND THE MOON; Jean Anouilh, translated by Christopher Fry; HEALD GREEN THEATRE CLUB; *20-27*

November 1993. Director: *Mary Crowth*.

249. RUN FOR YOUR WIFE by Ray Cooney; HEALD GREEN THEATRE CLUB; *29 January - 1 February 1994*. Director: *Jean Cox*.

705. SHADOWLANDS by William Nicholson; HEALD GREEN THEATRE CLUB; *19-26 March 1994*.

706. SEMI-DETACHED David Turner; HEALD GREEN THEATRE CLUB; *14-21 May 1994*. Director: *Geoff Reyner*.

707. AN EVENING WITH GARYU LINEKER by Arthur Smith and Chris England; HEALD GREEN THEATRE CLUB; *8-15)ctober 1994*. Director: *Andy Smith*.

708. DOUBLE DOOR by Elizabeth McFadden; HEALD GREEN THEATRE CLUB; *26 November - 3 December 1994*. Director: *Jean Cox*.

709. JACK AND THE BEANSTALK, a Youth Production; HEALD GREEN THEATRE CLUB; *15-17 December 1994*.

THE PLAYHOUSE, Anfield Road, CHEADLE HULME, SK8 5EX; **061-485 8084.**

686. ROUND AND ROUND THE GARDEN by Alan Ayckbourn; PLAYERS DRAMATIC SOCIETY; *2-9 October 1993*. Norman: *Mark Bennett;* Tom: *Joe*

Simpson; Sarah: *Jane de Vince;*
Annie: *Alison Pope;* Reg: *David
Ward;* Ruth: *Tina Wilkinson.*
Director: *Alan Simpson;* Stage
Manager: *Mike Rhodes;* Assistant
Stage Manager: *Rod Lambert;*
Set Design & Construction: *Mike
Rhodes, Jack Ince, Jeff Wint;* Set
Décor: *Beryl Burnett, Audrey
Smart;* Sound: *John Cooper,
Matthew Wagster;* Lighting: *Helen
Jackson;* Properties; *Anne Burns;*
Continuity: *Ann Melling;* Make-
Up: *Marg Hime +.*

704. **ABELARD AND HELOISE**
by Ronald Millar; PLAYERS
DRAMATIC SOCIETY; *20-27
November 1993.* Peter Abelard:
Ian Wilkinson; Heloise: *Helen
Clark;* Alaine: *Martin Pope;*
Gerard/Jehan: *Anders Thompson;*
Phillippe: *Peter Taylor;* Robert de
Mont Boissier: *Peter Grieve;*
Guibert: *Geoff Reyner;* Gilles de
Vannes: *David Burns;* Fulbert:
Jeff Wint; Belle Alys: *Deborah
Burnett;* Abbess of Argenteuill:
Jean Cox; Sister Laura: *Sheila
Gidley;* Sister Godric: *Ena Wint;*
Sister Constance: *Irne Minshull;*
Mariella: *Alison Pope;* Gisella:
Hilary Jarvis; Alberic of Rheims:
Jeff Wilson; Bernard of Clairvaux:
Martin Whitworth; Denise: *Haylet
Burgess;* Hugh: *Martin Pope;*
Whore: *Jane de Vince;* Nuns,
Monks, Students: *Hayley Burgess,
Ann Vale, Martin Pope; Anders
Thompson, Peter Taylor, David
Williams, Jeff Wilson.* Director:
Brian Seymour; Stage Manager:
Eric Ward; Assistant Stage
Manager: *Rod Lambert;* Assistant
Stage Manager: *Beryl Burnettl;*
Set Design & Construction: *Mike
Rhodes, Jack Ince, Jeff Wint,
Brian Seymour;* Set Décor: *Beryl
Burnett, Audrey Smart;* Sound:

John Cooper, Lighting: *david
Wayne, David Ward;* Properties;
Anne Burns, Val Humphreys;
Continuity: *Peter Taylor, Jean
Cox;* Make-Up: *Marg Hime +.*

710. **A BED FULL OF
FOREIGNERS** by David Freeman;
Karak: *Alan Simpson;* Heinz: *Carl
Birkenhead;* Stanley: *David Burr;*
Brenda: *Jenny Hilton;* Helga: *Jane
de Vince;* Claude: *Lee McGregor;*
Simone: *Jo Moor.* Director:
Geoff Reyner; Stage Manager:
Mark Hilton; Set Design &
Construction: *Mike Rhodes, Jack
Ince, +;* Sound: *Jeff Wilson;*
Lighting: *David Ward, Debbie
Burnett;* Continuity: *Rhoda Hills;*
Properties: *Den Fisher;* Costumes:
Audrey Kinder +, Make-Up: *Marg
Hime +.*

711. **A VOYAGE AROUND
MY FATHER** by John Mortimer;
PLAYERS DRAMATIC SOCIETY;
12-19 March 1994. Father:
Joe Crossland; Son: *Geoff
Reyner;* Mother: *Val Humphreys;*
Elizabeth: *Tina Wilkinson;* Son (as
a boy): *Dan Sharpe;* Headmaster/
George: *Ian Wilkinson;* Ham/
Boustead/Sparks/Mr Morrow:
Mark Bennett; Miss Cox/Doris/
Social Worker/Miss Reigate:
Geraldine Grieve; Miss Baker/lst
ATS: *Sarah Price;* Matron/
Witness/2nd ATS: *Alison Pope;*
Ringer Lean/Thong/Film Director:
John Cooper; Japhet/Film
Technician/Doctor: *Martin Pope;*
Judge: *Les Hill;* Reigate: *Mikey
Hindle;* Iris: *Christine Bottomley.*
Director: *Peter Taylor;* Stage
Manager: *Alison Pope;* Assistant
Stage Manager: *Martin Pope;* Set
Design & Construction: *Mike
Rhodes, Jack Ince, Jeff Wint;* Set
Décor: *Beryl Burnett, Audrey*

Smart; Sound: *Ray Rodwell;*
Lighting: *Helen Jackson, David
Ward,* Continuity: *Mary King;*
Properties: *Moira Hindle;*
Costumes: *Audrey Kinder +,*
Make–Up: *Marg Hime +.*

712. STEEL MAGNOLIAS by
Robert Harding; PLAYERS
DRAMATIC SOCIETY; *7–14 May
1994.* Truvy: *Wendy Patterson;*
Annelle: *Jack Quest;* Clairee:
Margaret Williams; Shelby:
Heather Butterfield; M'Lynn: *Val
Miiddleton-Egan;* Ouiser: *Ann
Melling.* Director: *Peter
Thornburn;* Stage Manager: *David
Wayne;* Set Design: *Mike
Rhodes;* Construction: *Jack Ince,
Jeff Wint;* Set Décor: *Beryl
Burnett, Audrey Smart;* Sound:
Jeff Wilson; Lighting: *Helen
Jackson, Dan Sharoe;* Continuity:
Margaret Cole; Properties:
Pauline Rhodes, Audrey Kinder;
Make–Up: *Marg Hime +.*

713. OUTSIDE EDGE by
Richard Harris; PLAYERS
DRAMATIC SOCIETY; *1–8
October 1994.* Miriam: *Deborah
Burnett;* Roger: *Mark Bennett;*
Bob: *Ray Gidley;* Dennis: *David
Burns;* Maggie: *Geraldine Grieve;*
Kevin: *Martin Whitworth;* Ginnie:
Anne Wint; Alex: *Carl
Birkenhead;* Sharon: *Alex Bell.*
Director & Design: *David Ward;*
Stage Manager: *Mike Rhodes;*
Set Construction: *Mike Rhodes,
Jack Ince, Jeff Wint;* Set Décor:
Beryl Burnett, Audrey Smart;
Sound: *John Cooper, Anne Burns;*
Lighting: *Dan Sharp, David Ward;*
Continuity: *Margaret Williams;*
Properties: *Moira Hindle;* Make-
up: *Marg Hime +.*

714. VERONICA'S ROOM by

Ira Levin; PLAYERS DRAMATIC
SOCIETY; *19–26 November
1994.*

REDDISH VALE, beyond
Vale Road, SK4 3DU.

302. JUST SO STORIES by
Rudyard Kipling, dramatised by
STOCKPORT YOUTH THEATRE;
19 June 1994.

**REDDISH VALE HIGH
SCHOOL,** Reddish Vale
Road, SK5 7HD; 061–447
3544; **AZ:** 74, B1; **XAZ:**
119, H2.

298. SHAKESPEARE'S
GREATEST HITS; MANCHESTER
ACTORS COMPANY; *18 January
1994.*

THE RIDGE COLLEGE,
Hibbert Lane, MARPLE,
SK6 7PA; 061–427 7733.

ROMILEY FORUM,
Compstall Road, ROMILEY,
SK6 4EA; 061–430 6570.
AZ: 76, B4; XAZ: 134,
A1. **W**

715. LYSISTRATA by
Aristophanes; EYEWITNESS
THEATRE; *14 October 1993*

**716–719: FIRST DRAFT
93;** NEW WRITING
PROJECT, 9 & 16 November

1993. Project Director: *Bill Taylor;* Co-ordinator: *Dave Campbell;* Tutors: *Cheryl Martin, Jane Hollindson, Bill Taylor;* Technical Direction: *Jon Morris, Simon Tipping;* Props/Costumes: *Neil Blakeman, Andrew Holland, Emma Marlborough:*

716. **GLASS ROOTS** by Emma Marlborough; FORUM COMPANY; *9 November 1993.* Archibald: *Mark White;* Lillian: *Jane Camp;* Captain: *Graeme Urlwin.* Director: *Howard Clark.*

717. **TEA AND KISSES WITH LOVER JANE** by Bill Doran; FORUM COMPANY; *9 November 1993.* Johnnie: *Eddie Criag;* Dirga: *Charlotte Jones;* Memory: *Dave Francis.* Director: *Alex Carter.*

718. **TOO CLOSE TO THE LINE** by Elvera Harkawenko; FORUM COMPANY; *16 November 1993.* Kev: *Jason Lee Ferrington;* Barry: *Marcus Davis;* Woman: *Jolie Hilton:* Anne: *Katie Allerton.* Direction: *Adam Colclough, with company.*

719. **PARADISE** by Aidan McGrath; FORUM COMPANY; *16 November 1994.* Steph: *Claire Ellis;* Jo: *Kate Hampton;* Critic: *Jo Yates.* Director: *Amanda Price;* Producer: *Glen Arrow Smith;* Music: *Craig Weston.*

720. **CAN'T PAY, WON'T PAY** by Dario Fo, translated by Lino Pertile, adapted by Bill Colvill and Robert Walker; LIVESPACE THEATRE COMPANY; *10 November 1993.*

693. **PINOCCHIO,** adapted by PLAYTIME PERCUSSION from Carlo Collodi; *14 November 1994.*

721. **OTHELLO** by William Shakespeare; CUSTARD FACTORY THEATRE; *17 November 1993.* Emilia: *Caroline Coleman;* Desdemona: *Jaq O'Hanlon;* Othello: *Christopher John Hall;* Iago: *Michael Murphy;* Brabantio/Cassio /Roderigo: *Robin St Bastian.* Director: *Julie-Anne Robinson;* Musical Arrangement: *Carol Pemberton;* Lighting: *Juliet Cavell;* Design: *Lyndon Mallinson;* Costumes: *Rossie Russon Costumiers.*

722. **WAITING FOR GODOT** by Samuel Beckett; SOLENT PEOPLES THEATRE with FULL BELT THEATRE COMPANY; *25 November 1993.* Director: *Mollie Guilfoyle;* Design: *Liz Ashcroft.*

725. **THE SNOWMAN** by Raymond Briggs; SNAP THEATRE COMPANY;

726. **FISHING FOR PIGS;** OILY CARTE; *25 January 1994.*

184. **THE MAGIC FINGER** by Roald Dahl; OPEN HAND THEATRE COMPANY; *8-9 February 1994.*

36. **PEACOCK;** DOO COT; *10 February 1994.*

727. YOGI BEAR AND THE MAGIC LAMP; FUNTIME PRODUCTIONS; 20 February 1994.

723. RICHARD III by William Shakespeare; THIRD PARTY PRODUCTIONS; 24 February 1994.

168. THE END OF TEDDY HEDGES by Alastair Goolden; NATURAL THEATRE COMPANY; 25 February 1994.

630. BRETEVSKI STREET; THEATRE CENTRE; 9 March 1994.

724. ANIMAL FARM by George Orwell; adapted by Peter Hall, Music by Richard Peaslee, Lyrics by Adrian Mitchell; FORUM COMPANY; 17-19 March 1994. Boxer/Farmer: Jason Ferrington; Benjamin/Farmer: Neil Blakeman; Cows: Caitlin O'Brien, Melissa Mellor, Bethan Lewis; Clover: Charlotte Jones; Cat: Claire Ellis; Mr Whymper/Dog: Alex Carter; Hens: Nicola Kenyon, Mandy Mason, Jo Yates; Mr Jones/Moses /Farmer: Mark White; Napoleon: David Francis; The Narrator: Katie Allerton; Minimus: Kate Hampton; Old Major/Mr Pilkington/Dog: Howard Clark; Mollie/Young Pig: Jane Camp; Muriel: Anna Pickard; Pigeon/Stable Lad/Sheep: Greg Nixon; Young Pig: Jenny Darragh; Snowball/Farmer: Marcus Davis; Squealer: Amanda Price; Sheep: Sarah Whillance, Helen Bardsley. Director: Graeme Urlwin; Producers: Graeme Urlwin, David Francis; Design: Tabitha

Dickenson; Musical Director: Nic Rands; Musical Input: Mel Gibbons; Movement: Jo McGrath; Lighting/Technical Director: Jon Morris; Stage Manager: Simon Tipping; Props: Glen Arrowsmith, Tabitha Dickenson et al; Mask Design and Construction: Jo Brewerton +; Stage Management Crew: Danny Barlow, Jonny Stuart, Jeanette Barber, Mark Peace, Claire Collister; Set Construction: Tabitha Dickenson, Serena Worsdell et al.

184. THE SOUND COLLECTOR by Roger McGough; QUICKSILVER THEATRE; 8 April 1993.

735. HANS ANDERSON; MARPLE OPERATIC SOCIETY; 18-23 April 1994. Hans Anderson: Barry Aspinall; Jenny Lind: Diane Moss; Rector Meisling: John Harrison; Otto: Peter Bowker; Also: Matthew Fletcher, Joan Sargent, Alf Clark, Robert Atkins, Carole Wood. Musical Director: Simon Gray. Press: AR: 7 & 10/4/94

185. PANCHATANTRA; CHITRALEKA AND COMPANY; 1 May 1994.

86. YOUNG COTTON MATHER'S WONDERS OF THE INVISIBLE WORLD; THE GLEE CLUB; 4 May 1994. Cast: Eddie Aylward, Catherine Kies, Ursula Lea, Mark Whitelaw; Music composed and arranged: Steve Mead; Cello: Olwyn Jackson; Trombone: Sue Auty; Trumpet, Flugel Horn: Bob Dinn; Double Bass: Nicky Dupuy;

Clarinet, Bassoon: *Caroline Gee;* Drums, Percussion: *Colin Seddon, Ken Leigh;* Soprano and Tenor Saxophones: *Paul Smyth;* Violin: *Helen Summers;* Voice: *Jill Taylor;* Guitar, Double Bass, Accordion: *Steve Mead;* Set Construction: *Neil Robson.*

85. COTTON MATHER'S WONDERS OF THE INVISIBLE WORLD; THE GLEE CLUB; *4 May 1994.* Cast: *Eddie Aylward, Catherine Kies, Ursula Lea, Mark Whitelaw;* Music composed and arranged: *Steve Mead;* Cello: *Olwyn Jackson;* Trombone: *Sue Auty;* Trumpet, Flugel Horn: *Bob Dinn;* Double Bass: *Nicky Dupuy;* Clarinet, Bassoon: *Caroline Gee;* Drums, Percussion: *Colin Seddon, Ken Leigh;* Soprano and Tenor Saxophones: *Paul Smyth;* Violin: *Helen Summers;* Voice: *Jill Taylor;* Guitar, Double Bass, Accordion: *Steve Mead;* Set Construction: *Neil Robson.* Journal: 4/5/94

728. RATS - THE MUSICAL; lyrics by Mike Rooke; TAMESIDE COLLEGE PERFORMING ARTS; *25-28 May 1994.* Director: *Alan Keogh.* Press: AR: 26/5/94

76. ROXANA by Daniel Defoe, adapted by Peter McGarry; EYE WITNESS THEATRE COMPANY; *9 June 1994.*

729. JESUS CHRIST SUPERSTAR by Tim Rice and Andrew Lloyd Webber; TAMESIDE COLLEGE PERFORMING ARTS; *22-24*

June 1994.

95. B-ROAD MOVIE; LIP SERVICE; *21-22 October 1994.*

730. A TALL POLICE STORY; CREDO AND ARIEL; *27 October 1994.*

STOCKPORT SCHOOL, Mile End Lane SK2 6BN; 061-483 3622; AZ: 84, C3; XAZ: 132, B6.

298. SHAKESPEARE'S GREATEST HITS; MANCHESTER ACTORS COMPANY; *21 January & 10 February 1994.*

STOCKPORT TOWN CENTRE, out and about

WOODFORD COMMUNITY CENTRE, Chester Road, WOODFORD, SK7 1PS; 061-439 3118. AZ: 95,3E; XAZ: 144,5D.

731. KINDLY LEAVE THE STAGE by John Chapman; WOODFORD COMMUNITY PLAYERS; *18-22 November 1993.* Charles: *Terry Simms;* Madge: *Pat Ralls;* Sarah: *Melloney Lenk;* Rupert: *David Rushton;* Mrs Cullen: *Beryl Horton;* Angela: *Margaret Bentley;* Nurse: *Dorothy Bayman;* Edward: *Fred Ford.* Producer: *Derek Blunt;* Stage Manager: *Trevor McKelvey;* Lighting: *John*

Ethell; Effects: *Graham Scurfield;* Properties: *Heather Braddock, Jo Ethell, Beth Lucas;* Continuity: *Patricia Platt.*

732. PARDON ME, PRIME MINISTER by Edward Taylor and John Graham; WOODFORD COMMUNITY PLAYERS; *21-23 April 1994.* The Rt Honorable George Venables MP: *Charles Pope;* Rodney Campbell: *Mike Swann;* The Rt Honorable Hector Crammond MP: *Derek Blunt;* Miss Frobisher: *Melloney Lenk;* Sybil Venables: *Rene Shaw;* Shirley Springer: *Fiona Hudson;* Jane Rotherbrook: *Jo Ethell;* Dora Springer: *Patricia Platt;* A Man: *David Rushton.* Producer: *Stan Shaw;* Stage Manager: *John Ethell;* Lighting: *Trevor McKelvey;* Effects: *Graham Scurfield;* Properties: *Margaret gregory, Malcolm Gregory, Melloney Lenk;* Continuity: *Heather Braddock.*

TAMESIDE

Evillene

Dorothy

The Wiz

TinMan

Scarecrow

Lion

THE WIZ: Although its lively script clearly suggests that it would be most naturally performed by Black actors, this vivid 1975 updating of The Wizard of Oz is becoming increasingly popular for local performance. TAMESIDE saw two notable productions this year: by NORTHERN KIDS at the HIPPODROME (777) and, shown here, MOSSLEY AODS (754). The latter continued their winning ways, not only with the GMDF Trophies for BEST PRODUCTION and BEST MUSICAL DIRECTOR (ANDREW WHITE) but with the ADJUDICATOR'S AWARD for "The Quartet" of Dorothy (DENISE GREASELY), TinMan (HOWARD CARTER), Scarecrow (CARL MORGAN) And Lion (COLIN WARD), seen here under the baleful gaze of Evillene, The Wicked Witch (ANN ATKINS) and The Wiz himself (DAVID HEWITT).

COPLEY COMMUNITY CENTRE, Demesne Drive, Huddersfield Road, STALEYBRIDGE, SK5 2QG; **061-338 6230.**

DROYLESDEN LITTLE THEATRE, Market Street, M35 7AY; **061-223 4014.** AZ: 52,C3; XAZ: 90,B4.

741. IT'S A MADHOUSE by Alan Bleasdale; *29 November -*

4 December 1993. Pete: *Richard Jackson;* Eddie: *Sean Worrall;* Christine: *Sheila Casey;* Ben: *Colin Smith;* Marie: *Michele Pownall;* Vera: *Connie Brooksbank;* Jimmy: *Keith Johnson.* Director & Design: *Melvyn Bates;* Consruction: *Ralph Wilkinson, David Miles, Sue Thorp, Kath Wood, Rick Wood, Nicola Phillips.* Co-ordination & Properties: *Pat Hatton, Steve Hussey.*
Press: AR: 25/11/93

742. THE CORN IS GREEN by Emlyn Williams; *24-29 January 1994.* Director: *Charles Alty.*
Press: AR: 25/1/94

761. HOLIDAY SNAP by John Chapman and Michael Pertwee; *21-26 March 1994.*

762. GHOSTS by Henrik Ibsen, translated by Michael Meyer; *9-14 May 1994.* Mrs Alving: *Jean Nicholson;* Oswald: *Colin Smith;* Regina Engstrand: *Sheila Payne;* Also: *Jack Platt, Michael R Grimshaw.*
Press: AR: 10/5/94

763. BIG BAD MOUSE Philip King and Falkland Carey; *4-9 July 1994.*

764. ABIGAIL'S PARTY by Mike Leigh; *3-8 October 1994.*

DUKINFIELD ASTLEY HIGH SCHOOL; Yew Tree Lane; SK16 5BL; 061-338 2374; **AZ:** 55, 4C; **XAZ:** 106, C1.

129. GROUNDED by Eileen Murphy; M6 THEATRE COMPANY; *22 February & 22 March 1994.*

EGERTON PARK COMMUNITY SCHOOL, Egerton Street, DENTON, M34 3PD; 061-335 0097, 061-336 1630/ 2039. AZ: 63,2E; XAZ: 105,3E.

FESTIVAL THEATRE, Corporation Street, HYDE, SK14 1AB; 061-320 0542/336 8840. AZ: 64,3B; XAZ: 106, B5.

GEORGE LAWTON CENTRE THEATRE, Stamford Street, MOSSLEY, OL5 0HR; 0457 832705; AZ: 45, E2; XAZ: 80,E2.

753. SNOW WHITE AND THE SEVEN DWARFS by Ron Hall; MOSSLEY AODS; *17-22 January 1994.* Fritz: *Malcolm Neild;* Snow White: *Victoria Hopton;* Chamberlain: *John Ross;* Prince Valentine: *Angela Ashworth;* Queen Lucretia: *Lisa Kay;* Dame Dumpling: *John Fletcher;* Fairy Dewdrop: *Scott Lees;* Olga: *Sandra Kenny;* Leo the Lion: *Glyn Ward;* Chief Housemaid: *Jenny Godfrey;* Chief Courtier: *Victoria Boshell;* Doc: *Oliver Watton;* Sneezy: *Nicola Fogg;* Happy: *Garth Hunt;*

Grumpy: *Ben Godfrey;* Bashful: *Emma Chapman;* Dopey: *Emma Leaver;* Sleepy: *Rowena Preger;* Tiny Tots: *Richard Beswick, Hannah Carlin, Emma Cooney, Katie Cox, Nicola Disdale, Lucy Godfrey, Amy Leaver, Layla Moores, Rachael Moss, Stephanie Powell, Lorna Ryder, Michelle Scott;* Senior Chorus: *Victoria Boshell, Amanda Combs, Jenny Godfrey, Mary Manock, Donna Nield, Emma Pitman, Sheila Redfearn, Stella McDevitt;* Senior Dancers: *Vicki Mills, Emmah Preger, Jenny Ross, Stephanie Rowley, Malyn Ward, Gemma Worrell, Sarah Preger;* Junior Chorus: *Michelle Armitage, Claire Beswick, Richard Carlin, Sarah Cooney, Rachael Cox, Kirsty Dinsdale, Leanne Edge, Katie Fletcher, Lynsey Fletcher, Geoffrey Hunter, Louise Kenworthy, Elizabeth Marsland, Roxanne Moores, Sarah Redfearn, Jaclyn Storey, Samantha Taylor, Emma Walton, Michelle White, Tracy White;* Junior Dancers: *Emily Carlin, Dionne Clarke, Joanne Cox, Sarah Holdich, Georgina O'Rourke, Lauren Wood.* Director: *Graham Young;* Musical Director: *David Chatman;* Choreographer: *Gillian Hughes;* Stage Manager: *Robert Godfrey;* Assistant Stage Manager: *Frank Webster;* Stage Assistants: *Nigel Banks, Gary Wright, Richard Ryder, Barry Rushton, Ross McLaren, Ian Maiden, Brian Whittaker;* Scenic Artists/Design: *Nigel Banks, John Buckley;* Lighting: *Martin Ogden;* Wardrobe: *John Ross et al;* Accompanist: *Elaine Chatman;* Make-up: *Jean Sheridan, Elaine Clarke, Joan Hodkinson;* Prompt: *Ann Broadbent;* Sound: *Glen Knight.*

Press: **AR:** 13&20/1/94; **MR:** 23/12/93

754. **THE WIZ,** adapted from *The Wizard of Oz* by Frank L Baum; Book by William F Brown; Music and Lyrics by Charlie Smalls; MOSSLEY AMATEUR OPERATIC AND DRAMATIC SOCIETY; *25-30 April 1994.* Aunt Em: *Avis Billington;* Dorothy: *Denise Greasley;* Addaperle: *Kim Bennett;* Scarecrow: *Carl Morgan;* Tin Man: *Howard Carter;* Lion: *Colin Ward;* The Wiz: *David Hewitt;* Evillene: *Ann Atkins;* Glinda: *Roberta McIntosh;* Uncle Henry: *John Ross;* Messenger: *Andrew Ryder;* Gatekeeper: *Scott Lees;* Mice Squad: *Lisa Kay;* Lord High Underling: *Malcolm Neild;* Crows: *Andrew Ryder, Scott Lees, Malcolm Neild, John Saxon, Paul Hulme;* Body Beautiful: *George Allan, Julian Davidson;* Female Chorus and Dancers: *Lisa Kay, Angela Ashworth, Amands Combs, Pauline Slate, Mary Manock, Gillian Hamer, Katrina McDonald, Catherine Lyles, Julie Banks, Sheila Redfearn, Patricia Reynolds, Karen Elward;* Male Chorus and Dancers: *David Owen, Paul Hulme, Scott Lees, James Schofield, Andrew Gibson, John Saxon, Michael Powney. Nigel Banks, Andrew Ryder.* Director: *Nita Bennett;* Musical Director: *Andrew White;* Choreographer: *Janice Hughes;* Stage Manager: *John Buckley;* Assistant Stage Managers: *Clive Darbyshire, Frank Webster, Robert Godfrey;* Stage Assistants: *Richard Ryder, Ian Maden, Barry Rushton, Brian Whittaker, Gary Wright, Ross McClarnon;* Design/Scenic Artist: *John*

399

Buckley; Lighting: *Martin Ogden, Stuart Redfearn, Mark Lynch, Dan Russell, Greg Ambler;* Wardrobe: *John Ross, Tracy Chadwick, Aileen Whittaker;* Properties: *Patricia Furness, Linda Sanderson;* Make-up: *John Fletcher, Jean Sheridan, Joan Hodkinson;* Prompt: *Stella McDevitt;* Sound: *Glenn Knight.* **Press: AR** 7,14,21&28/4/94; **MEN:** 29/4/94; **OC:** 19/4/94.

755. JUNE EVENING by Bill Naughton; MOSSLEY AMATEUR OPERATIC AND DRAMATIC SOCIETY; *5-8 October 1994.* Liz Sedwin: *Eileen Gorman;* Harry Sedwin: *Albert Jackson;* Olive Whittle: *Jenny Swinbourne;* Sarah Kippax: *Marion Datson;* Albert Kippax: *Stephen Timms;* Beattie Kippax: *Linda Adshead;* Jack Harwood: *Michael Newsom;* Polly Harwood: *Joanne Belle;* Fanny Brighouse: *Sheila Mills;* Miss Pratt: *Stella McDevitt;* Children: *Victoria Boshell, Emma Chapman, Kerry Rushton, Katie Fletcher, Lynsey Fletcher, Ben Godfrey, Lucy Godfrey, Sarah Redfearn.* Director: *Jessie Wright;* Stage Manager: *Ross McLarnon;* Assistant Stage Manager: *Frank Webster;* Stage Assistants: *Barry Rushton, Richard Ryder, Brian Whittaker, John Buckley, Robert Godfrey, Clive Derbyshire;* Scenic Design: *John Buckley;* Lighting: *Martin Ogden, Stuart Redfearn;* Properties: *Linda Sanderson, Tricia Furness, Alan Maley;* Wardrobe: *John Ross;* Make-up: *John Fletcher.* **Press: OC:** 4/10/94

GUIDE BRIDGE

THEATRE, Audenshaw Road, AUDENSHAW, M34 5HJ; 061-330 8078. AZ: 53,E3; XAZ: 91,E5.

743. SLEEPING BEAUTY; *4-11 December 1993.* Director: *Stuart Needham.*

744. GASLIGHT by Patrick Hamilton; *22-29 January 1994.* Detective Sergeant Rough: *Johnny Barlow;* Jack Manningham: *Allan Gauler;* Bella Manningham: *Jane Tonge.* Director: *Bill Klieve.*

745. TRIVIAL PURSUITS by Frank Vickery; *26 February - 5 March 1994.* Nick: *David Fielding;* TeddyL *Kevin C Howarth;* Also: *Sue Byrom, Sheila Gregory, Liz Openshaw, Mike Smith, Kath Cole, Dorothy Hynes, Keith Johnson.* Director: *Melvyn Bates.* **Press: AR:** 10/3/94; **OC:** 8/2/94

746. OUR TOWN by Thornton Wilder; *2-9 April 1994.* Cast of 30, including: *Jane Parker, Sheila Casey, Jane Tonge, Bryan McGuiness, James Robert Dunne;* Choir, including: *Barbara Anderton.* Director: *Ian Townsend.* **Press: AR:** 31/3/94

747. THE SUNSHINE BOYS by Neil Simon; *4-14 May 1994.* Willie Clark: *Johnnie Barlow;* Al Lewis: *Lyn Hudson;* Also: *Jerry Lakeman.* Director: *Carla Stokes.*

748. GHOST TRAIN by Arthur

Ridley; *11–18 June 1994*.
Director: *Constance M Smith*.

**749. THE CREATURE
CREEPS** by Jack Sharkey; *23–30 July 1994*. Mord: *Stephen Timms;* Baron Von Blitzen: *Ian Townsend;* Gretchen Twitchill: *Sheila Gregory;* Daisy: *Siobhan Peters-Meredith;* Frank: *Colin Smith;* Babsy: *Judith Howarth;* Frau Von Blitzen: *Wendy Hudson;* Quadruplets: *Mike Symmonds*. Director: *John Meredith.*
Press: AR: 4/8/94

750. SHIRLEY VALENTINE by Willy Russell; *3–10 September 1994.* Director: *Carla Stokes.*

751. FIVE FINGER EXERCISE by Peter Shaffer; *15–22 October 1994.* Director: *Alan Kenworthy.*

752. TOM THE PIPER'S SON by Norman Robbins; *3–10 December 1994.* Director: *Stuart Needham.*

LIVINGSTONE PRIMARY SCHOOL, Old Brow, MOSSLEY OL5 0DY; 0457 832495; AZ: 45, 2E; XAZ: 81, 2E

759. SPAGHETTI ISLAND by Mike Harris; LIVINGSTONE PRIMARY SCHOOL; *December 1993.*
Press: MR: 16/12/93

OLD CHAPEL, Dukinfield.

757. SLEEPING BEAUTY; *February 1994.* Queen: *Frank Thomas;* King: *Michael Hilton;* Princess Beauty: *Emma Wilcox;* Prince: *Katie McDonald;* Toffee Nose: *Beryl Peace;* Lady Pamela Tooth: *Kirsten Andrew;* Prince of Iceland: *Bronwyn Lowe;* Prince of Ceylon: *Barbara Farrow;* Prince of China: *Jennifer Moody;* Prince of Mexico: *Susan Hilton;* Carabosse: *R. Helen Phillips,* Dum Dum: *John Quarmby;* James: *Matthew Hilton;* Cagney: *Garry McCann;* Fairy Queen: *Amanda Farro;* Fairy of Happiness: *Victoria Ogden;* Fairy of Beauty: *Lisa Nathaniel;* Fairy of Love: *Jane Olchak;* King of the Spiders: *Shirley Edwards;* Vitriolic Vulture: *Susan Quarmby;* Courtiers: *Christopher Postings, David Maddocks, Michael Hilton, Christian Sandres, Patrick Smith, Jane Olschak, Victoria Ogden, Louise Ogden, Ami Robinson, Sarah Nathaniel, Lisa Nathaniel, Zoë Nathaniel, Susan Powers;* Fairies: *Victoria Peart, Claire Maddocks, Jill Quarmby, Victoria Jones, Mara Sandres, Sophie Hobbiss, Kimberley Hill, Emma Loe, Rachel Edwards, Vicki Olschak.* Director: *John Holland;* Musical Director: *Jim Cheetham;* Percussion: *Philip Cheetham;* Choreographers: *Christine Thomas, Samantha Thomas.*
Press: AR: 24/2/94

OLD RECTORY HOTEL, Meadow Lane Haughton Green, DENTON, M34 1GD; 061–336 7516; AZ: 76, A1; XAZ: 121, G1.

152. PERKINS' PROMOTION by Liz Lees; GREEN LIGHT THEATRE COMPANY; 6 November 1993.

PARK BRIDGE: Medlock Valley Visitor's Centre, OL6 8AQ; 061-678 4072. AZ: 44,B2; XAZ: 79, G2.

627. HOW THE COYOTE STOLE THE FIRE; MEDLOCK VALLEY WARDEN SERVICE; 20 February 1994

760. HORROR SCOPE; PROPER JOB THEATRE COMPANY; 29 October 1994.

ST MARKS CHURCH HALL, 2 Church Square, DUKINFIELD, SK16 4PX; 061-339 9010; AZ: 54,A3; XAZ: 91,H4.

STALYBRIDGE METHODIST CHURCH.

758. JACK AND THE BEANSTALK; February 1994. Fairy Fortune: *Catherine Milestone;* Button: *Liian Cullen;* Frederick: *Natalie Owen;* Isobel: *Gemma Cooper;* Malodorous: *Alexandra Harrison;* Blood and Thunder: *Sara Cresswell, Lindsay Vare;* Giant's Wife: *Karen Owen;* Anna: *Claire Young;* Ruth: *Sarah Cullen;* The King's Fool: *Sally Sheppard;* Connie the Cow: *Charlotte Harrison, Louise Taylor;* Also: *Louise Briggs, Jill Cove,*

Katy Cullen, Sarah Cullen, Victoria Harrison, Kayleigh Jervis, Lindsay Johnson, Jennifer Large, Jennifer Murray, Amy Williams, Angela Ashton, Harriet Bailey, Lauren Beard, John Cove, Sarah Cove, Laura Cullen, Alexandra Harrison, Paul Johnson, Philip Maden, Neil Sholes, Claire Young. Dancers: *Katy Cullen, Laura Cullen, Sarah Cullen, Alexandra Harrison, Claire Young;* Tinies: *Amy Cooper, Calum Coogan, Amy Kavanagh, Joseph Wilock, Rosie Williams.* Producer: *James Schofield;* Choreographer: *Laura Cresswell;* Musical Director: *Jacqui Dawber;* Guitar: *Martin Sholes;* Drums: *Ellis Bowker;* Flute: *Linda Owen.* Press: AR: 24/2/94

SCOUT GREEN, Manchester Road; MOSSLEY; AZ: 45, F2; XAZ: 81, E3.

765. GAWAIN AND THE LOATHLY LADY by Jane Rogers; MOSSLEY COMMUNITY ARTS; 8-10 October 1993. Sir Gawain: *Dave Jones;* Loathly Lady: *Dyllis Wolinski;* Cast of 35, including: *Amy Roberts.* Organiser: *Dave Moutrey;* Maker: *Mike Green.* Press: MR: 14/10/93

756. KISS THE FROG, devised and wriiten by the group, with Jane Rogers; MOSSLEY COMMUNITY ARTS; 13-16 July 1994. Frog Prince/Man: *Gordon Banks;* Fool: *Julie Clays;* Craven: *John Clifford;* Giant: *Terry Cowley;* King/Woman: *Michael McKrell;* Princess/Mrs Cosy:

Melanie Rogers; Mayor: *Jane Rogers;* Mr Doom: *Dyllis Wolinski;* Dancers: *Janet Collett, Kate Berry, Tracey Bingley, Ben Callaghan, Emily Callaghan, Laurie Clifford, Lucy Collett, Kim Connor, Caroline Ingman, Nicky Mason, Lindsey McKenna, Anna Moutrey, Hilary Williamson;* MUSICIANS: Musical Director, Composer, Saxophones, Vocals, Zukra, Mbira, Keyboards: *Mole Beale;* Vocals, Percussion: *Anne Blomeley, Janet Collett, Lucy Collett, Sam Collett;* Guitar: *Danny Blomeley;* Drums, Percussion: *Dave Walsh;* Guitar, Bass Guitar: *Chris Williams;* Percusion: *Kim, John.* Director and Producer: *Dave Moutrey;* Choreographer: *Janet Collett;* Design and Making: *All the foregoing + Alex Baker, Linda Callaghan, Mike Green, Jillian Harrison, Dave Jones, Annie Wright;* Stage Management: *Ben Proctor, Paul Wolinski;* Fireworks: *Gordon Banks, Terry Cowley, Lynn Proctor, Michael McKrell, Dave Moutrey, Tom Thompson, Ben Proctor, Lucy Proctor, PaBoom Phenomenal Fireworks.*

TAMESIDE COLLEGE,
Beaufort Road, ASHTON-UNDER-LYNE OL6 6NX; O61-330 6911, Ext: 2160. AZ: 54, BS; XAZ: 92, B3.

278. A STRANGE AND UNEXPECTED EVENT; GORSE AND BAMBOO THEATRE COMPANY; *2 November 1993.*

TAMESIDE HIPPODROME
Oldham Road, ASHTON-UNDER-LYNE, OL6 7SE; 061-330 2095; (Cards: 061-242 2505; Fee: £1) AZ: 54, A2; XAZ: 9I: H3.

766. SOOTY'S WORLD CRUISE; VINCENT SHAW ASSOCIATES; *20 November 1993.* Presented by *Matthew Corbett* and *Connie Creighton.*

767. MUSIC HALL AND VARIETY; HISS AND BOO; *24-27 November 1993.* Featuring: *Ruth Madoc, Franklyn James et al.*

768. THE FANTASTICAL LEGEND OF DR FAUST; script probably adapted from Johann Wolfgang von Goethe by Michael Bogdanov; ENGLISH SHAKESPEARE COMPANY with JACINTO THEATRE OF VISUAL ARTS; *29 November - 4 December 1993.* Faust: *Peter Holdway;* Mephistopheles/Wrath: *James Barton;* Gretchen/Witch's Familiar: *Joan Morris;* Valentine/Archangel/Covetousness/Gluttony/Witch's Familiar/Earth Spirit: *Charlie Folorunsho;* Witch/Earth Spirit/Sloth/Envy/Pride/Lechery: *Lisa Harley;* Musician: *John Pinter.* Director: *Kate Beales;* Consultant Director/Sculpture, Puppet and Mask Design: *James Barton;* Composer: *John Pinter;* Desgn: *Claire Lyth;* Lighting: *Michael Bogdanov;* Production Manager: *Graham Lister;* Company Stage Manager: *Adrian Dow;* Technical Manager: *Guy Stafford.*

403

Press: OC: 29&30/11/93; **TES:** 3/12/93

769. **99 HEYWORTH STREET** by John and Tony Bryan; OFF THE SHELF PRODUCTIONS; *13-18 December 1993.* Sheila: *Maureen Ann Bryan;* Lizzie: *Paula Bell;* Laurie Baldwin: *David van Day;* Molly: *Suzanne O'Keefe;* Father Flynn: *Tony Booth;* Stan: *James T Mawdesley;* Joe: *Nick Lamont;* Michael: *Stevie Wharton;* Sadie: *Anita Owens;* Bridget: *Catherine Walker;* Jessie: *Amelia-Jayne Stephens;* Mrs T: *Lindzi Germaine;* Cathy: *Claire Robinson;* Uncle Robert: *Iggy Navarro, Brian Gibson;* Rosie: *Jenni Nolan;* Girl in Street/Girl in Hospital: *April Bryan;* 2nd Girl in Hospital: *Dannielle Cook;* Uncle Tommy/Accordionist: *Bernie Nolan;* Andolini/Doctor Strelitz: *David Zalud;* Policeman: *Rob Watkin;* Altar Boy: *David Watkin;* Dancers/Ensemble: *David McGrouther* (Dance Captain), *Leroy Law, Julie Alltree, Deborah Elliott, Vicky Faithful, Jenni Nolan, Emma Williams, Nicki Willis;* Children: *Kerry Byrne, Hanna Bywater, Rosie Clark, Miriam Conroy, Natalie Edwards, Naomi Etchels, Jenny Gawley, Francesca Gibson, Amy Greaves, Hayley Kelly, Katrina MacDonald, Gillian Nolan, Claire Russell, Rachel Ryan, Lisa Stelfox.* Director: *John Bryan;* Producers: *Tony Bryan, Maureen Ann Bryan, John Bryan;* Assistant Director: *James T Mawdsley;* Music: *John Bryan;* Vocal Coach: *Amanda;* Original Choreography: *Diane O'Neill;* Choreographer: *David McGrouther;* Children's Choreographer: *Jenni Nolan;* Stage Manager: *Lisa Davies;*

Deputy Stage Manager/Properties Master: *Tony McCarthy;* Assistant Stage Managers: *Kris Kross, Stuart Flemming;* Design: *Jocelyn Meall;* Set Construction: *Mark Scott, Gary Hesketh, George Smith, Ralph Davod, Jayne Bell;* Lighting: *Mark Richards;* Wardrobe Mistress/Costumes: *"Amanda" Designs;* Wardrobe Assistants: *Joanna Louise, Laura Mansell;* Wig Mistress: *Vincenza Miele-Brown;* Production Manager/Company Manager: *Mu Ali.* **Press: OC:** 10&14/12/93

770. **ALADDIN;** BIG RED HEN PRODUCTION HOUSE; *24 December 1993 - 22 January 1994.* Aladdin: *Simone Robertson;* Wishee Washee: *Andi Peters,* alternating with *Toby Anstis;* Slave of the Lamp: *Treva Etienne;* Widow Twankee: *Gordon Peters;* Emperor: *Les Want;* Abanazar: *Chris Hennen;* So Shy: *Bonnie Hassell;* Princess Balroubadour: *Stella Czerniawskyi;* Pekin Police: *John & Jim Lavelle;* Also: *Stutz Bear Cats, Nellie the Elephant.* Director & Lighting: *John Redgrave;* Choreographer: *Josie Ashcroft.* **Press: CL:** 12/1/94; **MEN:** 23&29/12/93

696. **SNOW WHITE AND THE SEVEN DWARFS;** *14-16 February & 4 June 1994.*

771. **PINOCCHIO;** PRESTO PUPPET THEATRE; *17-18 February 1994.*

772. **BOUNCERS** by John Godber; HULL TRUCK THEATRE; *22-26 February 1994.* Director: *Damian*

Cruden; Design: *Robert Jones;* Lighting: *George Morris.*

773. HIGH SOCIETY; Music and Lyrics by Cole Porter; Book by Richard Eyre, based on the play *The Philadelphia Story* by Philip Barry; ASHTON-UNDER-LYNE OPERATIC SOCIETY; *14-19 March 1994.* Mike: *John Rawson;* Dexter: *Bill Nicholson;* Liz: *Pat Battle;* Tracy: *Julie Colson;* Also: *Ann Atkins, Adele Buckley, Malcolm Parker.* Producer: *Nita Bennett;* Choreographer: *Lyn Jones;* Musical Director: *Andrew White;* Chorus Numbers Set: *Kay Lilley.* **Press: AR:** 28/10/93, 10 & 17/3/94; **OC:** 15&22/3/94; **SR:** 6/1/94;

774. UP THE BLUE STALK: THEATRE ROYAL HANLEY; *21-26 March 1994.* Cast: *George Roper, David Darby,* Fairy: *Sarah Davidson, Nigel Peever,* Obsession, Tartlettes, Singer: *Aubrey Phillips.* Director: *Simon Ellingham;* Choreographer: *John Cumberlidge.* **Press: MEN:** 22/3/94; **OC:** 23/3/94

695. TALES FROM THE JUNGLE BOOK; PAN PUPPETS; *27 March 1994.*

775. OLDE TIME MUSIC HALL; *5 April 1994.* Presenter: *Aubrey Phillips;* George Forby/Al Jolson: *Steve King;* Mrs Shufflewick/Jack Pleasance: *Johnny Dallas;* The Great Levant: *David Paul;* Danny La Rue/Judy Garland: *David D'Arby;* + The Gaiety Girls.

776. POSTMAN PAT'S ADVENTURES by Charles Savage, from the stories of Joihn Cunliffe and the television series by Ivor Wood; Music and Lyrics by Bryan Daly; POSTMAN PAT PRODUCTIONS; *24-28 May 1994.* Director: *Charles Savage;* Costumes and Design: *Carol Foot;* Lighting: *Lawrence T Doyle.* **Press: AR:** 19/5/94

777. THE WIZ; Book by William F Brown; Music and lyrics by Charlie Smalls and Luther Vandross; NORTHERN KIDS; *27 -30 July 1994.* Aunt Em: *Catherine Hill;* Dorothy: *Jenny Gawley;* Uncle Henryl. *Richard Holden;* Addaperle: *Anna Jerram;* Scarecrow: *Simon Topley;* Tin Man: *Jon Clay;* Lion: *Dominic Stannage;* Gatekeeper: *Richard Holden;* The Wiz: *David Bowman;* Evilene: *Deborah Torr;* Lord High Underling: *Darren Stannage;* Messenger: *Matthew Watton;* Monkey: *Andrew Moss;* Glinda: *Jenny Spence;* Chief Mouse: *Adam Wilson;* 1st Munchkin: *Krystal Brown;* 2nd: *Carly Jones;* 3rd Munchkin: *Laura Evans;* 4th Munchkin: *Hazel Swan;* 5th Munchkin: *Tiffany Robinson;* 6th Munchkin: *Dawn Wrigley;* Other Munchkins: *Ryan Badderley, Kate Bailey, Nicola Bevington*

LIVINGSTONE PRIMARY SCHOOL, Old Brow, MOSSLEY OL5 0DY; 0457 832495; **AZ:** 45, 2E; **XAZ:** 81, 2E

759. SPAGHETTI ISLAND by Mike Harris; LIVINGSTONE PRIMARY SCHOOL; *December 1993.* Press: MR: 16/12/93

OLD CHAPEL, Dukinfield.

757. SLEEPING BEAUTY; *February 1994.* Queen: *Frank Thomas;* King: *Michael Hilton;* Princess Beauty: *Emma Wilcox;* Prince: *Katie McDonald;* Toffee Nose: *Beryl Peace;* Lady Pamela Tooth: *Kirsten Andrew;* Prince of Iceland: *Bronwyn Lowe;* Prince of Ceylon: *Barbara Farrow;* Prince of China: *Jennifer Moody;* Prince of Mexico: *Susan Hilton;* Carabosse: *R. Helen Phillips,* Dum Dum: *John Quarmby;* James: *Matthew Hilton;* Cagney: *Garry McCann;* Fairy Queen: *Amanda Farro;* Fairy of Happiness: *Victoria Ogden;* Fairy of Beauty: *Lisa Nathaniel;* Fairy of Love: *Jane Olchak;* King of the Spiders: *Shirley Edwards;* Vitriolic Vulture: *Susan Quarmby;* Courtiers: *Christopher Postings, David Maddocks, Michael Hilton, Christian Sandres, Patrick Smith, Jane Olschak, Victoria Ogden, Louise Ogden, Ami Robinson, Sarah Nathaniel, Lisa Nathaniel, Zoë Nathaniel, Susan Powers;* Fairies: *Victoria Peart, Claire Maddocks, Jill Quarmby, Victoria Jones, Mara Sandres, Sophie Hobbiss, Kimberley Hill, Emma Loe, Rachel Edwards, Vicki Olschak.* Director: *John Holland;* Musical Director: *Jim Cheetham;* Percussion: *Philip Cheetham;* Choreographers: *Christine Thomas, Samantha Thomas.* Press: AR: 24/2/94

OLD RECTORY HOTEL, Meadow Lane Haughton Green, DENTON, M34 1GD; 061–336 7516; AZ: 76, A1; XAZ: 121, G1.

152. PERKINS' PROMOTION by Liz Lees; GREEN LIGHT THEATRE COMPANY; *6 November 1993.*

PARK BRIDGE: Medlock Valley Visitor's Centre, OL6 8AQ; 061–678 4072. AZ: 44,B2; XAZ: 79, G2.

627. HOW THE COYOTE STOLE THE FIRE; MEDLOCK VALLEY WARDEN SERVICE; *20 February 1994*

760. HORROR SCOPE; PROPER JOB THEATRE COMPANY; *29 October 1994.*

ST MARKS CHURCH HALL, 2 Church Square, DUKINFIELD, SK16 4PX; 061–339 9010; AZ: 54,A3; XAZ: 91,H4.

STALYBRIDGE METHODIST CHURCH.

758. JACK AND THE BEANSTALK; *February 1994.* Fairy Fortune: *Catherine Milestone;* Button: *Lilan Cullen;*

Frederick: *Natalie Owen;* Isobel: *Gemma Cooper;* Malodorous: *Alexandra Harrison;* Blood and Thunder: *Sara Cresswell, Lindsay Vare;* Giant's Wife: *Karen Owen;* Anna: *Claire Young;* Ruth: *Sarah Cullen;* The King's Fool: *Sally Sheppard;* Connie the Cow: *Charlotte Harrison, Louise Taylor;* Also: *Louise Briggs, Jill Cove, Katy Cullen, Sarah Cullen, Victoria Harrison, Kayleigh Jervis, Lindsay Johnson, Jennifer Large, Jennifer Murray, Amy Williams, Angela Ashton, Harriet Bailey, Lauren Beard, John Cove, Sarah Cove, Laura Cullen, Alexandra Harrison, Paul Johnson, Philip Maden, Neil Sholes, Claire Young.* Dancers: *Katy Cullen, Laura Cullen, Sarah Cullen, Alexandra Harrison, Claire Young;* Tinies: *Amy Cooper, Calum Coogan, Amy Kavanagh, Joseph Wilock, Rosie Williams.* Producer: *James Schofield;* Choreographer: *Laura Cresswell;* Musical Director: *Jacqui Dawber;* Guitar: *Martin Sholes;* Drums: *Ellis Bowker;* Flute: *Linda Owen.* Press: **AR:** 24/2/94

SCOUT GREEN,
Manchester Road;
MOSSLEY; **AZ:** 45, F2;
XAZ: 81, E3.

765. GAWAIN AND THE LOATHLY LADY by Jane Rogers;
MOSSLEY COMMUNITY ARTS; *8-10 October 1993.* Sir Gawain: *Dave Jones;* Loathly Lady: *Dyllis Wolinski;* Cast of 35, including: *Amy Roberts.* Organiser: *Dave Moutrey;* Maker: *Mike Green.* Press: **MR:** 14/10/93

756. KISS THE FROG,
devised and wriiten by the group, with Jane Rogers; MOSSLEY COMMUNITY ARTS; *13-16 July 1994.* Frog Prince/Man: *Gordon Banks;* Fool: *Julie Clays;* Craven: *John Clifford;* Giant: *Terry Cowley;* King/Woman: *Michael McKrell;* Princess/Mrs Cosy: *Melanie Rogers;* Mayor: *Jane Rogers;* Mr Doom: *Dyllis Wolinski;* Dancers: *Janet Collett, Kate Berry, Tracey Bingley, Ben Callaghan, Emily Callaghan, Laurie Clifford, Lucy Collett, Kim Connor, Caroline Ingman, Nicky Mason, Lindsey McKenna, Anna Moutrey, Hilary Williamson;* MUSICIANS: Musical Director, Composer, Saxophones, Vocals, Zukra, Mbira, Keyboards: *Mole Beale;* Vocals, Percussion: *Anne Blomeley, Janet Collett, Lucy Collett, Sam Collett;* Guitar: *Danny Blomeley;* Drums, Percussion: *Dave Walsh;* Guitar, Bass Guitar: *Chris Williams;* Percusion: *Kim, John.* Director and Producer: *Dave Moutrey;* Choreographer: *Janet Collett;* Design and Making: *All the foregoing* + *Alex Baker, Linda Callaghan, Mike Green, Jillian Harrison, Dave Jones, Annie Wright;* Stage Management: *Ben Proctor, Paul Wolinski;* Fireworks: *Gordon Banks, Terry Cowley, Lynn Proctor, Michael McKrell, Dave Moutrey, Tom Thompson, Ben Proctor, Lucy Proctor, PaBoom Phenomenal Fireworks.*

TAMESIDE COLLEGE,
Beaufort Road, ASHTON-UNDER-LYNE OL6 6NX;

407

O61-330 6911, Ext:
2160. AZ: 54, BS; XAZ:
92, B3.

278. A STRANGE AND
UNEXPECTED EVENT; GORSE
AND BAMBOO THEATRE
COMPANY; *2 November 1993.*

TAMESIDE HIPPODROME
Oldham Road, ASHTON-
UNDER-LYNE, OL6 7SE;
061-330 2095; (Cards:
061-242 2505; Fee: £1)
AZ: 54, A2; XAZ: 9I: H3.

766. SOOTY'S WORLD
CRUISE; VINCENT SHAW
ASSOCIATES; *20 November
1993.* Presented by *Matthew
Corbett and Connie Creighton.*

767. MUSIC HALL AND
VARIETY; HISS AND BOO; *24–
27 November 1993.* Featuring:
*Ruth Madoc, Franklyn James et
al.*

768. THE FANTASTICAL
LEGEND OF DR FAUST; script
probably adapted from Johann
Wolfgang von Goethe by Michael
Bogdanov; ENGLISH
SHAKESPEARE COMPANY with
JACINTO THEATRE OF VISUAL
ARTS; *29 November – 4
December 1993.* Faust: *Peter
Holdway;* Mephistopheles/Wrath:
James Barton; Gretchen/Witch's
Familiar: *Joan Morris;* Valentine/
Archangel/Covetousness/Gluttony/
Witch's Familiar/Earth Spirit:
Charlie Folorunsho; Witch/Earth
Spirit/Sloth/Envy/Pride/Lechery:

Lisa Harley; Musician: *John
Pinter.* Director: *Kate Beales;*
Consultant Director/Sculpture,
Puppet and Mask Design: *James
Barton;* Composer: *John Pinter;*
Desgn: *Claire Lyth;* Lighting:
Michael Bogdanov; Production
Manager: *Graham Lister;*
Company Stage Manager: *Adrian
Dow;* Technical Manager: *Guy
Stafford.*
Press: OC: 29&30/11/93; TES:
3/12/93

769. 99 HEYWORTH STREET
by John and Tony Bryan; OFF
THE SHELF PRODUCTIONS;
13-18 December 1993. Sheila:
Maureen Ann Bryan; Lizzie: *Paula
Bell;* Laurie Baldwin: *David van
Day;* Molly: *Suzanne O'Keefe;*
Father Flynn: *Tony Booth;* Stan:
James T Mawdesley; Joe: *Nick
Lamont;* Michael: *Stevie Wharton;*
Sadie: *Anita Owens;* Bridget:
Catherine Walker; Jessie: *Amelia-
Jayne Stephens;* Mrs T: *Lindzi
Germaine;* Cathy: *Claire
Robinson;* Uncle Robert: *Iggy
Navarro, Brian Gibson;* Rosie:
Jenni Nolan; Girl in Street/Girl
in Hospital: *April Bryan;* 2nd Girl
in Hospital: *Dannielle Cook;*
Uncle Tommy/Accordionist: *Bernie
Nolan;* Andolini/Doctor Strelitz:
David Zalud; Policeman: *Rob
Watkin;* Altar Boy: *David Watkin;*
Dancers/Ensemble: *David
McGrouther* (Dance Captain),
*Leroy Law, Julie Alltree, Deborah
Elliott, Vicky Faithful, Jenni
Nolan, Emma Williams, Nicki
Willis;* Children: *Kerry Byrne,
Hanna Bywater, Rosie Clark,
Miriam Conroy, Natalie Edwards,
Naomi Etchels, Jenny Gawley,
Francesca Gibson, Amy Greaves,
Hayley Kelly, Katrina MacDonald,
Gillian Nolan, Claire Russell,*

Rachel Ryan, Lisa Stelfox. Director: *John Bryan*; Producers: *Tony Bryan, Maureen Ann Bryan, John Bryan*; Assistant Director: *James T Mawdsley*; Music: *John Bryan*; Vocal Coach: *Amanda*; Original Choreography: *Diane O'Neill*; Choreographer: *David McGrouther*; Children's Choreographer: *Jenni Nolan*; Stage Manager: *Lisa Davies*; Deputy Stage Manager/Properties Master: *Tony McCarthy*; Assistant Stage Managers: *Kris Kross, Stuart Flemming*; Design: *Jocelyn Meall*; Set Construction: *Mark Scott, Gary Hesketh, George Smith, Ralph Davod, Jayne Bell*; Lighting: *Mark Richards*; Wardrobe Mistress/Costumes: *"Amanda" Designs*; Wardrobe Assistants: *Joanna Louise, Laura Mansell*; Wig Mistress: *Vincenza Miele-Brown*; Production Manager/Company Manager: *Mu Ali*. **Press: OC:** 10&14/12/93

770. ALADDIN; BIG RED HEN PRODUCTION HOUSE; *24 December 1993 - 22 January 1994.* Aladdin: *Simone Robertson*; Wishee Washee: *Andi Peters*, alternating with *Toby Anstis*; Slave of the Lamp: *Treva Etienne*; Widow Twankee: *Gordon Peters*; Emperor: *Les Want*; Abanazar: *Chris Hennen*; So Shy: *Bonnie Hassell*; Princess Balroubadour: *Stella Czerniawskyi*; Pekin Police: *John & Jim Lavelle*; Also: *Stutz Bear Cats, Nellie the Elephant.* Director & Lighting: *John Redgrave*; Choreographer: *Josie Ashcroft.* **Press: CL:** 12/1/94; **MEN:** 23&29/12/93

696. SNOW WHITE AND THE SEVEN DWARFS; *14-16*

February & 4 June 1994.

771. PINOCCHIO; PRESTO PUPPET THEATRE; *17-18 February 1994.*

772. BOUNCERS by John Godber; HULL TRUCK THEATRE; *22-26 February 1994.* Director: *Damian Cruden*; Design: *Robert Jones*; Lighting: *George Morris.*

773. HIGH SOCIETY; Music and Lyrics by Cole Porter; Book by Richard Eyre, based on the play *The Philadelphia Story* by Philip Barry; ASHTON-UNDER-LYNE OPERATIC SOCIETY; *14-19 March 1994.* Mike: *John Rawson*; Dexter: *Bill Nicholson*; Liz: *Pat Battle*; Tracy: *Julie Colson*; Also: *Ann Atkins, Adele Buckley, Malcolm Parker.* Producer: *Nita Bennett*; Choreographer: *Lyn Jones*; Musical Director: *Andrew White*; Chorus Numbers Set: *Kay Lilley.* **Press: AR:** 28/10/93, 10 & 17/3/94; **OC:** 15&22/3/94; **SR:** 6/1/94;

774. UP THE BLUE STALK: THEATRE ROYAL HANLEY; *21-26 March 1994.* Cast: *George Roper, David Darby*, Fairy: *Sarah Davidson, Nigel Peever, Obsession, Tartlettes*, Singer: *Aubrey Phillips.* Director: *Simon Ellingham*; Choreographer: *John Cumberlidge.* **Press: MEN:** 22/3/94; **OC:** 23/3/94

695. TALES FROM THE JUNGLE BOOK; BARRIE STACEY PRODUCTIONS, PAN PUPPETS; *27 March 1994.*

775. OLDE TIME MUSIC HALL; *5 April 1994.* Presenter: *Aubrey Phillips;* George Forby/Al Jolson: *Steve King;* Mrs Shufflewick/Jack Pleasance: *Johnny Dallas;* The Great Levant: *David Paul;* Danny La Rue/Judy Garland: *David D'Arby;* + The Gaiety Girls.

776. POSTMAN PAT'S ADVENTURES by Charles Savage, from the stories of Joihn Cunliffe and the television series by Ivor Wood; Music and Lyrics by Bryan Daly; POSTMAN PAT PRODUCTIONS; *24-28 May 1994.* Director: *Charles Savage;* Costumes and Design: *Carol Foot;* Lighting: *Lawrence T Doyle.*
Press: AR: 19/5/94

777. THE WIZ; Book by William F Brown; Music and lyrics by Charlie Smalls and Luther Vandross; NORTHERN KIDS; *27 -30 July 1994.* Aunt Em: *Catherine Hill;* Dorothy: *Jenny Gawley;* Uncle HenryL *Richard Holden;* Addaperle: *Anna Jerram;* Scarecrow: *Simon Topley;* Tin Man: *Jon Clay;* Lion: *Dominic Stannage;* Gatekeeper: *Richard Holden;* The Wiz: *David Bowman;* Evilene: *Deborah Torr;* Lord High Underling: *Darren Stannage;* Messenger: *Matthew Watton;* Monkey: *Andrew Moss;* Glinda: *Jenny Spence;* Chief Mouse: *Adam Wilson;* 1st Munchkin: *Krystal Brown;* 2nd: *Carly Jones;* 3rd Munchkin: *Laura Evans;* 4th Munchkin: *Hazel Swan;* 5th Munchkin: *Tiffany Robinson;* 6th Munchkin: *Dawn Wrigley;* Other Munchkins: *Ryan Badderley, Kate Bailey, Nicola Bevington, Stephanie Brotherton, Caroline Brotherton, Dean Butler, Salauddin Chowdhury, Mahuiddin Chowdhury, Tina Deakin, Lauren Earith, Jane Earith, Hayley Eddlestone, Catherine Etchells, Kelly Fitzpatrick, Sarah Flanaghan, Sarah Gregory, Keighly Harding, Amanda Hennis, Katrina Ingham, Teena Jackson, Emily Lang, Hannah Lang, Rebecca McDermot, Karis McIntyre, Kieran McIntyre, Natalie Meadows, Claire Mehan, James Moorhouse, Carly Murphy, Sophie Poulson, Jennifer Riley, Danielle Roberts, Heather Robertshaw, Kay Slater, Becky Spence, Leanne Spencer, Karl Smith, Jamie Sumner, Sarah Thorpe, Dominic Tryczynski, Nicholas Ward, Michael Ward, James White, Adam White, Paul Willocks, Rebecca Willocks, Adam Wilson, Mark Young;* The Mice Squad: *Ryan Badderley, Dean Butler, Salauddin Chowdhury, Mahuiddin, James Moorehouse, Kieran McIntyre, Dominic Tryczynski, James White, Adam White, Paul Willocks, Mark Young;* Tornado/Addaperles Spirits: *Lauren Brown, Rachel Burton, Grace Burton, Carla Day, Sam draper, Sara Gould, Emma Gould, Emma Jodrell, Andrew Jodrell, Ben Ledwich, Emma Lomas, Jodie Lomas, Sam Maxwell, Adam Musson, Rebecca Christian, Suzanne Oates, Christine Pridding, Charlotte Payce-Drury, Shelley Phillips, Siane Phillips, Lauren Phillips, Rachel Stanton, Katy Sherwood, Lauren Veevens, Kirsty Wilson, Morgan West, Toni Walker, Ami Worrall, Becky West, Arrianne Winslow, Erin Winslow, Tina Wilks;* The Yellow Brick Road: *Nicola Bailey, Amy Bigwood, Kerry Clarke, Sian*

Deakin, Joanne Evans, Diane
Evans, Kerrie Fish, Katheryn
Holden, Kimberley Hibbert, Kelly
Hay, Ruth Hodgsonm Hannah
Hodgson, Natalie Hibbert, Louise
Kenworthy, Jane Lyons, Sarah
Lennox, Corrin Orm, Louise
O'Reilley, Louise Platt, Emma
Parker, Lise Spencer, Rachel
Sutton, Lucy Travis, Anna
Turner, Abby Wright, Michelle
Wilkinson; Kalidahs/Monkeys:
Philip Brown, Daniel Bigwood,
Eve Dugdale, Adam Evans, Emma
Forshaw, Matthew Hutchinson,
John Harrison, Gerard Jackson,
Neil Kvasnik, Andrew Moss, Lisa
Nathaniel, Lyndsey Nathaniel,
Melissa Poulson, Danielle Smith,
Simon Schofield, Oliver Watton,
Matthew Whitworth; Crows/Slaves
/Citizens/Escorts: Martin
Beddows, Steven Bickley, Richard
Holden, Darren Stannage, Oliver
Watton, Matthew Watton; Poppies
/Citizens/Slaves: Carolyn Bowler,
Louise Coffee, Julia Cooper,
Emma Dearn, Sara Davis, Lisa
Duncan, Abigale Emery, Tara
Hooley, Rachel Harrison,
Catherine Hill, Tatum Lane, Sam
Oldale, Kerry Oakford, EMMa
PErry, Annette Platt, Julie
Powell, Gemma Richardson, Adele
Sherlock, Caroline Young.
Director: Mike Day; Musical
Director: Colin Ward;
Choreographer: Angie Draper;
Keyboards/Guitar: Mike Gresty;
Company Choreographer: Lesley
Buckley; Tutors: Jackie Baddley,
Debolrah Bennet, Pete Curran,
Mike Day, Christine Evans,
Hayley Gibson, Emma Perry, Ann
Platt, James Stannage, Shirley
Watton; Junior Dance Tuitors:
Rachel Harrison, Annette platt,
Adele Sherlock; Stage Manager:
Deborah Bennett; Assistant Stage
Manager: Pete Barber; Deputy

Stage Manager: Jane Jones;
Stage Crew: David Platt, Brian
Hill, Alan Young, Andrew Bates,
Martin Bates; Make-up: Colin
Ward, Jane Parker; Properties
Manager: Sam Jones; Assistant
Properties Manager: Peter
Edwards; Wardrobe Supervisor:
Jean Powell; Costumes: Thelma
Gibson + Parents; Back Stage
Supervisor: Pete Curran; Assistant
Back Stage Supervisors: Jenny
Curran, Ann Platt, Jenny Rogan.
Press: AR: 4/8/94

**778. AN EVENING WITH
GARY LINEKER** by Arthur Smith
and Chris England; MAVERICK
THEATRE COMPANY: 22-27
August 1994. Ian: Paul Brady;
Birgitta: Sarah Hague; Dan: John
Marquez; Bill: Andrew Pasqual;
Monica: Donna Stapleton.
Director: Marcus Goodwin;
Producer: Nick Hennegan; Sound:
Robb Williams; Lighting: Tom
Popley; Design: David Palser.
Press: MEN: 23/8/94; OC:
23/8/94; P: July/August 1994

**779. OLD MOTHER RILEY'S
MUSIC HALL;** 7 September
1994. Peter Lindup, Barbara
Ray, Betzee Clewlow. Musical
Director: Colin Hilton.

**780. RITA, SUE AND BOB
TOO** by Andea Dunbar; FLYING
GEESE PRODUCTIONS; 12-17
September 1994. Sue: Lisa
Marie Allen; Rita: Sherry
Ormerod; Bob: James Healy;
Michelle: Amanda Whitehead;
Mum: Sylvia Gatril; Dad: Andy
Abraham. Producer/Director: Jeff
Longmore.
Press: MEN: 13/9/94; OC:
26/8/94, 2&13/9/94; RO:
17/9/94

411

781. PINOCCHIO; BARRIE
STACEY PRODUCTIONS; 2
October 1994

782. THE HISTORY OF
AMERICA (Abridged) by THE
REDUCED SHAKESPEARE
COMPANY; 10 October 1994

404. FEVER PITCH by Nick
Hornby; 11 October 1994.
Nick Hornby: Steve North.
Director: Paul Hodson.
Press: CL: 5/10/94; S:
16/6/94

790. 42nd STREET; Music by
Harry Warren, Lyrics by Al
Dubin, Book by Michael Stewart
and Mark Bramble; DUKINFIELD
AMATEUR OPERATIC AND
DRAMATIC SOCIETY; 17-22
October 1994. Director:
Melvyn Bates; Choreographer:
Jean Ashworth; Musical Director:
Paul Firth; Associate Musical
Director: Roy Brook.

783. THE LORD OF THE
RINGS by J R R Tolkien,
adapted for the stage by
THÉÂTRE SANS FIL, THE SAUL
ZAENTZ COMPANY; 25-30
October 1994. Director &
Puppet Master: André Viens.
Press: CL: 19/10/94; MEN:
5/10/94

789. BILLY BRADSHAW'S
STRANGER DANGER SHOW;
GREATER MANCHESTER
POLICE; 3 November 1994.

784. THE GOOD OLDE
DAYS; DUGGIE CHAPMAN
ASSOCIATES; 9 November

1994. Chairman: Duggie
Chapman; Star: Danny La Rue.

785. A CHRISTMAS CAROL
from Charles Dickens; 11-12
November 1994. Scrooge: Dave
Peters.

786. SOOTY'S WILD WEST
SHOW; VINCENT SHAW
ASSOCIATES; 15-19 November
1994. Presented by Matthew
Corbett, Connie Creighton.

787. UNDERNEATH THE
ARCHES by Patrick Garland,
Brian Glanville and Roy Hudd, in
association with Chesney Allen;
22-23 November 1994.

360. teechers by John Godber;
HULL TRUCK THEATRE
COMPANY; 5-10 December
1994.

788. CINDERELLA 16
December 1994 - 15 January
1995.

TRAFFORD

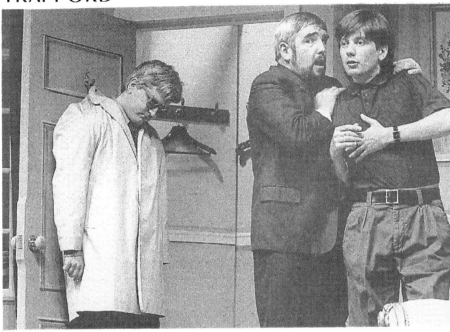

In the varied programme of the ALTRINCHAM GARRICK, pure farce is always a regular feature. Here, in OUT OF ORDER's bedroom with too many doors, STEVE WILLIAMSON's Right Honourable Member (centre) not only has to cope with the arrival of his seductee's husband (MARK JEPHCOTT) but the constant re-appearance of The Body (NICK EASTHAM). (809)

ALTRINCHAM GARRICK,
Barrington Road, WA14 1HZ; 061-928 1677.
AZ: 79,D3; XAZ: 125,F5. H

800. DANGEROUS OBSESSION by N J Crisp; ALTRINCHAM GARRICK; *25-30 October 1993.*

801. THE PYJAMA GAME; Book by George Abbott and Richard Bissell, Music and Lyrics by Richard Adler and Jerry Ross; TRAFFORD MARGARETIANS; *8-13 November 1993.*

802. SIDE-BY-SIDE-BY-SONDHEIM; ALTRINCHAM GARRICK; *15-20 November 1993, 17-22 October 1994.*

413

816. PLAZA SUITE by Neil Simon; ALTRINCHAM GARRICK; 22-27 November 1993.

803. ALADDIN by Derrick Kay; ALTRINCHAM GARRICK; 17 December 1993 - 3 January 1994. Aladdin: *Linda Townson;* Princess Jade: *Trish Francis;* Princess Jade: *Trish Francis;* Widow Twankey: *Brian Howlett;* Ab-Anana: *Don Poole;* Wishee-Washee: *John Keen;* Mee-ow: *Di Davies;* Pong: *BRianm Stoner;* Ping: *Andrew Cleal;* Abdul: *Tom Thistleton;* Opal: *Cathy Lawrence;* Slave of the Ring: *Janet Slade;* The Emperor: *Frank Boylan;* So-So: *Nick Eastham;* Adult Chorus: *Becky Haden, Joanna Bridge Water, Zoë Davies, Kate Warwick, Nick Eastham, Eric Vogel, Andy Davies;* Children's Chorus: *Emma Sails, Rachel Smith, Anna Metcalfe, Gemma Bookbinder, Anna Pylypczuck, Mandy Forest, Lydia Coulthard, Angela Grayson, Mathew Connell, Damian Zuk, Mark Wagstaff, Adam Ferina, John Woodcock, Rosie Moylan.* Director: *Celia Bonner;* Musical Director: *Robin Coulthard;* Choreographer: *Janet Slade;* Design: *Margaret Norris;* Stage Manager: *Phil Rawlins;* Deputy Stage Manager: *Steve Butler;* Chief Assistant Stage Manager: *John Newton;* Lighting: *Robin Watkinson;* Sound: *Dave Healy, Janine Shaw;* Wardrobe: *Mike Shaw, Pam Hunt, Noel Watson, Pam Nolan;* Properties: *John Newton, Marion Eaves;* Workshop: *Kevin Pearce, Ken Currah;* Set Construction: *Steve Butler, Mike Rawlins, Julia Leach, Jeff Butler, Ann Rawlins, Phill Rawlins, Steve, Trevor;* Stage Crew:

Steve, Drew, Julia Leach, Joanna Bridgwater, David, April, Trevor, Mark, Matt, Jeff Butler, Steve; Scenic Artist: *Margaret Norris;* MUSICIANS: Violin: *Rachel Coulthard, Jim Flattery, Robin Gill, Paul Morris.*

804. BLUE REMEBERED HILLS by Dennis Potter; ALTRINCHAM GARRICK; 7-12 February 1994. Angela: *Pam Nolan;* Audrey: *Val Watkinson;* Peter: *Barry Spencer;* Willie: *Neville Roby;* Raymond: *Stuart Harrison;* Donald Duck: *Gary Collins;* John: *Steve Williamson.* Director: *Helen Parry;* Design: *Steve Bradshaw;* Stage Manager: *Mark Wetherill;* Deputy Stage Manager: *Julia Leach;* Prompt: *Ros Greenwood;* Lighting: *Geoff Scullard;* Sound: *Janine Ruth;* Properties: *John Newton;* Workshop: *Kevin Pearce, Ken Currah;* Set Construction: *Steve Butler, Mike Rawlins, Jeff Butler, Ann Rawlins,* Scenic Artist: *Margaret Norris.* Press: SAM: 10/3/94

805. MOVE OVER, MRS MARKHAM by Ray Cooney and John Chapman; ALTRINCHAM GARRICK; 7-12 March 1994. Joanna Markham: *Angie Wetherill;* Alistait Spenlow: *Andy Cleal;* Sylvie: *Trish Francis;* Linda Lodge: *Janet Sladel;* Philip Markham: *Hugh Everett;* Henry Lodge: *James O'Gara;* Walter Pangbourne: *Mark Edgar;* Olive Harriet Smythe: *Stella Sails;* Miss Wilkinson: *Joannna Bridgewater;* Director: *Rita Howard;* Design: *Peter Coatman;* Stage Manager: *Dave Healy;* Assistant Stage Managers: *John Newton , Marion Eaves;* Prompt: *Brian Stoner;*

Lighting: *Nick Weetman;* Sound: *Chris Wetherill;* Properties: *John Newton;* Workshop: *Kevin Pearce, Ken Currah;* Scenic Artist: *Margaret Norris*
Press: SAM: 24/3/94

806. THE STUDENT PRINCE; Book and Lyrics by Dorothy Dinnelly, Music by Sigmund Romberg; TRAFFORD MARGARETIANS; *18-23 April 1994.*

807. WOMAN IN MIND by Alan Ayckbourn; ALTRINCHAM GARRICK; *2-7 May 1994.* Susan: *Maureen Casket;* Bill: *Michael O'Hara;* Gerald: *Hugh Wolfson;* Muriel: *Maureen Peacock;* Rick: *Andrew Cleal;* Andy: *Robin Wheeler;* Tony: *MArk James Edgar;* Lucy: *Ros Greenwood.* Director: *Alison Benefield;* Design: *Magaret Norris;* Stage Manager: *Mike North;* Deputy Stage Manager: *Irene North;* Assistant Stage Managers: *Melissa Naylor, Susan Stringer;* Lighting: *Robin Watkinson;* Sound: *Richard Honeyman;* Properties: *John Newton, Marion Eaves;* Workshop: *Kevin Pearce, Ken Currah;* Set Construction: *Ste Butler, Phill Rawlins, Jeff Butler, Ann Rawlins, Mike Rawlins, Bill Norris, Mike North;* Scenic Artist: *Margaret Norris*

808. A FUNNY THING HAPPENED ON THE WAY TO THE FORUM by Bert Shevelope and Larry Gelbart; ALTRINCHAM GARRICK; *23-28 May 1994.* Pseudolus: *Terry Chandler;* Senex: *Geoff Noar;* Domina: *Val Lynch;* Hero: *David Beddy;* Hystirium: *NEv Roby;* Erronius: *Peter Howe;*

Lycus: *Derek Cleal;* Phylia: *Jill Chamberlain;* Miles Gloriosus: *Dick Sails;* Gemini: *Di Davies, Cathy Lawrence;* Vibrata: *julie Hanson;* Gymnasia: *Many Flude;* Tintinabula: *Anne-Marie Davies;* Panacea: *Beverley Buxton;* Proteans: *Gary Collins, Barry Spencer, Derek Stuart-Cole.* Director: *Diana Harker;* Design: *Steve Bradshaw, Phill Rawlins;* Musical Director: *Robin Coulthard;* Choreograpoher: *Mandt Flude;* Stage Manager: *Phill Rawlins;* Deputy Stage Manager: *Ste Butler;* Assistant Stage Managers: *John Newton, Carol Gibson;* Prompt: *Pamela Knox;* Lighting: *Alan Morgan;* Sound: *Kevin Heap;* Wardrobe: *Mike Shaw, Noel Watson, Pam Hunt, Pam Nolan;* Properties: *John Newton, Marion Eaves;* Workshop: *Kevin Pearce, Ken Currah;* Set Construction: *Ste Butler, Phill Rawlins, Jeff Butler, Ann Rawlins, Mike Rawlins, Bill Norris, Mike North;* Scenic Artist: *Margaret Norris.* MUSICIANS: Keyboard: *Paul Fletcher;* Bass Guitar: *Tony Anderson;* Percussion: *Andrew Bold.*

815. THE CARETAKER by Harold Pinter; MALAPROP THEATRE; *24-25 June 1994.* Director: *Geoff Holman.*

809. OUT OF ORDER by ray Cooney; ALTRINCHAM GARRICK; *5-10 September 1994.* Richard Willey MP: *Steve Williamson;* George Pigden: *Mike Shaw;* Jane Worthington: *Anne-Marie Davies;* A Body: *Mark Jephcott;* The Waiter: *Bill Platt;* Pamela Willey: *Sonia Dykstra;* The Manager: *Mark James Edgar;* Ronnie Worthington: *Nick Eastham;*

Gladys: *Tina Chester.* Director: *Rita Howard;* Design: *Peter Coatman;* Stage Manager: *Noel Bowes;* Deputy Stage Manager: *Peter Coatman;* Assistant Stage Managers: *John Newton, Marion Eaves;* Lighting: *Andrew McIntee, Rob Gill;* Sound: *James Townson;* Properties: *John Newton, Marion Eaves;* Workshop: *Kevin Pearce, Ken Currah, John Stockwell;* Set Construction: *Ste Butler, Noel Bowes, Bill Norris, Ken Currah, Peter Coatman, Jeff Butler, Brian, Phil, Steve;* Scenic Artist: *Margaret Norris*

810. THE SECRET RAPTURE by David Hare; ALTRINCHAM GARRICK; *19-24 September 1994.* Isobel Glass: *Celia Bonner;* Marion French: *Carol Carr;* Tom French: *Dick Sails;* Katherine Glass: *Hazel Earnshaw;* Charles Cook: *Irwin Posner;* Rhonda Milne: *Di Davis.* Director: *Helen Parry;* Design: *Mike Stocks;* Stage Manager: *Jeff Butler;* Deputy Stage Manager: *Ann Rawlins;* Assistant Stage Manager: *John Keen;* Lighting: *Geoff Scullard;* Sound: *Steve Cox;* Properties: *John Newton, Marion Eaves;* Workshop: *Kevin Pearce, Ken Currah;* Set Construction: *Ste Butler, Brian Stoner, Phill Rawlins, Jeff Butler, Mike Rawlins, Mike North, Irene North, Graham Simmonds, Matt Wetherill;* Stage Crew: *Brian Stoner, Graham Simmonds, Mike North, Irene North, Matt Wetherill, Eric Vogel, Steve Williamson, Mike Rawlins, Peter Lawless, Nick Weetman;* Scenic Artist: *Margaret Norris*

811. FINIAN'S RAINBOW; Book by E Y Harburg and Fred

Saidy; Lyrics by E Y Harburg; Music by Burton Lane; SALE OPERATIC SOCIETY; *3-8 October 1994.*

812. THE WINSLOW BOW by Terence Rattigan; ALTRINCHAM GARRICK; *31 October - 5 November 1994.* Director: *Val Lynch.*

813. AN EVENING WITH GARY LINEKER by Arthur Smith and Chris England; ALTRINCHAM GARRICK; *28 November - 3 December 1994.* Director: *Alan Rothwell.*

814. HUMPTY DUMPTY by Roland Peake; *15-30 December 1994.*

ALTRINCHAM ICE RINK, Devonshire Road, WA14 4EZ; 061-928 1360, 061-926 8549. AZ: 79, 3D; XAZ: 125,F5.

CLUB THEATRE, 17 Oxford Road, ALTRINCHAM, WA14 2ED; 061-928 3542; AZ: 79,4D; XAZ: 137, F2.

798. AN INSPECTOR CALLS by J B Priestley; *9-12 March 1994.* Sybil Birling: *Janet Reidsma;* Sheila Birling: *Rachel Tucker;* Gerald Birling: *Richard Ellis;* Eric Croft: *Duncan Walker.* Director: *Garth Jones.*

799. THE CRUCIBLE by

Arthur Miller; *18-23 April 1994.*

DUNHAM MASSEY, WA14 4SJ. 061-941 1025. AZ: 88, A1; XAZ: 136,A2.

796. THE MAJESTIC MOAT WITH TWINKLING STARS; CHOL THEATRE, pa-BOOM PHENOMENAL FIREWORKS, BASHIR MAKHOUL, LOSTOCK HIGH SCHOOL, STRETFORD HIGH SCHOOL, DEWBURY COLLEGE, OLD TRAFFORD COMMUNITY GROUPS; *11-12 June 1994.*

97. THE WONDERLAND ADVENTURES OF ALICE, adapted from Lewis Carroll by Simon Corble; LIBRARY THEATRE COMPANY with MIDSOMMER ACTORS; *21 June - 2 July 1994.*

207. THE TEMPEST by William Shakespeare, adapted ODDSOCKS PRODUCTIONS; *11-14 August 1994.* Antonio/Caliban: *Andy Barrow;* Sebastian/Trinculo: *Simon Bridge;* Alonzo/Stephano: *David Hudson;* Ferdinand: *Russell Layton;* Miranda: *Elli MacKenzie;* Prospero: *Barry Shannon;* Ariel: *Nina Sosanya.* All aspects of production, including direction, "a team effort" but including: Script Adaption and Direction Co-ordinator: *Andy Barrow;* Company Manager: *Elli MacKenzie;* Stage Management Co-ordinator, Ship Construction: *Nick Palmer;* Musical Co-ordinator, Arrangement and Composition: *Barry Shannon;*

Choreography: *Nina Sosanya;* Costumes: *Julie Connolly and the Company;* Caliban's Costume: *Peter Kenny.*
Journal: 12/8/94
Press: CL: 10/8/94; MEN: 12/8/94

797. THE DUNHAM MANTICORE FOLLIES by Tony Lewery, DODGY CLUTCH THEATRE COMPANIES and numerous local artists, sculptors and performers; *3-4 September 1994.*

SALE CIVIC THEATRE, Tatton Road, M3 1EB; 061-980 8387, 061-962 2290; AZ: 70,A3; XAZ: B4.

793. 5 'n' 9; caberet by SALE NOMADS; *9-14 May 1994*

STRETFORD HIGH SCHOOL; 061- 876 4734.

TIMPERLEY CONGRERATIONAL CHURCH.

794. DRAMATHON '94; NUMEROUS COMPANIES; *24 continuous hours, 8-9 July 1994.*

TRAFFORD WHARF; MS FITZCARRALDO.

815. WATERWAY; WALK THE

PLANK; *20-25 June 1994.*
Press: MM: 9/9/94

**URMSTON LEISURE
CENTRE,** Bowfell Road
M41 5RR; 061-746
8443; **AZ:** 56, B3; **XAZ:**
96, 5C. **G, W**

795. THE CHALLENGE;
DYNAMO THEATRE; *7 May
1994.*

418

WIGAN

From TYLDESLEY LITTLE THEATRE's lively season: their production of
C P TAYLOR's AND A NIGHTINGALE SANG: (left to right) LYNN
SCOTT: The Babe in the Wood (sitting), DAVID HADCROFT: The
Tailor's Dummy, GAIL CRAVEN: The Cripplel, FRANK BOWDLER: The
Old Soldier (sitting), TONY THOMPSON: The Coalman, IAN TAYLOR:
The Lost Boy; WINNIE BEATTIE: The Saint. (822)

HAIGH HALL, Haigh, WN2
1PE;

97. THE WONDERLAND
ADVENTURES OF ALICE,
adapted from Lewis Carroll by
Simon Corble; LIBRARY
THEATRE COMPANY with
MIDSOMMER ACTORS; 21 June
- 2 July 1994.

LEIGH BEDFORD HIGH
SCHOOL, Market Street,
WN7 1DS; 0942 608471;

298. SHAKESPEARE'S
GREATEST HITS; MANCHESTER
ACTORS COMPANY; 21 January
1994

LEIGH DRAMA CENTRE,
Railway Road, WN7 4AH;
0942 605258.

PARK TEACHERS
CENTRE, Park Road,
HINDLEY WN2 3RX

419

651. HERO by Neil Duffield;
M6 THEATRE COMPANY; *3
October 1994.*

**PEMBERTON
COMMUNITY HIGH
SCHOOL;** Montrose
Avenue, WIGAN WN5
9XL; **0942 212507.**

TURNPIKE CENTRE, Leigh
Library, Civic Square,
LEIGH, WN7.

**TYLDESLEY LITTLE
THEATRE,** Lemon Street,
TYLDESLEY, M29 EHT;
0942 897149.

818. SPRING AND PORT
WINE by Bill Naughton; *27
September – 2 October 1993.*
Daisy Crompton: *Jenny Orman;*
Florence Crompton: *Karen
Seddon;* Betsy Jane: *Winnie
Beatty;* Wilfred Crompton: *Eamon
Doherty;* Harold Crompton: *Ian
Taylor;* Hilda Crompton:
Samantha Williams; Rafe
Crompton: *Jeff Stott;* Arthur:
David Hadcroft. Director:
Margaret Speakes; Stage
Manager: *Wallace Taylor;* Props:
Winnie Evans; Make-up:
Samantha Williams; Lighting: *Phil
Peacock;* Sound: *Craig Anderson.*

819. MOTHER GOOSE by
John Morley; *2-11 December
1993.* Mother Goose: *Frank
Bowdler;* Jack: *Gail Craven;* Silly
Billy: *David Hadcroft;* Sir Jasper
Moneybags: *Brian Hadcroft;* Jill:

Kim McArdle; Mangle Wurzle: *Ian
Taylor;* Hayseed: *Shauna Doherty;*
Duke of Dartmore: *Tony
Thompson;* Duchess of Dartmoor:
Margaret Speakes; Priscilla:
Louise Graham; Fairy Happiness:
Elaine Lomax; Devil Discontent:
Winnie Evans; King of Gooseland:
Mike Jeffries; Stephanie
Strongbow: *Winnie Beattie;*
Chorus: *Kirstine Anderson, Lesley
Clarkson, Lindsey Davies, Karen
Dean, Danielle Henry, Gemma
Higson, Suzanne Horrocks,
Andrew Houghton, Michael Roach,
Hannah Seddon, Catherine Smith,
David Stott, Dawn Stringer,
Natalie Todd, Elizabeth
Worthington.* Director: *Pam
Hadcroft;* Stage Managers:
Wallace Taylor, Jenny Orman;
Continuity: *Winnie Beattie;*
Lighting Design: *Phil Peacock;*
Lighting Operation: *Phil Peacock,
Paul Whur;* Sound: *Craig
Anderson;* Wardrobe Mistress:
Dilys Bromilow; Wardrobe
Assistants: *Barbara Worthington,
Hilda Taylor, Hilda Todd;* Make-
up: *Colin Grime, Catherine Jones,
Donna Park, Hannah Seddon;*
Dance: *Sandra Robinson, Karren
Morris;* Set Construction: *Glyn
Morris, Ron Griffiths, Ron Hayes;*
Set Decoration: *Bill Darlington,
Frank Bowdler.*

820. THE HOUSE BY THE
LAKE by Hugh Mills; *12-19
February 1994.* Janet Holt:
Linda Davies; Maurice Holt: *Alan
Hewitt;* Colonel Forbes: *Jeff
Stott;* Stella Holt: *Margaret
Speakes;* Brenda: *Karen Morris;*
Colin Holt: *Ian Taylor;* Iris Holt:
Elaine Lomax; Mr Howard: *Ian
Hunter;* Nurse Thomson: *Sandra
Robinson.* Director: *Mike
Jeffries;* Stage Manager: *Wallace*

Taylor; Continuity: *Winnie Evans;* Make-up: *Samantha Williams;* Lighting Design: *Phil Peacock;* Lighting Operation: *Phil Peacock, Paul Whur;* Sound Operation: *Craig Anderson;* Sound Origination: *Paul Whur;* Wardrobe: *Winnie Evans et al;* Set Constrction: *John Hayes, Ron Griffiths, Glyn Morris;* Set Decoration: *Bill Darlington;* Make-up: *Hannah Seddon, Lindsay Davies.* **Press: BEN:** 18/1/94, 8&15/2/94.

822. AND A NIGHTINGALE SANG by C P Taylor; *12-16 April 1994.* Helen Stott: *Gail Craven;* Joyce Stott: *Lynn Scott;* George: *Tony Thompson;* Peggy: *Winnie Beatty;* Andie: *Frank Bowdler;* Eric: *Ian Taylor;* Norman: *David Hadcroft.* Director: *Pam Hadcroft;* Stage Manager: *Wallace Taylor;* Continuity: *Jenny Orman;* Properties: *Jean Johnson;* Make-up: *Colin Grime, Hannah Seddon;* Lighting Design: *Phil Peacock;* Lighting Operation: *Phil Peacock, Sound Operation: Craig Anderson;* Sound Origination: *Paul Whur;* Wardrobe: *Winnie Evans;* Set Constrction: *John Hayes, Ron Griffiths, Glyn Morris;* Set Decoration: *Bill Darlington;* Set Dressing: *Margaret Speakes.* **Press: BEN:** 1/3/94

823. STAGS AND HENS by Willy Russell; *28 May - 4 June 1994.* Bernadette: *Jean Johnson;* Carol: *Sarah Seddon;* Linda: *JO Boyle;* Maureen: *Lesley Clarkson;* Frances: *Karen Dean;* Robbie: *Ian Taylor;* Kav: *Mark Farnworth;* Billy: *Paul Morton;* Eddy: *David Hadcroft;* Peter: *Craig Walker;*

Roadie: *John Heyes;* Dave: *Paul Ward.* Directors: *Ian Taylor, David Hadcroft;* Stage Manager: *Jenny Orman;* Continuity: *Winnie Beatty;* Assistant Stage Manager: *Wallace Taylor;* Make-up: *Colin Grime, Hannah Seddon;* Lighting *Phil Peacock;* Sound Operation: *Craig Anderson;* Sound Origination: *Paul Whur;* Set Constrction: *John Heyes, Ron Griffiths, Glyn Morris;* Set Decoration: *Bill Darlington.*

821. OUR DAY OUT by Willy Russell; *12-13 August 1994.* Cast: *Natalie Allison, Emma Darbyshire, Gareth Davies, Lindsey Davies, Nicola Dean, Shauna Doherty, Michelle Ellis, Mark Farnworth, Louise Graham, Debbie Green, Jennifer Harris, Linzi Helps, John Hodson, Laura Hodson, Karen Morris, Sarah Morris, Hannah Seddon, Dawn Stringer, Siobhan Wallwork, Daniel Ward, Paul Ward, Elizabeth Worthington, Reanne Worthington.* Director: *David Hadcroft;* Stage Manager: *Jenny Orman;* Continuity: *Jenny Orman;* Sound Operation: *Craig Anderson;* Sound Origination: *Paul Whur;* Set Constrction: *John Heyes, Ron Griffiths, Glyn Morris;* Set Decoration: *Bill Darlington*

824. CAT AMONG THE PIGEONS by Duncan Greenwood; *4-8 October 1994.* Ernest Jowett: *David Hadcroft;* Edna Jowett: *Ingrid Folkard-Evans;* Alfred Tinsley: *Tony Thompson;* Grandma: *Eileen McArdle;* Nora Tinsley: *Margaret Speakes;* Joe Hammant: *Jeff Stott;* Annie Hammant: *Lesley Clarkson;* Bill Tinsley: *Paul Morton;* Yvonne Chartreuse: *Karen Seddon.*

421

Director: *Ian Taylor;* Stage
Manager: *Jenny Orman;*
Continuity, Properties, Costumes:
Winnie Beatty; Lighting: *Phil
Peacock;* Sound Operation: *Craig
Anderson;* Sound Origination: *Paul
Whur;* Set Constrction: *John
Heyes, Phil Peacock,Ron
Griffiths, Glyn Morris
;* Set Decoration: *Bill Darlington;*
Make-up: *Samantha Williams,
Hannah Seddon.*

825. ALADDIN; *1-10
December 1994.*

WIGAN LITTLE THEATRE;
0942 42561.

826. WHEN WE ARE
MARRIED by J B Priestley; *23
February - 5 March 1994.*
Ruby Birtle: *Leslie Kellet;* Gerald
Forbes: *Ken Talbot;* Mrs
Northrop: *Jenny West;* Nancy
Holmes: *Wendy Walker;* Fred
Dyson: *Paul Griffiths;* Henry
Ormondroyd: *John Churnside;*
Alderman Joseph Helliwell: *Jim
Stirrup;* Maria Helliwell: *Rita
Benson;* Councillor Albert Parker:
Chris Norris; Henry Soppit: *Colin
Magenty;* Clara Soppit: *Margaret
Finch;* Annie Parker: *Margaret
Kinley;* Lottie Grady: *Debbie
Norris;* Rev Clement Mercer:
Stanley Hollywell. Director:
Clive Green; Stage Manager:
Brian Marsh; Set Design: *Clive
Green;* Set Painting: *Elizabeth
Dodd;* Set Construction: *Bill
Marsh, Bill Mayers et al;* Sound
and Lighting: *Andrew Everett,
Chris Wilcock et al;* Properties:
Jackie Skelhorn, Christine Seddon;
Wardrobe: *Pat Wilson, Clive
Green.*

827. CABARET by John
Kander and Fred Ebb; *6-16
April.*

828. KISS ME KATE; Music
and Lyrics by Cole Porter; Book
by Sam and Stella Spewack;
HINDLEY AND WIGAN
OPERATIC SOCIETY; *25-30
April 1994.*

829. THE ODD COUPLE by
Neil Simon; *May 1994.*

830. LORD ARTHUR SAVILE'S
CRIME by Constance Cox, out
of Oscar Wilde; *15-25 June
1994.* Director: *Bill Collins.*

817. ARMS AND THE MAN
by George Bernard Shaw; *9-19
November 1994.*

Section 4

ARTISTS INDEX

4. ARTISTS INDEX

A

425

427

428

431

432

435

436

438

439

N

O

446

S

447

451

Section 5

PLAYS INDEX

5. PLAYS INDEX

461

Section 6

COMPANIES INDEX

6. COMPANIES INDEX

3D Theatre Company; 45 Woodhouse Lane, Norden, ROCHDALE, OL12 7SD; 0706 31353; 39, 222, 648

Abraham Moss High School; Crescent Road, CRUMPSALL M8 6UF; 061-740 5141; 489

Access Theatre, Santa Barbara, USA; 010-1-714-220-6707; 366

Ace Puppets; 429

ACT (American Community Theatre); 702

Action Space Mobile; PO Box 73, BARNSLEY S75 1NE; 0226 384944; 634

Active Performance Society; 519, 520

Alarmist Theatre Company; Top Offices, 13a Western Road, BRIGHTON BN3 1AE; 9273 208739; 640

Albermarle; 74 Mortimer Street; LONDON W1N 7DF; 071-631 0135; 699

Alchemy Theatre Company; c/o Blackfriars Arts Centre, Spain Lane, Boston, Lincolnshire, PE21 6HP; 0205 355621; 506

Het Alibi; 413

Allégresse, 071-437 3647; 377

Altered States Theatre Company;

48 Rodney Street, LIVERPOOL L1 9AA; 051-709 3895; 74,

Altrincham Garrick; Barrington Road, WA14 1HZ; 061-928 1677; 800, 802, 803, 804, 805, 807, 808, 809, 810, 812, 813, 814, 816

Anthea Hall Theatre Company, 447

Apollo Leisure Group, Palace Theatre, Oxford Street, MANCHESTER M1 6FT; 061-228 6255; 83, 699

Apples and Snakes; Unit A11, Hatcham Mews Business Centre, LONDON, SE14 5QA; 071-639 9656; 383

Arden BTEC Performing Arts Course; Sale Road, Northenden, MANCHESTER M23 0DD; 061-957 1719; 294

Arden School of Theatre; Sale Road, Northenden, MANCHESTER M23 0DD; 061-957 1715: 5, 6, 7, 50, 55, 56, 88, 89, 90, 94, 111, 291, 292, 293

Arena Theatre Company; 5 Granby Road, Walton, WARRINGTON, WA 4 6PH; 217

Artaud's Blueprint; Contemporary Performance Research Group, Centre of Media, Performance and Communications, Adelphi Building, Peru Street, SALFORD, M3 6EQ; 061-834 6633; 262

Bolton School; Chorley New
Road, BL1 4PA; 0204 849475;
586

Booster Cushion Theatre; 394

BFP; 436

Bradshaw Drama Group; 211

Brighton Theatre Events; 404

Brookdale Dramatic Society;
Brookdale Club, Bridgelane,
BRAMHALL, Stockport, SK7
3AB; 061-483 1441; 238, 248

Burnage Garden Village Players;
29 East Avenue, MANCHESTER,
M19 2NR; 061-224 1584;
303. 304, 305, 306

Burnage High School; Burnage
Lane, MANCHESTER, M19 1ER;
061-432 1527; 296, 484

Bury Actors Company; The Met
Arts Centre, Market Street,
FREEPOST bl 5162F, BURY,
BL9 0YZ; 061-761 7107; 164,
196,

Bury Theatre Works; The Met
Arts Centre, Market Street,
FREEPOST, BL 5162F, BURY,
BL9 0YZ; 061-761 7107; 80,
81, 206

Bush Theatre; Shepherds Bush
Green, LONDON, W12 8QD;
071-602 3703: 51

Cameron MacKintosh; 1 Bedford
Square, LONDON WC1B 3RA;
071-637 8866; 458

Cartwheel Community Arts; c/o
Hamer County Primary School,
Albert Royds Street, ROCHDALE

OL16 2SU; 0706 31703; 474

Carver Theatre; Church Lane,
MARPLE SK6 7AW; 061-427
3183; 679, 680, 682, 683,
684

Celesta Players; 6a Gatley Road,
CHEADLE, SK8 1PY; 428
3091; 236, 356, 357

C'est Tous Dance Company: The
Black Horse, 15 The Crescent,
SALFORD M5 4PF; 061-743
1388; 547

CHADS Theatre Company; Mellor
Road, CHEADLE HULME, SK8
5AU; 061-439 2924; 241,
245, 685, 687, 688

Charlatan Theatre; 373

Cheek by Jowl; Alford House,
Aveline Street, LONDON, SE11
5DQ; 071-793 0153/4; 351

Children's Showtime; PO Box
127, REDHILL, Surrey, RH1
3FE; 0737 642243; 149, 691

Chinese Arts Centre; 36
Charlotte Street, MANCHESTER,
M1 4FD; 061-236 9251; 263

Chitralenka and Company, 185

CHOL Theatre Company; Friends
Meeting House, Church Street,
Paddock, HUDDERSFIELD HD1
4UB; 0484 424045; 796

Chorlton Youth Theatre; 4
Needham Avenue, CHORLTON-
CUM-HARDY M21 8AA; 061-
860 6797; 510

City of Drama; 2-10 Albert
Square, MANCHESTER; M2
6LW; 061-832 1994; 264,

DynamO Theatre of Montreal;
795

EADI (English Amateur Theatre in
Israel); 700

East Cheshire Amateur Operatic
Society; 734

Eclectic Pelican; 15a Gurdon
Road, LONDON, SE7 7RN;
081-858 2512; 91

Edible Theatre Company; 061-
724 0422, 061-248 0846;
452

Edinburgh Puppet Company; 26,
186

Edward Lam Company; 380

EEIc Theatre Company, Abraham
Moss Centre, Crescent Road,
CRUMPSALL, Manchester, M8
6UF; 061-795 4186; 279

Egg Rock Theatre Company; c/o
English Department, University of
Manchester, M13 9PL; 061-275
3144; 12, 419

El Inocente Theatre Projects, c/o
Independent Theatre Council, Old
Loom House, Back Church Lane,
LONDON E1 1LU; O71-488
1229, 071-481 9968; 119

Ellen Wilkinson High School;
Hyde Road, ARDWICH M21
6BA; 061-273 2793; 493

Empire Theatre Company; 437

English Shakespeare Company;
was at 38 Bedford Square,
LONDON WC1B 3EG; 768

English Touring Theatre; c/o The

Century Theatre, Lakeside,
KESWICK, Cumbria CA12 5DJ;
07687 72282; 653

Experience Playback Theatre;
435

Eyewitness Theatre Company;
Radley Common Centre, Grasmere
Avenue, WARRINGTON WA2
0NA; 0925 820628; 76, 715,

Fame Factory Productions; 601

Fanfara, La; Catalonia; 638

Farnworth Amateur Operatic and
Dramatic Society, 50 Saint
Williams Avenue, Great Lever,
BOLTON, BL3 3EW; 0204
654113; 130, 272

Farnworth Little Theatre; Cross
Street, FARNWORTH, BL4 7AG;
0204 840217; 144, 145, 146,
147, 235, 269, 273

Fifth Amendment Ltd; 0905-
424657; 18

Fifth Floor; 071-226 2555;
497

Fin de Siècle; 628, 629

Flying Geese Productions; 0457
873427; 642, 780

F Multi Media: 408

Forced Entertainment; Unit 102,
The Workstation, 46 Shoreham
Street, SHEFFIELD, S1 4SP;
0742 798977; 25, 428

Fortune Youth Workshop, 208

Forum Company, The; Romily
Forum, Compstall Road,
ROMILEY SK6 4EA; 061-430

6570; 716, 717, 718, 719, 724

Foundation Theatre Company, Abraham Moss Centre, Crescent Road, CRUMPSALL, Manchester, M8 6UF; 061-795 4186; 281, 290

Foursight Theatre; Performing Arts Site; Dunkley Street, WOLVERHAMPTON WV1 4AN; 0902 714257; 791

Freehand Theatre; 134 Harrogate Street, BRADFORD BD3 0LE; 0274 640072; 171

French Department; University of Manchester, M13 9PL; 061-275 3210; 324, 324

Full Belt Theatre Company; 722

Funtime Productions; 4 Haywood, BRACKNELL, Buckinghamshire, RG12 7WG; 0344 53888; 727

G&J Productions; 071-437 3647; 424

Gay Sweatshop; Holborn Centre for the Performing Arts, 3 Cups Yard, Sandland Street, LONDON, WC1R 4PZ; 071-242 1168; 28

German Society; University of Manchester, M13 9PL; 061-275 3182; 320

Geysher Theatre Company; Tel-Aviv, ISRAEL; 329

Girdle and Hose; 434

Glee Club Performance Company; c/o The Green Room, 54/56 Whitworth Street West, MANCHESTER, M1 5WW; 061-

236 1677; 17, 85, 86, 385

Gloria, 23, 327

Glorybutts Theatre Group; Hon Secretary, Mrs C A Cheethem, 26, Holcolme Village, BURY, BL8 4LZ; 0706 82 6536; 176

Graeae Theatre Company; Interchange Studios, Dalby Street, LONDON, NW5 3NQ; 071-267 1959/3164; 417

Greaves Street Players; 542

Green Candle Dance Company; 388

Green Light Theatre Company; 6 Chelford Road, OLD TRAFFORD, M16 0BJ; 061-860 6887; 152

Guide Bridge Theatre; Audenshaw Road, AUDENSHAW, M34 5HJ; 061-330 8078; 247, 743, 744, 745, 746, 747, 748, 749, 750, 751, 752

Hallé Orchestra Education Department; Heron House, Albert Square, MANCHESTER, M2 5HD; 061-834 8363; 162

Halliwell Road Methodist Drama Group; Harvey Street BL1 8BG; 590, 600

HATS; Honorary Secretary, Mrs H Hadden, 215 Kingsway Park, DAVYHULME M31 2EE; 061-755 3382; 172, 792

Hats and Tea Theatre Company; 389

Haveley Hey Junior School; Broadoak Road, BENCHILL, M22 9PL; 061-437 2151; 488

MANCHESTER, M14 7PQ;
061-848 8398; 95

Livespace Theatre Company; 720

Living Room Theatre; 210

livingstone Primary School; Old
Brow, MOSSLEY OL5 0DY;
0457 832495; 759

Liz Gamlin Puppets; 431

London Mime Theatre; 170

Lovely Plays; 657

Ludus Dance Company; Assembly
Rooms, King Street, LANCASTER
LA1 1RE; 0524 35936; 624

Lyceum Players; Union Street,
OLDHAM OL1 1QG; 061-633
1860; 603, 604, 605, 606,
607, 608, 609

Lyric Theatre; King Street,
HAMMERSMITH, W6 0QL; 081-
741 0824; 327

M6 Theatre Company; Hamer CP
School, Albert Royds Street,
ROCHDALE OL16 2SU; 0706
355898; 110, 129, 173, 174,
197, 646, 651

Macatashnik Theatre Company;
University of Manchester, M13
9PL; 061-275 3347; 48

Macclesfield Amateur Dramatic
Society; 228

MacLennon Dance Theatre; 190

Maiden Theatre Company; 364
Dickenson Road; MANCHESR
M13 0NG; 368, 369, 370,
371

Major Road Theatre Company;
29 Queens Road, BRADFORD,
West Yorkshire, BD8 7BS; 0274
480251; 283

Malaprop Theatre Company;
Lancaster; 815

Maly Drama Theatre of St
Petersburg; 77, 78

Manchester Actors Company; 414
Canon Green Court, West King
Street, Trinity, SALFORD, M3
7HB; 0204 884 830; 124,
298, 299, 300, 301

Manchester Athenæum Dramatic
Society; 18 Moorland Road,
DIDSBURY M20 0BE; 061-445
5829; 507, 508, 509, 525

Manchester Grammar School;
Telfer Road, M13 0XS; 061-
224 7201; 490

Manchester Metropolitan
University Drama Society; 37

Manchester Metropitan University
School of Theatre; The Capitol,
School Lane, DIDSBURY, M20
0HT; 061-434 3331; 49, 93,
105, 107, 296, 307, 308,
309, 311, 315, 316, 317,
544, 545

Manchester University Drama
Department; 503, 514

Manchester University Drama
Society; 516

Manchester University Stage
Society; 36 Spring Bridge Road,
MANXCHESTER, M16 8PW;
061-226 4023; 243

Manchester Youth Theatre; Unit
52, Cariocca Managed

Dalby Street, LONDON NW5 3NQ; 071 482 1576; 189

Riverside Players; 227

Roar Material; India House, 73 Whitworth Street, MANCHESTER MI 6LG; 15, 16, 348

Rob Frost; Raynes Park Methodist Church, Tolverne Road, LONDON; SW20 2RA; 361

Romiley Operatic Society; 692

Rose English; ArtsAdmin, 195 Kentish Town Road, LONDON, NW5; 071-482 3749; 322

Rossendale Youth Theatre; 230

Rough Magic Theatre Company; 5/6 Sough Great George's Street, DUBLIN 2, Republic of Ireland; (010 353) 01-671 9278; 73,

Royal Court Theatre; Sloane Square, LONDON SW1W 8AS; 071-730 5174; 378

Royal Exchange Theatre Company; St Ann's Square, MANCHESTER M2 7DH; 061-833 9333: 2, 3, 4, 47, 58, 82, 117, 287, 449, 500

Royal National Theatre, The; South Bank, LONDON, SEI 9PX; 071-633 0880; 32

Royal Shakespeare Company; Barbican Centre, LONDON EC2Y 8DS; 071-638 4141; 59, 286

Rumble Theatre Company; 46

Saddleworth Players; Players' Theatre, DELPH, Oldham OL3

5DY; 01457 874644; 242, 258, 259, 610, 611, 612, 613, 614, 615, 616

St Anne's Church, Turton Youth Theatre Group; 0204 852583; 585

St Catherine's Amateur Music Society; 0204 77451; 592

St Clement's AM&DS; Sandy Lane, ROCHDALE OL11 5DR; 647

St Clement's Junior School; Abbey Hey Lane, MANCHESTER M11; 061-301 3268; 486

St Joseph's School, Chorley New Road, HORWICH BL6 7QB; 0204 697456; 581

St Joseph's Players; St Joseph's Social Centre, Walmersley Road, BURY, BL9; 0204 592684;

St Mark's Stage Society; Waterloo Street, GLODWICK OL4 1ER; 061-652 3546; 636

St Osmund's Productions, Blenheim Road, BL2 6EL; 0204 32866; 157, 595

St Paul's, Astley Bridge, AODS; 0204 385432; 582

St Paul's RC High Schoolk; Firbank Road, MANCHESTER M23; 061-437 5841; 483

St Peter's Methodists Church Amateur Dramatic Society; Church Hall, St Helen's Road, BOLTON, BL3 3SE; 0204 20334; 150, 580

St Philip's AODS; Parochial Hall, Bridgeman Street, BOLTON BL3

6TH; 0204 595086; 584

St Simon & St Jude's Amateur Dramatic Society; Newport Road, GREAT LEVER BL3 2DT; 0204 26165; 602

St Vincent de Paul High School; Victoria Park; 482

Sale Nomads; 51 Manor Avenue M35 5JQ; 061-962 7407; 793

Sale Operatic Society; 11 Bollin Drive M33 3GL; 061-973 2621; 811

Salem Community Theatre; Moravian Church Hall, Lees Road, OLDHAM OL4 3AJ; 061-626 3908; 619, 620, 621, 622

Salford Open Theatre; 24 Orama Avenue, SALFORD M6 8LL; 061-789 6644; 439,

Salford University Theatre Company; Chapman Theatre, University of Salford, M5 4WT; 061-745 5000, ext 3248; 64, 65, 96, 674, 677

Salisbury Playhouse; Malthouse Lane, SALISBURY, Wiltshire, SP2 7RA; 0722 20117; 131

Sandbach School Theatre; Crewe Road, SANDBACH, Cheshire, CW11 9EB; 0270 7673231; 123

Sandpiper Productions; Flat B, Abingdon Court, Allen Street, LONDON W8 6BP; 071-937 9593; 261, 297

Sangbarta Group Theatre of Calcutta; 355

Saul Zaentz Company: 783

Scandalous Productions, 539, 540

Semblance; 381

SHADES; St Herbert's Church Hall, Broadway, CHADDERTON OL9 0JY; 061-633 9059; 635, 643

Shakebag and Will Theatre Company; 139 Cale Lane, New Springs, WIGAN WN2 1HB; 0942 37987; 122

Sharples School, Hill Cot Road, BL1 8SN; 0204 308421; 589

Shena Simon Theatre Studies; 34 Whitworth Street, MANCHESTER M1 3HB; 061-236 3418; 109, 296

Short and Stocky Theatre Company; 22, 397

Show of Hands Theatre; 284

Singh Theatre Company; 632

Sleeping Giant Theatre; 10, 225, 364

Slyne With Hest Drama Group; 233

Smilin' Mongoose Theatre Company;   c/o Nia Centre, Chichester Road, MI5 5EU; 061-226 6461: 45,

Snap Theatre Company; Unit A, Causeway Business Centre, BISHOP'S STORTFORD, Hertfordshire, CM23 2UB; 0279 503066/504095; 191, 725

Solent People's Theatre; The

Doncaster Avenue, M20 1DN;
061-445 5432; 487

Wigan Little Theatre; 0942
42561; 817, 826, 827, 829,
830

Wild Pink Turkeys; 061-737
5349; 250

Willpower Theatre Workshops;
593

Wilmslow Guild Players; 1 Bourne
Street, WILMSLOW, SK9 5HD;
0625 533843; 240

Wirral Hospital Players; 234

Woodford Community Players;
Woodford Community Centre,
Chester Road, WOODFORD,
SK7 1PS; 061-439 3118; 223,
731, 732

Wot No Boots! Theatre Company;
051-726 1433; 20

The Wrestling School; 344

Wright Robinson High School;
Abbey Hey Lane, MANCHESTER
M18; 061-370 5121; 491

Yer-Wat-Say Theatre Company,
543

Yorkshire Theatre Company; 35
Lupton Street, HUNSLET LS10
2QW; 664

Young Theatre Church Workshop;
Seymour Road, Astley Bridge,
BOLTON BL1 8PU; 0204
304332; 160

Peter Zegveld; 385

Section 7

1994 AWARDS

7.   1994   AWARDS

DAVID HADCROFT (left) and IAN TAYLOR, representing TYLDESLEY
LITTLE THEATRE collect the GREATER MANCHESTER DRAMA
FEDERATION DESIGN AND TECHNICAL TROPHY for the second year
in succession, on this occasion for STAGS AND HENS (823)

The following organisations do much do support the theatre
in Greater Manchester in many ways.   These include the
making of annual Awards in recognition of outstanding work.
Those for 1993–94 are republished on the follow pages.

| (000): Production Numbers from Section 2; (000'93): Production
Numbers from A YEAR IN THE THEATRE: Greater Manchester 1993 |

BOLTON EVENING NEWS DRAMA AWARDS 1993/94; 21 October 1994

BEST DRAMA: THE CAINE MUTINY COURT MARTIAL; Marco Players **(583)**

BEST MUSICAL: ROBERT AND ELIZABETH; Walmsley Church AODS **(831)**

SPECIAL AWARD FOR CHORUS WORK; BOLTON CATHOLIC MUSICAL AND CHORAL SOCIETY for Guys and Dolls **(740)**

GREATER MANCHESTER DRAMA FEDERATION;
Hon Secretary: Mrs Viki Williams, 24 Hazlemere Drive, CHEADLE HULME SK8 6JY; 061–485 2762; **Newsletter:** 2 Whitegates Close, Timperley, ALTRINCHAM, WA15 7PD; 061–980 8572

ONE–ACT PLAY FESTIVAL; 22 May – 4 June 1993, at Theatre Royal, RAMSBOTTOM.

SECTION A (Youth Under 16):

Andrew Winton Trophy: PADOS for **Juvie (232)**

Certificate of Merit: Summerseat Youth Theatre for **The Happy Man (215)**

Brenda Gillatt Trophy: David Livesey for **Andrew** in **Juvie (232)**

SECTION B: (Youth Under 21)

Nan Nuttall Trophy: Farnworth Little Theatre **The Valiant (235)**
Certificate of Merit: Tameside Youth Drama Group for **Other Side Story (239)**

Bertram Holland Trophy: Karen Ellery of Tameside Youth Drama Group for **Lucy Fer** in **Other Side Story (239)**

SECTION C: (Adult)

Settlement Players Trophy: 3D Theatre Company for **Gosforth's Fête (222)**

Stanley Harrower Cup: CHADS Theatre Company for **An Englishman Abroad (241)**

Certificate of Merit: Summerseat Players for **the Long Christmas Dinner (244)**

Robert L Goodwin Trophy (Outstanding Actor): Stephen Keyworth of Increasingly Important Theatre Company for **Picking Bones (225)**

Cyril V Hines Trophy (Outstanding Actress): Dianne Jenkins of Heald Green Theatre Company for **Aurora Bompass** in

How He Lied to Her Husband
(226)

SECTION D: (Original Play)

Playwrights Workshop Trophy:
Philip Stagg for Letter From
America (217)

ALL SECTIONS:

Vicki Lane Award (Meritorious
Director): Lynda Burton of
PADOS for Juvie (232)

Cliff Walker Trophy (Stage
Presentation): Celesta Players for
The Orchestra (236)

OPEN SECTION:

City of Drama Cup (Best
Production): Riverside Players for
Cecily (227)

Dick Morron Trophy (Runner Up):
Macclesfield ADS for The Actor'S
Nightmare (228)

Manchester Evening News Cup
(Highly Commended): Beacon
Drama for Facing the Wall (213)

Best Adult Performer: Derek
Garside of Slyne with Hest
Drama Group fof Bernard in Last
Tango in Little Grimley (233)

Best Young Performer: Thomas
Allen of Summerseat Methodist
Primary School for Ernie in
Ernie's Incredible Illucinations
(218)

FULL LENGTH PLAY
FESTIVAL 1993/94

Athenæum Rose Bowl
(Outstanding Achievement): Muriel

Goodwin

Lawrence Roberts Trophy
(Outstanding Contribution to
Drama): Harold Onions

SECTION A

Best Actress: Connie Walker of
Increasingly Important Theatre
Company for May in Salt of the
Earth (210'93)

Best Supporting Actress: Rita
Mayo of Farnworth Little Theatre
for Isabelle's Mother in Ring
Round the Moon (146)

Best Actor: David Reynolds of
Wilmslow Green Room for David,
King Edward VIII in Crown
Matrimonial

Best Supporting Actor: Harold
Smith of Farnworth Little Theatre
for Joshua in Ring Round the
Moon (146)

Platt Shield (Best Young
Performer: William Ash of
Increasingly Important Theatre
Company for Billy Fisher in Billy
Liar

Certificate of Merit Young
Performer): Richard Jackson of
Increasingly Important Theatre
Company for Arthur Crabtree in
Billy Liar

Design and Technical Trophy:
Stags and Hens, Tyldesley Little
Theatre (823)

David Lane Trophy (Front of
House Management): Tyldesley
Little Theatre

Edward Jones Cup (Best
Director): Colin Snell of

Increasingly Important Theatre Company for **Salt of the Earth (210'93)**

John Alldridge Cup (Adventure in the Theatre): Farnworth Little Theatre for **Second from Last in The Sack Race (147)**

Stockport Theatre Guild Trophy (Adjudicator's Award): Northenden Players Theatre Club

Lowry Trophy (Runners Up): Wilmslow Green Room for **Crown Matrimonial**

DRAMA SHIELD (Best Production): **Players Dramatic Society** for **Abelard and Heloise (704)**

SECTION B

Ian Armstrong Trophy (Best Male Performance): Ian J Parratt of Uppermill Stage Society for **Emile** in **South Pacific (618)**

John Garner Trophy (Best Female Performance): Lynsay Astin of North Manchester AODS for **Anna** in **The King and I (505)**

Best Supporting Male Performance: Martin Bradbury of Uppermill Stage Society for **Cabe** in **South Pacific (618)** and at Lydgate Music and Drama Society for **Pharaoh** in **Joseph and Thh Amazing Technicolor Dream Coat**

Best Supporting Female Performer: Rosie Wilson of Carver Theatre for **Fungus** in **Pinocchio (684)**

Geoffrey Kellett Trophy (Most Promising Young Performer): Sally Ashkenazi of Junior Stage 80 for **Miss Adelaide** in **Guys And Dolls**

Nan Nuttall Trophy (Originality): Phoenix Theatre Company for **Happy Jack/September in the Rain**

Wyn Davies Cup (Best Director): John Rawson of Uppermill Stage Society for **South Pacific (618)**

Ronald Ashworth Trophy (Best Musical Director): Andrew White of Mossley AODS for **The Wiz (754)**

Irene Rostron Trophy (Choreography): Sale Nomads for **5'n'9 (793)**

Joyce Pomfrett Trophy (Costume: Design and Creation): Altrincham Garrick for **Aladdin (803)** and **Red Hot & Cole**

John Evans Cup (Best Presentation): Altrincham Garrick for **Aladdin (803)** and **Red Hot & Cole**

John Blackburn Trophy (Adjudicator's Award): Denise Greasley for **Dorothy**, Carl Morgan as **Scarecrow**, Howard Carter as **Tim Man** and Colin Ward as **Lion** – The Quartet in mossley AODS' **The Wiz (754)**

June Leech Trophy (Adjudicator's Award for Youth): Sarah Yates of PADOS Junior for **Flo** in **Andy Capp (181)**

DAVID LANE TROPHY: Best Production): Mossley AODS for **The Wiz (754)**

SECTION C

Best Actress: Joanne Devlin of St Clements Drama Society for **Laura** in **The Glass Menagerie** **(647 //39)**

Best Supporting Actress: Jenny Handcock of Bolton Little Theatre for **Webbo** in **Shakespeare Country (133)**

Certificate of Merit: Carrie Alker of Lyceum Players for **Joe** in **A Day in the Death of Joe Egg (604)**

Best Actor: Jeff Gartside of CHADS Theatre for **Malvolio** in **Twelfth Night (688)**

Best Supporting Actor: Geoff Sword of Summerseat Players for **Warnie** in **Shadowlands (529)**

Frank Hillson Award (Stage Design and Decor): Saddleworth Players for **Madame Butterfly (427'93)**

Philip L Edwards Trophy (Best Lighting Design): Stockport Garrick for **The Ghost Train**

Frances Hargreaves Trophy (Outstanding Wardrobe): CHADS Theatre Company for **Twelfth Night (688)**

Monica Yeomans Trophy (Best Director): Grahame Humphries of Summerseat Players for **Shadowlands (529)**

Pat Phoenix Trophy (Adjudicator's Award): Carver Theatre for **Hard Times (682)**

Muriel Goodwin Trophy (Runners Up): St Clements Dramatic Society for **The Glass Menagerie**

(647 //39)

NATIONAL WESTMINISTER TROPHY (Best Production): CHADS Theatre Company for **Twelfth Night (688)**

MANCHESTER EVENING NEWS THEATRE AWARDS 1993/94

The date of these Awards has this year been changed to a month later, to **4 December**, in order form part of the final, climactic month of **City of Drama 1994**. This is too late for inclusion in this volume. The Awards should be published in the MANCHESTER EVENING NEWS on that date and will be reprinted in next autumn's volume of this record, A YEAR IN THE THEATRE – Greater Manchester 1994-95; ISBN 0 9521502 2 0. Contrary to previous practice, Nominations for this year's awards were not included with the other early announcements of the ceremony, so they cannot be included here either.

NATIONAL OPERATIC AND DRAMATIC ASSOCIATION (North West Area) Area Secretary: John Owen, Gwynfa, St Asaph's Road, The Willows, Great Sutton, SOUTH WIRRAL L66 2GP; 051–348 0004. Professional Theatre Accolades, adjudged by

Stephen Isaac Gregory.

BEST NEW PLAY: STRANGE ATTRACTORS by Kevin Fegan (319); Contact

BEST PRODUCTION OF A PLAY: LOST IN YONKERS by Neil Simon (421); directed by Roger Haines; Library

BEST PRODUCTION OF A MUSICAL: ASSASSINS by Stephen Sondheim and John Weidman; (248 '93); directed by Roger Haines; Library

BEST ACTOR: DAVID THRELFALL, Edmond Dantes in The Count of Monte Christo (117); Royal Exchange

BEST ACTRESS: JOSETTE BUSHELL-MINGO, Polly Peachum in The Threepenny Opera (75); Contact.

BEST MUSICAL PERFORMANCE: PETER BENSON, Charles Guiteau in Assassins (248 '93); Library

BEST COMEDY PERFORMANCES: ROSS McCALL aND MOHAMED MUKHLIS, Jay and Artie in Lost in Yonkers (421); Library

BEST SUPPORTING PERFORMANCE: DAVID FLEESHMAN, Samuel Byck in Assassins (248 '93) and Uncle Louie in Lost in Yonkers (421); Library

BEST DIRECTOR: RICHARD GREGORY, for Game Challenge - Level 7 by Kevin Feegan (208 '93) ;Contact, Nia Centre

and in between

BEST DESIGNER: RICHARD FOXTON, for Game Challenge - Level 7 by Kevin Fegan (208 '93), at and beyond Contact, and Blood Wedding, Lorca, translated by Henry Livings, Bolton Octagon (71)

Best City of Drama Production: THE MAN WHO ..., directed by Peter Brook (60)

Best Actor in a City of Drama Production: YOSHI OIDA in The Man Who ... (60)

Best Actress in a City of Drama Production: LILO BAUR, La Cocadrille in The Three Lives of Lucie Cabrol (35)

THEATRE MANAGERS ASSOCIATION/MARTINI REGIONAL THEATRE AWARDS 1992/93

Awards Officer: Andrew Leigh, Bedford Chambers, The Piazza, Covent Garden, LONDON WC2E 8HQ; 071-928 2651. The following Nominations were made for productions originated or performed in Greater Manchester. Those actually receiving Awards at the ceremony in Manchester on 21 October are printed in **bold**:

BEST ACTOR: Ian McDermid, Dancer in Hated Nightfall (344);

CITY OF DRAMA,visiting Dancehouse

Bucharest **(346)**; CITY OF DRAMA, visiting Dancehouse

BEST OVERALL PRODUCTION:

THE MAN WHO ...(60); CITY OF DRAMA, visiting Contact

BEST NEW PLAY:

HATED NIGHTFALL by Howard Barker **(344)**, CITY OF DRAMA, visiting Dancehouse

BEST MUSICAL:

ASSASSINS by Stephen Sonheim and John Weidman, directed by Roger Haines, LIBRARY THEATRE **(248 '93)**

SCROOGE, THE MUSICAL by Leslie Bricusse **(460)**, visiting Palace

OLIVIER AWARDS, London; April 1994;

PRODUCTIONS SEEN IN GREATER MANCHESTER:

BEST ACTOR: Mark Rylance, Benedick in MUCH ADO ABOUT NOTHING **(82 '93)**; premiered at TAMESIDE HIPPODROME

BEST ACTOR IN A SUPPORTING RÔLE: Joseph Mydell, Belize in ANGELS IN AMERICA **(32)**; CITY OF DRAMA; visiting Contact

BEST TOURING PRODUCTION:

THE THREE LIVES OF LUCIE CABROL **(35)**; CITY OF DRAMA, visiting Dancehouse

RICHARD III, Odeon Theatre of

Also Available:–
A YEAR IN THE THEATRE:–
Greater Manchester 1993

"It really is an excellent publication," **Sir Robert Scott**

"Highly useful, ... all encompassing, ... a snip," **City Life**

"Fascinating Journal, ... indispensable work of reference,"
NODA NorthWest

"It looks good ... A wonderful record of people's
achievements,", **SW, Northern Moor**

"A really Interesting Reference and Handbook ... Lovely
Journal Review of A JUBILEE," **Stephen Boyes, MAC**

"I was greatly entertained by the Journal," **BE, Northenden**

"Excellent value for money," **AC, M14**

"It deserves to sell very well indeed," **Geoffrey Clifton,
Proprietor of Manchester's Performing Arts Bookshop '67-93**

"A Great Record ... I am delighted to hear that the next
edition will be called A YEAR IN THE CITY OF DRAMA,"
Christopher Barron, City of Drama Director.

ISBN 0 9521502 0 4   £ 4.95

Available November 1995: **A Year in the Theatre –
Greater Manchester 1994–95; ISBN 0 9521502 2 0**

Obtainable through any bookshop (quote ISBNs) or direct
from **Broadfield Publishing, 71 Broadfield Road, Moss Side,
MANCHESTER M14 4WE   061–227 9265**